S

King Henry roared, "You tell me such lies, when all along there is another stands between us! Look you, Madam!"

He seized Kathryn by a caul-full of blonde-brown hair and flung her down. At first she saw nothing but the surrounding acres she and John had ploughed together, working to break up the earth a final time before winter froze it solid. The ground was therefore freshly thrown-up and easily received impressions of what had passed over it.

Everywhere she saw a series of shallow *V*'s set close together to form the Windsgeat *W* that marked all de Gael stock. John's stallion, Finnvarra, had left his unmistakable hoofprints everywhere!

"Do not give me your stories of Boleyn and Seymour, Madam," the king roared. "The truth is, you had rather be John de Gael's whore than my wife and queen of all England!"

Kathryn:
In the Court of Six Queens

Anne Merton Abbey

BANTAM BOOKS
NEW YORK • TORONTO • LONDON • SYDNEY • AUCKLAND

KATHRYN: IN THE COURT OF SIX QUEENS

A Bantam Book / May 1989

ISBN 0-553-28011-2

Published simultaneously in the United States and Canada

Bantam Books are published by Bantam Books, a division of Bantam Doubleday Dell Publishing Group, Inc. Its trademark, consisting of the words "Bantam Books" and the portrayal of a rooster, is Registered in U.S. Patent and Trademark Office and in other countries. Marca Registrada. Bantam Books, 666 Fifth Avenue, New York, New York 10103.

PRINTED IN THE UNITED STATES OF AMERICA

O 0 9 8 7 6 5 4 3 2 1

For the Criswells:
Barbara, Cindy (Sis), and Tom.
Family.

PART ONE

CATHERINE OF ARAGON
(The Valley of Gold)

"In greater feast than Priam's sons of Troy,
Where each sweet place returns a taste full sour;
The large green Courts where we were wont to hove
With eyes cast up unto the maiden's tower,
And easy sighs such as folk drew in love."

—Henry Howard, Earl of Surrey,
1517–1547—

"It was wonderful to see her courage; nothing seemed to frighten her."

—Thomas Howard, third Duke of Norfolk, said of Catherine of Aragon—

1
Ludlow Castle, Wales
April 1502

She was Catalina of Spain and she was not afraid to die.

No, no longer Catalina of Spain, the fevered princess reminded herself, struggling to sit up; she was Catherine of England now, Prince Arthur's bride.

And Arthur was dead. They had not told her yet, but somewhere in her heart she knew and accepted the truth. Why else the long faces, why else speak to her as though she were parchment-thin glass and might too easily shatter? It was not merely for the sake of her illness, she knew, for she was foreign to them, and the English were not sentimental. No, her Arthur had died and none dared tell her. That frail, ruddy-haired boy with his endearing shyness . . . the hacking cough that often woke her in the night; she had not heard it from the northwest tower today and knew full well that Arthur could never lie down without coughing.

Catherine tossed on her rumpled bed, the room swirling before her. *Arthur*. Frail, not like her. She was strong; she had come to bear the heir to the English throne many fine, strapping sons who would rule after him, and daughters who would marry distant princes, as her parents Isabella of Castile and Ferdinand of León had sent her to do.

Lying, burning, she thought how much healthier than her delicate husband she was. Chances still seemed good to her that she might fight off this infection raging through her body, filling her lungs, making her blood seem to sizzle in her veins. She might live, while poor Arthur . . . poor, poor Arthur. She held very little hope for his survival. And, as time passed and she was left parched and writhing, very little hope for her own.

"Will no one tell me of my husband's fate?" Catherine cried out. Her words seemed to race around the chilly room, faster and faster, encircling her. So hot, so thirsty, and a dim recollection that the room had once seemed damp and drafty . . . blessedly drafty, stirring the stale air of the place. . . . "What of my husband?" she shouted, and the sound stabbed her ears, made her wince and cringe.

Many heard the cry. But none at Ludlow spoke or understood her peculiar Castilian Spanish: councillors, ladies-in-waiting, men-at-arms in the armory, all heard and shivered, thinking the Princess of Wales in her death throes.

A blue-eyed woman, far along in pregnancy, struggled up from her bed in the Edward the Fifth tower. "Holy Mother! Will no one help the Spanish girl?" Lady Joanna Chase demanded of her maidservant.

Young Tansy, supposedly mending but actually dozing, jerked awake in her window seat. "Eh, Milady? Oh, it's nothing. Just the princess with the fever, going to die of it same as the prince."

Joanna stared, agape. "The prince died? And no one is doing a thing for the princess? Fetch out my brown taffeta and a coif to tuck my hair into, I cannot leave the princess of Wales to shriek out her life alone! Where are her Spanish women?"

"Probably gone to fetch more cool water for her. Now Milady Joanna, you must not go, it will endanger the child and His Lordship your husband will be furious."

Joanna lumbered from bed, crossed the room, and shoved Tansy toward the nearest trunk. "Oh, who cares what Hal thinks? Now kneel and fetch my gown from the trunk, you know full well that I cannot bend over to do it myself!"

It seemed impossible that she could still get into the ancient silk taffeta gown, but Tansy had let all the seams out half a dozen times and loosened the laces, and now between the two of them, they managed to squeeze her into it. Clad, coiffed, and irritable that she could only find her second-best shoes, Joanna now started down the steps. She had to grope her way along the clammy, too-cold walls, for she felt totally off-balance in this, her ninth month. *Already a week late*, she thought, cursing Ludlow Castle, cursing Hal her husband and last night's midnight journey here. *I have been called to the Welsh Marches*, he had said in his brief way, and told his bodyservant to pack for him.

Her handsome husband leave her and go to a household teeming with slender ladies-in-waiting and maids of honor? Leave her to have this second child all alone? *I am going, too!* Joanna had cried, fists on hips. He had a glimpse then of her true breeding. Not her father Thomas Howard but her grandfather, John Duke of Norfolk, dying at Bosworth Field for then-king Richard Plantagenet, even though he had been warned that Richard could not win. The notice on his tent had read: "Jackie o'Norfolk, Be not too bold, For thy master Dickon Is bought and sold." John had torn it down, donned his splendid German armor, and was dead within hours. Those were the Howards, fearless to the point of idiocy, warriors all, even the women. And Joanna was popularly acknowledged the strongest-willed of the lot. Maybe it was her being named after her grandfather John, Hal would never know.

Hal himself was dead Richard the Third's nephew. His father had been Edward the Fourth, king of England before brother Richard; Hal's mother had been one of many pretty ladies-in-waiting to catch the roving royal eye.

Plantagenet had faced Howard last night about a nine-months' pregnant woman journeying to Ludlow from Chester.

The Howard won.

Tansy started down the stairs after Joanna now. "Oh, stay put," Joanna fairly snarled. "Little Kathryn needs you more than I do! And if Hal comes back, lie to him about where I am. You can lie, can you not, Tansy? Or is that beyond your meager capabilities?"

She slammed the door after herself upon reaching the bottom step. Tansy sighed, shaking her head. A small, shrill voice behind her piped up, "*Mama?*" Little Kathryn Chase sat rubbing her vividly blue eyes as though intending to remove all trace of color.

"Mama is gone, but see what Tansy bought for you this morning!" the maidservant greeted her, bringing out a wooden apple. The beet-dye hue of it fascinated the two-year-old and she at once put it to her mouth to gnaw. Tansy, smiling affectionately, sat back down with her sewing.

Joanna found Doña Alvira, Princess Catherine's duenna ("A duenna is a governess with fangs," Hal Chase had explained to his wife last night), seated on a low bench before the armory fireplace. At least, since her coif and apron were snowy and crisp, and her gown the proper funereal black, and as she was carrying on mightily, Joanna surmised her to be the dreaded Doña Alvira and approached her as such. "Why are you out here? Why are you not with the princess?" Joanna demanded. But the Spanish woman only wailed and continued to rock herself on the bench. Joanna did not understand Spanish so could not tell that the woman was reviling the English climate and the dead prince, who had not even consummated his marriage with her little Catalina. Now there would be no kings of England sprung from Spanish seed and they must all go home in disgrace. Disgrace or worse if the princess died, and Doña Alvira was certain she would.

"Where are the other Spanish ladies?" Joanna Chase asked a man-at-arms lounging in the nearest doorway.

"The prettiest one—Maria de Salinas—is still ill. They say she will live. The others have gone for more water, the princess complains of a terrible thirst."

Just as her shiftless maidservant Tansy had said. "And have they gone *alone*?" Joanna demanded shrewdly. "Unprotected noblewomen, speaking nary a word of anything but Spanish, turned loose in a land of wild Welshmen? I suggest you find them most promptly, and I suggest you fetch them to me. *Now!*"

The man-at-arms hesitated. She was only an attaindered Earl's daughter, banned from Court because of her husband's blood. Besides, if that fearsome Plantagenet countess who had already harassed him discovered he had left his post—

Joanna's keen blue eyes said she was prepared to spit and roast him. He fled at a gallop.

It took her one-quarter hour to locate Maria de Salinas, wrestle her into suitable clothing, and bully her onto her feet. As Maria spoke no English and Joanna no Spanish, Joanna made the situation apparent by clutching her own throat, wheezing, fanning herself, and repeating the princess's name as she had heard Doña Alvira say it: "*Catalina.*"

Maria's great dark eyes went wide. Grasping the situation—as well as Joanna's hand—they rushed from her room. One woman in early labor, the other narrowly rolled back from Death's rim, they stumbled up icy stone stairs to the State Apartments, next to where the dead prince lay. A flurry of activity burst into being all around them as two exquisite but weary looking women toting leather water buckets approached. "Beatrix! Francesca!" Maria greeted them tearily.

Men-at-arms scurried this way and that. Ladies-in-waiting collided; cooks and priests snapped at one another. Two greyhounds ran yipping from the room. From the midst of the milling crowd an imperious woman appeared, dressed excessively for the hour, weather, and place.

Margaret Pole, Countess of Salisbury, was niece to two Plantagenet kings and daughter to the dead duke of Clarence; her blood was far bluer than the king's own and she was first cousin and closest kinswoman to the queen. An odd trinket dangled at her wrist—a miniature wine cask, for her father had purportedly been offered his choice of execution mode and had chosen drowning in a vat of expensive malmsey wine. The tiny barrel had begun as a child's wooden toy, gaining coats of gold leaf and jewels along the way. *She only wears it to twit my Hal because his father murdered hers,* Joanna thought irritably. She forced herself to curtsy as slightly as possible.

"Why are you stirring up the entire garrison?" Margaret Pole demanded. "And why is that vilely ill Spanish maid-of-honor up and about? Let her lie down and perish quietly as the others are doing."

Sir Richard Pole, unfortunate husband to the barrel-wearer, laid a restraining hand on his wife's jeweled arm. "I thank you, Lady Chase, for any concern you feel for the princess of Wales, but all is under control now. Return to your chambers and bear your child."

As if, Joanna thought, *that is all I am good for!* She smiled, and spoke through gritted teeth. "If everything is so well controlled then why is the princess shrieking for a husband no one has told her is dead? At least I *presume* that is what she is doing; his name is the only word I recognize in the Castilian tongue. Sent word to the king yet about his son and heir, Richard?"

She had him there and knew it. No man in the kingdom would willingly tell grasping, burning-cold Henry Tudor that his eldest son lay dead in a drafty Welsh castle. And as for the pretty Plantagenet queen, no one would want to break her heart with the news, either.

Confident that he would not stop her now, Joanna marched past Richard Pole, herding Catherine of Aragon's ladies before her. She pushed them into the sickroom and shot the bolt home behind them. Beatrix was rudely shoved forward and handed a poker to stir up the fire. Francesca knelt to feed more wood to the flames. Maria stood unsteadily, weaving to and fro until Joanna half knocked her onto the bed. "For Jesu's sake, Madam, talk to the poor girl!"

Joanna poured some of the fresh water into a pitcher and sloshed the rest into a basin to be warmed for bathing. What a wretched room; she shuddered to regard it. The Poles must have had Catherine moved here after Prince Arthur worsened; they had given the girl no tapestries to keep out drafts, and no down-stuffed mattress, only louse-riddled straw in bursting bags for her bed. Not even decent blankets, but the dregs from Ludlow's storerooms. Moth-eaten, infested—Catherine of Aragon was of no import to them with the prince dead, and these people obviously expected her to die as well, or at least be shipped home to Spain to remarry.

Maria de Salinas was heaping dusty blankets on the princess, five or more. Joanna had to stop her and signal *No, not too many*. Too much heat and the fever would burn up Catherine's brain; too little and she would shiver herself to death. It seemed to her, glancing at Catherine's ladies, that only Maria had wit and intellect. *Send me only your handsomest women that my lords may be eager to wed them and so further seal our alliance,* Henry Tudor had written Ferdinand of León. Pretty girls, hardly a featherweight of sense amongst them.

With the exception of Maria. She was clucking over the princess like an underaged mother hen, fluffing pillows, tenderly stroking the scorched forehead. So this one was a personal friend, not merely a glorified servant; this one cared very deeply, Joanna approvingly observed. With motions and an occasional clout she received Maria's assistance in stripping Catherine of her dirty shift, finding a clean one in a humpbacked Spanish trunk of black and vermillion leather. A thought struck Joanna then, seeing how Catherine of Aragon cried out from the fever's heat. She took the clean shift, threw open the shutters, and weighed the garment down with a wash basin, letting it flutter outside. Much-needed fresh air entered the room that way, too. When she and Maria finally ladled Catherine into the cool shift, the grateful sighs and murmurs told her that this consideration was much appreciated.

Meanwhile Beatrix and Francesca emptied the slop jar, stoked the fire, and made a delicious salty broth, which the four women took turns feeding Catherine. They bathed her twice that afternoon from a basin, then spooned broth and hot clove water into her as she half-sat, propped by pillows. Two light blankets covered her; Joanna allowed a third, and it happened: a sudden glistening on the princess's forehead signaled the fever's attempt to break.

A brisk, hard sweat followed. Joanna joyfully added another light coverlet, though by now she could feel labor contractions coming closer together. She urged another cup of broth down Catherine, watched perspiration plaster the linen shift to the girl's body. The princess's auburn-and-ivory head dropped to Joanna's shoulder as a child's might have done, so she rocked her as she did her two-year-old Kathryn, crooned a lullabye, and stroked the sticky face and matted hair.

It was nightfall when the sheets and woolen blankets lay soaked. Joanna unbarred the door then, certain that the princess would live now despite anything the doctors could do to her. She and Maria were changing the bed linens when an old man entered at the head of a gossiping group. He at once drew a long bodkin and a jar of leeches from his bag. Laboring or not, she could not allow him to do this, so Joanna waddled forward and gave him a hearty shove in the chest that sent him reeling into Richard Pole's arms. "You let him bleed her, she will die. Look at her, My Lord, is she not much improved? She will live now unless you let this barbarous blood-letter drain her dry."

Richard Pole thoughtfully stroked his beard. "Well, she does look better. I gave her up for lost last night when I saw her. . . . I have sent a messenger to inform the king of his loss. The messenger says he will find a chaplain at Richmond Palace to break the news, no one else dares."

Joanna opened her mouth to volunteer her husband, then thought the better of it. Henry Tudor had married one Plantagenet and murdered most of the rest—he would not wish to be told of his son's demise by one of that clan. "A most auspicious choice, a chaplain," she said, forcing herself to lower her gaze and look humble. *There*. Another contraction, quite close to the last one. She had better get to her chambers before she dropped this child in front of all present. But the princess's translator had been found and he was roughly, with no consideration of Catherine of Aragon's grave illness, telling her that Prince Arthur was dead and she would be sent home as soon as she could travel. At this, Catherine paled and fell back, arms held beseechingly out to Joanna. There was no outcry from her, no self-pitying wails, only enormous gray eyes and those terrified hands, reaching for solidity, strength.

The pains were less than three minutes apart. Joanna sat on the bed and gathered Catherine against her. She pulled Maria into the embrace as though together they could erect a wall between Catherine and harsh reality.

When Catherine had drifted into an exhausted sleep, Joanna freed her skirts of the desperate little hands and rose unsteadily.

"Now then, we will talk about disrespectful women not even invited to this Court, women not wanted as ladies-in-waiting here or anywhere else in England," said Margaret Pole, waiting harpylike at the door.

"We cannot talk of such people at the moment unless you intend to deliver my baby yourself," Joanna snapped. Margaret blanched. It was difficult to duck under that harpy-arm (or was it a *wing*, Joanna wondered crossly), but it was nonetheless possible . . . across the armory, her water breaking, drenching her one good gown, staining it for all time. Up those stairs . . . Sweet Jesu, there were a thousand stairs this evening and all of them a mile high. Wet skirts dragging, Joanna finally reached the top and flung the door open.

Little Kathryn greeted her from the curtained bed. The child's face and hands were smeared with gore, the bedclothes likewise. Joanna screamed and lunged forward, labor pains forgotten. She seized her blue-eyed daughter under the arms, held her up. An object about the size of a man's fist dropped away from the child's skirts, and rolled across the floor until it struck a parquetry trunk.

Joanna gaped. Look though she may, she could find no wound on the child; Kathryn, in fact, thought that being held and shaken was great fun and cooed for more. No wound, no hurt place—her frantic gaze fell upon the round scarlet toy against the trunk. "What is that thing?" she demanded of Tansy.

The young maidservant crouched back against the window seat. "Wooden apple, Ladyship. Nice and soft for little Kat to teethe on."

It was nearly impossible to set the child down, to squat, groaning, and pick up the apple. But Joanna did so and flicked out her tongue to taste the faded wooden surface. "Beet dye. A harmless beet dye. She's sucked it all away on one side," she said. A moment later she pitched forward onto all fours, crying out with pain.

People burst into the room, having heard her screams. Margaret Pole led the brigade, calling for the castle's crusty old birthing sheets, yelling for Tansy to fetch this and that. "All men out of the room," she roared, and one of them thought to take the two-year-old girl on his shoulders. But he soon fell asleep by the armory fireplace.

The sound of sobbing from behind a nearby door drew her away. Crying people liked little girls, it seemed to Kathryn Chase; Tansy and her mother always hugged her while they wept. So perhaps there was someone behind that opened door who would hold her.

She toddled through the narrow opening and surveyed the room. Two exhausted young women lay willy-nilly on the hearth, softly snoring. The crying was not from them, then. The bed, perhaps. A very high bed with all its velvet drapes drawn shut to keep out the cold. It took a footstool to reach it and climb inside, but the child did.

Kathryn landed on the amazed princess. "I Kathryn!" the little girl announced, and flung her arms around the widowed bride's neck.

"I Cat'rin," Catherine of Aragon echoed. The child's eyes were violently blue, like a field of cornflowers in bloom—that nice English lady who had been here had the same eyes. This was her daughter, then, and the cries echoing through Ludlow Castle must have come from that woman, laboring to bring forth the other child she was so large with.

"You stay here with me," Catherine of Aragon said, tucking Kathryn Chase in between her and Maria de Salinas. The child spoke no Spanish nor did she understand it, but she knew a warm berth and kind voice, so she promptly, comfortably, fell asleep.

Catherine of Aragon continued weeping softly. There would be no child like this for her and Arthur, he had never lain with her as a husband did. Every laundress at Ludlow knew it was a marriage in name only. Her sweet Arthur gone . . . no children, no child of her own . . . back to Castile and León in disgrace, no child, no husband . . . The crown of all England was her least concern; she could never expect to wear it now that Arthur—*oh, Arthur!*

In the teeming courtyard amidst horses, hounds, and hawkers with various wares, a carpenter stood carelessly banging a coffin together. The receipt was marked *For Owain Tyddier*, dead Prince Arthur having been originally named for that wild Welsh great-grandfather who founded the Tudor dynasty by loving a queen he could never marry.

"My Lord Salisbury, are you certain you do not want a second box just in case the Spanish girl dies?" the carpenter asked, pausing a moment with hammer poised in midair.

Richard Pole shuddered and crossed himself. "I pray not," he said.

2

Prince Arthur's funeral procession began on the twenty-third of April, called by all involved "the worst day of the year." Wind blew alternate torrents of rain and snow, first northwest, then south, sawing across swearing riders and skittering horses.

Lord Hal Chase sat with the other riders, refusing to wave good-bye to his wife. Joanna did not mind, her attention being turned to a more important matter. She had her daughter's future to think of and so held little Kathryn up to wave good-bye to the Spanish princess. Catherine of Aragon, in her mule-borne litter, cried out, begging her gentlemen-at-arms to hand her out into the dreadful weather. Disapproving, they signaled Joanna and Kathryn forward instead.

"She very to grateful to you," said the interpreter as they neared. "She say Arthur is very fine name for your new son and she pleased you named little girl for her upon first hearing of marriage negotiations two years ago."

That was a blatant lie but Joanna saw no reason not to take advantage of the coincidence in names. She curtsied very low and kissed Catherine's hand. "You tell her that I am so pleased she stood as godmother to my son, it is too great an honor for me to ever fully repay. But in an effort to thank her, my daughter is hers. Tell her that. Whether she returns to Spain or marries elsewhere, my daughter will come to her in a few years as a maid of honor."

The princess, he said, agreed. The women embraced, then the mules bore the litter away. "Send your child to Spain! As well as to the wilds of Africa," Margaret Pole called out disapprovingly from her own, finer litter, carried by better-bred mules. "You will never get back to Court by snuggling up to a Spaniard about to be sent home!"

"Oh, I do not know," Joanna said wickedly. "If they will take you back, they will accept *anyone* at Court!" She snatched up Kathryn and took her into the round Norman chapel where Prince Arthur's heart had been buried. "We are going to pray for guidance," she told the child. Kathryn obediently knelt, bright blue eyes squeezed shut, head in its white coif bowed. It was dark, there were no candles, but she obeyed her mother's commands even in this frightening place.

Look at her, Joanna thought proudly. *She is a model child, she knows how to follow orders. If I can get her into Court—any Court, even a Spanish one—she will make a good marriage. The princess is already fond of her. . . .*

Next year Kathryn would be old enough to start sewing, by age four embroidering and reading Greek. By six she could be sending Catherine of Aragon pillowcases she had embroidered for her, perhaps night-coifs or tapestry book-covers for prayer books. The Spanish girl was very religious, it might pay to have Kathryn learn some Spanish. Drill her in Latin, teach her prayers, hymns. Then perhaps the princess would keep her word to take Kathryn into her household at court.

The dank walls sweated and stank about her. Joanna knelt before the altar, hands clasped so tightly in prayer that her cheap rings bit into her flesh. *Guide me,* she pleaded. *Send me a sign, give me knowledge how best to escape this genteel poverty of my husband's.*

Henry Tudor had seized all Lord Hal Chase's lands upon taking the crown; Hal had spent ten years in the Tower before release. Joanna cursed her father for marrying her to the man. He was so unambitious, so content to drift through life robbed of all life's old glories. Well, she was not. She remembered the last years of Plantagenet glitter and gorgeousness, the excessively masculine Edward Fourth dying unexpectedly before his queen could reach him. Beautiful, treacherous Elizabeth Woodville—everyone said she was a witch. Elizabeth's children by Edward were then bastardized because Edward had married her after secretly betrothing himself to another woman as means of entry to her bed. When the news leaked out at his death, the princes and princesses were reduced to Hal Chase's status—bastards. Richard the Third took the throne then, for two brief years before Henry Tudor came. . . .

Joanna shuddered. She had met Henry Tudor only once, when she had been called to Court to see her father released from the Tower. Amazing that Henry had allowed her father out, for he had fought at the side of his own father, Jack of Norfolk. Also amazing that Henry had let him live and now hold office. *Eh, there will always be a place at Court for a Howard,* her father had said modestly. And Joanna had cried out, *But not for me! You had to marry me to a Plantagenet bastard, and now I shall never be allowed into that glittering circle! I will spend the rest of my life banished in wretched Wales!*

Inspiration struck her with an almost physical blow. Joanna gasped, opened her eyes. She craned her neck to see if Kathryn had bumped her, but the little girl still knelt where she had been told to, chubby baby-hands clasped.

Idea. Heaven-birthed inspiration. Realization that she had heard fleeting bits of gossip at Ludlow and could now piece them together. Ferdinand had not paid all of the Princess Catherine's dowery. If she was sent home to Spain, Henry Tudor would never receive it. And Henry Tudor loved money more than God, the crown, or a piddling thing like his family. Henry would no more give up sixty thousand crowns than a she-wolf surrender her cubs to the hunter. Therefore Catherine of Aragon would remain in England until King Henry had the rest of the dowery.

Meanwhile, he had another brat. A son named Henry, still far too young to marry. What was he, ten? Eleven? Give him five years and he could marry Princess Catherine, gain the dowery, and maintain the political alliance between countries. It should not be difficult to keep Catherine busy at court, cooling her valuable heels for another five years. Of course she was six or more years older than young Prince Harry, but no matter. When a crown hung in the balance, such things did not matter.

Mary, Mother of God, make the Spaniard Queen of England, Joanna prayed passionately. *Make her queen and my next daughter will be named for you and sent to a convent at birth. My next son goes for the priesthood, too. But you cannot have Kathryn or Arthur, they will be the wedges I drive into the unfriendly wall of Court.*

To gain a foothold at Court was to have the world spread before oneself. If a woman embroidered with the queen, gossiped with her, tucked her into bed at night, then it was easy to whisper political recommendations in the royal ear. Easy to accept bribes, gifts of land and gold from lords and ladies desperate to gain an audience with the queen for this or that. Knighthoods . . . the advancements of women from public Presence Chamber to the so-intimate Privy Chamber . . . Titles for sale, and noble families anxious to have their boys set to work in a king's treasury or law chambers.

Grasping, tenacious, cold-blooded Henry Tudor took no mistresses, had no bastards. But he would not live forever, perhaps his son would be friendlier. And she would have a daughter of the proper age by then, perhaps several daughters. That shy little Spanish princess already liked her and Kathryn, it would be so easy to worm their way into Catherine's household.

Young kings were always lusty; when old Henry Tudor died Young King Harry would take note of handsome ladies-in-waiting, grant their parents estates, titles. Old Henry himself had married a Plantagenet; might not a grandson of his one day do the same? There could at least be bastards, kings often preferred their natural children to their legitimate heirs.

Kathryn with her Courtenay, Howard, and Plantagenet blood—might not blue-eyed Kathryn win a prince's or king's approval some day?

Joanna swooped down on her daughter, seized her, and tossed her high in the air. There were no squeals of terror or even surprise from the little girl, she only smiled, watched her mother catch her and hold her close. "You are going to be a lady-in-waiting to the next queen of England, little Kat. What do you think of that?"

"Gaw bless Mama," the child agreed.

Joanna laughed, hugged Kathryn even tighter. "God bless your mama indeed; she is going to make of you a very great lady. Come along, let us write my father for all the latest gossip concerning the Spaniard's dowery. In return I shall tell him that the marriage was never consummated and Princess Catherine is therefore free to marry little Harry Tudor. We shall be subtle, you and I, we shall not say this outright, but through many months of insinuations so Father thinks it his own doing. Men never like to be told we are cleverer and more treacherous than they are—"

With the exception of Henry Tudor, she thought, suddenly sobered.

"We will get through this together," Elizabeth of York, queen of England, told her husband upon news of Arthur's death. "God willing, we are strong enough to bear up under such sorrow and young enough to make more children."

And so they made another and she died of it ten months after Arthur's death. The infant outlived her a scant few days.

A widower now with only one precious son and two mere daughters, Henry Tudor found himself with much to think about. Within a month of the queen's death he was heard to ask his Councillors, "Why return the Spaniard if her marriage to my son was truly unconsummated? We have not yet wrung all her dower lands and monies from wily old Ferdinand; perhaps it would be better if this rich marital prize joined with me, rather than moving on to France or the Netherlands. Yes, I think I should marry my daughter-in-law. What say you?"

Catherine fainted when Doña Alvira told her the news. Upon recovery she at once wrote her formidable mother Isabella, who dispatched a swift ship to take the princess home. "By God, she will to home and I shall never wrest her monies from Ferdinand!" Henry Tudor lamented. "If only I had someone reliable to place in her meager household, someone who would report to me what goes on in that girl's head!"

Richard Pole, stroking his short-clipped beard, murmured, "My wife's cousin, Your Grace."

Bony, parsimonious King Henry stopped his pacing to cough wrackingly. "Which Plantagenet traitor do you dare speak to me of?"

"Hal Chase is married to Joanna, the daughter of Tom Howard here—."

Thomas Howard the Elder groaned and put his head in his hands.

"Joanna Chase, that evil-tongued scold!" Henry burst out. "What has she to do with this?" He would never forget how insolent she had been when he released Howard from the Tower—as if marrying a dead king's bastard gave her some pretense at royalty! He glowered at Howard, who sank a little lower on his bench.

Richard Pole said, "She befriended the Spaniard. Saved her life, Your Grace, and her children were named for the prince and princess of Wales. She is desperate to return to Court, so I am certain she would, shall we call it, 'report' on the inner workings of the Spanish household if we put her in it. Besides, she is presently with her sister, Elizabeth, who married Thomas Boleyn. Joanna finds the Boleyns and their Hever Castle deadly dull."

King Henry tightened the belt of his floor-length coat with its shawl collar and squirrel-lined, turned-back sleeves. He coughed again. "I need that dowery from Spain and I am not like to get it with the girl a virgin widow. I could marry her myself, but a queen costs something to maintain—you would be surprised at the money I save with my wife dead."

Pole did not shudder, though he greatly desired to. In the

long, thought-filled silence that followed, Howard shifted his bench away from the wall. Benches—and very low ones at that—were the only seating allowed in a king's presence. *As if,* he thought coldly, *Howard blood were not bluer than that of this upstart Welshman who is too niggardly to light fires and wear ermine as a king ought*. "Your Majesty," he began gently, with a tact few other Howards possessed. "The people have already heard rumors that you intend to marry the princess. They regard it as . . . unseemly. But a treaty asking her hand for young Prince Harry would keep her here, although the treaty could be broken later at some convenient time."

"Treaties cost money. I should have to send special ambassadors to Spain, outfit a ship," Henry Tudor protested. "Well . . . I suppose I could send the ambassadors on a passenger vessel and keep it down to, say, three emissaries and servants they themselves shall pay for. Treaties are indeed expensive." He brightened slightly. "But, oh, how my wealth shall increase with the payment of that dowery! Indeed, Howard, let us dangle my son as a marital prize before old Ferdinand, lure him into sending the monies and land grants. When we gain all that and then break the treaty it may mean war, but . . . And by all means, get that Spanish girl out of Richmond and into her own household at her own expense. I refuse to pour money into her coffers while her father deals with me in so miserly a fashion. And Howard, tell your bitch-faced, sword-tongued daughter that I would not have her underfoot for all the gold in Christendom. But she may be useful to me if she joins the Spanish household at her own expense and keeps me informed of certain matters. It is not a return to Court, but it is a step up from the Welsh Marches; I think she possesses sense enough to see it in that light."

Both men knew a dismissal when they heard it approaching. Pole and Howard came creaking up off their benches and bowed low with many subtle flourishes. "Oh, and, Howard," the king continued, eyes narrowing, "tell Joanna that she is not to marry off her Plantagenet brats without the express permission of the Crown. After all, they will be first cousin to a king of England when my Harry sits on the throne."

Beads of perspiration started up on Thomas Howard's forehead despite the chill of the king's council chambers. He bowed very low and backed from the room.

Joanna, he knew, would be only too glad to spy on Catherine of Aragon.

* * *

A papal dispensation was required before Prince Harry could be betrothed to Princess Catherine. Henry Tudor and Ferdinand of León, in perfect agreement for once, decided that the word of an eighteen-year-old girl could not be relied upon, and so phrased the document that even if Arthur had consummated the marriage, Catherine would still be free to marry Arthur's brother, Prince Harry.

In later years, amidst the most famous divorce trial of all time, no one remembered the existence of this document to bring it to light.

Henry Tudor, meanwhile, was not content to leave the fate of this hard-earned nation to one personable young son and two contrary daughters. There was that splendid Scottish match for Margaret, and many offers for little Mary so far, but there should always be a Duke of Richmond to back up the prince of Wales in case of—oh, accident, disease, any number of things that might befall a twelve-year-old boy.

He himself was still young enough to remarry and beget a duke of Richmond, he announced to his council, and promptly cast his eye on Catherine of Aragon's freshly widowed sister, Juana. Thomas Howard the Elder spent days plucking up the nerve to murmur, "But, Your Grace, that time she and her husband visited England, did she not strike you as a bit . . . *odd*?" Henry said he had not noticed. Howard continued at a faster clip. "Servants report that she talked to herself and fell into shrieking rages if her husband so much as glanced at another woman. In Spain they call her Juana the Mad and say that she carts her husband's embalmed body about in a box, takes it wherever she goes. Lifts the lid, kisses him, and sleeps atop the box at night."

He hated being the one to always break bad news to the king; it seemed to him no way to win back the Howard lands and ducal title lost at Bosworth Field. But the other Council members pushed him into it, for with Richard Pole now dead, he was the only one who could so approach the king.

Henry Tudor pulled at his long jaw. "Eh, Howard, you dither. Being mad won't prevent Juana from breeding. As long as she gives me more sons to back up Harry, I shall not care if she babbles like an ape and bays like a hound. She is for sons, not companionship."

Prince Harry, chubby, cherubic-looking, and an excellent eavesdropper, listened at the keyhole and thought that his father spoke uncommon good sense.

To reach the prince's chambers one first had to pass through the king's own rooms. *The King is so protective of his heir,* the Court said, or else, *He does not want the boy corrupted by outsiders.* The truth of it was that Henry considered his son too young to sit in on meetings but not too young to learn the inner workings of a reign through eavesdropping.

The boy settled back on his heels, wondering if he would hear more of interest. But for several minutes there was only a low murmuring from his father, interspersed with much dry, raspy coughing that Catherine of Aragon would have recognized and been alarmed at.

Harry had never listened at the door while his mother yet lived. He remembered her as pretty, high-strung, and totally ineffectual, and he knew his father had married her only to strengthen his own feeble claim on the throne. It never occurred to him to wonder why a woman who had been the spoiled darling of a generous monarch would agree to marry the coldest, tightest-fisted man in England. *Oh, well, she probably wanted to be queen. Women always do,* Harry thought with a shrug. Women were chattels and ornaments to men of the still-young Tudor Court, and he took it for granted that he would one day be married off to some wretched German or French broodmare with jowls and rolls of fat.

Not that he wanted such a wife. No, what Harry Tudor wanted was something far different. Some shy creature, someone auburn-and-ivory who would defer to him, modestly avert her gaze in his presence. No one did that to him that he was aware of, for between his father and formidable grandmother—he thought of Margaret Beaufort Tudor as *The Dragon*—he was utterly sheltered.

Auburn and ivory . . . Harry sighed to himself. He had been in love with Catherine of Aragon since he had, at age ten, danced at her wedding. She was just as pretty now as then, still wearing the same golden brocade gown. He wondered why she rarely wore anything else; no one told him that in six years she had not been able to afford making a new gown. While his mother yet lived, she would take him to the princess's grim Durham House with her ladies—the only time he had been much in the company of women—and he had not forgotten picnicking on the riverbank with the princess.

The boy sighed to himself. One week he was betrothed to Catherine, the next it was called off. His father yanked him around like a weathervane and he was tired of it. Tired of The Dragon, too. Sweet Jesu, if his father should die while Harry was a boy, The Dragon would be Regent and have more power over him than ever! She would have the power of the king as she had always craved. Four marriages and only the one child, for King Henry had been born while she was hardly more than thirteen, a child not yet fit to bear children of her own. All of her passion and ambition had gone into that one son, and he had repaid it by letting her walk next to him in the coronation parade while his Plantagenet wife, Elizabeth of York, trailed far behind, forgotten in the rush.

Harry stood and strode over to pick up the age-spotted mirror at the bedside. He was young and healthy; maybe Father and The Dragon would die soon so he could have it all. *I am growing,* he thought, pleased with his reflection. Losing some of that annoying puppy fat that had plagued him so long. Tennis, horseback riding, hunting, and the tiltyard had begun rewarding him with a new, finer, harder figure. Girls were beginning to regard him differently, he was sure of it. Some day, when he was king, when he was slim and elegant, he would dress in gold and white, ride up to Durham House. *She* would be waiting, very pretty and flustered as he swept his plumed hat off and bowed low. *Madam,* he would say—here he allowed himself the luxury of imagining his adult voice as deep, resonant—*Madam, will you do me the most singular honor of becoming my wife now and forever?*

She would agree. Then, even before the wedding, they would hold hands and run off to do whatever lovers did in haystacks behind houses. They would make many more sons than his father ever had, every last one of them named Harry like himself.

Puffed with pleasure at the notion, he stuck his chest out, *I shall outdo that miserly prig in every way,* he thought. *I am already a far better horseman than he, for Father has no sense of sports whatsoever. I am clever, more graceful; I shall be handsomer.* All of his shirts would be of the finest snow-white linen, his doublets of silken velvet. Ermine, too, not moth-eaten squirrel. Cloth of gold instead of threadbare wool. And far more sons than that thin-haired, bloodless old goat had ever gotten on Harry's repulsed mother.

He laughed slowly and deliberately into the mirror without making a sound. *They are very good teeth. The finest teeth I have ever seen,* he told himself, practicing expressions of merriment for the benefit of his future subjects.

3

Durham House, London
22 April 1509

Kathryn Chase took the crumpled letter from her wadded-up handkerchief one more time. She scanned each hastily scrawled line, hoping against hope that she had been mistaken, that it would not read the same this time. But there it was, from her mother to the king—every last intimate detail of the princess's private life, of conversations between Catherine of Aragon and her ambassador.

She had not meant to read the letter. Catherine of Aragon had asked her for more black silk thread, and Kathryn knew her mother kept several skeins in her willow basket. So she had gone rummaging amidst the yarns and threads in the rotting linen lining, and there, between linen and willow, felt the parchment. It seemed so totally unlike her outspoken mother to hide anything that Kathryn presumed the letter had slipped down there by accident and shook the basket out to retrieve it.

Now she knew: her mother was spying on the princess. Had it been anyone but her own mother she would have rushed to Catherine's side with the proof. Split loyalties tugged her to and fro; love for Joanna warred with love for Catherine and the knowledge that, should her mother be sent from Durham, Kathryn would probably have to accompany her. Not for anything would she leave the princess—no, not even to go to her wonderful Aunt Elizabeth and her children, Kathryn's Boleyn cousins. Anne was too little to be much fun, but Mary was charming and George—well, every time she saw George he incited her to some mischief, though she was the elder of the two. On her last visit to Blickling Hall and Hever Castle he had persuaded her to help him dye the household linen with woad, and there were half a dozen blue sheets before they were caught.

Of course, she would never dream of doing such a thing again. She was nine years old now, not a frivolous child of seven. Too, there lingered the memory of a whipping with a birch wand . . . *I will never marry you to your cousin George now, the Boleyns think you are a troublemaker*, Joanna had shouted, shaking her.

She had been sent back to her father. Her brother Arthur had joined his Howard cousins at Kenninghall, while their younger sister Mary went to a convent in Kent. The convent, Joanna told Kathryn, was because of a deal she had struck with God's mother.

Kathryn grimaced, remembering. That was just like her mother, to bargain like a fishwife with the Virgin Mary.

She took the note to a hedge-shrouded corner of the courtyard, folded it flat, and shoved it down the front of her too-tight bodice. The motion forced her to glance down at her gown, seeing it as it was—twenty years out of date, with a too high waistline and tight sleeves that came clear down to her knuckles. *Goblet-cuff sleeves*, Joanna had called them, letting out the last of the seams six months ago. *From my girlhood.*

It was uncomfortably tight these days. Kathryn was already so tall that her ankles showed, as did the creased places where the hem had been let down five times. Other children mocked her old-fashioned dress. *Do not talk to me of your friends' laughter, we are all poor in this God-cursèd house!* her mother had cried out one afternoon. *I want to have a funnel-sleeved new overgown, or anything else that has not been let out, taken in, mended, patched, pressed half to death! The princess herself has not had a new gown since she arrived in England eight years ago; why should you think yourself any better than she?*

And yet her mother was betraying the princess's confidences to the king. Odd that she would do so after vigorously holding up Catherine of Aragon as a role model. It astonished Kathryn that her mother could be so like the Roman god Janus, possessing two faces, each wearing a different expression and contradicting the other.

She thought of the letter again, thought of the hateful, horrible bodice covering it. Divided loyalties—other children and even servants mocking her gown—the king, the letter—she hated her dress, wanted to burn it, burn it and the letter—*Doux Jesu,* she could not even turn to her father for advice. She had used fabric meant for two new shifts to make him a finely pleated shirt with broad bands of fashionable black embroidery. It had taken her ten months to make that shirt, and here her one white shift was in tatters. . . . He had not even written to thank her. She had not seen him in over a year, at which time they had started past each other like strangers, neither recognizing the other. Like any normal eight-year-old girl she had already learned Latin, Greek, and a smattering of French; a year later her black embroidery was better than any but the princess's. And her father had patted her on the head like a terrier, given her a baby's wooden whistle, and gone his way without mentioning the shirt.

No, she could not turn to Hal Chase for assistance. Nor was there anyone in the quarrelsome Durham household she could trust. Maria de Salinas, surely, but Catherine mattered so greatly to Maria that Joanna would be instantly flung out like a chamberpot's contents into the streets.

Kathryn was not old enough to realize that the constant bickering at Durham House was due to overripe virginity. The only married women were Joanna and Doña Alvira, neither of whom slept with her husband any more. All the others had entered Catherine's service as marriageable-age virgins, eagerly awaiting this husband or that. But the household was too poor to provide doweries; Maria had already lost a splendid match for lack of money. Joanna and Doña Alvira, envious of youth and past-its-prime-for-plucking virtue—or perhaps remembering those too-few nights of marital passion now sorely missed—rode brutal herd on the maids of honor.

So the household simmered. There were no physical outlets, for Catherine could not afford horses for sight-seeing and hunting, or even a bowling green or tennis court. Even had any of the women been invited to Court functions, they could not go, on account of being so shabbily dressed. So simple occurrences like dropped pin-boxes and borrowed combs led to screeching fits, even blows. No outlet for bursting energy, no hunting, dancing, making love; there was only the ceaseless embroidering and mending, remaking gown after gown, longing after the fashionable funnel sleeves and gable-shaped headdresses one saw on women passing in the street.

The prince must marry Catherine or we shall all go on like this forever—snapping at our dearest friends, pacing our bedchambers like lions in a menagerie, Kathryn thought.

Two years ago the household had still been whispering that the dowery would save them all. Then sixty-five thousand crowns of it was paid and Henry Tudor hardly gave the princess a crumb. She had sold her plate,* jewelry, clothing, and horses in order to remain in England and show good faith in the betrothal with Prince Harry. Her ladies, cooks, and laundress had not been paid in years. So they all waited,

*gold and silver dishes

hoping against common sense that the marriage would happen, that one day a rider would race to the house and—

Kathryn squeezed her intensely blue eyes shut with the fantasy of the princess's marriage. But the string of images became so real that she could actually hear hoofbeats—

You fool, she scolded herself, opening her eyes. There really *was* a rider approaching; she could see the dust he was kicking up on the parched road. Oh, tut, just a messenger from Court to tell them the betrothal was off again, no doubt. Everyone knew the king was currently courting one of Catherine's buxom young Spanish nieces. If he succeeded, Catherine and her ladies would be sent back to Castile on the next fishing vessel. *A good thing I can speak some Spanish,* Kathryn thought, and raced across the courtyard into the house. She did not want to be the last one to hear the bad news.

A wooden door flew open somewhere as she entered. She could hear it bruise the poorly paneled wall. A boy was crying out for Catherine of Aragon in English, and as she still spoke precious little of that language, he would be a long time finding her.

Kathryn rounded a corner and saw him then—a towheaded boy two or three years her senior. "In the Great Hall," Kathryn said politely and pointed. He made as though to doff his hat but was running too fast to actually do so. Sweet Jesu, something really *was* wrong, she decided, and picked up her skirts to run after him.

He was already on one knee before the princess, panting, as she arrived. "Yes," Maria de Salinas was repeating to the pale-skinned Catherine in Spanish, "he says the king had been spitting blood and coughing like your husband Arthur, and that it much worsened this season."

At mention of the dead prince all present crossed themselves, even the young messenger. He caught Kathryn watching him and winked conspiratorially. "Maria," Joanna Chase said impatiently, "tell her the rest. Tell her that he says the king is dead!"

Henry Tudor, dead? That meant young Prince Harry was on the throne now. That also meant—*Saints and angels be thanked,* Kathryn thought rapturously—that Joanna's letter to the old king could be burned and forgotten now.

"Betrothal? And betrothal?" Catherine asked in English when Maria had told her of the king's death. "Betrothal, yea or nay?"

The boy hung his handsome head. It was being said at

Richmond that before the old king was cold, the new king would take a Hapsburg bride. The Dragon, Margaret Beaufort, had her heart set on it. And as Henry Tudor had, with his dying breath, bequeathed the regency and therefore all of England to her, the underage king would be hard put to cross her. There remained two months before young Harry achieved his majority, but the old harridan would no doubt give him merry Hell should he try to cross her in that time. So the messenger hung his head, chewed his lip. Said nothing.

A thudding of many hooves along the riverbank. Riders were all but on the front steps suddenly, shouting, "The king approaches, prepare! The king approaches!"

Every woman in Durham House froze. A moment later Kathryn sucked her breath in and thought to tug at her mother's wrist. "Mother, your headdress is newer than the princess's. Could she wear it?"

The spell of amazement broke. "I have pressed your best black wool velvet gown," Maria was saying to Catherine of Aragon. "Come along, we will put you in it."

"She can have my silver girdle!" a girl cried.

"And my false pearls, they look very real! And Joanna's headdress and—"

Catherine of Aragon swayed slightly. At once her women seized her, rushed her through room after adjoining room to her own chamber. There, Kathryn knew, they would pinch her cheeks until pink, splash rose water on her, and dress her in the best of their pathetic assembled finery. Kathryn glanced over her shoulder and saw the boy watching her. "Why do you not rush to aid them?" he inquired.

"I am the smallest and youngest. In a panic such as this they all tread on me and swear that any mishap is my fault. I shall do better to avoid the crush, I would only be in the way."

The other messengers were now in the courtyard, their horses trampling the princess's meager roses and pinks. "The king is coming by river! The king draws near!"

Kathryn considered the fact that two separate messengers had arrived within minutes of each other. She cocked an eyebrow at the boy, asked, "If they come from the king, then who sent *you*?"

"Your grandfather Thomas Howard. You and I are related; Howard is my grandfather's . . . let me think . . . cousin's cousin, or something similar. At any rate, he thought the princess should know what had happened."

She adjusted her plain linen coif, tied with strings under

her chin. How she longed for a gable headdress, or a flat German thing like he wore, very saucily dipping over one eye. "I am Kathryn Chase, as you already seem to know," she announced solemnly.

"I am Edmund Howard. What is that screen over there? Let us hide behind it and listen. The king shall have to walk past it to enter."

He caught her by the hand and dragged her into the hiding place. Later she would realize there was something odd about spying on a scene they could have witnessed openly, but for now all she could think was that she had not talked to a boy in ever-so-long, and he was almost as much fun as George Boleyn.

They were scarcely crouched behind the pierced-work wooden screen when the doors banged open. Boys blew trumpets and hautbois; a herald bellowed the name and many titles of the new king. A party of lushly dressed men burst into the Great Hall, making Kathryn gasp to herself. She had never seen such clothes, such fabrics: tawny taffetas, lush crimson-on-crimson damasks, silks, and embroidered linens with blackwork that far eclipsed her own. *Ermine.* She had only read about ermine until today. Jeweled buttons, massive golden chains of office across padded shoulders, and broad, self-assured chests—these were not men, but gods, and the king, the godliest.

He entered last. He had flung away the floor-length robes of his father's reign and wore a short-skirted doublet showing the length of his muscular thighs. *All in gold and white like an altar-side angel of enameled wood,* Kathryn thought, seeing afternoon sunlight gleam on the metallic threads in his doublet and ermine-lined coat. The diamonds, the pearls on the cunning flat German cap . . . the longish hair, shining like new copper . . . "He is Apollo," she whispered, and beside her Edmund Howard chuckled.

"You had best learn not to speak your opinion aloud. No one at Court ever does. Here comes Catherine of Aragon," he warned her. The new king smiled broadly, flashing perfect, pearly teeth at the approaching princess.

"Do you think we shall all go to Court?" Kathryn whispered.

"Little goose, do you think he has come here in his finest to say that he will *not* wed her? You are still a baby, you have no sense at all!"

Catherine of Aragon was very nearly beautiful this afternoon. The black gown turned her skin white as milk, made her pale auburn hair seem to blaze. The borrowed silver girdle showed off a tiny waist, false pearls exhibited her slender throat. "Your Grace," she said, curtseying low.

Young Harry Tudor caught her hands, pulled her upright. "Nay, madam, it is I who should be bowing and scraping. Catherine—Sweetheart—will you do me the most singular honor of becoming my wife now and forever?"

Maria had to translate. All color left the princess at a rush. She swayed, one hand to her bodice-front, then pink flooded her cheeks. "*Si, si!* Yes, Your Grace—oh, *si*!"

Around them, courtiers and ladies-in-waiting burst into cheers. Kathryn rocked back on her heels, ecstatic. This was a blessed moment, she would always remember it, she told herself. An afternoon of such warmth and sunshine—

Edmund Howard shattered it. "Eh," he said sarcastically. "The king asked her to be his wife 'now and forever.' " Here he mimicked the king's voice a moment before continuing. "Huh, even a king should know nothing lasts forever."

Shadows across the sun, a sudden cold creeping into her bones. Kathryn cried out, "But you're wrong! This marriage *will* last forever!"

"Men change their minds," he said loftily, "and what is the king but a man? You place too much faith in human constancy. Ah, well. Court will cure you of your innocence. It will cure Catherine of Aragon, too."

No, Kathryn thought, viewing the princess' rapturous face. *No, nothing will ever rob my lady of her glow.*

But a child growing up at Hever Castle would one day do just that.

4

All seemed fairy tales and gilded enchantment in the first years of the new reign; to the end of her days Kathryn would always wonder when the gold leaf first tarnished and began to peel, showing cheap brass beneath.

But there were no such thoughts now. There was only the awareness that all England seemed to have fallen in love with the royal couple, even as Henry and Catherine fell in love with each other. They might have been any lovers learning to unfold before the other's adoration, not merely a king and queen hoping to further a dynasty through their lovemaking.

Yet by the time Catherine of Aragon was far gone in her first pregnancy, Henry had taken a mistress. The royal daughter was born dead, and for a while Catherine's life was despaired of. But she was young and determined, so soon recovered. Another year, another mistress, another dead child. And still Henry rushed to her side with the first fruits and flowers of spring, and lay in bed with her well into the morning, laughing, talking, making love, bringing her each tidbit of Court gossip and international intrigue with as much delight as if he had personally caused it for her benefit.

He consulted her on matters of State, sought her advice on his attire, deportment, the handling of the King's Council. The Dragon had long since sickened and died, satisfied that her seed now sat on the throne of England securely, so there were no disapproving old voices to condemn the young king's sumptuous food and garb, the late hours and merriment. Catherine alone could check his extravagances, and yet she chose not to, doting on him too much to deny him anything.

The bond between king and six-years-older queen deepened, for as 1510 drew to a close she was again heavily pregnant. Seers and astrologers hastened to assure the king of a son while England prayed for a safe delivery.

Joanna Howard Chase was alone in clucking her tongue and saying, "Three pregnancies in under two years! She shall breed herself into an early grave trying to please that man!"

New Year's Day of 1511 Catherine was delivered of a lustily squalling son. He was immediately named Henry after his beaming father. London went wild. Such merriment was not to be seen for another twenty-six years, at which time the next Tudor son was born.

Kathryn leaned open-mouthed from a window, watching Londoners light bonfires in the streets and dance around them. Cannons were fired; all church bells in the city rang for hours on end. At dawn the king appeared on the lawn to announce an upcoming eve of feasting and revelry at Westminster, with free ale provided for all the crowd. There was such cheering and commotion upon his announcement that the prince woke, and seemed to bellow his approval, too.

Carpenters set to work on artificial bowers of trees. Seamstresses' needles flew over acres of green-and-white cloth, the Tudor colors. Embroideresses and goldsmiths worked together to produce hundreds of bullion *H*'s and *K*'s.

"A prince at last!" Kathryn exulted, helping lace her mother's gown the morning of the royal christening. She and Tansy were hindering more than helping each other, so she finally stepped back and let the maidservant finish the chore.

Joanna placed both hands over her abdomen and pushed in. "Mary Mother, this is the last gown I can still get into and I find it ugly! Ah, well, the wages of sin . . ." She did not seem at all disturbed by said wages and was in fact preening before the hand mirror her daughter held out to her.

Kathryn's horrified gaze fell to her mother's swelling stomach. "You have not seen Father in quite some time," she ventured.

Joanna yanked the mirror away from her, smiled into it, and picked at her teeth with a green stick dipped in salt for this purpose. "No, of course not. It is the king's child. There is no need to look thus, I am not so very old that men find me unattractive."

Kathryn opened her mouth, remembered Edmund Howard's admonition never to speak one's mind at Court, even to intimates, and shut it again. Her mother observed the effort. "Very good. You are becoming discreet. *And* very tall. You are nearly out of your new dress already. How grown-up you look, but you are only what, ten?"

"Eleven."

"Eleven and as tall as I am. Time to betrothe you to someone who needs good blood more than money, some Sir Nobody recently come into a minor fortune and anxious for acceptance at Court. You rather have your heart set on that toothy brat of my cousin's—what is his name? Edmund? You are too well born for him, but his father Adam has a London town house, a small estate in Surrey, and surely some gold. . . . Of course, I should prefer you marry my sister's boy George. His father is going places. The King made Thomas Boleyn a Knight of the Bath at the coronation, and they say he shall be Sheriff of Kent before this year is up. Still, he has no money and no breeding; his children will surpass him, coming as they do from my sister. Perhaps we should promise you to George Boleyn after all. But he is some three years younger than you and that will keep you from the bridal bed so long."

Kathryn bit her lip and handed Tansy her mother's new gable headdress. Joanna sat, holding the mirror to watch as Tansy and Kathryn parted her hair in the middle and smoothed it back into a black silk bag and pins. The striped hood went over this, though only an edge of it would show in the end; all was topped by the stiff, peaked headdress that critics unkindly said was shaped like a dog kennel. More pins, the strap in back to hold it in place . . . arrange the long black velvet tails . . . "Here. Look at yourself, not me," Joanna said when they were done. Kathryn glanced at herself disinterestedly. Same too-blue eyes, same snub nose, same old face and that damnable hair of no definite color. An ashy light brown or even dirty blonde, a color with no light or life of its own.

"You are tall as a grown woman and becoming pretty, despite the snub nose. Oh, well, it could be worse. You could have that dreadful Howard beak like the rest of us. If you would only learn to smile and make dimples, but you are so stark, so serious. So tall . . . you must learn to bring your age up in conversation with men or they may think you older and take liberties. . . . Are you still learning to dance?"

Kathryn handed the mirror back to her mother. "Oh, yes, two hours a day—" *to make up for those years at Durham House* hung unspoken in the air between them.

"Only six women are being chosen to dance at the Court revel. I shall approach the queen and see that you are one of them—if you can prove to her satisfaction and mine that you are indeed a dancer. I must say, you have extraordinary posture and carriage, you shall do well with the adult dancers."

Because she was Joanna and the queen adored her, she had her way about Kathryn joining the dance. Kathryn was so excited she could hardly eat or sleep once the news came. There were frantic four-hour dance sessions with the other five young women, trying to make up for what she had missed, and rushed meetings with seamstresses. All the dancers were to wear old fashioned parti-colored gowns, white down one side, green on the other. Each gown was square necked and funnel sleeved, with sweeping skirts; bullion *H*'s and *K*'s were scattered here and there. Instead of gable headdresses there were splendid masks of gilded papier mâché, covering the upper face; Kathryn's mask was of a lioness, with her as yet unmet male partner's a lion. All too soon it was the night of the masque.

When she had finished dressing with Tansy's aid, her mother applied red Spanish liquor to Kathryn's lips, then wiped most of it off so that only a blush remained. "There. I want to see you betrothed, not ravished. Your hair reaches the small of your back, did you know? Of course, it's such a mousey color . . ." Here Joanna vigorously blew her nose on the cutwork handkerchief she had used to blot Kathryn's lip paint. "You are so tall and so pretty, you shall make me a grandmother in very little time. Dowery or no, men are going to seek you out. But remember: Not at this age and not without your marriage lines in your hand. Do not behave like a trollop."

"I will remember that," Kathryn promised, trying not to stare at her mother's expanding waistline.

Westminster was in a great uproar as Kathryn arrived. She squeezed onto a beer wagon with the five other female dancers, for there was no other mode of transport left at this late hour. Costumes were wrinkled, masks were jostled. Tempers flared until Maria de Salinas soothed everyone with her soft, accented English, laughingly pointing out that even the horses were in green and white with gold initials all over them. "The king is very proud of our mistress and their son," she said, and all of the women felt as pleased as if they had personally caused the child to be a boy.

Footmen handed them down off the barrels, and led them by torchlight to an antechamber off the White Hall. An octagonal bower of artificial trees awaited them, pretty golden things with green damask leaves; the six masked men waiting onboard the wheeled "forest" helped them up into it. Kathryn found her lion-masked partner drunk and very spritely; the third time he pinched her she dented his mask with her fist. The blow rocked him back on his duck-billed slippers while everyone held their breath for fear of retaliation. Then a tall man in a stag's mask burst out laughing and the others, even Kathryn's partner, joined in.

The laughter, conversation, and music in the White Hall came to an abrupt halt. There was a fanfare of hautbois and trumpets, then velvet curtains were thrust back from the antechamber. Henry Tudor stood framed in the doorway, long and elegant in cloth of silver and emerald green velvet. "See what I bring you, my courtiers and ladies!" he shouted, picking up a ribbon attached to the "forest" and starting forward. The servants beneath the wheeled platform struggled to keep up, though to the amazed onlookers it seemed the king drew the whole display after him with one hand. Applause rocked the candle-lit hall.

The king halted in mid-room, bowed, and returned to his seat on the dais with Catherine of Aragon. At that all six women pressed fingertips to those of their green-and-white-clad partners and started down the small steps. Lutes, vielles, and rebecs plucked a sweet, slow tune that speeded as the dancers finished their procession of the hall and began to form a wheel. They circled as wind instruments joined the stringed ones, musicians heartily puffing into crumhorns, sackbuts, and shawns. The tune became quicker, merrier, almost reckless; onlookers stamped their feet in time, shouted for more.

The twelve dancers had not been instructed beyond those first two dances. In confusion they repeated the last set of movements, then the musicians segued into a lively bransle. This was a common dance known by all present: step, kick, jump, with the women being half lifted into the air and passed to the next man in time for the following step. *One-two-three, one-two-three,* Kathryn chanted to herself. But instead of a half-lift, her drunken partner seized her by the waist and flung her high.

The intoxicated man in the lion's mask stumbled, fell flat beneath her as she started down. Kathryn knew a moment of petrifying fear, then strong, sure hands caught her. The bransle continued. She glimpsed pale blue eyes behind the stag mask that had saved her; eyes so light-colored that they made her think of milk in a blue glass goblet. He grinned conspiratorially at her, showing crooked front teeth; she liked him the better for that flaw.

Lords and ladies sprang to join the dance. King Henry himself descended the dais stairs, trying to tug the queen with him. But it was too soon after childbirth for Catherine of Aragon to dance, so she laughingly signaled him on without her. He turned in a thrice, caught Joanna Chase by the waist, and dragged her in amidst the dancers.

There was no time for Kathryn to grind her teeth and think that the king was flaunting her mother before the whole Court. There was scarcely enough time to see Catherine of Aragon stand, forehead creased, as she watched her husband and dear friend press each other indecently close. Kathryn was suddenly seized from behind, tossed from man to man as were the other women. Life was madly exciting of a sudden—dancers and musicians excelling themselves, men tossing off their caps and women their headdresses, to dance with streaming hair. But all those with masks maintained them, fearing such mementos would be stolen or smashed in the commotion; the stag mask alone stayed on for private reasons.

Dirty faces, unwashed hands pressed against windows. Merchants, guild members, and their wives had been allowed in to watch and had invaded the tables and dance floor, while outside, the poor of London eagerly observed. So many torches and candles—flickering golden light on fabulous velvets, damasks, taffetas—the jewels and gold and their own beloved king dancing light-footed as any lad at a fair.

A window was smashed, then another. "Hurrah the king, hurrah the queen!" "Hurrah our little prince!" "Hurrah Great Harry, long may he live and reign!" came the shouts as they entered.

The night's irresistible tempo swept over them. They poured onto the dance floor, ripped down the cloth of state over the dais. Two dancers were tossed in it, then the king himself was handed in with decorous bows and flourishes—and flung hilariously up and down.

One last toss tore the golden cloth. Fifty hands steadied the king, caught and righted him before he could be injured. Somehow a bullion *K* was unmeaningly ripped from his doublet. The man who had done it stared, horrified, and dropped to his knees to beg forgiveness. He never had the chance. Suddenly he was trampled, everyone craving a souvenir of this golden night. People fell on the king, kissing him, plucking first at the letters, then at his entire clothing. Hugged, pummeled, and laughing, he was finally stripped to his hose and half a shirt. At that he ran, still laughing, and caught up the queen to bear her safely away.

With the royal couple gone, the crowd's good humor vanished. All present wanted a gold initial and the dancers were covered with them. There was food, too, such as they had never seen: pickled eel on beds of chestnut pudding, roast peacocks stuffed with fruit and nuts, then sewn back into their feathers so they sat on the tables in fantailed splendor. Fountains of claret and malmsey, wines the townspeople could never afford to so much as taste on their own . . .

Chairs were kicked to splinters, tables walked upon and broken. Women broke each other's knuckles and noses over choice joints of beef. Two boys drew daggers and fought for a lemon-basted heron.

Everywhere Kathryn turned there were hands. Plucking, punching, ripping at her. Yanking away the bullion letters and landing on her until she went down under the mob. Her mask was knocked awry so that she could neither breathe nor see properly. *I shall be smothered, they are trampling me to death!* she thought, terrified.

A man atop her bellowed in rage and pain, was flung roughly aside. Her ribs were no longer breaking, she could sit, right her mask, and—

A strong, warm hand delved down in the pile of bodies and drew her forth. A glimpse of milky blue eyes, then she was flung over a broad male shoulder and carried away from the madness. Through room after riotous room he took her, the crowd's sounds finally dying away. Still onward, taking her to the crypt. She was finally set neatly on her feet near old Henry Tudor's marker.

"What, no effigy?" he asked, leaning over the tomb and chuckling.

"The king is bringing in some Florentine sculptor to do a gilded silver one," she said solemnly.

He made a strange noise in his throat at the sound of her piping, childish voice. Kathryn stepped back as he spun around, unfastened her chin-strap, and raised the lioness mask. "Why, you are a child! A green little girl! What the devil were you doing amidst the Court ladies?"

"I carry the queen's embroidery basket, I am in training as a maid of honor," she said.

He snapped his fingers. "Then that is why the burning blue eyes are familiar. Your parents would be—"

"Lord and Lady Chase."

"You were blessed not to receive the Howard beak," he said, still laughing. He touched a forefinger to her snub nose as he would have a little child; she slapped his hand away.

"I am not a baby, sir, please do not treat me as such."

"Neither are you the adult your height would imply. Now what shall I do with you? You are far too young for what I originally had in mind. But if I let you wander back into that crowd, my last sight of you will be people seizing each of those delicate little ankles and making a wish."

She caught her jaw just before it sagged. He had brought her here to seduce her until her voice gave away her youth!

She said, after two false starts, "I have not thanked you for helping me twice tonight. May I see your face?"

His slightly lopsided teeth showed in a fleeting grin. "No, my young friend, it is better if you never know who I am. My family was attaindered, I am not received at Court."

"Then why did you attend the feast tonight?"

"A family has no political power if it cannot represent itself at Court. I suppose I hoped to see some dimly remembered friends who might speak to the king for me. Or meet some charming ladies."

She opened her mouth, then shut it quickly. "No, no, speak your mind," he urged.

"Were you wishing to meet ladies for marriage or mere sport? Because I can list you which ones are best for which purpose." She did, too, as cold-blooded as any Howard was when discussing sex, marriage, or death.

"You are, what, twelve years old and cheering me on to both whoredom and marital disaster?" he inquired, voice echoing in the golden stag mask. "Not that I do not need a wife, but—"

"I am trying to repay the favor you have done me this evening. There are no rich members of my family to steer you to, so I can only advise you on women."

"Are you certain there is not some Borgia blood alongside the Howard?" he asked through gritted teeth.

"None whatsoever. Had either of my parents been to Italy they should never have returned, but fallen in love with the politics and poisonings. You may leave me to continue on to your evening's sport, I would not deprive the ladies of your presence."

She stuck out her tongue at him and they both laughed. He bent courteously over her hand, kissed it as he would have a great lady's, and said someone would come back for her. "Good-bye," she whispered to the green-and-white back disappearing down the aisle. It was a broad and dependable-looking back and made her fancy one could turn to this man when in trouble.

Kathryn plopped down on Henry the Seventh's tomb, chin in hands. It was damnably chilly sitting on cold stone in little but her shift and half a gown, he could at least have loaned her his—

A man's wolf-lined velvet coat landed across her lap. "A stranger gave me this. He said you would be cold and told me to fetch you," Maria de Salinas said, watching Kathryn struggle gladly into the coat.

"Who was he? Do you know him, Maria? He was nice, he saved me—"

Maria snorted. "*Nice?* Who knows about *nice*? But those shoulders, *Madre mia*, he is built like a god! Even better than the ki—do not go repeating my words, Big Eyes."

"No, Maria, I will not. I am learning to be discreet," Kathryn promised, and hurried out to a waiting mule-carried litter with her friend.

5

The infant prince died within the month.

Catherine of Aragon took to her bed. Not the king nor all her ladies could comfort her in her sorrow; she lay staring at the empty cradle when she was not doubled over with weeping. "You must not break your heart, Kate, there will be other sons, I promise," the king said, kneeling to kiss his wife's hands.

One evening he at last turned to Maria de Salinas. "The doctors say she is neither ill nor insane like her sister Juana. Tell me, then—for I know how you women have secrets—what ails her."

Maria curtsied very low. "She fears you will not love her—"

"What twaddle, I shall always love my Kate!"

"—will not love her if her sons die and Lady Chase's live."

So she knew. Subtle though Henry had been, his queen knew Joanna was pregnant. "You will send the lady to her home in the Marches at once," he said coldly. "We must not have our Kate troubled by her fecund presence."

Maria was not in charge of such affairs, but she knew better than to point this out to a king in a foul mood. "Will Your Grace be sending her off with anything . . . in particular?"

She meant an estate or title. Henry considered it. "That shall wait until we see whether she bears a son or daughter."

Such little value the world placed on daughters, on women! she thought. And yet without them there would be no political alliances settled by marriage, no well-tended home with a fireplace always glowing and a pleasant pot of something on to simmer. No nursing of the ill and aged, no childbearing, no compassion at day's end, no lust in the dark hours. Court would not sparkle and scintillate; Maria could not imagine a Court without women. Their prayers, their laughter, their friendship and learning . . . courage amidst adversity, kindness in sorrow.

"Yes, Your Grace. Shall I tell Lady Chase immediately?"

"No, wait until Court has settled for the night."

She narrowed her long black eyes as he left. He had not forbidden her to warn the girl. For Joanna she cared naught, but Kathryn had become dear to her. Because the mother had played the whore did not mean the daughter should suffer as well.

Maria rose from her almost-a-crouch curtsy. She smoothed her dark gray skirts of sarcenet—a cheap, coarse taffeta—and went to find Kathryn.

She was at her daily lute lesson, too-long fingers attempting to master the rebellious strings. Her instructor was pulling his beard and looking dismayed. The look he exchanged with the approaching Maria said: *A lucky thing she dances and sews beautifully.*

"Excuse me. I must steal Lady Kathryn away," Maria said, taking lute in one hand and Kathryn's nearest elbow in the other. She dragged the girl to the closest bay window. "Why, Doña Maria, you look quite troubled. How may I help?" Kathryn asked earnestly.

"I am not troubled for my sake but yours. Listen now and do not cry out: your mother is being sent from Court. Do you know what this means?"

Kathryn scanned the young woman's face. "Yes, it means I shall be expected to go with her. I have been dreading this day, knowing it must come; her condition is becoming apparent to all."

"His Grace the king thinks your lady mother's . . . *condition* . . . has made the queen feel threatened. You must not go, Her Grace would miss you very much. I, too. But I cannot think of a way to keep you here when your mother goes. Do not tell her yet, promise me? The king has ordered me to inform her late tonight when he is abed so she cannot disturb him. It is hard, asking you to go against your own mother, but—"

Memories of Joanna's secret letter to Henry the Seventh flooded Kathryn. Memories, too, of her mother preaching virtue and committing adultery with the king. "I will not warn her," she said shakily.

The court was retiring for the night when the word went out that Queen Catherine was unable to sleep for the second consecutive evening. She was reported to be sitting at the window, staring listlessly out, not even bothering with her needlework.

Needlework! Kathryn thought joyously, catching up her willow basket. She ventured a glance at Joanna, drowsing near the fire, and crept softly from the room. The door clicked shut behind her. Straight to the queen's bedchamber now—waiting, ear pressed to the crack, to hear who was inside. If it was the king she stood no chance, but to her relief she recognized Margaret Pole's voice.

Margaret, being the highest-born woman in England after Catherine of Aragon, was not actually a lady-in-waiting with duties and chores to attend to. Instead she was referred to as one of the Great Ladies at the Court, which meant she did little but show up divinely dressed at State functions. Therefore it was a surprise to hear her voice, but a welcome surprise nonetheless; she loved children, even those born of the hated Joanna.

Kathryn listened intently, heard Margaret trying to coax the queen to bestir herself, to eat, walk, anything but sit brokenhearted in her stiff box-bottomed chair at the window. It seemed to Kathryn that she could have been given no better cue, so she knocked lightly and waited with thudding heart. To her relief Maria de Salinas answered the door and gestured for her to enter. She and Margaret Pole were the only women attending the queen tonight; after unsuccessfully performing the nightly ritual of readying the queen's bed and tucking her in, the other ladies-in-waiting had been dismissed.

"Good evening, Doña Maria. I do not wish to disturb Her Grace but I have come for the king's shirt."

Kathryn said it in a stage whisper, as she had heard an actor in a morality play do. Her words carried well without seeming deliberate; she watched Catherine of Aragon flinch in her chair. "The king's shirt," Maria repeated carefully, brow furrowing in confusion.

"He wanted his shirt finished by week's end and Her Grace is not well enough to see to it. As one of the Gentlemen of the Wardrobe stopped me and spoke rather sharply about the king's need for the shirt, I thought perhaps I could work on it, with your help and that of some other—"

Catherine of Aragon twisted and looked over the arm of the heavy, box-bottomed chair at her. "Is that little Kat, come finishing my husband's shirt for me? Very sweet, little Kat."

Kathryn curtsied gracefully. "Your Grace, my stitches are very long. The king will not like it, he will recognize that it is not your own work. He—" She put a quaver into her voice. "He may shout at me."

The queen considered it. "You embroider nice-fine. Better than me. But seams—yes, stitches long. Just a little. Maria? Maria, where is shirt? Let us work on it," she suggested in heavily-accented English.

In the manner of women everywhere, they could not sew in a group and remain silent. Catherine's three companions made all the conversation at first—trifling family matters, humorous anecdotes of this courtier or that lady. Maria at last excused herself, saying with a significant glance at Kathryn that she would be back soon. Kathryn rose from her cushion at the queen's feet. "Your Grace, I fear I, too, must leave you. My mother is being dismissed from Court and I will be told to accompany her. I must go pack."

Catherine's golden needle savagely stabbed the crisp linen shirt. "Lady Chase go; you stay. You do nothing to wrong me."

Kathryn knelt, held her hands out for those of the queen, which she then clutched and kissed. "I shall never disappoint or wrong you! If I do, you must send me away at once, Your Grace."

The door banged open. Everyone jumped as Henry Tudor strode jauntily in, wearing a fur-lined wrapper of stiff, heavy, satin samite over his nightshirt. "What ho, Kate, I see you have busied yourself and so bettered your mood. That is my sweetheart."

He bent to kiss her, then glared at Kathryn. "And what are you doing here, little Chase?" His tone of voice said: *You damned Howard, you double-damned Plantagenet—how dare you remain?*

The queen clutched his hands and said in broken English, "Oh, please, My Lord Husband, do not make her go! She bring me sewing to take my mind off our prince—I lose three children of my own, do not take little Kathryn away, too. She named for me—she lucky for me."

Henry growled, but Catherine looked very fetching in white satin with her auburn hair spilling down. It had been nigh on six weeks since their son's birth; the queen was finally beddable again. "All right, Wife, she may stay at Court. But only on the condition that she and the Countess of Salisbury leave us at once."

Queen Catherine went delightedly pink-cheeked, looking up at her husband with such awe and devotion that Kathryn was ashamed to witness so intimate a scene. She and Margaret Pole took their baskets and hurried out with curtsies and flourishes. Once they were in the next room, Margaret thumped her lightly on the head with a thimble-clad finger. "You imp, you are Joanna's child after all! I thought you were trying to cheer the queen when all you intended was to beg staying on at Court!"

Kathryn, remembering—always remembering—Edmund's advice, met Margaret's gaze levelly and did not defend herself. She merely said, "It was rewarding to see the queen absorbed in something besides sorrow, Madam."

"Be off with you before I thump that turned-up sprite's nose of yours next! I shall keep a keen eye on you from now on, Child; I shall see to it that you are left in my care here at Court."

Kathryn groaned to herself, curtsied, and fled at a trot. "*Hsst!*" someone said ahead of her. Hesitating, she watched Edmund Howard pop from an alcove. He raced to meet her. "I heard the news. Are you going?"

"No, staying. Only Mother is to go."

"Hooray!" He seized her by the waist, swung her around and around until peals of childish laughter rippled through the room. At last, setting her down, he said very gravely, "I shall not marry anyone else. Plight your troth to me, Kat."

She sucked her breath in. Such agreements, even between children their age, could prove legally binding in a court of law. "I cannot, without the permission of my parents," she answered, squeezing his hands.

"But you love me, Kat, you must! I love *you*!"

Yes, she thought, *I love him.* But if she could only hurry this tedious process of growing up, if she could only be fourteen and marriageable instead of what seemed an eternal eleven. Perhaps if she were fourteen she could—

She blushed. It was not Edmund she was thinking of. "When I am a little older," she said, and permitted him to kiss her on the cheek. Those last few weeks she had thought of little else but the man in the stag mask. She dreamed that he would wait for her, that he would hold out for marriage until she was ripe for it. Sometimes he was dark-haired in her fantasies, sometimes fair. Perhaps he would return to Court after all. . . . Kathryn looked for him around every corner, felt her heart leap up when she heard male footsteps approach. At eleven she was in the throes of her first infatuation, and it made her affection for Edmund pale in comparison. On cold nights she even slept in the stranger's wolf-lined coat, which was by now falling apart.

Add to those romantic entanglements the fact that she was about to start life without her mother for the first time, and she felt very small and frightened. Seeing her shiver, Edmund placed an arm about her shoulders. "Nothing to be afraid of, I shall protect you, My Lady."

As the king protected the queen, leaving her at the first sign of pregnancy to sleep with other men's wives? As Hal protected Joanna, fleeing in the night each time she located and moved back in with him? "Perhaps I should learn to protect *myself*," she said worriedly.

"You will never get married speaking thus, Kat. Remember to keep your thoughts to yourself," Edmund warned.

A man's world, a man's words, though he was but fourteen. "You will not tell me what to do," she answered, jerking away. She could feel him stare after her as she went, but he made no move to stop her. She felt small again, and open to many dangers.

"There is going to be a war."

"Really? With France or Spain?"

"The king has not decided yet."

Henry Tudor was in a foul mood and wanted everyone to know it. He was currently allied with Catherine of Aragon's widowed father, Ferdinand, also the Holy Roman emperor, Maximilian, and the pope, all of them against France. A more uneasy set of allies never existed, each ruler circling the other warily, catlike, up on toes with backs humped and whiskers straight back. In particular the others mistrusted Ferdinand, whom Henry Tudor privately referred to as "that damned weathervane, always changing his direction." Told that Louis the Twelfth of France had complained of being lied to by him twice, Ferdinand cried out in offended surprise, "He lies, the sot! I have duped him *five* times!"

He had also duped Henry countless times. On days when her vacillating father struck yet another harmful blow at Anglo-Spanish relations, Queen Catherine was learning to take to her bed. She had little choice, as otherwise Henry turned on her in public, belaboring her savagely for her father's behavior. Ferdinand's latest treachery was to sign a secret pact with France while loudly proclaiming that country his enemy; Catherine lurked in her chambers for most of a week before Henry could forgive her the error of possessing Spanish blood.

And for not becoming pregnant again. There were many false alarms, for her monthly courses were irregular and she skipped them altogether some months. So the royal couple's hopes would rise, then plummet and always there seemed to fall the shadow of politics between them.

Joanna Chase's bastard was born female and dead. So there were no estates or titles for her, only a necklace that had once belonged to dead Queen Elizabeth of York. As her husband had left her once again, Joanna had little to live on, so she took the necklace to a jeweler, intending to pry the stones out and sell them one at a time before having the gold melted down. But the jeweler only examined the piece and guffawed at her. " 'Tis naught but glass and brass," he explained. She remembered with a sinking heart that Henry the Seventh had rarely bought jewels for his queen, so Elizabeth had been reduced to having fakes made.

Paste jewels. Joanna had nearly died delivering the king's stillborn child and all she had to show for it was a handful of—well, he had a paste heart, too, but he would call her back to Court. She was certain of it, and so dressed in her best each day, waiting for a messenger with her summons.

It never came. Within the year she had to write Kathryn for money, which her daughter dutifully sent.

Kathryn had a good living as a maid of honor. She was allowed one servant (her mother's Tansy), a lapdog (which she did not have), and a chamber she shared with several other girls her age. They were fed handsomely on beef, bread, and ale, allowed a small fortune in clothing, candles, firewood, and bed linens, on top of which they made seven to ten pounds per year. It was a fine salary, considering a master mariner might make only half that, and tutors considerably less. The salary enabled Kathryn to support herself as well as her mother, though it considerably reduced the dowery she had thought to save for herself. Now she would have nothing to offer Edmund or . . . the other. But surely the king would allow her mother to return to Court soon; the queen had remembered Joanna nursing her at Ludlow and was wistfully saying she missed her most outspoken lady.

But Henry had no desire to be faced by a second woman who could not produce live sons for him. His lack of male offspring seemed to him—indeed, to most of Europe—an insult to his manhood. Anxious to prove otherwise, he hotheadedly let himself be goaded into war against France.

The newly rebuilt English fleet was sent out under Kathryn's uncle Edward Howard, Lord High Admiral. He found the French a chivalrous enemy—so chivalrous, in fact, that when they defeated him and found him dead on deck, they embalmed the body and paid to have it shipped home to his father. The old man broke down in the arms of his other son and namesake. "There is only you now, Thomas," he said. "You are all I have left to count on, the other children are of no use."

In the morning Thomas Howard the Younger went to the king and implored on bent knee to be sent against the French. Encouraged by this show of spirit, Henry sent him to harry the enemy in the Channel and along the French coast. Each time a report reached the king of a French ship sunk or disabled, he would clap Kathryn heartily on the back, saying, "You Howards are a fighting breed, and your uncle the finest of the lot! Send your old grandfather to me, I would congratulate him once more!"

Henry told Thomas the Elder in front of a packed Court that he felt strengthened by the many Howards fighting for him. Regaining the family lands and titles no longer seemed such a fantasy; Howard accepted the compliment with as great a show of pleasure as if it had been the ducal coronet returned. In Joanna's next letter she told Kathryn that as the Howard star seemed firmly fixed on the ascent, she granted her permission for the betrothal to Edmund. *Dear Mother,* Kathryn thought, *always with political power on her mind!*

Maria de Salinas, blushing, announced her betrothal that spring. "Dearest Doña Maria! But who shall it be!" Kathryn asked.

"Lord Willoughby."

The pink cheeks told her it was a love match as well as a sound marriage for a foreign lady-in-waiting of no high birth or fortune. Kathryn hugged her, wishing with all her thirteen-year-old heart that she might be a year or two older and making the same announcement. But Joanna was so strict, saying that girls ought not to start breeding before fourteen years of age.

Willoughby went to war at King Henry's side against the French that summer. "We should have married first. If anything happens to my betrothed—" Maria said to Kathryn, and closed her eyes to pray.

The queen prayed, too. Catherine of Aragon had been made regent in Henry's absence, with the Thomas Howards left to advise her. "The old one's dependable as a rock, but too ancient and weak to take to war," Henry had told her before leaving. "You may rely most sturdily upon his advice. The young one is hot-tempered but good-hearted; if there is any trouble he shall lead the troops."

He kissed her good-bye, pausing for a glower at Kathryn and Margaret Pole before leaving. "What have we done?" Kathryn anxiously asked the countess.

"Not we, but our Plantagenet relatives. France has recognized Richard de la Pole as king of England. Richard is the oldest son of old Edward the Fourth's sister, Elizabeth."

But Kathryn and Margaret were both descended through the male line, which put them far closer to the throne than Richard de la Pole, Kathryn thought. She did not speak it, she knew better, but the glance she shared with her father's cousin was one of real fear.

Catherine of Aragon was so newly pregnant that she did not know it until Henry was gone. She had suspected but dared not raise false hopes before he left. She wrote him now, and promised him a healthy son in winter.

Pregnancy and battle—double proof of masculinity, Henry thought, and shouted for his armor.

The moment it was known that he was out of the country, rebellious Scots poured over the Border into England. The Thomas Howards grimly packed up their fine Missaglia armor and knelt before the queen to receive their orders. "My Lords, we must haste northward. The fate of all England lies in your capable hands; what men, what horse and monies you need, you shall have. I have had the remaining Council summon all the foot soldiers and cavalry we have. They shall join us on our journey. May God's Blessed Mother keep us safe," Catherine said, tight-throated with emotion. She was taking forth the dregs of England: the few soldiers who had been considered unfit for service in France because they were too young, too old, too undependable, or infirm. Thomas Howard the Elder was so aged and crippled with gout that he had to make the journey in a litter slung between horses, but he went nonetheless. Catherine meant to take the field with her army, but part way there, her pregnancy stopped her. The Howards sped for the Border. Upon arrival Thomas Howard the Younger offered personal combat to King James of Scotland, King Henry's brother-in-law; James shrank back from the challenge.

Together the Howards led their troops forward and fell savagely upon the Scots. They obliterated some six thousand enemies to a mere fifteen hundred of their own men dead. At day's end King James lay dead together with the very cream of Scottish nobility, while English priests sang Te Deums in the gore-soaked field.

The news roared deafeningly through England. Upon receiving the messenger, Queen Catherine called for Kathryn Chase. "It was your grandfather and uncle who did this marvelous thing, you shall bring my inkwell and portable desk and sit with me while I write His Grace of the news," she told Kathryn. "The queen of Scotland—My Lord's sister Margaret—I must write her as well, tender my sympathies and say we English support her in her regency for the child-king."

We English. Forgotten was her Spanish blood, her proud heritage of centuries. This was her husband's country and through him it was hers, too.

Kathryn raced to obey. Soon she stood at the queen's elbow, rapturously listening as Catherine dictated to a scribe, then signed the letters. The queen was nearly finished when the sound of cheering burst upon them, growing louder and louder. People scaled the garden walls, flinging flowers and shrieking for their queen in a frenzy of devotion.

Catherine of Aragon rose majestically from her chair and went gliding through open doors to the gardens. All in sight grew silent, many falling to their knees. "Yes, my people," she called out in her Castilian-accented English. "We have beaten them roundly at Flodden. We have done it—we English!"

They cheered her again, flinging their caps into the air. Several bricklayers knelt to kiss the hem of her gown; one woman called her, "A fearless warrior-queen like dead Queen Isabella, God rest her soul!"

A cluster of merchants stepped forward and knelt to take the queen onto their shoulders. Catherine demurred, stepping back with both hands protectively clasped over her belly. "No, no, good people, you must not jostle your prince and heir."

At this news they knelt again, shouting, cheering, many weeping for joy.

"God Himself could not save any known mistress of the king's who showed her face in this place today," Maria de Salinas observed to Margaret Pole with satisfaction. Kathryn overheard and nodded. The crowd was quieter now, respectful of the queen's condition. They began filtering out in soft-spoken groups. But once outside, the merriment returned in force. Church bells pealed for hours, people danced around bonfires in the streets. As much ale flowed as if Catherine had personally led the English into battle and then given birth to a son.

King Henry won a small battle after an insignificant siege. Lest his own accomplishment look small in the face of the queen's, he proclaimed his military engagement the fiercest fighting known to history and promiscuously knighted everyone he could get his sword on.

Fifteen-year-old Edmund Howard came home early, wounded and a knight. Kathryn flew into his arms lightly, mindful of the bandages on his side, and kissed him heedless of who saw. "I hear I must address you as Sir Edmund now. Were you terribly brave?"

He shrugged, embraced her, and winced from the effort. "Yes, but mostly he knighted all of us so his battle would seem as big as that at Flodden Field. And besides, he felt sorry for me. My brother was killed. *Older* brother, so I am the heir now. Next year I marry you."

Catherine of Aragon, frazzled with the strain of regency, battle, and fear for her husband's sake, gave premature birth to a stillborn son. One month later the king returned unexpectedly, surprising her at Richmond Palace. He scooped her up, flung her over his shoulder before the cheering Court. Hats were thrown in celebration, women tossed their expensive gable headdresses. "Make a son, Your Grace!" called out Charles Brandon, the king's boon companion.

The king did not halt, only shouted over his wife's rump, "I intend to, Charles . . . with or *without* your encouragement!"

People laughed fondly. In the ensuing feasting and dancing, Charles sought out the king's pretty little sister, Mary, and bowed very low. "Will you dance with me, Majesty?" he inquired.

She hesitated. He had a very bad reputation and had been married many times. Eyes wide, she laid her hand on his arm. "I believe I shall," she admitted, to her own surprise.

6

A lusty winter ensued, and a lustier spring. Marriages sprang up, immediately followed—or, too often, preceded—by pregnancy. Courtiers pursued flirting ladies, who chased rich old lords no longer sprightly enough to flee.

Kathryn's grandfather Thomas Howard was reinstated in the family's attaindered Earldom of Surrey. With added time and martial prowess he regained his father's title, Duke of Norfolk, and passed the Earldom to Thomas the Younger.

The roving Charles Brandon was named Duke of Suffolk; rumor had him infatuated with Mary Tudor. "It will not do him any good," Margaret Pole said at the evening sewing circle. "He has been married more times than a dog has fleas. Twice to the same woman, with a broken betrothal before and an elderly, annulled wife in between. No matter how often the king drinks and wenches with Charles of Suffolk, he will not, I repeat, *not* allow him to marry his sister."

"Especially not with King Louis of France sniffing after her, making apologetic noises about last year's war," said Kathryn's aunt, Elizabeth Boleyn.

Maria crossed her eyes a moment. "King Louis is old enough to be the princess's *grandfather*!"

Kathryn, winding herself a fresh skein of red silk thread, said nothing, only cranked her ears out another notch.

Margaret Pole knotted a thread and snipped it expertly with a tiny jeweled scissors. "Age is a matter of no concern whatsoever in royal marriages. Nor is compatibility or disposition or anything else save the usefulness of the impending match to both countries. But I hear Mary Tudor is no fool. She is trying to wring a deal from King Henry that allows her to marry whomsoever she pleases once she is Queen of France and old Louis dies. Says it is the only way she will let her brother marry her off to a drooling dotard. Hmph, imagine what this world would come to if we let all young girls pick their own husbands! They would marry for lust and infatuation, and the noblest blood in the land would die out. There would be no more political matches, no matings between great houses. We should all become no better than curs, breeding mindlessly for personal enjoyment."

There was a sudden uproar in the adjoining rooms, Queen Catherine's chambers. A man was bellowing, bearlike; crockery shattered and a woman screamed. Every lady in the room cast down her sewing and ran to defend the queen—until they saw the cause of the noise.

Henry Tudor stood inside, swollen with a red-faced Welsh rage. "Your father again, Madam! I will no more be duped by your Spaniards; you cannot be trusted at the treaty table nor in the bedchamber—he gives me no useful allies and you give me no living sons!"

For once Catherine of Aragon did not retreat before his wrath. Eyes shining, she plucked the ornate dinner dagger from his belt, knelt, and offered it to him. "I am English through my love of you and our people, English through our children that God has chosen not to grant long life to. You find a Spanish part of me, you may hack it from my body. I am not Spaniard, I am English to the core, My Lord—*I am all English!*"

He had no choice but to pull her to her feet and embrace her in front of so many onlookers. "Oh, Kate, what a pother you make about words ill-chosen in the heat of anger," he murmured. But her behavior rankled with him for days afterward. She had never crossed him in any way nor called his bluff before, and it unsettled him to find her so set on her own way that she would make a scene. He had forgotten that she was daughter to the wiliest king in Christendom and was a queen who led troops into battle while pregnant. Some dormant spark of fanatic Isabella glowed even in the recesses of Catherine's gentle soul, and he was now afraid that Time would fan it into full flame.

Six days before her wedding Kathryn was stopped by a smartly dressed man in the gardens at Richmond Palace. "Are you Lady Chase the Younger?" he asked, and there seemed something familiar in the twinkle of his blue eyes.

"Yes, Papa," she guessed correctly, holding out her hands to him.

He gripped them tightly. "Why, you are almost a woman, I am surprised at how grown you are. Turn around, let me see you." He spun her slowly by one hand, letting her show off her red silk-and-linen gown. "Yes, Kathryn, you are grown and marriageable at fourteen and one half. Come sit and talk with me about this wedding."

"Papa, the queen is sending me for thread and cambric shirting, I cannot wait."

"Then I shall accompany you," Lord Hal announced, escorting her out through the gardens. Shadows of Richmond's many spires and turrets fell across them as they walked through the late afternoon sunshine, light bouncing off golden weathervanes and copper onion domes. Surveying the palace, Hal Chase said, "I never realize how greatly I miss my father's Court until I see such a place as this."

He was a king's son, she often forgot that. It seemed so unreal to Kathryn, those dead, hated Plantagenets who were always posthumously getting her in trouble. "It must hurt to be away from the glory and activity," she said, gentler than she had ever been with him.

"Aye, Kat—the glory, activity, and *money*. I should be a duke by now had my father . . ." He never finished the sentence, but took her by the elbow to help her along the stone path to the queen's barge.

"Do you have permission to be at Court for my wedding?" she asked suddenly. No reply. Very well, so he had not thought it meet to ask the king. She would have to go on her belly to Adonis Tudor this evening, and approach the queen, too.

Hal handed her onto the barge, climbing in after her. The polesman held out his hand for the seven shillings due him, and Kathryn paid, counting the amount out from the queen's velvet drawstring purse. Then she and her father settled back against the cushions for the pretty river journey. "Now tell me your news," she ordered suspiciously. It was unlike her father to suddenly drop out of the blue for her wedding and she wanted to know what he was seeking from her.

"Your mother and I wish to be divorced."

He sat in the shade of the awning so she could not read his expression—a deliberate move, she suspected. Suddenly she was heartily tired of her parents' eternal bickering and politicking and turned a face as guarded as his own on him. "I do not care what you and Mother do so long as you do it after my wedding. As I have no dowery, all I can bring into this marriage is my family name and honor. Please do not besmirch it so that Lord Adam Howard refuses me his son, as I am not likely to get another offer, penniless as I am."

He indicated her crimson damask skirts. "A pretty gown for one pleading poverty."

"I am supporting your wife, Sir, that is why I have no

dowery. As for this, it is one of the queen's hand-me-downs. She is very generous to me."

Had she really said that? How the child's heart in her longed to cry, *Queen Catherine is more a parent to me than either of you!* If she could only hurt him as his abandonment had hurt her! But in a moment she had mastered her emotions once more and sat with hands neatly folded in red silk-linen lap.

"It is the queen's generosity to you and your mother that brings me here," Hal began.

"Not a shilling," Kathryn answered, horrified. "You shall not get a one from me!"

"No, not a shilling. A bishop or two who might plead the divorce to Rome."

Catherine of Aragon help a married couple divorce? Lord Hal was obviously not acquainted with Her Grace's views on the married state. Kathryn nearly told him so before reflecting that her father might be perverse enough to proceed with the divorce straightaway and ruin her chances with Edmund. Pretending to consider it, Kathryn studied her hands a moment. "Please let me think about it," she said at last, and glanced guardedly up at her father.

He had lost all interest in her and stood staring up at the riverbanks of Windsor Castle. As he looked, he swore a long, appalling string of oaths, ending with, "And the cheeky bastard dares doff his hat to *me*!"

He threw his own hat off and stamped on it. Kathryn rose and peered out from under the awning. Even at this distance she could see a fine white mare ridden by a man in garish red, green, and gold. He was extending a rude gesture toward her father, then, spotting Kathryn, bowed low in the saddle with a flourish of his plumed hat. She saw chestnut brown hair, then the white mare wheeled and galloped into the Windsor oaks. "Calm down, Father, he was not waving his hat at *you*. This is the queen's barge, after all; perhaps he expected her to be on it."

Lord Hal regarded her with his face queerly reddened. "*You!* He was flapping his cap at *you*! How do you know that man?"

"I—I do not know him. He is not at all familiar to me," she answered, falling back from him.

He lunged, caught her by the shoulders, shook her until her gable headdress fell to the striped cushions. "Do you swear before God Himself that you have had aught to do with him?"

"I have never seen him before."

He released her, spat into the Thames. "I believe you. Him and those cold moonstone eyes—"

Moonstones were a milky blue-white. Kathryn's heart plummeted to her shoes. She raced to the side of the barge, looked eagerly up to the cliff. But there were only trees waving where his horse had gone. "Who is he?" she demanded. "Why is he so bad?"

"Let us call him a relative of sorts," her father said tersely. "Let us also call him a heretic, a blasphemer—and decidedly wealthy. I believe he is the wealthiest man in England, after the king."

"More money than Archbishop Wolsey?"

"A *lot* more."

She wanted to cry out, *Is he handsome, too?* But that would give it away. Moonstone eyes. She was so close to getting his name out of her father, if she could only—"Why are you looking at me thus?" she demanded of Lord Hal.

"You are of a sudden very interested in this man you do not know."

"And you, Sir, are of a sudden quite interested in a child you have abandoned these last fourteen-and-one-half years. I will not have it."

His mouth dropped open. "Not have it! I should box your ears, Child!"

She picked up an unused barge-pole, stood braced with her feet apart. "You may *try* to box my ears, Sir. But as we are strangers to one another, I shall take it as an attack on my person and defend myself most readily."

Hal Chase did the most unexpected of things—collapsed on the striped cushions, laughing. He laughed until tears came from his eyes and he could not breathe. "*You!*" he gasped out. "I believe you are your mother's child after all! I keep looking for my gentle mother in you, or my pleasure-loving father, and instead I see before me an old man in Italian armor. What a granddaughter you are to old Norfolk! Do the other Howards know how like them you are? Worse thought—does Edmund suspect?"

Kathryn set the barge pole down. "I hope not," she admitted guiltily. "And I pray you, do not tell him."

The morning of the wedding Maria de Salinas and Margaret Pole helped Kathryn dress. She had just finished making a high-necked shift for herself, resplendent with blackwork and silver stitching at collar and wrists, and her father had uncharacteristically provided a length of heavy black wool velvet, just enough for a gown. "Of course it is a trifle warm for May and rather mature for you," fussed Margaret Pole, tucking Kathryn's hair into a new peaked headdress she had given the bride. "But then again, you will no longer be a mere maid of honor but a lady-in-waiting with your father-in-law's private Court apartments. No more sharing a room and bed with three other girls! You will have your own rooms and young Edmund's knighthood honors."

"With the promise of Lord Adam's title some day," Maria added, smiling fondly.

There was a knock at the door, then Joanna Chase and her sister, Elizabeth Boleyn, entered. "Good morrow, Daughter!" cried the one. "A merry wedding to you, Niece," called the other.

Hookéd and laced into her new gown, Kathryn crossed the tiny room to embrace them both. "Mother, Aunt Elizabeth. I am so glad you are here!"

Elizabeth Boleyn kissed her cheek. "In your place, I would be equal-glad to see my new horse." Seeing Kathryn's blank stare, she added, "The magnificent white mare in the stable. The boy said she was yours when we rode in. He also said the queen herself had not a finer mount. Well? Who has sent her? The tag on her bridle read, *For the little Howard bride*, and no more. But there was a funny kind of mask on the stall door."

"A stag's mask. Papier mâché," Kathryn said weakly. So he knew she was marrying and this was as close as he would approach. *But I am old enough now!* she wanted to cry out. *He could marry me himself if he but asked!* Perhaps she was still a child to him, no matter her age. Or perhaps . . . perhaps she did not please him and the mare was merely a stranger's kindness to a little girl he had once rescued.

"So you know who sent the horse? But how odd . . . I thought only the de Gaels of Windsgeat had such white horses, and they are no friends to my family," Joanna said, puzzled.

"I am certain it was a Windsgeat White," Elizabeth Boleyn told her sister. "That faint dappling, almost a blue-gray along the throat and rump . . . that indicates one of Windsgeat's finest horses. They rarely sell the blue-whites, only the off-colors, the creams and grays. She must be one of their best. Jesu, Kat, she is a beast out of fable, ought to have a unicorn's horn on her forehead. When did you meet and befriend that heretical nest of de Gaels? And why the golden deer-mask?"

Kathryn was backed into a verbal corner now and could think of nothing to say. It was Maria who defended her, loyally saying, "Many years ago at a masque a man pulled Kat'rin from the crowd. The little prince's christening, recall? The stag mask rescued her, that is all there was to it. I assure you nothing untoward ever happened. If he has sent a fine horse it is only out of fond rememberance to a child whose wit once impressed him."

"There best *not* have been anything untoward. He is related to her twice over, and is some kind of religious heretic. A house that size, so rich, and *no chapel*!" Joanna shrilled.

"They say he is one of Richard the Third's bastards, with steely Plantagenet eyes."

"Oh, no, my dear, he is the spitting image of his father, Kenneth de Gael. Old friends of my family."

"Those heretics! Really, Countess!"

"I hear he is the handsomest man in England, saving only the king."

"I hear the richest."

"I hear he is ugly and squints and limps."

"His grandmother, Red Emma, inherited Windsgeat over male cousins. A woman, inheriting!"

"I was told he is one of Edward the Fourth's bastards."

"No, but his mother was my aunt. Blessed Mother Mary, she was a shrew!" Joanna exclaimed.

From there the four older women launched into genealogy and Who Was Executed When for Which Treason. Kathryn, despairing, fled the room. She hoped to visit her new mare in private but found the queen and an admiring flock outside the stables, watching Edmund trot the animal back and forth on a lead rope. "Ho, Bride! Whence comes this beast?" he inquired.

She had never even met an unmasked de Gael, nor knew who and what they were, except that they seemed to stir strong feelings in people. And most of those feelings were negative. So Kathryn only smiled, looked blank, and stroked the mare's velvety muzzle. The queen said, "I have not seen so fine a white horse since my coronation with the king. Someone anonymously sent me two white mares and a cloth-of-gold litter, and when he saw them, the king went purple in the face. Something about Plantagenet upstarts, he said."

Kathryn turned and dropped a neat curtsy. "And did he tell you more so you could write and thank the man, Your Grace?"

"No, no, he said the horses came from a nest of sorcerers and blasphemers and he sold the mares after the crowning. I was very sad to see them go, they were so lovely, so gentle. I have always wanted a white mare since then, perhaps some day I can buy a sister to this one. Oh, here comes the bishop."

Kathryn and Edmund were taken to the chapel and married. Afterward the king, fresh from signing treaties, joined them with a toast. "To a fine little bride and a fine white mare for her to ride the morning after—that is, if she is capable of sitting at all!"

After a wedding there was always a wedding night; Kathryn had not thought of it until now, with all the men laughing at the joke and clamoring to kiss her. The king did so before any of them, swinging her up in his arms for a hearty avuncular smack on the lips. The entire wedding party, including the royal couple, then escorted them to her father-in-law's Howard House on the banks of the Thames.

In the torchlit parade Kathryn found her uncle Thomas Howard, Earl of Surrey, riding next to her. "You are too quiet, Niece," he said.

She smiled quickly. "Among other things I was thinking that I had been very rude to you, my uncle of Surrey."

"How so?"

"I asked that you present me to the bridegroom at the altar, and then my father showed up to claim the privilege. I had rather have had you."

He said in his gruff way, "Now do not become sentimental on me, Kat. You know I like you best of all the family because you are so levelheaded." But he smiled nonetheless.

Married to Ned Howard and regretting it already because he was not a blue-eyed man on a white mare like her own. And her uncle thought her levelheaded! *You do not know everything, Surrey,* she thought, and blew her nose heartily.

Surely they would be rushed into the house, bedded, and on to the next day, she thought. But no, Adam, Lord Howard's entire household turned out on the lawn for them; cooks, housekeepers, valets, stable boys—some two dozen in all. Poor for a lord, but miraculous to Kathryn, whose family had never had more than Tansy and Lord Hal's old manservant.

"Now, Ned, you must carry her over the threshold," Lord

Adam told Edmund. So the boy lifted her, but he stumbled slightly; the queen cried out that it was bad luck and insisted they do it again.

It took Edmund two more tries; Queen Catherine covered her mouth with her hand to hide a moue of alarm.

A feast and gifts waited inside. The first window-grown fruits of late spring lay piled on pewter trenchers flanked by bottles of ale, malmsey, muscatel, claret, and sack. Tables groaned beneath a whole roasted veal-calf, which, when cut into, released a flurry of songbirds to the hammerbeam ceiling. Flayed eels lay stuffed with leeks, chestnuts, peppercorns, and oranges; nearby sat saffron rice, and salads of endive, cress, tarragon, garlic, spinach, rosemary, and dill weed. Marchpane fancies of pounded almond and sugar had been shaped, baked, and then gilded; raw oysters were pickled in lemon brine. It was some time before Kathryn learned that Adam, Lord Howard had virtually bankrupted himself to provide a wedding feast for the king to attend. At the time all she could think was that she had never seen such splendid food outside the king's Court and that Lord Howard must love his son a great deal. Later she would find the old man had sold his property in Surrey and auctioned off many of the household furnishings to cover the feast, so there was little left for Edmund to inherit but the house.

There was dancing after the feast, not bloodless two-steps, but boisterous bransles where women were flung so that skirts swirled and showed an indecent amount of petticoat and stocking.

Presents were opened afterward. Books from the Boleyns and their three children, and sterling bridal goblets from Maria de Salinas. *Counterpanes and lambswool blankets from the Chases, and clothing and their very own Court apartments from Lord Howard. The king gave them a black oak bed that had reportedly belonged to his grandmother, the witch, Queen Elizabeth Woodville during her first marriage; sure enough, the initials *EW* and *JG* were carved on the headboard, amidst a profusion of wooden herbs and flowers.

Kathryn's Surrey and Norfolk relations gave her three of dead "Jack o'Norfolk's" tapestries, woven with the family crest and his personal badge of lions, Margaret Pole handed over a small, exquisite Turkey carpet, and the queen, beam-

---

*used as a bedspread, or uppermost coverlet

ing, presented a set of black-embroidered linen sheets she and the maids of honor had painstakingly stitched for the bridal couple over the past eighteen months. "It was difficult to do in secret, you were always underfoot, working for me," Catherine of Aragon said, and kissed her.

New mattresses, too, the upper stuffed with lambswool, the lower with sweet clover. "Gentlemen, if you will hammer the bed together, we ladies shall make it up for the bride and groom," Joanna Chase announced, and the men cheered.

Only Thomas Howard the Younger gave Kathryn a sympathetic glance. He chucked her under the chin. "Tut, tut, 'tis not so bad, and the lad loves you. Do not look so pale, Niece."

He went on to assist the other men. All too soon the bed was prepared, heaped with its new finery. The women undressed Kathryn, handed her into her best shift, a semi-sheer cotton one the ladies-in-waiting had made. She had never owned anything so fine and soft before. It was nearly transparent, it seemed, as she gazed down to see her fair skin showing through. She blushed as the women tucked her in amidst crisp new sheets and dried rose petals.

The men pounded impatiently at the door. In came Edmund, red-faced and strutting in his nightgown, a loose outer garment for informal wear not sleep. How silly and dear he looked with his thin legs showing, trying to act like a grown man but with that little-boy-blush giving him away.

The king stripped Edmund to his nightshirt, popped him under the covers like a cork and sang out, "To it, children! God's blessings on you both and may you make many fine sons!"

A glance at the embarrassed queen, then he strode out, calling, "Adam! Tell me, Lord Howard, have you any more of that splendid old malmsey left? . . ."

Trampling feet, blown kisses, crude comments as everyone filed out merrily. The door clicked shut.

Edmund pounced. Laughing, pretending to wrestle, the newlyweds rolled over and over. Pillows flew, sheets tangled about them. Kathryn diplomatically let him win. They burrowed under the covers together, giggling and kissing until all giggles were forgotten. He was touching her barely-budding breasts through the cotton shift and that was pleasant; she stroked his chest down the low neck of his nightshirt and that was pleasant, too. Now he was drawing up the hem of her shift. Frightening but delightful. His legs were hairy and the feel of them against her naked flesh made Kathryn laugh in delighted anticipation.

Open-mouthed kissing. She did not know if she liked that or not. Something rigid poked her thigh. Kathryn had seen animals mate and knew what it was, so boldly placed her hand on it. Edmund yelped as though she had struck him and laid between her legs.

He had barely penetrated before he gave another yelp and collapsed on her. "Is that all there is to it?" he asked at last.

Kathryn kissed his nearest ear. "Do not worry, the countess of Salisbury assures me that it gets better with practice."

Margaret Pole was right, at least for Edmund. The second time lasted longer, chiefly because neither of them knew what to do. At last he said, "I think one of us is supposed to move," so they both did. Kathryn found it uncomfortable bordering on painful, but made no protest out of love for Edmund. There followed more movement, pain, and sweating, but it was not as bad as she had heard, only boring. At any rate, being sprawled out in the Woodville bed was far more comfortable than cramming in four abed with the other maids of honor.

She thought marriage might be tolerable.

Most of the guests were still there when Kathryn and Edmund descended for breakfast. There was no morning meal of mulled cider, kidney pie, fruit, and bread laid out on the sideboard, for the plentiful remains of last night's feast were still strewn about. Kathryn's mother and Aunt Elizabeth Boleyn had curled up like kittens together in the windowseat, reverting to childhood days when they warmed their feet on each other during sleep. Margaret Pole snored contentedly in a nearby box-chair.

Thomas Boleyn, dark hair tousled and red beard a-bristle, opened bloodshot eyes at them. He fumbled for and found a goblet, raised it in a toast. "To the newlyweds. Would that I were sixteen again and could ride all night after riding all day, eh, Ned Howard? I always knew you Howards could drink, but I never thought of you as romancers to boot! Now go reel your father out of the fishpond, Lad, he was baring his soul to an eel last I saw of him. Sit you down here, little Lady Howard." He patted his knee.

It took Kathryn a moment to realize he meant her. "Yes, Uncle," she said obediently, smoothing her blue-gray sarcenet skirts and perching on his knee.

"Want to go to France, Niece?" Boleyn barked.

"Why do you ask, Sir?"

"Because King Harry's about to ship his pretty little sister, Mary, off to marry Louie the Twelfth of France. She is going to need experienced ladies-in-waiting amidst the new girls—new girls like my own Mary, though her sister Nan is an experienced maid of honor. Nan stayed at the Imperial Court in Flanders last year when I was ambassador. The Lady Regent liked her."

He was an ambitious man as she well knew, and it was generous of him to include her in his latest plans. "Thank you, but no, Uncle, my place is with Queen Catherine and my husband."

"Think of it, girl—French Court is not like here, a girl with your wit and face could go far."

She stood and brushed off her skirts. "Sir, I think if you want a promiscuous relative at the French Court you should look elsewhere."

He yelped with laughter as she walked away, head high, spine stiff. *Well*, she thought, *giddy little Mary Boleyn will do well enough in decadent France, she is pretty enough and too eager to be liked. But Nan is so young and so serious, she will never fit in. I am surprised to hear she was appreciated in the Low Countries.**

What would the Boleyn girls wear in France? she asked herself, stopping at the garden door. The family had little money, while she herself had three new gowns—she would give Mary her prettiest brown wool while the queen's old red silk-linen damask, her own favorite, would flatter Nan's dark, gypsylike coloring.

Thinking of that one solemn, dark little crow amidst the cheerfully tweeting Boleyn sparrows made her pity Nan fiercely. With a bride's big-hearted generosity, she decided she would not make over her old dresses to wear another year, but give them all to Nan.

Then she went out into the garden to make sure her husband had not been talked into going to France.

---

*Holland, Flanders and their general vicinity

7

Mary Tudor proved her lineage to the world that winter.

She did not flinch when her royal brother ordered her to France, did not openly display her repugnance to a gouty and near-toothless groom thirty-four years her senior. But as her quill hovered over the marriage lines, she regarded her brother with round eyes, and murmured, "You *did* say that when King Louis died as he is sure to in the near future—"

"That you could choose your own second husband. Yes, yes, now sign," King Henry urged frantically.

Mary announced that the quill tip was dull and called for a knife to sharpen it. By now beads of sweat were popping out on Henry Tudor's forehead. "You are certain?" she pressed him.

Yes, yes, of course he was. Over his head she made eye contact with the passionate Charles Brandon, newly created Duke of Suffolk. He was nodding nearly as insistently as the king was. So Mary Tudor languorously signed, leaving the observant Thomas Howards wondering what all that hesitation had been about.

Kathryn, newly pregnant, need not have worried about clothing her cousins—Mary Tudor's entourage was gorgeously arrayed to prove to France what sumptuous wealth King Henry had. Charles Brandon went enviously along. He could not seduce the new queen so he jousted viciously in France, defeating all comers.

Mary Tudor, whatever her personal feelings, kept her emotional cards close to her bodice and went unprotesting into Louis the Twelfth's hoary arms. He mightily bestirred himself to enjoy her favors three times on the wedding night; a prelate named Peter Martyr wrote a friend, "If he lives to smell the flowers of spring, you may promise yourself five hundred autumns!"

As Court critics had never yet seen five hundred autumns, Louis expired scarcely eleven weeks into the marriage. He perished on the first and most violent storm of the new year; all that wind came from Heaven laughing at the love-besotted old fool, courtiers said.

Mary Tudor ordered the Boleyn girls to start packing for her, only to be told that she must go into seclusion; the new king, saturnine François the First, wanted to be certain she was not carrying a child with a better claim to the throne than his own. While she was virtually locked up, François perused her at length and offered her the position of his *maîtresse en titre*—official mistress. She bounced a chamber pot off the royal chest and began shrieking that her brother would have his head on a platter.

François, only slightly dissuaded, withdrew from the scene.

The Boleyn girls wrote their relatives all about it, Nan being of the discreet, wardrobe-dwelling variety of eavesdropper. Her father rushed the news to King Henry, who, bellowing and stamping his feet, roared for someone to "Get the devil over there and fetch my sister home!"

This was Charles Brandon's cue. Newly arrived from the French wedding-turned-funeral, he dropped to his knees at Henry's feet, doffing his cap. "Your Grace, allow me."

Both Thomas Howards, Norfolk and Surrey, started forward to protest. Then the old man remembered the scene at the marriage-signing and halted, signaling Surrey to do the same.

By the time Mary Tudor next set foot on English soil she was Brandon's Duchess of Suffolk and Henry was purple with fury.

The Court, Kathryn included, fairly rolled on the floor with hilarity. Send Charles Brandon to fetch home the most beautiful Englishwoman alive! Charles of Suffolk, who had been widowed, divorced, and remarried often enough to make a living at it! "And the king is surprised? He might as well be surprised that a starving wolf let into a sheep pen makes off with the most succulent lamb," Margaret Pole whooped, and they all doubled up laughing again.

Not in the king's presence, though. "She was supposed to marry your nephew Charles, they were even betrothed once. She rejects the future King of Spain!" Henry railed at Catherine of Aragon. She nodded into her mending, struggling to maintain control of her features.

Henry paced faster and faster in front of the fireplace. "Well, it is too late to have it annulled now, the entire French Court has heard them consummating the marriage these many weeks."

Catherine made a helpless snorting sound and edged his half-mended shirt closer to her twitching face. The king continued. "There might even be a child on the way. Any move to break the marriage would leave my sister appearing to have borne a bastard, and that is unthinkable. But she was to have brought me another alliance, another—wife, what ails you?"

The half-mended shirt had come up over Queen Catherine's face by now and her stitches were an inch long. "A head cold, my lord," she managed, jerking with repressed laughter.

"Head cold! Are you laughing at me, Kate?"

She gave up, threw the shirt over her head, and burst into peals of breathless laughter. Wounded, Henry said, "Really, Kate, I fail to see what is so amusing about all this."

"It is just that she is so very like you! She, too, will have no master but herself."

That tickled Henry's touchy vanity at first, but as she went on cackling his feelings were hurt. So even his own wife thought him a fool to have sent amorous Charles after sweet Mary! "A divorced man! How could she?" he asked hotly, and stamped his foot.

Catherine of Aragon yanked the shirt off her head, suddenly sober. "A divorced man, it is unthinkable. You must fine him heavily since you cannot break up the marriage without impugning Mary's honor."

"That is a very good idea, Kate, I was wondering how to express my disapproval. And I believe I shall deny them coming into the royal presence for a while, too. Think how they shall suffer!"

To be forbidden the Court was very serious indeed. He must be even angrier than she suspected, to forbid them that magical sphere of influence, that center of all that mattered most in England. "Yes, you are very right to do this," she soothed her husband. "But think how you will enjoy having your beloved sister back in England again."

"That is true enough. But they are going to have a very public wedding at Court because there were so few witnesses to that furtive match in France. No one is going to call Mary Tudor a trollop!"

Meanwhile his other sister was hardly doing better by him. Margaret Tudor, widowed at Flodden Field, had remained in Scotland as regent to her infant son. She, too, married for love the second time, and she, too, did it without consulting Henry about her choice of bridegroom. Her second husband, the fiery Earl of Angus, was such a difficult spouse that the uproarious English Court took to calling him the Earl of

Anguish. More indelicate snorting into mending followed. It trebled when Margaret Tudor wrote Henry with the word *divorce* underlined.

Henry strode into his wife's rooms, flapping the latest letter and shouting, "Both of my sisters have married vile rogues and so blackened England's name at home and abroad! *Divorce!* How dare she write that word to me? I shall see her in a nunnery first, I shall lock her up on bread and water, I shall tolerate no divorces in this family!"

He halted, glancing with concern at his placid and heavily pregnant wife. Her widowed father, Ferdinand the Fox, had married an eighteen-year-old niece of Louis the Twelfth and worn himself out hunting, dancing, and lovemaking. Peter Martyr, who had commented so acidly on King Louis's own May-December marriage, hastened to pen, "Ferdinand expired of hunting and matrimony, either of which is fatal to most men at age sixty-three."

Henry had allowed no one to tell Catherine of her father's death, lest it endanger this latest pregnancy of hers. "I have disturbed you with my rumbling and stamping," he said softly.

Catherine stood, hands to the small of her aching back. "No, My Lord, it is only this great son of yours, wanting to be born," she said, and smiled.

"It *will* be a son," Henry said flatly, kissing her damp forehead.

"Oh, yes, a squalling, lively son such as little Kathryn Howard has."

"I will have her bring him in to see you. What did she name him? Oh, yes, James. The sight of little James Howard will reassure you that you shall bear me a healthy son."

A contraction shook her. Gasping, Catherine burst out, "There is no time to fetch any sons but our own, Husband! Where are my ladies? Where are the doctor and midwives? Your son approaches!"

The son was a daughter, christened Mary. She was lusty and vociferous, but then, so had been dead Prince Henry, the intended Henry the Ninth. "At least this one was not stillborn or miscarried or too premature to live as the others had been," Henry comforted himself by saying. He was afraid to touch Mary at first, fearing she would go the way of the others, but as weeks past and she grew strong and cheerful, he took to carrying her about with him. "The greatest jewel in the kingdom," he named her to visiting ambassadors.

Kathryn and Maria de Salinas Willoughby, both with children of their own, leaned over the royal cradle and shook gilt rattles at Mary. "Grow and prosper, little queen!" Kathryn whispered.

"You must not call her that, the king will be angry. She will have brothers and then she shall not be queen," Maria said firmly.

Dark Spanish eyes met blue English ones over the cradle, not daring to speak doubts aloud. Catherine of Aragon rarely had her monthly courses any more; what if this delicate girl-child was the last born to her?

"We will all have more children, you, the queen, and myself," Maria announced, and reached to hug Kathryn.

To her surprise she saw tears start up in Kathryn's eyes, and so hurried her from the royal nursery. "What is it, dear girl?" Maria asked, offering an embroidered handkerchief.

"I shall not be having any children for a while."

"That last miscarriage?"

Kathryn nodded. "The doctors have ordered me to sleep apart from Edmund for six months. It has only been six weeks and already he is . . . he is . . ."

Did she mean he was forcing himself on her or—worse to Spanish Catholic Maria—seeing another woman? Maria crossed herself. "You still have James and he is healthy. When the six months are over you will start more sons."

Kathryn bit down on a wad of handkerchief. She longed to spill the entire story but could not bring herself to do so. In the first place, Edmund had changed since their marriage. Now that he possessed her he no longer treated her as a valued friend and confidante, only as a bedmate and housekeeper. Upon receiving the doctors' orders he had immediately interpreted them as permission to commit adultery, and was doing so far afield.

And her baby did not like her. It seemed ridiculous to say of a year-old child, but James screamed and fussed constantly at her. He was only quiet for his father; not even dear Tansy could seem to calm or amuse him.

At least, she thought, letting Maria hug her, Ned was not doing his philandering openly, publicly.

But one week later he began courting Lord Mountjoy's pretty fourteen-year-old niece, Bessie Blount. Bessie shoved him away and boldly cried out, "I shall not be wasting my maidenhead on a mere knight, Ned Howard! Water those spurs until they grow into a ducal coronet and then mayhaps I shall consider it!"

The story went all over court. Kathryn kept her head up, though she rushed to her mirror to see if she appeared old and ugly at age sixteen. She explained to none but Maria that Edmund slept apart for her health's sake; let the others think what they may, she refused to defend herself. Soon people were saying that she was a cold wife, and it was no wonder poor Ned Howard sought comfort elsewhere. He would be lucky to get a second son out of that thin, stiff-necked prude.

"Here now!" the Earl of Surrey roared at her one morning when they passed in the king's antechamber. "Why are your eyes so puffy, Niece?"

She glowered at him for drawing attention to the fact that she had cried herself to sleep again last night. Surrey, after studying her a minute, asked, in softer tones, "Shall I take that young rascal out and thrash him within an inch of his life?"

Kathryn smiled affectionately. Everyone thought Thomas Howard the Younger gruff and unfeeling, but she knew better. "No, but thank you," she answered.

"Ned's behavior is unpardonable, a man should be discreet. And that Blount girl—there is a strumpet in the making if I have ever seen one! She wants money or a title for her maidenhead. She is no honest woman, you shall see. Better not to worry about the likes of her. Why, you are better company than that girl any day!"

"Most men do not care for conversation, uncle. They care for beauty."

"You would be pretty enough if you only ate once in a while," Thomas Howard informed her, lightly pinching her arm and finding no spare flesh there.

At a court pageant in honor of the Princess Mary's birth, Bessie Blount appeared in blue velvet and gold tinsel-cloth, which splendidly set off her golden tresses. Her witty refusal of Edmund was repeated until it reached the king, courtesy of Thomas Boleyn, who, had he been female, would have been known as the Court Gossip instead of King's Advisor. "She said, Your Grace, that she would not be wasting her virginity on a knight or perhaps even a mere duke."

Henry Tudor sat forward on his high-backed chair and picked at his teeth with a scrolled golden stick. "Think, then, how a king would please her, eh, Thomas? You are a whoremaster, one hears how you allow your daughter Mary to peddle her charms the length and breadth of the French

Court. And yet why shove Elizabeth Blount at me? What benefits it you if I bed the girl?"

Boleyn bowed very low—too low, Henry thought, watching from the corner of his eyes while Bessie Blount danced before him. She curtsied extravagantly, showing him her boiled leather corset and all that firm white flesh compressed by it so that her breasts had a deep, tight cleft between them.

Thomas Boleyn murmured, "I am benefited by witnessing your pleasure in observing so beautiful a subject, Your Grace, no more."

Henry gnawed his toothpick a moment before answering. "Boleyn, you are a sycophant and a pander. I have always admired that in a man! Think you I should enter the dance?"

Bessie was dancing enticingly near the royal dais again, flashing all that pulsing white cleavage. Boleyn said, "If only to prevent all the other men at Court from trampling each other to death in an effort to reach her first, Your Grace."

Henry, laughing, stood and smote Boleyn on the back. "Yes, decidedly a sycophant and pander. Did I get that speck of cress from between my front teeth, Thomas?" Assured that he had, he descended the dais and joined the dancers.

Early next morning, Bessie Blount moved into larger and grander rooms at Court, taking those next to Kathryn's. Hearing furniture bumping and scraping and people creeping about in the pre-dawn gloom, Kathryn yanked a rabbit-lined nightgown on over her sleeping shift and stumbled next door. "Why, greetings, Bessie. What is happening?"

The blonde, dressed for hunting, pulled on one prettily perforated green kid glove. "I am directing the decorating of these rooms I have just inherited."

Kathryn rushed to the maid of honor's side, forgetting her jealousy over Ned's attention to Bessie. "Oh, I am so sorry! Who has died?"

"My virtue," Bessie announced, looking about the multi-room suite with its many windows. "Yes, my virtue," she repeated, satisfied with this latest turn of events. She went out switching her taffeta skirts and whistling "Me Liketh Ever."

Within a week she was sporting a new gown in the Tudor colors, green and white, slashed in the German fashion to show her sheer linen shift beneath, which was then drawn out in large puffs of fabric. She rode the finest bay gelding at Court and took it to heart that Kathryn's white mare, Mask, surpassed him. From there on the mare was a bone of contention between the two girls. As Bessie could not have the finer mount, she was forced to settle for finer trappings. Mask had been delivered with a scrolled silver sidesaddle, but Bessie must have a gilt one, edged in jewels and set on a cloth-of-gold blanket. When even that did not satisfy her, she covered her mount in green-and-white trappings stitched all over with gold *H*'s.

Kathryn retaliated by putting *C*'s (for Catherine of Aragon) all over Mask with lip paint and leaving her tied in the Greenwich courtyard. Her grandfather Norfolk laughed so hard that his servants feared he would have a stroke and begged him to settle himself. "That child!" he gasped out. "She is so like my father Jack—so pig-headed, so unswerving in her loyalties! I will wager you the Blount wench bursts her bodice strings when she sees that horse!"

Bessie did worse than that. She exploded into Kathryn's bedchamber at dawn, dressed for riding and carrying a leather riding crop, which she brought whishing down on the bedclothes. Kathryn woke to a harpy's shrieks and the feel of blows landing through thin coverlets and sheets. Spotting that familiar blonde head in the dim light, she sat, threw the covers over Bessie, and rode her to the floor.

Greenwich Palace awakened to such a screeching as it had never heard. "You whore, get out of my room!"

"Whore, am I? You could use some whoring yourself, Kat Howard, after the way your husband crawled to me on his belly—"

"He was only trying to approach you on your own level, you bitch!"

"Look who is talking, you with your slut mother! Which Plantagenet pretender to the throne *really* sired you? Or did all of them? And we all know what you did to get that horse from de Gael!"

Listeners, gathering blurry-eyed at the door, reported that they heard glass shattering, a riding crop descending many times, and the hard smack of fists on flesh. Squeals of feminine pain and outrage, such curses as few men uttered—"And our niece was the worse of the two! I had no idea she *knew* such words," Elizabeth Boleyn admiringly confided to her husband later.

Kathryn was distinctly heard to cry, "So you wear the king's initials on your gown, eh? I will show you what they did to our initialed gowns the Night of the Twelve Dancers!"

Open-handed slaps were followed by cloth being ripped and shredded. Shrieks, more blistering oaths. Suddenly the door burst open, releasing a half-dressed Bessie Blount on a flock of eavesdroppers.

Kathryn, hair coming out in clumps, blood streaming from both nostrils, stood triumphantly brandishing the broken riding crop. "How dare you betray our mistress the queen? You, you, you—" She had used "whore" overmuch, she thought, and must seek for some new way to insult her rival. She finished a long string of invectives with, "And we all know you *bleach your hair*, you shameless trollop!"

Bessie, hands to her false golden roots, fled screaming.

That night Elizabeth Boleyn delivered to her niece a dismissal from the king. But morning found Kathryn turning back the queen's bedclothes as she did each day and handing her a steaming cup of clove water while Margaret Pole threw open the shutters. "Good morning, Your Grace," the bedchamber women chorused.

Catherine of Aragon sat, stretching. "Good morning, ladies. Why, Kathryn, I heard you were leaving us for—" She gasped, and spilled clove water in the act of taking a sip. "Your face! My dear girl, your face, who has—oh, men can be such brutes!"

Kathryn said darkly, "A woman did this, Your Grace."

"A woman! Who?"

"It would scorch my lips to say her name in your presence."

"The whore Blount?" Catherine of Aragon demanded, and all her tense ladies dissolved into giggles. The queen laughed, too; after a moment even Kathryn followed suit. "Lady Howard, you need not defend me with your fists and paintbrush. Did the, er, initials ever come off the horse?"

"Yes, Your Grace."

The queen smiled fondly. "That is good. Now, you must go back to your husband's bed and end all this gossip and bad feeling. And I will in turn prevent the king from sending you away."

It was phrased with the best of intentions, but it was a royal ultimatum nonetheless. Queen Catherine did not know about the doctors' orders; it had only been half of the allotted six months.

"Yes, Your Grace," Kathryn said weakly, and knelt to kiss the proffered white hand.

8

The court rode a-Maying that spring as it did every year, for May First was England's most favored of the old pagan holidays. Fairs in London eagerly awaited King Henry's annual "surprise" appearance amidst the Morris dancers with their beribboned staves and garland-heaped hats, for the king often joined them after picnicking and hunting all the day.

This year's festivities took the Court to verdant riverside Windsor, seat of England's kings since the days of William the Conqueror. Queen Catherine insisted on bringing little Mary along lest the baby die while they were gone, as Prince Henry had; the child necessitated her early return to the dank castle while the day was yet young.

Bored, the king cried out, "Let us hunt without her, then! Boleyn, Surrey, Suffolk, awaken and arise! To horse, My Lords, and your ladies as well!"

The drowsy picnickers bestirred themselves, dropping bits of fowl they had been gnawing, lifting their heads from each others' shoulders or laps. Bessie Blount, with a simper, adjusted her gloves and struck a pretty pose near her gelding. As the king hoisted himself aboard his own horse, Edmund Howard rushed to aid Bessie. Kathryn, burning with humiliation, stepped back in time to see the king lean from his saddle. He tapped Edmund with his crop. "Let Surrey do it, boy; you will not do any poaching on *this* particular preserve."

The Earl of Surrey turned, saw Kathryn standing alone and clench-fisted, unable to mount Mask because of tight bodice and trailing skirts. Affecting not to hear the king, he said, "Here, Niece, let me help you." He hefted her up to Mask's silver saddle, slipped the bit into the mare's mouth, and handed Kathryn the reins. She gave him a quick, grateful glance.

He aided the infuriated Bessie next, flinging her gracelessly aboard so that she momentarily went rump-up, ripping out her hem and smacking herself in the face with her riding crop. By that time the king had ridden on ahead, leaving her no one to complain to; all riders hurried after the royal presence.

Up ahead the huntsman's horn blew amidst oaks and willows, pied hounds yipping in shrill tenor tones. Lords and ladies spurred after those sounds, eager to catch up to the king.

They traveled many miles in his wake without sighting prey. The horses finally stood back at Windsor once more, huffing and blowing in exhaustion; Mask alone, Kathryn noted with pride, was not winded. King Henry noted that, too; she found it odd that a king should be jealously glaring at her mount. Then a nearby horn blew. A magnificent rack of antlers flashed in the fecund valley below, and vanished into a thick grove of oaks. The hounds roused themselves, went baying in pursuit; riders spurred their weary mounts a final time. Kathryn sent Mask after the others, catching glimpses of an ancient house, nearly hidden by the valley's trees, as she rode. Down the slope now, hooves skidding on damp turf, horses sliding on their haunches. And still that enticing rack of antlers bobbing in the brush. "Look at him! I have never seen finer antlers!" Charles Brandon shouted. "Fifty points or more!"

King Henry had caught up to the hounds. "Ho, lads, the shot is mine," he shouted. Kathryn watched him draw his gorgeous yew-bow and fit the arrow to the nock. He held that pose long seconds as his horse obediently stopped. Another man would have shuddered with the strain of holding the huge longbow, but Henry was in his violent prime; as the sweat of strain ran into his eyes he squinted, perfected his aim. Let fly the feathered arrow.

The stag screeched like a woman, then staggered, fell. The hunting party gazed in astonishment as he rose on forelegs alone. His hindquarters looked paralyzed from the feathered shaft in them. He was dragging himself gallantly, as if by supernatural effort—they would lose him if he gained those trees ahead. . . .

He crept beneath the largest oak, shuddered, and died sitting upright. The slender forelegs buckled, the heavy tree of antlers sank to the ground. "A brave animal," Elizabeth Boleyn said, and crossed herself in superstitious awe.

Everyone rode after the victorious king, then reined in their steaming mounts, calling congratulations. Kathryn jerked her head up, hearing too many hooves pounding around her. *Other riders are approaching*, she thought in confusion.

"Strange how the animal cried out when struck," Surrey observed.

"Yes, like a woman," his wife agreed.

Thomas Boleyn grinned at them. "Perhaps he was calling for help."

"Rather belatedly," the king announced proudly. There was a ripple of feminine delight as Bessie Blount agreed with her lord and lover.

Henry Tudor threw his reins to Edmund Howard and swung down from his golden saddle. A quick gesture brought his huntsman scuttling forward. The small, hooded man had no sooner drawn his voyding knife to gut the stag than the surrounding grove exploded into action. Two dozen mounted archers in black-and-gold livery burst out at the hunting party; yew-bows laid on laps voiced a silent threat. Bessie screamed, Charles Brandon reached for his own bow.

"I would not do that, M'lord," rang out a deep voice.

A late arrival rode from behind the ring of archers. He reined in a spirited white mare, near-twin to Kathryn's Mask; the horse shied and curvetted between standing king and dead stag.

Her rider had apparently rushed from bed or bath as he was tousled, shockingly hatless, and only half-dressed. Long, expensive boots of chestnut leather had not been fastened and so slid down about his calves; he wore no breeches over his brown silk hose and no doublet, jerkin, or cape. His magnificent shirt boasted twice the black embroidery of the king's own and the silk of it was nearly transparent, reminding Kathryn of winter's first thin ice on a pond. There was a half-year's work from three embroideresses in that shirt; the king himself boasted nothing so elaborate.

Neck and wrist strings fluttered, untied. The shirt hung open to the stranger's waist, slid halfway off one broad shoulder. Kathryn caught up her breath. A fine figure of a man with his craggy face and rumpled chestnut hair. Something familiar about—oh, Sweet Jesu, those milky blue-white eyes and he was riding a white mare—her heart hammered so loudly she feared those around her must hear it.

"*You,*" he snapped with regal aplomb, jabbing an accusatory forefinger at the kneeling huntsman. "You touch that stag and I shall hang you higher than Haman."

At the sound of his voice the white mare reared, but he brought her down effortlessly, one-handed. Elizabeth Boleyn, glancing from his mare to identical Mask, whispered, "Spirited horse."

Bessie Blount, visually devouring the rider, murmured, "I

would buck and plunge if *I* were under John de Gael, too!" Nervous giggles crept through the clustered women.

So he had a name and was indeed one of the Unmentionable de Gaels. *Why, you are a child!* rang in Kathryn's head. *Are you certain there is not some Borgia blood alongside the Howard?* . . . He was younger than he had sounded, not even a decade her senior. How arrogant of him to call her a child five years ago when he had hardly reached adulthood himself!

He was not as handsome as in her dreams. But there was something vital about this man, something proud and feral, like the lion she had once seen in the royal menagerie.

King Henry—at a disadvantage, for he was on foot—threw back his copper-and-ivory head and planted a meaty fist on each hip. "Who the devil are you, to countermand an order to my huntsman? I take it, Sir, that you do not know who I am!"

That infuriated de Gael forefinger now jabbed in the king's direction. "No, I take it that *you* do not know who *I* am! You have crossed from your land to mine and killed my king-stag, not one of your own. *Show him.*"

It was not lost on a person present that he gave the king no title of respect, not so much as the "sir" offered a stranger. Henry Tudor's face was more purple than red at this point.

A little blond archer dropped from the saddle, knelt, raised the dead stag's left forefoot. A neat double wedge had been nicked in the hoof, forming a *W*. "Thus we mark all of our stock to distinguish them from yours. Our stags are smaller than yours and darker, with more points per rack; the difference between yours and mine is obvious at one hundred yards on so clear a day," John de Gael snapped.

Henry, hands fisted on his hips, scanned his opponent's face. "I take it you are the present head of this nest of heretics and Plantagenet by-blows known as the de Gaels."

Satisfied that he had regained lost honor with such an insult, he turned to his companions with a smug face. The chill voice behind him rang out, "And I take it you are one of those parvenu Tudors from up the hill. Tell me, have they ever found Katherine of Valois' marriage lines with your great-grandfather? Or proved Margaret Beaufort's first betrothal was annulled before she married your grandfather?"

Nearly all present gasped. Henry the Seventh had based his claim to the throne on a mésalliance between once-queen Katherine of Valois and Owain Twydwr; none but the Tudors had ever claimed matrimony blessed the affair. And Margaret Beaufort *had* been betrothed elsewhere before marrying Owain's son, Edmund—

John de Gael had just called the Tudors bastards.

Henry royally purpled as he swung to face de Gael again. "By God, you are saucy, Sir! You dare not speak thus to your king amidst his own courtiers!"

"No? My ears must mislead me, then, for I would vow I already *had*. Now listen to me and listen well, King of Nothing: as I have no title left and your father made my Windsgeat an independent duchy with its own laws, you cannot hurt me. You are poaching on private land and if you do not remove yourself and your companions, I shall, for starters, have my archers quill your huntsmen and pack like porcupines. I won my case against the last hunter who poached on my land; *you* would presumably not face the noose, as you can reputedly pay the fine. But I would insist on coinage, not a promissory note."

Not one of the twenty-four Welsh longbows was raised, but the king's hunting party began retreating. King Henry seized his reins from Edmund and attempted to remount. His horse evaded him three times before he managed to swing aboard—a poor showing in the light of de Gael's horsemanship. The little blond archer from Windsgeat had to help him. "By God, Sir, I shall see you in the Tower!" Henry bellowed.

John de Gael looked utterly unperturbed. "I think not. Ask Hal Chase or Norfolk why you cannot touch me; they will tell you. As head of an independent duchy I am not answerable to the Crown, regardless of my lack of titles. Your own father saw to that; we received the writ from his hands."

"—my father!" the king snarled, and turned his horse for Windsor.

The blond archer fell in alongside Kathryn as she rode. He murmured in a Flemish accent, "My Lady, De Lord of Windsgeat requests dat you circle back. He would speak wid you, if he may be so honored."

He spoke as though of a king or god. Kathryn, a-tremble with conflicting emotions, slowed Mask so that the others far outstripped her. When she had fallen far enough behind, she reined in beneath a stand of willows so that John de Gael was forced to ride after her and not the other way around. He did so, reining in at her side.

As if he had earlier heard her mental assessment of his looks, he smiled and was suddenly, unbearably, handsome.

"I deeply regret your having to witness that disagreeable exchange. Well! So you have grown up, I am not certain I approve. You *are* Kathryn Chase . . . ? The azure eyes—I am certain it is you. Speak up, I know you have a reputation for holding your tongue at awkward times, but anyone who shrieks "whore" at the king's mistress cannot be all that shy."

Unwillingly, she felt her lips curl up in a smile. "Five years ago you complained that I was a child. Now you complain because I have grown up. Make up my mind for me, My Lord. Surely there is some brief, fleeting moment in a woman's life when she is an acceptable age?"

John de Gael's smile widened, showing the slightly crooked teeth she remembered—his one unlovely feature. Oddly it only endeared him to her the more; her heart seemed to turn cartwheels in her breast. He said, laughing, "I had forgotten what spirit you showed the night of that riot. Not afraid to fight half of London nor be left alone in a crypt. Gods, you were a peppery little creature! Still are. Would you consider returning with me to Windsgeat for supper?"

"What, and come home with a Plantagenet by-blow of my own? What a pretty compliment, and you newly wed to my father's sister!"

She could have bitten her tongue off for that one, and colored with embarassment. He reddened, too. "I meant no harm. You are still a child to me, though married and with a child of your own. As for your aunt, I married her out of love and she came to me with her false, bright smiles and winning ways, bearing the king's bastard. All men are fools, my young friend."

He had called her friend before. "Are women any better?" she countered.

"Do you refer to my inestimable wife—who, by the way, is fighting divorce tooth and claw for the sake of my fortune—or to yourself, because you married Ned Howard?"

"You have never been to Court, what do you know of me or my husband?" she demanded.

"I know he is a wencher and becoming a drinker as well. But as it troubles you, we will say no more of him. . . . How do you like the mare?"

"She is sweet, my lord, and responsive to the slightest signal."

"She *should* be, I gentled her myself, starting within a few minutes of her foaling. I wanted to give you something that would be all your own, as your family gave you so little. . . .

If you ever let your husband touch her, I will take her back," he threatened.

"Oh, no, never! I never let anyone else handle her, only the stable boy and myself," Kathryn hurried to say. She realized that he was smiling then, that all the gruffness in his voice had been teasing. What an odd man; he had threatened the king, insulted him, and yet thought to give a rich gift to a child he had met once.

A sudden, unbearable thought struck her: *Oh, if I only had not rushed to marry Ned! Ned hates me now, while this man considers everything—*

The fantasy that had sustained her these five years popped inaudibly. Dreams were of no use, she could not change the past. She had married, so had he. "I named her Mask," she said quietly. "And I cannot thank you enough for her, she is the most precious thing I have and she knows it. No one at Court has a finer horse; the queen covets her."

"Then you must give the queen my prettiest compliments and tell her I have many more horses, some of them very nearly worthy of her. Will you do that for me, Kathryn?"

He had called her by name without a title or any formality. It shook her to the core, made her suddenly angry with him, with herself, with the way her life had turned out. He was no fairy tale prince after all, he was mere flesh, though still as distant as any dream. "Yes, I will pave your way with the queen. But only if you tell me what you and your family did to have Windsgeat declared an independent duchy even without the title's restoration. Everyone knows your father fought at Bosworth."

Those slightly crossed teeth showed again in the merest hint of a grin. "My family specializes in deeds that no one else will sink to. My man will see you back to Windsor. Pieter, be so good as to escort the lady."

He turned and rode away with a flick of the reins. Kathryn stood up in the stirrups, dangerously unbalancing the mare; Mask snorted disapproval and stamped at pine needles.

Damn the man! He was not neat, precise, and perfumed like the dandies at court, he smelled of leather, horse, and hot silk. Tight male muscles in close-cut hose, a cynical laugh, an uneasy mouth, and yet there was a sparkle to his eyes. His chestnut hair was inches thick and, oh, the tantalizing bare shoulder in that untied shirt! . . . She had been able to see all of his chest in that shirt, the fine golden-brown hairs and his nipples. Kathryn found herself suddenly, violently alive, and hungry for things she had never known.

"My lady?"

She turned to Pieter van der Hüm, the little blond archer, and saw him regarding her with understanding. "I will ride far behind you so dat I seem a passerby and not an escort. If dey find you have spoken wid De Lord, dey will assume de worst," the Fleming warned her. "*The Lord,*" she thought, *as if John is Christ Himself!* He took off his easily recognized black-and-gold, followed her discreetly back.

No one but Bessie Blount seemed to notice she had been gone. Suspicious and envious, Bessie glared at her as they rode behind the king, who was saying, "To the devil with my father, and to the devil with that Plantagenet bastard's duchy! I will take one thousand acres of his precious Windsgeat, that should crease his monstrous pride! I shall clap him in irons, place him in the Tower of London, and . . ."

Henry took the thousand acres but he never had John de Gael arrested; the Duke of Norfolk labored all night to talk him out of it.

It was years before Kathryn found out why.

9
Howard House, London
June 1519

"Visitors from Wales, milady," announced Tansy.

Kathryn took the baby from her breast, covered herself and smiled. "Wales! They must be family, then. Please send them in."

Tansy fluffed her pillows, deposited a shawl around Kathryn's shoulders, and went on out. A young couple soon shyly approached the doorway, hanging back with lowered heads and scuffling feet. Both had blond-brown hair and eyes that looked blue even at this distance; the boy was seventeen or so, the girl somewhat younger. "Come in," Kathryn called out cheerfully. "Forgive my not rising but I only had the baby yesterday. You two are—?"

"Arthur and Mary Chase, Milady," the boy said.

Her brother and sister! She had not seen them since early

childhood. Kathryn exclaimed with pleasure, shifted her new son to one arm that she might use the other for an embrace. Mary hurried into the caress—what a pretty girl she was, Kathryn thought proudly—but Arthur hung back shyly.

They sat on dead queen Elizabeth Woodville's curtained bed with her, warming by degrees until they all laughed and chatted like old friends. "But I am so surprised to see the two of you," Kathryn said at last. "I thought Mary a nun by now and Arthur, the last I heard you were managing Father's estates in the Marches. Tell me, did our parents' divorce ever go through?"

Mary Chase laughed with a sweet, chiming sound. "No, Mother and Father are still together, quarreling and making love." Arthur said her name disapprovingly but Mary continued, dawdling with a pillowcase. "And I have no wish to be a nun. Mother cannot force me. The nuns did not like me, anyway. Father sold the estates so there was nothing for Arthur to do. There we were, no acres to ride, no social life, terribly boring. So Mother suggested we come to you."

Kathryn chuckled, bouncing the drowsy baby so that he gave a mournful gurgle. "In other words you two seek my help finding positions at Court. Very well then; you, Mary, shall apply to Mistress Stonor, the 'Mother of the Maids,' as she is called. She reviews and trains prospective maids of honor. And Arthur, I am not certain about you. What is your speciality, dear brother? Horses, the law, estate management?"

"Horses," Arthur quickly answered.

"Then we shall see if the Master of Horse can find work for you. That is where Ned is making best use of his talents these days."

When he was not out wenching, that was.

A few minutes later, Edmund himself entered for his first sight of the baby. He pecked Kathryn dispassionately on the brow; she did not bother asking where he had been all night. "Another fair son, madam?"

"Another son. What shall we name him, Ned?"

"Adam, for my poor old father. Two sons in five years, Kat; not bad, but we must do better."

He stepped back, smiling as she introduced him to Mary and Arthur. Edmund was far from the boy she had met at Durham House, Kathryn thought, watching him bow over Mary's hand. Oh, the freckles were still there, and the impudent eyes and strong Howard nose, but the inner Edmund seemed gone forever. This new man could only drink, whore, and wait for his father to die that he might inherit what little remained.

"Another fair son," he repeated, then added, eyes twinkling, "but, by God, a fairer sister! Shall I show her and Arthur the sights of London this night?"

How uncharacteristically generous of him. "Yes, Ned, please do," she said, surprised.

He sent her brother and sister on out and turned back to the bed. "Why have you not asked me for the latest Court gossip? Bessie Blount has borne the king a son and been rewarded with a promise of dull country living, a dull estate, and an even duller husband."

"In other words, glorified banishment."

"Exactly. While the king has named the boy Henry Fitzroy and kept him to be reared as an heir in case the queen bears no more—"

"Oh, but she will, Ned. Queen Catherine will have sons, you shall see."

"Would that all of us had your blind faith in her reproductive abilities," he said, and went on out. Not a single inquiry as to her health and hardly any mention of the baby, Adam, except to name him. And the king keeping Bessie Blount's bastard at Court right in front of the queen—men could be so thick-skinned, Kathryn thought irritably. Oh, well, at least Catherine of Aragon would no longer have to tolerate Bessie's daily presence now. And the thought of self-centered Bessie drummed out of Court into the arms of some gentleman farmer, far from the center of action, had a satisfying ring to it.

Tansy brought little James in just then, leaving Kathryn too preoccupied with her sons to dwell on Bessie Blount any more. "The queen should have sons like yours," Tansy observed.

"Yes, that would make all of England rejoice. Have you asked the housekeeper to set places for two more, late tonight?"

"Oh, no, your husband says he is taking Mary and Arthur out with him."

It was late when they returned, drunk and boisterous. Kathryn met them at the door, her face streaked with tears. "Ned, it is your father," she began.

"It can wait. Help me to bed, Wife, I can scarce stand upright."

Arthur collapsed in the nearest chair and began snoring almost at once. Kathryn called old Lord Adam's bodyservant to put her brother to bed and signaled Tansy to lead the tittering Mary away. "Please come into the solar, Ned. We need to talk," Kathryn repeated.

He threw his hat and gloves on the nearest oak breakfront. "Very well, I promise not to get Mary and Arthur intoxicated again or—"

"Your father is dead."

She had to blurt it out in an effort to capture his attention. Edmund's sole reaction was to bellow for his father's bodyservant to hurry back to him with a bottle of ale. Once he had finished tucking Arthur in, the old man arrived wet-eyed and stoop-shouldered, for his lord of forty years' service lay cold in the bedchamber above.

"Here is your ale, Sir Ned," he said almost inaudibly.

"That's Lord Howard to you."

"Yes, My Lord," the old man agreed, depositing the ale on the oak breakfront and bowing on his way out.

Edmund wrested out the cork and drank freely from the bottle. He looked around himself fixedly. "I believe I shall throw out these old tapestries, have some new ones brought from France. What do you think, Kat?"

She understood that he was not asking her opinion, only thinking aloud, so bitterly held her tongue. He continued, "And I shall pull down the back of the house, glass it in for fruit trees. The queen has planted some very fine plum and cherry trees, you must get slips from her gardeners for me. Yes, I think the tapestries should go, and all these doddering old family retainers. I wish to fill my house with young people and much merriment."

At this she could no longer keep silent. "Ned, some of these servants have been with your family forty years and more. They will be unable to find other work, they are too old. Their fathers and grandfathers worked for Howards—"

"Then let some other Howard support them. Do not tell me what to do with my inheritance, wife, you are nothing in the eyes of the law. Now that I am lord, you must never contradict me again."

She fetched him a ringing slap that knocked him against his great-grandfather's portrait. "You are not Henry Tudor, milord, to so lecture and despise your wife! You are no king, merely my husband and the father of our children!"

He remained against the portrait, hand to scarlet cheek. "Am I, Kat? Am I their father?"

Kathryn gasped. "I have ever been a faithful wife to you, Ned, you know that!"

"Then perhaps you would like to explain this long friendship of yours with John de Gael? The entire Court buzzes about your visits to Windsgeat."

"I have taken the queen three times to see his horses, that is all. I rode with all the other ladies in Her Grace's retinue and the men-at-arms. Surely you can find no scandal in taking Queen Catherine to buy horses. You are drunk and ridiculous, Ned, and I object to your accusations."

"*Are they my sons?*" he cried out, lunging forward and catching her by the shoulders.

Kathryn yanked free. "Your father lies dead upstairs and all you can think of is squandering your inheritance and making insane accusations! Yes, James and Adam are yours! Look at that painting of your grandfather behind you and tell me those boys are not yours! The same eyes, same chin . . ."

She left him then and went upstairs to finish dressing and laying out her father-in-law. Old Adam Howard, who had been so kind to her—she prayed her newest-born, his namesake, would be like him and not like Ned.

Kathryn's cousin Mary Boleyn, having been passed from lord to lord like an old wineskin, was finally sent home from France in disgrace; chaste little Nan stayed behind. Nan wrote Kathryn, "And while I shall miss my sister for the long years' affection I bear her, I find myself hoping the French Court quickly forgets her existence that they may cease equating the words 'Boleyn' and 'whore.' "

Elizabeth and Thomas Boleyn quickly appealed to Kathryn's sense of family and she found Mary Boleyn a place in the queen's household. Almost at once King Henry sampled the blonde beauty's charms; within months he had married her to a member of his household that he not again be accused of debauching unprotected virgins as he had with Bessie Blount. Not that anyone on either side of the Channel was foolish enough to believe Mistress Boleyn innocent; there were more obscene songs about her than any woman since Eleanor of Aquitaine.

As for the other Marys, Mary Tudor Brandon, Countess of Suffolk, was still happily married to her adventurer and producing children at regular intervals. The king's daughter Mary Tudor remained an only child; Queen Catherine lost a full-term son after Mary and no other pregnancies followed. The Court held its collective breath, waiting to see if the nation's future was to depend on this one slender girl-child.

Mary Chase was dismissed by Mistress Stonor, Mother of the Maids, in precisely six weeks. When Kathryn pressed the stalwart woman for a reason, her only response was, "Eh, Lady Howard, your sister be not much like you. Let us leave it at that so you and me might remain friends, eh? Your sister is too pretty, for one thing. . . . I much prefer the mousey little girls like Jane Seymour and Anne Parr, they are so plain, so good."

England and France, playing at on-again, off-again war, decided that this year they should be allies. King François the First invited his "brother-king, Henri" to France for feasting, diplomatic neck-wringing, and jousting, and Henry Tudor, who could no more resist festivities than open bedroom doors, agreed.

The English Court flew into a panic. What to pack, what to wear? Which servants to take and which to leave behind? Should their children accompany them? Only those of marriageable age, the king answered. What about taking mistresses along? Henry Tudor found some piddling task for William Carey to perform, that his bride Mary Boleyn might accompany him to France.

"They are building grand pavillions and making cloth-of-gold tents," Arthur Chase told his enthralled sisters. "Carpenters are already in France and artists have been called in to design costumes and gowns for Court masques. I am glad to have been taken into the king's banquet planners, though I wanted to work with the horses; I hear so many more interesting things this way."

"Is the queen going?" young Mary asked.

"Oh, yes," Kathryn answered. "She has asked me and Aunt Elizabeth to dance for the French king. I only wish Maria de Salinas—Lady Willoughby—were going. How I miss Maria, she hardly ever leaves Parham House any more, and she has the sweetest little daughter named for the queen. . . ."

Mary caught at her sister's hands. "Oh, take me with you, Kat! I will do anything—take care of your gowns, be your servant, anything, only you must not make me stay home and miss the adventure of a lifetime!"

"The very idea of a young girl having adventures!" Kathryn marveled aloud. "What you should be having is a betrothal, and soon!"

"Oh, Kat, you are so old, all your living is done. You never think of anything but babies, horses, and helping the queen. You are an old married woman who cannot remember being young and alive."

Edmund told her she was dull, too. Kathryn swallowed too hard. "There is no need to be cruel to me, Mary, because you disagree with the way I live my life. Nevertheless, I will see if Ned and I can take both of you with us."

Mary squealed and applauded.

The next morning Catherine of Aragon called her women together. First came the unmarried maids of honor, glorified chambermaids who cared for her bed and body linens; the only women at Court below them in rank were the actual chamberers who swept, cleaned, and folded. Then the Ladies of the Presence Chamber filed in from the royal audience chamber where they aided Catherine of Aragon in handing out money and food to various charities and receiving visitors and petitions.

Ladies of the Privy Chamber entered next, looking down their noses at the others. These women were those allowed to wait on Queen Catherine in her private solar, music rooms, and chapel, the usual personal quarters of the monarch's wife as she moved about her daily householding out of the public eye.

Kathryn entered with the last and most select group—Ladies of the Bedchamber. These were in the position of greatest intimacy with the queen, bringing her a nightly posset and taking away her fur-lined nightgown, turning back the bedclothes, reading or sewing with Catherine of Aragon while she waited to see whether the king would or would not attend her that evening. They dressed and undressed the shrinkingly modest queen and so spotted pregnancies as soon as she did; they checked the state of the royal sheets each morning to see whether the queen was breeding, bedding the king, or having one of her irregular monthly courses that caused such distress and pain.

She was greeted by them each morning as they opened the shutters, drew back the bed curtains and coverlets, and brought her something to drink. They helped her into slippers and nightgown or handed her out of them into a bath; they dressed the queen's hair with golden cauls and jeweled gable headdresses, noting as the first gray hairs made their appearance. Combing, bathing, dressing, undressing the queen, reading, sewing, praying, and gossiping with her, these select few were Catherine of Aragon's closest companions and therefore the most powerful women in England.

Kathryn was the only woman among them born lower than a countess, now that Maria was away from Court. Surprisingly, the high-born women were gracious and not condescending to her, for not only was she a king's granddaughter, but they could hardly recall a time she had not been with the queen, first toddling amidst her spaniels, then carrying their royal mistress's embroidery basket after her. That had been her first task; her second had been to rip out stitches the queen deemed too long. She was still officially in charge of the queen's sewing supplies and longed for the day a daughter of hers would toddle after Catherine of Aragon with a split willow basket of threads and the treasured old tortoiseshell needle box with its entwined *H*'s and *K*'s.

Standing, waiting for the queen to speak, she noted how giggly the maids of honor were today. "They say Frenchmen are the handsomest and best-dressed gentlemen in the world!" exclaimed little Anne Parr.

Pale-faced Jane Seymour replied, "Nonsense, no one is handsomer or better-dressed than the English."

And Ned calls me *a prude and a bore!* Kathryn thought, delighted at being capped by a mere child.

Margaret Pole, Countess of Salisbury, imperiously shook out a roll of paper and began reading who would go to France and who would remain as an honor guard for the royal daughter. Most of the maids were staying home, for Queen Catherine wanted no accusations of immorality and especially no mésalliances producing half-French bastards nine months later. Several of the younger girls wept with disappointment, but, Kathryn observed, prosaic little Jane Seymour only shrugged and kept at her embroidery.

Kathryn had no doubts about being chosen herself, so did not react to hearing her name called off. She was the queen's, body and soul, and knew Catherine of Aragon knew it, so why trouble herself wondering like the others? The queen would never leave her behind. "It must be nice to be so certain," Elizabeth Boleyn whispered, and gave a little gasp of relief as her own name was read from the scroll.

Margaret Pole then read how many servants women of each rank could take, and what manners of gowns they must have made: black cotton velvet of such-and-such a cut, silver tinsel for the dancers (here Kathryn and Elizabeth clasped hands, knowing they were included in that number), green-and-white satin for hunting, red damask for this, gold brocade for that. Kathryn wrinkled her nose, knowing gold brocade showed her to her worst advantage. Her coloring was not strong enough to stand up to such garishness; silvers, reds, steel blues, and blacks were far kinder to her cornflower blue eyes, fair skin, and ashy hair. In fact, had she not been blessed with slanting black brows she knew she could not wear red or black at all.

When the women were finally dismissed in a gossiping, excited mass, Kathryn heard a familiar voice call her name. She turned, saw Edmund stomping toward her with a face like a thunderhead. "What is it, Dear?" she quickly asked.

"The king wants a white stallion to ride in France. The Master of Horse and I rode over to Windsgeat this morning and—" He seemed unable to finish the sentence.

Kathryn drew him by the sleeve to an alcove away from the crowd. "*And*?" she pressured none-too-gently. John did not like the king and he despised Howards, saving only herself; naturally he would have told his visitors to go to the Devil in a handbasket. But smarting from Edmund's inference long-ago that she had been unfaithful, she wanted to hear the story from his own lips.

"You know perfectly well what happened," Edmund grumbled. "Now how do we get a stallion for the king?"

"Why, I do not know. There are a great many white horses in England, I am sure someone will sell one to His Grace."

Edmund audibly ground his teeth, took his velvet cap off, and turned it inside-out. "I am very sorry I accused you of . . . misconduct with that man."

In other words he wanted her to ask John for a horse for the king. "Pray, continue," she ordered coolly. But she thought, *Squirm, Ned, squirm!*

"I said I am sorry and—and it will not happen again. Now will you and the queen visit Windsgeat? No one has finer horses than that man, and the king of England cannot ride through France on some plodding cob!"

"You consort with every bawd in London, accuse me of adultery, hardly bother to mourn for your own father, and now wish a favor of me? I will consider it, Ned. When I think of something you can trade me for such a service, I will let you know," she said coldly, and moved away.

That evening at dinner the king made a similar move to influence her. "Wife," he said loudly, "you love Lady Howard, do you not?"

Kathryn twitched.

"Yes, Your Grace," Catherine of Aragon agreed.

"Do you regard her as obedient to her king and queen?"

"Oh, yes, very."

Diners were beginning to hesitate in mid-bite, waiting to hear where this exchange was headed. Kathryn's ears burned.

"Tell me, Wife, do you suppose that unyielding Howard pride of hers could unbend enough to do her king and country a service?"

"I am certain of it, Your Grace," the queen said amiably, putting little tidbits of baked swallow and roast heron in his trencher. By now the other diners, having heard rumors, were staring at Kathryn with thinly veiled grins. As the king did not continue, Queen Catherine made the mistake of gently asking, "Why, my lord? What service do you need, pray tell?"

Henry's sizable fist smashed down on the long table, making soup bowls leap and dance. "I—" *Wham!* as he struck the table again. "want—" *Wham! Wham!* "a white horse!" *Wham, wham, wham!*

Mary Boleyn, about to lose control, took the honorable way out and fell in her soup. No one dared laugh, but several dozen scarlet faces showed the strain. Surrey and Norfolk were making inarticulate mewing sounds into their goblets; several maids of honor slid under the table where they lay kicking and convulsed with silent hilarity.

The king compounded his error. Glaring from face to twitching face, he burst out, exactly like a naughty child, "I want a bigger and better white horse than the king of France has!"

Mary Boleyn saved the day. Unable to help it any longer, she snorted hysterically, sucking soup in and spraying it everywhere. At this, half the company fled, falling over benches and one another. Everyone else leapt to pound on Mary's back and pretend she was the reason they laughed and gasped. "Whatever ails that Boleyn girl, do you suppose?" the king demanded.

Catherine of Aragon took excessive pains with her linen napkin, trying to wipe away her smile. "If you want a white horse, Your Grace, I am sure Lady Howard will do all in her power to aid in finding you one. I will, too. In fact, she and I shall ride out tomorrow from Windsor and see if we cannot locate someone with white horses."

But Queen Catherine and her ladies rode to Windsgeat alone the next day, for Mary Chase fell mysteriously ill and Kathryn rushed to Howard House to nurse her. For hours the girl tossed and moaned, eyes bright with fever. Kathryn, trickling cool water into her sister's mouth from a clean rag, suddenly noted that the bedclothes were turning red beneath her. "Mary, what have you done? Answer me, Mary—*what have you done?*"

Her sister's blue eyes fluttered open. "Forgive me, Kat. I could not allow myself to further disgrace you by bearing a bastard child."

Well, the Church called it a sin, but with a girl as pretty as Mary, Kathryn knew she should have been forewarned. "There, Sweetheart, no need to cry. Mary, how do you consider you have 'further disgraced' me?"

She dipped the rag in the basin, wrung it out, laid the cool cloth across her sister's hot brow. "I did not willingly leave the abbey, I—I was flung out for . . . immoralities with my confessor."

Kathryn bit her lip, forced down a cry of chagrin. "Oh, my poor little sister," she said loyally.

Mary burst into fresh tears. "No, you must not pity me! I have so severely wronged you that I deserve no kindness, no further love from you. Because, Kat, the father of my baby promised to leave his wife and marry me and I believed him. And he was—your husband Edmund!"

Ned. Ned was the father of the child Mary had just aborted. The entire room spun for a moment while Kathryn considered vomiting into the basin she held. Then her head cleared. She said rigidly, "You should have confided in me earlier instead of poisoning yourself in secret. I might have been able to find some gentler way to help you."

"Shall I die now?" the panic-stricken girl cried out.

"Probably not, now that I know what ails you. I shall have Tansy fetch some nettles and raspberry leaf, they say the juice stops bleeding . . . you poor, silly girl, you are my sister. How can you think I would not stand by you, no matter your mistakes?"

Now she knew why Mistress Stonor had drummed Mary out of the maids of honor—she must have caught her with Edmund or some other man.

When she was certain that Mary was out of danger, Kathryn went to stand in the new 'solar' where sun streamed in through long, mullioned windows. It hurt to look straight up into that dazzling warmth but she did, wishing it might burn her blind. Then she would never need look upon her husband's face again.

10

"The Field of Cloth of Gold" was the grandiose name given to the Anglo-French camping event. Anybody who was remotely important went; both countries were so stripped of their peers that a stableboy seated himself on Henry's vacant throne and commented, "Did a cannonball land on the Field o' Cloth o' Gold, I should be declared King o' the World by morning!"

The English monarchs took a mere five thousand retainers to that shallow dip between Guînes and Ardres, forever after called the Val d'Or—Valley of Gold. Amidst striped tents of painted fustian and rainbow-hued cloth of gold lay an open field for jousting and tilting, and there the two kings had arranged to meet.

Both men fussed like virgin brides over their appearance. Henry wrestled his way in and out of seven doublets, while François so waxed, trimmed, and tinkered with his beard that he mowed it down to a mere fringe.

"My crown, do you think?" Henry asked Catherine of Aragon, who stood holding a mirror up to him in his dressing tent.

She smiled beatifically. "No need, my lord, he will know you by your clothes and bearing. Now! How about the white-and-gold flat hat with the seven ostrich plumes?"

"My crown, do you think?" François asked Queen Claude, who held the mirror he primped in.

"No need, my lord, he will know you without it. Might I suggest the silver cap with the ribands and feathers?"

Both kings had ambassadors and spies in each other's camps, by which means they discovered when their fellow sovereign left his tent, when he mounted his horse, and how soon he approached the broad, grassy field. They arrived at opposite ends of the field at the same time and reined in their mounts, waiting to see what the other man would do. François's gorgeous black charger raked the ground with a splendid forefoot; Henry Tudor's magnificent Windsgeat White half-reared, allowing his rider to exhibit a showy mastering of him.

Both kings waited another nerve-wracking minute. Then, laughing, Henry spurred his stallion foreward. Not to be outdone, François also nudged his own horse over the low fence. The kings rode toward each other at a breakneck pace. Trumpets and hautbois blew, men cheered and shouted. Henry laughingly flung his cap into the air and François returned the gesture. Their horses skidded to a halt together, sinking back on muscular haunches while the kings impulsively reached across their necks to embrace.

That night each king dined with the other's queen. The banqueting hall was redolent with heady scents and soft music; lutes played mildly, boy tenors singing of heartbreak while royalty feasted.

Outside, the pecking order was being violently established. Bigger and better tents were grabbed by the highest ranking until it occurred to a master of protocol that while Kathryn and Edmund had very little rank, she was a Lady of the Bedchamber, which put her far above countesses and even many duchesses. At that, servants blacked eyes and bloodied noses; Charles Brandon had to sit on Edmund to keep him from fistfighting the Earl of Surrey.

No one listened to Kathryn wearily announce, "I do not care where we sleep so long as we sleep *soon*."

Edmund lunged out from under Brandon, Surrey swung a fist at him, and the night erupted into violence. "*Men!*" Kathryn hissed to herself and stormed out for a walk about the camp.

It was unseasonably brisk for June and she was immediately sorry she had not worn a cloak. Hugging herself and shivering, she suddenly heard a familiar male voice hail her not twenty yards from the embattled tent. "*John de Gael!*" she said, pleased, and hastened to join him.

He hung back in the shadows so she could hardly see him. "I hear you missed the Queen's last visit to my Windsgeat because your sister was ill. Is she better now?" he inquired.

"Yes, in fact I brought her along with me. How did you hear about my sister?"

"Oh, money buys all manners of things, especially information."

"Edmund continually tells me how old-fashioned and boring I am, John. How then do I interest you enough that you would buy gossip about my household?"

A drawn-out "hm" from the shadows between tents. "I like you," he said frankly. "You are one of the few women I know who never simpers or coquettes. You talk to me exactly as you would a friend of any age or gender; you were the same as a child. It is a refreshing change from all the giggling fools hereabouts. I have always appreciated women of common sense and forthrightness."

Kathryn shivered. "And I appreciate a man with a fur-lined cloak. Let me have a corner of yours, John, it is very cold out here."

She sensed, rather than saw, his answering crook-toothed grin in the dark. "I would love to, my dear, but you would react with great shock and outrage. You see, there is a good reason for my lack of chivalry: the cloak is all I have on."

"John, I am shocked indeed. Shocked that anyone would throw you out of bed at this early hour! What happened?"

He sighed. "Let us say an earl re-entered his tent at an ungodly clip and his countess only barely delayed him. I wonder if he has yet noticed that he has a new scarlet doublet and some excellent Turkish boots."

First Kathryn laughed. Then, without knowing why, she felt tears racing down her face. Although she laid her hands over her eyes she could not stem the flow of tears and stood sobbing and swaying until John caught her by the arm. "I am as bad as Edmund, is that what you are thinking?" he asked savagely. "Well, my marriage is still no marriage at all; if I bed the bitch I cannot divorce her. I see nothing wrong with taking some willing woman if I cannot have the one I *really* want. Kathryn, you are breaking my heart. Come here."

He crushed her against him, rocked her, let her sob. "You poor creature, stuck with Edmund who ruts after everything in sight. Why he would do that when he has you is beyond me."

"That is kind of you," she snuffled against the velvet cloak. "But I am not—not—*hotblooded* like other women. Edmund says I am a dull, boring prude. But I prefer that to being another Mary Boleyn, with everyone sniggering and telling filthy jokes at my expense."

"People are like that, Kathryn. A man's a great seducer, a woman's a whore."

She pulled back. "Do you believe that, too?"

"Oh, no, how could I? I am one of the worst whores I know."

"You are not so bad, John, you simply have not found the right woman," she said and blew her nose on a blackwork hanky.

He chucked her under the chin. "Yes, and I never *will* find the right one if I stay busy with you married women. If you were mine I should never get out of bed again."

"Oh, stop ruffling me under the chin and patronizing me, I am *not* eleven years old any more," she growled.

"Yes, I was noticing you have grown up quite nicely."

Kathryn halted suddenly. This was getting dangerous, he was no longer holding her as one held a sobbing child. The sable-lined cloak had slipped down from one of his broad, bare shoulders; she pressed her hand there, then her cheek. The throb of his pulse filled her. She felt his lips at her brow, thought, *Yes, why not?* and turned her face up to be kissed.

He was gentle with her at first. It was not a boy's sloppy kiss as with Edmund, careless teeth cutting her lips. No, this kiss was slow, exploratory, his tongue stroking hers lightly. Kathryn clung to his neck, let him go deeper. A shudder passed through her as he opened the sable-lined cloak and pulled her under it with him. His skin felt velvety and scalding-hot and the kiss was more demanding now. More needful. All of her life had been spent in ignorance of such a moment; she wondered how she could have lived and breathed all those years, ridden to the hounds, danced, talked, laughed, given birth, and never guessed herself capable of such lust.

They were gasping together as he unfastened the neckstring of her shift and bent to suck her throat. Kathryn moaned, stepped closer in order to feel all of him against her. John laughed a little. "And Edmund thinks you cold? The boy is stark mad. Kathryn . . . if you intend to stop me, you had better do so immediately. I have only wanted you the last few months, but I have wanted you very fiercely."

She ran a finger along his lower lip; he bit it. "When did you finally stop seeing me as a child?" she asked in amazement.

"March of this year. I was on a barge on the river, going by Howard House. You had the baby slung in an apron on your hip and your other little boy chasing butterflies nearby. Your hair was down, nearly to your waist, and you had only a kerchief tied over it. No shoes and a tawny-colored gown . . . you were picking flowers into a basket on your arm and tickling the baby's nose with an occasional one. Everyone was laughing and you looked like a country girl, not a Court lady. I saw that you had grown up and were very beautiful and . . . I wished you and the children were mine."

"We are both very lonely people, John," she admitted. "By

the way . . . is that your *blinding* scarlet doublet just flew out of that blue tent?"

"So it is. That rare scoundrel, where is my other boot?"

"I shall go find out."

"No, Kathryn, wait!"

But she had already pulled free and was stooping over his clothes. The tent flap came sailing open again. A man's surly voice said, "I ought to—Lady Howard! Is that your husband's—"

"Welcome to the Val d'Or," she answered placidly, and continued picking up John's belongings. The tent flap was lowered with a resounding slap of painted canvas.

John was breathless with laughter when she returned. "Now people will think Edmund's taste has improved—from tavern whores to countesses."

"It will improve his reputation and do hers no harm, as she is twenty years Ned's senior," Kathryn said.

"You are absolutely priceless. I wish you were mine," John said, smiling as she handed over his clothes.

She did not have to stand on her toes to kiss him, she was tall enough next to him. Her damp lips grazed his. "Then we are even, sir. I have wished you were mine ever since I met you."

And, picking up her taffeta skirts, she fled before he could say another thing.

Edmund never once wore her favor in the days of jousting that followed. A handkerchief from this girl, a feather from that one, even a garter from John's middle-aged countess, who now pursued him. But Edmund never fought for Kathryn. She swallowed her bitterness and clung to Catherine of Aragon like a silent, reliable shadow, always waiting to help with a cloak clasp or a sleeve, always rushing to mend and fetch. At least in that capacity she learned how John had come to be at the Field of Cloth of Gold. "Your friend with the horses, have you seen him?" Catherine of Aragon asked one morning.

"Briefly, in passing, Your Grace. I am astonished the king let him come."

Queen Catherine dimpled. "It was my idea. De Gael has been more than generous with me—fine mules for my litter, two mares, and a gelding he broke himself for me—so I told him to tell the Master of Horse that the king could not have his best stallion unless an invitation to the Val d'Or was forthcoming. Of course," she added ruefully, "I had no idea the king would *explode* quite like he did . . ."

Kathryn, curiosity satisfied, watched lovers stroll by together and felt her heart scorch her. Claret ran from all the fountains, sterling cups were stacked in rows for people to use and then take home. Paths were planted with rosemary and chamomile that, when walked upon, released delicious scents into the air. But what good was that when she had no one to tread those paths with? When there was no hand but her own to raise the silver cup to her lips? Of what use the flowers, the wine, the heady summer nights when she could not share them with—

The queen went out. Kathryn sank onto a hassock with the royal mending and resentfully jabbed a needle into King Henry's best shirt. "Lady Howard?" came a musical voice. A moment later a dark, slender girl peeked in. "Yes, I am Lady Howard," Kathryn said, rising.

"I take it you do not recognize me?"

Something familiar about the blue-black hair, the sloe eyes and defiant chin. Strong features for a woman, with more than a hint of the overpowering Howard nose, and yet the girl was saved from unattractiveness by the extreme femininity of her bearing and attire. She was also willow-slim and graceful-looking as a doe.

The sleeves finally gave her away. They were too long and not turned back to reveal their lining. The way she held her hands, too—even as a child she had insisted on too-long sleeves and a nervous laying of one hand over the other to hide the deformity of a second nail on one bent little finger. "Cousin Nan Boleyn!" Kathryn sang out, delighted.

"No, no, not Nan but Anne now. It is good to see you, Kat!"

They embraced, crying out with delight. "You are so grown-up that I scarce know you, Anne! What a pretty gown and what a cunning headdress, so much more flattering than these English dog kennel ones."

Anne, pleased, touched the curve of her headdress. "They call it a French hood, I like them far better than the English ones. Dog kennels, indeed! I like French gowns better, too, longer and softer without so many bulky gathers, and hardly any buckram in the bodices at all."

"So much for French fashions. Now what of French *men*?" Kathryn asked, meaning, *Are you betrothed yet?*

Anne's dark eyes flashed fire. "I am not like Mary, I am not! The entire world laughs and mocks at her for spreading herself out like a Turkey carpet for every man who—"

Her voice had risen to a screeching peak of hysteria. "There, there," Kathryn soothed. "I only meant to ask if you had married yet, cuz. I know your father has his eye on one of your Butler cousins."

"I would rather not marry one of the Butlers, they are wild Irish and everyone knows there is even less fashion in Ireland than England. And forgive me for snapping at you, but there have been so many sly digs about my sister! King Henry will drop her just as King François did. . . . How very *foolish* women are to give themselves away for free, how silly they are to allow themselves to throw away a good name, which is all any woman has! I warrant you I shall not be so stupid, Cuz, I know my own value. By the way, we are dancing together tonight, did you know? We ladies of the French Court are dancing with you English ones. It will be you, Mother, and King Henry's sister Mary Brandon against us. Oh, I love Mary Brandon, she is so sweet, all of France wept when the old king died and she went home."

Anne considered her own words. "Funny how things work out, Kathryn. Mary Brandon was supposed to stay married and in France and now she is married to an English earl. My sister and I were sent here to get betrothed in her Court and Mary's ended up with a terrible reputation and a nobody husband while I am still unmarried. And you wed that dreadful Ned Howard, I always hated him! But at least you are at Court, though everyone knows Queen Catherine is so boring: it's *pray, sew, pray, sew* all the livelong day. Almost as bad as Queen Claude, they are so poisonously good and so very old! But I hear that does not bother you, everyone says you were born middle-aged, possessing all the old-fashioned virtues of loyalty, fidelity, and close-mouthedness. Oh, well, I shall see you at the banquet tonight. At least everyone says you dance well!"

Old-fashioned virtues. *You are wrong,* Kathryn wanted to cry out. *Two nights ago a man held me and I felt so wanton, so unsure of myself . . .*

Instead she clenched her fists in her full skirts. "Yes, Anne," she said politely. "I shall see you tonight when we dance."

11

"Damn this cloth of silver!" Kathryn swore aloud.

Her sister Mary laughed sympathetically. "Yes, I hear cloth of gold does not tarnish and rub off all over one's skin and body linen as this stuff does." She pulled Kathryn's lacings tighter.

Kathryn gritted her teeth. "When I think of all the jewelers who sit pounding metal into strips and then give it to some poor woman to weave into cloth, I want to weep. All that work for something this untrustworthy, every seam fraying and in need of mending when I have not even worn this damned thing yet! Ouch, that is too tight, you will break the strings!"

Her gown was of the lightest weight cloth of silver, called tinsel. Metal formed the warp, with the weft being a pale blue; as the fabric was semi-sheer, the dancers had lined it in a pale blue silk samite, giving it body and more sheen so that the effect would be of women garbed wholly in sterling.

"It is beautiful. So are you. But I have never known you to be so short-tempered," Mary observed mildly. "Is there something on your mind? Something like a man?"

Something very like a man, though she did not say so with the memory of John's kisses still burning her mouth. Whenever she caught sight of him she trembled like a sapling in a high wind. "You are rather glowing-faced yourself," she told Mary.

"Yes, but everyone expects such behavior of me. Nothing they say can hurt me any more. But you, Kat . . . you will be careful?"

"Help me with that caul and headdress," Kathryn answered irritably. She had spent these three days in France having to talk herself out of going to John's tent.

The feasting pavilion was ablaze with torches and lavender-scented candles when she arrived. People were already dining, jugglers finishing a splendid show, while two jesters were waiting impatiently to go on next. Kathryn hastened to join her aunt Elizabeth Boleyn and Mary Tudor Brandon, both perspiring in their silver gowns. Anne Boleyn and the two Frenchwomen wore gold and claimed it was even hotter as the six of them rehearsed their steps. Elizabeth, mopping her lovely brow, said, "Goodness, but it is not a night for dancing or sleeping on furs, is it?"

Kathryn suddenly thought of John's sable-lined cloak and how he had pulled her under it. "Goodness, you have gone pink in the face. You are not breeding, are you, dear?" her aunt asked solicitously.

"No fear of that, Ned has not been within plate-throwing range for weeks," Kathryn answered, cheered by the thought. Her uncharacteristic frankness made the other Englishwomen all stop and gawk at her.

There was a lull in the banquet hall as the jesters left, gathering up the coins flung at them. In the near-silence, François the First's melodious voice rang out, "Where is my cousin Jean?"

Everything ground to a halt. "Jean who?" the unsuspecting Henry Tudor inquired.

"My cousin Jean, he is one of the finest dancers I have ever seen. After our ladies are finished you must allow him to show you some steps, *mon frère* Henri."

"Jean who?" Henry repeated.

"Jean de Gael! Have you never heard the one about his grandfather and my great-aunt . . . ? Oh, very scandalous. It seems the old man visited Sorbonne in his wild, irresolute youth and—someone go fetch Jean, will they?"

There was a loud gnashing sound from the English royal table as a page raced to fetch John. Musicians took advantage of the pause in conversation to strike up a pavanne; the six women entered to dance. Silver danced, then gold, then the women split into couples: Mary Brandon with the French king's sister, Elizabeth Boleyn with a French duchesse, and Anne and Kathryn together. "Your sister, Henri, is still oh-so-beautiful it steals my breath away," King François commented.

"Yours is lovely, too, Francis, my brother," Henry Tudor managed to say grimly.

"But I confess I like the last couple. Who is the so-elegant light-colored one? Not truly pretty by any means, but such gracefulness!"

"Kathryn Chase, Lady Howard, married to a minor branch of the family. Her father is a bastard Plantagenet, and her mother is one of old Norfolk's daughters. That lady there, Elizabeth Boleyn, is the other."

"She is light as a feather, this slender English mare. But can one ride her at will?"

"Not even her own husband, one hears," Henry grumbled. François laughed so loudly that it startled the princesses, who fumbled their steps. "Who is the thin dark little girl with her?" Henry asked, gnawing a lark's wing.

"I am surprised you do not know. That is the younger Boleyn girl. As cold a flirt as ever batted her eyelashes at a codpiece. She does not ride, either."

"All mares must be broken to saddle some time," Henry observed nonchalantly. The other king found this so funny he choked on his turkey leg, and Henry had to hammer enthusiastically on his back. He enjoyed the hammering; François had spent the last three days out-wrestling, out-riding, out-jousting, and out-romancing him in the tiltyards and tents.

The dance was ending when John de Gael entered, hastily buttoning up a blinding gold doublet. "*Merde*, what *shoulders*!" Anne Boleyn murmured.

"*Merde*, what a *doublet*," her mother wincingly answered.

"Cousin Jean!" King François roared out. John leapt half a foot into the air and twisted to see who the French monarch was talking to. "Yes, you, Cousin Jean!" François greeted him. "Come sit with *mon frere* king. We are discussing dance steps. How is the family?"

John had caught himself by now, and, bowing low, suavely answered that everyone was fine. "And your sisters, my *belle cousines*? I hear they are still *ravissantes*. Come, Jean, come sit."

He warily regarded Henry Tudor, whose facial veins were standing out like stevedore's knotted ropes. Kathryn shot John a curious, adoring glance; he winked encouragingly and went to attend the kings. Her aunt Elizabeth caught the exchange of glances and tucked it away for future reference.

"And how is that splendid white stallion King Louis gave your grandfather to start his stud farm? I hear you have many splendid colts of him. Stop bowing, Jean, you will crinkle that . . . *astounding* jacket of yours."

François promptly shoved a chair forward with his nearest foot, granting John permission to sit down at the head table in the company of kings. Henry Tudor was breathing like a runner; John's face was very white as he gingerly lowered himself to the chair. "Jean, I was just telling my brother-king here that you and I could outdance him and any man of his Court," François then bragged.

"That would be difficult, as His Grace is notoriously light-footed," John said diplomatically. "Besides which . . . in a bransle you would be a bit harder than the ladies to throw up in the air and catch."

Henry Tudor shoved back his chair. "I will take you up on that wager! Charles Brandon, where are you? Charles is the best dancer after me in all of England. We challenge you two! But I warn you, Francis, a peer can always outdance a commoner."

John went impossibly whiter but François only shook his long, dark head and picked at his teeth. "There are no commoners at this table, *mon frère*, just because you have not forgiven John's father supporting Richard at Bosworth Field; his blood is bluer than mine. He is related to every known king of England including your illustrious self, and in fact, he is descended from the last Anglo-Saxon one as well. What was his name—Harold Godwinson, I think. Died fighting a Frenchman, Guillaume le Bâtard. I am not ashamed to dance with so well-born a man, are you?"

This time John blushed and Henry Tudor went pale. "Choose your ladies," Henry barked.

"Your sister," François said.

"Lady Howard," John murmured, making Kathryn go hot all over.

"The tall dark child, she is a marvelous dancer," Charles Brandon said.

"I prefer Lady Boleyn myself," Henry answered as the men began casting off their doublets to dance. Everyone ended up staring at John again, his shirt being equal to the garish doublet; instead of being trimmed in blackwork with a little gold, the entire shirt was crusted with bullion.

"That man could never sneak up on anyone," Elizabeth Boleyn observed, shaking her head. "They would hear his clothes approaching!"

Henry Tudor, looking his enemy up and down with mingled envy and offended fashion sense, murmured, "Who the devil dresses you, Man?"

John, who saw nothing wrong with his clothes, answered, "Why, *I* do, Your Grace."

Henry, no quiet dresser himself, said, "*Oh.* For a moment

I thought I understood why you were divorcing that wife of yours!"

The couples lined up, women extending their hands. As John's fingers folded over Kathryn's, she trembled. *I cannot look at him,* she thought, *or they will all know how I feel. I cannot disguise it.*

"You are breathtakingly beautiful tonight," he told her. "Is it too early in the evening to make indecent proposals?"

There seemed no safe answer for that, so she made none. When the bransle music began he swung her up easily by the waist. "You are still light as a child. Come to me tonight," he urged, letting her slide through his hands to the floor.

She had been about to say no when his hands traveled down her body in that seemingly innocent caress. "I—I do not know," she stammered. Out of the corner of her eye she saw Edmund, staggeringly drunk, leave the banqueting hall on the arm of some pretty stranger.

The men exchanged partners in the bransle, Kathryn ending up with Henry Tudor awhile before going on to Charles Brandon. Henry was flirting outrageously with Elizabeth Boleyn, for he favored buxom women; her arrow-slim, dark daughter found no favor on his arm.

When the women in their tight corsets and trailing skirts were danced to exhaustion, the men danced together. Sweat ran, seams popped, tempers flared. Catherine of Aragon and Queen Claude finally put their heads together, loudly proclaimed the dancing a perfect draw, and descended the dais to drag their husbands back to chairs.

A draw after so many little defeats; Henry Tudor would have none of it. The fact that François was taking it so well especially goaded him—that and John de Gael's very presence. Henry caught up a napkin, wiped his face. "If I cannot convince you that I am a better dancer, My Lord, then you must at least admit that my men are very fierce fighters," he loudly announced. François allowed that this was so. "Well, then, I say the meanest water boy from our side can outjoust the meanest from yours. We English are born fighters."

"And we French are born lovers, but I will grant you a *pont de guerre*. I shall choose a boy from your camp, you choose one from mine. But no water boys, they must be lads who know how to ride at least, though not how to fight. Otherwise we shall have needlessly cracked skulls strewn about the field, very messy. What say you, Jean?"

Addressed on the verge of slipping out the door, John found himself trapped and considered it. "I say that is no contest at all, Your Grace. If you would prefer real riding at the tilt* with lances, I should like to fight for England against all comers."

Henry looked him up and down. "You have never been to Court or on any campaign that I know of; what makes you think you can fight, Man?"

The corners of John's mouth twitched. "I have my own tiltyard and was a professional soldier for five years before I came into my inheritance," he said. Kathryn's jaw sagged. Would this man never cease surprising her?

Both kings agreed, but wanted the squires to fight as well. Henry Tudor went one direction by torchlight and came back with some French lord's third son; François returned with Arthur Chase. "I choose a good one to give England a fighting chance," François said pointedly to Henry, who had grabbed the spindliest lad he could locate. "Now let us find armor for them. My lords are lined up waiting to fight de Gael. He met a few in some war several years back."

Kathryn swallowed too hard. John and Arthur both to fight? It seemed too much to take in at once. There was a touch at her sleeve, a softly spoken, "My Lady?" She turned, saw John's valet, Pieter van der Hüm, waiting on her. "My Lady, Windsgeat says to fetch your brudder along and he will arm and horse him. He also suggests dat your husband's armor might work for Arthur wid some adjustments, and asks dat de two of you attend him."

She found Tansy and sent her and Pieter to collect Edmund's joust gear before taking Arthur to meet John.

The two men got along splendidly—perhaps, she thought, because John, who had so much, was not condescending about helping Arthur, who had nothing. He talked tactics with the boy, showed him how to hold his lance, taught him which knee movements and sounds guided the horse. "Now help me armor up, I joust before you and you need to see how all of this goes on," John directed, peeling clothes off. Kathryn, wide-mouthed with admiring shock, caught things as they fell.

He stripped down to his hose and held muscular arms out for the sleeveless quilted gambeson Pieter quickly laced him

---

*a wooden barrier between riders. Jousting was usually called 'tilting' because of it.

into. There was a very young squire helping, too, a fiery-haired boy with freckles and wide green eyes. Despite his age he functioned as part of John's fighting team, handing things to Pieter, who eased John into them.

The velvet-lined armor went on from the ground up—stark, angular stuff, the color of new sterling from so much polishing. "I have never seen armor like that," Arthur murmured, watching as Kathryn helped buckle John into his breastplate.

"It is old German stuff, that is why. My great-grandfather wore it at Bosworth Field and died in it."

"How? I see no perforations."

"When armor is struck hard enough it fans out the pressure from the blow. Internal bleeding killed him. Hand me the pauldrons, will you? Good lad."

Great-grandfather. Odd, Kathryn had always heard it was his *grand*father who died at Bosworth. She started to say something, thought the better of it, and closed her mouth. John caught the motion and smiled at her. "You have an excruciatingly beautiful sister, Arthur," he said.

Arthur did not hear. "Is this antique armor? Why do you fight in old armor? I thought you of all people could afford a new suit."

"This is German, and one of the finest suits in existence. You will understand why it is my favorite when you see me ride against the French; theirs is flimsy Italian, not the so-excellent Missaglia suits, and graven with scrollwork that catches the lance tip too easily. Richard, Boy, the bracket for the *sallade*, please, I cannot find it. This helmet requires a brace or riding at the tilt could break my neck."

Pieter brought out his cloth coif. "Let me. Your hair is caught at the back," Kathryn said softly, and ran a hand through the thick chestnut stuff to free it. John felt the tenderness in her touch and blessed her with his eyes as Pieter slid the coif on for him. The young squire, Richard, brought out the *sallade*, a weirdly long-tailed German helmet of the kind not fought in for thirty years; Pieter eased it on over his lord's head. "Why are the sides planed away like that? To keep from catching the lance tip?" Arthur demanded. "Is the bracket really necessary for the helmet? Is a *sallade* safe to joust in? I read somewhere that . . ."

John grinned through his immovable visor and beaver at Kathryn. "You have not given me your favor yet."

He was asking for something of hers to wear in front of all of them. After a moment's consideration, Kathryn asked for a dagger and reached for the velvet tails of her headdress. "Nothing more personal than that?" John asked, watery blue eyes flicking over her.

"If I give you a garter, everyone will say I am a whore. And then my stockings will fall down!" She could not decide which result would be worse.

"Oh, give him a garter! You are such a prude!" Arthur chastised her. So Kathryn brazenly, defiantly flipped her skirts up, untied the embroidered, bias-cut strip of velvet, and knotted it on John's arm just above the elbow.

He looked over her head at Arthur. "Now go with Pieter and Richard and get into your brother-in-law's armor, I would speak with your sister alone."

The de Gael servants did not loiter, but bolted at a trot, dragging Arthur with them. "What is it?" she asked breathlessly.

"In case they crack my skull out there and I am not capable of saying so afterward, I thought you should know that I love you. And that in case you ever need anything, go to Windsgeat and ask it of my sisters. Jacquetta will be the best friend you ever had. She is the jewel of the lot and runs Windsgeat now that she is widowed and back at home."

She pressed damp palms to the front of his gorgeous German breastplate. "John . . . do not let them hurt you. I—I—" She could not say it, so lamely stood on her toes to kiss the fixed visor he could not lift. He grabbed her, driving cold metal into her tissue gown and marring it permanently. It was frightening and weirdly erotic to be embraced by a man in a full suit of armor; when he left her and strode away she had to sit down and catch her breath. He loved her, she thought dizzily, head between hands. John de Gael loved her, and she was sitting here like a fool! She should be cheering him on to victory! *John, oh, John . . .*

Kathryn scooped up handsful of silver skirts and ran to the spectators' box on the field.

John defeated three French knights and a duke of the royal house. Their lances splintered off his armor while he unhorsed them methodically one at a time. She disloyally allowed that the armor and horse helped some; his old white gelding leaned coolly into each blow while the fractious French mounts shied and swerved.

Afterward, when he rode to the box to receive the kings' accolades, Henry Tudor suddenly demanded to know whose garter he wore. Elizabeth Boleyn, seeing Kathryn's blushing face and remembering those hot glances in the banqueting hall, said, "It is mine, Your Grace."

Mary Tudor Brandon took in the situation at a glance. "No, it is mine, brother," she said. John's crooked front teeth flashed through his pierced-work visor in appreciation of their loyalty to Kathryn.

"Cousin Jean, I am offended," François announced, hand over heart. "You dance for France but fight for England and humiliate my so-brave *gentilhommes*. What am I to think? Your Englishness has overwhelmed your better blood. Nonetheless, it was *très gallante* a fight. Dismount, Jean."

It took two squires and Elizabeth Boleyn to get weary John off his wearier horse. "Kneel, Jean." François called out for the nearest sword and, before Henry Tudor could more than squeak with alarm, knighted John.

Not to be outdone, Henry then had to duplicate the performance, smiting John so hard on the shoulders that he was driven down into the turf and had to be handed back up.

François, laughing, asked, "Have I earned a white horse yet, Jean?" The stands echoed with laughter.

It was not a return of the de Gael ducal coronet but it was a start, Kathryn thought, thrilled. A light hand landed on her back. "Guard your face," Elizabeth Boleyn warned. "Anyone looking at you will know you are in love with that man."

John said quickly, "If Your Graces continue to so extravagantly admire my bloodstock, I shall soon have none left to share with you."

"We would accept some of your so-beautiful de Gael women in their place," François teased hopefully.

John shook his head. "But de Gael women are harder to break than the horses, Your Grace! They were all born with the bit between their teeth, there is no controlling them. Jacquetta's husband expired between the sheets, loudly lamenting that he was not more man—or she, less woman."

People laughed again, suddenly sorry this man was not accepted at Court. Thomas Boleyn was approaching him with a tankard of something frothy, half a dozen hands reached to help him out of his gauntlets and heavy *sallade*.

Henry Tudor observed and simmered.

Kathryn ran to see her uncle of Surrey boost Arthur onto his borrowed mare's back. Prick-eared with excitement, the Windsgeat White pawed the ground, pulled at the reins. "You lean like so, lad," Surrey was saying, remembering his moment of blazing glory at Flodden Field. "Do not brace that lance against your gut, grip it here. Leave your visor up until just before you spur the mare, you will need to see the field to memorize the lay of it. She seems a bonny, brave mare, lad, so treat her well; I doubt you can afford to so much as bring her home bruised."

The French boy, in blue-and-gold enameled armor on a rearing bay colt, caught the eye of the crowd. But no one looked askance at Arthur's mélange of equipment, having seen how thoroughly John de Gael had humiliated his opponents in armor presumed obsolete decades before.

Thomas Howard the Younger, Earl of Surrey, dropped an arm around Kathryn's narrow shoulders. "Niece, you are white as bleached sheets. The boy will be all right."

"Aim true, lad!" Henry Tudor bellowed as Arthur rode toward the end of the field. "Hold that mare steady!"

"Ride safely," Kathryn whispered, hands clasped. She had a moment to wish that her sister Mary could be found to see Arthur's ride, then Queen Claude dropped a handkerchief and the horses lunged forward.

Surrey did a thing that amazed the onlookers. He leapt the rail like a boy of eight-and-ten, ran shouting onto the field. They understood when he screamed, "Stop, Arthur, stop! The visor, lad—*the visor is up!*"

Too late. The bay and white sprang fiercely at each other, jousting lances crossed. Propelled by thirteen hundred pounds of galloping horse, the French lance splintered, flew up at Arthur's unprotected face. There was a shriek of agony as the force of the blow snapped the visor shut.

To Kathryn's abject horror, a foot of lance protruded from beneath the face shield.

Feeling her reins drop, the white mare stopped as she had been trained to do. Arthur Chase swayed and toppled to the turf beneath her.

Kathryn reached him mere moments after her uncle. Together they grasped for the hinges that fastened helmet to gorget, and started to unscrew and draw it off.

The shattered lance protruded from the boy's left cheek, just beneath the eye. Arthur was blue-faced and wide-eyed. "I am sorry, Niece, the lad is dead," Thomas Howard said, and started to draw Kathryn away.

"No, he is not!"

There was a clanking and rattling of armor as John de Gael laboriously hefted himself over the striped rail and barreled toward them. He sank to his knees on the matted grass, raised Arthur's head to his lap. "He is alive but he cannot breathe, Tom—hold him down!"

There was none of a doctor's careful groping or hesitance; John grasped the wooden shaft and yanked it out. Together he and Surrey then rolled Arthur over onto his knees. He was still not breathing, so John reached down his throat, drew out splinters of wood and bone. Arthur's nostrils and the wound in his cheek yielded up dangerous pieces, too.

Pink returned to Arthur's face. He inhaled with a great rasping sound and collapsed, spitting blood. "Is there a lady with a sewing basket present?" John demanded, craning his head. "I need a needle and some strong silk thread, along with some strips of very fine silk to pack his cheek and nose. And some aqua vitae to wash the wounds."

Catherine of Aragon, never without her tortoiseshell sewing box thanks to Kathryn, dashed forward with the necessary supplies. The king of France held out his brandy flask, the queen and Kathryn cleansing the hideous wound and shakily assisting John as he worked. "You should have been a doctor, Cousin Jean," François observed.

"No, Your Grace, but my brother Tom is. He has often told me that jousting men are killed by things knocked down their throats or into the air pockets on either side of the nose, and Arthur's color clearly said he was choking."

"How did you and he know about those air pockets, Sir?" Henry Tudor demanded belligerently. Dissection was still forbidden by the Church, bringing with it the penalty of death at the stake. John, finishing his work, cautiously answered, "Master da Vinci wrote some splendid treatises on the workings of the human body, and my brother and I studied them."

Henry crossed his muscular arms. "This da Vinci sounds a proper heretic."

"He probably was," François agreed cheerfully. "He was my unofficial court painter and philosopher until he died last year. So he is now beyond the stake, my brother-king."

Two men arrived with a litter for Arthur, who was now capable of hoarse words and hand signals. "Take him to my tent, I will sit with him," Kathryn said quickly. She looked at John with love deepened by gratitude, and saw that he was exhausted and that her brother's blood dappled his gorgeous armor. His chestnut hair was smashed flat by coif and helm; as she watched, he self-consciously ran a hand through it, leaving blood-stripes that made it stick out in all directions. As if on cue, little Pieter van der Hüm materialized with Richard the squire. John said, washy blue eyes never leaving Kathryn, "Do not let the doctors disturb him too much. Sleep would help Arthur more than anything now. If Their Majesties will excuse me now to get out of this infernally hot German suit . . . ?"

The crowd quietly parted to let him through. "I have a confession to make, *mon frère,*" François began. "I never saw that man before tonight. I asked my spy—*ambassador* who I could best tease you with and he told me all about Jean de Gael."

Henry Tudor, a magnificent actor, raised a tawny eyebrow at him. "I know. I allowed you to do so because I knew he was anxious to prove himself on the field, and I knew he could beat any five men in France. De Gael is a magnificent fighter. But I still loathe the man."

"But *Mon Dieu,* he has the most beautiful sisters and horses in Christendom! His half-sisters, I should say. Their mother was Flemish, she passed through our Court with three so-exquisite blonde girls some years back. But his grandfather was never here."

"Which is how I caught you in your lie, brother-king. His maternal grandfather died at Bosworth and the paternal one at St. Albans, so neither was in France at the right time. Tell your ambassadors to research your next joke more carefully."

François clapped Henry on the back. "Then you are not angry with my little jest, *mon frère*?"

The Tudor king, who wanted nothing so much as to shove the broken lance down François the First's throat, forced his gleaming teeth to show in a broad smile. "It was very amusing," he said through gritted teeth.

Now Kathryn knew why John had looked so startled at being addressed as the king's cousin—it had been a total surprise to him. Clasping Arthur's sweaty hand in hers, she signaled for the litter-bearers to start away, Elizabeth and Anne Boleyn coming with her. Both kings sent their physicians, but remembering John's advice, she did not allow them to poke and prod Arthur.

The women slept in shifts to watch Arthur. Toward morning Kathryn woke to the feel of her head cushioned on a soft lap, and felt her aunt pat her face. "Hello, dear. Tansy has brought us some food and wash water and I have had her press out your wine-colored sarcenet."

"Why?" Kathryn asked suspiciously, sitting.

"You *do* intend to thank John de Gael . . . ? Arthur is still sleeping, but he seemed much improved the last time I woke him. Now here is our food. . . ."

"Aunt Elizabeth, are you trying to throw me into John's arms?"

Wide, innocent eyes met hers. "Me? I am only thinking that when two people love each other and one of them has saved the other's brother, a visit would not be out of order."

Anne Boleyn reentered the tent just then, a scarlet cloak over her arm. "Here is Mary's cloak, Mother. Now will you tell me why you asked me to fetch it?"

Kathryn laughed helplessly. "Aunt Elizabeth, you are the dearest, wiliest, most interfering woman I have ever met!"

Elizabeth beamed. "Thank you, Dear, I was not sure you noticed. The queen sent word that we need not wait on her today, so I shall sit with Arthur and make excuses to Edmund if he ever returns."

An hour later, fed, washed, changed, and combed, Kathryn crossed the English camp in Mary Boleyn's notorious red cloak. Lounging men-at-arms cheered and whistled as she passed, lords blew kisses, and women glared disapprovingly. She kept her head down, face hidden beneath the deep red cowl, as a result of which Pieter van der Hüm refused her entry. "Pieter, it is Lady Howard!" she hissed at the Fleming.

He fell back, both eyebrows up. "Milady, Milord is still asleep."

She blushed furiously beneath the cowl. "I shall wake him up," she murmured. He cuffed Richard the squire then, told him to be off attending the horses. "I will guard de door," Pieter announced to Kathryn, moving a discreet distance away from it and taking up John's *sallade* to polish. But she noticed he was grinning broadly as she entered.

Not liking those tents provided by the king, John had brought his own, a huge striped pavilion stuffed with all the comforts of Windsgeat: a heavy table supported by dog-faced sea-sphinxes, scarlet and azure silk carpets piled four deep on the floors, even a few tapestries and paintings of his ancestors. But the chief thing that caught her eye was the bed, towering massively over trunks, armor, and carpets. Other lords had brought traveling beds or simple pallets; John had brought his best black oak bed, heaped with furs, embroidered linens, and a lynx-lined velvet counterpane done up in the black-and-gold of the de Gaels. His only accession to travel had been to leave off the ten-foot top with its fifty yards of velvet curtains.

Kathryn grinned to herself. The ostentation of the man was truly astounding; not even the king of England had brought a fancier bed to the Field of Cloth of Gold. *What a peacock you are, John,* she thought, and went to see if he was lost somewhere in the heaps of bedclothes.

He was. She found him three layers down, courtesy of a foot sticking out one side. Judging by the state of the bed, he had not slept well; when she uncovered his face she saw that he slept frowning and so bent to kiss the lines away. He stirred slightly then, murmured something that sounded like her name.

Now might be the only chance she ever had with him. There seemed nothing dishonorable in it after the traumas of the night; she had been drawn inescapably close to him through adventure and near-tragedy. She loved him, loved his stubborn pride and courage, the way he helped Arthur, the way he had honorably let go of her. Another man would have bullied or pressured her but John had let her slip through his arms, laughing, instead of forcing the issue. Since childhood he had been a silent friend in the background, watching over her; she had built fantasies about him only to discover the real man was infinitely dearer. No, there could be no dishonor in bedding such a man.

Trembling with emotion, she remembered an annoying fact: she had never undressed herself in her life. It was the mark of a lady that there was always someone to lace her in and out of her gowns—servants, husbands, daughters, sisters, cousins. But if she woke John she might shy away, lose her courage.

So Kathryn took up his jeweled dinner dagger from the sea-sphinx table and slit the lacings up her back. The gown sprang open. Layers of petticoats, corseting, garters, stockings—finally she was down to the last layer, a light cotton shift. She timidly edged the covers back, drew the garment off over her head, and lunged into bed. It seemed appropriate to her that she wore a shift to make love with her husband but not her lover; she had the feeling John would not tolerate anything like clothing between them. The thought made her dizzy with anticipation.

The motion of her hitting the bed woke John. "Wha's'it?" he asked sleepily.

"Do you not think '*who*'s'it?' would be a better question?"

"*Kathryn!* What are you—"

She rolled over on him, stopped further silly questions with her open mouth on his. Another squawk, some mumbled words, and he surrendered. Strong arms wrapped around her, pressed her closer. She clung to him, reveling in the hard body beneath hers, the latent force that would make it so easy for him to hurt or crush her. And yet she had faith that he would not treat her roughly. His delicacy of touch surprised her, and the fact that he seemed in no hurry. Everything was rushed with Edmund, hurry-up-and-get-it-over in the marriage bed. But John was so deliberate, so patient.

Stroking his throat now with both hands, timidly touching his chest, the hard, wide shoulders with their bunched muscles and faded old scars . . . kisses that still tasted of the morning's hot clove water and smelled of her ginger and rosewater mingled with his leather, metal, and silk.

His hands caressed her back, the neat slope of rump and thigh. At last he rolled her over, kissing the hollow of her throat, the curve from throat to shoulder. Her pink-tipped breasts, down over her ribs, prominent hipbones . . . Edmund had never kissed her there, never lain between her legs, kissing and stroking her to a shuddering ecstasy like this. She climbed, crashed, climbed again. Hung gasping in his arms, frightened but trusting in him and this wild new sensation.

John moved back up into her arms. Crying out his name, she twined her long legs with his, thrust up against him. Penetration made her moan, surging with him. They drove together slowly at first, seeking out and prolonging little moments of pleasure. Fed, the need grew; Kathryn clung to his neck, dug close-clipped nails into his back, wildly urged him on to completion.

Passersby, hearing the cries, paused a moment. "I gather someone was impressed by your lord's fighting last night," Charles Brandon called to Pieter. The little Fleming only grinned and started polishing his master's greaves.

"I love you, I love you," Kathryn whispered as they sank

down into the covers afterward. "Not only for this but for so many things."

"Only love me for being myself, Kathryn, that is the only constant. I love you, too."

She whispered into the thick hair that had fallen over his ears, "No one has ever loved me before. Not my parents, not my husband . . ."

John rose up on his elbows, smiled down into her beaming face. "Then I shall have to love you the harder to make up for the empty years."

"Oh, yes . . . love me again, John. And again and again!"

They laughed until she drew him down into her again. Then there was no more laughter, only violent passion . . .

12

"Lady Howard has suddenly become beautiful," Henry Tudor observed, tipping his chair back against the wall of the pavilion.

"The thin, light one? Ahh, she must be in love," François said, scratching at the underneath of his beard where he had clipped too close last week. The two kings pulled their chairs-of-state closer to gossip.

"With whom? She is the Court prude," Henry marveled.

"My brother-king, it must be Jean de Gael. When she danced with him she was pink as a cherry, and there was so-great devotion and fire in her blue eyes when he saved her brother. I am willing to wager it was Lady Howard who visited him this morning in Mary Boleyn's red cape."

"It certainly was not Mary, she was with me all morning, complaining that her younger sister had stolen her cloak. Now why would . . . ahh, Elizabeth, Mary's mother. She raised Kathryn for several years and loves her dearly, I would wager Lady Boleyn is behind this. The interfering bitch!"

François smacked his sensual lips at an approaching platter of meat pies, bottles, and enameled Venetian goblets. "But a beautiful interfering bitch nonetheless," he said approvingly as one of his lords knelt to pour the kings' wine. "I can see where Mistress Mary gets her so-fine looks. The other daughter, the bony dark one, is not so fair. But she dresses strikingly and carries herself like an empress. I wonder if she will have a bosom like Mary's when she grows up."

"What, her? Not enough meat on her bones to satisfy a full-blooded man, Francis. Nor enough wit and sparkle, she seems very ordinary. Besides, she is a virgin at the most lascivious court in Europe! The chit must have ice water in her veins!"

"Not like Mary Boleyn, eh?" leered François, who had sampled the abundant Boleyn charms long ago. He dug his elbow irritatingly into Henry's brocade-covered ribs, knocking Henry's chair down so that wine splashed and food flew.

Henry could not decide whether he was being laughed at or not.

Edmund lay asleep beside her at last, snoring rhythmically. Grateful that he had not turned his hated attentions on her, Kathryn smelled the ale on his breath and prayed that he would sleep until morning. She rose softly from bed, donned a plain gray cloak over her shift, and crept into the night. Leaping over tent pegs, tiptoeing between pavilions where merriment continued despite the late hour . . . John's voice from his tent startled her. "Damnation! He will stop at nothing to strike at me, will he? First my land, now my stock—I should never have crossed him that day of the hunt, not even for the sake of the King-Stag!"

A woman's voice, mellifluous, foreign accented like Pieter's. Flemish, then, though the accent was slighter. "You must keep Kat'rin safe from him, too. Warn her of this latest outrage."

"I believe she is safe from him. He mistrusts her Plantagenet blood for one thing, and he prefers his women buxom and blonde."

"Like me?" the woman asked, and laughed prettily.

No matter who the woman was, that sounded like as good an entrance cue as any. Kathryn drew back a dozen paces and proceeded to break every twig between her and the tent. No need to scratch at the flap this time—John met her, whisked her under his arm and into the tent. "I missed you," he said, and kissed her so fiercely she could neither breathe nor think.

Behind him, heavy silk taffeta rustled in leaping torchlight. "Could you introduce us before you get started, John?"

The kiss to Kathryn's mouth abruptly ended, but there were others showered on her brow, hair, fluttering eyelids.

"This is Kathryn Chase, Lady Howard. Kathryn, meet my half-sister Jacquetta de Gael, the widowed Countess Courtenay."

The woman rising from a lavish leather seat was at the peak of her beauty and charm, twenty-five years old with golden hair and John's same pale moonstone eyes. She had not been cursed with the craggy, overpowering de Gael features so handsome on men and unflattering to women; the best of her Flemish mother and Plantagenet ancestors showed in every magnificent pore.

She was absolutely ravishing. Kathryn, regarding her with dropped jaw, supposed men walked into walls everytime this golden Aphrodite sauntered past. "Countess," she said, and started to drop a curtsy.

Jacquetta yanked her back up. "Stop that, you are practically family. I wondered how long it would take my knuckle-brained brother to realize he was in love with you. *I* have known it for quite some time. We must talk, come, come." She drew Kathryn forward by the hands, bade her sit in the nearest chair.

"The king has claimed my breeding stock at Windsgeat and forbidden me to ever return to England," John announced hurriedly. Kathryn gasped, hands over heart. "Actually he phrased it more politely than that, said that since King François and I get along so well I should stay here as an ambassador with him. He could find no reason to exile me outright so he found this way to banish me, God damn him! And in my absence he sent justiciars to remove the horses."

"But Windsgeat—your family—" she gasped out.

"Jacquetta will manage it all. But I cannot return to England, Kathryn, it is forbidden."

The room swam before her. Kathryn dropped her head into her hands, fighting tears of blackest despair. "John, you are too rough," Jacquetta chastised, putting her arms around Kathryn. "Poor, dear John, he is only a man and they are so unthinking, they do not know how to break news to a woman. . . . Kat'rin, you could stay here in France with him."

"There would be no honor in it," John burst out.

"Hang your honor! Does love mean nothing to you men?" his sister asked.

Kathryn raised her streaming face. "No, Jacquetta, he is correct. I have my family to think of . . . my sons, my mother to support, my brother and sister. I am a Lady of the Bedchamber, I need the money and position. I—I cannot abandon my responsibilities any more than John can."

"Ask me to," he argued bitterly.

"How can I?" she cried out. "If we ran away somewhere together you would come to hate me, to hold me responsible for your losses, always measuring my worth against your family and estates. Perhaps the king will allow you to return some day if you only perform well in France."

"I should never blame you for anything that happened! Never!"

Kathryn smiled sadly. "But if you think about it, you will see that I am right."

"I know you could never bear to leave the Court."

Was there a reproach in his words? Sitting suddenly straighter, she said, "As a carter makes carts and a miller grinds flour, so I, too, have my lifework. Would you reprimand me for having no less ambition than a *man* of honor?"

He held her while she wept softly into his broad, comfortless shoulder. "Well!" Jacquetta exclaimed busily. "I cannot get your exile reversed but with real effort I may perhaps get some of our horses returned." She collected her cloak and peacock feather fan from the sea-sphinx table.

"You go near Tudor and I will cut your throat," John snapped. "I will have no more of his bastards in my house!"

Jacquetta thumped him on the nose with her fan handle. "Your wife has finally given up and agreed to a divorce, and I know how to keep from breeding little Tudors. And do not spew forth on me about family honor, you know perfectly well that we have none left. Your wife will claim you impotent and the Court will learn to call me whore, but we three in this tent know what matters: *family*. I will do anything, anything at all to protect my family and hold Windsgeat intact. Kat'rin, I would have words with you in private. John, go look in your horses' ears or some place similarly exciting."

He glared but went. Jacquetta, flourishing her fan, said, "Now then, when you return to England, Kat'rin, I shall expect you to become a steady visitor at Windsgeat. That dreadful woman—pardon me, I keep forgetting she is your aunt—will be gone by then, and people cannot gossip when there are no men there for you to be visiting. John shall be here in France and Tom our brother moved north years ago. So your romantic reputation will be quite safe at Windsgeat, though I cannot vouch for your religious one."

"Thank you for the invitation. Now what is it you really

want to tell me?" Kathryn asked, wiping her face on her sleeve.

"Your sister Mary. You must disown her to the king or risk arrest."

"Why?" Kathryn demanded stiffly.

"Because last night she secretly married her lover, the man the French have long accepted as rightful king of England."

Dear God in Heaven—Richard Pole, the Plantagenet Pretender! And it was illegal for their family to marry without the king's permission! Kathryn said blankly, "Perhaps I could talk her into an annulment."

"She has already fled the Val d'Or with him. I met them on the way here, she heard my name and gave me this letter for you."

Kathryn broke the seal and scanned it. When she had finished, she said, "Mary says she wrote this at your instigation. You took a great risk carrying this for me."

"I did it because you are dear to John and we de Gaels are close as fingers on a hand, even when we quarrel. Now I will let John back in; come morning you will know what to do."

Kathryn rushed into his arms when he returned. They clung together all night, passion fed by fear and the expectation of being parted too soon, clung like failing swimmers in a sea of intrigue.

In the morning she rushed back to her tent and woke Tansy, demanding to be laced into her most becoming crimson gown. After all, she might have to beg the king for mercy, and a woman wishing to appeal to Henry Tudor's mercy must first appeal to his eye. "And the gold-trimmed headdress and the chains and all the damned jewelry I have," Kathryn burst out, kicking her cloak to one side and digging in a trunk for her embroidered stockings.

Dressed, painted, poised, she started for the queen's tent. On the way she met a lute player and paid him to follow her and sweetly play Catherine of Aragon awake. The boy settled on the grass near the men-at-arms; soon enough the queen woke and called out. "It is Lady Howard, Your Grace," Kathryn answered, heart hammering. "Are you ready for your morning cup of clove water?"

"Yes, please enter. Are the others with you?"

Kathryn stepped inside, hurried to draw back the bed curtains and hand the queen her clove water. "I am alone, as you can see. Please pardon me for waking you so early but we are in grave trouble—my family and I."

Catherine of Aragon sat, copper hair tumbling about her shoulders as she accepted the morning-cup. "What offense could you have committed?"

"I have not controlled my family as I should have. My sister has eloped with Richard de la Pole."

The queen gasped, spilling clove water on her cloth-of-gold counterpane. "Oh, my Kathryn, this is very bad! The king will clap you in the Tower—you must cast yourself at his feet and beg forgiveness, he can never resist a plea to his huge heart!"

Not his huge heart but, rather, his gargantuan self-opinion, Kathryn thought disloyally. "Yes, Your Grace is right. I must rush to the king at once."

"For what?" boomed that too-well-known voice from the doorway.

As Kathryn was already kneeling, it was not too great an effort to fall prostrate at the royal feet. "I knew nothing of it ahead of time, Your Grace, but my disloyal sister has run away with Richard de la Pole and married him."

"I know, the King of France just told me. I am having a warrant drawn up to convey you and your entire family to the—"

"Oh, no, Your Grace, please!" Kathryn cried out, shaken to the core. Her mother dragged from Wales, her infant sons raised in captivity—perhaps even her uncle of Surrey and grandfather Norfolk would lose their titles to disgrace! The Chases and Howards both—the king would welcome any excuse to execute her Plantagenet father—

"Oh, please, Your Grace!" she pleaded. "Negligence was my only crime, forgive me for not paying closer heed to my household. My sister is young and foolish only, not malignant, but I say to you that I shall sever ties with her as surely as though she lay dead. For she *is* dead to me, Sire, to have committed so foul and treasonable an act against you! I can say in my defense that I had no suspicions, that is all. Oh, do not take my sons away and lock them up! I would die!"

Henry Tudor harrumphed. After all, Kathryn was pretty despite her thinness and he liked having pretty women ask him for favors. When she cried out for her little boys and not her own sake, he found himself deeply touched. "How then did you discover your sister's perfidy?" he demanded, trying to sound suspicious.

"Jacquetta de Gael, Countess Courtenay, brought me this

letter, Your Grace—she met my sister on the way into the Val d'Or."

He accepted the proferred letter, read it, placed it in his doublet as Catherine of Aragon joined Kathryn on the floor. The sight of his wife's tear-streaked face softened him, as it always did, though he secretly welcomed this chance to take Kathryn and her Plantagenet pride down a peg or two.

"Lady Howard, your sister is a whore of the first degree," he announced coldly.

"Yes, Your Grace, you are correct. I should have sent her back to the convent, I should have—"

"A whore, and your husband a whoremonger. Still . . . as long as I have known you, *you* have been regarded as chaste. As a prude, in fact, Lady Howard. None of us were surprised that your husband had to seek elsewhere for warmth."

Kathryn glared nervously at his white suede shoes. "That is so, Your Grace," she forced herself to say, to deny those precious few nights with John. "I am old-fashioned and prudish, and I beg you not to mistake my friendship with the de Gaels. They only wanted to use me to bring your attention to their horses."

Henry tapped his soft-shod foot, treading down upon her little finger. "De Gael's horses are mine now."

Kathryn dared throw her arms around his ankles, pressing her lips to jeweled trim. "Take my horse, too, Your Grace, imprison me, smite my head off. But I beg you spare my sons!"

He idly prodded her with the side of his foot. "I cannot even levy a fine on you, everyone knows you have no money. Someone must tell Surrey and Norfolk what has happened so they do not unknowingly take your treasonous bitch of a sister in."

Was he going to let her go, then? Trying to keep the ecstatic relief out of her voice, Kathryn said, "Please allow me to tell them of our family disgrace."

She and the queen knelt up, kissing his be-ringed hands. "You have the lovely, long neck of the Howards, Lady Kathryn, it would be a shame to cleave through it. Therefore I will expect you to inform me should you hear from your sister again. Do not stop to gain my wife's assistance but come straight to me."

He took her by the elbow and ushered her to the door. There his voice dropped to a whisper. "Is it true what King François said about the de Gael women?"

"No, it is not, Your Grace," she answered craftily. "He undervalued their beauty—the countess is a lush golden Venus of a woman. She makes Mary Boleyn look like a *boy*!"

He released her, looking contemplative.

Kathryn went twenty feet and fainted in a heap.

"Our last night," John whispered, drawing Kathryn under his sable-lined cloak with him.

She nestled her head against his shoulder and brought him to a halt. The lights of camp were distant, like fireflies in the night. "Here," she told him softly. "Out here where we can breathe, John, not in a tent where we need fear discovery at every moment. Dear God, but I love you!"

He caught her by the waist, pressed her against him so that she felt all of his body and the strength of his desire. "Divorce Edmund and I will find some way to come home to you," he said, and he sounded angry. "You are related to him within the degrees of consanguinity—it will cost dear but I will pay for it, send to the pope and king—do it, Kathryn! I wish to marry you!"

She thought: *He is pushing thirty and has no heirs of his body, only nephews; it is this voice I hear speaking*.

"I have not proved especially fertile, My Love," she told him.

"Damn the children, I do not care whether we make none or a dozen! It is you I want—I cannot bear the thought of Edmund touching you, possessing you—"

He was kissing her too hard, bruising her mouth as though through violence he might convince her. She made a mewing sound of fear, twisted half out of his arms. "Stop it, John, I am not the enemy!"

Kisses all over her face, gentler now. "Forgive me, forgive . . ." Softer kisses on her wounded mouth now, tasting of the malmsey they had shared while walking from camp. His hands were expertly unhooking her gown and she did not know whether to be pleased or annoyed that he had had so many women to be so sure of himself.

Kathryn untied his shirt and slid her hands down the front. He had goosebumps from excitement and the chill night air; his nipples were very stiff. She unfastened the clasp of his cloak, let it fall to the ground and them on top of it. "I cannot bear to let you go," he crooned in her ear. "Cannot bear it . . . love me, Kathryn. Love me now. You are my Val d'Or, my Valley of Gold."

Dark, fevered kisses in the blackness of night; distant campfires dancing on the ridge. John's hot hands gathering back her heavy skirts, sliding up over bias-cut cloth stockings, and finding the vulnerable place above, that when caressed, made her buck and shudder. And then she was pulling him atop her, into her . . .

"Is someone murdering a woman out there?" one camp sentry asked the other.

His companion grinned toothily, spat into the fire. "Aye—with a very familiar sword."

When Kathryn returned to camp at dawn, she did not care who saw her. Only a kerchief held back her hair, which tumbled to her waist like a slattern's; there were grass stains all over her old crimson damask gown and the hem was muddy halfway to the knees. Such was her bearing that not a single sentry challenged her; her chin was too defiantly high, eyes too hard and bright.

Kathryn wore John's sable-lined cloak flung across her narrow shoulders, the weight almost too much for her to bear. She told Edmund that she had traded some gowns and needlework for it and he never thought to price Muscovite sable, that rarest of furs, and discover such a trade impossible.

She did not look back over her shoulder at John, for she had no regrets. Six weeks later when her monthly courses still had not arrived and morning nausea started, she ladled ale into her husband and seduced him. She did not regret that, either, for it would protect her child—hers and John's.

Four days after the Field of Cloth of Gold ended, a freak windstorm slashed through the Val d'Or, reducing tents and pavilions to piles of rags and kindling.

Within two years the "brother-kings" had declared war on each other. By order of King François, all English were sent from the country. John, taut with excitement, opened his orders from Henry Tudor only to discover he was being sent to Spain.

But a heretofore insignificant girl named Anne Boleyn came home.

PART TWO

ANNE BOLEYN
(The Pillar Perish'd)

"The pillar perish'd is whereto I leant,
The strongest stay of mine unquiet mind:
The like of it, no man again can find,
From East to West still seeking though he went."

"And 'round her neck is writ . . .
Noli me tangere. For Caesar's I am,
And wild to behold though I seem tame. . . ."

—Sir Thomas Wyatt,
cousin to Anne Boleyn—

"The Happiest of Women."
"Me And Mine."

—mottos of Anne Boleyn—

13

Anne Boleyn clasped her hands together lest she rise up out of her chair and smack the good cardinal across his pudgy jowls.

"So you see, Mistress Anne, you cannot marry Harry Percy. His father—perhaps you have heard of the mighty Duke of Northumberland?—has taken him home to the girl he was betrothed to in early youth."

Just as I was to have married my Butler cousin before they took one look at my eleventh fingernail and the strawberry mole on my neck, screamed "Witch!" and dragged him back to the wilds of Ireland, Anne thought furiously. There had been one major difference, however; she had cared not one whit for James Butler, while she loved Harry Percy with all the dark, steaming possessiveness of her highstrung nature.

She had been called the last virgin at the French Court and now that she was home seeking to end that state in matrimony, the chosen one had been forbidden her.

She fixed her unwavering black gaze on Cardinal Thomas Wolsey. "Pray tell, My Lord Cardinal, why did Northumberland object to me?" she asked very softly. He mumbled something about lowness of birth, forgetting she was Norfolk's granddaughter; something about previous betrothals, never mind that there were none. Well, Anne told herself, she would have some satisfaction from this man. "Did Harry Percy at least fight for me?" she asked bluntly.

"Very little," Wolsey replied with relish. He waited for her to blush or weep, though he had heard she did neither. Anne, true to form, remained as outwardly unshaken as a glass-smooth stream. *Blush or weep?* he asked himself with an ill-concealed grin. *Nay, this peppery little shrew would rather smite me with both fists until I fell down bleeding!* He said, "Perhaps you two would have been ill-suited. Everyone knows Harry Percy is a meek lad."

"So he is, but a woman in love can overlook such flaws."

So she regarded meekness as a flaw. "A woman of wit can always seek elsewhere for a man of quality," he informed her.

But Anne only snapped, "Oh, My Lord Cardinal? And who might that man be? Your august self?"

He went crimson. "You wrong both of us, Mistress Anne," he said curtly. "This audience is at an end: go now."

She rose with as little show of effort as a swan from its bed of rushes. A willow in the wind, this black-eyed girl; she gave him no satisfaction of an emotional scene.

Anne curtsied and left, flawed hand fisted into a ball. *God!* she thought hotly. *Had I been born a man I would lay about me with a sword rather than be refused the one I love! But as I am only a woman I have no weapons. No, none at all. My bloody father could have spoken to Northumberland, could have bargained for me, could have done something. Everyone knows his star is rising at Court and the king likes him.*

Yes, the king liked him. People claimed King Henry had been fond of Thomas Boleyn even before Mary Boleyn came home, but Anne sourly doubted it. *Revenge,* she thought, striding away from the archbishop's offices. If only she could find some way to hurt Wolsey, hurt Northumberland . . . ! But the only one she could imagine how to hurt was her father, and there were only two methods for that: go a-whoring or refuse every would-be bridegroom he brought her. Not that there were likely to be any more after two botched betrothals in a row.

And she had too much sense to end up like her sister Mary, selling virtue cheap, buying respectability dear. *Not I,* Anne told herself staunchly. *I will not sell myself so cheap as Mary.*

A thought struck her so that she had to lean in the nearest doorway for support. *Sweet Jesu! I am already the oldest virgin I know!*

It was a bad time to be a Plantagenet.

In 1513 Henry Tudor had executed John de la Pole lest there be a rising in his favor while Henry was out of the country. Before the Field of Cloth of Gold Henry had briefly toyed with the idea of trying the Duke of Buckingham for treason, but waited until the next year when Buckingham and Wolsey fell spectacularly out. Cardinal Wolsey being Henry's trusted High Lord Chancellor of England, Buckingham lost the argument and his head on the pretext that he stood too near the throne in blood.

There stood a male far closer to the throne, a son of Edward the Fourth, though bastard; Kathryn's father, Hal, Lord

Chase, was confined to the Tower within days of Buckingham's own arrest. The fact that his daughter Mary had married Henry's archenemy, Richard de la Pole, "the Last Sprig of the White Rose," made it unlikely that Lord Chase would ever taste freedom again.

It was only their Howard blood that kept Kathryn and Joanna Chase from joining him, for the Howards stood very high at Court those days. But the Chase blood was so suspect that Edmund insisted their sons be sent to safer homes; Kathryn, weeping but knowing he was right, saw six-year-old James taken to Norfolk's household at Kenninghall and three-year-old Adam to the Boleyns at Hever.

That left the baby, Isabella, who, being female, was not in such danger as her brothers. Henry Tudor decreed she not marry without his express permission, that was all. Chances seemed slim that she would ever end in the Tower or on the block.

Although Margaret Pole, senior surviving female Plantagenet, said, "I would prefer the block to the Tower—that damned place is so unbearably drafty!"

Little Isabella was Kathryn's darling. James had been trouble and Adam by far her favorite until Isabella's advent. She would have been anyone's chosen daughter, for she was a sweet-natured baby, but to Kathryn she was made doubly dearer by being female and John's child. Kathryn persisted in nursing Isabella herself, to the horror of the Court, and went on worshiping and dandling her long after the thrill of motherhood should have worn thin. Confused, the other ladies-in-waiting put their heads together and decided that as she appeared immune to men, she must be one of those women who put all their passion into maternity.

Catherine of Aragon, who had noted a new glow and determination about her favorite, wisely thought that a man stood alongside the child in Kathryn's affections. But she said nothing; there had been no brothers and sisters for her own dear little Mary, so she knew how besotted a mother could be with her daughter, bound by fierce ties of gender and affection.

The queen wore a hairshirt beneath her damask gowns now, and though the king upbraided her for it, each time he left the bedchamber she donned the loathsome garment again. Henry said it was ruining her fair Castilian skin and he was right, but as repeated childbearing had already thickened her figure and he came rarely to her bed these days, he did not protest unduly.

Catherine of Aragon no longer prayed for sons. Three successive years with no pregnancy caused her instead to pray that she might accept God's iron and unforgiving will. She prayed also that Kathryn Chase's Howard blood would keep her safe and that God might forgive Henry Tudor his ever-increasing adulteries. At age thirty-seven her monthly courses were little better than nonexistent, so she could not bear him sons, but she could give him the affection and understanding any woman bore her liege-lord.

Sons, she would think. *Had I borne him sons he would not wander so far afield.* But hope of them seemed as remote as her girlhood home. Magnificent, unrelenting Spain . . . the Moorish towers of Castile and León, her indomitable mother riding in armor at the head of ten thousand men-at-arms . . . Ferdinand and Isabella, both dead now, living on through their children and grandchildren. Catherine was raising little Mary Tudor with memories of Isabella, teaching her to prove a fierce woman warrior in defense of her faith and dazzling birthright—a birthright she could only realize if there were no sons. And with Henry's dwindling visits and her own scant monthly courses, sons seemed unthinkable.

Mary Boleyn had already begun to pall with the king, she knew. Mary had no wit or fire as Bessie Blount had, which was why the queen liked Mary and had despised Bessie. And why she mortally feared Jacquetta de Gael.

Oh, the countess smiled at the proper times, curtsied lower and more respectfully than any woman at Court, but she never should have been there in the first place. She had managed it very cleverly, of course, visiting Kathryn at Howard House on a Sunday when the king took the royal barge upriver, as was his habit. The two women happened to be picking flowers at the water's edge that particular Sunday. . . .

How the afternoon sun had glistered on that dazzling profusion of honey hair! How enticing the swell of cleavage above the low, square neckline as Jacquetta curtsied in obeisance!

The king had immediately ordered the barge to land at Howard House though there was no wharf and he had to wade ashore to meet Lady Howard's dazzling friend. There had been no simpering, no coquetting from the direct Jacquetta, who had boldly regarded Henry Tudor with such frankly erotic promise that he felt quite the lovestruck schoolboy.

She led him a merry chase, however. Maybe, maybe not

was her song and she sang it so prettily that Henry lingered at an impassioned pitch for months. She made no pretense of virtue standing in the way; no, that was not what kept Jacquetta de Gael from the king's bed. Instead she said bluntly, "My brother would not like it, after you exiled him and took our horses. And my sons would be shamed, shamed! It is *unthinkable*! Though of course," she would add, flicking her pale blue gaze over Henry and voluptuously licking her lips, "I think of it all the time."

The price, when she changed her tra-la-la'ing to plainsong, was high enough: the return of all the de Gael breeding stock. She even thought to specify that Windsgeat would be flattered if the king considered his own any foals born the de Gael horses since their "Babylonian captivity."

Henry shook in his shoes at that one. He had never met a blunter woman, nor one who made him feel less like the virile seducer of legend. No, with this wildly experienced widow he knew himself to be a rank amateur and hungry for her instructions.

Then one morning Kathryn was awakened by a resounding series of knocks at the door of her cramped Windsor Castle quarters. When she sleepily answered, a breathtaking blonde stood there, munching an apple; she thought it Bessie Blount and braced herself for the attack. Instead she heard Jacquetta say, "What ho, Kat, you slugabed! Don riding clothes, have Mask saddled, and join me for a sight you shall never forget. To chamber pot, to wash basin and wardrobe! Send your manservant to the stables and Tansy for water, I shall tight-lace you myself; Henry Tudor can vouch for how tight things can be with me! What, do I see a faint blush in the first glittering of dawn? I thought you proof against embarrassment after that morning you came sauntering barefoot into the Val d'Or with a cat-licking-cream-off-her-whiskers look! Hurry, Boy; hurry, Tansy! Faster, everyone! When Jacquetta plans an adventure, nobody sleeps!"

Half an hour later they sat on their handsome white mares in Windsor Great Park. "Is the king going to be here? He usually likes to hunt all morning after—er—you know, all night," Kathryn mumbled.

Jacquetta tossed her second apple core of the day to the turf. "Harry Tudor couldn't ride a *feather-bed* today."

"You are very proud of your evening's debauch."

Jacquetta smiled broadly and smacked her lips. "With this tender white body I have accomplished things a man could not do with pen, sword, or politicking. If a de Gael woman cannot best a man at his own game, no one can. After all, it is our stock-in-trade. Here! Hist, Kat, here they come!"

Thunder in the distance. Kathryn thought that odd as the morning was cornflower blue, with a froth of mist dallying about the trunks of whispering oaks and willows. Dawn was striping the sky with broad bands of crimson, gold, and ripest peach; night fell back before the gorgeous onslaught. Then the mist blew furiously on the next knoll as two hundred tossing white heads broke through it. *Like Neptune's steeds through a rolling white surf,* Kathryn thought in awe.

The Windsgeat Whites were coming home.

They leapt and sprang with the sensual pleasure of freedom. Unbridled, fenceless, some bucked riotously. Young stallions jealously nipped necks, brood mares who should have known better curvetted like foals. Every shade of white was there—pale, pearly grays, faintly yellow whites, and the true, blue-white few that legend said the Devil in horse-form had gotten on a de Gael daughter centuries before.

One sturdy mare led them, a cold-eyed, calculating beast with a bell braided into her mane. She swerved straight toward the waiting women, and all the men riding herd could not turn her. "Home, Dia!" Jacquetta cried to the mare with shining eyes. "Home to Windsgeat!"

She spurred her mount toward the lush valley beyond. All the horses caroused after her as she kept pace with the bell mare, but Kathryn found herself caught in mid-herd. She had never seen such power and spirit as in the thundering white clan, capricious as girls frolicking on May Day. Manes streamed, plumed tails bespeaking Arabic ancestry bannered in a horse-created breeze. The mist fled them, rolling away from flashing hooves to the sanctuary of mistletoe-draped oaks.

Through the two miles of Windsor Great Park that had long ago been part of the original Windsgeat, they curved downhill. The estate waited their arrival, shining like a verdant gem. Through shallow ponds now, splashing them dry, past flocks of John's Manx sheep with their insolent black faces and six horns each. Past the little dark de Gael deer, past the peeking foxes and flapping owls aroused from their naps.

Home to Windsgeat.

Kathryn's eyes streamed as she rode. God willing, someday Windsgeat might be her home, too, if she only dared dream. She and Isabella and John . . . The white herd could be no dearer to her had she already owned them and overseen their breeding at John's side, making marks in the ledgers Jacquetta had shown her, registering this sire with this dam. And as for the plush emerald grass, the streams, lakes, the rough-hewn manor house with its brick corkscrew chimnies . . .

Mask trumpeted like a battle charger as she galloped. *Like a rapacious stallion, not a lady's mount,* Kathryn thought, surprised into laughing aloud. Her twelve-year-old mount, usually so stately, was rearing, squealing, and lashing out at any horse that came too near. The long white mane streamed back, engulfing Kathryn; she leaned into the pose, understanding what it was to be a centaur.

As if they had never been away, the horses poured back onto de Gael land. Out of Windsor Wood into Windsgeat proper, past the ancient stone maze, down into the flat green valley. Led by Jacquetta—now riding Dia, the bell mare, Kathryn saw to her amazement—they swerved at the stone-and-timber house, fanned out before the great sickle-moon-shaped lake. Frenzy of freedom spent, the herd slowed. Some fell to quibbling, some waded into the lake to quench their thirst. Others cropped grass. Several young stallions, suddenly discovering their masculinity in the thrill of the moment, took off after chosen fillies.

Jacquetta was bellowing like a fishwife. Grooms and stable-boys spurred to obey her lashing voice as another three dozen servants raced from the house. "Get those colts out of the lake, they are too hot to drink! Cut out the mares who are in season and put them in the broodmare barn before we have a full-fledged orgy on our hands! Cut out the breeding age colts 'til I decide who to geld and who not to and—you there, I said *get those horses out of the lake*! No, no, you addlepated fool, can you not tell a stallion when you see him? You have let Cernunnos at the mares!"

Kathryn knew Cernunnos by reputation only. *He has a neck like an ox and is wilder than the wind,* John had told her. *There is no rope that can hold him and he has never been ridden. The last time I tried he threw me down and danced on me. The king's own men could not catch him when they stole our stock; he lives, wild, in the greenwood, and always has.*

Cernunnos had a Roman nose, massive neck, and the wickedest little black eyes Kathryn had ever seen on a horse. Effortlessly eluding grooms, he plowed through the herd, coming straight at . . .

Her!

Jacquetta rode by just in time. "*Jump!*" she shouted. And Kathryn, gathering up her skirts from the silver sidesaddle, did. Cernunnos's wicked little raisin eyes were fixed lustfully on Mask, who shamelessly presented herself, with tail raised in invitation.

Laughing, the two women rode, Kathryn mounted behind Jacquetta, to the nearest door, slid off with a ripping and rending of fabric, and sat down too hard on each other. By the time they scrambled back to their feet, the necessary horses had been separated with the exception of Cernunnos, who mounted four more mares before streaking off across the lawn, trumpeting defiance at his out-classed pursuants.

When things had settled somewhat, Jacquetta took Kathryn indoors. "I love every stick, every hearthstone and window of this place," Jacquetta said passionately, arms wide as if she could embrace the old Anglo-Saxon Great Hall they stood in—Windsgeat's first room. A forty-foot stretcher table ran down the middle of the massive room, flanked by some three dozen box-bottomed chairs in an era when houses possessing four chairs were considered wealthy. There were three fireplaces with Italian marble facings from the last century; one green with gilt, one black with silver and semiprecious stones, and the last, hunched with jasper mermen and lapis caryatids. The checkerboard floor was marble, too, black and white, and suits of armor lined the walls.

"I love this place, too," Kathryn said warmly.

"You should. You shall be mistress of it some day," Jacquetta predicted.

"Oh, no, no, this is your home, it will remain yours."

"I will marry off it again some day. After all, I cannot have a husband of mine here, he would not wish to be subject to John's rules. Nor mine, and Windsgeat will always come first to me. Over John, over my sons, over any man I choose to wed. Windsgeat will always come first."

"You and John are very passionate about your ancestral home."

Jacquetta smiled suddenly—a very disarming smile that Kathryn found herself mistrusting. "Windsgeat is sacred to us, Kat. *Sacred*. It is not merely a place, it is—well, the rest will have to wait until you have married my brother."

Amused at Jacquetta's assumptions, Kathryn answered, "Even did I ask for a divorce and even did Edmund agree, chances are poor that the king would allow me to marry his least-favorite subject. Especially since we both have so much Plantagenet blood."

The beautiful blonde shrugged. "All the better. That way perhaps the de Gaels can put a Plantagenet back on the throne some day."

"That is very dangerous talk; I am afraid I cannot listen to any more of it."

A servant brought them a cloisonné tray bearing delicate glass goblets of wine. The two women raised their drinks in a toast, then started out through the gardens. "I have something to show you. John wants it to be a surprise but I think you need some encouragement. Come along, Kat."

Kathryn threw a hand up in the air with a gesture of resignation. "Must you take charge of *everything*, 'Quetta? You have your finger in everyone's pie, I will wager. Why, you are a witch when it comes to minding the business of others!"

They followed the herringbone brick walk to the carpenters' shed, where loud noises of planing and hammering filled the air. "A witch?" Jacquetta asked and laughed. "Yes, of course, Dear, has John not told you? All the de Gaels are witches. Now come see."

Her laughter twinkled, gemlike, as she kicked the door open. Inside, craftsmen scurried in sawdust, repairing chairs, making tables, wrestling pieces for a hammerbeam ceiling. Jacquetta led Kathryn to the rear of the shop where a bed-of-state was being constructed. Its cup-and-cover posts were broad as a big man's waist; the towering headboard scraped the ceiling of the shed. Amidst half-carved oaken foliage, capering sprites, bearded Pans, Diana and the Three Graces were interwoven *JG*'s and *KC*'s.

"John's divorce is final. He waits only for yours to present this to you as a betrothal gift," Jacquetta announced proudly.

It astonished her when Kathryn clapped both hands over her mouth and ran from the shed, sobbing.

14
March 1522
York Place

"I loathe and despise England," Anne Boleyn said darkly.

Kathryn considered the statement with a total lack of sympathy. "I know, Cuz, and it is a shame you must be here against your will. Now please help me fasten my mask, will you? The trumpets and hautbois are starting up." They shifted in their toy "castle."

"King Harry and his boring old masques! Why did I ever let my father yank me away from the French Court?"

"Because war was declared and François the First promised to personally hang anyone of English blood remaining on French soil. And, Anne, sweeting, your neck is already long enough."

They fell silent while the gabbling of the six other women in the canvas-over-wood "castle" overwhelmed them. At last Anne murmured, "I apologize, Kat, I know how it hurts you to think of the French war. You thought John would come home because of it and there he is, stranded at the Imperial Court in Spain. Rest assured we shall hear his name tonight as these are the emperor's ambassadors Cardinal Wolsey is entertaining. By the way, the gossip is so conflicting and I know you are very high in the queen's favor, can you tell me who the king's latest mistress is?"

Every gold-and-white clad woman in the Castle Vert turned to look at them. "I *wonder,*" Jacquetta de Gael said, and Anne had the good grace to blush.

Two days ago at the joust staged for the Imperial ambassadors, the king had ridden a silver-swathed horse whose trappings showed a pierced heart with the caption, *Elle Mon Couer à Naverra*—"She Has Wounded My Heart." Kathryn swallowed hard, thinking, *The king's passion shows no signs of abating; one time Jacquetta admits him to her chamber, the next she locks him out, crying that she compromises her family honor. Perhaps her machinations will get John home yet.*

Anne, eye-to-eye with tall Jacquetta, said frostily, "I beg

your pardon, Countess, it is so difficult to tell the king's blonde whores apart."

A button dropping would have sounded loud as cannonfire. Jacquetta smiled broadly. "No, little girl, it is not so difficult. I only sleep with the king; your sister is the one who sleeps with Sussex, Essex, most of the North, and two-thirds of France. Also, your sister was fool enough to get no better than a farm and untitled husband, while I had two hundred horses and five hundred acres returned me, not to mention gaining two new manor houses in the process. So you see, I am the clever, *selective* blonde whore; it is how you can tell me from the ones you are related to."

Anne went crimson beneath her sallow skin. She was opening her mouth to fire a return volley when the toy castle gave a sickening lurch that toppled the ladies-in-waiting inside it, sending them bobbing like ducks after bread crumbs. In the ensuing flurry they could hear the onlookers at Cardinal Wolsey's York Place crying out with delight at the sight of the Castle Vert they inhabited being wheeled in. A herald was bellowing, "Hark you, my lords! What place is this that such beauty defends it?"

There was no beauty to be seen, however, for Kathryn was kneeling on Elizabeth Stafford Howard, her uncle Surrey's wife, while Anne had gone down under the other five thrashing women. Gowns tore, headdresses toppled as women fought to regain their footing in the rocking castle.

The herald weakly tried again. "Hark, my lords! What place is this . . ."

The crowd tittered. *"Get off my lap!"* Surrey's wife hissed at Kathryn, and gave her such a shove that she fell over Jacquetta again. Someone knelt on Anne Boleyn's stomach, and fists flew. Had Maria de Salinas not been present on one of her rare visits, the entire evening would have been at a standstill.

Maria flung Kathryn to one side and gave Elizabeth Howard a shove. "Stand up and identify yourselves!" she ordered in a hissing voice.

The Countess of Surrey straightened her mask and popped up above the canvas battlements. "I am *Gentleness*," she announced, with a savage kick at her nearest niece.

Kathryn narrowly refrained from sticking a headdress pin in her aunt's well-cushioned rump. "I am Loyalty!" she announced, leaning out over the far left battlement. Maria appeared in the middle, identifying herself as Honor. The other women likewise named themselves, with Jacquetta at last arriving under the name Beauty. She wore her fair hair down tonight, powdered with gold dust; candles fastened to either side of her mask burned brightly, which had caused a delay in her appearance, for Anne was standing on the flint needed to start them.

Jacquetta spoke further, identifying the inhabitants of Castle Vert as "Honest English virtues brought to life for their proud country's sake." At once eight women in she-devil masks and Italian gowns rushed in, proclaiming themselves such things as Jealousy, Scorn, Danger, Spite, and Wantonness. "We shall never allow the Castle of Truth to be captured by further virtues!" they shouted.

But trumpets and sacks sounded again as eight masked knights rode into the hall. Henry Tudor led them in scarlet velvet slashed to show the snowy linen beneath; his diamond-studded hat waved with dozens of plumes and his mask showed Eros pursuing Psyche so that his small blue eyes were hardly visible. "Who is this that would keep us from Castle Vert?" he roared in his resonant actor's voice. "Do you not know that I am Ardent Desire and cannot be stopped by Jealousy, Discord, and their like?"

Behind him the other knights shouted their names. Kathryn's heart gave a mad leap in her breast as she saw a stag mask at the rear. Had John managed to sneak home with the embassy? No, it was not possible, she warned herself, feeling the evening sour. This man was far too short to be John.

At first she had missed his wit, his jokes and understanding; now, lying nightly awake and unfulfilled by her once-a-month-or-less sexual grapples with the appalling Edmund, she remembered only John's body on hers and that blotted out all else. It was not his mind or his heart occupying her thoughts after nearly two years without him, trying to pretend her husband was him in the dark. *I am wanton,* she thought, and the pounding in her breast seemed to echo throughout her body. *I want John so badly I can concentrate on naught else. I throb, I burn; a priest brushing against me at chapel makes me start with lust because he is male like John. In time I will be another Mary Boleyn, taking on the hoards to slake my lust.*

She could wait forever . . . if she could only be certain that John would return. But after so many months, hope had begun to fail her.

King Henry and his knights dismounted, horses quickly led

away by pages before they could soil Cardinal Wolsey's fine parquetry floor. The "Italian" women cried out, "Gentlemen, you must not advance for we defend the castle against your goodness!"

"Is this war, then?" Henry yelled. "Gentlemen, *lay on!*"

To the delight of the crowd, the weapons were brought out: dates, figs, and orange slices for the men, while the evil ladies defended themselves with sugar plums and cinnamon comfits. The battle was hugely enjoyed by all, Henry's knights feigning terror and clustering behind him, venturing out only to be met with a hail of candy.

"You are dripping wax in my hair, Madame Whore," Anne acidly observed to Jacquetta, who tilted her head, letting more run down as she spoke. "*Move,* then. Or is movement forbidden the world's oldest virgin?"

Anne had started toward her with clenched fists when a roar from the crowd alerted her. The men had won. The evil "Italians" had broken ranks, scampering away while King Henry and the knights set miniature silver ladders against Castle Vert and started up.

The king was first, of course. None dared best him at anything. He threw a muscular leg over the top, copper hair gleaming from under the edge of his scarlet cap as he seized Jacquetta by the waist and held her high. "And so Ardent Desire conquers Truth and achieves, at long last, Beauty!" he announced. The crowd cheered lustily.

The women descended the stairs at the rear of Castle Vert, each helped down by a knight. At the bottom Kathryn found herself met by the stag mask, though the eyes behind it were disappointingly brown. "Lady Howard, I have here a letter for you from De Lord," said a familiar voice—that of Pieter van der Hüm, John's Flemish valet, long exiled with his lord. "Here, take it, please, for I must get dis costume back to George Boleyn—he charged me a small fortune to borrow it!"

The feast lasted hours. It seemed forever before people were engrossed enough in politics for others to begin slipping away to lovers, chamber pots, and more comfortable chairs; others went to sleep in window seats until the dancing was announced.

Kathryn bunched up her skirts in one hand and took the precious letter to the garden, not caring who saw her legs as she ran.

There was a bitter surprise awaiting her in the letter. John was angry she had not attempted to divorce Edmund and insisted that she start proceedings at once or he would relinquish all claim to her. "I would wait the rest of my life for you could I but be certain you were sincere and meant to marry me. But there is no sense in two lives hovering on the brink indefinitely because you cannot make up your mind," he wrote. The missive ended with his usual passionate farewells but Kathryn detected a note of panic in them. He had not signed with his usual *W* cipher for Windsgeat, either, only sketched a lady amidst a maze—a lady resembling Kathryn herself.

I cannot blame him, she thought sickly. *He is living like a monk and he is no bloodless man to bear that well. He has his family and lands to care for, he has to think of marriage and children. But he knows that if I divorce Ned I will not be accepted at Court, and my salary is supporting my entire family.*

It never occurred to her that with a wealthy husband she would be able to provide bounteously for her family; she never thought of asking John's financial help, while for his part he erroneously presumed she knew him well enough to be certain he would not let the Chases and her Howard children suffer. Kathryn was too proud to ask and John too proud to voice the offer, each thinking they knew the other too well.

"I will take that, Milady," a voice boomed.

Cardinal Wolsey snatched the letter from Kathryn's hands. "I have waited for this a long time but I never thought you so foolish as to bring unauthorized correspondence from abroad here, in my own house! It is against the law to receive such letters, Lady Howard; now you will go to the Tower with the rest of your treacherous Plantagenet kin. And de Gael will be recalled only to lose his glorious head while the king and I share Windsgeat's riches!"

"Why should *de Gael* die for a letter *I* wrote?" came a puzzled-sounding male voice.

Victim and persecutor whirled to face a jaunty-looking George Boleyn. Her cousin had grown very tall, Kathryn thought with a rising note of hysteria, then, *God's Saints! If he gets me out of this one he can put all the spiders he wants down my back!*

"You lie, Sir," Wolsey countered, jowly face folding into a sneer.

"Were you not a man of the cloth, Cardinal, I should call

you out and cut you into collops," George said pleasantly, folding his arms. "Everyone knows I have courted Lady Kat since we were brats at Blickling Hall together and I first put spiders down her shift."

"I—I—I shall take this matter to the king!" Wolsey threatened.

"*Do,*" George agreed. "Only allow me to do this first." He drew his fancy little dinner dagger, pricked his finger to draw a bright bead of blood, and insolently left his print at the bottom of the page. Wolsey, dark-faced with rage, left the garden.

"You risk too much for me, Cuz," Kathryn said, knees giving way. She sank down onto the nearest marble bench, stays suddenly too tight.

"I did not risk it merely for the sake of our childhood romps, Kat—de Gael's man saw Wolsey stalking you and gave me another fifty sovereigns to help you. Though frankly, I believe that was a hundred-sovereign job; I must remember to go back and demand fifty more."

Both hands pressed to her tight bodice front, Kathryn gasped out, "George, I owe you a favor."

He considered it. "Then let us dye the tail of the cardinal's favorite mule, shall we?"

He looked sincere. Kathryn groaned to herself; suddenly they were eight years old again and at Blickling or Hever Castle in Kent. "It is good to find a friend," she said, holding a hand out to her cousin.

George took hold of it. "And it is good to *be* a friend, Kat. Remember I am still around if you need me."

"I want a divorce."

Kathryn, embroidering a Spanish-style smock for Isabella, plunged her new silver needle straight into her finger. "Edmund!" she cried out, dropping her sewing and putting the wound to her mouth.

"I mean it. I am divorcing you for Bessie Blount's sister. As you and I are cousins it should not be too difficult."

In the light of the fireplace his fair hair suddenly seemed silvery, like spun sterling. "But—but we were granted a papal dispensation!" Kathryn argued hotly.

"A different pope has his arse in Saint Peter's chair now. The request is already on its way, funded by the last of my inheritance."

Kathryn heard him with a rising knot of hysteria bubbling

in her chest. Five months earlier she had written John, "With my father in prison I must regard myself as head of the Chase family and wholly responsible for its welfare. As a divorced woman I should be removed from my position at Court, losing the queen's favor and through it the king's protection. It seems a miracle that my brother and sons have not been sent to the Tower. . . . You must believe that my love for you has never faltered, but I cannot abandon my folk. . . ."

But with Edmund in the position of plaintiff she would not be condemned at Court. She would still be allowed to serve the queen, even if she married John—John, whom she had not heard from since sending that letter, though she wrote a dozen more times. Or perhaps she could take her children to John at the Imperial Court at Spain and be a lady-in-waiting there. . . . *Aye,* argued her conscience. *And the moment you go, they will put your father's head on a pike over Tower Gate.*

Kathryn did not know why that should matter so terribly to her. Lord Hal had never raised a hand to help her, never sent money, never given love or encouragement to any of the family. Her mother wrote only to demand money, Mary was still married to de la Pole and breeding sons in France, and Arthur was worse than no help at all. He was also a pederast, which meant she could not even count on him making a good marriage with a wife who would support him and take him off Kathryn's hands. But at least his lovers had made a much-feared jouster of him.

To hell with my father or my brother! she thought wildly. *I can take the children and join John in Spain, I can—*

Leave Jacquetta, the Boleyns, and the queen? Let her father go to the block, leave her mother languishing in Wales?

Confused, anguished, Kathryn threw down her embroidery and rushed to the cradle where Isabella slept. The little girl was drowsy and mumbled some new word Tansy had taught her that day, fussing as she clung to her mother's neck. Kathryn felt braver holding her favorite child, John's daughter; she drew deep, steady breaths, calming herself. "Yes," she said at last. "Yes, Edmund, a divorce is an excellent idea. I shall not interfere with it."

"Good, that is sensible of you." He nodded into his ale, suddenly glanced up at her from his fireside chair. "I will take the boys with me, of course."

She had not seen them since Christmas; they were due

home to visit within the week. Adam had not known her last time and had cried when she kissed him. "Oh, no, Ned," she said sickly.

"The Howards have never stood higher at Court. Living with me, people will forget the boys have Plantagenet blood, they will remember only that they are Howards and so they will be safe. Perhaps I will thus gain the king's favor."

"Bah, you know the king does not like divorced people at Court! Charles Brandon is the only one he ever tolerated; do you not recall how furious he was when his sister Margaret wished to divorce the 'Earl of Anguish'?"

"I am still a Howard. King Henry will favor me."

She did not know why she bothered arguing with him. He was nothing to her now, only a stumbling block between her and her beloved sons. And yet here he was, about to remove himself from her life. It seemed such outrageous luck, the good mingled with bad like fine wine atop stagnant water, that she laughed ironically, hand to mouth. "You are still pretty, Wife. Wouldst to bed?" Edmund asked hopefully.

Kathryn buried her face in Isabella's downy chestnut hair. "No, Ned, I will not risk making a child that will either have no father or be taken from me. And I would like to keep Isabella and Adam both. *Please?*"

Now she could write John, now she dared hope for the first time in two years. Now she could have everything, even if it meant living in exile abroad. Leaving England.

Why the pain, why the tugging at her heart? Surely she loved John no less than at the Val d'Or, and yet why was she still dragging her feet, still frightened of shadows?

Why?

Unexpectedly, things began to go in Kathryn's favor. At Court she was viewed as a much-wronged woman, Edmund being widely known as an infamous whoremonger.

Arthur announced his betrothal. "I thought you did not like girls," Kathryn said, and watched him blush furiously.

"Well . . . she is much more tolerable than most of them, and we both want children," he said. But he picked a bride with no money, the sister of William Brereton, a lowly but well-liked young Court chamberer. The bride was a merrily tweeting nut-brown creature who scarcely came up to Arthur's armpit. *I hope I do not end up supporting the two of them and their children,* Kathryn thought, relieved at Arthur's decision to marry.

Kathryn's sons James and Adam came home filled with news about the Howards and Boleyns. James, age seven, had just been given his first horse by his great-grandfather Norfolk and was insufferable about it as only a son of Edmund's could be. Adam, nearly four, solemnly asked Kathryn, "Shall I continue to see you when I have a new mama?" In the end, Edmund decided to take James and leave her Adam, which pleased Kathryn greatly.

George Boleyn came calling. "You are going to need new quarters at Court now that Edmund is divorcing you," he pointed out cheerfully. "Want mine?"

"Why, thank you, George, but people would talk."

"They have been gossiping about us ever since Wolsey grabbed that letter. You silly woman, I am offering you my rooms because I am proposing marriage."

She opened her mouth, let it hang unflatteringly a moment before snapping it shut. "I see," George mused. "So the rumors about de Gael are true after all. Well, no hard feelings, you and I are not in love but we have always had fun together. Say, Sweet Cuz, ride out to Hever with me some time, Annie has gone home in a snit again. I believe it broke her heart when the cardinal forbade her to marry Northumberland's boy."

"Harry Percy, yes, I know. They are currently trying to force him into marrying some girl they claim he was precontracted to long before he met Anne. Poor boy, he was always ailing; I fear Wolsey did the proper thing, not letting them marry. Anne is so fiery and Harry so frail, she would consume him."

"Yes, he should have burned like tinder struck by lightning and been gone within the year. But it broke her heart, and though she tried to stay at Court, she could not bear the merriment and has slunk home to mope. Spends all day in bed staring at the walls; Mother cannot do a thing with her. Are you certain you will not marry me and save me from the clutches of Jane Parker?"

"Is that who your father has picked out for you? God's Saints, George, she is all wrong for you! Thin-lipped and dried-out as an old twig."

George twisted his cap in his hands, stared down at it crushed in his fingers. "Have you never heard," he began, looking up at last, "the new saying around Court? 'What Boleyn wants, Boleyn gets.' Father is very hard to refuse."

Thomas Boleyn was Household Treasurer to the king this

year, having pulled himself up to that, Sheriff of Kent, and Knight of the Bath all in a few years. *An ambitious man, my uncle*, Kathryn thought. *All my uncles are*.

George went on his way, leaving Kathryn to wonder what she *would* do for rooms at Court now that her divorce was approaching finality. Of course if she went to John in Spain . . . But John had not answered her letters in so long, had not acknowledged being told that she would marry him as soon as Edmund was gone. The long-awaited news drew no response from him and she was panicking more each day as no letter arrived.

Jacquetta had not heard from him either. "Not in seven months or more. And yet earlier this year the gossip was that he was still alive and well."

It was Thomas Boleyn who finally cleared up the mystery of why John had not been heard from. Henry Tudor sent Boleyn on several brief diplomatic missions and Thomas, upon his return, immediately sought Kathryn out at Richmond Palace.

She had just finished preparing the queen's bed for the night when a note arrived saying her uncle wished to see her that evening. When the tedious nightly process of bedding the queen down had been finished, Kathryn slipped away to the Boleyn chambers and found Thomas in front of the glowing fireplace. "I have something of yours, and something for your friend the countess, too," he explained, and handed her a large bundle of letters addressed to John in her own scrawling hand. Not a one was opened.

"What is the meaning of this?" Kathryn demanded shakily.

"You mean, what is that packet's significance aside from the fact that you entered into forbidden and therefore treasonable correspondence? It means John de Gael is no longer in Spain, nor has he been for some time. He received secret orders from the king to attend our English embassy in the Low Countries at Margaret of Austria's court. Your letters were stacked up in Spain, never having reached him."

Then John did not know she was divorced and waiting for word to join him. Kathryn said nothing but she paled.

Thomas Boleyn gnawed his lip. "Do you want the rest of my news?"

"Please, Uncle."

"Very well, then. I confess I interfered in your affairs. Finding your letters to him told me that Wolsey was right, you had had an *affaire de coeur* with de Gael. I sent a messenger to him via a very swift courier service asking his intentions and I received letters in return. He confirmed that he had not heard from you since you last wrote to say you would not leave Edmund, and he said that none of his correspondence was getting out of the Low Countries. His man Pieter van der Hüm told me this personally. Kathryn . . ."

Why did he sound so sorry for her? She stared at him, thinking it odd that Thomas Boleyn did not rail at her about lost virtue or family honor. "There is also a letter for you and one for his sister. *Kathryn*. He did not hear from you, he thought you had deserted him so he gave up on you. He married elsewhere."

No. John would not do that to her, especially not when she was so near freedom. "I do not believe you," she said, smiling nervously.

"Do you know his writing? Read the letter."

"He does not know you, he would not have confided in you. This is some trick of the king's."

"Kathryn, he wrote me to ask that I help break the news of his marriage—and because he wanted you to know he thought you had abandoned him and had never written. He thought you had given up on him."

To show him that she could not be fooled so easily, she ripped open the letter in front of him and read it twice. It was John's script and John's wording; John's bitter, stiff-necked apologies for having doubted her and surrendered hope. He had married one of Jacquetta's Flemish cousins, he said, thinking he could not possess Kathryn and being tired of waiting for something he could never have.

She did not cry. There were no tears large enough, damp enough for so great a shock. Thomas Boleyn had to fetch Jacquetta to take Kathryn away and put her to bed, where she lay listlessly staring at the ceiling. In the night little Isabella cried out; Jacquetta rose, put the child in Kathryn's arms.

"At least you still have his child, Kathryn, while I—I have nothing. I still cannot marry and install some other man as lord of Windsgeat; I must live *in-between*, Kat, struggling to protect my home from the king. I am so tired of living in-between! So tired of waiting!"

"John was tired of waiting, too," Kathryn whispered hoarsely.

In the royal bedchambers, Henry Tudor was tired of waiting also. Tired of Mary Boleyn's bland, blonde complaisance, tired of Jacquetta outwitting him at each turn. Like John de Gael he wanted a family life, wanted a woman and sons to call his own in the eyes of the law. Looking around he saw an ailing, prematurely aging queen, figure plump, complexion muddy, religious impulses running rampant. The seed was planted in his mind by physical distaste that she was not really his wife, she was his brother's widow.

And then there was his daughter. Frail, bright-eyed Mary who, no matter how often he jounced her on his knee and called her "the greatest jewel in the kingdom" was only a girl after all. The only other queen regnant in England's history had plunged the nation into civil war.

If Mary married abroad, some foreign power would expect to rule Henry's England through her. If she married at home it would foment rebellion, the lords vying for power amongst themselves, his son-in-law coveting the crown.

Two men, two enemies: Henry Tudor and John de Gael. Both were thirty-two years old and without sons. Both grasped desperately for some measure of success and family security, both craved love and the keeping of their respective kingdoms from attack.

In the process each crushed the woman who loved him best.

15

There was nothing prettier than Hever Castle in the autumn.

It was far smaller than any royal residence termed "castle," yet it was exquisitely built and placed. Three-storied, rectangular, it perched delicately in a moat that reflected its crenellated towers and patterned brick chimnies to perfection.

Ivy, columbine, and honeysuckle climbed the walls and paused halfway up, green and brown stems woven together. All around the moat, trees stood in flaming scarlets, yellows, and oranges that seemed bright enough to glow in the dark; their fallen leaves cast brilliant blotches upon the browning verdant lawn.

The royal party's outriders reached Hever one scant hour ahead of the rest, yet Kathryn still marveled at how much Elizabeth Boleyn could accomplish with only sixty minutes' notice. The servants' aprons and work smocks all bore fresh marks of heated pressing irons, and the castle's base showed white marks where floating greenery had been stripped away from the stones. Everything bustled: rhythmic whackings bespoke mattresses, Turkey carpets, and mats of woven rushes receiving the beatings of a lifetime.

Thomas Boleyn bowed very low before the king, in the courtyard, Elizabeth dropping the most elegant curtsy Kathryn had witnessed to date. "What brings you hither, My Liege Lord?" cried out bluff, bold Thomas. "Not some long-faced, grievous political news, I hope, else you would be too busy to grace my humble house. No, My Lord, I insist you tell me this is a pleasure outing, that I may rush to make your stay a merry one."

Henry, hand on hip, surveyed the pretty place with pleasure. "Thomas, I hear you have worked miracles on this house since taking it over. Actually, my Lord Treasurer of the Household, I was loitering about Richmond, bored and restless, when I observed your niece, Lady Howard, packing up her gowns and children to come visit you. As she was about to travel with only one maidservant and your son, George, I thought I had better come along to lend the outing an air of respectability. Then the countess wanted to come along and some of my boon companions who heard you had a splendid bowling green and tennis courts and . . ."

He brought some fifty-two persons in all, and Hever was none too large or well stocked. Thomas Boleyn swallowed so hard he could not find air or voice for half a minute. "Your Grace honors me too much," he managed, cheeks as red as his beard.

"We have brought some venison to ease the burden of our arrival and, God willing, we shall have good hunting in Kent Wood tomorrow," Henry said. "Saint Mary, but I have been in this saddle too long! Give me a hand down, Thomas, and let us see those tender young stags on a long spit over the fire, eh?"

A groom handed Kathryn down into Elizabeth Boleyn's effusive embrace. "Greetings, Dear! And these are your boys; they have gotten so big! Give me Isabella—I am surprised Ned let you have James."

"Ned is freshly married and wished to be alone with the bride. James, Adam, greet your aunt like proper gentlemen."

Adam performed admirably, neither too grave nor too merry, but James overdid it with a rakish bow and too big a kiss on

Elizabeth's cheek. "That will be enough of that," his great-aunt announced. "There is no need to go overboard as your father always does. Now you lads run along with Tansy while I see to your mother. . . ." Slipping her arm through Kathryn's in the old, familiar way, she started her across the noisy courtyard. "Let us find you a washbasin and have your clothes beaten, hung, and pressed, you are dusty from your journey. Jacquetta, Dear, please go with my steward, he will show you to the master's chambers where you and the king shall stay."

Jacquetta thanked her with a jaunty touch of riding crop to feathered cap and snapped her fingers. A dozen servants in the de Gael black-and-gold livery sprang to seize her baggage and follow, toting clothes, carpets, sheets, and pieces of her best bed.

"It is an odd friendship between the two of you, you are so unalike," Elizabeth murmured, watching Jacquetta sweep imperiously up the stairs.

"The differences between us are precisely why we get along so well. We are such opposites that we never argue, already knowing where the other stands. Now, how are you, Aunt Elizabeth?"

"Very well. Your mother was here last month, on her way to join the princess Mary's household under Margaret Pole's thumb. She was fine, fine, as I am, but my Anne . . ."

"I know," Kathryn said. "George told me how poorly she is doing, that is why I took time away from the queen to visit."

Tears started up in Elizabeth's eyes. "I thought she would be all right when she went to Court but she returned looking a mere wraith of herself. I am worried out of my wits for her sake; she has taken to bed and will not rise. And you know how pigheaded Thomas is, no compassion, he yammers at her constantly about finding a husband until I have to step in between the two of them. At first she argued back, even shouted at him. But now she just lies there and tolerates his abuse. That frightens me, it is so unlike Anne!"

Kathryn went straight to her cousin's room. Anne indeed looked a wraith. Never sturdy, she had lost an alarming amount of weight and her skin had gone sallower than ever, almost yellow. There were gray hollows around her lackluster eyes and even her wealth of blue-black hair seemed dingy. It had not been washed in recent memory and her gown—oh, that horrible yellow dress, so gruesome with skin that color, and large enough to fall off her, should she rise and walk.

When Kathryn hugged her, she could gather up handsful

of fabric at the dark girl's waist. "Nan, you shall die!" she cried out in alarm. "Wither and die! Shame on you to lie so dispirited when it is not your body that is ill but your mind! Autumn has come to Kent, the trees are magnificent, hunting has never been better—your mare is pawing at the stable door to join the chase and your riding habit needs only to be aired and taken in. Rise, Anne! Fight this heartbreak! There are two brace of fat bucks turning on spits—"

"Fight heartbreak! Had you ever suffered a broken heart you would know that to be impossible!"

Kathryn stood, hands at waist. "No, of course I know nothing of pain. My sister is renegade, I have not seen Mother in years, and Father is in the Tower with a virtual death sentence hanging over his handsome head. And John de Gael, whom I have loved nigh my entire life gave up on waiting for me and married just when I was free of Edmund. Not know about heartbreak? Reconsider your words, Cuz."

Anne sat, face puckered with concern. "I apologize, I had not realized so much. But Kat—if men really love us as much as they claim, why do they never fight for us? Never wait for us? Why can we never depend on their supposedly undying devotion?" She covered her face with bony hands and sobbed wrackingly.

Kathryn sat on the narrow bed, wrapped her arms around Anne's emaciated body. She had not felt fierce or hearty since learning of John's marriage, but now the desire to heal her wounded cousin made her strong. For months now she had not wanted to ride, to hunt or dance. But if she and Anne were to get over their anguish, they must do exactly those things, must hurl themselves back into activity, into *life*.

She had not really been living these last months. It astonished Kathryn to realize that. She had gone through her daily paces, mouthed the expected sentiments, curtsied, served the queen, sewn, and eaten. But she had felt none of it, had been beyond letting reality penetrate that thick layer of shock John had left her in. Well, the shock-layer, like so much wool-felt between layers of a counterpane, was being stripped away by Anne's greater need.

It *was* autumn, their mares *were* chafing to hunt. The air smelled of smoke and cider and it was cool and brisk. The meaningless clichés she had mouthed at Anne were suddenly brought to life for Kathryn; she realized she wanted to live after all, to laugh, dance, revel in pretty gowns and sumptuous food.

Kathryn began stacking pillows up against the headboard and propped Anne up against them. "Now, you just sit there while I take care of everything," she said, and kissed her cousin's wan cheek.

Sweet Jesu, but it was good to be needed again!

Anne did not emerge from her rooms, but she ate all the food Kathryn brought to her, steaming on a silver tray. Little delicacies prepared by the cook traveling with the king—jellied eel in madeira, capons in lemon, a salad of shallots, purslane, garlic, and cucumbers, baked apples stuffed with candied violets, a cup of clove water, and a tall goblet filled to the brim with hot, hard cider.

She watched her cousin's eyes close in bliss. "I had forgotten what Court food tastes like," Anne marveled.

"For the next course I will fetch you pear pastry with caraway, scraped cheese with sugar, and hippocras, the best spiced wine in Christendom."

Anne, who had nibbled daintily at first, wolfed down the last scraps. When finished, she stealthily wiped her hands under cover of those trailing sleeves, hiding, as always, the little deformity of her extra nail. "Why are you good to me? You always were, even when we were children. Other women have never liked me; why do you?" Anne suddenly challenged.

Taken aback, Kathryn could only stammer, "Why, I—I do not know. But I have always liked you, Nan—I mean, Anne. I suppose part of it is because you are so plainspoken, I never have to guess with you."

"Do you like King Harry, too?"

"He is the king. A good subject always loves her king."

"That is not what I asked," Anne replied archly. "I asked did you *like* him. Well, I loathe him. I find him a great, lusting beast." Noting Kathryn's expression of horror, she raced to finish before she could be slowed by interruption. "Do you know the real reason that rutting rooster is here? He wants me. Told me so the night of Wolsey's masque with Castle Vert. I suppose that is why I was not allowed to marry Harry Percy, the king had cast his fancy at me and wanted me to remain at Court. I left against his strictest orders to remain, you know. And now he is trying to tempt me downstairs with his fine French delicacies. Well, I shall not go. He likes buxom blondes; I suppose I only interest him because I am so different from his usual mistresses. He has already had my sister countless times, even chased Mother, and he had your mother, my aunt, years ago. Well, let him slake his lust on the rest of my family or on that damned de Gael woman, I would not have him were he the last man in England! It is only my difference from the rest—and my *in*difference to him—that intrigues that rutting monster. The more I refuse him, the greater his desire, like dangling a carrot before an ass. No thank you, I will remain in my room! I had rather been Harry's countess than Hal's queen!"

She giggled, a high-pitched, grating sound that made Kathryn want to slap her. "Calm down, Anne, and do not speak that way with Hever full of the king's friends. Walls have ears."

Anne flung off the comforting hand on her arm. "So what if they do? I shall tell no lies, I know well enough what that hulking brute wants of me. Well, let him ride my sister and the de Gael mare, he shall not get a leg over me! If I am not fit for Harry Percy's bridle then I shall not be broken by any man!"

She refused to see the king or leave her room all that week. "A shrewd child," Jacquetta observed, unruffled by thought of competition. "Harry never wants what he can gain too easily, that is why four times out of five I refuse him, and on the fifth, ride him senseless. But when he receives the goods he has so long sought after, they had best be prime: he has no patience with a chase that ends in less than sublime satisfaction. You should tell your hysterical cousin that. She had best avoid Court completely or she shall further pique his interest; if she wishes, she could also lead him a merry dance before surrendering. But she does not seem warm to me, not sensual; taste, texture, scent, sight do not arouse her finer instincts. He would find her, I think, cold as Cararra marble."

Words Kathryn would recall in later years.

She had looked her last on youth and trust, and bid goodbye to Howard House, custody of her eldest son, the familiar old quarters at Court. Gone marriage, gone household, gone the last hopes of John and joining Jacquetta as second mistress of Windsgeat.

At age twenty-four Kathryn stood unbowed by disappointment and the slow freeze of celibacy. That she did not remarry surprised much of the Court, for although she was reputed to be sexually cold, she was well born and adored her children; such a woman's duty was to marry again and quickly, beget more sons, be a wife. Yet she only continued with her chores at Court, becoming more and more the queen's favorite with Maria de Salinas gone to Parham House. As instigator of the divorce, Edmund was no longer acceptable to the king and so lost his minor Court appointment, so she no longer need deal with him, which seemed one small relief in her loneliness.

And there was Jacquetta. Thank God for Jacquetta! She could make anything bearable with her laughter, her loyalty, her cutting wit. Even Catherine of Aragon had begun liking Jacquetta against her will, for Jacquetta brought her such superb gifts and regularly terrorized lesser ladies of the Court into performing their duties with a promptness not even the queen could wring from them.

It was Jacquetta who suggested Kathryn sell Mask's magnificent Cernunnos colt to Charles Brandon for a large sum of money; Jacquetta who found her a weaver to repair Jack of Norfolk's tapestries; Jacquetta who turned to her for help when aborting the king's latest bastard, which made her frightfully ill. The bond between the two women was no looser for not being related through John; they were not sisters-in-law as they had hoped, but each was as close to the other as a blood sister. Kathryn's steadier temper balanced Jacquetta's pomposities and rages, so that together they provided a formidable united front against enemies.

Except Anne Boleyn. Kathryn found herself caught in the middle between the two warring women and announced to each in turn that she would not give up the other. Both grumbled, but in the end found her friendship too precious to risk. Thereafter they were better-behaved, at least in her presence.

The three of them were an uneasy trio, deprived of love and marriage. Anne refused to wed, Jacquetta craved to and dared not, and Kathryn thought desperately that she must not end up with another man like Edmund. Then, too, her memories of John had not been lessened much by time. She still woke upon occasions, feeling the sun on her face, and thought she had overslept at his side in the Val d'Or.

She wished a thousand evil fates upon him and feared lest they come true.

Meanwhile her family seemed to have settled down. Arthur had replaced Edmund in the Master of Horse's employ and gave Kathryn no worry, though he and his Brereton bride still had no children. Her mother, Joanna, being gainfully employed in the little princess's household, no longer wrote constantly begging for money, and Kathryn's children were well behaved, though she had to prevent Jacquetta and her tall sons from spoiling them.

On Sundays she visited her father in the Tower. It seemed odd to finally be close to her father, but the fact remained: now that he was the king's prisoner and she came to him once a week, they got along splendidly.

One particular Sunday she brought him a bigger basket than usual, having been given three kinds of wine by the queen and finding herself loathe to keep it all when Lord Hal was subsisting on poor ale. She found her father in fine fettle. He was fifty years of age now, and his ruddy Plantagenet hair was streaked with silver so that it had softened to the hue of a ginger-colored old cat. "Daughter!" he exclaimed, starting up from his desk as she entered.

She kissed his brow, pushed him back onto his bench, and seated herself on the narrow camp bed. "See what I have brought you," she said proudly. "Port, malmsey, and hippocras from the queen. Some anise comfits, plums in green ginger, a dozen roast sparrows, and some lemons and limes. You are looking very fit, I think you will make short work of all this food."

"I shall. Every day they let me onto the Tower Green to walk, and I go around as many times as they let me—it fights the fat of a long captivity. The fat which I would not have, did you stop bringing me such food! I am just back from today's walk, in fact, and am writing your mother. Oh, and you just missed Arthur, he came and walked with me. Said his wife was with child; he was as proud as if he had done it himself!"

They both shrieked with laughter before Kathryn managed to say, "Well, perhaps he did. He seems very fond of her, though he cannot bring himself to avoid men. I expect to see him at Westminster this evening, so I shall act surprised when he tells me his news."

Hal took the basket from her, picked through it with a child's glee. "How are Isabella and the boys?"

"I hear James is doing fine with his father. Isabella has just turned four and is carrying the queen's embroidery basket for her as I once did. Adam is a wonder at his lessons, the tutor says he is going to be a Latin scholar."

"It is not too early to think that the boy may be ripe for the priesthood."

Kathryn made a moúe of annoyance. "He is too young to

think of such things. Besides, I have not gotten over having him taken away from me after Mary eloped with de la Pole; I am going to keep Adam with me this time as long as I possibly can."

Her father smiled fondly. "It is funny how greatly you care for your children, considering how little time your parents spent with their own. It has taken you and Arthur reaching adulthood for me to recognize you as independent human beings and friends. I am sorry I was so slow to love you. As for Mary, well, had she not been sent off to an abbey as a child, had she grown up in a loving home, she might not have become so wanton. But gossip has her a faithful wife to old de la Pole now, and with sons. God help the girl, she can never come home now that she has sons. . . . So! How go things with your Boleyn and Howard cousins?"

"The Howards are just getting used to the changes wrought by Grandfather's death. Surrey—Uncle Thomas—is Duke of Norfolk now his father has died. He is very close to the king. He takes all affronts to the crown personally, you would think he was the king's mother! I loathe his little boy, Henry, who is Earl of Surrey now; a pomous, affected brat with scant sense of humor. Grandfather's funeral was very stately . . ." She paused here, reflecting on it. "I cannot say I was close to the old man, though of course I miss him. My uncle of Norfolk is very good to me, he has given me his old quarters at Bridewell, Richmond, and Westminster. He says he can afford to be generous because he is taking three new sets of chambers to befit his new title. The Boleyns do well, Sir Tom is full of himself, per usual."

Hal bit into a gingered plum and made a face of pleasure at the sharp taste. "They say he sells his daughters to the king in exchange for favors."

"Father, Uncle Thomas was a Knight of the Garter and a Knight of the Bath long before King Henry even knew there were Boleyn daughters. He has been working steadily to advance himself; he is very ambitious, sometimes that frightens Aunt Elizabeth."

Hal shrugged. "She is a Howard, she cannot frighten too badly. All you Howards are made of fine-tempered steel, remember that. There never was a Howard could be broken; remember your great-grandfather Jack being warned at Bosworth that the king was betrayed and fighting to the death for him anyway. And your grandfather was there, attaindered and clapped in the Tower, but within ten years he was a peer again and free, made Earl of Surrey and Lord High Treasurer. Commander of the field at Flodden and finally getting the Norfolk titles and lands reinstated . . . well, his son is a staunch man, he will keep the family together, though to Thomas Howard the Younger the crown comes before all else. Everything regained, not thirty years after Bosworth . . . ahh, Bosworth Field and the fall of the Plantagenets . . ."

"Do you remember your father the king?" Kathryn asked softly.

"Vaguely. I was a very young lad, and his queen, Elizabeth Woodville—do you still have her bed?—did not wish me at Court. I recall a great bear of a man with brown hair that turned yellow-striped from riding long hours in the sun. . . . Queen Elizabeth Woodville, now there was a woman! They called her a witch; perhaps she was."

"Whatever became of her sons, the two Little Princes? Everyone says your uncle, Richard the Third, killed them, but—"

"Well, of course 'they' say that, 'they' are the Tudors who took the throne. Besides, my uncle Richard had no need to murder them, they had already been bastardized because of my father's precontract with another woman." He moved his rough bench closer to the bed, dropped his voice to a low murmur. "And Henry the Seventh wanted to marry their sister Elizabeth of York to seal his bid on the throne, but he could not marry a bastard, so he had the *Titulus Regulus* naming all the children 'Bastard' revoked. Which again made the princes kings of England and a danger to him."

"So you are saying the elder Henry Tudor had the boys killed. But some henchman of Richard's was named—"

"Named but never rewarded for so important a murder; does that make sense to you? Think, Kat! Who besides the Howards survived supporting Richard at Bosworth? Who, in fact, gained an unheard-of boon the very week of Bosworth? A thing not seen in England since the days of John of Gaunt?"

Saints! He meant an independent duchy—he meant Windsgeat! "Are you saying John de Gael's father, Kenneth, did it to save Windsgeat?"

"Bah, John is not Kenneth's son. But he *is* a great-grandson of Jack of Norfolk, I will wager he never told you that. It is that murder performed for Henry the Seventh that keeps Windsgeat intact; there are documents, witnessed deeds pertaining to it. He was a fox, old Kenneth, I rather admired him for having so few scruples." He took hold of her hands, looked deep into her cornflower-blue eyes. "I am glad you never married John de Gael. It took me work and you may hate me for it, but I helped keep your letters and his from crossing paths."

"Why?" she cried out, jerking back. "Because he is a bastard?"

"Oh, no. He is legitimate heir to Windsgeat, his parents were married. But he is the most dangerous man in England, I could not have you doomed for his sake. It is his blood, his beliefs."

John claimed to have loved her, but he had never told her of their blood ties through Jack of Norfolk. "I do not understand," Kathryn stiffly informed her father.

"The de Gaels are witches, surely you know that by now. And as for their bloodlines . . . well, you must understand that I acted for the best. I did not want to see my best and brightest child at the stake or in the Tower cell next to mine. Will you hate me now?"

"A little," she admitted, standing and gathering her cloak about her.

"Ahh, that is my straight-spined little Kat! Give me a kiss and go back to your royal mistress; some day you will understand all."

She rapped at the iron-bound door, called to the guard. At the last moment she turned back to Lord Hal. "Why have you suddenly told me all of this?"

"Call it a premonition."

"I do not believe in premonitions. You have had some kind of news; they say prisoners hear things first."

He took her by the shoulders. "Go, Kat, and know that I love you best of all. Congratulate Arthur again for me."

So Kathryn returned to Westminster, puzzled and curious about her father's unexpected news. She set off in search of Jacquetta, who had charge of Isabella and Adam for the day, and heard she was in her rooms, which adjoined the king's Painted Chamber, a room so vast that two or more peasant cottages would have fitted within. The ceiling fresco portrayed the coronation of Edward the Confessor, with his long white beard flowing down over the royal robes. In the background stood his mother, Emma, who had been queen of England twice. Over the years Emma's paint had peeled, which led to the queen still being dressed in Anglo-Saxon robes while her wimple had become a gable headdress. Most incongruous of all, she teetered on wooden chopines of the last century, stiltlike shoes that kept hems and slippers out of mud.

The same thing had happened with the Old Testament wall scenes. The Israelite army wore a mad mélange of Tudor, Plantagenet, and Angevin clothing, and how anyone could sleep with David gorily beheading Goliath three feet from the bed was beyond Kathryn.

Doors to the Painted Chamber as well as Jacquetta's rooms stood open, for the weather was fine and servants were airing rooms. Shutters banged back, glass was wrested up. Carpets flapped over Westminster's gardens, brooms flew across floors.

She did not mean to eavesdrop but kings never lowered their voices; Kathryn could not help hearing Henry Tudor boom out, "So you would still marry your mother's nephew, the Emperor Charles?"

"Oh, no, Your Grace, not if you do not wish it. I am ever obedient to your will," little Mary Tudor, heir to England's throne, dutifully answered her father, for she was home from her own household and basked in his presence.

"Well, then, you are no longer betrothed to him or anyone else at the moment. Yet I think that, like your mother of Spain, you have some leanings toward that country."

"Your Grace, I am but fond of all things my esteemed parents hold dear."

Nine years old and already a skillful diplomat! Kathryn smiled to herself and started past the Painted Chamber. Just then she heard the king ask, "And where will *you* marry, Isabella Howard?"

Only four years old but tractable, praise God, and very quick to mind her elders. Heart hammering, Kathryn heard her daughter lisp, "I shall marry where Your Grace and my mother wish me to."

Henry laughed. "And what if I order you to marry some enemy of England, say, a Frenchman?"

Saints! Hard questions for a baby just now mastering her alphabet and embroidery stitches! Kathryn bunched up her skirts and started in to rescue her child.

Isabella, though, needed no help. "Well then, Your Grace, if you ordered it I would go and let the evil French cut my head off."

At this Henry and Catherine of Aragon laughed together, praising the little girl's presence of mind. *She never got that obedience and subtlety from her damned father,* Kathryn thought savagely. For a moment she wanted John so fiercely she could almost smell him, feel his velvet shoulder under her cheek. But age had faded remembrance; she had forgotten his smile, the exact shade of his hair.

She hastened on in, knocking first then curtsying so low that the king had to hand her back up. He was picking Isabella up, holding her poised on one brawny arm. Bless the girl, she was keeping her head respectfully bowed, not daring look him in the face. "Lady Howard, I remember when you were plain Kathryn Chase and no bigger than your daughter here. Tell me, how did you rear such a marvelous child? She could give lessons to all my courtiers and ladies."

"Your Grace, all I have done is what any mother should: taught her that you are God's annointed representative on earth and that she is to fear and honor you above all else."

"So you are raising a philosopher! I see that you are wily Norfolk's niece after all. What say you, Wife?"

Poor Catherine of Aragon, so plump, so faded and matronly. She smiled, showing new gaps in her teeth. "What pleases my lord pleases me, as well you know. I love whom you love, but as Lady Kathryn is my especial favorite, I am delighted she has brought you joy."

"So she has, by raising a model daughter. Pray God the girl does not end up with the Howard nose, though. Oh, well, her mother did not, so . . ." He peered at Isabella's chestnut hair, so unlike that of most Howards.

Kathryn caught the gesture and panicked. "Do you think her hair will go even more reddish, like my uncle of Norfolk's? Here, Your Grace, allow me to take her from you."

Isabella came unwilling to her mother, for she had discovered a particularly fascinating ruby on the king's neck chain and wished to peruse it at length. "What do you hear from your Howard and Boleyn cousins?" Henry asked suddenly as he was relieved of the child.

Mary Boleyn had born a son who might be his, yet Kathryn knew he was thinking of black-eyed Anne. She carefully answered, "Truthfully, Your Grace, both the Boleyns and Howards owe me letters and have for many weeks, so I have heard nothing new of them."

"You surely knew that George Boleyn had married, though. I must say, I never thought you would wait so long to take a second husband with young George chasing after you. He seems an able enough fellow, though I wonder if the Boleyns are breeders. After all, your aunt only has three children."

"True, Your Grace, but she lost several babies, as did I."

"Ah, yes, you Howards get children quickly enough, and I daresay you would have plenty more had Edmund not strayed so far afield. And yet they say he has no family started, and his bride two years with the ring a-finger."

The Howard breeding potential—where was he headed with all these suspicious questions? He was going on in some detail while she and the queen both blushed faintly.

Around them, Westminster erupted into sound. Duck-billed slippers came slapping along wood and marble floors, silks rustled, whispers echoed. A woman cried out and that seemed the signal for several men to start shouting.

"Where is His Grace the king? Where the king? A messenger from the Low Countries, Sire!"

The Low Countries, where John was. Kathryn lowered Isabella to the floor but kept a tight grip on her, lest she wander off into the approaching crowd.

King Henry put on splendor like an ermine cloak. He actually stood taller and broader than before, sticking out his chest and extending one foot in an attitude of negligent power. Thomas Howard strode anxiously in, knelt at his feet. "Your Grace, I have had the messenger searched. He bears no weapons, only news, and has the proper credentials. And such news it is!"

Behind him, all of Westminster clustered at the doorway. "Very well, Norfolk, send him in," Henry said with a calm he did not feel.

The messenger was shoved forward, muddy, sunburnt, hollow-eyed from lack of food and sleep. He more collapsed than knelt at Henry Tudor's feet. "Rise and say your say," Henry ordered.

There was something familiar about the bony, intelligent face, Kathryn thought. Where had she seen this green-eyed young man before?

"Your Grace, forgive me, I cannot rise," he gasped out. "Your ambassador to the Court of Margaret of Savoy in the Low Countries, Sir John de Gael, bids me tell you that there was a very great battle fought at a place called Pavia. There fell Sir Richard de la Pole who called himself the Earl of Suffolk, mortal enemy to yourself and England. My Lord received the body and can testify to this; also that the king of France was taken captive by the Imperial forces of Charles, who is King of Spain and Holy Roman Emperor."

Richard dead—*Poor Mary,* Kathryn thought compassionately while the crowd droned and buzzed.

Henry Tudor let out an ecstatic whoop. "Now are all of England's enemies gone! Fetch me a sword of state someone—no, no, 'twill take too long. Norfolk, give me yours."

It was only a short dress-sword for Court and had never been out of its ornate new scabbbard, nor should it have been worn in the king's presence, but Norfolk was glad he had it now. He brought it out with a hissing of steel on leather and laid it proudly across the king's open palms.

"Your name, lad," the king said.

"Richard Stoneleigh, Sire."

John's little squire, grown near to manhood now! Kathryn thought, craning her head for a good view of the proceedings. Yes, that was him, she could make out freckles and coppery hair beneath the mud now.

The sword came to rest first on one weary shoulder then the other. "Arise, Sir Richard Stoneleigh," Henry briskly announced. Then added over his shoulder to Norfolk, "This is spectacular news. Send to the Continent to see if it is true. If so, tell de Gael he is now Baron Windsgeat and may have his other five hundred acres back. To think that England's last Plantagenet enemy may be dead!"

Richard Stoneleigh had fainted across the king's feet but in his preoccupation Henry did not notice. A steely voice from the rear of the crowd called out, "Not *all* your Plantagenet enemies, Your Grace. There are those who stand closer to the throne than de la Pole ever did."

Kathryn's heart seemed to plummet to her feet. *No, no,* she opened her mouth to shout, but no sound emerged.

Henry Tudor stroked his new beard. "How so, Cardinal Wolsey? Do you mean de la Pole's two infant sons?"

"I mean his father-in-law, Edward the Fourth's last surviving son, though a bastard," the cardinal said.

Lord Hal Chase. The room spun as Kathryn speechlessly slid to her knees in the voiceless, age-old attitude of supplication. "Lord Chase has a son and grandsons, too, Your Grace," Wolsey pointed out.

Catherine of Aragon joined Kathryn on the floor. "I beseech you, my husband, if someone must die let it be only the old man. Spare the boys—Arthur Chase chose a low-born wife to prove to you that he has no designs on the throne—"

"Be still, old woman! I will not be lectured to by my own wife!" The crowd buzzed at this shocking unkindness shown their beloved queen. Henry, gazing down, saw two pairs of blue eyes burning beseechingly into him—Kathryn's too-blue, like an azure sky, and Isabella's watery, like moonstone. The mother could think of no words, could only gaze at him thunderstruck; the child looked on in fear because of her mother's behavior. Isabella tried to smile at the glowering face so far above, stretched her chubby little arms out in hope that he might pick her up again and let her dandle his ruby.

Kathryn released her child to slowly, gracefully prostrate herself. She dared touch the king's slashed red velvet shoes, which Norfolk had pulled Richard Stoneleigh away from. Down here she could see every fine stitch in their heavy samite lining pulled through the slashwork; could make out intricate details of golden embroidery that did not show from above. The table-cut diamonds sparkled in between hump-backed cabuchon rubies. So beautiful a shoe encasing so fearsome a foot; every detail of that red shoe stayed with her through the last day of her life.

Kind, strong hands landed on her back. "Aye, execute old Chase, then," Norfolk said gruffly. "But only put Arthur in the Tower, though he is a harmless lad. And place the two lads in my household, I will vouch for them."

"You are none too greatly in the clear, Tom; these are all your folk named here," Henry Tudor snapped.

There was a saying in England: *As English as the town of Tottenham*. Even London did not so pride itself on its nationality as that town did.

Thomas Howard snapped, "If you doubt my loyalty, you have there a sword to smite my head off, Your Grace—but know you that I will turn traitor the day Tottenham goes French!"

Henry chuckled, pleased at this show of spirit. Taking its cue, the entire Court laughed very discreetly. "Very well, Thomas, you shall take the boys into your household at Kenninghall, far from here. And see that you nurse no vipers there!"

" 'If thy right eye offend thee, pluck it out,' " Thomas Howard quoted. "There shall be no treasonous right eyes at Kenninghall."

People began to drift away from the scene to gossip. Norfolk tried to lift Kathryn and could not; Henry Tudor continued to stare down at little Isabella Howard, her arms held up to him in silent pleading. At last, disturbed, he pulled the queen to her feet and led her, protesting, away.

"You must get up, Niece," Thomas Howard said gently. "Do not despair; we have lost your father but saved Arthur and your sons. They will be well seen to by my wife, and they will enjoy being with young Henry my son. Please, Kathryn."

She did not move, was hardly breathing. Stooping, he turned her over and picked her up. Her eyes were open but she did not seem to see him; he started out the door carrying her. Halfway there he saw that Richard Stoneleigh, the new knight, was sitting looking at Kathryn worshipfully. "Come along, Lad," Thomas Howard said kindly. "You need food and a bed, do you not? Come along."

16

Sunday, June 18, 1525
Bridewell Palace

Anne Boleyn giggled. It was a habit she had when nervous or overexcited and she had every cause to be excited today. "My father is being made Viscount Rochford. I shall be Lady Anne now," she said to Kathryn and burst into a fresh round of giggles.

On the other side of the gallery, Jacquetta regarded her with venom. "One more tee-hee-hee from you, you addlepated bitch, and I shall box your ears until the rest of us have cause to laugh, too. And leave Kat alone, she has too much on her mind to worry about you getting so tiny a title."

"Some day I shall be in a position—" Anne began.

"Yes, under His Majesty, and you expect to then rule the world through him. Well, it does not happen that way, little girl. You think bedding the king would afford you a means to revenge yourself on Wolsey and me, but remember: Wolsey acted on the king's orders. Revenge yourself on *him* if you dare."

Per usual, Jacquetta got the last word in by simple virtue of telling the truth. Kathryn remained silent, far removed from the argument. Her father was to be executed tomorrow and her sons were already far away at Kenninghall; what did she care for petty quarrels?

The ceremony began. King Henry's bastard son by Bessie Blount, Henry Fitzroy, was being elevated to the peerage today as were many others, Anne's father among them. There was a great stir and guesswork about which titles Fitzroy would be given; all others knew theirs ahead of time.

Knights of the Garter had already been installed in a long and tedious ceremony. Moving upward through the ranks now brought Thomas Boleyn and several other knights the title of viscount. Barons came next, John de Gael honored in absentia; Kathryn's ears paid his name dull, uncaring heed. Earls included the king's nephew Henry Brandon, son of Charles Brandon and the king's beauteous sister Mary.

Bessie Blount's son was last. Courtiers and ladies held their collective breath, for only the title of duke remained below that of king and Prince of Wales. No one had guessed Henry would rate the child so highly.

The greatest shock came when the slender, pale boy with his coppery Tudor hair knelt and was pronounced Duke of Richmond—the title reserved for Tudor heirs. First Prince Arthur then Henry himself had borne that title. No one dared gasp. Other titles ensued for the boy: Duke of Somerset, Earl Nottingham, Lord High Admiral of England, Ireland, and Wales, Knight of the Garter, though all these seemed an anticlimax after the Richmond name. The lowest title on the list was unprecedented advancement for the bastard son of a base-born woman, mere niece of a minor lord.

Elizabeth Boleyn sighed, whispered, "A good thing Bessie is not here, she would lord it over all of us until we expired of it. My own daughter has borne a son probably sired by the king, but it is uncertain so she gets nothing for the boy."

"I wonder the queen did not attend the ceremonies," Anne said. "But she is of course furious about the boy's preferment, even if her daughter *is* being made Princess of Wales and shipped off to Ludlow. Serves that dowdy old witch right."

In the silence that followed, Kathryn's slap across Anne's face rang out startlingly. Every person at Bridewell twisted to look up at the spectators' gallery.

Elizabeth Boleyn lunged against the rail, pretending to have stumbled. She beamed down at the glowering king, curtsied to show cleavage, which made him grin appreciatively despite himself. The ceremonies then continued.

In the jostling and bustle that followed the investitures' end, Anne started for Kathryn, fingernails out, but her mother seized her. "Anne, Anne! Her father dies tomorrow, can you not forgive?"

Kathryn said in a raspy voice, "I did not strike her out of worry for my father, I hit her for insulting my mistress the queen. And if she does so again, I shall knock her down and tread upon her."

"I hate you," Anne burst out to no one in particular.

Her mother roundly boxed Anne's ears as though she were a small, disobedient brat. "Now listen to me," Elizabeth said flatly, not bothering to raise her voice. "You are a Howard. You will behave with the dignity expected of a Howard or I will drag you by the ear back to Hever, lock you in, and drop the key down a well. You forget how good the queen has been to take me as a lady-in-waiting and you as a maid of honor long before we had titles; you forget how Kathryn tenderly nursed you when your heart was sore wounded and you were trying to starve yourself to death. And here you are making a scene on the day your father and the King's son join the peerage—I am not surprised that Bessie Blount's boy is made a duke and your nephew has nothing! To witness your behavior, one would think the Howards rotten stock, not fit to breed from."

"No, Mother," Anne whispered, black eyes flashing fire. "We may be rotten stock but we Howards are capable of breeding a great many fine sons, which is more than the queen can do."

Richard Stoneleigh arrived just in time to prevent further altercations. Hat in hands, he gently said, "Lady Howard? Your horse is waiting. I have here the letter you need to visit the Tower." His gaze never left her, as though sight of her somehow nourished him.

Kathryn numbly thanked him, accepted his offered arm, and started out with him. "Oh, no, you do not," Jacquetta exploded, racing after them. "People will talk if you two go alone. I will accompany you."

Richard glanced back over his shoulder at her. "I thought so. I saddled Circe for you."

"Well, stop that. You are a knight now, not a mere squire, you must not run around saddling people's horses. You two wait for me, I will see if Elizabeth Boleyn will keep Isabella and see my boys home."

The ride jarred Kathryn's senses until she felt raw. Her father would die tomorrow, her sons had been taken from her; there was only Isabella left her. She could not bear the thought of anything endangering her children, especially that littlest and most precious one.

Oh, John, she thought and felt exhaustion overwhelm her. *I should never have lain with you, never have given them one more child they could use as a weapon against me. I have Isabella but I have constant fear for her sake, too; you spend your nights beside a loving wife while I—*

While she felt dry and withered as an old apple core. Desire, terror, and loathing had so mingled in her that they became one passion; she had refused John in order to remain in England, protecting her family, and had ended by losing both the man she loved and her scant family security. Or had she ever really loved John? The Val d'Or was so far away in time and space and she had no pillar to cling to in her despair. Her family—yes, they had been her pillar, her strength. Even though she had emotionally and financially supported them and not the other way around, being needed had strengthened her; now there was nothing. She was helpless as a newborn child, she had no cloak of protective invisibility to wrap around those she cherished.

She did not observe Richard Stoneleigh's eyes as he rode in mute adoration behind her. Because of Kathryn he had chosen to remain in England instead of returning to John's lucrative service; Jacquetta had made some minor use of him at Windsgeat.

A pretty lad, Jacquetta thought, observing his wide mouth, the frank green eyes, high cheekbones brushed by copper hair. *Not a day over eighteen and mad for Kat. If she does not take him, I shall.*

She had turned thirty a few days ago—middle age to her contemporaries. Her eldest son was in his teens now and the other close behind. Her childbearing years were vanishing by leaps and bounds; being the king's mistress brought no further benefits to Windsgeat nor did it return John that she might be free to marry. And yet marrying would take her from adored Windsgeat, and de Gaels withered away from their sacred land with its dark, wooded secrets and festivals of fire.

It occurred to her that it was time she retire from Court to pay closer attention to Windsgeat business. Sooner or later Anne Boleyn would name the price for her maidenhead; the king was already fascinated by her black moodiness and unpredictability. Better to go now instead of waiting for that sloe-eyed bitch to replace her, shame her, drive her out.

Somewhere there must be a man for her, an equal—but one who would not seek to seize control of the rich de Gael estates. John's lordship of the land was holy to his family and tenants; a stranger would never be accepted in his place. *A husband*, Jacquetta thought passionately. *How I long to be loved again, how I long to be with a man who knows I have not only a body but a mind.*

But until that paragon rode into her life, there was long-legged, green-eyed Richard Stoneleigh, grown near to manhood and pretty as an unbroken stallion.

It shamed her to realize she thought of such things when her dearest friend's father was to die in the morning. She urged Circe on after Mask.

Hal Chase died as a king's son should. Standing in his collarless cambric shirt that Kathryn had made him specifically for this day, he thanked the onlookers for attending, paid the executioner, and said he lived as he died—a loyal subject of King Henry's. He asked that his family be spared any further punishment and knelt gracefully.

So noble was his appearance and speech that none cheered when the handsome, gory head was held up. "Thus perish all enemies of the king!" the executioner shouted, but there were no murmurs of agreement.

Kathryn rose, wild with grief and rage, but she was abruptly pinned from behind, a hand over her mouth. "Stop it," came the familiar voice of her cousin George Boleyn. "You will only make it worse for the family and yourself. Here, Stoneleigh, take her home. Norfolk sent me with a cart to claim the body."

The hand over her mouth was lifted when she ceased struggling. "You will not place him in a pauper's grave," Kathryn said.

"Jacquetta is waiting at Windsgeat, she has a place for him there. Now go on, I will take care of things."

Her mind seemed abruptly to clear of its terrible fog that had hung over her these last weeks. "No," she heard herself say calmly. "No, I am not going to let a man do my dirty work. I thank you and Richard both, but I will see to Father's body."

She did, too. She spoke with the officials and took the winding sheet to wrap the mutilated body in. Together she and the men lowered what remained of Hal Chase into his narrow wooden box; she cried out as the body bumped the sides, as though Hal could still feel the pain of it. Murmurs of sympathy rose from the crowd. When she swayed on the wheel well of the cart where she was posed to lower the coffin lid, dozens of hands reached to steady her.

"God bless you, My Lady Plantagenet!" whispered an old man. "I remember the other king, your grandfather."

"God save you, Mistress!"
"A brave death for old Hal—you teach your sons to remember him, Lady Howard! He were a king's son, he were."
"We pray for your children every night, M'lady—such a sweet little girl you have, I seen her with you at market."
"We hear your brother, Prince Arthur, is in the Tower. We will send him food and drink every week, just as we did your father, Milady."
"You must not say these things," Kathryn whispered hoarsely. "But I thank all of you—all of you. How kind you are in this dreadful hour."
Even before the sun had gone down, Lord Hal's head had disappeared from its pole over Tower Gate. The grave at Windsgeat remained unfilled until young Sir Richard showed up carrying a small, round bag, barked palms and shins bearing evidence of a hard climb; dozens of sympathetic Londoners formed his torchbearing bodyguard on the trip upriver.
It was never reported at Court where Lord Chase's body lay, nor did King Henry seek to answer the riddle of the missing head. "She is a tough woman, your niece," he told Norfolk. "I would not be surprised did I hear she climbed that pole herself to take it down. Tough as old chestnuts, your Howard women, and even more difficult to crack. Tell her I will not punish her. In fact, I will let her Isabella join my Mary's household in Wales, that should show that I still hold her in esteem. It will protect her from harassment from the Court, who will seek to prove me their loyalty by persecuting her."
Take his niece's favorite and last child away! And the king thought that would please Kathryn? By God, she would break, would shatter like a glass goblet flung to a marble floor. Norfolk's stomach lurched; he placed a damp hand over the growing ulcer there. "It is very good of Your Grace to so consider treatment of Kathryn," he said weakly.
A wise man knew when to accept defeat and retreat. Thomas Howard, being a wise man, bowed and backed from the royal presence. Outside the Presence Chamber he stopped a moment, hammered one taut fist against wooden paneling. *He is my king. I must support him, I must!*
But it would cripple Kathryn, and he liked her better than even his own children. He dreaded telling her the news.

No, Kathryn maintained, they would not take her daughter from her. Isabella was all she had left in the world; she would stay with her mother. Kathryn did not care if she was sent from Court at this point, did not care how she was punished. She sent the queen a note, packed in the night, and fled for her aunt Elizabeth at Hever. Catherine of Aragon read her note to Henry, who said, "Poor woman! Tell her I will not take Isabella, she may come back."

It seemed nearer three hundred than thirty miles from Windsor. Mud mired Mask and the pack mules down, one of the latter breaking a leg and having to be shot. Bandits struck the last day of the journey, during which attack Kathryn's manservant fled, leaving her and Tansy alone and unarmed except for their dinner daggers. The two women stood back-to-back, weapons out, Isabella sandwiched silently between them. "Tell yer whot," the bandit leader said. "Yew doan cut me an' I will na cut thee. Yew doan look rich, got no jewels nor fancies, so give me the white mare an' we call it quits."

Mask against her daughter, Tansy, and the bundle containing her only gowns and silver plate. Mask against violence and knowing they must lose. Kathryn slowly nodded, slipped the reins from her arm.

She had thought her last vestiges of childhood dead with Lord Hal at the scaffold, but it was not so. Light and sweetness and innocence went with her precious Mask, veteran of a dozen hectic years together. The virgin bride on her wedding day finding the white mare in the stable, the colt sired by Cernunnos who had brought her money she put away for Isabella's dowery . . . Mask the Faithful, who never set a hoof wrong, never failed her, and had driven all the other ladies-in-waiting wild with jealousy. Especially Bessie Blount.

Kathryn blew her nose violently as the mare's long white tail fanned out behind her in the snowfall; it was the last thing she could see of the departing bandits. "Good horse, good-bye," she called out softly.

"At least we are all safe," Tansy pointed out. "She were a good horse, Lady Kat, and she saved us when we needed it most."

That was true, and Hever was only another few miles up the river. The ground was freezing rapidly so there was no more mud to slide in; as if knowing the journey's end neared, the two remaining pack mules stumbled eagerly along after the women.

Elizabeth Boleyn was shocked at their appearance when they arrived. Even Anne forgot she was supposed to be angry with Kathryn and threw her arms around her cousin's neck with cries of sympathy and alarm. George and half a dozen servants set out with cudgels to retake Mask but never found her, returning hours later chilled and exhausted.

That night Kathryn could not sleep. Her tossing kept Isabella awake, so she slid out of the big bed and left Isabella curled up with Tansy beneath the mountain of wool counterpanes and sheepskins. She yanked her heavy old felt nightgown on over her shift and stumbled outside to catch her breath. It hung suspended on the night air like white puffs of cloud; walking a little farther she stumbled against a wooden bench and sat tearlessly sobbing upon it.

Warm, reassuring hands dropped on her shoulders. "Sweet Jesu, you will freeze out here, Cuz," George Boleyn said, picking her up easily and wrapping her in his coney-lined coat. Kathryn acquiesced, burrowing her nose into his hot neck.

He hesitated at the door of *his* chambers, not hers. "You have not forgotten I have that bitch of a wife at Court," he attempted.

No, she had not forgotten. But she had known nothing but pain for so long, had spent day and night struggling just to place one foot after the other and draw a breath; what did a minor thing like committing adultery matter in the light of that? She had lost the fear of losing her immortal soul for such sins at the Val d'Or, and surprised herself by responding hungrily when George opened her mouth with his, breathed heat and passion into the kiss.

He carried her into his room, kicked the door shut behind them. Whitewashed walls glowed orange, reflecting flames in the fireplace; there was a stag's hide on the floor with a silverpoint picture of a man in Italian armor of the last century hanging over the narrow headboard.

George drew back the wool coverlets and top sheet with its border of black embroidery, laid her down, unbuttoned her shift. "Am I taking advantage of your mood on what has been a disastrous day?" he inquired, kneeling on the bed beside her.

Kathryn managed a watery smile. "George, I have not been with a man in so long I cannot remember how it feels or what to do. My heart has dried up, my body is frozen. Thaw me, George—take advantage of my mood. It will be the nicest thing anyone could do for me."

She pulled her shift off over her head, giving him no chance to undress before she pulled him down. It struck her as odd that she could feel this need with George whom she was fond of in a cousinly way but did not love; she had thought love a neccessary requirement for good lovemaking.

They caressed awhile, murmured, touched, shared a cup of spiced wine from the hearth and spilled it on each other to lick off the excess. But as passion spiraled there were too many images in Kathryn's mind, she could not fight them all. Her father's head on the scaffold floor, John's sturdy, bare shoulder beneath her tear-streaked cheek, her little sons being taken away . . . the cell in the Tower where her brother lay awaiting the headsman's axe. Jacquetta, always Jacquetta there when she needed her . . . Kathryn's open palm smacking across Anne's dark cheek. A Court masque, groveling to the king . . .

George saw the struggle in her, knew she needed more help to lose control. He rolled, threw her down. Pinned her wrists to the headboard and rode her until she moaned, screamed, shattered in a brief, brutal peak that released the stored madness of months.

They shared another goblet of hot spiced wine, then Kathryn led him to the only other piece of furniture in the room—a heavy chest, requiring three strong men to move it. She threw down pillows on it for padding, sat the wondering George on them, and straddled him. He had a hard-muscled young body, firm and ready for more, and she found herself running her hands all over him in admiration. Then they began to move together, up and down, striving for perfection. Their sweat mingled from exertion and nearness to the blazing hearth; she took him until there was no thought of anything but this awful, animal need she had not quenched since the Valley of Gold.

He woke alone on the deerskin next morning, in a heap of coverlets, wondering if it had all been some wild erotic dream. Kathryn was very polite when he saw her, but she was as remote as Florence from London. He took her riding with Anne and his mother and nothing in her bearing indicated that there had been the ultimate intimacy between them.

But at midnight she crept through his doorway, witchlike and fey in black, finger to lip beseeching silence. Every night for the month of her stay she arrived thus, after treating him no differently during the day. The last morning, knowing she was to leave in a few hours, he lay with her golden-brown hair spread across his chest and watched dawn bluing and peaching the white walls. "You are the most marvelously discreet woman I have ever met, and the least coquettish. And yet all of these things you know to do to a man . . . you never got that knowledge from Ned Howard. Who, then?"

She sat, stretched with an odd voluptuosity for so slender a woman. Childbearing had not thickened her figure; in fact, he thought, she looked thinner than ever. Not healthy. He awaited an answer.

Kathryn only said, "Thank you for helping me learn to live again, George. In my grief and loneliness I kept myself isolated; you brought me warmth again."

He propped himself up on one elbow, watched her reach for her nightclothes. "I should have told my father to go to Hell. I should have carried you off and so disgraced you that you had to marry me."

"George," she said patiently, adjusting buttons and ribbons, "driving the headboard through the wall is nothing to base an entire marriage on."

With the fire behind her he could see through the thin linen of her shift until she disappointingly pulled on her heavy nightgown. "Kat, you should know better. We get along as friends, too, and that could last a lifetime. You should have married me instead of leaving me stuck with Jane Parker."

Kathryn shook her head, long hair spilling down over the dark robe. "I was not ready for marriage then, George, and you were. I can never ask a man to wait for me again, it is not fair. Thank you for reminding me that life goes on, Cuz." She stooped, kissed his brow.

He watched her sweep from the room with the poise of an empress. *I wonder,* he thought, watching the door click shut behind her. *I wonder what the devil my lady cousin intends to do next*.

Later, after he had slept, he wandered into the Great Hall to discover Kathryn gone. Anne was sitting at the table, idly paring an apple she had no intention of eating, so George sat down with her. "Did Kathryn get away safely?"

"Yes, Mother loaned her two men-at-arms and a horse. You should have married Kat, I can see you thinking it. Well, and I should have married Harry Percy, Brother, but all that is over and done with, we cannot change the past. We can, however, consider the future."

He took the apple from her, gulped down a half-chewed bite. "Go on. You are plainly headed somewhere with this train of thought."

Anne tossed her long black hair. "I am heartily sick of you, Mother, Hever, Blickling Hall, and being bullied throughout Court by that damned Jacquetta de Gael. Not to mention the thousand other shrews at Court who think they have one up on me. I have decided to set my cap for the king himself."

George smashed the apple down on the table. "I will not have another sister play whore!"

Anne's arm shot out. She grabbed George's nose and twisted so hard that he was glad to sit on the hearthstone where she placed him. "Now listen you, George, and listen well: the king wants sons and I want to rise to a position of power in this world. I would also have revenge on Wolsey and the de Gael bitch. I am old to start breeding for the first time but it has kept me from being ruined in my prime like the king's grandmother Beaufort, a mother at thirteen and never capable of childbearing again. Or the queen, made an old woman by constant pregnancy . . ."

She was conveniently forgetting that Catherine of Aragon had started breeding late in life, too. "Pray, continue," George said, nursing his nose and glaring up at her where she stood.

"The king and I have discussed my becoming his mistress but I quoted Elizabeth Woodville, his other grandmother, and what she said to Edward the Fourth when he made a similar proposition, '*I may not be good enough to be your wife but I am far too good to be your mistress.*' "

"Wife! How dare you speak of wiving with him, and he a married man!"

Anne clasped her hands, unconsciously weaving her fingers so that the malformed one was bottom-most and hidden. She had been hiding the spare nail for so long that the gesture was as unthinking as breathing or swallowing. "Our uncle of Norfolk said the king has been toying with the notion of putting the queen aside. *Leviticus* says that a man who takes his brother's widow to wife shall remain childless."

George, who knew as much biblical scholarship as any well-reared young man of his day, argued, "Yes, but *Deuteronomy* says it is the duty of a dead man's brother to marry the widow! Besides, the marriage is not childless, there is the princess Mary."

"Who is only a girl-child. When Eleanor of Aquitaine was queen of France she was able to divorce the king because they had only daughters."

"Christ, Anne! You have gone so far as to mention divorce to the king?" George demanded.

"No, no, I only quoted Elizabeth Woodville that the thought might appear to be his own. He is always commenting to me how fertile we Howards are; I have told him that any husband of mine shall have a dozen fine sons."

He had always known her to be devious, but George had not guessed Anne to be so damnably clever. He cleared his throat faultily. "He has always been so outspoken against divorce."

"If he was never really married to Catherine of Aragon, then there need *be* no divorce. She will be sent to an abbey and Mary bastardized. And I shall not be his mistress, for his pride would never allow him to marry a woman the world named 'whore.' Besides, his interest never holds long. Jacquetta is the only woman to maintain his attention so long, and it is because she is clever and keeps him waiting, doling out her favors sparsely then running for home. But I will not dole them out at all, only give him a nibble here and there to keep him snapping at the bait."

George shook his head. "You gamble hard. And I had always thought you would marry for love! You do not love His Grace."

"Love him?" Anne spat the words out as though they had been rinsed in vinegar. *"Love him?* He is putting on weight, he will be fat in five years. Fat and forty. He parted me from Harry Percy whom I loved, he is a conceited, swaggering, vicious tyrant and I loathe the sight of him! But he can make me queen of England, George; that makes him seem slender, mild, sweet-and-twenty."

Picking up her skirts, she fled the room, hysterical giggles fanning back over her shoulder.

17

Anne Boleyn, King Henry discovered, had the most enchanting laugh. It was more of a chime, really, a clear but muted tone that made him think of tiny gilt bells tickled by a spring breeze. And those bewitching glances from the corners of her black eyes, luring him on until he seized her and she cried out in alarm. That made him gentle then, gentler than he had ever been with anyone; she made him feel broader, more manly than he already did, which was aplenty. After all, God put men on earth to rule and protect delicate little women like her. When Anne fluttered against his chest it shook him to the roots, made him feel she was some haunted woodland creature fleeing to him for sanctuary from the huntsman's bow.

Yet she was not one of those pale, pasty girls, unable to lift a knife unaided, meek and spiritless. No, his proud Anne saucily tossed her head, sprang away from his hands and into her sidesaddle as though she had little need of his strength. She spurred her mare side-by-side with his great stallion at the hunt, both of them wearing out their horses until they needed to call for a second set of mounts, then a third. Her slender silver arrows flew, true as a strong man's shots; she was the only woman he knew who hunted so well, so fearlessly, though she usually remembered to judiciously lose to him.

The fragrance of her, dark as her hair and doe-eyes—not for her the insipid gillyflowers, violets, and rose water of colorless English ladies. No, his Anne wore civet and spice and something with a mossy green undertone, mysterious, individual. Blindfolded, he could have picked her from a crowd by scent alone.

She dressed so sumptuously, too, better than anyone at Court except his Jacquetta—and Jacquetta had gone home to Windsgeat. Only in France had he seen women dressed like Anne. Every day a new gown: thick, prickly, dull wool velvets with patterns seared into them, limp silk velvets that clung to her slender figure. Black and silver brocades that caught the kingly eye from across a garden. Forest, pine, and lush emerald greens. Dark rose samite, that stiffest, heaviest, and most costly of satins. Russet damask that made her tender skin glow; bright scarlets, snowy whites.

Henry even found himself fascinated by her headgear. Not for his modish, spunky Anne those damned things that made a woman look like she was peeking through the door of a dog kennel. Anne wore French hoods, curved things that followed the shape of her head and showed several inches of sooty black hair. Flat pancake caps in the German style, too, prinked and slashed with the lining pulled through to hang in prettily arranged folds. Pretty little pearls, little garnets. *She needs emeralds*, he would think, watching her dance with Kathryn or one of the other ladies in a blue-green gown that banished all sallowness from her skin. *Emeralds for her green gowns, rubies for the reds*. Huge, immodest golden collars to show off her long swan-neck. One stone half the size of her fist to rest at the hollow of that pulsing, vibrant throat . . .

It never dawned on him to wonder how the Boleyns dressed her so spectacularly on Lord Rochford's meager income. He did notice, though, that her second-rate gems were vastly inferior to her blazing gowns. One morning when she breakfasted with him on Windsor lawn with its towering oaks, he noted that she wore no jewels at all. "Where are your pretties, my love?" he asked, raising her blunt Howard chin with a gem-studded forefinger.

She cast her eyes down, then glanced seductively up at him through a veil of coaly lashes. "I thought my gowns pleased you more than my baubles, so I sold the baubles to try and pay for the gowns." She stuck her lower lip out just enough to show its frail pink lining.

She had huge square-cut diamonds from him within the week, flashing white fire from her uncommonly long and slender neck. He noted that even in the evenings when she might have worn her hair down in the relative privacy of her family's Court apartments, she kept it up in silver cauls to show off that neck. Its only flaw was a flat, strawberry-shaped-and-sized mole on the nape, which she kept covered, usually with a velvet riband when there was nothing better at hand.

It never occurred to him that she played him as a fisherman played "a fine, fat trout," as she told her uncle Norfolk.

"Very well, Niece, but do not play so near the fire," Thomas Howard warned her. "And as for the gowns, I cannot buy you a single more."

"Do not worry, Uncle Norfolk, the gifts have begun to roll in at last." His honest Northern face looked so dour that Anne, laughing, bent over his chair to kiss his brow. "What ails you, Uncle? Do you not believe he will make me queen?"

He shrugged. "I believe that he will make you his sole mistress for at least a few months; I dare hope for no more."

She clapped her hands gaily together. The gesture threw back her long funnel sleeves, exposing the bent finger with its second nail; horrified, she flung her sleeve back down. "Never fear, My Lord Uncle, I will not give into him until the ring is on my finger."

Giggling, she stuck out her ring finger. "The marriage band will go right *there*."

Norfolk stood solemnly, removed her black velvet cap so that the waterfall of glossy hair spilled out. "But do not forget the crown sits *here*, Niece, and how heavy it is, how hard to bear."

He tapped her on the head to make his point. *Saints,* he thought as she giggled irritatingly, *if only she had Kathryn's good sense and steadiness! Then I could trust her to see this thing through.* But Kathryn was incapable of flirting or teasing; she was wife material, that one, not cut out to play whore.

She had been single long enough, too. He decided to ask around and see to whom he might marry her off; a nobody would satisfy the king, a nobody of no family who was obviously after Kathryn for her own sake and not that of her proximity to the throne.

A name popped into his mind. Christ, one could hardly go lower than that messenger boy, the one he had fed and housed after he brought news of de la Pole's death at Pavia. Everyone knew he was smitten with Kathryn. What was his name again? . . .

Sir Richard Stoneleigh sat at Kathryn's feet, letting her wind freshly dyed yarn about his hands. It was cool in the shade of the fountain and surrounding trees; he thought there was no place he had rather be today. Looking up at her he saw that Kathryn's eyes were a shocking sky blue, nicely set off by her slanting black brows, and that the hair peeking from beneath the stylish French hood (a gift of her cousin, the Boleyn trollop) looked fine as silk embroidery floss. Nice color, too, blondey-brown as a little girl's often was before it decided which color to be.

He cleared his throat twice before she noticed. "Yes, Richard?" she asked in what seemed to his ears the most musical voice in the kingdom.

"I was remembering how bonny you looked when you first returned from Hever those many months ago. You look like that again, now you have recovered from your illness."

She twitched slightly. Had he guessed the nature of her illness, or that she had remembered Jacquetta's words about choosing not to have children and had gone to her for an abortion? "Whatever do you mean, Sir?" she asked softly, carefully.

"I just mean that it is good to see you looking so hale and pretty again."

He caught himself in time; he had been about to say, *Like you looked at the Field of Cloth of Gold.* How well he remembered her face when his lord had jousted, the glow about her when she emerged from Windsgeat's tent at dawn. One did not say such things to a lady; one did not refer to past indiscretions, old heartaches. *I was the lowly boy by the fire, adoring you, and you were a woman in love with a great lord. . . .*

Equally well he remembered his lord's increasingly short temper when Kathryn would not divorce to marry him; by the time Windsgeat discovered she was free, he was married with a child on the way. What a storm had broken then! Richard hoped he never witnessed such a rage of pain again. John de Gael, so icy, so masterful, had taken Jack of Norfolk's broadsword and destroyed two rooms as well as the sword. He might never have stopped had he not put his arm through a window and nigh bled to death. Richard shuddered remembering the slashed draperies, smashed glass, upended tables, and Windsgeat himself lying in a scarlet huddle amidst the wreckage.

His baroness, Margrethe, great with child, had remained unflinchingly calm. She wrapped John's arm, sent Pieter for a doctor, and read Thomas Boleyn's crumpled letter. Lifting John's lacerated face from her shoulder, she had said in her thickly accented English, "If you will grow to hate me because of this letter, I will go now. . . ."

Richard could not imagine Kathryn so calmly accepting evidence of her man's love for some other woman. Kathryn probably would have picked up another sword and . . . He smiled to himself.

"What is it?" Kathryn asked.

"So many questions! Can I not smile because it is a lovely day and I am sitting with the prettiest lady-in-waiting Queen Catherine has?"

He liked being able to say the queen's name because it was the same as his lady's. But there was a lull in the conversation now, the compliment had made her go pink-faced. Richard realized he had embarrassed her and fumbled for a way to achieve his point. "I mean," he began anew, "I mean that you look like you did after Hever. Your aunt Elizabeth must have brought you out of your shell."

"I adore my aunt. I know I already have an Isabella, but my next daughter will still be named Elizabeth for my aunt, though it is but the same name in another language."

That gave him the opening he wanted. He artlessly said, "Lady Howard, I should like your Elizabeth to be my daughter as well."

In a flash of chestnut taffeta she was on her feet. The ball of yarn she had been winding went rolling down the brick walk, bumping to a halt against the fountain.

The wind changed; a sand-fine spray from the fountain spangled both of them. "You *what*!" Kathryn squeaked, forgetting her manners. "You damnable rogue!"

"I mean that I would like to *marry* you, Lady Howard!"

"*Oh!* . . . Richard, can you not find some sweet young girl? I must be at least seven years your elder and I have a crop of children—"

"If you want more, you need a strong young man from the country, not one of the old Court lords."

"That is twice you have mentioned fathering my children. Do you men think of nothing else?"

"Holy Mother, Lady Kathryn"—there, he had used her first name and she had not reprimanded him—"I can *talk* with you, too. The 'sweet young girls' as you call them have no brains, no wit—and I have loved you since I first saw you." He knelt, kissed her slender hand. No response. Not daring look up lest he see scorn, he managed, spine stiffening, to add, "Of course I realize I cut a pathetic figure after Lord Windsgeat, I am but a boy with no money or great name or—"

"Hush, Richard. Do you think money or a lack of family matters to me? You are my friend and I have forgotten John's face these six and more years. It is only that I think your devotion a boy's infatuation that will wear off quickly. And I am older and very set in my ways, I am not tractable."

He could not help grinning against her hands. "I know that well enough, I still remember how you bounced a plate off your husband's head in the Val d'Or! Pieter and I laughed until we ached."

Kathryn laughed, too, remembering. It was poor timing for the laugh; at hearing staid Lady Howard giggle, the king rounded the fountain with his greyhounds. Seeing him, she tried to shake Richard off but only succeeded in amusing Henry Tudor. "Milady, is this knave bothering you?" the king demanded.

She curtsied low, unable to free her fingers from that possessive grasp. "No, Your Grace. Not exactly," she gasped out.

"I see. Then the lad has come a-courting? What have you to say for yourself, Stoneleigh?"

Richard released her, flung himself at the king's feet. "Your

Grace, I seek your permission to court Lady Ka—Lady Howard with an eye to marriage."

"Pish, boy, judging from her face, you had better convince the lady before applying to me."

"And if I convince her, Sire? She requires your permission to marry."

Henry regarded the earnest boy, the furiously blushing woman. He seemed to see again before him little Isabella Howard, beseeching him silently with uplifted arms and those weirdly pale blue eyes he had seen somewhere before. Not her mother's eyes, Kathryn Chase had fine, azure eyes.

He stroked his short beard. "Stoneleigh, you are a nobody, you have nothing. Your knighthood is only honorary and will not be passed down to your sons. She has offers from two earls, did she tell you? Or that her cousin, Lord Rochford's son, wanted her? She has no dowery but she is perhaps the highest-born woman at Court after the Countess of Salisbury."

Richard inclined his handsome coppery head, green eyes pleading. "It is because I am such a nobody that I would be an ideal husband for her ladyship. I am of too low a station to have ambitions concerning her bloodline, I am a farmer's fourth son. There is no threat in my family tree, Sire. I am a safe match. Love is the only reason I seek her hand."

"Hmph, prettily said, but how will you live? On your wife's salary?"

Richard managed to kneel somewhat taller. "Your Grace, I have had offers of positions with both Suffolk and Sir Thomas More."

The greyhounds whined and fawned on Henry, who stood resplendent in green and gold. "That will not do," Henry said. "Both the queen and Milady Boleyn are too fond of Kathryn, they will howl recriminations at me should I allow her to leave Court when you enter private service. Have you ever had two shrieking women dogging your footsteps, Stoneleigh? I tell you, they will make my life a merry hell. I cannot allow you to marry Lady Kathryn and take her away."

The young man's face fell.

The king considered it. "I can, however, see if there is not some suitable job here at Court for you. That should ensure domestic tranquility for *me*, but as for you . . ." He flicked his small blue gaze over Richard. "You have no high-born relatives, nothing of the sort? You are not some base-born de Gael?"

"No, Your Grace, I am just plain country folk."

"By God, sir, you have courage to think to wed the lady when Windsgeat himself could not catch her! If she wants you she can have you and the two of you will not remain penniless for it, I shall see to that. Take her, take her if you can. You have my permission to pursue, woo, catch, marry, and bed Lady Howard—if you can!"

It pleased him to be generous and banish the memory of a staunch little girl with her arms held out to him in a plea he could not fulfill. Far better were the days he could make someone love him for permission to woo. Henry was so pleased with himself he kissed Kathryn and, yanking Richard to his feet, shoved him at her.

The king went whistling on his way, greyhounds trotting behind. Kathryn wiped her hand across her mouth. "Now see what you have done! You made it so he *kissed* me!"

"Then he is succeeding where I have failed. Will you marry me?"

She stuttered, she stammered, she could not find her tongue. "Very well," Richard said. "I will take that as an affirmative that I may at least begin courting you. But before we go into all of that, I feel I must tell you about the countess and myself."

"What, Jacquetta? I know all about it. And you, I suppose, remember all about me and John. Do you know Isabella is his child?"

He considered it. "I can see it now, she has his exact coloring. I thought it was old Norfolk she took after, with the ruddy hair, but it was John's Howard blood showing through. So we are both well acquainted with the de Gaels, Milady, what of it?"

"Can you not interest yourself in little Jane Seymour or Anne Parr?"

Richard took her hands again, less grasping this time. "Kathryn," he said, and smiled at the luxury of being able to use her name instead of title. "I do not love you *despite* our age difference but *because* of it. I love your fire, your wisdom, your knowledge of things I have as yet no notion of. I do not want some little prig or a dithering coquette. I want *you*, flaws and all. And I adore Isabella, if I cannot be her father then let her think of me as an uncle. Agree to let me court you or—" He tried to think of the worst thing he had to threaten her with. She could not tolerate vulgarity, sloppiness, or having a scene made, Jacquetta had warned him, so he said, "Or I will loudly serenade outside your Court apartments every night and embarrass you!"

He did, too. The first night he and his lute were baptized from a washbasin. The second night, ladies and courtiers threw old shoes and apple cores, yelling for silence or a less-warped lute.

The third night Anne Boleyn loaned him a freshly tuned lute, decided the evening looked entertaining, and joined him on the lawn with her brother and another lute. By night four Kathryn had two dozen courtiers and ladies lustily downing metheglin and ale and belting out lovesongs in English, German, Welsh, Latin, and French. By week's end it had become a nightly lawn party, complete with velvet cushions and hawkers selling toasted nuts and spiced cider. The king's sixty personal musicians joined in with seven-part harmony on a song Henry had written himself.

"Such a lot of fuss, Mama," Isabella complained, rubbing her eyes. "Are you going to marry Dickon Stoneleigh so I may get some sleep?"

Kathryn, perched in a bay window over the singers, softly asked, "Would you like a new papa all that much?"

"I would like whatever pleased you, Mama," answered her perfectly affable child.

"No, Isabella, tell me what *you* would like."

"I would like to know why you never married the man who looks just like me."

Kathryn's heart seemed to freeze in her breast. "Whatever do you mean, Sweetheart? What man?"

"Aunt Jacquetta's brother. I saw a miniature on ivory of him at Windsgeat."

If the child was that quick-witted, it was time to be honest with her—or as honest as one could be with a child. Kathryn told her a carefully expurgated story, wondering how much of it her daughter understood. When she had finished, Isabella sat up against the pillows, nodded. "I thought he must be my papa. I do not look like Edmund Howard. Well, if we cannot have my real papa, perhaps we could have Dickon. He is ever so nice and he has promised me a spaniel if I talk you into marrying him."

"Bribery!" Kathryn laughed until it hurt. She came over to the Woodville bed, gathered the leggy little girl into her lap. "You know too much, my angel. Now you must promise never to repeat what I just told you."

"I promise, Mama. I really am very fond of Dickon, and not just because of the spotted spaniel."

"I like him, too. He is so natural, so unaffected. But he is so terribly young, not quite twenty. Are you sure you will not fuss at me if I marry Sir Richard instead of some rich old man who would buy you lots of silk dresses and ponies?"

Isabella sleepily wrinkled up her nose. All this talk of fathers was beginning to bore her. She answered, "I do not care about silk dresses. But Aunt Elizabeth Boleyn is teaching me brewing and Aunt Jacquetta says she will teach me to distill herbal potions. I can still do all of that if you marry Dickon, no?"

Herbal potions like the one that had swept George Boleyn's unborn child from her womb. *Saints, but I would love to have my own man, own husband, and more children,* Kathryn thought, closing her eyes. *And Richard is a delight to be near, he makes me feel almost light-headed. When I am with him I remember I am a woman, and not an ugly one, either. And he is a good, reliable friend.*

"Besides," Isabella said sagely, "love and friends matter more than silk dresses and ponies, and Dickon is just about the best friend you have next to Aunt Jacquetta."

"My little philosopher! Would you like more brothers and sisters?" Kathryn asked, kissing her daughter.

"I would rather have that spotted spaniel."

Laughing, young again, Kathryn carried her child piggyback to the bay, flung the windows wide. Musicians faltered, bracing in expectation of flung garbage. "Richard! Sir Richard Stoneleigh!" she shouted boldly. "The answer is yes, Richard!"

Someone found a blanket and they began throwing the overwhelmed Richard up and down in it. "I never thought I should hear Kathryn Chase shrieking out windows like a fishwife," Henry Tudor said approvingly.

Jacquetta de Gael placed her elbows on her pretty gold leaf desk and let her head sink into her hands. The last of her sisters had married and moved north; she and her boys were alone at Windsgeat with their many servants and farmers. Henry Tudor had graciously allowed her boys to start at court this week but she could make no time to join them; managing the estates was a full-time job and weighed too heavily on her.

Beauty remained but youth was gone. Her fertile years were slipping away in service to the sacred land of the de Gaels. She was thirty-two and overwhelmed by the bookwork, the records, the plantings and reapings that had taken her and John together to manage. Her whole being cried out for a husband; Windsgeat cried out for a second hand at its helm. It had always been too great a load for one person; John himself could not manage it alone.

She picked up her quill again, dipped it, and continued to write. *You know how we have always been taught that as Windsgeat goes, so goes England? The lake is drying up; a brown blight has begun spreading out from it. Most of the lambs were stillborn this spring.*

She must risk all and be frank with him, franker than she had ever before dared be on paper. *John, the fertility of Windsgeat lies in the fertility of its Lord or Lady. You know I will not bear bastards so you must either come home or send me some suitable husband.* Hesitation, then, *If The Lord does not come home, they will want my boys. There must be fertility or The Lord of the Dance must die and my darling Edward is the eldest de Gael male at Windsgeat. Save my boys, John. Come home!*

There. That was enough to see her burned; the references to earth-magic, the old, forbidden pagan titles. Jacquetta signed, writing at a furious rate, then added the postscript: *Your squire Richard is marrying Kathryn Chase. If you have one bit of decency and compassion left you, you will rejoice in her good fortune and that the child will have a loving father.*

There was more she wished to add but the quill was too dull for further use and she could not remember where she had placed the knife used to sharpen it.

Jacquetta sealed the letter and trudged wearily upstairs to bed. *Alone,* she thought. *Alone again.* It came to her that to save the land and her sons she should have taken Richard as official consort, given him a year and a day, and then sown him into the ground to ensure a healthy crop.

I am losing my touch, she thought, and giggled hysterically.

Gods of her mothers, she was starting to sound like Anne Boleyn, she thought, and made the old crescent moon sign against evil.

Jacquetta, gleaming in her new golden tissue gown, outshone the bride. Kathryn did not mind; she was proud of her best friend's frank, sensual beauty and would never dream of trying to dress up to Jacquetta's standards.

Isabella beamed up at her splendid aunt, gripped her hand a moment. "Mama says that she and Dickon want to be alone a few days and that I shall stay with you at Windsgeat. I love Windsgeat, Aunt 'Quetta, it will be so nice to be there with you."

"Yes, it will. Now run along and get a drink from Norfolk, I must talk with your mother."

Kathryn approached, arrow-slender in her new blue-and-gold brocade gown, a gift of the queen. "Jacquetta, darling," she said, and embraced her friend. "You are ravishing as ever. Perhaps you will choose a husband from amidst all these swains? I invited all the unmarried men I could find. By the by, could you tell me what is wrong with Isabella?"

"What, is she jealous of Richard?"

"No, no. Other children have been teasing her unmercifully, calling her names, but I never arrive fast enough to discover what the names are. I fear 'bastard' may be among them."

"It is not. 'Witch' is what they call her, knowing she spends much time with me at Windsgeat."

Kathryn was happy tonight but there remained a faint, troubled echo somewhere within. "You joked with me about being a witch once," she said uncomfortably. "And my father said all de Gaels were witches."

"I was not joking, nor was he."

"Is that why my parents always referred to the de Gaels as heretics? You and John worship the Devil?" she asked wildly. Surely she could not be hearing these words!

"We are not Christian but we do not worship your Christian Devil, either, so calm yourself."

Kathryn struggled to stay calm, though she wanted to scream. "Are you Moslem then?" A crowd of dancers swirled past, signaling for her to join them, but she shook her head and tried to act broad-minded.

"No. We worship the All-Mother and All-Father who preceded Christianity, Islam, and Judaism. We do not eat unbaptized babies or fly about on broomsticks, so stop looking so shocked."

Jacquetta, who in her loneliness had imbibed rather more wine than usual, continued talking. "Do you know why Catherine of Aragon's first husband, Prince Arthur died? The blight began at Windsgeat and it would have spread to all of England. Kenneth—Father—went to Henry the Seventh and told him. No one had to tell the old Plantagenet kings, they knew all about such stuff. But those damnable upstart Tudors—"

"Had to tell old Henry Tudor *what*, dear?"

"That a king had to die, had to go willingly to the sacrifice to save England. Tudor cast him out but Prince Arthur overheard. You see, first with Arthur then with Harry, the old king let them listen at the door to hear politicking firsthand. So Arthur heard and knew England was in danger. He believed, he had some kind of sign. The Old Dark Ones spoke to him. He laid out in the rain that night and took the lung ailment that eventually killed him. And the blight ceased. Now the blight has come again and I cannot tell the king, it is not a woman's job. Can you imagine me trying to tell Great Harry that England is imperiled and a king must die? He would not bother with the ecclesiastical courts, he would burn me himself in the fireplace! What a muck John made of things when he first angered Harry. It has kept me from marrying and started the blight again."

She was starting to sway. Kathryn rushed her outside, stood shivering beside her in the brisk air. "Of course," Jacquetta started up again, "there is always Isabella. You and The Lord made her on Midsummer and she was born at Spring Equinox when the thaw begins and the fields are first broken for planting. Were she ten years older she could go to Windsor Wood and offer her maidenhead to the god, but she is still a child and so I have nothing to buy back the *greenth* with. Nothing but my boys; the priestess never dies for the land, I cannot offer myself. There's only my Edward and Robert."

Kathryn knew what Midsummer meant. It was no longer so popular with otherwise God-fearing Christians as May Day, but she had still seen her share of villagers leaping over bonfires on Midsummer that their crops might ape them and spring high into the air toward the sun.

She sucked her breath in, hard. "Jacquetta, this is all a little too much for me to take in just now."

"Yes, and on your wedding night, too. My poor Kat, I had thought you would marry John and your children rule Windsgeat after this current generation; I had thought to spring all of this on you gradually. Now you probably will not let me take Isabella, who must be the next Lady."

"Jacqui . . ." She called her that so seldom that its use now made both of them very gentle. "I am not a very good Christian. I pay it all lip service but I no longer think I believe in a Heaven or Hell, for I have seen too much Hell-on-earth in mankind's inhumanity to fellow man. All I ask is that Isabella be allowed to decide for herself and that you do not teach her things to endanger her with the authorities yet."

"She already knows things I never taught her, but yes, you are right. I will answer questions she asks but I will not preach at her. It is hard for me, though; I thought to have a daughter of my own to be Priestess, Lady, and Keeper after me but there is only Isabella. I will go now, I know I have had too much wine and my tongue is loose. Give me my niece and go on to your wedding night."

Kathryn was standing in the doorway watching them leave when a coat landed around her shoulders. Richard sprinted past her to tell Isabella good-bye, then the little girl was gone into the night, gazing adoringly at her beloved aunt. "You look frightened, Kat; what is it?" he asked, coming back toward her.

"I just had the most extraordinary conversation with Jacquetta." she said slowly.

"What, about the de Gaels being pagan? She said she would tell you but I never thought it would take so long."

Kathryn wagged an indignant finger under his nose. "Sometimes I think the whole world knows every last detail about that family and I am the only ignorant fool!"

"You are no fool, Wife."

He had not called her that before. Pleased, she gave a little shiver as he reached under the tails of her French hood to caress her cold neck. They stepped closer; his arms were around her now and it felt as though she had come home. He was nice to hold, not gangly or clumsy as she had expected. Kathryn rubbed her nose in the neck slit of the new shirt she had embroidered for him. It seemed beyond comprehension to her that she could be married again, and as excited as a virgin.

"Promise me one thing, Kathryn," he said. "Promise we will have only daughters so King Harry does not feel threatened by them."

"All right," she agreed, "but only if we get started on them right away. *Richard* . . . I am ready to do married things."

He chuckled at her boldness. "I have a room reserved for us at an inn. It is not so fine as you are used to, but it will save us being constantly disturbed as I understand often happens on a Court wedding night. Wait while I fetch your cloak and muff."

There was a surprise waiting her in the palace stables—a pretty pearl-gray jennet bearing her old silver sidesaddle. "I wanted to get you a mare but could not," Richard said defensively.

Kathryn went straight to the mule, held her hands out and found herself snuffled all over. "Oh, Richard, she is sweet. Lift me up, will you? I want to ride her as soon as possible!"

He put her on the mule, swung up on his gelding, and led her out. The inn he took her to was miles from Court, as Richard could not afford any of those nearby, but Kathryn did not mind. The evening was crisp and snowy but her new husband had brought her velvet cloak with its rabbit fur trim so she was comfortable. She found her mount well broken, not young but not past her prime, and a pleasure to ride. Kathryn did not allow herself to think of Mask or anything else in the past; she was starting over, she told herself, and kept her chin high. Besides . . . she was growing more and more excited at the thought of being alone with Richard.

The innkeeper welcomed them in with a round of drinks in the taproom before leading them up the narrow steps to their room. "Here you go, Sir and Lady. There is water in the washbasin and a pot of mulled cider on the hearth. God's blessings on you this night."

Richard thanked the man, tipped him as well as he could, and stood nervously awaiting some show of approval. He and Kathryn both knew she was used to better places; seeing him bristle in expectation of criticism, she thought with affection: *He is still a boy at times. Does he think I will insult him on this, our wedding night? Does he think I presume myself so far above him?*

She remembered her own parents once being too poor to afford an inn on their travels and so asking a farmer's permission to sleep in his stables.

"It is a very nice room," she announced. "Very clean, and the innkeeper has made it cozy for us." There was a mat of woven rushes on the floor and when she furtively stamped on it, nothing came running or flying out. The bedclothes were clean, though much-patched and mended; she should have thought to bring her own sheets. Lavender somewhere . . . She turned back the covers and saw bags of lavender with loose stuff and chamomile sprinkled on the rush matting below.

Everything passed inspection. She turned and saw Richard jittering against the wall. Poor lad, he did not know what to do. After all, this was his first wedding night. "Be a dear and warm your hands at the fire before unlacing me. I shall not be in an amorous mood if your hands are like ice," she suggested gently.

He nearly backed into the fire. At Court there were always women to undress the bride; she supposed he had not expected to do so himself. Richard opened his mouth to answer, but all that came out was, "I—I—I—"

"Do not act so shy, I know you and Jacquetta did not play *cards* all night, and she is not the sort to simply let you throw her skirts over her head. Now, the laces are knotted at the top and tucked into the back of the gown, Richard. Come along."

He thrust his trembling hands nearly into the fire, rubbing them for warmth a half-minute before turning back to Kathryn. It was several moments before he could bring himself to touch the straight, slim back she presented; another few moments fumbling the knot before he found his pace at unlacing her.

At last the gown was loosed. Kathryn thanked him nonchalantly, took the warming pan from the hearth, and ran it all over the sheets. Then she handed it to him to set back down, for by now she was wriggling out of her gown and had that to busy her.

In a thrice the gown was folded on a low red chest, with her damp shoes on the hearth to dry. Kathryn sat back on the bed, flung her shift up to her knees, and began untying her silver-stitched cross-garters. On to the ill-fitting bias-cut stockings which came off to reveal nice legs, though very slender. Richard had always wondered what kind of legs she had; now he knew.

Stockings and petticoats gone, she sat in the center of the bed. There was a flash of bare shoulders and breasts as she drew the linen shift off over her head, then the shift went sailing and she was hidden under the covers. When he still did not move, she said, "Richard, it is our wedding night. Am I to spend it alone?"

He broke every lacing string, eyelet, and hook on his own clothes; Kathryn, smiling to herself, realized that the wedding breakfast would be spent in mending. She held her arms out to him. He came into them hesitantly, both of them starting back at the first touch of silken flesh on its like. Realization followed that fear was unneccessary; he folded her into his embrace as though he had protective wings. She laid her cheek to his heart, amazed at the wild beat of life within. "I did not expect you to be like this," he said. "Aloof, perhaps; the royal lady condescending to marry one of the new household treasury secretaries for who-knew-what reason. But you are very sweet and gentle."

"Not so sweet, Richard. I need very fiercely."

She kissed him, marveling that a man's lips could be so soft. In turn his hands were careful on her, not hurried or rough. But this was not a night for excessive carefulness, she had waited too long. Kathryn drew his head to her breast while she stroked his long back and the fine dark hair on his thighs.

Jacquetta had taught him well. When he lay between her legs and pressed his mouth to the burning core of her, she shattered not once but twice before seizing hold of him, guiding him into her. They moved together furiously before he fell across her, spent.

She had forgotten how young he was—at nineteen a full seven years her junior. Long before the hour was up he had remounted, and shortly after that when she rolled on top, he was ready again. He found a place on the side of her throat that when licked or sucked, maddened her; "Do you like this, Kat? Is it better when I do this? Oh, Kathryn, Kathryn!" he cried out.

Toward dawn, exhausted, they slept.

The gray jenny had little to do but eat and be walked by the innkeeper's boy that week; it was a full seven days before her mistress could sit a sidesaddle again.

Within two months Kathryn was pregnant and shockingly, unfashionably in love with her own husband. She had never been so happy even with John, for loving him had seemed a doomed thing from the start. But love with Richard grew and grew; he courted her like a lad with his first girl, dropped bunches of spring violets into her apron, fed her choice tidbits from the table. And he made her laugh as she had never laughed before, even with Jacquetta.

Four months later she lost the child. "She is too thin to make healthy babies," the doctor told Richard, shaking his head. "You must give her rest and nourishing food, plenty of red wine, red meat, thick soups and stews."

Richard spoon-fed her the next week. Even Jacquetta came to Court with herbal potions and a fetching new nightgown for the invalid. It amazed the Court to rap at Kathryn's door and find the fabulous, the dazzling Countess Courtenay in a linsey-woolsey housegown and apron, brewing herb liquors and sweeping the sickroom floor for her friend.

Catherine of Aragon visited as she always did when a favorite was unwell, and as Kathryn was her especial darling, she attended her nearly every day. She and Jacquetta struck a truce to work together caring for their friend, as a result of which Kathryn mended quickly. But she remained alarmingly thin and the slightest exertion wearied her so that she had to sit down at once.

Finally, wracking her loving brain for a way to help, Catherine of Aragon hit on an idea. She summoned Richard and said, "I have here a writ with the king's signature allowing Lady Howard's sons to come from Kenninghall and join you and her at Woodstock, the old royal hunting lodge. It is rather run-down but very private; I will send a chamberer, housekeeper, and cook with you to care for Kathryn and she will get better there. You are both excused from your duties here—*with* pay—for as long as it takes to completely heal her."

There were mornings lying late abed after that, though Richard had to use other ways to please Kathryn and himself, lest lovemaking find her too soon pregnant again. They had romps in the fields with her three children, hunting, riding, playing Hoodman's Bluff in the woods. James he could not bring himself to like; at twelve the boy considered himself near manhood and would take no instruction nor accept friendship from his stepfather. But Adam, eight years old, small, dark, and serious, blossomed under Richard and Kathryn's attention. And they all loved Isabella.

Soon Kathryn had color in her cheeks and gained enough weight to require letting all of her gowns out. She sparkled again. When the doctors allowed, she and her husband resumed lovemaking, and lay awake afterward, laughing over the day's many little occurrences and planning the future of all their unborn children.

In early summer they returned to Court only to discover that there had arisen the fearsome matter of the king's conscience.

18

27 June, 1527

"Out, out, good ladies, I would speak to the queen your mistress alone," King Henry said, flinging wide the doors of the queen's Presence Chamber. Kathryn and the others picked up their mending and lutes, curtsied, and left.

There was nothing for George Boleyn's wife, Jane Parker, Lady Rochford, to do, as she had been playing the virginals and could not carry them away single-handed, so she helped herself to some of Kathryn's embroidery and followed to the nearest solar.

The ladies grouped beneath the oriel window. One sent a page for cushions which they then settled themselves on in the streaming sunlight. "I know what the king wants," Jane Rochford said. Everyone leaned closer as she knotted her thread. "He is going to ask the queen for a divorce."

"Milady, it cannot be so!"

"Jane!" Kathryn reprimanded.

"What have you heard? Tell us, tell us!"

Jane folded her ring-studded hands a moment before taking up scissors to cut her thread. "Some days back, the king went before an ecclesiastical court at York Place to answer a charge of living with his brother's wife."

"Tame gossip, and old. All of that was taken care of before you were born," harrumphed Lady Rutland.

Jane took a few mincing stitches and allowed herself a smirk. "Yes, but this time the king agreed, said that his conscience had been smiting him mightily. He says he believes the marriage is invalid and that is why he has no lawful-born sons."

"*Sons!*" snapped Lady Rutland, temper aroused. "My mistress the queen bore him aplenty sons! It is not her fault they died!"

"While those of his mistresses live," Anne Parr said gently. "So are we to believe he actually thinks the marriage unlawful?"

Jane's thread knotted. She slowly straightened it with little tugs of teeth and nails—*Like a cat feasting on a still-living bird*, Kathryn thought with a shudder. Jane said, "Ladies, think what you wish, but the fact is that my husband's sister intends to be queen of England and the king has agreed to put his wife aside for her."

There were gasps, outcries of dismay. From the Presence Chamber voices could be heard: the king's growing louder, shriller, more insistent, the queen's steady, curiously unruffled refrain. *I wish Margaret Pole were here,* Kathryn thought desperately. *She would know the truth or falsehood of this rumor. She would know how to straighten things out and put us all in order.* That vicious old woman who had once had legal care of her—how she longed for her imperious ways now, bullying everyone into line!

Doors flew open, splintering against prettily frescoed walls. Henry Tudor came barreling out of the Presence Chamber, face as violet as his slashed Italian doublet and coat. The ladies-in-waiting sank into abnormally low curtsies as he passed, afraid to draw his wrathful attention by not appearing respectful enough. "He is gone!" Anne Parr whispered at last. Mending flew to the ground, lutes sank onto abandoned cushions. A rosary broke, beads scattering as the women bunched up skirts and petticoats and raced to the queen's side.

They found her pale but composed, standing with white hands folded. "We will go to chapel," she said, Spanish accent noticeably thicker due to stress. "Lady Howard, you will please tell the London representatives in the audience rooms that I will be one-quarter hour late, I must go pray for my husband's soul. Afterward please tell my secretary I will wish to dictate a letter to my nephew, the Holy Roman Emperor. *And* to the pope, who has been his virtual prisoner since the Imperial troops sacked Rome. It was bound to happen, with so many godless Protestant mercenaries in the Imperial army. Shame on my nephew for allowing them to riot and attack the Pontiff!"

The queen swept from the chamber with as much majesty as though she stood Henry-tall and broad, not little and faded. Her skirts fanned out around her, rounding the corner with a silken *whoosh*! Women scurried to keep up.

God's Own Saints, the Emperor and the pope! And saying she must pray for her husband's soul . . . *Jane Parker was right,* Kathryn thought sickly. It struck her as ironic that for once she had beat Jacquetta, with her well-paid spy system, to a choice bit of news. She would have to send word to Windsgeat, let Jacqui know.

In the meantime she went to hunt down Catherine of Aragon's secretary and give him his orders.

Cardinal Thomas Wolsey was exhausted. It had been a long and fruitless trip across the Channel to approach the pope concerning "the king's Great Matter" and now he found himself wondering what all the effort had been for. Which of the big-eyed court whores had Harry Tudor cast his eye on? After all, no matter what he said, this could not be a simple case of conscience reawakened by biblical study; no, there must be some scheming bitch at the bottom of it all. Oh, well, as long as the king had chosen anyone but that icy Plantagenet bitch, Kathryn Chase; that would call for a double divorce, plop the Plantagenets back on the throne, and absolutely stagger Pope Clement. Maybe it was her friend, that dazzling de Gael heretic . . .

Wolsey's feet ached intolerably. Rocking in a litter between two sets of mules who were gorgeously bedecked in crimson cardinatorial cloths, he pondered on the unjustness of being sent on a mission as gout struck him. There was an annoying stuffiness in his head, too, and eyestrain from pouring over legal documents. *All this fuss about a divorce,* he thought indignantly. *It is not a divorce if it was never a genuine marriage*. Good old Harry Tudor and his resilient conscience, expanding and shrinking as necessary. *You serve a wily master,* he reminded himself as the mules halted on command.

He was taken by torchlight to the Privy Chamber where his king sat, strong-shouldered, muscularly-calved, though Wolsey noticed fat had begun creeping in. All of that ermine and padded gold-on-white brocade did not make the king's majesty look any slimmer, either.

Wolsey came to a dead halt. Behind the king's low dinner chair, leaning familiarly on the spindles, was that black-haired, goggle-eyed bitch King Henry had ordered him to yank from Harry Percy's side. *Oh, no, not Anne Boleyn,* he thought, grinding his teeth. *She will not even sleep with His Grace, surely he is not so great a fool as to be drawn into endangering his immortal soul for the sake of a few nights with her!*

"Your Grace, My Lady," the cardinal said, bowing so low that he wobbled on gouty feet and nearly stumbled. When he straightened, the arrogant bitch was still there, dark deer-eyes staring holes in him. He took his chances. "My Lady, if you would be so good . . . ? I would speak with the King's Majesty alone."

She leaned forward, wrapped possessive arms about the king's oxlike neck. "Where else would I be but where the king is? Speak, My Lord Cardinal. *I command it!*"

Wolsey, beaten, knelt and obeyed.

Catherine of Aragon faced the foe with grace and aplomb. She began demanding lady-in-waiting Anne Boleyn as her partner at cards most nights, making the notoriously highstrung young woman sit through round after repetitious round of Imperial or Pope July. One night when Anne drew a king and cannily held her hand for another round, Queen Catherine leaned across the table and tapped her opponent's wrist. "You show great good sense at stopping at a king," she said levelly. "But I know you, Lady Anne, you are not like the others: you will have all or nothing."

When finally released from this bondage hours later, Anne could not stop giggling. She giggled wildly throughout the night until women in surrounding rooms took their pillows to friends' rooms and pled for sanctuary.

A few months later the pope was freed from Imperial captivity and all England rejoiced. Now that Boleyn whore would see how solid the royal marriage was! The pope would save the old queen, Londoners said. Dairy wives coming to market heard the latest gossip and said to butcher-wives, "If he can divorce a bluidy queen, wha' will become o' the lot o' *us*? Wha' tis to stop any man from gi'ing his old woman the shove and taking a new one if our pious Queen Kate is flung out?"

Men said, "I remember when the king was in France and she beat the Scots at Flodden Field. She ordered the gates opened and we come a-running in—man, man, a real mob we were! But she only stepped out, unafraid-like, and stretched her arms out to us. Said 'we English' like she been born and bred with us. Said she would give us an heir and, by God, she did—little Mary Tudor! A fine little princess!"

Those who had been lads eleven years before crossed themselves when a potter said, "I was young and wild, I took part in the Apprentices' Rebellion where we all ran wild in the streets, attacking foreigners. Course, we did not consider the queen one, we never thought of her as Spanish. . . . You did not know me then and mayhaps you do not recall how all the apprentices they could catch were chained together like beasts, under sentence to have our bowels and hearts drawn from our living bodies before we were beheaded and hacked to quarters. And good Queen Kate, she come straight from bed in her shift and nightgown, hair a-flowing. She flung herself down at Great Harry's feet, begged him to spare us because we were only lads and they two might have reckless lads of their own some day. He ordered our chains struck off, our lives saved. She be a very great lady."

The next time Catherine of Aragon's barge was seen moving downriver, people by the thousand raced to the Thames embankment. Flowers and fruit were thrown to her, voices joined to scream that she was their queen and they would have no other.

That summer she dared hope, for June First found the dreaded Sweating Sickness oozing through London, dropping victims so quickly that they died at dinner, in the bath, mounting horses. King Henry, always in horror of disease, ordered Court to break up under pretense of taking his usual summer progress through the countryside. By mid-month London business was slowed to a crawl by the disease; the next day Anne Boleyn's maidservant staggered and fell to the tiled floor at Greenwich.

Henry Tudor summoned courage to speak to Anne. "You will have to go home, Sweetheart, I cannot risk taking ill. I will ride on to Waltham in Essex, you must return to Hever."

Instead of kissing her robustly or squeezing any of the tenderer portions of her anatomy as he usually did, Henry stretched a hand out, wincingly brushed her fingertips with his, and fled. Anne, swearing like an old farmwife, shook her fist at him as the servants packed for Hever.

She was ill by the time they arrived. It began with a headache, then her lower back pained her, as it did at the onset of her monthly courses. Nothing unusual there, so Anne tried to ignore it. Nausea followed, too severe to be normal even at this time of month, and next came stabbing pains in her liver. She alternated between chills and a stinking sweat, so crazed by fever that she seemed to float up above herself, looking down on the pain-wracked Anne below.

The illness spread to her father and brother. Several servants died; through it all Elizabeth Boleyn remained mysteriously unscathed, nursing them, washing bed and body linen, providing cool sips of water and soup. Thomas recovered but Anne and George lay shuddering and shivering, sheets darkening with profuse sweat. "They will sweat themselves dry!"

Elizabeth cried out, standing between their sickbeds. "I cannot keep water in my children! Oh, Sweet Jesu, help my children!"

Henry Tudor, safe away from the Sweat at Waltham, tied a handkerchief over his mouth and nose when Anne's letters arrived. "Open them for me and read them from over there lest the illness leap onto me," he directed his secretary. "Well? What says my lady?"

"She wrote this as she was being taken ill with the Sweat. An enclosed note from her mother says she does not know whether Milady will live or not."

"Faugh! She will live, she *must*, now that I have set so many wheels in motion for her sake. Send me Doctor Butts, he will go heal her."

Anne and George lived anyway. Their sister Mary's household was not so lucky; her husband, the newly knighted Sir William Carey, died after a scant twenty minutes of symptoms.

In the archbishop of Canterbury's house eighteen strong men died in four hours.

The Sweat struck Kathryn's tiny cottage outside London while she yet had custody of her sons. Adam died in her arms, reciting his Latin lessons to the end. Isabella's life was despaired of for days; only healing her saved Kathryn from collapsing over her beloved little Adam's loss. She found herself disloyally wondering why God could not have taken James, who whined, complained, cheated, and lied. James was his father all over again and there seemed nothing she could do to change him; she was only too glad to reflect that soon he would be returning to either Edmund or Norfolk's wife at Kenninghall.

In the Tower, the Sweat killed Arthur Chase's wife and son and nearly Arthur, too, though he recovered.

Thin, worn out by doctoring, ill, Kathryn miscarried again. She rose from her sickbed to find that James was ill, which smote her conscience for wishing him dead instead of Adam; she lavished so much attention on healing him that he protested being smothered. They had all begun recovering when they had an unexpected visitor.

Pieter van der Hüm. "Richard, look who is here!" Kathryn called out, wiping her hands on her apron before reaching to embrace Pieter. "Saints, Pieter, I had no idea you were back in the country. Is—"

"No, Milord did not return. He cannot. Lady Howard, I have been everywhere looking for you, you must come to

Windsgeat. De servants have been sending to you and His Lordship seeking help for De Countess. She took de Sweat and near died of it, dough she is somewhat better now. But her young Edward and Robert died."

"*Oh* . . . oh, *no*, Pieter! Not her boys!"

"De Lord sent to her sisters but dey could not help her. Dere is only you, as *he* cannot come back to England. Lady, she has lost her mind, she runs drough de house screaming for her boys to come back. She curses De Lord, curses de gods. She will die!"

Richard entered the room; Kathryn threw herself into his embrace. "It is Jacquetta, I must go to her! If I ride on ahead, will you follow with Isabella and James when they are all better?"

His concerned green gaze flicked over her. "Yes, of course I will. Let me saddle Gray Jenny."

"I have brought Circe for her, she goes like de wind. Hurry, lady, I think Jacquetta will break into little bits and die. Hurry!"

There was time to kiss her husband and children, and wrap up some cheese and bread in a knapsack. Then Richard flung her on Circe's back and she was riding from the cottage, bursting out onto the dirt track that led toward Windsor and therefore Windsgeat. Halfway there Pieter's gelding gave out so they rode double until reaching fresh mounts he had left at an inn. It was night by then; they rode relentlessly through the starless dark.

At Windsor ridge above the valley she thought she heard Jacquetta screaming. Her horse picked her way clumsily down the slope, staggering and broken-winded. *I can go faster on foot*, Kathryn thought, and slid from the saddle. Her skirts ripped, she stumbled, fell, skinned her face. Yes, they *were* screams, and that was Jacquetta's voice! Kathryn flung her skirts over her arm, ran blindly, madly to the glow of golden candles through multipaned windows. Behind her the horse fell, gasping. She would have killed all of Windsgeat's magnificent Whites if only she could reach Jacquetta in time to save her, she thought as the sound of a merciful shot rang out behind her.

The stone maze loomed up white and stark on her right. Something huge and pale burst from it, ran with her; she recognized the Roman nose and bunchy ox-neck of Cernunnos. Oddly, she was not frightened. The stallion ran alongside her, as though urging her on; lent speed and courage by his presence, she made it to the house and burst inside.

A knot of frightened servants clustered before her. Elbowing through, she saw Jacquetta huddled in a corner, hugging herself. Pieter had not exaggerated her grief. In fact, he had understated it.

The russet-and-gold gown hung on her in dirty tatters, white silk shift blotched with wear. One muddy shoe was on, one not, and her silk stockings were full of holes and briars. Jacquetta had torn at her hair, leaving one side of her scalp blood-crusted and half-bare; her moonstone eyes were unfocused.

Kathryn knelt, tenderly lifted the ruined glory of that golden head. "Jacquetta. Dear, wild Jacquetta. You will not die or stay mad, I will not allow it. You are my friend, my sister; I shall not leave you comfortless."

The housekeeper sobbed into her apron. "Oh, if only The Lord be here!"

Kathryn's head snapped up. *Aye,* she thought savagely, *when was he ever here to help her, yet they call for him now!* "I can read a label just as well as John of Windsgeat," she snapped. "Fetch me the countess's Spanish leather trunk and its key. I want her books, too."

"Books, Milady?"

She stood, fists clenched. "God's wounds, do de Gael retainers play the same stupid games as their masters? I know who and what you people really are; get me her magic book, her pagan Book of Hours,* and get it *now*! I want hot wash water for her, fresh sheets, and a room with no glass or sharp objects. Get me her oldest and most comfortable clothes and find me that trunk of medicines. And I do not mean two bloody damned days from now!"

Generations of servility in the de Gael servants had left them without much initiative. Relieved at hearing a masterful voice shouting orders, they raced to obey.

She bathed and changed Jacquetta, guessed at how much mandrake to give her, and put her to bed. Sitting, watching her friend, she heard a rap at the door and watched as Pieter entered. "Here is what you seek, Lady Howard. It was kept locked away in De Lord's chambers, under de floorboards."

He laid it across her lap; its weight was that of a three-year-old child. Leather-and-gilt-bound, inches of parchment and older vellum . . . *Wyg's Geat Book of Shadows* read the

---

*Book of Hours—an illuminated private missal, or prayer book.

faded gold lettering. "Dat is its fifteenth or sixteenth cover. 'Book of Shadows,' dat is what we call a Book of Hours in our religion. I will fetch you a table, dat is too heavy for your lap."

In a few minutes a dozen men, panting and struggling, had brought her John's sea-sphinx table. She hefted the book onto it, tucked the sleeping Jacquetta more firmly in, and turned to Pieter. The door shut as the others left. "Why 'Wyg's Geat'? I thought it was 'Wind's Gate.' "

"Wyg or Hraeg or Waendle was some form of Woden or one of de udder, earlier, Old Dark Ones. Some sort of Saxon word. And it is not 'gate,' but *geat* the Saxon word for way, path, street, or even temple. A magic line of power runs drough dis land. *Wyg's Geat*. God's Path, or Way."

Now she understood the family's motto, Guarding God's Way. This land was sacred to them. "Stay with me, Pieter," she urged, afraid to open the book by herself.

"I cannot remain alone wid two ladies of quality!"

"Master van der Hüm, you and I are practically family, we have seen each other at our worst. If you leave now, I shall—I shall—I shall tell John you neglected your duty by his sister!"

His spine stiffened with an audible snap. "Richard will not like our being closeted alone like dis, Milady."

"You have my permission to roll Richard down a flight of stairs if he tries to interfere with my helping Jacquetta. And my name is *Kathryn*, not Milady, damn it."

She dared open the frightening book. The first pages, of ancient calfskin vellum, were dry and curling up at the ends. "What is this peculiar writing?" she demanded.

"Pictish, dey dink. No one can read it now."

Drawings of herbs, ceremonies, animals. "And *this* writing?"

"Anglo Saxon for de next few dousand pages."

Exquisite writing, sharp and slash-like. An occasional word was close enough to German or even English that she could pick it out, translate it. But the family's history was not what she needed. Rather, she must find something about healing.

Something strange occurred to her. "Pieter, *women* wrote all of this! Dozens and dozens of women. There is not a man's hand on a single page!"

He shrugged, unconcerned. "Women are de priestesses, de records keepers, de healers and growers."

She blurted out, "Then what good are the men if the women do all the work?"

"Dey make children and die dat de crops may grow. My great-great-grandmudder, she worked for de Gaels here in England. She said hundreds of years ago when De Lords were yet young, dey were torn apart bare-handed and sown wid de crops to make dem grow. Dis is no longer done, dough an occasional Lord must give himself over to de god's judgment to save de land. Milord John had to kill his uncle to regain Windsgeat when he came home from his days as a mercenary; mortal combat by torchlight in de stone maze. And now De Countess's two boys have died of de sweat. She had dem burnt and deir ashes scattered on de land; de blight immediately ended. Windsgeat is green again, de rain comes, de lake rises once more. England is saved. It is a sacred ding, Lady; I do not pretend to understand it all."

She felt a sense of fascinated horror with all of this. It sounded very much like animals and the natural order of things: one king-stallion scattering his seed far and wide, dying before his prime ended that the herd remain fertile. A male could get many children in one night, a woman only one per year; John de Gael might ride and plant his own acres when he was home, he might keep breeding charts on the livestock and even decide who did what when, but his real purpose was as fertility god. And while fertility gods were often murdered, priestesses were not. The real religious power at Windsgeat was Jacquetta's, not John's.

"Where do the Tudors and Plantagenets come into all of this?" Kathryn gasped out, repulsed, intrigued.

"De Plantagenets were de ones meant to die for de land; somehow it accidentally ended up being de Gaels. Dey wish to have a Plantagenet king back on de drone to take dis duty from dem."

Thought. "Did John only take me to try for a Plantagenet heir?"

"No. He would never try for dat without it being a legitimate heir. He took you for love only. De countess's recipes and herbals are at de back of de book, in de most recent section, you might look dere for someding to help her."

She leafed through until she came to Jacquetta's delicate, spidery scrawl. "This is not her private book, this is a family thing. Where are her private herbals?"

"Dis should have everyding you require. It is a dangerous book, I do not know why dey keep it. It could burn all of dem."

Kathryn read awhile in silence, lifted her head to find

faithful Pieter still there. "Lady," he said carefully. "We cannot lose Jacquetta. She is goddess-on-earth to her tenants, dere is no one to replace her. She has no daughter. I do not mean dat she is not important to you and De Lord and me for her own sake, but . . . she has no daughter to replace her."

Yes, she did. A daughter of the spirit, not flesh, though Isabella was her niece.

A bargain seemed to be drawn up before her. Kathryn was not sure how harmless any of the de Gaels' religious beliefs were, or how pure at heart, but in those moments, looking at Jacquetta's bandaged head on the pillow she reached a decision. She said, "If Isabella wishes it and I am certain that no harm will come to her, my daughter is free to choose the de Gaels' path. I will not let Windsgeat and England fall; the de Gaels will not perish because I denied them my daughter's free choice."

"You would do all of dis for De Lord?"

Kathryn's face clouded. "In seven years, did John de Gael tend my wounds, feed me when I was ill? Did he help rear my daughter, did he find me a loving husband, was he here for me to weep on? Did he bury my father, did he take me in when all the world was against me? Does he remember my birthday, my saint's day? No, Master van der Hüm, but that woman there does. I will help Windsgeat, but I will do it all for her; I will save these people for Jacquetta's sake."

She had seemed pliable to him at twenty; sweet, unaffected, and too totally average to be wordy of John de Gael's fervent love. Now, looking at and listening to her, he saw that at twenty-eight she was hard as green wood was hard, and supple enough to bend before springing back and fighting. *Gods, gods,* he thought regretfully. *De Lord should have waited for her, she is more dan wordy of Windsgeat now.*

In fact, she seemed a sight too good.

19

It was a brutal fight for Jacquetta's life and sanity. "A race wid de Devil, only he does not exist," Pieter murmured after one particularly trying night.

First there was making out Jacquetta's careless scrawl. "For sleeplessness, three drops of Number three-seven-five per twenty pounds of body weight, in medium-sized goblet of water."

Kathryn stripped Jacquetta down to her shift, cocked an experienced seamstress's eye at her to calculate size. Very well, eighteen drops of the stuff in a glass, stirred widdershins, that was, left to right. The potion was no sooner down than Jacquetta had one of her attacks and had to be tied to the bed with soft toweling. That was the hardest part, having to restrain her dearest friend as though she were some ravening animal. But soon Jacquetta's twitching feet relaxed, then her legs, and so on up until she lay peacefully drowsing.

Now back to the book. Number three-seven-five was a blend, not a straight exact or distillation. Limeflower, chamomile, linden, and mandrake. Three-seven-six had a drawing of a flea next to it and smelled violently of lavender, pennyroyal, rosemary, and something else she could not make out. All of the three hundreds were blends, she soon discovered; the next eleven were abortificants for varying stages of pregnancy, and after that . . .

She fell asleep on the beautifully illuminated Book, dreamt of burning at the stake and feeling no pain in it. It was time to dose Jacquetta again, when she woke, wondering if there were herbs to treat the root of the problem and not merely its symptoms. Kathryn drifted off again in the four hundreds, head on the Book, elbow in Jacquetta's little leather chest of bottles. Someone was shaking her, it must be those men who meant to burn her . . . "My lady, your husband and children are here," a maidservant said.

Richard and Pieter were hugging and thumping each other on the back when she entered the Great Hall. Her husband came striding toward her and picked her up in an embrace that made her ribs creak. When he set her down, Isabella came into her arms. Only James stood back, thinking himself too old for motherly embraces at age thirteen.

"How is she? How can we help?" Richard asked quickly.

"I want to help Aunt 'Quetta," Isabella chimed, round-eyed.

James said huffily, "I wish I had not been dragged here, I do not wish my chances at Court ruined because we stay with a lot of goat-kissing heathens."

Kathryn only had to raise her hand halfway to him. "She is my dearest friend and higher born than any Howard; you will not speak so of the countess."

He glowered but backed down, apologizing and even tolerating an embrace.

James offered no aid to Jacquetta but Richard and Isabella were a godsend. Isabella knew all about potions and distillations and even brought out Jacquetta's private Book of Shadows, which would be buried with her at death. Richard and Pieter took turns physically putting Jacquetta on her feet and making her walk with them. Both men read to the invalid, took turns feeding her, trying to call her back into herself.

Summer progressed and she showed little change. Potions kept her from reaching a peak of shrieking and flailing; now she did not speak at all, never fought, was tractable and vague. But when Kathryn lessened the dose, the old violence came back upon Jacquetta.

By mid-July she could press embroidery into Jacquetta's hands and be rewarded with painstaking stitches, but she had no personality, none of the spark that made her Jacquetta de Gael, Countess Courtenay, imperious, spirited, witty. "It is as though the real Jacquetta is gone and we have a changeling here or an empty husk," Kathryn miserably told Richard one night.

And then she spoke. It was the last night of July and Kathryn had seated Jacquetta in a window bay. They looked out upon thousands and thousands of emerald acres, all covered with crops that had been unable to grow until the deaths of two fair-haired boys. Thinking of that made the midnight fields seem bleak to Kathryn. How odd it was that de Gael men—aye, and women, too—would cheat, fight, fornicate, steal, and murder to protect their land. It was only dirt after all, some grass, some barley and rye, with horses, six-horned Manx sheep, and surly red cattle grazing around this house. And yet without the land they had no food, no crops to grow, no animals to work the ground and provide meat. There was the family history to consider, too, all summarized in that one dangerous book.

Jacquetta gasped. Turning, Kathryn saw her friend pressed to the mullioned windows, eyes wide, mouth open. "The Lammas fires. They are bringing me the harvest but I—I cannot go out there. Could not bear it."

Kathryn dropped her sewing, rose from her chair to place an arm around her friend's trembling shoulders. "You do not have to go out there, Jacqui. No one will force you."

"They will congratulate me on the loss of my boys and sowing the ashes. They will think me pleased, they will say what fine lads I had to go so willingly. And then they will give me the first cuttings from their fields and ask, 'Where is our next priestess?' The mother-on-earth is always shown them and I have no one . . . no one . . ."

Pinpoints of light came prickling across the flat valley, drawing steadily nearer. The animals fled before them, dark little deer, those demonic-looking sheep from the Isle of Man, several calves. Last came a wicked-looking white outline.

Cernunnos stopped before the window, trumpeted expectantly. The little triangular head tossed up and down, Roman nose dipping at the glass.

"What does he want?" Jacquetta whispered. She had her answer a moment later as another, far smaller white shape shot across the midnight lawn. There was a flash of pale gown and pale skin; Kathryn saw her own oval face and Jacquetta's washy blue eyes in the night as the girl who had them both held her arms up to the wild stallion.

He dipped his head again, pushed it against the thin chest. He stood patiently while she seized handsful of mane and climbed up them onto his bulging withers.

Cernunnos wheeled, ran toward the torches with Isabella on his back.

"My baby!" Kathryn shrieked, and scrambled out the nearest door after them.

She yanked her voluminous skirts up to her knees, sprinted like an athlete. One tiny figure in white, riding a wild horse—the torches up ahead—God's Holy Saints, her baby, her only daughter! Adam was dead, she could not bear to lose Isabella, too. Sowing ashes in the field, tearing the Old Lords apart—her baby girl, what would they do to her?

Thousands had come to the ceremony. Surely there could not be so many servants and tenant farmers on the de Gael estates. Some of the people looked exhausted, as though they had traveled many miles to be here.

Kathryn fought through the curiously quiet crowd. They seemed to be grouped around something. . . . "The princess Kathryn," someone said, and they all parted for her like the Red Sea. *Princess*. At her father's execution someone had called her brother Arthur a prince—

They had made an altar of fresh green boughs. Isabella sat atop it, arms wide, accepting their stalks of herbs and corn.* She had been crowned with berries and rosemary and was receiving the first cuttings with as much solemnity as an empress.

"The mother," a man said, and they all turned to regard Kathryn with calm interest. Someone lay sprigs of rowan and stalks of barley across her arms, too. "The Plantagenet princess," a woman informed the crowd; many bowed or curtsied to her. Then the offerings continued. After each was made, the offerer retreated; hours later the last of the crowd had withdrawn deeper into the valley, where torches burned brightly and ale flowed.

"How were you able to ride that horse?" Kathryn demanded, pulling Isabella toward the house.

"Why, it was easy. He told me to meet him there and go with him, so I did. He is a very nice horse."

And a little child shall lead them.

Richard met them a little ways on and hefted Isabella onto his shoulder. "I did not know you two would go to the ritual without me."

"She ran out into the dark—she rode *Cernunnos*!" Kathryn exploded.

"Well, we will all talk about it in the morning. Jacquetta is fine now, she is sitting in the kitchens drinking cider and talking about what kind of bread the housekeeper is to bake for tomorrow. Come along, I shall put this little one to bed and then we will talk, Wife."

As panic ebbed, weariness settled in. Kathryn dully followed him, unlaced Isabella out of her gown, and watched Richard tuck the little girl in. Afterward, he unexpectedly seized Kathryn by the waist, flung her over his shoulder. "Let us go upstairs and make another daughter to prevent Isabella thinking she is the center of the universe. What say, are you up to it at last?" he queried.

---

*corn—not North American maize, but any cereal crop such as oats, barley, rye.

Her chin thumped comfortably between his shoulderblades with each stair. "Up to it? I am blind and *screaming* for it."

The top of the stairs and on to a dark, curtained bed. Richard flung her down, mock-wrestled her awhile. "Daughters only, remember?" he asked. "That was the deal." He laughed until she stopped it with kisses. The long, slow strokes of his tongue in her anxious mouth—the sweetness of sliding her hands under his shirt, finding all that bare, familiar skin.

They did not bother to undress, only pushed her skirts up and untied his codpiece. Richard pinned her wrists down, playing the conqueror; she arched to meet him. "Oh, that is *good*," he gasped out. "You are so ready!"

"Very," she agreed, clasping him to her heart where he belonged.

The teasing and coquetting had not yet worn through for King Henry. It had for Anne Boleyn, though. She found it increasingly difficult to maintain her facade in the face of so much blatant hatred shown her by the city of London. She was a favorite target of their chamber pots or other refuse when she rode in town; none yelled "gardy loo"* before flinging their garbage down when Nan Bullen rode the streets. The king's heavy-handed overtures were grating on her nerves, too; she felt invaded, assaulted. He had put on weight these last few years and while not yet obese, seemed bulky and lumbering as a bear to her in his hugely padded coats and doublets.

He never touched Anne without her thinking: *I can bear this for the weight of a crown on my head. I can bear anything for a crown, even this hulking ape.*

The king's self-pride was so touchy! Anne could never cross him, never outhunt or outgame him, though in reality she could outwit, outthink, and outreact him a dozen times a minute. Always having to appear smaller, weaker, and stupider galled her; in a year or two when she was queen, she would *show* him, she thought. When she was queen she would eat as much as she wished, swear all she liked, ban from Court those who mocked her. And she would let Great Harry know her mind at last.

No more being humiliated by the Spanish dowd, either. Anne had stayed at Bridewell Palace for the holidays and

---

*From the French "Gardez-l'eau," meaning look out for water.

Henry had bedecked her with gowns, jewels, and gifts (she had paid Norfolk back at last). He had looked splendid in a new coat of gold brocade lined with lynx; the first time she had actually found him physically appealing. How the two of them sparkled together, she could well remember it. Anne had gathered her partisans about her, the courtiers and ladies who saw her star rising and came courting her to gain the king's ear. How they danced, what music they made!

But it was still Catherine of Aragon who sat beside Henry at Christmas Court beneath a gorgeously embroidered cloth of state. Still Catherine whom the crowds lined up to see, screaming, "God save Her Grace!" Catherine they called the most English of queens—*One has to go back to John of Gaunt to find her English blood,* Anne thought spitefully. *I am all English! I have more of this country's blood in my veins than the damned king! I can give him the sons she cannot, and still they prefer her!*

The giggling spells were coming closer together now. She tried to work them off by riding, dancing, but her nervous energy only seemed to increase through exertion, making her pace Greenwich Palace's ceramic-tiled floors long after everyone else was abed.

In all of her worries and fancies she saw her cousin Kathryn Chase before her. The queen would be divorced and gone soon enough; the people could be brought around to loving Anne (she thought) through plentiful money and food granted them. But there remained a diehard group of the queen's supporters and they all seemed centered around Kathryn.

She was polite all right, but she never responded to Anne's dinner invitations. Never attended her intimate parties where the noblest-born in the land sought Anne's advice, her favor. Men had never objected to Anne, but their wives were harder to win over; she could have used a cooler, more experienced hand than her own on those occasions, would have loved to greet her guests alongside Kathryn, who was widely liked.

Mary Brandon, the king's sister, hated her. Mary's husband Charles backed Anne, but sweet-tempered Mary, who had never raised her voice or done an unkind deed, made Anne's life a merry hell whenever she visited Court. *Nan, fetch me this; Nan, fetch me that*. Snubbing her, ordering her about by virtue of far superior rank. And her aunt Elizabeth Stafford, Norfolk's wife and duchess, called Anne a whore to her face, "and no niece of mine!" She went so far as to say,

"Thank Jesu I was not born a Howard and am no real blood of yours, else I should hang the both of us in shame!"

But everyone liked Kathryn. If only she could win Kathryn over, Kat was so stodgy, so reliable, so respectable. With Kat back it would be more like the carefree old days when they ran and tumbled together, climbed fences, tore their skirts, were scolded in tandem. Kathryn had taught her to embroider, Kathryn was her cousin, flesh of her flesh. *Family*, like a pillar to lean on. Family should stick together whenever there was opposition.

Women liked Kathryn and hated Anne. Men were so easy to beguile, Anne could turn her smoldering dark gaze on them and wordlessly make them feel taller, stronger, more attractive, willing to wait hand and foot on her. But women saw through her ploys; only Kathryn had ever genuinely liked and loved her and now the *like* seemed gone.

She cried out to her mother one night, "Kat is the only woman who was ever my friend—I must have her back, I must!"

"She was reared by the queen, Dear, you must give her time," Elizabeth soothed.

But there was no time left her, for Wolsey caught Anne out and in desperation she knew she must turn to her cousin.

Some years earlier the then-pope had declared Henry Tudor "Defender of the Faith" for a book Henry had written lashing out against the heresies of Martin Luther. Anne was a secret Lutheran, though Henry despised the outlawed faith. She dared not let him know where her religious sympathies lay and so had forbidden tracts and books smuggled to her at Court in sewing baskets. One day the inevitable happened, because of Wolsey's spy service and huge bribes: a servant spilled the secret to the cardinal.

Wolsey himself crept to Anne's deserted apartments one afternoon, plucked from its hiding place *The Obedience of a Christian Man*, one of her many proscribed books. To make matters easier for him, he found that the telltale servant had used Anne's initialed falcon book stamp to mark the inside leaf.

That night the servant confessed to Anne, fearing she might be burnt or hanged because of him. "Burnt?" Anne shrilled. "Hanged? That has not happened recently to heretics in England, fool! But they are forced to do public penance, publicly recant, and they are never, ever crowned queen of England! God help me, I am ruined! That damnable, interfering Wolsey has ruined me. . . . Well, I shall fix My Lord Cardinal. It shall be the dearest book he ever bought, I shall have him assassinated, boiled in oil, shot, strangled . . ."

The manservant fled into the night while Elizabeth Boleyn took her daughter by the shoulders. "Calm yourself, Anne, you are overreacting again. Kathryn has been at Court since childhood, I shall go ask her opinion on what to do."

"No—no, I must be the one to go. Give me your gray velvet cloak with the fox fur; perhaps no one will recognize me. I do not want Wolsey arresting me before I can speak with the king, and I do not wish to be seen attending Kathryn and thus compromise her with the queen, or she will hate me. Lock up after me, lest they come with a writ."

She fled in her mother's gray cloak, scratched frantically on the Stoneleigh apartment's door until admitted. "Kat, are you alone?"

Kathryn, pregnant and drowsing before the fire, nodded and let her in. "What is it?" she demanded. Anne spilled the news in a torrent of tears and babbling.

"You are in very grave danger, Wolsey hates all the Howards, and you and Norfolk most," Kathryn told her.

"What shall I do?"

"First thing, get a grip on yourself. You must stop the weeping and giggling or the king will have nothing to do with you. Take deep breaths, Anne, like this—yes, that is good, like that. Now listen to me: you must go straight from me to the king or else Wolsey will beat you there. Burst right in on him, throw yourself at his feet saying you have done a foolish thing, and must seek his sage advice."

They sank down on the warm hearthstones, holding hands as they had done in childhood. "Must I really say *sage*?" Anne asked irritably, wiping her cheek on her shoulder.

"*Yes*. When he asks how he can advise you, tell him that you have been curious about his religious viewpoints but did not dare ask him about matters of such import. He will like that, discussing religion fascinates him, makes him feel good. Tell him that in private you began trying to read various books he was for and against; admit to having forbidden books but say they are a muddle to you, that you do not understand them and need help. At the very end, explain that your manservant, book stamp, and a book have vanished and you fear the man will attempt blackmail. *Then* burst into tears."

"He likes to feel merciful, does he not? And he likes to

lecture on God's word, as though he learned it at God's own knee. But must I appear so weak and witless?"

"Why not?" Kathryn asked wryly. "The rest of us have to."

Anne squeezed Kathryn's hands so tightly they hurt. "If this succeeds," she said fervently, "you shall have titles, a manor house—you are my cousin, you must have something better than a tiny cottage and a knighted husband—"

"Hush, I will not be rewarded for being disloyal to the queen!"

"—or perhaps I could get Arthur released from the Tower where he has languished so many years," Anne gabbled on. She climbed to her feet and helped herself to Kathryn's washbasin, splashing away signs of tears. Then she used her cousin's paint pot, adjusted her French hood, and stepped boldly outside.

Anne followed her instructions with several spectacular embellishments, not the least of which was letting the king go sexually farther with her than ever before, though still denying him the main prize.

It ended with her more firmly entrenched than ever in his favor, while Wolsey's short, swift decline commenced.

20

On Monday, the twenty-first of June 1529, Henry the Eighth, by grace of God, King of England, Ireland, Wales, and Calais, and his wife Queen Catherine of Aragon, faced each other at last in the legatine court.

It was Midsummer and their twentieth coronation anniversary.

Catherine's pleas to have the case tried in Rome had come to naught. Henry, furious with Rome's years of dawdling, had demanded the prelates of England call their own court. Not daring refuse, they did.

Henry opened the legatine court that morning at the Blackfriars' Priory in London. Seated beneath a red tinsel cloth of state, he announced, "I have a greater desire for justice concerning this matter than any man alive, My Lords, but I must be delivered from doubt concerning the sanctity of my so-called marriage to my brother's widow, as it endangers the legitimacy of my said heirs and the future of the crown of England."

Catherine of Aragon entered too soon. Little, square-shaped, she looked indomitable in a gown of plush blue velvet she had worn when her nephew Emperor Charles the Fifth visited England several years earlier. It had been made in the German style to commemorate Charles' German holdings and was slashed all across the bodice and upper sleeves, each ribbon of fabric held together by a thumbnail-sized diamond. In between a heavy silk samite shift peeked out, crusted with white-on-white embroidery.

The effect on the court was audible, for she owned no more queenly gown. *I have not been the king's harlot these twenty years,* she had exclaimed when digging through her wardrobe for a suitable ensemble. *They will not make of my daughter a bastard! I want none of my pious blacks and dove-grays, I want a gown to proclaim that I am and shall ever remain rightful Queen of England!*

She wore a broad, flat German cap of silver tissue drawn through blue velvet slashings; a diamond near the size of a baby's fist pinned the brim back from her face. Beneath it and two dozen white plumes her hair hung loose, waist-length, a pale, grayed ginger.

All attention leapt to her. The king forgot his closing comments to the court, though his wife had not yet uttered a single syllable. Her mere presence, so gorgeously gotten up, so defiant, unhinged him, and it was all he could do to grind to an incoherent halt.

When the court lay silent, she went straight to Henry, knelt at his feet. "I kneel before you under this cloth of state where according to the laws of God and man I have the right to sit at your side. My hair is worn as a virgin bride's is to remind you of what you already know: that I was a very maid when first I came to you, and no true bride of Prince Arthur's. I pray thee, for all the loves that have been between us, to let me and our child of my body know justice. . . ."

The audience hardly drew breath while she spoke at length. When finished, Queen Catherine stooped lower, kissed each of the king's twitching shoes in turn, and glided from the courtroom. The legatine herald finally remembered his duty, hammered with his staff on the floor, shouting out, "Catherine, Queen of England, come into the court! Catherine, Queen of England—"

The daughter of Isabella the warrior-queen halted in the doorway, jabbed a majestic forefinger at the unfortunate herald. "You hear, My Lords? This man at least still knows my rightful title! I rest my case."

The crimson-cheeked herald, wilting beneath the king's gaze, whispered, "Catherine, Queen of England, come into the court. Catherine, Queen . . ."

Waiting Londoners flung open the outer doors of Blackfriars' for the queen. Women threw herbs and flowers, men cast down their caps and cloaks for her to walk on. "God bless Your Grace!"

"Fight for all us good wives, Queen Kate! If you fall, we all fall!"

"What God has joined together, let no man split asunder!"

"God bless the Queen's Majesty!"

"Yes, bless her!"

Catherine remembered suddenly that twenty years ago to the day, her husband had first said he loved her and made her his wife and queen. *Yes, what God has joined let no man dare sunder!* she thought, crossing herself as she descended the stairs into the midst of her loyal ladies-in-waiting. The proud tilt of her chin said she had given as good as she got. *She might win yet,* Kathryn thought, hurrying to keep up with her royal mistress.

The legatine court, uneasy at opening without papal authority, adjourned until October without accomplishing much. Long before October, however, there arrived word from the pope that Henry's prelates had no authority to try the case and it must come before Rome.

"It is that wretched Wolsey's fault, he would not see me queen," Anne shouted at Henry. She had never shouted in his presence before; he had thought her incapable of such untoward anger. "He did not even try to see the pope that time he journeyed toward Rome," she continued. "He defies your wishes with his sloth and negligence, he undermines your authority and if you are too great a fool to see that—"

She had gone too far. His eyes told her that. With all of her highstrung actress's abilities, Anne wept very easily and so turned on the flow now, casting herself down at Henry's feet. She laid her head on his knee, knowing how that softened him. "Forgive me, Your Grace. It is just that I am frustrated, being stopped again like this, when I so love and desire you and would be your wife."

"Be my wife in all but name then," Henry urged, running his hands up her soft French bodice, so delightfully unencumbered by stays, buckram, and corsets. How little her waist was, how tender the flesh he pressed through scant layers of velvet and linen!

Anne was so relieved that she allowed him to chiefly undress her, caressing her slender body both over and under her shift. Stopping him proved difficult, and afterward she avoided him days on end, fearing he would take her by force. She must not lose that jewel she bargained with and he must not think her too close to giving in, she told herself. Back to arm's length for the time being. In response, fearing he had offended her, Henry came wooing more tenderly than ever, fetching along stacks of opulent gifts.

Though Anne did not at first realize it, he had heeded her accusations against Wolsey. It began to seem to him that indeed the cardinal overreached himself in many matters and persecuted Anne.

The case against Wolsey was furthered when time came for Henry's yearly summer progress. Trapped between two iron-willed women, the king had no choice but to take both of them along. Queen Catherine did not plead or demand, only showed up at his elbow, taking it for granted that she would accompany him. Anne had to beg, weep, and work the king's passion into an imploding frenzy before he allowed her along. In the end Catherine rode at his side beneath a cloth of state while Anne was forced to tag morosely behind, surrounded by the rest of Catherine's women. She did not even have the comfort of Kathryn's grudging company, for her cousin had recently borne a daughter and remained behind in London.

Cardinal Wolsey was not invited along, as had been the custom on numerous summer progresses prior to this one. He followed anyway, arriving at Grafton only to be told there was no room for him and he must leave. Still he made his way to the king's chambers, arranging to speak further with him the next morning.

Anne's spies informed her of the arranged meeting. She rose next day before dawn, had a sumptuous picnic packed, summoned fifty of the merriest lords and ladies. They woke the king with gentle madrigals and rounds outside his window, lured him out to his white stallion and on to the surrounding forest glades.

She kept him out all day, finally causing the waiting Wolsey to admit defeat and return to York Place.

In October he was ordered to surrender his chancellorship of England, the chancellor's Great Seal, and his properties.

But he beat the orders, sending all of it to the king ahead of time, of his own will.

In November a small council was sent to Wolsey at York Place, where he yet lingered with his last few loyal devotees. At Anne's request, her uncle Norfolk sent as head of the council the new Earl of Northumberland—her old suitor, Harry Percy.

Wolsey sat at his thick-legged dinner table, admiring the wood's sheen. Perhaps, he thought, he could take this favorite piece of furniture with him, wherever he was headed.

The double doors to the hall banged open. Wolsey, ripe pear in hand, stared up to see pale, implacable Harry Percy approach. The boy had aged and hardened, he thought at first, then: *He looks like death. Whose?*

"Yes, Northumberland?" he asked, none-too-concerned.

"My Lord Cardinal, you once separated me from something I valued greatly," said the hollow-cheeked man. "I am here to return the favor."

"What is left to rob me of?" Wolsey asked, sounding patient, but his rings bit into the half-eaten pear.

"Your freedom and your life, my Lord Cardinal. I have here a writ signed by the king to convey you to the Tower of London on charges of treason in accepting the pope's authority over that of King Henry."

The pear splatted to the floor, lay bruised and abandoned. It remained there as the dazed Wolsey was dragged to mule, then barge; it lay, furred with dust and dehydrated when the cardinal first writhed with the agony of dysentary in his dripping cell.

It was swept away the day dysentary killed the cardinal, sparing him the block and axe—the day the double doors were finally reopened to clean in preparation for the king's visit.

Wolsey's dying words were whispered all across England. Hoarse, gasping in pain, he had murmured to his confessor, "My only regret is that His Grace did not marry Boleyn two years ago. Then I should have had my revenge on that black-eyed bitch by now, for, upon finally achieving her, how swiftly he shall tire of her!"

The cardinal was not even buried before Henry took Anne to tour the deserted York Place. They walked through openmouthed, for even two people so used to splendor could not fail to be affected by the quarter mile of tapestries on the walls. "Half a ton of gold plate, too." Henry marveled at the cardinal's dishes, and he was not far wrong. Forty-foot trestle tables, hundred-year-old chairs inches deep with carved knights, maidens, and monsters—religious robes crusted with bullion embroidery and precious gems, so many that when the king tried one on he feigned tottering beneath its great weight. "Why, you would make a fine cardinal, My Lord!" Anne cried out, arms wide to him. "And I think you would make an excellent pope, too, with the authority to make the king of England my husband!"

He froze; she wondered if she had gone too far again. Henry's shrewd, small blue eyes narrowed, mouth puckering in thought. "Do you suppose," he began and stopped. "No, no, 'twas a frivolous notion. Help me out of this monstrous cope, pretty Nan, and let us choose tapestries with which to decorate your Court apartments. Is this not a fine house we now have?"

"It is like unto a palace," she agreed, relieved he was not angry.

Henry's face shone. "Then, Anne, let us make it *into* a palace! Even more huge and sumptuous than it is now . . . we shall clear the neighboring lands and cottages, build clear down to the water's edge . . . gatehouses, many long galleries to walk in—I despise these old-fashioned palaces where one room opens onto the next so there is never any privacy. Yes, several long galleries in which to hang paintings and walk in inclement weather and over at that end of York Place I shall . . ."

Thus was begun Whitehall, which eventually covered twenty-three acres.

And thus was planted the notion in Henry's head that he and not the pope should be the ultimate authority in England.

It was the child who woke them so that they discovered what had happened.

Windsor Castle lay dark and silent that July morning of 1531. But there sounded one last clink of spur on stone floor, startling little Elizabeth Stoneleigh. She stood up with a frightened wail in the cradle she had nearly outgrown, rubbing both fists into her eyes. Richard, the faster to awaken (for Kathryn had had a late day with the queen), stumbled from bed, hefted the child up. She tucked her little coppery head, so like his own, under his chin. "What is it, Sweetheart?" he asked and yawned. "Why do you—"

He stopped. There was a flurry of sounds, many horses

moving away from the castle through Windsor Great Park. "Kathryn?" he asked, puzzled. "Kathryn, wake up. Something is amiss."

She sat, rubbing her eyes as her nearly two-year-old daughter had done moments before. "Where are all those horses going? It is too early, too dark for a hunt," she mumbled.

Richard thrust Elizabeth into her arms. "I mean to find out what is happening. Here, Wife."

It was awhile before he returned. Kathryn and Elizabeth were both fully awake by then, and Isabella had joined them in the Woodville bed. They sat with candles lit, a golden haze haloing them, so that Richard, returning, thought at once how lovely his womenfolk were. "They are all gone," he quickly said. "The king, the Boleyns, their sycophants. All of their baggage, beds, and horses as well. Only those loyal to Queen Catherine remain. The chief porter knows nothing of this night flight."

"Every trunk? Every bed?" Kathryn demanded. "You mean—"

"Yes, they have moved on to some other royal residence or gone on summer progress without half the Court. Is Maria de—I mean Lady Willoughby—still visiting the queen? I think you had best wake her and then Her Grace."

He was right. It would be easier on proud Catherine of Aragon coming from her oldest friend. Kathryn said, "Richard, ride spying after the king to see where he has gone, I will take the children. My blue-gray linen damask, Isabella, please. Elizabeth, let me scrub your face before we go—" Richard kissed them all and left.

Maria de Salinas said, when informed, "This is terrible news. I think His Grace means to leave her behind forever and live openly with that black-eyed whore. Forgive me, Kathryn, I know she is your cousin but she is a whore and a bitch and breaking the queen's heart. Oh, this will kill my dear Catalina! How can I tell her of this insult, this blow to her pride and position?"

"I suggest you tell her in Spanish so that the others do not understand until she has had time to hear and assimilate. Maria, I wonder if they will take us from her."

Maria's thin, pretty face showed sudden strain. "Would the king be so unjust? Service to the queen is all I have to do with my life now my husband is dead and my daughter, Catherine, placed in the Brandons' household—where Charles

Brandon daily preaches at her about how wrong our royal mistress is to fight the king on the matter of divorce!"

In her excitement, Maria's voice had risen. "My ladies?" Catherine of Aragon sleepily called from the next room. "My ladies, what is it?"

They raced to her side. Several maids-of-honor slept on pallets near the bed; Kathryn and Maria stepped over them and drew back the bed curtains. The queen sat, gray-streaked hair tumbling over her trembling shoulders. Kathryn thought, *Why, she has greatly aged.* Counting on her fingers she realized her once-young mistress would be forty-six in the next winter.

Maria broke the news of the desertion in Castilian Spanish, which set the maids to sitting and whispering—all except Jane Seymour, Kathryn observed. There was a level-headed girl, and loyal to the queen. They exchanged worried glances.

Lady Rutland entered then, half-dressed, stumbling and bearing a letter with the king's personal seal on the back. No woman of the Court would consider setting foot outside of her private apartments so clad or with her hair undone. *Yet here we all are,* Kathryn thought grimly, *looking like dairymaids. These are serious matters indeed to make even Lady Rutland, the stickler-for-details, forget her cap. And she does not even know the root of the problem yet.*

The queen read, then fisted the letter in one quick crumpling motion. "It is not over yet," she said clearly. "They will see who is still queen and His Grace's wife! Whether she bears him children now or waits until he has gone through some form of marriage with her, the results will be the same: their offspring will be bastards while my Mary grows to rule England! She is great Isabella the Warrior's granddaughter, she was not yet three months old when she grabbed for the scepter the king held over her. They will not make of me a harlot and my child a bastard!"

She threw the letter down. Maria handed the queen into a brocade nightgown, following as she started from the room. "No, wait," Catherine of Aragon said, turning back. "Lady Howard—Kathryn—read the letter."

Kathryn stooped, retrieving it unwillingly. ". . . and in closing, Madam, let us say that we wish certain jewels and possessions of your person and say that you may take any thirty of your ladies to The Moore, excepting only the Baroness Willoughby who is to immediately return to Parham

Old Hall near Framlingham, while my lady Boleyn requests the presence of her cousin Lady Kathryn at . . ."

She dared not cast it into the fire lest the queen need to refer back to certain instructions in it later. So she dropped it and slowly stepped upon it, grinding her heel down. Behind her, Isabella gasped at this sign of her mother's scorn upon the king's seal.

Little Elizabeth toddled forward. "Bad letter! Lissy help!" And she stamped on it until she fell on all fours.

The queen fled in tears, Maria close behind. Kathryn picked Elizabeth up, smoothed the child's hair and looked into her green, slanting eyes, so like Richard's. "Lissy see queen!" her youngest daughter insisted merrily.

Dry-eyed with the awfulness of impending loss, Kathryn kissed Elizabeth. "Not any more, Lissy will not," she said softly.

Anne Boleyn turned on the king with a harpy's tongue, mocked his clothes, his riding and hunting abilities, even his virility. "Perhaps it was not Catherine's fault she did not bear living sons—perhaps it was the fault of a man who is not even sincere about leaving her and so dangles me on without honor, without accomplishing our ends!" she railed at Henry one night.

This was no longer the sweet-spirited girl he had fallen in love with so long ago. The nervous giggles had begun to grate on his nerves like hard cheese on metal slots—crumbling, breaking into annoying little clumps and bits. He saw her other side now—the satiric shrew who could never leave well enough alone.

"Oh?" he asked, cocking an eyebrow at her. "Perhaps you do not wish to wait yet a while longer and then be made queen?" He loosened the waist of his short half-breeches, unbuttoned a few more diamond buttons on his doublet. They had just partaken of a heavy feast and he found himself needing to stand and stretch. Odd, only last month when this suit had been made for him it had fitted well, but now he found himself thinking the tailor had scrimped on fabric, cut it too small. Same problem with his armorers, always squeezing him in, cheating on the amount of steel.

Anne stamped her foot at him. "Oh, no, I know your pride, your love of show. You would not have the whole world know you regret your choice before you have even bedded me or begotten—oh, my sweet Hal! Say you do not regret me!"

He had sworn to make her his sole mistress and he had; he, the most amorous of men, had not even slept with the queen in so long he could hardly remember the last time. Jacquetta de Gael had been the last. Remembering her now he missed her fiercely. That summer of the Sweat when she had lost her boys he had not dared send her so much as a trinket or one of his many doctors in case Anne heard and took it amiss. Through Kathryn Chase he had kept track of his favorite former mistress, though, for Kathryn saw through his seemingly disinterested inquiries and kept him up to date. So he knew the mistress of Windsgeat lived and once again prospered, though he dared not ride down Windsor Hill to see for himself.

Jacquetta had never screamed at him, never satirized his clothes or riding. In fact, she had always been so perky and witty with him, seeking his advice each day on what she should wear, asking would he prefer her in the red Spanish or golden Italian. She brought him such little niceties, too, horehound comfits when he had a cough, sugar plums, ginger suckets. Big gifts, too; once he had reached for his hat in the morning to find a whopping table-cut diamond pinned to it. Another time a new Windsgeat White had suddenly shown up in his stables, bearing princely trappings and accompanied by two matching white Russian wolfhounds—"borzois," she called them, assuring him that her couriers had smuggled them out of savage Muscovy at severe risk to limb and life.

And the tricks that glorious, golden woman knew in bed . . . !

He let Anne fret awhile longer, recalling Jacquetta's finer points while stewing in Anne's many petty unkindnesses. "Regret my choice?" he asked with a show of indifference. "Oh, perhaps I do. After all, I would feel cheated, did I wait so long for you only to find you barren in the long run."

"I will not risk having bastards! No king takes a queen trailing bastards behind her up the church nave!"

He stood, stretched, felt a keen sense of pleasure in her discomfort. Henry stuck his thumbs through the button loops on his ermine-lined coat, made a gesture of boredom. "I do not see how I can marry you without knowing you are fertile, Lady Anne."

She began to weep in earnest. "I know your ways! The moment my belly is big you will wed me to some stable-sweeper or lowly chamberer, I will never be queen!"

"That will not be, I will never desert you and a child of mine."

"*Mine*," not "ours." Was she really losing him then? *Hold some promise out to him, make him snap at the bait again,* she told herself in desperation. "My Lord," she said suddenly, craftily, "I would not so fear seduction by you, did I know I had something of my own to cling to, should you grow weary of my presence. I know you soon tire of the women's beds you have achieved and I do not wish to end like my sister and Bessie Blount, tucked away with an unwanted husband in the country far from the center of things. Of course, they were both widowed and able, then, to wed a man of their choice . . . But if I had something of my own, some lands, some title to cling to and support my child, should you leave me pregnant and alone . . ."

He was hurt that she presumed him so great a scoundrel, and seized her by her narrow waist. "I will never abandon you, Anne! No, nor any child of ours, for he will be king of England!"

Forcing her chin up, he kissed her deeply. *How long?* she thought, acquiescent in his heavy arms. *How much longer can I draw him on like this? How soon before he stops snapping at the bait?*

How long before he realized she hated being touched, resented the many attempted invasions of her flesh, her soul, her privacy? How long before he realized she feared him and so wavered under the strain of role-playing with terror, greed and anger ruling her entire life?

And yet . . . she enjoyed his companionship, for he invigorated her. *I could almost love him if only he did not let me twine him around my finger,* Anne thought, frowning against his cheek. But that was the opposite reason she had fallen for Harry Percy those eight long years ago: he had seemed so pliant, so easy.

Had things really changed so much? Had *she* changed so much that she hardly knew herself now? *The rules of the game are altered,* Anne thought, wild with dislike in the royal embrace. *I need help—I must make one last bid to hold him and thus gain the crown—*

21
1 September, 1532
Windsor Castle

Kathryn fidgeted as she awaited the ceremonies' beginning. It was difficult to be so old—thirty-two—and pregnant; her feet and the small of her back ached from dancing last night at Anne's eve-before-investiture ceremony. Now she stood in Saint George's Chapel in the heart of pagan green Windsor, wishing she could sit.

Her grandfather, Edward the Fourth, was buried to one side of the altar, and Elizabeth Woodville next to him. That made her feel better; family pride made her lift her head, trying to ignore the nagging pain in the pit of her spine.

"I told you not to dance so hard," Richard murmured, offering his shoulder for her to lean on. He added, "Can you imagine the king giving Anne a *man*'s title?"

"Of course. That way she need rely on no man to take it from her."

Anne Boleyn, hair streaming to her waist as befit a virgin, knelt on a golden cushion before the altar. Her deep red gown, of costliest Venetian velvet, fanned out behind her. *A good color,* Kathryn approvingly told herself once more. She had helped Mr. Scutte the royal tailor design it to best flatter Anne's figure and coloring and go with the investiture robes.

Bishop Stephen Gardiner, one of King Henry's new, favored prelates, with Wolsey dead, pronounced Anne Marquis of Pembroke with precedence over all other Marquises in England. That was not the sentence in the Letter of Patent that caused the crowd to murmur, though, it was slow realization that between the words "title to be inherited by" and "heirs male" the customary phrase "legally begotten" had been left out.

The king stepped forward amidst the murmurs and laid a neatly scrolled coronet upon Anne's dark head. She beamed up at him. The Duke of Norfolk then handed Henry the ermine-lined red velvet mantle of a marquis, which Henry lowered across her slender shoulders.

Kathryn, groaning, kissed Richard's cheek. "Excuse me, Dear, I have to walk out with all the other ladies. At least I am fortunate in not being a peer's wife, that saves me carrying her heavy train."

He smiled but mention of titles made him feel bad. She was still Kathryn Chase, Lady Howard to the Court; he had no real title to give her his name. "Stop it, Richard, a Letter of Patent will not make me love you any more," she scolded, and moved ahead to join the others. She walked with the "mere-ladies" as Jane Seymour called them, being one herself; the two of them mouthed those words at each other, grinned, and maintained their snail's pace far behind the duchesses and countesses.

Poor, dear Jane, Kathryn thought, eyeing her young friend. *She has no money, little title to speak of, and she is chinless as a rabbit. I have known her since she was hardly tall enough to help lace a gown and I like her. She would make a fine, steady wife for my James.*

She had suggested it and James had turned his nose up at the idea. Edmund and his Blount wife had had no living children in their years of marriage; James had his eye on being Lord Howard of Howard House some day, and too good for mere-lady Jane.

They moved on to the all-day festivals. Kathryn was required a dozen places at once, first at Anne's side, then running here to fetch some countess, next giving orders to a steward, for Anne had made her Mistress of Protocol. The receiving line had to be closely guarded, lest some viscount and baron fight it out over who came first; ladies-in-waiting had to go *here*, not there—

By evening Kathryn was having mild contractions, months early. She was not unduly alarmed, as she had suffered them throughout pregnancy with Elizabeth and still delivered a healthy child, but it was an uncomfortable annoyance on so busy a day. There was no slipping off before midnight, either; Anne called her ladies-in-waiting to usher her to bed.

Anne went with the assurance of a bride. Her sallow skin was radiant, the dark doe-eyes sparkled. Once in her apartments, she insisted Anne Parr brush out the famous black Boleyn hair, then snapped at her for taking so long at it. "Give me that brush, I can do better myself! Rutland, fetch me my new black velvet nightgown with the fox lining. Aunt Elizabeth of Norfolk, I should like my silk shift with the white-on-white embroidery." She eyed Kathryn in her lavish gilt hand-mirror. "Well, Cuz, what think you of all of this?"

Pale, beginning to sway, Kathryn said, "I think it all a fine show, Anne. Now, if you would excuse me, I am not well. The child—"

"Hang the child! I am sick of hearing about everyone else's children, I will make my own now and then he must marry me! Get out, all of you—get out—no, Seymour, you stay. You are good with clothes and things and I wish to look my best for His Grace tonight."

Kathryn and the others started for the door. "What time should we awaken you?" Kathryn asked, voice slurred by pain.

"You shall not awaken me at all, I shall finally have the king in my bed. Get out, all of you, except Jane Seymour!"

Pale little hands, stronger than they looked, eased under Kathryn's nearest arm. "Lean on me, Kat," Jane Seymour said. "That is it, like that. Easy now. Lady Rutland, please help me with her, I cannot hold her. She is slipping away—"

Yes, slipping away, Kathryn thought as the room spiraled.

Slipping down into darkness, into a buzzing giddiness that sounded like so many bees . . .

"Get back in here, Seymour!" Anne shouted.

"There is blood everywhere," Lady Rutland whispered to Jane.

Eleven-year-old Isabella Howard came running from a pack of maids of honor. She shouted for her stepfather, who soon arrived, little Elizabeth on his shoulder. "Richard, she is losing the baby," Isabella cried out. He slung the child into her arms; she lowered her to the marble floor.

Isabella knelt, that she might be her little sister's size. "Listen to me, Lissy: do you know that little blue casque of mine? The blue leather one Aunt 'Quetta gave me?" The little girl nodded. "It is on the chest in Mother's apartments. How are you with your numbers? Can you read Numbers twenty-two and two-seventeen for me and bring them here at once?"

Still nodding, the three-year-old toddled away to obey.

Blood of a too-soon baby on the marble floor, Jane Seymour thought worriedly as Richard Stoneleigh scooped his wife up. In one room this happening, and in the next, a king about to blood himself on the virgin he had pursued so long.

She made the sign of the cross before rushing to get the door for Richard.

By January the entire country knew Anne Boleyn was pregnant. How could they help knowing when she had gigglingly announced as much in front of so large an audience? "I have a great craving for apples," she had cried to her cousin Thomas Wyatt upon meeting him in the Long Gallery at Greenwich one day. "The king says it means I must be with child—what do you think?" And she had cackled wildly, triumphantly—*Just like a witch's shriek,* Jane Seymour reported to her two favorite brothers.

What all of England did not know, however, was that the king, wearying of the wait for divorce, had married Anne in secret. Even Thomas Boleyn found it a ridiculous gesture and said as much to his brother-in-law, Norfolk. "Peace, Tom," Norfolk answered, swirling malmsey in his cup. "She will achieve the crown yet, you will see. Then all our waiting will be done with. King Henry is about to declare himself spiritual head of England, independent of the pope's power. Now reel your jaw in like a proper—what did he make you this time? Oh, yes, Earl of Wiltshire. Sit up straight, Tom, act like a proper earl. And listen to this. . . ."

It seemed that a priest named Thomas Cranmer had long held that Henry's marriage to Catherine was invalid. He was about to receive confirmation from Rome on his appointment as Archbishop of Canterbury, which would make him chief prelate of England; Henry Tudor would then declare himself head of the English Church with Cranmer as his next-in-authority.

Upon being made archbishop that spring, Cranmer called his trumped-up court, announcing that Henry's marriage to Catherine was invalid and had been from the first. Therefore the king had been a bachelor and free agent when he married Anne Boleyn at midnight in Saint George's Chapel: therefore this new marriage was valid.

After eight years of plotting and five of convoluted legal maneuvers, Anne Boleyn was about to be crowned queen of England. "I must have a grand coronation to make up for that miserable, sneak-thief wedding," she informed her husband. "To convince the people that I really am queen, I must have a coronation such as England as never seen! When they see me carried in state through the streets of London, great-bellied with their future king, they will learn to love me. They must!"

"How will you make them love you when your own cousin does not?" Henry asked coolly. "How will you make Kathryn Chase show you the kind of loyalty she bore Catherine?"

"I will raise her higher—oh, say I may, My Lord! We must

make something of her husband, give him some title and place that she is ranked with greater ladies than before. I must put her in debt to me!"

Sir Richard Stoneleigh was abruptly yanked from the king's offices where he was spending a miserable day trying to decipher Thomas Boleyn's handwriting in the household expense ledgers. "Congratulations. They are making you a baron," George Boleyn informed him.

"Why? I have not done anything. Has Kathryn performed some especial favor to A—to Her Grace?"

"No, it is the fact that she will *not* perform. The two of you are now proud possessors of Whitbourne in Kent, which makes you Lord and Lady Whitbourne. Now you will not have to listen to her called by Ned Howard's title any more."

"That is the nicest part of it. 'Baroness Whitbourne,' hm, I hope Kat likes it."

George grinned. Despite jealousy, he liked Richard. "She will hate being indebted to Anne, she will kick and scream."

"No, just get very pale and quiet. But later on I will hear doors slamming and perhaps something breaking. When is the investiture?"

"Coronation week in May. Are you still hard at work in the tiltyard? As a baron you will be expected to joust in the tourney celebrating Anne's crowning."

"Yes, as a matter of fact your uncle Norfolk *and* your lord father have both given me some thundering wallops to the head. I have gotten very good at ducking."

George threw his head back in a hearty laugh. "That sounds like both of them. By the way, Anne is also having Arthur Chase released from the Tower. He will be expected to joust, too, though with his father's attainder and execution he has no title left. Still, word is that the king will create a great many Knights of the Bath to celebrate, so you and Arthur may expect membership."

Richard kept smiling but there was little color in his face. "I know," George said drily. "You are thinking that the Garter dues and robes will break you financially, even with income from the baronial lands. Well, that cannot be helped, you will have to go into debt as everyone else does. At least Whitbourne is very fertile land, though the manor house is rather old and crumbling. Cheer up, man, you have a thousand acres to support your family now."

But Richard had a job at court, leaving him little time to ride thirty miles to Kent every time crops needed planting or reaping. Absentee landlords needed stewards, which cost money. Richard shrugged. "I suppose the first thing we will need to do with Whitbourne is sell half those acres. Otherwise we will have nothing to fund us for the coronation."

"You and Arthur have to come up with horses and armor, too," George said softly. "Go see Norfolk, will you? He is famous for helping those he likes. And it need not be an outright gift, if you are proud; if you like, he can loan you what you need. Of course, you will not find decent armor so quickly; you will have to get some flimsy, locally-made stuff."

Armor tragically was the least of Richard's worries. He found himself thinking how ironic it was that joining the peerage would bankrupt him, who had never had enough money to worry about such a thing before. He groaned at George. "I guess I had better go tell Kathryn before she hears about it from A—Her Grace," he said. "It was very nice of the king. I wonder what he wants."

After doing so much to please Anne and her family, King Henry looked about him and decided to now please himself. As Anne was too pregnant to risk riding on horseback, he decided to go hunting without her and leave coronation plans to reliable Norfolk.

Already he was weary of Anne's alternate moods of frenzied excitement and black sarcasm. She had not proved the prize he expected in bed, either. The first few months had been warm enough, for he had waited long to possess her and the thrill of the chase had whetted his appetite. But she was no sooner pregnant than he realized all her passion had been playacting. She stared at the painted ceiling in bed, grumbled, sighed repeatedly, mocked him if he tarried, laughed if he was quick. No matter how he tried he could not thaw her out. There had never been a woman he did not please, never one until now that he could stir no more than if she had icy spring water in her veins. *Cheated,* he thought angrily. *She cheated me, she is not upholding her end of the bargain.* Worse, what if she had only led him on for the crown, the child? Were all her words of love and passion false? Was this all he mattered to her—a circlet of metal set on her long black hair and a future king in her womb?

One bright May morning he crept from the royal apartments with a bow and full quiver of arrows. He called for his youngest de Gael colt to be saddled—Lugh, one of old Cernunnos' get. To saddle, to reins, and away through Windsor Great Park, the silent Muscovite hounds at heel. It seemed to Henry that he had never seen a bluer sky nor greener turf, like cornflowers and emeralds spread before him. Clouds loomed huge and white as palaces overhead, a good omen for his building Whitehall, he thought.

There was no disappointment in him when the dogs failed to catch anything he flushed from the woods. He loosed his peregrine at some doves, only to have her return empty-taloned; he laughed, stroked her downy breast and rehooded her. A strange excitement possessed him this glittering morning.

"It is so beautiful," he said aloud. Startled sparrows fled the sound of his voice; the hooded bird on his wrist screeched in longing and was still. The mossy oaks spread shade overhead, dappling horse and rider with blotches of silver. *I will wager Windsgeat is verdant as a lapful of emeralds this spring,* Henry thought, remembering. *Like emeralds worn on green velvet . . . I wonder if Jacquetta's hair still pops out of its jeweled caul with one flick of my wrist, and does it yet flow down to her naked rump? She must be but few years short of forty; I wonder, is she still buxom, golden, and steaming?*

As though Henry had spoken aloud, Lugh turned for Windsgeat. Perhaps he scented home or caught a whiff of his dam or old stablemates; perhaps he merely heard activity in the valley below and, horselike, wished to investigate. Or it could have been the call of a sorceress . . .

Without knowing how it happened, Henry Tudor found himself galloping for Windsgeat. From the Waendles, the Windsor lakes, he caught his first sight of her in years: a splendid woman whose brilliant amber hair reached past the waist of her gown.

Henry gave Lugh his head. Jacquetta came forward to greet them, sank in a curtsy. "Up, Countess!" the king merrily ordered. "You will ruin that gown of yours in the dew!"

She rose. He was astonished at the richness of her lands and apparel; crops had grown nearly to the house and all the trees were one-third again as large as on his last visit. (When had that been? In Twenty-four or five? Twenty-six? He could not recall.)

Her emeralds were as large as the last joint of his thumb, each framed in cloisonné plaques; the necklace wrapped around her neck twice before falling to her thighs. He saw that the whole of her slashed green velvet gown—a wonderful green, like new grass—was lined in gold tissue and that the silk shift pulled out through the slashwork was sheer as a thin glaze of ice. He could see the creamy mauve-gold of her flesh shine through, the violently pink nipples and pulsing blue veins. "You—you are a witch, madam. You grow younger and more beautiful while I age," he said almost humbly.

She leaned against his leg, his horse, caressed the heavy swell of calf and thigh muscles. "No, you will never age," she purred, and put her lips to his knee.

A boy appeared as if from nowhere, took the bird and Lugh. Henry dismounted without knowing he did so, watched his own hand picked up by Jacquetta and tugged toward the house. He followed with no will of his own.

The servants, all fabulously liveried in the de Gael black-and-gold, were lined up on both sides of the Great Hall as he entered. In one smooth motion they bowed, curtsied, cried out, "God Save His Grace the king!"

Who yells that in my own household? Henry asked himself. *Since when did anyone rush out to meet me without being ordered to?*

When had Anne last dressed for him and not herself? Jacquetta's dull green cotton velvet was all for him. So, too, the emeralds and transparent shift, the subtley applied face-paint and her hair scarcely drawn back from her face and falling to her rump in ringlets. She walked him across silk carpets, inches thick—only the de Gaels could afford to put their Turkey carpets on the floor instead of on tabletops, he mused to himself—through frescoed rooms, down a long gallery with breathtaking hammerbeam roof. The scent of everything overwhelmed him: Jacquetta's musk and eglantine, boughs of evergreen hanging from the ceiling beams, chamomile and lavender spread beneath the carpets. There was not a rush mat in sight, only acres of jewel-toned silks and wools on parquetry and marble floors.

Henry had never been toured through Windsgeat. He found himself dazzled. The many suits of armor going back four hundred years, the ancestral portraits, the dozens of brilliant new tapestries, all featuring erotic scenes from mythology. Queen Maeve sported with a dozen lovers, Leda leaned back in ecstasy as the swan ravished her. The Rape of Europa was graphic and literal; Dido straddled Aenaes in a manner never committed to tapestry before.

Through the fog of bedazzlement it came to Henry that Jacquetta was making a statement: *You can see I am not helpless, nor poor, nor weak, nor any kind of supplicant. I have power of my own; I only bring you here because it pleases me. I do not need you.*

She took him up broad stone stairs remaining from the days when Windsgeat had been an Anglo-Saxon abbey. Gargoyles leered at him, sheila-na-gigs squatted and exposed themselves from the stone rails and doorways. Up still farther, to a chamber of glowing auburn wood. Clouds of frankincense encircled him, brilliant brocades and tinsels gleamed on the enormous bed.

There were two maidservants awaiting them. They undressed Jacquetta slowly before his ensnared gaze, leaving her in silk bias-cut stockings and emeralds; he watched as they caressed her, rubbing precious unguents all over her cream-and-pink body. Then they turned to him, undressed him also, lingering even longer on his body.

Then they were gone and he was alone with her. She had not forgotten a single of her harem-tricks; he lingered in rapture's galleries a long time before she took him to its privy chamber. *Emeralds on velvet*, he thought at the first of many peaks. *She sent me that image, she called me here. They are right, she is a witch. Thank God!*

He was king, he need please no one but himself. But for once he wanted to give as much as receive, so he brought her to a pitch where she screamed his name, drew blood with nails and teeth. Afterward, lying exhausted across his chest, she murmured, "I have had nothing but boys in so long. What a great stallion of a man you still are."

Oddly, he sensed that she meant it and this was not one of her many ploys. Drained, released, drugged with pleasure, Henry chuckled. "There is no one like you, Jacquetta. I want you back at Court in time for the coronation." She raised her drowsy golden head to protest; he stilled her with a finger across her coral lips. "But I know running Windsgeat is a full-time occupation. So, since you have not asked, I will bring your damned brother home. He may even come to Court. The two of you shall fight it out privately over who stays home to go over the ledgers and who dances the bransle at my palaces which night. Perhaps thirteen years is enough time for even your thick-skulled, pigheaded de Gael brother to learn his lesson."

She sat, beautiful bare breasts quivering with emotion. "Your Grace, you amaze me!" she exclaimed, and climbed back onto him.

Henry, staggered to find himself surging into action once more, cried out, "Aye, Woman—and I am amazing *myself*, too!"

22

John de Gael came home in no lesser state than if he were Grand Sultan and all of England his courtyard.

There was his newest red-and-gold doublet and coat for one thing; not even the king usually dressed so loudly, so spectacularly. Observers fairly winced, though they envied the money that had gone into the ensemble. He rode a Windsgeat White that made Lugh look spindly and he had aged well, with only feathery-fine lines on his face and little gray in his chestnut hair. His wife, two sons, and one-hundred-and-seventy-one servants came with him; the meanest of his lackeys dressed better than the average baron.

He brought the king nine Flemish paintings of indescribable beauty and two dozen Flemish shirts with intricate borders of blackwork, stitches padded with silk stuffing, and designs picked out in seed pearls. Two dozen servants followed, unrolling a wool, silk, and bullion carpet made to fit the king's Painted Chamber where he slept at Westminster; the king's gifts ended with a sapphire hat ornament Henry admiringly called "large enough to eat dinner off of!"

Anne, who had not been able to wring white mules from Jacquetta by bribery or threats, was presented with four flawless ones to carry her coronation litter. Each was decked in gold-and-white harness and blanket. John even provided the ornate white leather litter Anne was to ride in.

"We have been shamed, Tom," observed Thomas Boleyn.

"Worse, Tom, we have all been made to appear tight-fisted beggars," Norfolk replied. "If I sank into my gifts what my de Gael cousin did, I should not have so much as a half-loaf left at home. My estates do not provide such revenue in four years."

John, ablaze in gold-and-crimson brocade with its wolf-skin lining, bowed very low before his monarch. He swept his plumed hat off in a blaze of diamonds; the richly embroidered wrist ruffles of his shirt fluttered dramatically. Henry thought: *He must have practiced that bow for days!* Reflecting, the king laughed aloud in delight. He would be just as defiantly overblown were he in John's position; no proud man wished to appear humble or contrite.

"By God, sir! You know how to give a gift!" Henry praised. He could not resist adding, "Had I guessed you to be so generous, I would have spent these last thirteen years exiling and then recalling you every six months!"

John had the good grace to smile—*faintly*—as he straightened from his bow. He was forty now; all of his bows were strictly formal and a certain wariness never left his mouth even when he smiled, which was seldom. Any lingering youth or capriciousness had been beaten out of him by ambassadorial service. He could now smile through any news, no matter how unpleasant, and hold his temper through events that would have made him erupt ten years earlier. The last explosion to come out of him had been the day he learned of Kathryn's divorce; there had been nothing else he need express in such physical terms since. Yet his marriage was happy, his home life not allowed to be marred by anything he dealt with in the king's foreign offices.

"Thank you, Your Grace," he said, and the moonstone eyes were unfathomable. *(Good! I like that!* thought Henry. *He is going to be a magnificent opponent, though we both pretend not to know it!)*

"Your Grace, it was worth the wait to see you and the queen so flourishing."

Henry laughed, smote his throne's arm with a delighted fist.

"I am remembering how well you thrashed those three Frenchmen at the Val d'Or, and not a one of them ranked under duke. We are having some splendid battles to honor my wife's coronation; will you be entering the lists, Baron Windsgeat?"

John recognized an order, no matter how prettily phrased. "If it please Your Grace, I shall be honored to."

Anne Boleyn's eyes flicked over him. She thought: *I remember my first sight of de Gael in France. I thought to myself, "Now* there *goes a man." I was not surprised that Kathryn should love him.*

But Kathryn had married his former squire, who now held

rank equal to John. How things had changed from the old days when Kathryn had loved The Lord of Windsgeat and Anne herself had been a lowly nobody! Well, she was queen of England now she thought, and Kathryn happily married at last; strange how things turned out. Who could have predicted all of this when they had camped side-by-side in the Val d'Or thirteen years ago?

Anne lifted her chin, said, "Baron Windsgeat, we have not yet met your baroness. Please have her come before us. Your sons, too."

Henry glowered. He had wanted to give the order himself.

The call went out for Lady Windsgeat to enter the Court. When she did, she was smiling so unconcernedly that Anne caught herself smiling back. The boys followed.

Margrethe de Gael was scarcely shoulder-high on her husband. Her gasp-deserving hair was a pale, almost silvery blonde, wonderfully offset by eyes so dark a blue as to be considered black. Her figure was buxom bordering on round; she was pretty, rather than beautiful, and merry as a wren. Diamonds blazed at her throat, ears, fingers, dazzling with her silver German gown and cap. The boys, Payne and Francis, had her eyes and John's chestnut hair. They were eight and six, respectively.

Those should be Kathryn's boys, Anne thought. *She should have divorced Edmund for him and . . .* Well, all that was years behind them. The important thing now was that Windsgeat's sister and sons marry in England and keep the family money circulating where it could best benefit the crown. Such gifts they gave, too. She would keep them here for that alone. Margrethe, curtsying, was presenting Anne with a lavishly illuminated Book of Hours that had once belonged to the Borgias. Her Flemish accent was very strong but all of her words correct and said from the heart. *I am going to like her, and I never like women,* Anne thought, still grinning back at her.

After the formalities, John sought out Kathryn and Richard. There was a moment of awkwardness between the two barons, one of whom used to empty the other's chamber pots, then John stepped forward, laughing. "You have done very well for yourself, My Lad," he said, and embraced Richard. When the two men finally stepped apart, Kathryn offered her hand to be kissed. John took hold of it, held it long moments.

"Funny how things turn out," he said. Then, "Margrethe? Come meet dear old friends."

Margrethe hugged Kathryn, surprising her. "So you are Kat'rin! Just like family, my dear cousin Jacquetta says. The three of us must ride through Windsor like the Wild Hunt and terrify the men, shall we?"

It was impossible not to warm to her. Kathryn had noticed how even Anne could not resist Margrethe, and found herself thinking: *Does John's wife know? Does she realize what happened between us?* It did not seem possible, looking at John de Gael, that she had ever been twenty and loved him, lain with him, had her heart smashed to bits by news of his marriage. No, that had been some other Kathryn, some tender-souled girl she remembered as one might vaguely remember an acquaintance not met in many years. The Kathryn standing here today had never loved a man with opal eyes, sword-scars, and crooked front teeth that overlapped slightly as if trying to cross themselves for luck. It seemed to her that she had always loved Richard; John was hardly a memory and Edmund never crossed her mind at all.

By that evening, Kathryn and Margrethe were lolling on the hearth rug in the Stoneleigh family apartments, swilling spiced wine with their hair hanging loose. Their husbands had gone out with George Boleyn, Pieter van der Hüm, Jane Seymour's brother Thomas, and Arthur Chase—"As rowdy a lot as ever caroused together. Do you think they will get in trouble?" Kathryn asked.

"Woman-trouble, no. Fights, maybe. My poor husband has gone through life having to defend his doublets with both fists. You know, I used to blame Johan's color choices on being unable to distinguish certain hues. What do you English call that?"

"Color blindness."

"Yes. I thought, after marrying Johan and getting my first intimate peek at his clothes, that he could not tell red from green or blue from orange. But he *can*, that is the tragedy of my marriage. And so he wears all those colors together and people give me looks that say, 'Madam, how can you let your husband go down the street in a coat that has just blinded my best horse?' "

They were rolling on the carpet, choking with laughter, when the door banged open. "*Reinforcements!*" shrieked Jacquetta de Gael, and fell into their arms.

Jacquetta had her old apartments back, adjoining the king's. Anne Boleyn went wild with rage, drew Henry's sword of state, and slashed through Jacquetta's bedhangings. "You will not come in here!" she screamed at Henry. "You will not humiliate me by keeping a mistress!"

He peered ostentatiously down his nose at her. "You are nothing, I have raised you from a hovel in Kent to be what you are today. So shut your mouth and bear with your husband's mistresses, Madam, just as your betters did before you!"

He stormed from the room. But Anne still had her sumptuous coronation, even though the king's sister Mary pleaded illness and refused to attend. "Illness! She was never sick a day in her life, that deceitful Tudor sow!" Anne shrieked as her women prepared her for the coronation journey to the Tower. "I will teach Mary Brandon, she will never dare show her face in any Court of *mine*! I will take her lands and titles, I will—"

Kathryn and the Countess of Rutland rolled their eyes at each other. Was the new queen mad to think she could bring down Henry's darling, his favorite sister, his pet? They went on combing Anne's raven hair back from her brow, finally setting a jeweled coronet on top of her head. Then her other ladies handed her off her chair into a heavy gold overgown. "Will it be too hot, do you think?" she anxiously asked her mother. "I would not want to get overheated and endanger the chi—"

A button caught on a hangnail Lady Jane Seymour had neglected to trim for her. Anne swore with pain, lashing out with one fist. She caught Jane a ringing blow over the eye and knocked her headdress off. "You little cow, I shall kill you!" She advanced toward Jane, dark eyes wild with rage.

Kathryn neatly stepped in between, swung Jane behind her. "Here, Your Grace, allow me to help you with that sleeve," she suggested.

"Get out of my way, how dare you interfere when your queen seeks to punish someone? Have your wits become addled by the return of your lover to Court?"

Kathryn forgot her cousin was now queen of England. She forgot everything but that she had just been mortally insulted in front of sixty-some women who would repeat the slander all over England. It would come back at Richard, the girls. . . . "Look in the mirror before you name me whore, Madam!" she snapped.

Elizabeth Boleyn stepped in. "Ladies, I suggest that tempers always have short fuses at times such as this. Let us try to go on working together. Anne, dear, what you said was unjust and untrue. Kat, you must remember that your cousin is queen now and due your respect. Now hold your arms out, daughter, and I will fasten your sleeves."

Anne jerked back. "No. Not unless you call me 'Your Grace.' "

"You forget who I am," Elizabeth Boleyn said with a spine straighter than any castle battlement. "I am the daughter, granddaughter, and sister of the Dukes of Norfolk, premier peers of the realm. I carried you in my womb for nine months, gave birth to you, changed your diapers when you were a mewling, puking brat. You raise your voice to me and I will raise my hand to you—queen of England or no, you are still my daughter and I will bounce you off the walls do you speak to me thus again! Now hold your tongue and stick your arms out or I swear I shall rip your clothes away and leave you stark-naked, unable to lead your damned parade. And if you have any wits left you at all, you will know how greatly you have angered all women in this room and how willing they are to follow me, should I walk out!"

Glancing around the room, Anne saw every face there set against her. She screamed, threatened, protested, but the moment they started out the door, she shouted, "Mother? Please, Mother—help me with the sleeves?"

In a moment they had all returned, buttoning, lacing, hooking. Turning back the ermine-lined funnel sleeves, fastening them at elbow-length with cabuchon rubies on enameled plaques. Anne yanked down the ruffled ends of her shift sleeves, making sure the witch-finger was hidden.

A golden mantle, also lined with ermine, went over the two gowns, three petticoats, corset and shift. "It is so hot," Anne whined as she left the palace. Every stony face in her wake said, *Good! We hope you sweat half to death!*

She had claimed Catherine of Aragon's barge from the royal wharf, had it repainted with her badge of a white falcon rising from a branch of Tudor roses. Dozens of other barges waited to accompany it up the Thames to the Tower of London, the banners of their proud owners fluttering in the morning breeze. But it was so silent on the riverbank that Anne, puzzled, cocked her head for sound. There was none. "Where are the people? Where the cheering crowds?" she demanded. "Why is there no sound?"

Jane Seymour ran to the servants' barge, urged young Mark Smeaton to strike up a tune on his lute. Sackbuts and vielles joined prettily in as the queen's barge started upriver.

But from Greenwich to the Tower not a cap was flung, not a cheer sounded. No pedestrians lined the banks, tossing flowers down into the barges.

King Henry awaited them at the Tower. He greeted Anne with an embrace that placed his hands on either side of her protuberant belly, as though he held the child within. Cheered into pleasure that he had so greeted her, Anne became very merry. That mood lasted until Henry noticed whose barge she had appropriated and berated her soundly in front of everyone.

Jane Seymour, listening, crossed herself. Blood the first night Anne spent with the king and now quarreling so close to the coronation date. What evil omens accompanied Anne Boleyn!

The next day, sixty men were made Knights of the Bath. This required them to leap naked into a great pool with the king and already-existing knights, all of them quaffing massive amounts of wine. "Let no one remain sober!" Henry bellowed, signaling the stewards for another refill. Observing John de Gael being less than riotous, he added, "You there, Windsgeat! Why so glum?"

"Your Grace, you, *too*, would be glum to face a howling pack of twenty-year-olds tomorrow!"

Said twenty-year-olds descended upon John en masse, dunking him and threatening worse on the morrow. "I was wrong about him, he is a very entertaining fellow," Henry observed to Norfolk, watching John losing the water battle.

"Entertaining, yes. But dangerous, unless one has something to offer him," Norfolk observed.

"I am surprised at you, Thomas. He is some sort of cousin of yours, I believe."

John surfaced, yelled, "Whitbourne! Are you going to let them drown me?"

Richard Stoneleigh was not used to his new title, and had to be called again before swimming to the rescue. Battle challenges were then made for the upcoming joust, Henry drunkenly urging them on until the pack grew brave enough to dunk him, too. Afterward, Arthur Chase, half-carried out by Richard and John, said, "He likes us. It is going to be all right, lads, the king likes us!"

The next day's parade to Westminster brought Anne in her litter, dressed all in white tissue furred with ermine. There was a matching mantle which she cast off in the heat; her black hair, long enough to sit on, rippled free beneath a jeweled coronet.

Sunday, regal in purple, gold, and more ermine, she was crowned. Archbishop Cranmer, outlawed by Rome, performed the ceremony that placed Saint Edward's crown on her head. It was so heavy that Anne wobbled beneath it, nearly dropping her orb and scepter. Cranmer hastily annointed her with chrism, skipping words to hurry her on to the part of the service where she could don a lighter crown. But Anne stopped him, made him inch through all the proper words lest she be accused of not being fully made queen.

In the heat and stress she began to giggle. Cranmer's chief fear was that she would miscarry and he be held responsible, so sweat dribbled down his face. By the time he finished, Anne's giggles had become full-throated, raucous laughter.

The bulky crown bit into her brow, marring the tender skin Henry had once so lusted to stroke.

The lighter crown now, made especially for her. Down the long nave of Westminster Abbey, entering white sunlight blinking and dazed. Back into the litter, the rear mule centered squarely behind her so that his ears appeared to be rising from her head. The crowd shrieked with hilarity, making Anne and her escort peer about them for the cause. The Londoners lining the streets then spotted the entwined *H*'s and *A*'s on everyone's livery and jeered, "Look what it spells—*HA, HA!*" Hats remained so firmly placed on heads that Anne's fool yelled, "Methinks Londoners all have scurvy heads that they dare not uncover them!"

Anne sat stiffly in her gorgeous litter, ablaze with brocade, furs, and jewels. Men-at-arms, hastily directed by Thomas Boleyn, began passing out pieces of gold to make the crowd respond favorably. One little boy shouted, "Hooray the queen!"

His mother fetched him a ringing slap, overheard by all. "You will not cheer that whore!" she ordered.

What have I done that they should hate me so? Anne wondered, lump in throat. *What?*

"You boys will not thump each other too hard?" Margrethe de Gael anxiously asked her armored husband. When John leaned from his tall battle charger to embrace her, she tied a black-and-gold scarf to his arm. "Promise me?" she asked, and kissed his fastened visor.

"I promise, Sweetheart, that I shall probably fall off my horse the first time Arthur whacks me. Then I shall come limping back here, sore and irritable, and that will be that." He cocked an eyebrow over her shoulder at Kathryn. "For the gods' sake, tell my wife riding at the tilt does not hurt."

Kathryn hugged Margrethe. "It hurts. I make myself look at something else."

"Thank you for all your encouragement," John grumbled. "Your husband and brother have promised to knock me into the stands because I laughed when Norfolk held them under the water last night!"

John and Arthur rode to opposite ends of the field, servants rushing to make last minute adjustments in turning pins, visors, and lances. Kathryn went to her brother's side, remembering that awful night in France when he was nearly killed. "Oh, brother! You will be careful?" she pleaded.

His hand rested a moment on her shoulder. She knew then that he, too, was remembering. "I was allowed to practice while yet in the Tower. Place your money on me, not Windsgeat, who has not hefted a lance since the Val d'Or, except in practice. Of course . . . he *is* twice my size, and his wife *has* promised to break my legs if I hurt him!"

She stepped back. Arthur made a great show of lowering his visor so she would know there would be no such accidents as happened in France.

Lances were firmly fitted to their ornamental sockets in each breastplate. Squires still ran under horses' necks, giving everything one last examination, checking hooves for rocks, adjusting saddle cinches one last time. "Are you ready, My Lords?" rang out the herald's voice. Two "readies" answered him.

The queen dropped her handkerchief and both horses sprang forward. The crowd screeched approvingly. They might hate Nan Bullen the Whore but they appreciated free food, ale, and violence, and today offered plenty.

Driven by nearly two tons of horse and amored man, the point of each lance brought several hundred tons' worth of pressure to its impact point. Wooden shafts crossed, John's catching Arthur under the gorget* and snapping his head

---

*neckpiece

back. Lances flew to flinders; the horses, knowing there was no need for speed after impact, slowed to self-satisfied trots.

It took Arthur two or three minutes to collect himself for the next round. Again the queen signaled the charge, again the crowd shrieked as the two massive chargers leapt forward. Clods of dirt flew from platter-sized hooves, exploding across onlookers. John's white, eight hundred pounds heavier than a mere pleasure-horse, was the more experienced of the two mounts and leaned into the blow better than Arthur's borrowed gelding. Both men struck hard, snapped back in their saddles. John's lance broke while Arthur triumphantly trotted on, brandishing his undamaged weapon.

"Fifty golden sovereigns on Windsgeat!" Anne cried out delightedly. "He will strew Cousin Arthur's guts across the field!"

"And I say fifty on Arthur, he has had more practice as of late," Henry answered her. Excited by the wager, the royal couple kissed with reborn affection.

The last run waited. Both horses, knowing that fact and that fresh stalls and water buckets waited, snorted and raked iron-shod hooves through the dirt. Impatient for impact and the release that followed, impatient for feed buckets and being sponged down, they ran their fastest time on the last round. Arthur's gray, a loan from Norfolk, was younger and smaller. As a result the gray sprang in under John's blow, moving at a dead run the white could not match; Arthur's blow caught his opponent square under the arm and knocked him from the saddle. There were cries of alarm and delight all around.

John had unbracketed his old-fashioned *sallade* helmet and was sitting bare-headed by the time Pieter and the field marshals reached him. Blood streamed from both nostrils but he was smiling. "What a run! Did you see that gray come at me? He is magnificent, I must congratulate Norfolk on his training. And what an arm young Arthur has developed, I—"

He attempted to stand, crumpled to one side. "Broken ankle, Milord. Let us get you a litter," Pieter advised.

"No, no, just a sprain. Let me walk off the field or my poor wife will panic. Worse than that, she will not let me tilt again!"

Here came Margrethe, skirts flying up to show an indecent amount of stocking. She launched herself, sobbing, into John's arms. He started off the field, hobbling with one arm around her and the other around Pieter. "I will get Jacquetta. I think your nose is broken, Johan," his wife warned.

"No, Dear, leave her be, she is in the tent with young William Brereton. Not for all the bruise-salves in England would I interrupt. Ho, Richard is up next, I must see if he needs a hand."

The ankle splintered the rest of the way; he promptly fell over in a faint. Pieter caught him just in time to keep his head from striking a tent peg.

Kathryn found her husband being strapped, buckled, and hinged into his brand-new armor. Having it made had ruptured their household budget and taken half their thousand-acre baronial lands. And it was indifferent armor at best, ill-fitting, badly finished. "Keep John away, he howled and pointed when he saw this suit," Richard grumbled. "Said the armorer may have trained in Italy but that the only good Italian stuff comes from the Missaglias. Told me I had no business getting armor made without asking him or Norfolk for advice. I know he meant well, but he can be so God-damned overbearing at times—!"

She took his helm from George Boleyn, thumped it, and said, "At least this is a good, solid piece here and will not let you down. Now be nice and do not ride George's horse over my brother, it would be so bad for family relations." When he still scowled, she softly said, "I love you, Richard."

"I love you, too."

He slid on his quilted coif, stooped to let George ease the helmet on for him. The horse waited patiently. "Look, de Gael is just now sitting up. I wish they would let me fight the loser instead of the winner, John looks a fright," Richard said cheerfully. He rode off yelling, "This will be such fun—!"

Kathryn huffed, "Only a *man* would think that going out and getting his face broken was fun."

George gave her a fast hug. "No, it is only fun when you break the *other* fellow's face!"

"Milords Howard and Whitbourne! Ready?" cried the herald.

"Ready, sir!" came twin shouts. At the signal, the horses came tearing down rain-filled ruts on either side of the rail.

Tilt armor was smoother on the left than right, for lances met there. John's magnificent armor was so well made that neither sword nor lance could catch on it; only a rupturing blow for a mace had stopped Jack of Norfolk in it. But the helm and gorget of Richard's cheap suit did not fit together snugly enough and that was where the point of Arthur's lance caught.

Richard's chin touched his right shoulder. His entire body jerked to that side, unbalancing the horse. A flash of mane and armor, a blur of hooves as the horse staggered and fell back upon its rider. Richard, head lolling, was flung from the saddle to lie unmoving in the mud. His borrowed charger regained its footing, stood protectively over him as taught.

Silence lay upon the field.

Kathryn all but flew over the rail. Her daughters started after her but Elizabeth Boleyn seized them. *"You stay right here!"* she hissed. This was no sight for children to see. After awhile Isabella, sobbing, thought to hide little Elizabeth Stoneleigh's face in her skirts.

Richard was not moving. He lay on one side, helm half-off, one armored hand ground into the dirt. Kathryn knelt, wrested uselessly at the helmet without finding the turning pins to release it. "Help me!" she begged of the marshals. "Help me with him!"

No one moved. She began screaming Richard's name in the silent field, yanking at metal until her nails broke and fingers bled. "Help me with him, I beg you!"

The stewards reached her side with a litter, looked on, and did nothing. She heard Arthur scramble from the saddle and race toward her with armor rattling. "Oh, sweet Jesu, sweet Jesu," he babbled, and sank to his knees in prayer.

Why would no one help her? Why did they not answer her cries? *John*, she thought wildly. *John saved Arthur, he can save Richard, I know he can! He did it before—*

Here he came, half-masked with blood-stained bandages. His eyes looked at her with compassion from an armor-marked, suntanned face; she had met him in a mask and now he wore another, one of pity atop the gory gauze.

He did not so much as bend over Richard. Instead he hobbled, agonized, to a halt, placed both cold metal hands on her shoulders. So well made and flexible was the right-hand gauntlet that he was actually able to knead her shoulder with it. "Come back to the tent, Jacqui and Margrethe are there," he said simply.

"But, John, you have to save Richard! Nobody else can do it and you saved Arthur once—I know you can do it again!"

The pale eyes scanned hers. "Pieter, give me the pistol," he said. His valet obeyed, loaded and primed it for him. John could think of nothing to say so he turned Kathryn around into the shelter of Pieter's shoulder. There was a moment of fumbling as he placed the pistol's muzzle behind the ear of the crippled horse. A dull thudding sound followed with a shower of scarlet. The horse folded up, sank slowly to earth.

Where were the women? John thought. Why were they not coming forth to give her the news? *Let this cup pass away from me,* John thought, bitterly quoting Christian mythology to himself. *I am a warrior, a politician, not a woman or confessor—I do not have the proper, gentle words in me.*

Staunch, unflinching little Pieter was sobbing like a woman. He had raised Richard from early childhood and now sank to his knees by his friend, unashamedly weeping.

Only John's right hand was flexible; the left jousting gauntlet was more of a metal mitten. He wrested that clumsy one off that he might have a bare hand to offer Kathryn. It went solemnly onto the curve of her shoulder that he had kissed, bitten, stroked in passion; there was no feeling in him now but a great sadness for her plight.

"Save him, John," she urged, but her voice was a hoarse croak this time. So in her heart of hearts she already knew.

"Kathryn, friend, I cannot help Richard. He is dead."

"He cannot be dead. Richard is the most alive person I know, he would not die so easily. John—" A rising note of hysteria in her voice, but she fought it down. *"John, I have to see him to be sure!"*

He sank to the mud and torn grass then, broken ankle swelling to horrific proportions; he was going to have to be cut out of his right greave and solleret tonight. Blood was coming from his armor and facial bandages; he fought a wave of blinding dizziness for Kathryn's sake. Behind them, the stands murmured with sympathy.

Richard's treacherous helmet was finally lifted off, though not without a struggle. Forever young now, he lay with beautiful eyes wide and vacant. Memories flooded John of the starving urchin he had bought from a poor family up North. *I was young then, exiled from Windsgeat by Kenneth de Gael's brother, who had stolen it from me. I meant to leave Richard at some convent but when I crossed the Channel and met Pieter, he began training the lad as my squire . . . then the boy grew 'til he was entrusted to bring King Henry the news of Pavia and de la Pole's death, and he married Kathryn, who was once mine. It was all so long ago, and he was like a son or brother . . .*

"His neck is broken," he said softly. "Our Richard is dead." He reached to shut the glassy green eyes.

"No, not yet. I want to look at him awhile," Kathryn said, and lifted the limp coppery head to her lap. She lifted Richard's coif, smoothed his hair, cleaned his armor-grimed face with her handkerchief. Only after long study of the expressionless features did she close his eyes, kiss him, rock him against her breast. "Dear God," John heard her say. "Dear God, he only gave me one baby. And he promised to stay with me and love me long enough to give me a dozen! You lied to me, Husband . . . oh, sweet Jesu, you lied to me and left!"

John de Gael, who had not cried even as a child when his real father was murdered in front of him, wept now.

23

7 September, 1533
Greenwich Palace

Both of Kathryn's husbands died that year. Edmund passed away with no child of his second marriage, leaving Howard House and his title to James, who took over at once. Kathryn, still numb with grief, hardly noticed him go.

Meanwhile, Anne Boleyn discovered that Mary Tudor Brandon's illness had been very genuine. Mary died that summer, leaving her eldest son betrothed to Maria de Salinas's lovely young daughter, Catherine Willoughby. But within scant weeks Charles Brandon, the forty-seven-year-old widower, broke the betrothal to marry fourteen-year-old Catherine—and her fortune—himself.

The marriage was never publicly celebrated. The peers and king had no sooner gathered in the chapel at Greenwich than the doors burst open. "The queen has gone into labor!" shouted Norfolk's son, the poet Henry, Earl of Surrey. People ran in all directions at once, colliding and dropping hats, rosaries, wedding gifts.

It was a hard labor but not overlong. Somewhere between three and four that afternoon the long-awaited prince arrived.

Squalling, healthy, red-haired, and female.

So sure had the king been of the child's sex that birth statements and the chapel register already read "prince." There was scarcely room to squeeze in even one tiny *s* after that word on all documents.

Anne turned her face to the pillows, weeping and crying out that she had failed, was finished. When Henry entered the room she was too afraid to face him and so remained huddled. Her sheets were of the finest lawn, she thought, stroking them absently. No one had finer sheets or such counterpanes of fur-lined velvet and cloth of gold. So very fine a bed, too—proof that she was finally queen . . . her long, slender hands ran faster and faster over the sheets, nails finally splitting, fingers raking.

Henry paused at the foot of the bed as she continued to claw. *I would not want to face me with a daughter, either,* he thought. He swerved toward the cradle. It was long as a man was tall, swathed in crimson and gold. Henry and Anne's initials were carved, painted, and embroidered all over it along with their family badges and mottos. Dieu et Mon Droit read the Tudor family phrase—"God and My Right," Henry the Seventh's defensive cry upon usurping the throne and murdering so many Plantagenets.

"You were to be a son," he said idly to the mewing figure in the overlarge cradle. Kathryn and the other ladies-in-waiting shivered, waiting for the explosion to follow.

He bent over the child. She cooed, crinkling up her face. Henry recognized his own becoming-pudgy features on her as both wrinkled red fists flailed at the royal nose. "She is a fighter, a worthy daughter to Your Grace," Norfolk dared observe.

Henry considered it. "I could name her Henrietta or Edwarda," he mused, for she had been meant to be a Henry the Ninth or Edward the Sixth. He had not imperiled his immortal soul and caused a schism with Rome only to have more daughters, he thought. After all, even Anne's sister Mary had once borne a son, a fine lad named Henry Carey who might be his own. And look at Lady How—Lady *Whitbourne,* even she, thin as she was, had borne gorgeous brats, the first two of them boys and the ones still living, healthy as horses.

He stared at Kathryn so hard, so searchingly, that it chilled her. She alone in the room dared look at him with open sympathy in her eyes. *That is very brave of her, but she has always been brave with me,* he thought. She was his cousin as well as Anne's, he remembered, and had been at Court forever; she alone seemed to know how greatly this birth hurt him. *She is a good woman. We will have to find her another worthy husband soon,* he told himself, and unexpectedly smiled at her.

"Tell me, good Cuz, would you not say she is all Tudor? I do not see the Howard nose or chin on her. Come look," he directed.

He had never thus addressed Kathryn before. Honored beyond words yet still terrified of him, she approached carefully, dared bend over the cradle. "She is very like your beautiful mother that I barely recall. There is your ruddy Tudor hair and goodness, but she has a Tudor voice!"—for the child was wailing defiance and hunger to the world.

The king laughed. "Her eyes are all her own," Norfolk said. "They are not blue-gray like the Tudors' nor brown like the queen's. They are almost yellow, like cat's eyes. She is a beauty, Your Grace."

Delighted at their compliments, Henry leaned over, tickled the tiny pink chin. His daughter responded by suckling furiously on his signet ring. "By God's Wounds, Tom, she is a lusty brat! Such brothers she shall have!"

"Half a dozen, my liege. You are both young and healthy enough."

Softened, Henry plucked the child from her ornate wrappings. Norfolk clucked, but the king said, "Now Tom, do not make old-hen noises at me. I have fathered brats before, I know how best to hold them." He took the infant, properly supporting the back of her neck, and went to sit at the foot of the queen's bed.

Anne lifted her bedraggled head, eyes streaming. "A son next year," she timidly promised.

"Yes, Madam, and a son the year after that, and the next and next! But only if they are all howling, brave Tudors like this one. We will call her Elizabeth after both our mothers and my mother's mother, that indomitable Woodville witch. What say you, Wife?"

"Oh, yes, Husband! Elizabeth Tudor is a remarkable fine name!"

The royal couple embraced, leaving Norfolk and the ladies to quietly file out. The Duke stopped Kathryn outside. "You look dreadful, Niece, like an actor who has been in a play so long he goes on reciting the same, meaningless words without knowing or caring their meaning."

"I will live," she said listlessly.

"Look, Niece, you know I do not side with the old qu—I mean, the *Dowager Princess* Catherine of Aragon or her daughter, the Prin—I mean, the *Lady* Mary, but—"

"Lady Mary? The Princess of Wales is to become mere Lady Mary?"

"Surely you knew that the king could not allow a declared bastard to retain that title. The badges are being ripped from her servants' livery; she will be sent from Beaulieu to some smaller place. That is what I wished to tell you. And the qu—*Dowager Princess Catherine*—will go to Buckden. You need not scowl so at me, Buckden is a pleasant red brick place with turrets for her to look out from. A park with a garden to walk in, some pleasant fruit orchards, a fish pond—"

"It is a drafty, stinking place where the wind whistles clear through. God's blood, Uncle, do you men think women so stupid that we see and hear nothing? Well, let me tell you that for every man who thinks he knows all the privy information of this Court, there are five women worming it out of him. I know what a wretched place Buckden is, and I know all about the Act of Supremacy the king is about to proclaim, forcing the peers to acknowledge on paper that he is Head of the Church of England. Those who do not sign will be proclaimed treasonous and executed. That way Cousin Nan will stop her hysterical ranting about enemies at Court trying to undo her, and many of the king's dearest friends will have their heads stuck on pikes over Tower Gate as my father's so briefly was."

He never had witnessed such spirit from her before, so dumbly let her continue. "Well, the Act matters not to me, Arthur will sign it and James, too, and I have no other menfolk to worry about. If he wants women to sign, then I and my daughters will, if I have to drag them by the hair; there will be no martyrs in *my* family, Uncle."

"You have gotten very headstrong without a husband to keep you in line."

She snapped her fingers at him. "I am too old and neither rich enough nor titled enough for you to declare me your ward or a ward of the Crown and thus order me where to marry. As a dowager baroness I shall do exactly what I please and I do not intend to try and replace my irreplaceable Richard with some stranger in a forced bed!"

She was shaking. Norfolk impulsively said, "*Peace*, my dearest niece, let there be *peace* between us! I have spoken too harshly; you are not healed from your loss yet." He began walking her along Greenwich Long Gallery with its many windows between rows of portraits and tapestries. "I suggest you take the girls and go to Whitbourne House awhile, try to find your normal serenity again, and heal."

She leaned gladly against his velvet-clad shoulder, needing the physical support. "I never think of it as Whitbourne House. It is Vamplate Manor to me."

Norfolk gave a start. "Do you know what a vamplate is, Niece?"

"I have armored three men in my day; yes, I know. It is a jousting shield with a notch in it so that the lance protrudes without exposing the fighter's heart, as it would if the lance simply stuck out over it. Whitbourne House is my vamplate against the world, my one little protective notch . . . yes, Uncle, I should like to go there."

"I will have the king sign the papers before Anne finds out and protests. I will fetch them to you tonight."

He watched her move away down the gallery. *I wonder if my death would so affect my wife*, he thought, and grinned wryly. *Hardly likely, nor my mistress, either. Stoneleigh, you fool, how could you die and leave her?*

Kathryn's long white hand trailed along the oak paneling as if blindly seeking support. *Poor woman*, he thought protectively. Then, *Vamplate Manor, indeed! She needs it, that protective notch in her shield. A lance is rarely knocked out of a vamplate; that private farm is her weapon and protection against the entire world.*

He had never been so proud of her as in those moments she stumbled along the gallery, too fierce to ask for help, too strong to crumple.

Henry Tudor, thickened and slowing with ponderous maturity, remembered the many treasures of Windsgeat with envy and so called John de Gael to his privy chamber first of all the lords.

"Your Grace?" John asked, regal despite his green-and-orange doublet. *Damn him*, Henry thought, *he always bows too low. It is too showy, almost satiric. Yet there is something I admire about his arrogance, something about him that says: 'I am not to be bent or broken by the likes of you, king or no!' I would behave the same in this haughty knave's place. But I would not wear that doublet!*

"I have here a document for you to read and sign, Windsgeat."

John's washy blue gaze covered the Act in detail. "Such an honor. I did not expect to be first to sign so illustrious a thing." He took up the king's own crimson quill, dipped it with elaborate courtesy in Henry's favorite rock-crystal-and-gilt inkwell. Henry watched him sign his title, "Windsgeat," one ornate letter at a time. A series of flourishes followed.

"I never thought you would do it, man. Where is your loyalty to Rome, or is it true you de Gaels refuse to recognize Rome's authority?"

"De Gaels," said John, picking his words carefully, "recognize only the authority of the king of England."

"You say that with such complacent arrogance that I am led to believe you do not consider *me* king," Henry observed. He had the satisfaction of watching the quill quiver, spraying ink across the gaudy peas-and-carrots doublet. The craggy de Gael profile gave nothing away, though. There was no flicker of surprise or alarm in the eyes or mouth, though that jerk of the quill had spoken guilt loudly as words. *Look at him*, Henry thought, thrilling to the chase. It made him feel powerful to threaten John, who so reeked with power himself. And damn him, but de Gael was still built like a twenty-five-year-old, no spare flesh, few gray hairs. Only some deep laughlines at his eyes and that slightly askew nose, gotten in the tilt just before Arthur Chase killed Richard Stoneleigh. How dare the damned man hardly grow older, how dare women still turn when he passed, and him Henry's own age?

It took John a full minute to answer. "Your Grace, what an odd thing to say. You are everywhere acknowledged as king of England."

You clever bastard, I have you now. You will have to lie or die, Henry thought excitedly. He leaned forward in his leather-padded chair. "I did not inquire about how I was everywhere acknowledged, Lord Windsgeat, I asked how you regarded me. Come, Sir, we all know what great Plantagenet sympathizers the de Gaels are! So tell me who the de Gaels regard as rightful king. Tell me, Windsgeat." A stroke of genius illuminated Henry's mind, then face. He glowed with anticipation. "Windsgeat! Tell me, *who was your father*?"

The narrow opal eyes widened, but that was the only visible sign of alarm. John picked up the quill, dipped again, began adding more flourishes to his signature. "I am far too young to be a son of Edward the Fourth, if that is what you are thinking. Nor am I some by-blow of Richard the Third's. I am your same age within a few months, Your Grace, and I am who I am—my father's son."

"And I will lay you odds that Kenneth de Gael never sired you. Tell me, Windsgeat, is it true that witches cannot lie to a direct question?"

Like cannon fire, John straightened, said, "I have papers with Swiss, French, and Imperial bankers, signed by your father and Kenneth de Gael, whereby Henry the Seventh did order Kenneth to privately execute the Little Princes in the Tower, Edward the Fourth's sons. All three are originals and I have half a dozen copies to back them up. Only I know the location of all the papers; my bankers have instructions to publish, should I be incarcerated in the Tower, tried, or executed. I do not think Your Grace wants me at the stake or block badly enough to see papers ordering the murder of children printed throughout Europe."

It took Henry awhile to find his tongue. "He never told me," he murmured.

"He never told you about the Green King, either," John said drily. "He never explained to you what Kenneth told him: that in times of drought, blight, or famine, a lord of the ruling family must die to save England. King and country are inseparable. You have read classical mythology, you know how the king must die in his prime to save the land. Sometimes there need not be an actual death, only the ruling lord's acknowledgement that he is willing. If you think about it, Your Grace, you will see that at every crisis point in your father's life he executed a Plantagenet, and you have done the same. But you are forgetting that the Tudors, too, are half Plantagenet."

Henry's mouth went dry inside, as though swabbed out with a handful of dusty cotton. He knew John was not threatening him; somewhere deep within he accepted the words for truth. "Will my turn come?" he whispered.

"You will never acknowledge your role, so your sons and friends have long died in your place. We de Gaels have only been sentinels to the duty until now; it was always our plan to return it to those of proper blood sitting the throne."

He had called the man presumed to be his father "Kenneth." Yet he had said "we de Gaels," so what did that make the man? "Who are you, really? Who were your mother and father?" Henry asked, less threatening than curious this time.

John finished signing and drawing. He had taken up the

entire document with his signature and a well-executed drawing of Windsor Castle and Great Park flowing down into Windsgeat proper. There was an ornately embroidered handkerchief he pulled out to blot his fingers on before easing long red gloves from his belt. He slapped them absently against his thigh, then pulled them on one finger at a time. "I am The Lord of Windsgeat and all that stands between you Tudors and oblivion. My name is John Howard de Gael Plantagenet and my father is the young man who married my mother."

He bowed, caught up his hat from the king's desk, and left without being dismissed. Henry dug square-cut nails into his damp palms. He had once heard his brother, Arthur, cry out, "It is the Green King!" in his sleep. So Arthur had known and Arthur had died. . . . Funny, though, de Gael had not threatened him with the information. Had only stated it flatly, with no emotion, as though some kind of pact had been agreed to between them. *He never did answer a direct question and he never did lie,* Henry thought. Jesu! Were the rumors worse than true, were all the de Gaels witches to think king and Nature must rule in joint partnership?

I could have his head on Tower Gate in twenty-four hours, Henry told himself, frowning. He remembered de Gael's supposed bargain with his own father, remembered hearing of the Titulus Regulus bastardizing Edward the Fourth's children. But old Henry Tudor had reversed that Act to make Elizabeth of York legitimate and marry her, which meant the boys had to die; they were kings again. And that complacent, unsmiling man with the crooked front teeth had known all about it while Henry himself was left ignorant.

Who is he, really? he thought. *And why do I not know? Surely someone in my damned kingdom must know who sired John de Gael!*

Vamplate Manor, Kent, England
1534

Kathryn survived grief because she had always survived and knew nothing else.

The words "bend," and even "beg" were in her vocabulary

when it came to saving her family, but "surrender" was foreign to her. She knew darkness, knew despair in the wake of tragedy, but some indomitable spark she had not realized she possessed made her start up from bed each morning at dawn, go down to the kitchens of Vamplate Manor, and begin work for the day. She had bread to bake, floors to sweep, beds to make. The five Whitbourne cows needed milking, Lissy needed gowning, Tansy and Isabella must be awakened and set back to work mending the stone wall that kept Gray Jenny and Richard's nameless gelding out of the winter corn.

Work always kept her going. She had been a maid of honor since early childhood, tottering behind Queen Catherine with her embroidery baskets, and a lady-in-waiting since age fourteen, nearly twenty years previous. There was no other way of life for her than that of busy-ness.

Then, too, love of landowning had finally come to her. She had let most of Whitbourne to tenant farmers in exchange for a rent of crops and petty cash; a lamb here, a calf there, a dozen hens to start her own manor from little more than a stone shell and some wild, overgrown acreage. One morning she woke to realize that she was finished whitewashing the walls and patching holes in them; the old white stone house glowed peach and plum in the dawn, finally intimate and welcoming instead of foreboding.

Weed-pulling, milking, gathering warm eggs, currying mule and horse—she loved it all because it was her own, felt a warm thrill of satisfaction that two women and two girls could accomplish so much. But oh, how much more could she accomplish were Richard yet alive! He was so hard a worker, so knowledgeable about farm-things. The baking, cleaning, repairwork would have seemed so much easier, could she only turn to the shelter of his arms at night in the big Woodville bed.

He had only visited Vamplate Manor once before his death. They had ridden in on a brassy April morning of green and gold, sun shining on the foaming white stream that had named the place *Whitbourne* and given them their titles. "It will take years," he had predicted. "We will have to clear a few acres at a time, find a manager for our long absences at court."

She could not afford a manager now. There had been his armor to pay for, his funeral, too. Mourning clothes for the family; she had chosen white—French mourning—because he had always admired her and "their" girls in that color.

Gone, now, the pillar of love and strength she had never expected to find. Gone and yet something of his goodness and joy remained.

Isabella was brokenhearted. Richard had been the first father she had known, and to lose him and Edmund all at the age when people were first trying to shove her into marriage confused and depressed her. Only her mother seemed to understand, and her aunts 'Quetta and Margrethe. Kathryn was forever putting her arms around her, saying, "Thirteen is too young to marry. Fourteen or fifteen, too. I will never allow you to wed as a child, nor will I let anyone, not the king himself, order you into some stranger's arms. You will marry who you wish, when you wish, and *if* you wish. I shall never force you."

And now Isabella's third and real father was back, and that was confusing, too. John had finally sat down with her, Kathryn and Margrethe allowing father and daughter to become better acquainted. It was then that John brought out a packet of letters, yellowing with age and tied with a broken armor strap; he had written Isabella since before her birth and never sent the letters. Thus she came to know him through a sort of disjointed diary he had addressed to her over the years of her life.

In winter, the king summoned the Whitbournes back to Court. Kathryn dawdled at returning, wondering how she could possibly desert the farm now that it was limping toward minor productivity. How could she afford to abandon all her hard work, how could she afford to hire someone to—

Snow suddenly blew along the riverbank. She shaded her eyes, leaned with nose against the window. The approaching rider was on one of the lesser Windsgeat Whites; within moments she had recognized the golden Flemish head of Master van der Hüm. His horse skidded to a halt, stood huffing and blowing as she ran to catch his bridle.

"Hullo, Pieter! What is it? Something wrong at Windsgeat?"

The little blond man avoided her eyes.

"No, Milady Kathryn. De Lord and Lady told me you were summoned back to Court, so I volunteered to come watch over de farm for awhile."

"Pieter, I cannot pay you."

"Windsgeat pays me," he scoffed, then remembered her pride. "You and I can work someding out later on. We should trust each odder, you and I, after so long an acquaintance."

She did, too. "You look like a man struck to the heart,

Pieter; why not tell me the other reason you are so glad to leave Windsgeat?"

"I do it for you, you are *friend*."

"Pieter van der Hüm, if you do not tell me why you left Windsgeat, I shall not let you set one foot over my threshold!"

She spread her arms wide, blocking the door to prove she meant it. He slid from the saddle, eyes suddenly dark with hurt. "Eh, I fell in love wid De Lady and had to get away from dere before dey knew. She is so far beyond my reach, I could never dare aspire. And she loves elsewhere."

"Well, it is not unheard of for a man to fall in love with his lord's wife," she said in sympathy.

Pieter's head jerked up from contemplation of his feet. "De Lady Margrede? Oh, no, Kat'rin—" In his anxiety he had finally given her no title and the Low Countries pronunciation, which had trouble with *th*'s.

Her jaw sagged. "Pieter, it is *Jacquetta*! Oh, my poor, dear Pieter, come in, come in, and tell me all about it."

So Pieter had a place of refuge and she, an able steward for at least that winter. She refused any other help from Windsgeat, though. Her three friends wanted to send her workers and seed but she refused. "I have all I want from them now," she told Isabella and hugged her. "They gave me *you*!"

The king greeted her with an uncharacteristic embrace. "Welcome back to Court, Lady Whitbourne. You are looking improved from when you left."

"It was good of you to let me go. The land always helps; there is something healing in planting a thing and watching it grow."

"There certainly is. The queen is pregnant again!" He slapped his thigh, roared with laughter. *And so Anne will become the next Catherine of Aragon*, she thought, *exhausted and faded through excessive childbearing*. In five years the gorgeous black hair would begin to fade, teeth fall out, the skin become pinched and more sallow; there would follow painful monthly courses or none at all and a series of miscarriages and stillbirths. Such was the lot of queens. But living children were bound to come of it, and some of them future kings of England, so everyone would think it well worth Anne's broken health.

Kathryn curtsied low. "Congratulations, Your Grace. Now, how may I be of assistance?"

"You have such fine children and you grew up with the

queen. It comforts her to have you around. I would ask you to be especially tolerant of her vapors and whims now that she is carrying a prince and future king. In return the Crown will provide doweries for yourself and your daughters; when I gave you Whitbourne I knew it was rumored to be fertile land but I did not realize it had gone back to seed, so I feel shame at having given you so rough a home there."

He watched admiringly as she thanked him again, curtsied again, and backed away from the royal presence.

Henry shook Norfolk awake, for the duke had dozed off on his bench at the king's feet. "Thomas, I married the wrong one of your nieces. There goes a wife who stands behind whatever husband she has, there goes a woman I have never heard criticize a living being, nor contradict her betters. De Gael was mad not to marry her. But tell the two of them that should they try to wed, his head will be forfeit and she shall spend her remaining days in the Tower. A child of theirs would be too near the throne in blood. Speaking of Plantagenets, I want Margaret Pole removed as governess to my daughter, the Lady Mary. The countess stuffs Mary's head full of her own importance, encourages her to resist me as head of the Church. I wish the queen's aunt, Lady Anne Shelton, in her place."

A page ran in to tell him that the queen was miscarrying.

"They did not wait long enough. I have learned through my own experiences that a woman cannot go straight from childbed to wifebed again," Kathryn told Norfolk that night. "Anne needs rest, needs to have plenty of red meat and red wine, build up her strength again."

Norfolk ran a hand through his graying ginger hair, pulled his velvet cap back on. He stuck his hands closer to her fireplace. "It was not the king who had insisted on hurrying her back to bed. No, that was Anne's idea. Can you not tell she is desperate-mad to bear him a son? She is remembering that he shunned Catherine of Aragon and cast her aside for having only daughters. Our Nan Bullen is frightened half to death."

Kathryn harrumphed into her mending. Gone were the days when she followed Edmund's advice and held her peace even with her intimates. She and Norfolk knew each other too well to hedge issues any more. "He will not divorce her. He could never remarry with two former-wives in the background, all of Europe already saying there was no divorce and Elizabeth Tudor is a bastard. Not a monarch in Europe would give him a sister or daughter under such circumstances. And he would need a political marriage, did he seek another."

"I still remember how Catherine of Aragon faced King Henry in Court. God! Her courage was wonderful to behold, though I could not support her. My king comes first to me," her uncle admitted.

"I know, but I love you anyway," Kathryn answered with a shrug. She had more important things in mind than hashing over old issues; Isabella at thirteen was chin-tall on her mother and sprouting out of all her gowns and shifts. Kathryn was letting out the last possible girlhood gown, with an eye to cutting down things of her own for Isabella. "You know," she said, settling on the foot of the Woodville bed with scissors in hand, "if Qu—if the Dowager Princess dies, Anne will be unprotected. As long as there is a former wife in the background, she need not worry. He dare not have *two* former wives, it would endanger the Succession."

Norfolk had thought his position in life secure until now. But watching Kathryn's golden-brown head bow over her precise stitches, and hearing her commonsense words, he felt his breathing quicken. Sweet Mary Mother, the fortunes of the entire Howard family rested on the slender, undependable shoulders of a queen who had twice in one year failed to give the king a prince.

Worry stalked him now on quick, clawed feet.

24

Jacquetta did not cover up the letter quickly enough as Kathryn entered the de Gael family apartments, Jane Seymour at her heels.

"Why do you leap so? We knocked first," Kathryn said frowning. It was impossible to miss the fear in her dearest friend's eyes, or the way the long, knobby de Gael hands rushed to cover the page.

Jane shut the door firmly, leaned back against it. "She is frightened because she is writing the Princess Mary."

"*Lady* Mary," Jacquetta corrected cautiously. Sun streamed

through morning windows, gilding her flesh, loosened hair, and silver nightgown.

"*Lady* Mary!" Jane spat out. "You believe her to be rightful heir as much as I do, Countess. How do you think your letters reach her and the real queen, or how theirs come to be in your writing box? I am their messenger at Court."

Surprised at mousy Jane's loyalty and bitterness, Kathryn rushed to fasten Jacquetta's windows and draw the tapestries. It would muffle sound. "We are all for Queen Catherine and Princess Mary, then," Jacquetta whispered, holding both hands out to Jane.

The little maid-of-honor gripped the proffered hands. Both of them turned to regard Kathryn. "I have not survived thirty years at Court by entering into conspiracies. I will not do so now," she said flatly.

Jacquetta turned on her with astonishing rage. "And you were Queen Catherine's favorite, right alongside Maria! When did you become so spineless?"

"Since I do not have a man to throw in their path and sacrifice, should I commit treason! You have John to toss at the wolves, should they scent your trail; I have one poor house, some overgrown acres, and no damned man between me and the headsman's axe. I am all there is to protect my daughters, Mother, Arthur."

The conspirators unlinked hands. "The people will rise if the real queen asks them to," Jane whispered.

"If you think Catherine of Aragon will ask them to, then you do not know her. She sees Henry Tudor as God's Annointed On Earth; she will never lift a finger against him. And Mary will never cross her mother's desires. Now you must say no more to me, for it is treason. I have the girls, Arthur, and my old mother to think about."

She brushed out past them, trembling with hurt feelings and fear. Jacquetta had never crossed her before, let alone yelled at her and accused her of cowardice. *Yes,* Kathryn thought, clench-fisted, *I would be brave, did I have Windsgeat's vast wealth behind me as she does! And a brother expendable in years of drought!*

She agreed, in her heart of hearts, that Catherine was the real queen of England and Elizabeth Tudor a bastard. But for the sake of Isabella and Lissy, for the sake of lanky Arthur and dimly remembered Joanna, she would keep that opinion to herself.

* * *

The Act of Succession followed the Act of Supremacy. This time Kathryn's family was among those required to kiss the Bible and holy relics and swear to "maintain the Act" calling Anne Boleyn Queen and the children of her body, heirs to the throne of England. Mary Tudor now fell far below the bastard Duke of Richmond in the king's esteem, for she would not sign and acknowledge her mother a whore and herself base-born.

Anyone who now proposed a toast to the King's Great Whore or jokingly called Elizabeth "that little red-haired Tudor bastard" could be arrested, tried, and sentenced for treason.

Henry insisted John de Gael sign the Act in front of an entire Council of lords. John bowed too low, kissed the Bible and bones too emphatically, and again signed with an entire pageful of flourishes that made secretaries whimper, knowing they would be up all night having to make more copies of the Act. The king, observing the kiss on the Bible, said, "It is a miracle your lips do not burn off at the touch of a sacred object."

John, about to lay the quill down, found an entire inch of parchment he had not embellished and dipped the quill once more. "Does my drawing need sun and clouds, do you think?" he inquired of Thomas Boleyn. Henry Tudor burst out laughing.

"Windsgeat, are you afraid of nothing? Not of perjuring yourself before God who made us all, nor even of my wrath and that of my Council?"

"I am afraid of much," John responded cheerfully. "One day you and I shall go hunting alone in the greenwood and I will show you what de Gaels fear. In fact, I would be honored to have you attend Midsummer at Windsgeat. It will be a ride such as you never knew before. Something to tell the grandsons about."

A baker's dozen years as an ambassador had given John a perfectly unreadable face, though Henry thought there lay a challenge in the modulated voice. "It is a bargain. Approach, Windsgeat."

John did, kneeling so low that his chestnut hair brushed the ground. "Oh, cease the playacting," grumbled stiff-legged Henry, who could not bend to John's pose for all the gold in the Vatican. "You are not fooling me, though these idiots might think you passing civil." His gesture included the premier peers of the realm. "Now, then, Midsummer it is. But only if you do not let anyone else have that fabulous two-year-old Cernunnos colt, I want him gelded for the queen."

"Do you mean Phaëthon? He is too wild, and the best colt I have ever bred. He will be the next king-stallion, allowed to run free, repopulate my stables, and never know saddle or bit. He is too good to geld and too violent to try and break for riding; I would kill him in the effort. But I have a filly for Her Grace, so sweet, so spritely . . ."

He was furious by the time Henry released him. Anger only showed on John through a certain whiteness at jaw, bespeaking clenched teeth; he barreled through the door of his Court apartments in a rage, hissing for his man to saddle his mare. He would be glad when Pieter returned from Vamplate Manor and leapt to anticipate his needs once more.

The sight awaiting him brought him up short. Kathryn sat in the window seat, removed from conversation, plucking her lute and murmuring some melancholy tune to herself. Across the room, on the hearth, huddled his silver-gilt Margrethe with Jacquetta and Jane Seymour. The three of them sat so close their foreheads bumped as they whispered.

Margrethe sprang up so hastily that she nearly knocked Jane Seymour into the fire. "We are in trouble with the king?" she demanded, seeing the familiar white-jawed look on her husband.

"I kissed the bones, book, and his Goddamned ring. Pardon my language, Ladies. And I invited him to Midsummer's Eve at Windsgeat."

"Hunting?" Jacquetta hammered on the hearthstones with both jeweled fists, breaking a ring. "I will not have it, if the royal household comes calling they will stay and stay, eating up all this year's profits and—"

She envisioned a typical summer progress, the king and five hundred favorites with servants and horses staying a month. Eating every last crumb, hogging the best beds, stripping Windsgeat bare—

John was one of the few men in England whose personal wealth would have been thinly dented by a summer visit from the Court. But Jacquetta was right, it would strip the place of crops. "Calm yourself, sister, he is coming for a private hunt. Only a handful of companions."

"You will not take him to the woods that night," she countered warily.

"I most assuredly will. I wish him to know exactly where he and I stand in respect to the greenwood and each other. We have made arrangements to leave our men and go out alone with our bows. My, how alarmed you all looked when I threw that door open! So guilty, so fearful! Have I a nest of conspirators in my apartments, Ladies?"

To his consternation, none of them laughed.

Anne Boleyn announced that she was pregnant before the summer progress began that year. Six weeks later she had to deal with the advent of her monthly courses in the king's presence so there could be no lying to him. "But I was certain! It was nearly three months without them!" she cried out in desperation.

He was so disgusted he could scarce stand to look at her tear-streaked face. "You bore me, Wife," he snapped, and spun from the cloth-of-gold pavilion, shouting for his horse.

An unfamiliar horse was brought him, the finest Windsgeat White he had yet seen. White like snow, not milk, with blue dappling under his throat and across his muscular rump. Henry knew what this new mount signified and leapt to the jeweled saddle, laughing in expectation.

The summer Court was left behind in the dust. He signaled half a dozen men to follow, but spur though they may, he soon left them behind on the dirt road from Windsor. "Meet me at Windsgeat!" he shouted over his shoulder, and heard their assenting shout. "And do not allow the Court to follow!" he added.

Jacquetta met him a mile up the road. She gleamed in white-and-green, his colors, with a man's flat German cap trailing half a hundred plumes. No modest French hoods or gable headdresses for his Jacquetta, no high-necked English shifts; the hat let all of her honey hair tumble over one shoulder, ending in a triple love knot between her spectacular and half-bared breasts. Somewhere she had come up with fifteen equally blonde girls to accompany her, all of them also in Henry's colors. But, shockingly—delightfully—they wore boy's garb and sat their horses clad like archers. "Our bodyguard. You may have all of them if you wish; they are my gift to you," she said as he rode up and kissed her hand.

He might have guessed that with John overseeing the hunting, Margrethe the food, and Jacquetta the entertainment, it would be an unforgettable week at Windsgeat.

"The king is *where*?"

"Hunting with my father at Windsgeat," Isabella said complacently, and counted another stitch in her pattern-darning. Two down, one up, three down, two up—

"You are not to refer to John that way, it could put all of us in a great deal of danger," Kathryn said. "Why has the king gone to Windsgeat?"

"Because Fa—"

"Uncle John," they both compromised in chorus.

"Because Uncle John dared him to attend the Midsummer revels and Aunt 'Quetta took him fifteen blonde whores dressed as archers so he would keep his hands off *her*. She is in love with William Brereton, you know. He left the Boleyns, in fact the whole Court, behind. Only my cousin Surrey, the two Seymour brothers, and some others followed, and they have not been invited to join the private hunt. Mother? Will Uncle John hurt the king?"

"If he does," Kathryn answered grimly, "you will be the only child in English history to go through three fathers in a year. Hold me, Isabella, I am frightened!"

Her daughter flung down her sewing, raced to her arms. "So am I, Mama! What is happening at Windsgeat? *What are they doing?*"

Devout Jane Seymour accepted the bag of herbs, frowning. "It is not witchcraft, Countess?" she whispered.

Jacquetta smiled. "There are no spells on it, no sorceries. It is a mix of herbs to keep the Boleyn from conceiving for awhile, that is all. Leave the rest to me."

Jane still doubted. "I do not think he will put her aside and take Queen Catherine back."

"Of course not, Dear, that is not the plan."

"Then what is?"

A monstrous horn-voice sounded in the woods, signaling a journey the likes of which Henry Tudor had never known before.

Jacquetta's smile broadened. She leaned forward, pinched the other woman's cheek. "What an innocent you yet are, Jane! Our purpose, Dear, is to make you the next queen of England."

Minutes earlier, two men had sat atop the knoll on panting horses. Below them, exhausted archers and hounds sank to the vivid green turf. "They will never make the climb," Henry Tudor predicted, laughing.

"No, we have certainly outrun them. Let us to the greenwood now, Your Grace," John suggested.

The king put a hand out, caught John's horse briefly by the bit. "You would not take me off and murder me?"

"I intend for you Tudors to remove the mantle of Green King from de Gael shoulders; why should I kill you before you do so? A little farther on, Your Grace, let us hurry."

Midsummer fires blazed in Windsgeat valley below, dots of gold on the greened-black night grass. King and baron clucked to their horses, only to discover both beasts too tired to carry them. They dismounted, then, continued with reins over arms.

Half a mile later, deep in the thick heart of the wood, John suddenly said, "Here it is, Your Grace." He sounded excited.

"It" proved to be some sort of monstrosity, a spiraling, twisty horn longer than two tall men laid head-to-head. At its narrowest end, where it had been dug out for blowing into, it was the size of Henry's smallest finger; the other end would have admitted him on all fours. "What astounding beast did this once bedeck?" he whispered in awe.

"I do not know, nor do the legends tell. It has always been here to summon the Old Dark Ones. Would you call the Wild Hunt and ride with them, Your Grace? Then I will help you raise this end and you shall blow into it."

None but the Lords of Windsgeat had used the horn since their first forebearer arrived in England before the Norman Conquest. John said a quick prayer to deities thousands of years older than any now commonly worshiped, hoping against hope to be relieved of his family's burden. The king nodded, then both of them struggled to raise the horntip. "Three times," John directed fervently.

The sounds emerging from it were horrific, as though stags, bulls, and mad stallions all trumpeted their challenges at once. A horrid cacophony, chilling the royal blood—

A sticky blue mist began to rise about them, plucking at unhooked doublets and booted legs with greedy, hot fingers. Ahead of them, a long blue path seemed to open, leading down from the trees. "*What is it?*" the king demanded in a whisper.

"The god-path is opening." John said it so casually that Henry's nerve began failing him. There was a silence of some minutes before John added, "Your Grace, if you will give me a hand with that stag you took—?"

They handed the dead beast down from behind John's saddle. *And now they will make the proper choice at last*, he thought, relieved, and bent over the stag with his voyding knife. With a quick, practiced motion he opened the belly. "For the Hounds," he said simply, and Henry Tudor's blood ran cold. Then the knife flashed again, drew still-hot blood from the stag's throat. "I will buy you a new doublet and shirt," John de Gael said, and wiped blood on the King of England's brow and breast. Then he daubed his own brow and breast while the blue mist grew hotter, thicker, and the god-path swelled open. They remounted their horses. The Wish Hounds, voiceless black dogs who preceded the hunt, came creeping to feed on the stag.

"Did my father come here with yours?" King Henry whispered.

"No, he would not. But a son of mine will bring a son of yours, and so on down the line."

"I will have sons, then?"

"I am not a seer, Your Grace, I merely presume, as all of us do."

"Those hounds are big as calves. Windsgeat—*they have fingers*!"

The black dogs came first. Waist-tall on a big man, lion-maned, with paws like hands, they swarmed down the blue god-path and over the stag's carcass. Henry cringed back, eyes wild. "*What are they?*" he gasped out.

"Wish Hounds," said John. To *wit*, or *wist* meant to know, though centuries had corrupted the word to "wish." Henry, staring into the flat black gaze of the beasts, saw that they indeed knew all about him. Then the long black snouts dipped back into the deer's flesh.

No voice. What struck him as worse than their horrific appearance was their utter lack of sound. No howling, barking, or snapping at each other as they accepted the blood sacrifice. Only an almost human gravity, as though they ate a funeral dinner after a loved one's services. It chilled the king clear through.

The mile-long line of riders came then. On black stags, black horses, horned beasts the likes of which had never existed on earth. In armor of leather, and black, gleaming metal; in hides torn from living creatures, not all of them animals. Some of the riders were not yet born, some were dead. In their midst rode a horned and hairy beast-man, Lord of the Forest, God of the Dark—Cernunnos, Herne, King of Stags. She-Who-Birthed-All rode ahead of him in streaming black and red robes.

"Mother!" cried out the king as one dear, dead form amidst so many rode silently past. Then, "Mary! Sister! Mary, *wait*!"

They rode past him without a backward glance, unhearing, unheeding. Mad with grief, Henry spurred after them, joined the long line of human dead and old, dark gods whose number stretched across the horizon to infinity.

I am free. I have saved Windsgeat and my sons, John thought, chest heaving with strong emotion. *He will ride with them as The Lord always does, they will accept him and my family will be free at last. I need ride no more.*

They were nearly past in their black, silent parade when She-Who-Birthed-All turned to him. There was no mistaking the crook of her forefinger, the commanding though wordless presence; she had always loved the company of de Gaels.

His stallion sprang forward of its own accord. Swearing, John hauled back on the reins. To no avail; in seconds he was amidst the nightriders, enmeshed in the damp funk and rot of the Wild Hunt once more. Called to the Queen-of-All, accepted again as The Lord and High Priest.

Neither man returned to Windsgeat all that night. Toward nightfall of the next day they came back, tattered, blood-splashed, on foot. Both of their horses had been ridden to death and now lay glassy-eyed in Windsor Great Park, fodder to less majestic beasts—Nature returning its own.

The king never said where he had been that night. Nor did Baron Windsgeat, bitter with disappointment, offer the information to those who dared ask.

Anne raised so much fuss that Henry finally, reluctantly, had to ask Jacquetta de Gael to leave Court for a while. John, though, was now one of the king's boon companions and had him to Windsgeat often. So all the queen gained by her small victory was her husband's assured absence.

To combat it, she did something that provided gossip for months: brought her young cousin Madge Shelton to Court and paraded her before Henry, remembering his old fondness for teenaged girls.

As Madge was young, fresh, and without a single opinion of her own, Henry was intrigued. His wife and chief mistress were the strongest-willed women in England and he had not forgotten his paternal grandmother The Dragon. "With all those steel-spined ladies, a man of four-and-forty craves something more pliant upon occasion," he confessed to Norfolk.

The duke did not panic, since Madge Shelton was still family. Better to have the king sewn up between two of his nieces than yanked to and fro between Anne and that dazzling de Gael woman.

But the king tired of Madge's simplicity. "She is too easy.

No challenge, no thrill of the chase," he confessed to Jacquetta in her brother's chambers at Windsgeat one day. She bedded him no more, treating him with an almost sisterly concern, but such was his fascination that he still continued to visit.

"True enough, Your Grace, she sounds more the wife type than suitable mistress material. A man likes a good woman at home to manage things and a bad woman to play with. I, of course, am the mistress type. Faithful women like Kathryn Chase and Jane Seymour, who can hold their tongues under pressure and sew for hours without dying of boredom, are the wife sort."

"I have often admired Kathryn's coolness under fire and thought I married the wrong cousin. But Ned Howard always accused her of such coldness, and a man likes something warm abed, does he not, Sweetheart?"

She kissed him on the nose. "True, My Lord, just as a woman does. I have heard even little Jane Seymour complain to her brothers for not choosing her a husband; seems she is warmer than we thought."

Being Jacquetta and wise in the ways of men as Anne Boleyn had once been, she planted the seed and immediately changed the subject so that the matter would seem entirely of Henry's choosing. The entire Court, though, was surprised when, three days later at Whitehall, the king's greeting to Lady Jane Seymour was noticeably warmer than usual. Her eyes shone in reply.

Not two weeks after, Jane was seen fingering a handsome new portrait medallion of the king, set in diamonds. Elizabeth Boleyn finally mentioned the matter to her daughter, hoping Anne would immediately sign an order banishing Jane to her home of Wolf Hall. Instead, Anne went storming after her rival.

She found Kathryn and Isabella playing a duet on their lutes in the Long Gallery while other ladies danced, prettily partnering one another's steps. Jane was not there but a distant thread of her voice wove through the music; shoving dancers aside, Anne reached an alcove beneath an oriel window. The king sat there on an ornate chest, saying something that made Lady Jane blush. He reached out, she withdrew—he grabbed her arm, hauled her onto his knee—

Anne crossed the alcove in three strides. She seized hold of the medallion bouncing on Jane's flat chest, yanked it with an equestrienne's strength. Jane screamed as the chain bit into her white neck, then a link parted. The medallion came away in Anne's hand, blood-specked, while Jane dropped to her knees, sobbing.

"So this is why we have no sons, my lord!" Anne snarled at the king. "It is because you prefer to spend your seed on such sluts as this pious little fake! I married you to make princes, did I not? And all we have is one small daughter because you visit beds other than mine! Come back to me this very day, husband, and I will make you such a son as England has never seen!"

She always spoke in exclamation points. Beside the dark, dangerous, ravenlike Anne, Jane seemed a sweet-voiced little brown wren. "Silence your vicious tongue, Madam, and I may consider it," Henry said. Anne did, approaching to perch on his knee, caress his bearded cheek. Jane, knowing she had lost this round, fled weeping.

Kathryn saw her friend go by and rushed to her aid. "Jane, what has hap—your neck is bleeding! Here, my handkerchief—"

Anne left the king's lap, hurled herself out of the alcove at her cousin. "Aid that whore, will you? You are my cousin, you owe me your first loyalty! I will teach you to succor my foes—I will take your daughters from you! Yes, I will send them both from Court!"

Within the week Isabella and tiny Elizabeth had been sent back to join the household young Mary Tudor uneasily shared with Princess Elizabeth. "Ahh, well," Isabella gently told her mother. "I am of an age to take good care of Lissy so you need not fear. I will see to her Latin and embroidering, Mama. I will not disappoint you."

Her daughters, her only riches! Fighting to remain dry-eyed, Kathryn said, "You are of an age to make daughters of your own, not watch mine. Is there no young man you will mourn leaving behind? No one I may ask the king to allow betrothal to?"

"No, no, Mama, I am neither romantic enough nor willing enough to put my neck beside another's in a yoke. But I shall miss you—dear gods, I shall miss you so greatly! Tell Fa—Uncle John farewell for me, and Aunts Jacquetta and Margrethe. Payne and Francis, too," she added, naming John's sons.

Kathryn was left with none of her immediate family but Arthur and James now. Her brother was a man's man in all senses of the word, loving them and never women. He had none of the effeminacy she was accustomed to in such men;

all he could talk of were horses, arms, and hunting, as a result of which she found him boring and avoidable. But at least there was affection between them, which was more than she could say for herself and her only remaining son.

Whether God was bearded Jehovah or the de Gael's hornéd Herne, he had played a bitter jest on her in taking Adam and leaving James. There could be no more obnoxious son in the world, she thought, for he was twenty now, Lord Howard of Howard House, and certain that he never made mistakes. It was true that he was a devilishly handsome young man despite the Howard nose—women flocked around him and he even carried on a mild flirtation with Anne Boleyn, who adored clever young men about her these days. She was always surrounded by musicians and courtiers who flattered her, something the king never bothered doing any more.

"I know it is a harmless, chivalrous thing between you and Anne, but when the king notices it, he will be furious," Kathryn warned James one night when he visited her at Court.

He took a hothouse pear from the willow basket on her only table, said, "This is too green, can you not afford better? Mother, what I do with the queen is no more than Norris or Weston or even Jacquetta's secret lover William Brereton do."

"Yes, and very silly you all look, mooning after the unachievable! Are all of you in love with her?"

"Oh, no, it is only the fashion to appear so, as ladies do with the king."

He pitched the pear into her pretty fireplace, where it made an ugly, thudding sound like John shooting Richard's borrowed horse. Kathryn shuddered, remembering that last, tragic tournament. "There is a difference, son, between a queen's behavior and a king's. When a king takes a mistress it does not affect the succession. But did a queen bear bastards, she would be tried for treason and burnt."

"Mother, do not be such an old-fashioned ass of a—"

She slapped him so hard he staggered. "Ass? Get out, I am still your mother! You may not speak to me that way, I have done nothing to merit such disrespect from you."

"No, you have only been Windsgeat's mistress these twenty years or more! Did he father all of us, or am I really Ned Howard's?"

"You dirty-minded little monster! Yes, you are Ned Howard's, and no, I have not been Windsgeat's mistress twenty years! I married your damned father out of love and remained in love long after the mood passed him."

"Still, you cannot deny Isabella is Windsgeat's. She is the exact image of him. You know, the whole Court says you lie four abed: him, his whore-sister, his wife, and you, my sanctimonious mother."

The whole room reddened before her. *I will kill him,* Kathryn thought almost flatly, feeling the same taut Howard temper that made her uncle Norfolk mow down fifteen Scots singlehanded at Flodden. *I will cut his filthy heart out!*

Some dimly remembered voice at the back of her brain named him *son, child, family*. The only pillar in life, *family*.

Blind and wild with fury, she fumbled her way to the door, threw it open. "Get out and never come back here with your filthy lies. Whose mistress I was fifteen years ago for a fortnight is no affair of yours; I am chaste now and have been since Richard's death. The only whoring in the Chase family was done by your father, who probably left you a troop of bastard siblings all across England and France."

"It is different for a man, you said so yourself. It does not affect the succession. It is really fascinating, though; yesterday I saw you with Margrethe de Gael's sewing basket and this morning, her horse. Is there nothing of hers she does not loan you? I have always wondered, does John lie in the middle or do you two women—"

The Howard rage that Norfolk's wife so feared in her husband was upon her now. Kathryn, at hearing herself and her friends so slandered, picked up her earthenware washbasin and threw it, full of soapy water. It struck him square-on; his father could have warned him she had good aim. James rolled out into the Long Gallery in a hail of sudsy water and ceramic shards, hand to bruised chest.

Margrethe, who had come along in time to hear half the argument—as had everyone else in the gallery—shouted, "I will show you what your mother and I *do* share, you lout!" and cuffed him on his way for a dozen yards. "Forgive me, I know he is your son," she said when she returned, fists clenched. "But God help him, should word of this reach John!"

"John will not hurt him . . . ?" Kathryn asked, coming back into herself.

"Well," Margrethe said uncertainly, "I have only seen him angry once . . . when the Howard blood is upon you or him or Thomas Howard, it is a very frightening thing to see. What a rage all of you inherited from Jack of Norfolk—! Now come along, the queen is demanding you."

Kathryn dared not say it aloud of Anne Boleyn, but her expression read: *That bitch!*

Anne was sitting with Mark Smeaton, the lute player, at her feet and Arthur Chase at her side. Not even the king could fault her for keeping company with her cousin Arthur; everyone knew he did not bed women—"Tried it once with the wife and did not like it," was the joke at Court.

"You sent for me, Your Grace?" Kathryn asked very stiffly.

"I should like you to wheedle some dainties from the cook. You alone know what niceties I require—some neat's foot jam, maybe a small kidney pie, some shallots in oil and vinegar, a roast heron, some marchpane and comfits, and a pot of mulled cider."

"Your Grace has a very good appetite today."

"I should think so—I believe I am eating for two," Anne said and giggled. Her laughter suddenly ceased. "If so, then we are all saved. All we Howards will have something to bargain with after all. Will it be a boy, do you think? Oh, Kat, it must be a boy!"

And she tittered again, that grating sound that made Kathryn once again wish herself back at Hever a dozen years ago so she could slap that smug, hysterical face she had once loved.

PART THREE

JANE SEYMOUR
(The Thing of Light and Warmth)

"She stepped into my heart so vividly,
A thing of light and warmth!—
As, all unknown,
A princess having wandered from her throne
Might grace a peasant's hut with courtesy."
—Petrarch, 1304–1374—

"Bound To Obey and Serve."
—motto of Jane Seymour

25
January 1536

"The queen is dying."

Jane Seymour leaned forward, whispered it into Kathryn's ear. "The real queen, I mean. You must beg the Boleyn's pardon to leave court for your estates, tell her something, *anything*."

"Queen Catherine is—"

"At Kimbolton. Maria de Salinas awaits you at the Barbican, her London house. Jacquetta has horses, pack mules, Tansy, and Pieter van der Hüm awaiting you outside. Please! Queen Catherine is calling for you and Maria these many days!"

To her shame, Kathryn realized she had all but forgotten Catherine of Aragon. It all flooded back to her now, memories of early childhood at Court, the many kindnesses and gifts, all for love's sake alone, as Kathryn had nothing to offer in return but her dogged devotion. The dancing, the riding together, the lute-playing—the many gowns too new to pass on to a mere maid-of-honor that the queen gave her anyway, observing the many mendings on Kathryn's only garments.

She threw down a shift she was making Lissy and hurried to Anne Boleyn's Presence Chamber. No other excuses came to her, as she had always been a poor liar, so she pleaded melancholy. "I can well believe it." Anne bit off the words nastily. "A person would think you the only woman in the world to lose a husband, and that nigh three years ago! The least you could do is take a lover, but no, you are so poisonously pure nowadays that we have to put up with that long face born of your empty bed—"

"Insult me, hate me, only let me go," Kathryn said grimly, pale with concern for the old queen.

Anne swooped from her chair, flung thin arms about Kathryn. "Oh, Cuz, do forgive me! I am so short-tempered with this child and so afraid, so terribly afraid—please forgive me for lashing out at you, I never mean to hurt you but I always do anyway."

Stricken at so betraying her, Kathryn said, "I will hurry back as soon as possible."

"Please do. That nasty little Jane Seymour is beginning to dress *divinely*."

Kathryn impulsively kissed Anne's cheek. "You worry too much. She is too religious to settle for bed without marriage."

Anne shivered. "I know, that is what worries me. They say I am safe as long as old Catherine of Spain holds out, so I suppose we are all good for another thirty years' use, she always did have the constitution of an ox. Hurry back, Dear."

Kathryn intensely disliked herself all the way to the Barbican. From there it was sixty miles to Kimbolton with no signposts nor even any roads to follow. There was an occasional dirt trail from one farm to the next market, but no more. Luckily Pieter's sense of direction was excellent. Weather also favored them, being moderately wet but not too cold. Bandits only threatened them once, and when Pieter shot the leader dead from thirty yards' distance, the others fled at a gallop.

By the last few miles everyone was wet and dispirited, fearing they would not reach Kimbolton in time. The womens' skirts were muddy to the knees, their borrowed Windsgeat Whites, yellow-gray and brown with bedraggled tails. Pieter, Tansy, and two men-at-arms withdrew to the cover of forest, leaving Maria and Kathryn to go the last quarter-mile alone. One or two women might make it in; an entire traveling party would not.

Maria hammered on the door with both fists. A guard finally answered, wiping his nose on his none-too-clean sleeve. "What is it, Wummin?"

"Kindly address me with some respect, you blithering fool. I am Lady Willoughby and this is Lady Whitbourne. We have had an accident, can you not see the mud all over us? We wish to come in out of the weather and recover ourselves."

" 'No one may enter said pree—prem—*premesise* without express written permission of the king,' " he quoted proudly.

"Here is my permission," Maria said, and laid a purse of gold in his palm. "Now see to the horses before they catch their death of cold." She slipped in under his arm, pulling Kathryn after her.

By the time he thought to protest, they were halfway up the stairs, hand-in-hand like naughty children. "Me Ladies, you cannot go up there!"

Kathryn fumbled for and found all her buried family arrogance. "Do not say 'cannot' to a Howard or I shall flog you from the house, little man! Do you not know who we are? My grandfather was king of England!"

Even on flat ground she was tall for a woman—on the stairs she positively towered. The man froze in mid-protest; by the time he recovered, they were safe in Catherine's rooms with the door locked behind them.

The queen lay propped up against pillows. All the copper had gone from her long hair; it now lay gray and dull as her once-lovely eyes. Her confessor, secretary, and two Spanish ladies were with her, so the women all sorrowfully embraced and murmured news. Then the two newcomers approached the curtained bed. "Francesca, Beatrix, I have not seen you since Durham House."

"Kathryn and Maria? Can it truly be?"

"Your Grace? It is Kathryn Chase and Maria de Salinas come to see you," Francesca said.

Delight shone in weary old eyes. Catherine gestured for them to sit on the bed with her and took hold of their hands. "My very dearest friends—my very, very dearest!" It would have been unthinkable to sit on the queen's bed in the old days, but there was no such formality now.

"Well, how is he?" Catherine demanded eagerly. The two women looked at each other blankly. "My Lord, my light! How is my husband?"

Maria made a choking sound deep in her throat. Kathryn recovered the faster, hurried to say, "The King's Grace is well and sound."

"I hear he still has trouble with that leg ever since Charles Brandon unhorsed him at the joust back in twenty-six. I was there, I recall the blow. I ran screaming onto the field."

Yes, she had been there, but she had spies at Court to know the leg still troubled him. Kathryn knew Jacquetta and Jane Seymour must be those spies. "It is somewhat ulcerated but he does well on it, still rides much," she soothed. "He even tilts against Brandon occasionally."

"And the Great Whore?"

Maria answered this time. "He tires of her rages and vanities. They say if she does not bear him a son this time, he will put her aside."

The dying woman said nonchalantly, "Not while I yet live and breathe. But he will not have too long to wait. I knew he would soon enough tire of her, she is so shrill, so excitable. And His Grace likes peace of an evening, likes his shirts made just *so*. Oh, I hear she donates heavily to charities to gain his favor and plays a pretty enough lute, but that will not make up for screaming and nagging. His self-opinion is very tender; a man likes to think well of himself and cannot do so with a harpy to bed."

Only the nearness of death could force that whispered confidence from her. Unable to bear sitting another minute, Maria rose to tearfully fuss with the fire. "Have you any spices?" the queen asked wistfully. "I remember, Lady Kat, how you used to bring me hot clove water of a morning, even in France."

Kathryn reached in her drawstring purse, shook the bag of cloves at her. "As soon as Maria brings us water, we will set the cloves a-stewing, Your Grace. I even brought some metheglin, hearing from my mother how you enjoyed it at Ludlow."

"Metheglin!" Catherine of Aragon made a child's face of distaste. "I only drank it to flatter the kind Welsh, who brought me so many flowers!"

There was nothing they could do for her. Already her voice was weakening, breath coming harder. The next day she dictated a final letter to the king, ending, "Lastly, that mine eyes desire you above all things." She signed in a final spurt of defiance, *Catherine the Quene*.

Dying, she took an irreplaceable part of the lives around her. Lost youth, abandoned dreams, a valley of gold, and a pillar perished. When the body had been laid out, Kathryn sat before the downstairs fire, swollen-eyed, heavy-hearted. "May God forgive me, I was so enmeshed in my own pain that I forgot her these last few years."

"I am Spaniard, I never forget," Maria snapped back at the crackling flames. "I knew the queen from when we are tiny girls in Spain. So happy for her to marry the prince . . ." She glanced furtively about them, dropped her voice to a whisper. "They say King Henry waited only for our mistress to die. Now that she has, well, who can say? The Great Whore may meet with justice at last."

Kathryn was too miserable to hear the threat to Anne. "Oh, Maria, I cannot bear it! Even though I had not seen the queen in years, yet I felt strong knowing she was there, like the light and warmth of the sun; on rainy days the sun is still there, though one just does not see it. She was so kind to me from childhood on, gave and gave to me. . . . I should have fought my cousin's orders, should have insisted coming into exile with the queen!"

"Will you tell them at Court?"

"What, that she is dead? No, the messenger will beat me there. I paid him well not to mention we were here; I was at Vamplate Manor feeling melancholy, remember? I must return to Court pretending I know nothing of the news and not show the grief I bear. . . . Maria, I feel one thousand years old and wrung dry. My son Adam, my father, Richard, and now Her Grace—oh, it is so much to bear!"

"Yes, it is. My husband is dead, too, my daughter sold to lecherous Charles Brandon who is old enough to be her grandfather. . . . He always hungered after young girls, I remember his first few marriages. And I could do nothing; the days are gone when I was high enough in King Henry's favor that he named a ship the *Mary Willoughby* for me. Dear Kathryn, take care of yourself! I do not know when or if we shall meet again."

They embraced desperately. Then Maria went back upstairs to sit in vigil with the body while Kathryn started for Court.

She rode numbly, unfeeling after her explosion of grief. The many losses of her life suddenly made her feel beyond the pale of ordinary pain. Her children were of an age to survive without her, Richard and Adam were gone, her father gone . . . Well, she had friends at least, she thought, looking glumly at the back of Pieter's head. The little Fleming was the first male friend she had ever had who expected nothing of her, made no demands like family or aspiring lovers did. George Boleyn, wretched in his marriage to Jane Parker, Lady Rochford, had begun making overtures to Kathryn again, as had Thomas Seymour, Jane's handsomest brother. *I am through with all that. Dead to passion at age thirty-six,* Kathryn thought, closing her eyes. *I will not love again and so subject myself to loss and further pain. There will never be anyone to replace my Richard, anyway. Another man would be a poor imitation and I could not bear that.*

Many women of her age never remarried, never took lovers again. But they must have ice water in their veins, not pulsing red blood as she did, she thought, remembering. Dear God, how she missed having a man, her own, loving man in bed at night! She recalled how, with the children finally asleep, she would lie in the dark with her head on Richard's bare chest. They would laugh, talk about events of the day, tell little stories about their separate duties and the people they had come in contact with. It was a contest to see who could make the other laugh the hardest, thus relaxing after the stresses of Court. Then the laughing would turn to soft murmurs and cries, her long white limbs twining with his sturdier, browner ones—oh, for Richard's beautiful, withy body wrapping around her! Richard with his total understanding of her dark moods, her need for that laughter and moaning in the dark—

Tears squeezed out from her clamped eyelids. Pieter, glancing back, thought that she looked like a death mask of herself.

The king celebrated when he heard the news. Put on yellow satin and danced all night. Lady Rochford, among others, danced with him until she was breathless and dizzy. "You have worn me out, Your Grace," she gasped at him.

"You did admirably, Milady, but now I must have the two lightest-footed ladies at my Court. Wife, where is your mother and your cousin, Lady Whitbourne?" he demanded.

Anne, not daring dance for fear of endangering her unborn son, folded defensive hands over her beginning-to-swell abdomen. "Mother is quarreling with Father somewhereabouts. Kathryn claims a headache and is lying down but I know perfectly well what the truth is. She will not celebrate the old termagant's demise."

"By God, she will celebrate when I tell her to! Someone run, fetch that uppity Howard!"

But she was not to be found at Court that night, for she had ridden to Windsgeat. Margrethe received her propped up against too many pillows in bed; it made Kathryn think of the queen lying so and her heart contracted with panic. "I received your note. What is it?" she asked, stooping to kiss the serene white brow.

"Sit, sit, we must talk. I need your help," Margrethe said gently, as if to a wounded child.

"You are my friend, Margrethe. You know I will do anything within my power to help you."

They held hands tightly with worry. "Kat'rin, I need you to tell Johan and Jacquetta that—that I think I am dying."

"No!" The word slipped out.

"I have a pain here." She indicated her womb. "What I am growing inside is not a child, though it has stopped all my monthly courses. My mother and her sister died this way, it is one of those things that runs in families. Thank Heaven I had no daughters to pass it on to, eh? I will become weaker and weaker as they did, I suppose. Kat'rin, in the end, when the pain is too great—and it *will* be, I have seen two women die of this in agony—I will want one of Jacquetta's potions to ease me out of this life. My dear, my dear, you must not weep! I am not sad, how could I be? I have had a wonderful life, two husbands I adored, and you and Jacquetta have been inexpressibly dear to me. I am sorry to put this weight on you so soon after Queen Catherine's death, but where else can I turn? I have not the courage to tell my husband or sister-in-law. But you are always a good intermediary and I love you dearly, I beg you to help me."

"Perhaps Jacquetta has something to help you," Kathryn said, eyes stinging with tears that refused to fall.

"Yes, she can help with the symptoms but not its cause. I can no longer bear lovemaking, it pains me so; I know Johan is thinking I must no longer love him. Not love my husband! He is life and breath itself to me, he is my sun! But you and Jacquetta . . . you are my stars, you shine so brightly when all others fail me. What sweet sisters you two have been to me. Now blow your nose and wipe your eyes, I have more to say."

It was too awful for words. Margrethe was being too calm, too serene. *No, fight!* Kathryn wanted to shout. *Do not be like the old queen and give up with a smile, fight this specter of doom!*

She had to walk around the room awhile, then finally lay weeping in Margrethe's arms. Only Margrethe would have the strength to comfort a friend when she herself was the dying one; feeling guilty at that realization, Kathryn sat, straightened her posture. "I am ready to hear the rest," she said at last.

Margrethe smiled. "Surely you know how greatly I love my family and this place. I include you and your girls in my family, Kat'rin, we are all so fond. I look around me, see my husband, sons, possessions, Windsgeat—all that I love. And I know Johan must have a woman behind him, he is a marrying man. The fact is this: I cannot bear the thought of a stranger sitting in my place, sleeping in his arms. I want you to marry him when I am gone."

"*Jesu,* Margrethe! You must not talk this way—I could never—I loved him once so long ago but I could never—"

The blue-black eyes were untroubled, silver gilt hair neat and orderly. Margrethe patted Kathryn's trembling hands. "My dear, what you and Johan have now is more substantial than when you were lovers. You are good friends, the passion will return later, with luck. How could I leave him to anyone but you? He acts so hard, but inside, he needs love more than most people; I want to be sure he will have it. So I ask my big-hearted Kat'rin."

No. She was not going to lose one more person she loved. Kathryn kissed her friend's cool cheek, excused herself, ran, and found Jacquetta working in her herb garden by moonlight. Given the news, Jacquetta sat down very hard on a marble bench. "Oh, no. No, no, no . . . given that description, there is nothing I can do for her. Lose Margrethe! I cannot bear it, she is always so good-natured, always something kind or funny to say when the rest of us are irritable or sullen. *Gods*. This will kill John, he thinks she is invincible."

Jacquetta wiped her eyes and sat a long while in silence. "Kathryn, this is your night for de Gael family secrets. I think you should know that I have married."

"What! And kept it a secret?" She thought Pieter had been too quiet on the trip from Kimbolton; he must have been craving to tell her. God bless him, Jacqui could not have picked a finer man.

"I have had to keep it to myself until I am too pregnant for John to try to insist on an annulment or abortion. He would never forgive me for marrying William, low-born as he is, though he has a better position at Court now, is Sheriff of some place in Wales with a handsome little income."

She had married young William Brereton, brother to Arthur's dead wife! Kathryn sat down next to her on the bench as her knees gave way. "John will not begrudge you happiness at this late stage of life. Credit the man with some compassion," she said sourly. This news on top of Margrethe's impending loss on top of the queen's—it was all a little too much for her tonight.

"I will go see Margrethe, discover whether I am mistaken about healing her or not. Then we must tell John about her."

Jacquetta sprang from the bench, picked up her brocade skirts, and fled inside, light-footed as a doe.

I wish I was like her, Kathryn thought dully. *Wish I could love wherever I pleased and come out with a lusty young husband. But there I lie, virtuous and shriveled in that Woodville witch's marriage bed, night after night. She must haunt me, that I should have such sensual dreams, such memories and longings.*

She had started to cross herself out of habit before remembering she was on Windsgeat land. What heretical gesturing, what pagan signs was one to make for luck in the heathen greenwood?

Her eye caught a reflection of moonlight on the old stone maze where visitors were forbidden to enter. *Damn you*, she thought. Damn everything green and fertile about this place, making a mockery of the death, pain, and age awaiting them all! Windsgeat had brought her little but grief; she had meant to be mistress of it once, had made a child here with now-dead Richard, was about to watch Margrethe wither and die by inches . . .

"I have had enough of the de Gaels!" she cried to the night. Enough of them! She would saddle Richard's old gelding, ride for Court or Vamplate Manor. She would isolate herself from people so she no longer loved and therefore could not be hurt. She would run from them all, flee pain, run away—

Her great-grandfather, Jack of Norfolk, had not run when the note on his tent warned him certain death awaited anyone supporting Richard the Third—Richard her great-uncle who had charged Henry Tudor single-handed, mowing down a dozen knights and Charles Brandon's father before whole relays of men killed him. No, neither Jack nor Richard Plantagenet had run at Bosworth.

Her mother had not run and deserted Thomas Howard, her father, when he went to the tower after Bosworth. Instead she had gone proudly to the king, faced him alone to have her father and husband freed.

Howards and Plantagenets never ran, and Kathryn suddenly remembered she was both.

She pulled her French hood on straighter and walked back into the house to give John the bitter news.

"The king is dead!"

"I have just heard that the king has died!"

Whispers raced through red brick Greenwich.

"What is all that annoying muttering about out there?" Anne Boleyn demanded, glancing over her shoulder. She was seated on a leather-padded trunk in Greenwich's prettiest oriel window, watching snow fall. A lovely scene for a woman with child to contemplate, she decided. One should never look on unpleasant sights when pregnant, especially not with the heir to England's throne. Not England alone, either, but also *"Wales, Ireland, and Calais in France,"* she whispered to herself, smiling. A son this time. She was certain of it.

Kathryn, at her side, was making lace, winding and knotting silver threads around pins on a little sand-filled pillow. "Would you like me to go see what the fuss is, Your Grace?" she asked.

"Yes, but only if you shut the door on your way to block out the noise. It disturbs my viewing of the courtyard."

As she went, Kathryn heard Anne say, "I do not know why I keep that sullen bitch about me, I know she despises Us. Play louder, Smeaton, drown out those voices. Lady Rochford, if you cannot keep up with him on your lute, do not bother playing!"

Kathryn rounded a corner, found a babbling hoard flying toward her in Norfolk's wake. Her uncle was somber-faced as an executioner today. The long, slightly beaked Howard nose was drawn down nearly to his upper lip, brows pulled together. His hooded eyes suddenly seemed ancient to her. "Niece, where is the queen?"

"Straight ahead in the oriel. She sent me to—"

Without slackening pace, he caught hold of her elbow, strode along bringing her with him. "She will need women about her."

Stitches in her sleeves popped as he hauled her after him. It was then she heard the murmurs. *"He is dead . . ." "No, no, only badly hurt . . ." "In a coma, I saw him . . ." "Jousting. One sees a lot of good men killed that way, but the king of England! . . ." "Miracle his neck was not broken at once, like Baron Whitbourne's . . ." "Hush! That is Lady Whitbourne there, you fool!"*

Norfolk flung open the doors, stood staring at Anne. She sat perkily, cracking nuts into a little silver dish and observing the snow. "Yes, Uncle?" she asked, turning from Norfolk's reflection in the window.

"The king was jousting, Your Grace. He has taken a severe crack on the pate."

She shrugged. "He has taken aplenty before. Let us tuck him in bed and fetch Doctor Butts at once." She set the dish down, stood, and stretched.

Norfolk's steely gaze arrested her motion. *"Niece,"* he said.

He had rarely dared address her as such since her coronation, so use of the word froze her. "Niece, the blow was most severe."

"*How* severe?" she demanded in a hoarse croak.

"He is breathing finally but not responding to words. Brace yourself, Anne. He may not recover."

Anne began backing away from him. "The people hate me—his Councillors hate me—he burned a seeress who said *I* would burn, did I marry him, and I know all of you will do it! He must live, Uncle—if he does not, my enemies will murder me! He must live to protect me and my son!"

She broke and ran, tripping over her long skirts. Smeaton's lute twanged once, then he threw it down and started after the queen.

Kathryn plucked at her uncle's sleeve. "Send for Windsgeat, he has experience with tiltyard injuries. Quickly, while I help Anne!"

None of the other ladies-in-waiting pursued Anne. Instead they stood quibbling over which of Henry's daughters would end up queen by virtue of the most political backing. Probably Mary, they decided, for she was but thirteen months short of twenty-one, old enough to rule without Regent or Council. Little Elizabeth was not yet three, which would lead to a dangerously long regency.

Kathryn would not have found Anne but for the trail of blood the miscarrying queen left.

A messenger killed his horse riding five miles to Windsgeat at top speed. John, half-armored to instruct his sons Payne and Francis in the tiltyard, cast down his padded lance to bellow for Circe, Jacquetta's fastest mare. She was gasping but sound by the time he reached Greenwich, throwing his reins to the nearest lord and yelling, "For God's sake, man, have her cooled down proper and I shall give you her next foal! She is too good to lose!" Circe stood with head between her forelegs, wheezing and blowing.

Henry was still unconscious when John entered the royal bedchamber. "You moved him, you Goddamned fools! It could prove the death of a man wounded in the head, do you not know? Someone draw those tapestries and bed curtains against the light, take those candles away. Doctor Butts, get back from my view, if you would."

"I hear you trained with your radical brother who thinks amputations and battle wounds should be treated with medicinal oils instead of hot pitch."

The tone of the good doctor's voice implied that Doctor Thomas Gale (as John's brother had Anglicized his name) was a madman. "True, that is what his book says," John agreed, bending over Henry in the now dim room. He ran skilled hands over the king's silent body. "He will not live," Butts predicted in sepulchral tones. John thought: *Gods, give me strength not to crack this fool's pate like the king's!*

"Cracked ribs," he said suddenly. "Three of them."

"Your brother says cauterizing with hot irons or pitch 'traumatizes the system' and causes death after shock," Butts continued querulously.

"Yes, that is so." John covered the king up again, eased first one royal eyelid up then the other. So far so good. "Tom also recommends leaving victims of head injuries in quiet, nearly dark rooms. No loud noises like hysterical relatives, or the patient can go into fits and palpitations. He will live, Butts, though I cannot guarantee his soundness of mind when he awakes. There does not seem to be any swelling pushing against the skull, but we must watch, wait, and keep him as little disturbed as possible. Did you check his old leg wound while you were at it?"

"It was never an open wound, only a bone bruise, but I worry because so bad a bruise can sometimes cause clots long after the accident."

Very good. John graded him higher this time than before. "I will go make sure Norfolk keeps the screamers and weepers out, if you will guard the king."

"Milord! With my life!" Doctor Butts huffed.

I must not make an enemy of him just because he is a fool, John thought drily. *He will never find another employment this rich*. "Do you think the old leg injury will flare up again after this fall?" he asked. "Not last week I saw the king limping slightly and I wanted to ask your opinion as to whether or not . . ."

The door to Anne Boleyn's bedchamber banged open, marring the newly frescoed wall. Bled white, devoid of her half-made son, Anne cringed back against the headboard.

"You have murdered my son, Madam!" roared the king. He pointed at the cradle. "That lies empty as do you, Madam! Well, you shall lie empty forever now because of it. Good day and good riddance!"

Kathryn, horrified, watched him slam dizzily out of the room. She turned back to Anne just quickly enough to catch sight of Lady Rochford's face: Anne's sister-in-law wore a smirk of impurest delight. "You bloody damned bitch," Kathryn said darkly, and slapped the other woman. "Get out of here—get out!"

Jane Parker fled, babbling and weeping.

Kathryn climbed onto the royal bed, tenderly drew the sobbing Anne into her arms. Shrew or not, her cousin needed comfort. Backbiting, gossiping, tyrannical Anne—she was like any other terrified child facing punishment, and Kathryn's quick heart went out to her. "There, Cuz," she soothed, drawing Anne's disheveled head to her shoulder. "There, there, men are cruel when disappointed, he will apologize later."

"No, he will not! He loathes me now, I see it in his eyes! Oh, do not leave me alone in the dark, Kat! It is so black in here and I am afraid of going home for the last time in the dark!"

Kathryn, ever literal-minded, thought she spoke of riding to Hever Castle by night and was mystified that a woman in Anne's condition could think of travel.

Hours later she emerged from the chamber, stiff and aching from holding Anne while she slept. To her surprise she found John waiting for her just outside Anne's door. He had removed his breastplate, greaves, gorget, and gauntlets and now sat bare-armed in his sleeveless fighting gambeson and breeches. Someone had loaned him an ill-fitting cloak which he had flung around his shoulders to keep away the chill.

The washy blue eyes looking up at her from the bench were unguarded, pain-filled. "The queen is somewhat better. How is Margrethe?" she asked.

He shook his head, spread both hands wide in a gesture of helplessness. "I am the wealthiest man in England after the king, did you know that?" he asked. "I have become a friend of his and a member of his Privy Council. People call that 'having power.' I can even ride with the Old Dark Ones and, upon occasion, help someone who has been thumped too hard by a lance. But I could not save your Richard and I cannot save my Margrethe. What the Hell have I been devout for these many years when it leads to losing her? Is a life so much to ask?"

Margrethe was right, Kathryn thought. She and John were friends after all.

She drew his chestnut head to her side, laced her fingers in the thick hair. "Lean on me a moment, John, and I shall lean back. Perhaps that way we might hold each other up awhile longer and go on with our lives."

He patted her arm, smiling through misty eyes; she vaguely remembered all the reasons she had loved him sixteen years ago. "Funny how things turn out," he said.

"Yes, funny," she agreed, thick-throated with too many years of loss.

It was the day Catherine of Aragon was buried in Peterborough Cathedral. Many said her vengeful ghost had made Anne miscarry.

George Boleyn was not made a Knight of the Garter as expected that spring when a vacancy occurred in the ranks. The honor went to John de Gael instead. Windsgeat, once the king's worst enemy! The Court could not stop buzzing about it.

Jane Seymour's brothers Thomas and Edward were given fancy new apartments at Court. Jane wrote young Mary Tudor, "Be at peace. A little longer and you shall be returned to your father's forgiving presence."

Henry sent an impassioned letter and purse of gold to Jane at Wolf Hall. She knelt and kissed the letter but refused the purse, telling the messenger it would compromise her honor in the eyes of the world. "If His Majesty would so bless me with gifts, then beg him, let it be only upon the occasion that he and God send me some good and honest husband," she said. Her lips so caressed the word "husband" that the messenger, exactly mimicking her tone and expression, got the news across to Henry Tudor; Jane Seymour was not to be had without marriage.

Well, why not? Henry meditated upon how quiet and meek Jane was, how unobtrusive and adoring. Tiny, too, not long and gangly like that black-eyed bitch. Little Seymour would never shriek at him in public, saying he wore doublets as loud as Windsgeat's; would never accuse him of impotence until he found he could not perform with her. His worshipful Jane would not bring a crowd of clutching, rapacious relatives to Court, only her two clever and companionable brothers. The rest of her many siblings preferred quiet country life.

A neat little woman who would stay in the background as a wife should. No more emotional scenes and explosions. He would have no more unyielding foreigners, no more high-spirited viragos to sorely wound his tender male pride.

Sweet little chinless Jane with her sensitive mouth so like a child's, the short, pleasantly rounded neck his hand just exactly curved around to fit. And a virgin to boot.

He told Thomas Cromwell, whom the Court called "the new Wolsey," to get rid of Anne Boleyn.

"Any way possible," he added.

26

2 May, 1536

". . . amen."

"Amen," Anne's ladies echoed, kneeling to wait upon her at dinner. They rubbed her plates with soft cloths and salt, likewise polished her dinner dagger, spoons, and goblet before laying them out before her.

Kathryn was pouring watered wine for the queen when there came a curious sound outside, like a trampling of many feet. "Whatever they want, send them away, Whitbourne," Anne said and giggled wearily. "I am so tired from the May Day tourney yesterday that I can hardly keep my eyes open. Send them away. So—so *tired*." She yawned, then uncontrollable giggles came from her open mouth. Her women looked on in consternation as the slender shoulders shook with sobbing laughter.

Kathryn opened the door, saw Norfolk at the head of a small party of men-at-arms. Her uncle was queerly pale and looked suddenly old to her, like some aged bed sheet boiled and mercilessly wrung out. Thomas Cromwell, porcine-faced with his snub nose and tiny eyes, stood next to him, staring holes in Norfolk as though daring him to show any weakness.

"*Kathryn*," Norfolk said simply. She saw the exhaustion in his face, the slumped shoulders and too-bright eyes.

"My Lord Norfolk? *Uncle*?"

His voice, when he finally regained it, was very hoarse. "We have come to arrest the queen on charges of treasonous adultery."

Someone dropped a gilt plate. It banged to the floor, clattered in ever-tightening circles before finally lying still. Anne gave a sarcastic laugh. "Adultery? *Me*, whom he calls the least passionate of women? A joke in poor taste, Uncle. What is the real purpose of your visit? One of my ladies marry the wrong man?"

"The accused men have already confessed," Cromwell informed her smugly.

Anne tried to shove her chair back and rise, but as it and the table were of solid oak, neither gave way. She floundered, barking shins and elbows, ripping out her hem before she could stand. "*You lie!*" she screamed, clutching Henry's jeweled portrait at her breast. "I am His Grace's true and faithful wife, no man touched me before or after him! I came to him as true a maid as any novice to nunnery and I have not so much as held the hand of another man since! Who accuses me? You tell me who lies thus about his queen! Who is arrested?"

She was very much a Howard in those moments, seeming to stand far taller than she was.

"Henry Norris," Norfolk began tiredly.

"What, Sir Hal? One of the king's boon companions, a pleasant old fellow, due to marry my cousin Madge Shelton. Hardly the kind to inspire passion. Who else?" Anne asked almost gaily. *Such a ridiculous man they accuse me with for openers*, she thought. *If it is all no more serious than this—*

In the candlelight Anne's gray dress aged her sallow skin, made her look yellowed and already dead.

"Mark Smeaton."

Anne threw her dark, slender head back, roared with mocking laughter. "Poor little Smeaton, the lutist! I would not touch the fingertips of so base a fellow, no matter how prettily he plays! Go on, Norfolk, you afford me rare entertainment."

"William Brereton."

Jacquetta's husband, and the two of them about to announce the marriage! Kathryn, still holding the door open, felt her mouth go dry, knees weaken.

"Sir Thomas Wyatt—" The queen's distant cousin and old friend. "Sir Francis Weston—" Another old, passionless friend. "William Page—" Anne could hardly recall the man's face. "Sir Arthur Chase." *Cousin Arthur*! Anne thought "—and Lady Rochford has accused her husband of incestuous adultery with you, Your Grace."

"My dearest friends along with virtual strangers, a lute player, my cousin, and own brother? Uncle, you do much malign me!" Anne blasted back. She had to cling to her chair for support, but she drew her head back like a viper about to strike—her head snapped forward—she spat full in Cromwell's face. "This is your doing, Wolsey the Second. I know these foul accusations are your doing!"

Arthur, George, William. Kathryn slid down the back of the door, unnoticed by most in the room. She lay there in a heap while they took Anne away, ladies milling after her.

One yeoman of the guard, hat pulled low over his eyes, lingered in the shadows. "My Lady Whitbourne?" he whispered in a familiar voice.

She stirred, raised her head. Dizzily sat. The halberd he held above her head seemed to foreshadow the executioner's axe; she put a hand up to ward off the killing stroke.

He tilted his cap back, showed the handsome face of Jane Seymour's favorite brother, Thomas. Her lips formed the inquiry, "*Yes?*" to him, though no sound emerged.

Thomas Seymour handed her up. "Jane says to tell you: go home at once to your estates and remain there until she sends for you. Otherwise you will be charged by Lady Rochford with procuring lovers for the queen and will go to the block alongside Anne Boleyn and your brother. Within eight weeks or so Jane will have talked the king into seeing your innocence and you will be able to return."

"Would not flight be an admission of guilt?" she croaked. "And how can I not stay to defend Anne, George, my own brother? Oh, especially Arthur, everyone knows he has no interest in women! For him to be charged should prove all the adulteries equally fictitious."

She had refused to stand up for Queen Catherine, so recently dead. Instead she had been swayed by her passionate desire to protect her family. Well, a fine job she had done; her husband, father, second son dead, and Arthur threatened. Anne . . . George . . . Her children were no longer infants; even did they have to spend their lives titleless and landless, Norfolk and the de Gaels would never let them starve.

"Conscience has served ambition too long," she said, chin coming up, slanting black brows nearly meeting in the middle. "Let them arrest me; as I have been Anne's constant companion I can speak in her favor. A woman has honor as well as a man and can only be bought, bullied, and threatened so far. I will stand up this time—I will be heard!"

He considered it. "That is how my sister *said* you would respond. Forgive me, My Lady," Thomas Seymour said. And cracked his fist across the point of her proudly upthrust jaw.

Little pinpoints of light exploded around Kathryn. Reaching for his face, she grasped nothing and so pitched forward into oblivion.

"James? James Howard, you let me out of here this instant! *I am your mother!*"

Kathryn recognized the windowless wardrobe room at Howard House, courtesy of a strip of light penetrating under the ill-fitting door. She had rattled the knob, bruised her shoulders flinging her negligible weight against oak and brass, and now stood roaring for her son in a fine Howard rage.

Footsteps approached, blocking the light. "Shut up, Mother," said James, sounding delighted.

"Why are you doing this to me?"

"Because the trials have commenced this very day and are no real trials at all. You would only get yourself ingloriously decapitated and the Howards stripped of all rank and property."

"But your uncles—Anne—"

"There is no helping them. Henry Tudor wants Anne dead so he can remarry without any legal knotwork such as he went through with Catherine of Aragon. He cannot divorce and sire one more questionable heir, ending with the countryside whispering "bastard" as they do about little Elizabeth Tudor. And you know how King Henry can never bear taking the blame for anything—not even for marrying an unpopular woman he grew to loathe. So to clear his own good name he has let them accuse her of as many adulteries as Cromwell could invent in so short a time. Incest was of course the crowning touch; that violently revolts all decent folk. It was Jane Parker's contribution to the list of charges. Wyatt and Page have been released but the rest is all formality; the others have been found guilty and condemned to the block before they even go to trial."

Her mind tripped over those harsh words, sat unbelieving and hardly functioning. Kathryn leaned against the door, fingers braced as if she could dig through dark wood to the light beyond.

"I have passed the word," added James, "that all of this has stricken you gravely ill with brain fever and that I have taken you to Whitbourne to recover. So no one will come free you; only the Seymours know you are here, and they think I have a loving son's devotion toward you."

Begging would do her no good, she was slowly realizing

that. "Will you release me when the trials are done with?" she asked.

"You will be dead by then and never again humiliate me with your lovers, bastards, and politicking. Good-bye, Mother; I have sent all the servants away, no one will hear you scream. I shall return every few days to see if you have starved yet. Then you shall be pronounced dead of the fever at Whitbourne and I shall be free of you at last."

Scraping sounds of wood whining on its like. The door leaped back against her cheek with an impact from the other side; he had pushed some piece of furniture against it and was adding more. Bit by bit she lost the thin strip of daylight under the door, until finally there was nothing but her screaming repetition of his name.

Raw-throated, shut in stale blackness, she gasped to a halt. Another door thudded shut somewhere far away in the house, then another.

He had locked her up to die in Howard House. She had not so much as a dinner dagger to pry the lock open, not a hat pin nor a metal stay in her bodice nor—slapping her clothes frantically—anything else. He had removed it all.

Kathryn could hear her own panting fill the inky wardrobe room. The close-set walls pressed in on her—

None came forward to speak for the accused. Anne was closeted with her four least favorite women, excepting Lady Rochford; they even brought in Mistress Stonor, former Mother of the Maids to spy on her, for she had despised Anne since Anne's early days as a maid of honor.

At George Boleyn's trial he was ordered to silently scan a slip of paper bearing something he and his sister had supposedly said of the king. George, knowing he was doomed and wishing, George-like, to prick the famed Tudor pride on his way out, read loudly the words, "That we did accuse the king of utter impotence," thereby endearing himself to Henry-haters everywhere. François the First, hearing of it across the Channel, laughed until he gagged. "He was a so-brave man, that Boleyn. I will have three Masses a day said for his soul, all this next year!"

Anne was finally given the welcome word that she would be beheaded instead of lingeringly burnt. In fact, the king was so merciful that instead of a blunt axe requiring several strokes, she would have an excellent swordsman from Calais, guaranteed to kill with one clean blow.

She giggled wildly about it to the four hated ladies. "Why, 'twill be simple," she said. "The swordsman is said to be very good, and I have so slender a neck! I shall be known from now on as Queen Anne Lackhead! As for that Seymour bitch . . ."

They had accused her of witchcraft, to have so beguiled the king and blinded him to her wickedness. Anne closed her eyes until only slits of white frighteningly showed. "I pray that Jane Seymour die the most agonizing of deaths, to have so encouraged the king my husband to murder me and marry her."

Seventeen days from arrest to death. She was magnificent on the scaffold, a Howard to the end with her calm speech and majestic posture. Blindfolded, kneeling with her luxuriant black hair piled atop her head to bare the long swan-neck, she neither trembled nor wept.

The headsman's assistant tromped down upon the scaffold, startling her. Anne instinctively turned toward the sound, though she was sightless behind the rectangle of white linen. In that instant she presented a target that made for the headsman's easiest work, and her own least pain.

The sword swung in an arc of dazzling steel.

Henry Tudor heard the cannonfire announcing her death. "And the silver hat to go with it," he told his valets, smiling into the mirror. *Teeth look wonderful*, he thought, picking at them with his fingernail. Glorious new doublet and coat, too. Well, the bitch was dead now, so off to the barge, then downriver to dine with the Seymours.

Little Elizabeth Tudor screamed in her sleep, sat clutching nothing with both tiny fists. In a flash her door was open and Isabella Howard was there, gathering the child into her arms.

Elizabeth looked over Isabella's shoulder, pointed beyond her as though she could see something terrifying beyond a three-year-old's wildest imaginings.

"*Mama*," she said, and wept.

"You have until the count of five to tell me where she is and then I shall gut you like a stag," John de Gael said. "She is not at Court nor in the Tower nor at Vamplate Manor, and there are writs out for her arrest all over England. One, two, three—witnesses now say they saw you carry her out of here over your shoulder—*four*—"

The voyding knife pricked Thomas Seymour's quaking abdomen. "*Howard House!*" He screamed it, the sweat of fear soaking his fine, frilled shirt.

"You would not lie to me and expect to live, Tom?"
"God's Blood, man! The king will burn your bowels out for this!"

John's face was scant inches from his, crooked front teeth showing in a ghastly smile. "Your sister's betrothal to Henry Tudor makes you neither king, pope, nor headsman as far as I know, Seymour. Speak one word of this little interlude and I will be weeks in killing you."

He still held a handful of Seymour's shirt, twisting it so tightly that Thomas choked and sputtered. "I swear, Windsgeat, I never harmed her! My sister wanted her saved so I crept into the yeoman guards' chambers, dressed like one of them, marched to the queen's quarters with them. Jane knew Kathryn would speak up for her family and die along with them, so she ordered me to kidnap her and take her to James Howard for safekeeping until all this was over."

"The heads are on Tower Bridge Gate except for Anne Boleyn's, which was crammed into that arrow case with the rest of her and buried under Saint Peter Ad Vincula's floor. Face the bridge, Thomas: I see the heads, do you, too? And yet Kathryn Chase has not shown up, nor is James Howard smirking abouts. Oh, Seymour, I shall be many, many days a-killing you, have you lied. Such things I learned with the German army, such niceties of torture. . . ."

He moved amazingly fast for a big man. Thomas Seymour was thrust through the nearest window with the same motion that turned John out the door.

Seymour toppled six feet to the ground, lay screaming in a nest of brambles and glass shards. Courtiers rushed to help him. "What happened, man?" one demanded.

He could still feel the voyding knife against his belly. "I—I slipped," he sobbed out. Jesu, he had been trying to *help* the woman! What would Windsgeat do to him had he *harmed* her?

The outraged shouting become shrill screaming. Eventually the screams turned to pleas, then low, rasping moans. She was a hard woman to kill, his mother. Little gory scraps of gray fur told James she had lived on mice awhile but this was the last of her. He had checked on her last night, seen her cracked lips and swollen, almost black tongue. No pulse to speak of, chest only rising and falling shallowly. She would be dead by tonight and no one the wiser.

Horses passed the house. James was not startled; living so

near the river there were always travelers. She had no strength to scream for help any more, and the thick walls of Howard House would keep anything from being overheard from the bridle path.

He was therefore surprised when, a few minutes later, a voice behind him said, "Move, Howard, and you are a corpse."

John de Gael's voice was familiar to him, though never in this timbre. "Come in, Pieter, I have him covered," James heard him add.

The little Fleming entered, longbow drawn, arrow nocked. "We wish de honor of your lady mudder's company," van der Hüm said. *As though*, James thought wildly, *he is good enough to speak thus to a lord!* So he said nothing.

"On second thought," John said, "I must countermand my previous order. Move after all, Howard; turn very slowly toward me. I should like you to see something."

James did not leave his chair, only turned his head to regard John. The man was dressed in Lincoln green suedes, having come from hunting in the greenwood, but seeing him so uncustomarily informal was not what shocked James. No, it was the thing aimed at him. A rich lord's typical yew-bow, tall as a woman, the gold leaf half-rubbed away with use; no surprise there.

But the arrow had two monstrous heads, both barbed and fanged.

"I cannot miss from this range, nor can Pieter," John informed him with no emotion in his voice. "But whereas Pieter's arrow might be dug out, mine can not. The doctors will have to hammer it out the other side and it will not leave a single sound organ in your entire body. You have until the count of five to tell me where Kathryn is. One—"

"*Upstairs in the garderobe!*"

"You broke fast for a Howard; could it be possible your father was really a *Tudor*?" John asked. "Come here, Pieter, take my bow."

Incredible that a man the size of the little Fleming could pull that bow without help, but he took it, stood staunch and unshaken.

John bounded up the stairs five at a time. Chests, chairs, a table—he wrested them back, smashed through the lock with his pistol-butt.

Howard lied, was his first thought. This was not Kathryn, this was some dead old woman. The drab, filthy hair—the stench of confinement—skin puckered with dryness, clothes torn, a handful of hair plucked out. Bits of dead mice, blood, and wood under her broken nails from clawing to escape—

A shudder ran through her. Death throes, he thought, then saw a faint flicker of cornflower blue from beneath her lowered eyelids. Gods! It *was* Kathryn!

He lifted her. She might have been a bag of feathers, tiny, dry, and brittle. No flesh on her bones, wrist-joints sticking out through a thin layer of chalky skin. Her collarbone jutted above the ripped bodice; how could she be so thin and live?

"Sweetheart, darling, live for me a little longer. Live to eat and breathe. Just hold on a little longer while I fetch you some food."

She was trying to say something but there was no saliva in her mouth. John kissed the feverish brow, the sunken cheek. "There now, I have you, Kathryn. You will not be hurt any more."

There was so much food in Howard House's kitchens. Bacon, new cheese draining on a bed of nettles, fresh-baked bread. Ox-bone stew, which John watered down for Kathryn. But she could not drink it from a spoon, so he dipped a towel in the pot, squeezed a few drops at a time into her mouth. A crock of cream, some butter, pounded fruits rolled in honey and spices—James must have been to market this morning, sat gorging himself while upstairs Kathryn, his Kathryn . . .

John gave her watered wine the same way, his hands shaking while she nursed on a damp corner of the toweling. "I am going to leave you here on the table for just a minute, sweetheart," he said, laying her down and spreading his short hunting cloak over her.

Kathryn made heaving sounds, tried and failed to grasp the front of his suede tunic. "Do not worry," John said grimly. "I will not kill your son."

Pieter stood drenched in sweat, shoulders wobbling with the strain of keeping the bow trained on James for so long. "She is alive," John said. "At least for the moment. She weighs no more than a lady's brocade gown, Pieter, and she ate mice to live. She has no voice, no color, and candlelight blinds her. He shut her up to starve these seventeen days. But her eyes tell me she does not want him dead."

"Let me do dis ding, Lord, I beg you!" burst out the Fleming.

"Do not kill him and do not leave conspicuous marks, Pieter. Howard House has deep, thick cellars as I recall; I should not like Milady to be disturbed by this animal's howls."

Straight teeth showed in an evil grin. "Wid pleasure, Lord," Pieter said.

John was back in the kitchens with Kathryn when he heard the cellar door softly snick shut. He knew his manservant well; there would not be a sound from down below.

He talked to keep Kathryn alive. She was too frail to move and he must keep her alive until he could send Pieter for Jacquetta. A few hours to let her stabilize; Jacquetta could do nothing more than he could at this moment. Just to get a little moisture into Kathryn, warm her after the chill, closeted spring nights . . .

The mule-drawn litter had nearly reached Windsgeat before she spoke. "*Anne?*" Kathryn asked so softly that they hardly heard her. John, riding Morrighan alongside the litter, reined the mare in and answered. "She died bravely."

"To a man it would matter she was brave. A woman only cares that she died," Jacquetta snapped.

Kathryn asked, "Who died with her, and did you sit on the council of peers condemning them?"

"Oddly, Tudor did not ask it of me. Your cousin George died, young Brereton died." Here Jacquetta, riding ahead, gave a convulsive twitch of the shoulders. John listed the victims, finishing, ". . . and Arthur, too. Only Wyatt and Page escaped the block. Those who died were all granted peers' privilege and beheaded instead of drawn and quartered, even the commoners. Norfolk and Harry Percy had to sit on the Council and pronounce them all guilty; Percy broke down, had to be carried out and laid on the lawn. There is a man with death in his eyes! I can bear that Norfolk and Northumberland, who so loved her, would judge her thus; they have families to protect. But that Thomas Boleyn would sit so in judgment of his own children and convict them of that monstrous charge is unforgivable. He has gone home to face his wife, your aunt; let that be his punishment."

They traveled in silence down the slope from Windsor. John finally thought to add, "Tudor used Anne's nonexistent betrothal to Percy to annul the marriage and bastardize Elizabeth. In which case he executed a woman not married to him who therefore was not guilty of adultery. There are all manner of ways to bend the law to suit a king's purpose."

The trip had taken all color from Kathryn, left her looking much as she had when he first spied her on the filthy floor. Her lips formed the word *heads*.

John fussed with Morrighan's reins. "I could not get them down from the bridge, Kathryn. They were accused of something more serious than your father and there is a guard posted, not like for Lord Hal. I have had Arthur's body buried with your father. Some day perhaps we shall have the rest. George Boleyn's body I could not get. He is under St. Peter-in-Chains' chapel floor, like Anne."

He knew her next question and dreaded answering it. "Let her know she still has a son, unlike your sister who lost hers years ago, awaiting your return," Jacquetta said spitefully.

So he said, simply, "James lives."

Kathryn nodded weakly. It was more than she had dared hope for. Her tired mouth formed Margrethe's name. "She lives," he said. There was no way to detail in what suffering, nor how often she required painkilling medicines that left her mind fogged.

John was not ready for the last question. "Jane Seymour?" Kathryn whispered.

"Is queen of England now and praying as hysterically for sons as her two predecessors did."

"My girls?"

"Were never arrested. They are safe with the princesses at Hatfield."

The golden-brown head sagged back onto her pillow; he turned Morrighan away toward Windsor. "Where are you going?" Jacquetta demanded.

"To buy her life from the king; have you forgotten his writs against her? Queen Jane has not sent word that he has forgiven Kathryn for being Anne's cousin. My money will talk to him, it always does." He spurred for Court.

27

Had she bitten off too much to chew? Jane Seymour sometimes wondered. Had she reached too far above herself, dared too greatly, risked too much? This king she had married was nothing like they told her—easily wounded in his self-opinion, touchy in pride, in dire need of a good, religious woman. Her brothers and Jacquetta appeared to be wrong; Henry Tudor needed no one and no thing.

There was no one to tell her that he was a changed man. Freed of Anne's nagging and hysterical scenes he felt himself a dozen years younger and the swagger he walked with was pronounced. Those who looked at him with anything less than devotion were immediately ordered from Court; he would not be contradicted on even the smallest point.

Having declared himself Head of the Church of England, he regarded all priestly property as his and sent troops to sack abbeys across the land, thus fattening the Privy Purse. This became known as the Dissolution of Abbeys. When devout, God-fearing Jane timidly dared ask one night whether he might restore several of the older, most historic monasteries, he roared out, "'By God, Madam, you would do well to remember the fate of your predecessors and hold your tongue!"

That had been five weeks into the marriage.

So she could not approach him directly. She must work as she always had, behind the scenes, pulling strings while pretending to be but one more fascinated member of the audience. Her letters to the fanatically Catholic Mary Tudor brought groveling entreaties from that girl to her royal father but that was not enough for him—he demanded Mary sign the Act of Supremacy, naming him Head of the Church. In fear of her life if she did not, in fear of losing her immortal soul if she obeyed him, she finally broke down and signed.

Isabella Howard, from behind Mary's chair, murmured, "You could always write the pope explaining that you acted under duress, Your Grace. He would consider it better that you live to defend your faith than die and be unable to help."

"You must not call me 'Your Grace,' " Mary murmured. It was only later, when Isabella had gone to bed, that Mary realized the maid-of-honor had said "your faith," not "our faith."

It was not enough for Henry Tudor. He had broken Mary's will, forced her to commit the mortal sin of placing his authority over the pope's, had kept her from her mother's side and deathbed. Now, having suffered her recalcitrance so long, he demanded she attend him at Court and publicly beg his forgiveness. Here Isabella's mother was able to help her. Kathryn advised, "He loves a show of having been proved right and the world wrong. Because you see, Prin—I mean, *Lady* Mary, he so thoroughly believes it that he is outraged anyone should doubt him. It will be hard on your pride but the fastest way to win his mercy is to prostrate yourself. Yes, go flat on your face and kiss his shoes. I have done it many times myself. The knee bends like this, the other like so, and the arms go here to ease you down. He will love it and then feel very virtuous about helping you back up."

Lady Kathryn had become very cynical since her attack of the brain fever, Mary thought, rehearsing the prostration with her. Even five years ago she could not imagine Lady Whitbourne speaking so of the king. Perhaps it was true that she had gained much conceit through association with the so-arrogant and gorgeous de Gaels. It was certainly true enough that when that family bought her way back to Court, thin and wobbling, the king had commiserated with her on her loss, meaning her brother and cousins. Lady Whitbourne, looking him square in the eye, had dared reply, "And I with you on *your* loss, Your Grace." She had then prostrated herself so excessively that Henry had not known whether to laugh or have her arrested. In the end he had done neither out of embarrassment.

Mary went prettily flat on her face before her father that night and was taken back into his good graces. Yet she could hardly bear living with the sin; her entire life would now be spent trying to atone to a ruthless God for having so betrayed Him. Years later she would try to buy her soul back with the charred bodies of heretics; she would die as she had lived, with her convoluted Spanish soul thoroughly misunderstood by the uncomplicated English.

But then, Mary would have seemed foreign at any Court in Europe.

Imperious old Margaret Pole, Countess of Salisbury, was recalled to Court several weeks after Mary was sent away again. Hearing that the former royal governess was arriving and thinking Mary and Elizabeth might be with her, Londoners jammed the streets in a show of support. They so impeded the progress of her traveling party that the countess leaned from her curtained litter, cried out, "My good friends, make way for a tired old woman!"

"The princesses! Where are the princesses?" they cried.

"What are they shouting out there?" the king demanded.

Jane, who dared not tell him, answered that she did not know. Then she hunched lower over her embroidery. She was not as good a needleworker as Catherine of Aragon, though she had learned sewing from her and Kathryn, and feared that every miscounted stitch showed. "Over two, up three," she whispered to herself. Kathryn, on a cushion at the new queen's feet, glanced at her worriedly. Was Jane going to crack as Anne had done, and so quickly?

Henry went onto an arched stone balcony, shouted, "Good folk, what troubles you?"

"The princesses! Have the princesses arrived with Lady Salisbury?" someone cried.

Jane Seymour flinched at that forbidden word. *Princesses*.

"My bastard daughters will visit soon enough. Now disband, I tell you. Disband!" He turned irritably from the window, brightened at the sight of Jane. "Now! Who is jousting tomorrow to celebrate the reopening of Parliament? Your fine brothers, Wife?"

"Yes, Your Grace."

He eagerly turned to Kathryn. "Will Windsgeat fight? Of course, he is rather old for it."

"Nay, husband, Windsgeat is but your age and you are still plenty young enough," Jane hastened to say.

He chuckled. "Young enough for what, Little Wife?"

Jane crimsoned, a becoming shade in her marriage gown of deep red velvet with gold cording in a fishnet pattern all over her turned-back sleeves. *She looks so much nicer since Master Holbein the artist began designing her gowns,* Kathryn thought. After one too many blinding de Gael doublets, Margrethe had asked John to go to Holbein, too. But, in the manner of men everywhere, he took umbrage at the suggestion that his sartorial splendor was excessive.

She ventured a peek at the royal couple. Henry was making Jane drop her embroidery so he could kiss her tiny hands. Once Jane had worn flattering little French hoods; now, lest her headgear remind Henry of Anne Boleyn and her foreign clothes, she reverted to old-fashioned gable headdresses. Kathryn had convinced her to modernize them by pinning up one or even both of the heavy black velvet tails that normally hung down the wearer's back. This way it showed Jane's short but prettily rounded throat, necklaces, and the tops of her shoulders, for nowadays high-necked shifts were out of fashion. Shifts, in fact, showed only in wrist ruffles; there was nothing to cover a woman from her chin to the low, square neckline of her gown.

"I repeat, Sweetheart," the king said, caressing Jane's bare neck, "young enough for *what*?"

Jane Seymour reddened further. "For anything my good husband desires," she answered humbly.

Pardon me while I vomit, Kathryn thought sourly. Gathering up her willow basket, she curtsied and left unnoticed by Henry and Jane. The de Gaels were coming to Court tonight and she was looking forward to their visit, as Margrethe so seldom left Windsgeat any more. It would be so good to see her and John and the boys! "My cornflower blue velveteen," she told Tansy upon reaching her apartment. "And not one of these ugly damned gable headdresses, I want to look pretty."

"You dare not wear a French hood, it will remind the king of you-know-who," the maidservant replied, then snapped her fingers. "Ahh, Lady Kat, I have just what you need! That silver caul of your mother's with the glass gems set all over it. I shall polish it up for you. Start brushing your hair; I will arrange it for you."

A fresh shift and petticoats, her prettiest silver-gray stockings and garters. The cornflower velveteen, her plain silver chains. By the time Kathryn had brushed her hair one hundred slow strokes she felt like a cat in the sun, lazy and content. In fact she found a stray sunbeam to sit in while Tansy parted her golden-brown hair, drew it back into an intricate heap of braids, and snooded it. "Such hair you have, nor a hint of gray to it," Tansy said proudly. "There is not many of six-and-thirty can say they got no gray, Lady."

"And me without a single grandchild. I thought Isabella or James would have wed long ago," Kathryn lamented. She never heard the story of what John and Pieter had done to James, but word of his mistreatment of her had gotten around Court. And as he had no fortune to recommend him, either, parents refused to allow him to court their daughters. Norfolk had even gotten the king to ban him from the royal presence. So James could not marry, and Isabella had announced total disinterest in the subject. That left only Lissy, who had eight or nine years to go before she was marriageable. "I will be forty-four by then and unable to make babies of my own," Kathryn said aloud, closing her eyes in the warm sunbeam. "Mary has babies, but I am forbidden to write her and Arthur is dead. Poor, pederast Arthur, dying for a woman."

"Eh?"

"Nothing, Tansy, nothing. Just thinking aloud."

They were finishing when there came a knock at the door. All the de Gaels but Jacquetta stood there, smiling. Kathryn embraced frail, colorless Margrethe, greeted the boys. "Payne, Francis, how tall you are!" She embarrassed them both by kissing them, but John she did not embrace. They no longer hugged as she hugged other male friends, be they her own acquaintances or the husbands of women-friends; funny that this new awkwardness should spring up between them. She had held him the day the king nearly died jousting, and he had held her for most of two days at Howard House. She remembered sleeping in his arms during her convalescence and it discomforted her beyond words.

He was in one of his moods today; there was a white line along each side of his jaw. "Who just got the better of him?" she drily asked Margrethe.

"Jacqui. She will not tell him who the father of the upcoming baby is."

Payne swallowed hard and fled, muttering excuses. Francis, who was much harder to upset, sighed and slowly followed him while Kathryn led Margrethe inside, handing her into a softly padded chair. The dying woman sat with a sigh of closed-eyed gratitude. "Why should she tell him?" Kathryn asked, feeling antagonistic to John today. "It is none of his business."

"None of my business?" John meant to nudge the door shut with his foot but he kicked it so hard it banged deafeningly into the frame. "When my sister bears a bastard it is my business to know who the man is. Especially if he is the king of England!"

"Henry Tudor is not the father, and in case she has not told you, the child is legitimately begotten."

He bent, raised Margrethe's little feet to a hassock. "Oh, thank you, Johan, that is nice!" his wife whispered.

John chewed on Kathryn's information a while. He finally surrendered, let a smile flit across his face. "Well, the two of them could have trusted me. I know Pieter has loved her for years and I am glad she finally has the sense to see that titles alone do not make for worthy men. He is the finest—"

"It is not Pieter and do not ask me more. It is not my secret to keep."

He and Kathryn exchanged angry glares. "A person would think I sold you into slavery instead of—"

Kathryn countered, "Instead of buying my freedom from the king? You could have consulted me first, but no, you never asked my opinion! Now people slander me again because—"

Margrethe sighed. "Because they think you are his mistress again and that the two of you are just waiting for me to die. I would feel so comforted to know you two would have each other when I am—"

"Stop it!"

Neither of them had ever heard John shout as he shouted now. Kathryn quailed, but Margrethe only said, "Oh, stop it, Johan. You sound like Payne losing at cards! We all know I am dying but none of you ever allows me to mention it. Does it never occur to you that I can accept death and that you hurt me by not accepting it, too? Let me speak of it, let me release my grief and fears at leaving you."

They held her then, let her talk as she needed to.

A shock awaited the Court next day when Parliament reopened; Henry Fitzroy, duke of Richmond, the king's bastard son by Bessie Blount, preceded him into the parliamentary chambers at Westminster.

John, yanking at the confining neck of his heavy baronial robes, entered his family's apartments afterward. "There is a new Act," he began.

Margrethe groaned. "So you lords will all get writer's bump from signing again, eh?"

He sank onto the hassock at her feet, watched concernedly as she wincingly sat back. "This one requires no signing." Beyond her he could see Kathryn beating his sons at the card game of Pope July. How it would hurt those boys to lose their mother! They loved her nearly as much as he did.

"The new Act says the king can declare whomever he wishes his chief heir. In other words, he expects to make Richmond king after him if the Seymour bears him no sons. Your goddamned uncle—"

This was directed at Kathryn. "Do you swear at me, Windsgeat?" She vaulted up off her chair, hand raised. "By God, sir, I will box your ears as I would any other rude brat! You will not speak to me thus!"

"Pardon me, your *sainted* uncle, Norfolk, pushed him into it." He had conveniently forgotten he was related to Norfolk, too. "Ever since he married his daughter Mary Howard to Richmond, he has been itching to see them rule England together."

"That is a terrible cough Richmond has," Margrethe commented idly.

Kathryn sat back down. "A dry, hacking kind of cough? Mother said Prince Arthur and old King Henry both coughed like that."

They were all silent awhile, then John, regaining control, asked, "Have you heard from the girls?"

"Lissy and Isabella are fine. Isabella wrote to say that when messengers began tearing the royal badge off little Elizabeth Tudor's belongings, she turned to her household governor and asked, 'How haps it, My Lord; yesterday My Lady Princess and today but My Lady Elizabeth?' "

Margrethe flinched. "And she but three years old! What a queen she would grow to be, eh? But it may be Richmond after all."

Yet within a month the slender, pale Richmond was seen no more and young Mary Howard, Duchess Richmond, wept constantly. At this time Norfolk also vanished awhile and returned without a word of explanation—until Kathryn sauntered up to him.

"I see you have been in Thetford," she said innocently.

He clapped his hand over her mouth, dragged her into the nearest window bay, and roared for the occupants to get out. "How did you know that?" he demanded in a low hiss.

"Why, it is the pilgrim's badge on your cap, you have forgotten to remove it. That kind only comes from the Thretford shrine."

Cursing colorfully, he yanked the little sliver of stamped pot metal off, stuffed it in his money purse. "Not another word of it, Niece. I trust you to keep silence, as you are the only Howard ever famed for holding her tongue."

"That was yesterday, Uncle, and yesterday's gone. If you have broken the law you had best tell me now, that I may prepare to collect one more head from Tower Gate."

Christ! What had gotten into her? This was not his discreet, soft-spoken favorite any more; she sounded hard as horseshoe nails and bitter as brass. He snapped, "Anything I have done is at the king's express orders! If anyone asks, you must say that Richmond has gone on a summer progress to my castle at Kenninghall. I intend to send my daughter there tomorrow to join her bitch mother."

So the dry cough had killed the boy as it had so many other Tudors. Kathryn shrugged with brutal frankness; what was one more dead prince to her, who had seen too many these thirty-odd years at Court?

Norfolk was shivering as he left her. What the devil had gotten into Kat? She was starting to sound like Anne Boleyn! He crossed himself, thought, *Annie, Annie, I had to sign the judgment against you, else it would have been me and my children next*.

That night the princesses returned to Court. Both had the

ruddy Tudor hair and highly admired milky skin; twenty-year-old Mary entered solemnly matching her pace to that of tiny Elizabeth, who wordlessly clutched her hand. Behind them came Kathryn's fifteen-year-old Isabella, and Lissy, seven years old and almost a stranger to her mother.

King Henry observed as the welcoming ceremonies ended and Kathryn broke ranks to seize Elizabeth Stoneleigh and toss her in the air as though she were a baby and not a maid of honor. The little girl came down, giggling with pleasure, and wrapped her arms around her mother's neck. "Thank Jesu that shrew's brats are back! I have had enough of her black moods and tart tongue," Henry told Jane. He had not been able to get over the change in Kathryn since her return to Court. She who had always been the most obedient of women was suddenly so completely a Howard it unnerved him. One day she had dared walk straight up to him and demand the book he claimed to have written on *The Tragedous Fall of Anne Boleyn*. Her azure eyes had been so cold and piercing that it had made him go speechless—as though he had picked up a gentle hare by the scruff only to see it stare back with slitty, malevolent cat's eyes. Sometimes he woke sweating from dreams that upon Anne's death her soul had entered her gentle cousin's body.

It was good to see the woman acting like a doting mother again, he thought. In fact her behavior shocked many women, who gave her disapproving stares. Feeling guilty for the many wrongs he had perpetrated on this one thin woman, Henry caught up his own Elizabeth, tossed her high and made her squeal. His daughter had been looking at him with her enormous gold-and-brown hawk-eyes, starred with the biggest pupils he had ever seen. From across the room they seemed all black, like a ghoul's unwavering, soulless stare.

He threw a banquet for his daughters that night, allowed Mary to sit closest of all the guests to his new queen, thus signifying that only Jane outranked his eldest daughter. Mary was a credit to him this evening in a close-cut gown of gray-and-silver over one of crimson. Pleased with her elegance, he gestured at her with his two-pronged, crystal-handled fork. "Do you remember when you were small, Daughter, and I carried you on my shoulder? I used to tell foreign ambassadors that you were the chiefest jewel in my realm. To think that my councillors said my jewel would never acknowledge my religious supremacy, to think they desired I put you to death!"

He had reminded her that her soul was in jeopardy and that she had spent the formative years of her life beneath the headsman's shadow. Inarticulate with fear and pain, Mary started halfway up from her chair as Jane, thinking to help, said, "Oh, Husband, it would be the chief pity of your life to so lose the greatest jewel in your realm!"

Mary Tudor fainted dead away.

28

The queen remained late in bed the next day. She was still lying propped against the pillows when Kathryn entered with a morning cup of cool, fresh milk mixed with honey, egg and spices. Jane waved back her other women, whispered, "Kat, do you ever regret things you have done?"

"Not as much as I regret things I did *not* do, Your Grace."

"Please! Do not 'Your Grace' me, it is *I*, plain little Jane Seymour, the same Jane you taught to play the lute when I was no more than waist-tall! Tell me, Kathryn—tell what things you *did* do that you later regretted."

The round brown eyes were very disturbed today, the grip on Kathryn's wrists earnest. She sat down on the royal marriage bed. "I regret that I did not raise my son James differently. I regret my first marriage, for we were ever mismatched; I have vague recollections of regretting two fine marriages I *could* have made and did not. But I have had some very fine women-friends and I adore my daughters, so it all balances out."

"So women are security in your life; only the men have proved uncertain."

"Well, there was Richard. My only dependable man and an angel in so many ways. There will never be another like him. Why, Jane, what is it that ails you? What do you feel doubts and regrets about in your own life?"

In a flurry of motion, Jane threw back the sheets with their foot-wide band of embroidered trim. On the sheet below—and her new sleeping shift—a tiny patch of scarlet showed. "Again I am not with child. I do not want to die because of it!"

"This is not even your third month married, Dear. Sometimes it takes a little while."

"Little while?" Jane knelt up, clinging to Kathryn's wrists again. "It only took him three years to tire of waiting for a son from Anne Boleyn! You must go to—" Here she dropped her voice to even more of a conspirator's whisper. "To Jacquetta and ask for a potion opposite of the one I gave the Boleyn for so long."

Surely Kathryn was not hearing this. "You gave Anne a potion?"

"Nothing to harm her, just to keep her from conceiving. Whenever I could not get to her morning cup, she got with child. But I did not have courage to tamper with a possible already-begun child, not even to further help Princess Mary and the old queen. It seemed I could not face God on the Day of Judgment with that sin on my soul."

Kathryn said tartly, "If God forbade Heaven to women who tried to control breeding, the place would be all-male. Come, Your Grace, let us get you bathed and into something pretty and you will feel better."

She caught herself, thought, *I am speaking to the queen of England as I would a frightened child*. But the round brown eyes showing over the jeweled cup's rim *were* a child's, and haunted with thoughts of headless Anne Boleyn crying out for the sons Jane denied her.

Kathryn leaned forward. "Your Grace, Anne lost two children on her *own*; you had nothing to do with that."

"That is true," Jane said hopefully. There came a rat-a-tatting on the door that made her leap half a foot, spilling the milk cup's contents everywhere. "Do not tell the king—I beg you when he comes in, do not tell him I am not with child yet! I thought he was kind, I thought the Boleyn was all that made him touchy, short-tempered—"

None of the other ladies-in-waiting would beard the king's wrath. Kathryn thought grimly: *He dislikes me so much that at this point I can hardly make myself less popular*. She strode over to the door, opened it a crack. "Relax, Your Grace, it is only your obnoxious brother."

Jane, who had half a dozen brothers, said, "What, *Tom*? Tell him to give me an hour and I shall be out." Jane Seymour was taking no chances of being closeted alone with a favorite brother as Anne Boleyn had been; *she* would give the king no incest rumors. "Go on," cried Jane visibly relieved.

"You heard her," Kathryn said, and closed the door upon

Thomas Seymour's fingers. There was a sound as of beaten hounds baying, then his hand was hastily withdrawn.

She summoned the maids-of-honor from their dance lessons in the adjoining room, ordered the fire stirred up and fed, water heated in copper cauldrons. One girl set up the folding leather screen that shy Jane insisted on robing and disrobing behind. The bloodied sheet was handed out, set to soak while coverlet-sized sections of heated toweling were handed in. Another possett was sent for, and a breakfast of fruit, hard cheese, almond-paste marchpane fancies, and beef pie.

The wardrobe mistress and her assistants brought in two dozen gowns for Jane to choose from today. When the queen could not decide, Kathryn pointed out a gold-shot beige satin, flattering to Jane's muted coloring. "And perhaps the low-necked shift with the gold wrist-ruffles."

Jane gnawed on a bent forefinger. "You are right, that will be lovely. I can always trust you, Kathryn, to know the proper gown or phrase. I tell you what, I would like to know what the Lady Mary is wearing today so we look pretty alongside one another for the king. Yesterday her green clashed with my red; he said that, seated together, we looked like one of Windsgeat's coats!"

Kathryn grinned to herself as she stuck her nose outside. Good, no howling Seymours in sight. She rushed to Mary Tudor's rooms, found Isabella lacing her into an exquisite thing of russet samite—near the shade of her hair, for Mary's locks were far redder than those of the other Tudors, though darkening with maturity. "One of Windsgeat's coats," Mary marveled upon hearing the reason for the queen's request. "Yes, we did. For all that John has the best manners and most money at Court, he has also the most overly-vivid clothes. I have seen his poor wife shade her eyes and shudder when he went past. How goes that lady, Madam?"

"Poorly," Kathryn said, tight-throated. "The end is near; she is confined to bed now."

"Poor woman, you must send her a basket from me of all the finest fruits and candies in the kitchen. Here, I will write you an order for it."

When Mary and Isabella had continued on to Jane's chambers, Kathryn took the written order and a large willow basket and started out the door. Thomas Seymour fairly leapt out at her. "Let me carry the basket," he urged, tugging at the handle.

"If you do not stop springing at me from dark corners, I will tell your sister!" Kathryn huffed, trying to yank the basket back.

"Fine. Just do not tell your lover, I still have scars from the day he asked where you were."

"My lo—" She fetched him three ringing slaps across the cheek. "How dare you, I have no lover!"

Hand to stinging cheek, he appreciatively looked her up and down. "Good God, Madam, why not? It was a compliment, not an insult. I meant no disrespect. I merely wanted to make sure you were not Windsgeat's mistress before I asked you to dine with me."

"You mean before you made designs of your own upon what remains of my virtue," she snapped, both of them still hanging on to the willow basket. "Well, let me tell you, Tom Seymour, that I do not belong to you, Windsgeat the Uppity, nor any other man. So if you thought to ask his bloody damned permission—"

He had never had a woman, and a well-born lady at that, swearing at him before. He glowered hopefully at her. "Then I may appeal directly to you for your favor and not worry that he will throw me down and stomp on me?"

"My favor! You oaf, you churl, you struck me across the face and turned me over to my vicious son—"

He dared inch his fingers closer to hers so that they touched on the basket handle. She did not appear to notice. "I did it on my sister's orders, and I had no idea James would attempt to murder you. He assured me he would take excellent care of you, Kathryn. My deepest apologies."

He dared bend and kiss her hand. "That is 'Lady Whitbourne' to you. I have given you no leave to use my Christian name. And stop slobbering on my knuckles, someone will see."

Nevertheless, she gave up the tug-of-war, surrendering the basket to him. *Windsgeat will kill me,* he thought, blissfully walking eight paces behind her to the kitchens. *He will take up that gorgeous damascene blade of his and dice me into little cubes for his breakfast.*

And I do not care in the least!

Three days later, Thomas Seymour showed up at the royal hunt with one fist-blackened eye swollen half-shut. "Brother mine, what has happened?" the queen cried out, gloved hand flying to her little mouth.

"Oh, nothing, nothing. I ran into someone's nonexistent lover and his nonexistent fist."

Women giggled, glanced around to look for a guilty face. So Kathryn stood up in her one sidesaddle stirrup and looked around, too.

She had not survived thirty-odd years at the Tudor court by being a poor stage-player.

The huntsman blew his horn. Greyhounds sprinted across the blazing green turf, led by the king's two silent borzois. Kathryn, nudging forward Richard's old bay gelding, found her way blocked by a seething Thomas Seymour. "Madam, you have not been truthful with me. I should make you pay for the steak it took to bring the swelling down!"

Saints! What had that terrible eye looked like *before* the steak? She said, "Thomas, if I was Windsgeat's mistress, why would I ride this old bay instead of a Windsgeat White? He thinks to protect me, that is all."

She was not known for lying or coquetting, so Thomas found himself reluctantly believing her. Of course, she might really believe what she said about Windsgeat, but as for himself, he could see that John had gotten very possessive with her and that when in each other's company, she and Windsgeat quarreled incessantly. So there could easily be a revival of the old, rumored attraction that they were trying to fight, refusing to accept.

He grinned but it moved the right side of his face, made him wince. "Then next time *I* will be the one lying in wait, and *I* will strike the first blow! May I ride alongside you, Lady Whitbourne?"

"Only if you can maintain the pace. *Hee-yah!*" And she dug her soft little suede heels into the gelding's ribs. He shot forward as though cannon-propelled.

Thomas Seymour admiringly watched her perfect posture as she rode. That subtle curve of breast, the Howard swan-neck, the enticing ripple of her green skirts—*What a woman! I must have her*, he thought, and spurred after.

"You and I must talk."

Kathryn, hand on doorknob, squinted into her ill-lit room. The fire had burned very low, but she still recognized the craggy-faced silhouette in her tallest chair. "Get out," she coolly ordered, hauling her gloves off and flinging them on her only table. "I have had enough of your company,

Windsgeat. How dare you abuse my suitors and how dare you enter my rooms without permission!"

"I did not break in here, Tansy admitted me. And as for suitors . . . ! That word implies an eye to marriage and Thomas Seymour never marries, only debauches." John sat forward, entering the ring of light.

She dropped her money purse on the table, too. The drawstring gave way under the force of her blow, sent tiny copper coins—all she had—rolling everywhere. "Is it any concern of yours whether I plan to marry or debauch? You gave up any right to interfere in my life years ago, Milord. Now get out, I will not have idle gossip return to our Margrethe and so harm her."

He rose, kicked the door shut. *How odd to be frightened of John,* she thought, heart hammering against her bodice. *I know him, I have always known him, there is no need to fear him. And yet I do!*

Her slanted black brows went level in an effort to master face and voice. "You have ten seconds to tell me what you want and then I start screaming," she announced, chin up, standing her ground.

"You are going out of your way to hurt me with Thomas Seymour."

"I assure you, I never think of you when I am with Tom Seymour. That is God's truth, no matter what you choose to name that god."

"You have been uncommon sharp with me these last weeks. I had dared hope . . ." He slumped back against the door, said dully, "All the murders of your loved ones have been swift and sharp, you have never watched your chiefest treasure wither slowly, by day, by hour and long, loathesome minute. Gods help Margrethe, I cannot. The two of you are so different and yet I love you both, Kathryn, and I cannot ask you to wait for me. It would be too cold, too untrue to her. The fact that she wishes it only pains me the more. I feel very much caught between the two of you, between the king and my religion, between so many matters I never wanted a hand in."

She stood with her back against the tall chair he had so recently deserted. It was a solid, box-bottomed one and would not tilt, no matter how hard she leaned.

"*John*. Are you saying you have fallen in love with me a second time?"

There was a flicker of movement, an unmistakable nod in

the dim room near the door. Some spark of cruelty rose in her, some long-buried memory of lying heartbroken and near spiritual death at night because of this man's marriage. She said, "That is too bad, because I do not love you, nor even particularly like you these days. You are the last man in England I would have to-do with; I learn my lessons the first time. Not even for Margrethe will I mend your shirts, rear your sons, and share your bed. All that died for me long ago, John. Let it stay buried. Besides, even did I want you, the king has forbidden it because of our Plantagenet blood."

"We are more closely related than you know," he said, sounding wryly amused. "Kathryn, do not speak to me as to an enemy. I was your friend long before we were lovers and I have thought us to be friends ever since. Give me a friend's solace, if no more."

"I have always stood by the de Gaels; it was they who broke faith with me."

"You and your pride and honor, your Goddamned ambition that kept us apart!" he said. "It is all that holds you aloof now."

"Yes, you and I are very much alike in that way. You will not be master of my affections again, John, no man will. I shall love *where* I like, *whom* I like, but I will not be a mistress or a wife, only a free agent. I shall never belong to anyone again."

He started out, hesitated in the doorway. "You will come to Windsgeat when I see the end is upon her? For Margrethe, not me?"

"I will never fail anyone I consider family."

When he had gone, she eyed the door to the next room. Crossed to it in four swift strides, hauled it open. Tansy fell flat at her feet. "Hear enough to hang anyone?" Kathryn demanded.

Tansy stood, dusted herself off with more dignity than an eavesdropper should have. "You must be the only woman at Court who would refuse that man anything. They all know he is faithful to his wife and they all wait to catch his eye when that good lady is gone. But you—!" They had been together too long for the usual servant-mistress relationship, besides which Kathryn was notoriously easy on her hirelings. Where another would have clouted Tansy from the room, she merely said, "Go on. You obviously have more to say to me."

"I am finished. I am sorry."

"Not as sorry as I am going to be if we do not finish my

wine-colored sarcenet in time for the feast tonight. Hurry, Tansy, start on the hem while I heat the pressing irons!"

"I am not a marrying man."

Thomas Seymour, hand on Kathryn's, led her through the intricate maneuvers of a new Court dance. She said, "So say those three thousand harem virgins you debauched."

"Three thousand, by Saint Mary!" he marveled, one eyebrow raised. "And did I have a good time, Milady? I—Jesu preserve me, it is your overgrown watch-hound! He is not cutting in on us if I can help it!"

He braced himself to refuse John. But before the two men clashed, the king himself stepped between them. "Here, Windsgeat, be so good as to teach your queen that new step. I would dance with Lady Whitbourne. Seymour, you are odd man out; good-bye."

King Henry, Kathryn thought, was growing portly with age. His clothing did not lessen that image—hugely padded garments with yards of shirt-linen pulled through the slashes, and even in warm weather, bulky fur linings. He looked half bear and half man in his fuzzy brown-and-gold brocade tonight. Nonetheless, she curtsied with extravagant reverence, came up and placed her hand in his.

"You look damnable pert this evening, Madam," he informed her. "What new mischief is cooking in that sharp-cornered Plantagenet brain of yours this night? Some romance with Seymour, or is he but a cover for what goes on between you and Windsgeat? They say you are waiting for a certain baroness to die."

"Then they lie, Your Grace. Let us be frank: I find young Seymour by far the better man."

"He is ambitious; I could not let the lad marry a woman of your royal heritage. Still, he would be preferable to Windsgeat. You know of course that should Windsgeat ever place a ring upon your finger, you will both die for the deed."

She laughed merrily, like brook water tinkling over smooth stones. "Your Grace knows I am too old a campaigner to disobey your word; I prefer my head on my shoulders to marriage with any man."

"And you are clever enough to have survived the reigns of my three queens, I know, I know. Still, word has it that Baroness Windsgeat has elected you her successor."

"So may a woman choose a mare to mate to her favorite stallion, only to have the mare break and run."

Henry found himself liking her again. "By God, Madam, you are saucy tonight! It is a pleasure to hear your bright wit and yet I think you should be more like the queen. She is very tractable, is she not, and an obedient wife?"

"She is not a Howard," Kathryn said cheerfully.

He so bellowed with laughter that the other dancers faltered. "Madam, you need a husband to take the edge off your tongue!"

"I will make no more sons," she answered, meaning: *No more of my family to die beneath your headsman's axe!*

Henry considered it, leading her about him in the required circle. "I married the wrong Howard niece," he said, amused. "Norfolk has always said you were harder to crack than a green nut and I finally believe him correct. *Kathryn* . . ." He never called her by her first name if he could help it. Startled, she looked into his eyes as the circle ended and he handed her down into a brief curtsy.

"You shall never marry John de Gael while I live, dear lady, not even when you are too old to make him sons. You are Edward the Fourth's granddaughter and the de Gaels have much Plantagenet blood; married to you John would think himself quite good enough to be a king or make them. I would not have either of you so endangered. So if you like young Seymour enough, tell me and I will order him to marry you. But to become a de Gael is death to you."

He left her in the curtsy, unable to rise a moment. Then Thomas Seymour caught her hand, eased her back up. The music changed to something foreign and lively. "Will you show me this new Italian step?" he asked. "You have a reputation for being the lightest-footed dancer at Court."

"Yes, Tom, it goes like so . . ."

He stood behind her, hands at her little waist. "One-two-three, one-two-three-*four*."

Henry Tudor reclaimed his queen, leaving John to stand on the sidelines sipping hippocras and observing the dancers. As Seymour's fingers closed around Kathryn's middle, the enameled glass goblet exploded in John's tense grip. ". . . two-three-*four*," Thomas counted, and lifted Kathryn so high that she laughed and blushed.

Blood and shards of glass leaked from John's clenched fist. No right to love her, no right to ask her to wait. How could a man so love two women at once? How very bitter that he should grow to care for her again when it seemed a brutal disloyalty to his adored and dying Margrethe.

Gods. Look how little her waist was, like when she had been twenty. Seymour's hands nearly met around it. He could see the pale blue veins of her slender swan-neck from here, and the violent azure of her laughing eyes. The smoky burgundy gown against her ivory-and-gold skin, the tawny hair and thin, black brows. She made the other women look like cattle, he thought, watching how quick and feather-light she moved. That tantalizing sway of sarcenet skirts—

"Three years and Lady Whitbourne has not remarried. You know, I never thought her particularly pretty until tonight, but look at her, Man! She sparkles," a man at John's back addressed a companion.

"I have always thought she had a quiet sort of beauty, but she never coquetted or flirted so I presumed her cold. Still, one hears the most interesting rumors; all the Howard mares are said to ride comfortably."

A blind, unthinking rage. John had started to turn when light, cool fingers spread over his bleeding fist. "Drop the pieces into my cup, Baron," said Isabella. "You will do her good name no help, do you challenge a man for her sake."

She would be the next goddess-on-earth, he could feel the soft balm of her compassion spread over him, removing the fury. "Your eyes are so very fierce. Do I that closely resemble her?" she asked, prying his hand open and picking out bits of glass.

"You have her figure and height, but Jacqui's eyes. I see no touch of me."

"This is your own hair, worn woman-long on me; yours my opal eyes, my wrist-knobs, something of your laugh which one so seldom hears. But my face is very like your father's."

She could not know, even Jacquetta did not know. Buckingham, Hal Chase, and Thomas Howard the Elder had all signed witnessing that pact between old Tudor and old de Gael; those three had also witnessed another, more dangerous document Kenneth had drawn up. Two of them had died without telling their sons; the only living being who knew his secret might be Norfolk. Isabella had no way of knowing.

"You do not look like Kenneth de Gael," he said cautiously.

"Why should I? He is not my true grandfather," she said, picking out the last of the glass from his bloody hand. She then took out her feast napkin, wrapped his hand in it. Their pale eyes met. Isabella said levelly, "What I know, I know. You said there is no touch of you in me? Ahh, you lie, Lord. There is all your passionate love of Windsgeat in me; I am pagan as a Roman coin and more loyal than any horse or hound. I am part yours and part Mother's but I am wholly Windsgeat's—and wholly the Old Ones'. There is no sacrifice I would not make for the god-path; Windsgeat will never fall while I yet live and breathe to defend it."

"How did I make such a marvelous child?" John asked softly, wonderingly.

"With much love, I believe. People are beginning to look, you must excuse me."

Lump-throated, he said, "I long for the day I can publicly call you 'Daughter.' "

"Being unable to name me thus does not lessen what lies between us; a name does not make or un-make a thing except in magic ritual."

He had always been fond of his daughter but now there swelled in his heart love and immense pride. She curtsied, softly murmured, "Good-night, *Your Grace,*" and turning, was swallowed by the crowd.

Across the room his gaze met that of Kathryn. She danced with Thomas Seymour but her eyes were all for *him,* John. So her indifference was feigned, or else she lied to herself about her feelings; there was something in her eyes so desperate, so disturbed, that it was all he could do not to stride across the room and wrap his arms around her.

She watched him over Thomas's arm, noted John's flawless posture, the straight back unbent by adversity. His thick chestnut hair was graying more at the temples and the laughlines at the outer corners of his eyes had gotten very deep. She would always remember her first glimpse of those eyes through a stag mask, the first sound of his laughter when he was nineteen and daily knew joy in living.

The broken ankle he had splintered going to her aid when Richard died never made him limp in public, though she had seen him drag it awkwardly after him at home. *He is so unyielding,* she thought. *He has never been broken*. She had. Been broken, splintered, had to lie low like green wheat in the wind, then risen to greet the sun once more. His way was a man's and hers a woman's; in the end she realized their strength equal, if wholly dissimilar.

Thomas Seymour was not her equal.

Watching John, she was unable to bear his stare another moment, and so broke from the dancing embrace, fled the busy room heeded by few. Thomas fumbled for her in the crowd, found himself delayed by a woman in search of a dancing partner. Thus John, leaving by the opposite door, managed to reach her first.

Kathryn was nearly to her apartments before he caught her, spun her around by the shoulders. She was sobbing for air as she wrapped her arms about his neck, let him carry her a dozen steps into the deserted chapel.

He set her down, thought the better of it. Started away. Heard her whirl with a cry of anguish, turned to see her press herself face-first to a long painted window. Her hands were outstretched as if to snare the moonlight beyond. "Tell me to go and I will," John said, almost angrily.

"I cannot, I *will* not have you! Not even with Margrethe's approval!"

Was she crying? She had not wept in all her convalescence at Windsgeat this June. "Because the king forbids it or because you loathe me?" he demanded.

Her long white fingers spread across painted images of saints, everything made blue by the night. "Oh, gods, how I loathed you! I prayed for word of your defeat, torture, damnation! I loved first, knew pain second, and hatred third. And finally forgave all, forgot much. . . . Your wife is dearer to me than my own sister; I will not have her dishonored."

"I am not asking you to let yourself be taken on this chapel floor. *I* would not do that to Margrethe, *either*. Gods! Do you think me devoid of all soul or conscience?"

"*Yes*."

That word tore into him, added new wounds to the gory place Margrethe's impending death had dug. He wanted to hurt her, shake her, make her know fear—

But when he stood behind her, his hands came down lightly on the nearly bare shoulders. Her velvet headdress tails were pinned up in Jane Seymour-fashion, baring the long graceful neck; inclining his head he put his lips to her downy nape. "Good-night," he whispered, and left.

Gone. He was gone. So why did the kiss still burn mercilessly, why could she hardly breathe, see, think? It was only lust, after these three years alone; it could be nothing more. She could even feel pity for him, thinking he loved two women at once, unable to make love to his wife and unable to allow himself infidelity. And she had thought him without honor; how severely she underrated him once again.

"Kathryn?"

She whirled with a gasp, realized the figure in the doorway

was not John but Thomas Seymour. "I thought I heard you weeping," he said and drew near.

The lure of flesh to its like was very strong. When he pulled her into his arms she did not protest. His open mouth was on the side of her neck—the neck she would not lay on the block for John. Kissing her face now, her anxious mouth that had not been kissed in so many, hungry years . . .

It was exciting to hold a man again, to touch and be touched. She was tired of her life, tired of every day being a struggle, sick of watching other women with lovers, husbands, babies when her husband was dead and her children, independent of her. John—to be held like this—the kiss still burned on the feathery hairs of her nape—John—*Oh, Richard, forgive me—John, John—*

Right there on the chapel floor.

Afterward, lying dazed and amazed on a pile of discarded clothing, he asked, "Who taught you all of that?"

"The pope's entire Vatican guard, last time they were in town. What does it matter, so long as we enjoyed it, Thomas?"

She was up and dressing. Not lingering in his arms, not asking him to stay, only efficiently, emotionlessly garbing herself and preparing to leave him. He suddenly found himself hurt and angry; it struck him what women must feel when he left them this same way.

"You are a very strange woman, Kathryn Chase," he said as she kissed him on the brow and started out.

Yes, she thought, aching with new enlightenment, *and you are not John.*

29

Jacquetta bore a daughter that autumn. Until she named the child Wilhelmina, John did not guess who the father was. Now he knew why she had maintained her stubborn silence—not only because William Brereton was base-born, but because of his execution for adultery with the queen. All the truth came out now; how she had gone to the king to testify that the nights William supposedly spent with Anne had been spent with her, Jacquetta; how the king told her if she named Brereton "husband" and innocent of the charge, he would charge John for adultery with the queen, tear down Windsgeat and turn the land into a royal hunting preserve.

And John had thought he hated Henry Tudor before this news.

Margrethe died in his arms that week. Her last words were, "Take care of our Kat'rin. Her pride is too stiff to let her beg assistance when she needs it; you will need to watch her, and guess."

Jane Seymour never had her coronation. The dreaded Sweat returned to London, causing Henry Tudor to flee the city with queen in tow. Kathryn, safe at Vamplate Manor with her daughters, did not need fear the illness.

Thomas Seymour wrote her every day. "I hope you are not impressed," Isabella said. "His secretary turns those notes and poems out by the dozen."

Kathryn laughed. "I know Tom for what he is—superficially amusing and totally fickle. God help the woman who ever really loves him! Now, then: why did the king allow you to leave Court with me? Is it because you turned down those two betrothals?"

"He says he wants no unmarried women about Lady Mary because it attracts—and I quote him—'profligrate bachelors.' "

As though he himself had not scandalized all Europe with his romantic exploits and many marriages!

They both wore mourning for Margrethe, household gowns still smelling of the black dye pot as they kneaded bread dough side-by-side. Isabella wiped a flour-smudge off her mother's nose. "I miss her," the girl said suddenly.

"Margrethe or the Lady Mary, darling?"

"Them, the old queen, even Anne Boleyn. Richard, Uncle Arthur, Uncle George, Grandpapa Hal . . . Mother, are you going to marry Father?"

Kathryn's bowlful of dough came slamming down on the table. "You know I cannot, even did he ask. Even did I feel for him again. And you? Why do you refuse to marry?"

"I took a vow at Windsgeat two summers ago. I swore virginity, unless I needed to save the land."

Her mother was kneading the bread so pitilessly that the entire table rocked. "What did you swear it to? Something dark and hornéd in the woods?"

"No, to the All-Mother."

Kathryn seized the dough up in a flour-coated mass, slammed it down one time too many. Her one and only table that had traveled all over England by wagon and mule-back, as did the

Woodville bed, suddenly collapsed. She said a word Isabella had never heard before, even from John de Gael, and began kicking the traitorous piece of furniture.

When that display had ended, she looked up to see Isabella regarding her with John's level, expressionless gaze. "Must you look at me as he does?" she cried out.

"I think you are very unhappy, Mama."

"Unhappy! I am the most desperate of women! Henry Tudor is going to kill the queen, I know he is, and I cannot bear to see it happen again! Last night I dreamed Jane Seymour lay in a wooden box beneath the altar stones while the king paraded before the Court in a new yellow doublet, just as he did when Queen Catherine died!"

Understandable she would be upset, she had watched Jane grow from early childhood. "What else, Mother?"

"I am so tired of outliving those I love. My feelings are so mixed about Margrethe's death . . . I was never able to get my brother's head down from over the bridge . . . another few years and I will not be able to bear children, and you and Lissy do not need me anymore."

She was tired. She had been since the week she delivered Jacquetta's Wilhelmina and watched John bury Margrethe. How badly she had wanted to comfort him, how great had been the unexpressed sorrow in his white-lined jaw and too-stiff shoulders. He had held his sister and sons while they wept; young Payne had confided to Kathryn, "Poor Papa, he has spent so long hiding his feelings from kings and ambassadors that he no longer knows how to cry."

She remembered the boy's words now, shook her head at Isabella. Poor John. He had needed her as a sexless friend at the funeral and she had not been one, had stood stiff and aloof with her own pains and problems. Had he been a woman-friend, she would have thrown her arms around him until they both cried together; that night they would have gotten drunk in front of a blazing fireplace, lain on the hearth and reminisced about the dead beloved. But his being a man had held her back. *And here, in reality, it would not have mattered had I been male, female, or a thing of no gender at all—he needed to speak of her and I would not let him approach.*

"I failed your father," she said simply, and bent to pick up the bread dough.

"I know that," Isabella answered, equally forthright. "But you felt he had failed you, too, in the past, and I suppose you needed to balance the scales at last. But Mother . . . you were never bitter or bristling before."

"And now I am. Forgive me, dear, I have had to build walls to survive losing so much. But now . . . now it is time to build something new. I think it is time I returned to Court, faced some old ghosts and demons. What do you think?"

"I think you should take Lissy and go. I will stay here and mind the farm."

Kathryn looked at the unlined fifteen-year-old face and opened her mouth to protest, *But you are a child!* Isabella was *not* a child, she was of an age to be running her own household and bearing children, had she so chosen. Besides which she sometimes thought the girl had been born old, like little Elizabeth Tudor. "All right," she agreed. "I always feel better when I am needed; I will go see if Queen Jane needs me, and I will be kinder to John when I see him. I will make a point of visiting Jacquetta, too; in my private griefs I have abandoned her these last many months. I will go where I am needed."

Jane Seymour needed her indeed.

That winter at Court, Kathryn heard that Anne Boleyn's old flame Harry Percy, Earl of Northumberland, had died. He had been forced away from marriage with Anne, had tried to convince the Council she had been precontracted to him and so was not the king's lawful wife, in an effort to save her life. They had denied him, made him sit in judgment on her, and then divorced her from the king on grounds of that same never-existent precontract they had refused to let save her life. And then they killed her anyway. He had gone home to the northlands, turned his face to the wall, and died childless and deserted by his wife. The title went to a cousin.

Living in constant fear (though the king was painstakingly gentle with her), Jane Seymour finally let it be announced at chapel that she was with child.

"She is too old to be bearing her first," Jacquetta said one afternoon at Windsgeat as she walked muffled in cloth-of-gold lined sables, alongside Kathryn. "She is too little, her bones are too tiny and set too close together. Difficult for them to part enough to let a child through. The best she can hope for is to have it early, before the head is too big."

Kathryn came to a halt, wet-shoed, thin-cloaked. She held a hand out. "You are missed at Court by me and the queen. She asks for your return. Time and distance have drawn us apart, Jacquetta, *sister*; I would have you back at my side again."

"Not yet, not yet. Not with my loss so fresh upon me and that damned Henry Tudor having threatened me, making me choose between John and William. I am a de Gael through both my parents; I am more de Gael than even John, and we neither forget nor forgive. I hear Henry expects a son. . . ."

Daily, courtiers clustered about the king, crying out, "Your Grace, never fear! It will be a son!"

One day too many said it. Henry glared at them, said, "You self-declared soothsayers all claimed Elizabeth and Mary would be boys, too, and here I am with my only son a dead bastard! Make no more predictions to me, Sirs—take your Tarocchi cards home!"

That night in bed, Jane clung to her husband's arm. "Promise me, Your Grace!"

It was late but she so prettily said it and gave him his title that he was pleased. She made him think of something Windsgeat had quoted to him at his baroness's funeral . . . what was it, something by Petrarch about "a thing of light and warmth." "Yes, sweetheart, anything for my Jane," he said.

"Your Grace, I want no male doctors with their big, rough hands hauling at me during childbirth. Please—if I could have my dear Jacquetta back, if only for the birthing—"

Her Jacquetta! How well he remembered *his* Jacquetta drawing back from his hand when he made his last offer! The first gray had begun to speckle her hair so that it hung silver-gilt like Margrethe's or his dead Woodville grandmother's, according to the historians. Jacquetta's hair had hung loose across her heaving bosom and her pale eyes had been a viper's. "You have condemned my husband and now hold the axe over my lands and brother. You want me, too, My Lord? *Take me!*" And, seizing the neck of her gown, she had ripped it open to show the same magnificent body as always, beautiful even in pregnancy. "Go ahead," she had told him, "and I will lie as still as death, pretending you are my condemned husband all the while!"

And Jane wanted the bitch back! Well, one must always humor pregnant queens lest they lose valuable sons. "Of course, Sweetheart," he lied, patting Jane with genuine affection. "Now get some sleep for you and our prin—*child*."

She trusted him. She had no other choice. Yet as spring

passed and summer neared, bringing with it the Sweat, she grew fearful and fell to observing all the old, forbidden Catholic rituals and holy days. If the child was a girl—if she made no sons, as the Boleyn had made none—if she could not manage to bring him back to the Roman Church. England was crisscrossed with blackened, burnt trails from one sacked monastery to the next.

At least she had dear Mary Tudor back at Court, and Kathryn Chase, too. Kathryn would send for Jacquetta, if the king forgot. Jacquetta would deliver her of a son, she was certain of it. She must, she must!

At night sometimes she thought she saw Anne Boleyn in the shadows, head under her arm. Waiting for Jane to fail as Anne herself had failed, knowing in death about the sons Jane had kept her from conceiving month after month. Waiting . . .

Three days in labor. Three sweating, stinking, screaming days in the autumn heat at Hampton Court. Roughly, humiliatingly, painfully handled by dirty-handed men with no notion of what to do for a delicately-built woman trying to push out her too-large first child.

Henry was not with her. Afraid of catching the still-hovering Sweat, he had fled to nearby Esher, leaving her isolated, as was the royal custom, for the ensuing birth. Shut away as though she were something shameful, not bearer of the heir to all England. Shut away with that bitch Lady Rochford who had been allowed to return to Court, been given fine apartments and a position of honor by a king grateful to her for the charge of incest against his last queen.

At least Kathryn was there. Mopping Jane's brow, giving her cool water. But the doctors kept watch on Kathryn, would not let her send for Jacquetta or give Jane anything for pain or to help her push the baby out. So Jane Seymour lay shrieking, soaked in foul-smelling sweat; they would not even let Kathryn change her queen's sheets or body linen. Unable to eat, beginning to vomit even water, the queen screamed, "I will have your heads if you do not let Lady Whitbourne help me! Dear God, Kathryn, ride for Windsgeat! Bring me my Jacquetta before they kill me and the prince!"

A laboring woman's folly, they said, and pushed her back down. "Let her walk, damn you," Kathryn snapped. "It will help her! Let her walk, kneel, crouch, stretch her cramped muscles, bring the child forth!"

No, they declared. Flat on her back was the proper position for a birthing woman, and they had orders: no Jacquetta de Gael. Then they discussed opening her belly, which would kill her, to take the child.

Jane lay flat, held down, screaming. Her water broke and still no child; blood followed and still no child, though they did not tell her of the blood. Kathryn leaned down, put her lips to Jane's ear on pretext of kissing her pale cheek. "Jane, first count three, then make an effort to scream and flail as hard as you can. I have got to reach Francis de Gael, send him to Jacqui; I have just heard him outside in the gallery. Distract them for me."

The queen lay back, summoning the last of her strength. Colorless, pain-wracked, she gathered her last reserves, obeyed Kathryn in a series of blood-curdling shrieks. When the doctors leaned over her, Kathryn shot out the door and down the Long Gallery, shouting Francis' name. Of a sudden the ten-year-old was there. "Aunt Kathryn, they say the queen is in labor in there."

"They are keeping it secret because she has been hard at it three days—get your aunt Jacquetta and her red leather box and hurry! They speak of cutting Jane to get the prince out!"

He sprinted away; she was caught by a man-at-arms, dragged back into the royal bedchamber. Directly in front of the queen, the doctors were still quarreling about whether to cut her open now or wait until she died. Kathryn announced, "You had better give the king a choice; he is uncommon fond of her."

They grouped by the door, bickering; a tray of food arrived for them and the women. Kathryn accepted it, stared down at it and almost laughed aloud. A pepper grinder. No, it would not work. The pepper would not be ground fine enough, it needed to be a powder. She cocked an eye at the page who brought it, said, "Fetch me some finely ground pepper, please. Fine-ground as a lady's face-paint."

It might do. It was not much of a weapon, but it might do. When a different, oddly-familiar boy returned, the doctors were still grouped. If only the door remained open awhile longer—if they did not notice that the knife she took from the dinner tray was blunt and not dangerous. "Go see what the doctors are saying," she ordered Jane Parker, who was so affronted at this behavior that she obeyed without thinking. *Now,* while that bitch was huddled with the doctors—Kathryn sprang forward with a handful of loose pepper while the page cried out in a girl's shrill voice.

She flung pepper over the doctors. Kicked Jane Parker, Lady Rochford, square in the rump and knocked her through the open doors. Punched, shoved, herded the three medical men after her, pricking them with the dull knife all the way. "Close that door and bolt it," she ordered the page. "He" sprang to obey.

Poundings and yelling on the other side. Still some powdered pepper in the dish. "Forgive me, Your Grace," she said, and held it under Jane Seymour's nostrils.

A sniff, a snort, whimpering sounds. The sneezes finally came one after the other, violent as gunfire. "You could have told me what was happening; I should have helped you lock them out a little quicker," said a familiar voice.

The page's hat and moustache had come off, revealing Isabella's chestnut hair and grim face. "*You!*"

"I felt a disturbance, arrived, listened to gossip, and knocked the tray-boy over the head. Gods, you would think someone would notice how badly the clothes fit; a good thing we make flat-chested women in this family. Here we go, the contractions have started, Mama."

Jane was jerking and heaving. More powder, more shattering sneezes. "She is doing it, she is—wait, Mama, the baby is turned—oh, dear gods, the contractions are too hard and the baby, turned!"

Isabella flung down a shoulder satchel, dug through it. She hurled off her purloined doublet, tied her sleeves back, and greased her hands. "Hold her down, sit on her if you have to. Your Grace, hold back, hold on—Mama, it is a boy. Your Grace, a son, by the feel of him, and still alive! Hold it, hold it—there, I have him turned properly. I have the head. Push now, my queen, push, push!"

The head was "crowning," appearing from the queen. But Jane, fingernails tearing bloody trenches through Kathryn's sleeves, was too tired to keep pushing. Isabella stooped, fumbled in her satchel again, drew out a cloth-wrapped forceps. At the last minute she froze. "Dear gods, a king of England! Mother—Mother—"

Kathryn shoved her daughter down practically atop the queen. "You hold her. What do I—"

"Around the head, in the temple-hollows. A king . . . oh, my word, if we let a king of England die . . ."

So it was Kathryn, untrembling in her awful urgency, who forcibly drew out the child.

A big, wailing boy, almost purple-faced for lack of air. One whack on the rump, then half a dozen—all to no avail. The queen fell back, dying.

"Cut the cord and give me the prince," Isabella said, in control again. She held him up above her head a moment, said, "Bright Lady, Dread Lord, this is the Green King who will keep England young. I give him to you until such time as he will save England!"

Then she laid him on the queen's belly, breathed into his mouth and nose.

Behind her, axes bit into the door. Voices screamed, shouted that the queen was being murdered. Wood splintered—bright metal gleamed—

The prince's chest gave a convulsive heave. He shuddered, lay still as Isabella withdrew her breath.

Color abruptly flooded the tiny, wrinkled face. He screamed.

And screamed and screamed. Mother and daughter flew into each other's arms, hugging, kissing, slapping backs. The axes hesitated, voices stilled. "A prince is born to Their Graces!" Kathryn thought to cry out. "A fine, healthy son! Long live Their Majesties, long live the prince!"

Norfolk's voice boomed, "Back, you knaves! I command you to get out of my way! Kathryn, Niece, let me in there."

"Put a guard on those doctors first, they have nearly killed her. I will not have them in here, I want only Jacquetta de Gael when she arrives."

"Let me in that I may witness the condition of queen and prince, else what goes amiss will be blamed on you."

The prince was shrieking away; Jane's breast moved shallowly but steadily. "Uncle, if you lie to me and let men-at-arms in, I will cut your throat," Kathryn said coolly.

She turned to her daughter. "Have you a weapon in that magical bag of yours?"

"A pistol, Mother."

"Cover me when I let the old fox in."

He had been more of a father to her than her real father, but she had borne three days of watching the queen tortured; she would tolerate no more uncaring cruelty from men. "Kill only Norfolk," she loudly ordered her daughter.

Outside the door, he heard and chuckled. "She must have Isabella in there with her. Gentlemen, I value my hide and my niece's aim; kindly stand back when I enter."

He entered alone, coatless, stripped to shirt and hose to show that he carried no weapons. "The prince and queen live and prosper," he called out to the waiting crowd. "Now be good enough to send word to His Grace, eh? Put the pistol down, Isabella, and help the queen, she is a mess. To think you did not trust me!"

"I would not be a true-born Howard did I trust my favorite Howard relative," Kathryn said curtly. He laughed, turned his back for modesty's sake while they tended the unconscious queen. First, the filthy, matted shift was stripped away. A sponge bath, some water dribbled carefully into her mouth. When she woke, and began whimpering in pain, Isabella pulled out another sponge, this one hand-sized and an odd hue. "What is that?" Kathryn asked.

"A surgical sponge. They are soaked in opiates and dried out; water makes them potent again. Let me see . . . Aunt 'Quetta said three drops for minor wounds or a small woman, but this is major, so—" She lightly dampened the entire sponge, held it over the queen's mouth and nose.

"My father had marvelous apartments in the Tower; I hope I get the same ones," Norfolk said aloud. "If I am lucky, the king will let me write my wife for some pleasant books and tapestries . . . a few Holbein portraits on the walls would be nice. . . . They will probably build a special rack for three and torture us all together. . . . A cat would be nice, they keep the mice out of your cell."

"Mice in a cell can come in *very handy*," Kathryn said, remembering.

". . . really wonderful apartments he had, they let him paint the walls. Nice view out the window, he could see Tower Green. Of course, he had to find out ahead of time when executions were, or else it interfered with lunch . . ."

A clean, soft shift for the queen's ruined body, a basin to wash her matted hair in.

". . . of course, they are not too good about emptying chamber pots in the Tower," Norfolk continued with a sigh.

A clatter and fuss in the Long Gallery. "Get out of my way, you scum," said the most imperious woman in all of England. Blows landed, men yip-yipped like hounds. Ladies fled, silk skirts rustling.

"You had better admit your Aunt Jacquetta," Kathryn told her daughter.

She blasted in without a word, threw her leather casque and bags on a chest and opened them up. She felt the queen's pulse in her wrist, checked the prince's condition, began barking orders. "Get a wet nurse in here at once for that child. Lemon and barley water in here to bring down

Jane's fever—pour it for her, Kat, while I knead on her abdomen to bring out the rest of the afterbirth."

"It is out, I saw it."

"Not all of it; see her belly muscles contracting? Her cramps are too severe for normalcy, there are probably tiny bits of tissue left inside. Norfolk, stop mumbling about sewage at the Tower and start wadding up this gauze for me. Isabella, girl, *go*!"

She slapped her Book of Shadows open on a table right in front of Norfolk—her own, private Book, a thin, blue leather cover with drawing after drawing of herbs. "Let me see, nettle would stop the bleeding but she is parched for lack of liquid and it would further dry her out. . . . Body sloughs off all moisture with nettles. Plantain and peppermint, I think. Kathryn, make me a very strong infusion, use it all if you must, they grow more in the gardens here. Norfolk, I want the witch hazel, that is bottle fifty-six. Pour it in a dish, lay the rolled gauze in to soak. She must recover better before I sew her up."

So Kathryn delivered King Edward the Sixth while the Duke of Norfolk helped a witch save the queen's life.

Too soon the king was there, admitted with all his doctors. "Norfolk, you have sinned to let so much happen!"

"Your Grace, the doctors followed your orders and nearly killed queen and prince. I can testify that without these three ladies, you would have neither wife nor son. And a great, fine lad he is, too!"

Jacquetta stood, blue eyes blazing. "Do you know what they did to her? Handled her with dirty hands, let her perforate and hemorrhage. She must have nothing but thin, clear liquids for a fortnight—"

"Two Plantagenets, a heretic whore, and a babbling duke—is this the honor guard for my son? Norfolk, get these women out. *Now*!"

The king bent over the half-conscious queen. "Look, Jane, look at our son. You have done very well. Next year we shall have a duke of York to back him up, then a third son—mayhaps I shall make him archbishop of Canterbury—and a pair of little girls to marry into French and Spanish treaties. Childbirth is not so bad, sweetheart, you make a great fuss about nothing. We shall churn out one a year after this."

She fainted.

That she survived so much rough handling was a miracle.

Jacquetta had done all she could in the hours allotted her, brought Jane back from the grave's edge, but the doctors returned in force. Unwashed hands poked and prodded, then they ignored her until the next day.

Jane was a product of her times and tough; though she had to be carried, she attended the christening. That night, unbearably hot, she threw off all the coverlets, begged for cold water and rich, greasy foods. No one had listened to Jacquetta's warning of perforations into rectum and intestine; by mid-afternoon Jane lay cramped and convulsed, screaming that Anne Boleyn had come to snatch her soul away.

Twelve days after the birth of Prince Edward, Henry Tudor was a widower.

30

The king rode to Windsgeat one fine day, found the entire household still in white French mourning.

That impudent little Fleming, van der Hüm, informed him that John was in seclusion and would not see anyone. "Tut, Man, I lost my own wife, I know how he feels! Life goes on, he must see that. He lost his fine Flemish mare and I my little English one; we shall mourn together awhile and help each other."

Pieter remained in the doorway, arms stubbornly crossed. Henry thought, *I was wrong. Windsgeat is not the most arrogant man in the realm; he is a lord, high-born, he comes by it honestly. But for this rascal to so defy me, and he a nobody—!*

The Fleming saw danger in the royal eyes. "Your Grace, I would not approach Windsgeat just now did you dreaten to boil me in oil!"

This was ridiculous. He did not want to have John brought out by force from his own house, and yet he could clearly see that, yes, boiling oil would not budge van der Hüm an inch. He growled, "I know how to get him out here, Master Pieter. Tell him I have come to say I was wrong about something."

Pieter staggered, tripped over himself rushing inside. What seemed seconds later, he emerged with John at his heels.

The de Gael "laughlines" had perceptibly deepened this year, giving John the appearance of a constant squint. A little more gray at the temples, too, but still a ridiculously well-made man. *Some woman or other will sink her claws in fast enough,* Henry thought. He said, "Saddle up, Man, we have things to discuss."

The two widowers rode along the Thames, trailing archers and hounds. At water's edge Henry pulled up. It took four efforts, clearing his throat ostentatiously each time. "I was wrong to send the 'Three Graces' out of my wife's rooms and I was equal wrong to insult Jacquetta as I did. It is only now that people have proved to me that she saved Jane and would have left her hale and hearty at my side had I allowed her to stay. I should not have trusted medical degrees over woman-secrets and the old, herbal ways."

Shock left John speechless awhile. He was quite certain that Henry Tudor had never apologized to anyone before in his life, and wondered if he had had to inquire around to learn the proper words. "Your Grace did what he thought proper at the time. And there is no changing the past now at this late date," John said.

"True enough," Henry agreed, staring out at a line of barges bound for market. He started to say more, then hesitated.

John rubbed the stubble on his strong Howard chin and thought: *What the devil does he want from me? He is after something*. "You seem troubled, Your Grace. How may I assist in easing your mind?"

"Oh, do not be so Goddamned formal, de Gael! This is the two of us now, with no Court listening; you need not pretend to be a politician now, only Our friend."

I was never your friend. Your opponent, your whipping-boy, your glorified jester; never a friend. John waited, expression reined in as tightly as his nervous mare.

Henry slapped the reins back and forth between his gloved hands. "I need another wife and a duke of York."

John allowed himself a rare grin. "I am hiding neither in the rafters, Your Grace." Morrighan whinnied in agreement, pawing the grass.

"I know that, John." The use of his first name surprised both of them. "I need a woman of good birth—a woman born well-enough that many consider her a Plantagenet princess. A woman with dead Jane's common sense but some of your sister's spirit. An attractive woman, though not an immense beauty; a woman I cannot let you or any other decently-bred man in my kingdom marry. I know you were fond of her once, John, though I have never been certain how far it went."

God's Horns, he was going to propose to Kathryn! John kept his face steady, contemplative. "It is good of you to tell me, Your Grace, but the lady in question is no chattel of mine."

"Stop with the Your-Grace-ing when we are alone, John. I have a Christian name; use it."

He felt like a henpecked husband. "Yes, Henry," he said meekly.

"Of course, I will not tell Kathryn right away. I must have a decent mourning period, say, another six to eight weeks. Then I shall ride in state to her little place in Kent and ask her. No child of hers and mine could ever be king, of course, but she is still by all accounts young enough to give me a Duke of York. Beneath the Howard pride she is rather modest, so I expect her to be overwhelmed."

Really, Henry? I expect her to drop dead of shock, myself.

Kathryn wiped her flour-streaked face on a rolled-up sleeve and kept kneading bread. The dream had come true, Jane Seymour was dead and buried. It seemed that no one remained from the old days at Court, even little Anne Parr had long married and gone to her husband's Herbert estates. So many of the rest were dead.

Push, pull, turn, twist, start over. *Damn Death*, she thought, fighting tears. *Goddamn Death!* How could she ever face Court again without little Jane Seymour scurrying up to her in that quiet, solemn-faced way of hers—? Oh, well, there was no need of ladies-in-waiting where there was no queen; they had all been sent home so she need not worry about seeing echoes of Catherine, Anne, Jane in every familiar palace. And Arthur. Laughing George, dear cousin. Papa . . .

She shaped the loaves, popped them in the brick chimney shelves. Flour up the nose made her sneeze into her apron, hunt for and locate her handkerchief. "Is that a sneeze or a good cry coming on, Mama?"

She smiled down at eight-year-old Lissy, quartering apples into an earthenware bowl. "A little of both, My Angel. How pretty you are today, I must thank Tansy again for doing your hair that way."

Elizabeth was going to have trouble with men too soon.

Isabella was more handsome than pretty, even at sixteen; a certain evenness of feature and serenity of expression and bearing kept most men from interest in her. John's coloring was more flattering to a man than a woman, too. But Elizabeth had the best of both parents, Kathryn's long, thin black brows, sloping nose, slenderness, and height combined with Richard's coloring. Copper hair, blazing green eyes, skin like milk and a dusting of gingery freckles—boys and men were already whistling after her in the streets. She was a sparkling little creature, too, not solemn like her sister.

"Mama, is Uncle John going to answer the letter you sent with Iss'bella?"

"I have no idea, Lissy. In fact I—"

A rider in the night. Elizabeth, in mid-yawn, froze. "*Mama*?"

Hooves and the barking of her shepherd's dogs along the river marsh. *Who else has died, that they ride in the night to tell me?* Who was left? Already Kathryn found herself thinking, *If it is Isabella I will die, it will cut the heart out of me—*

Elizabeth, Tansy, herself, and the old man who kept the farm for her when she was gone: a handful of women, children, and one old fellow far past his prime. Anyone hearing of that household and that it was headed by a lady-in-waiting might expect riches worth stealing. She took Richard's arquebus down from the wall, along with its powder flask, some cotton wadding, and shot, and pushed it all down inside with a ramrod. "Lissy, light me a twig from the fire and then load your grandpa's pistols for me."

She stepped out into the night, away from the illuminated doorway so she would not present a framed and waiting target. The horse was very near now; the dogs went wild at the stranger's approach. Sheep bleated, her hens fussed in the shed. All of this she had fought for, worn calluses on her hands plowing like a peasant; she thought of the house being burnt over her head after all the patching, thatching, and whitewashing. Her gowns, greatly reduced in number, for half had been cut down for Isabella and Lissy, but they were all she had to wear; one broken table, her precious Woodville bed, and wedding linens . . . the last two pieces of silverplate . . . Her stock, her maidservant, but most of all her little girl, Richard's only child. "Stay inside and put out the candles," she barked, gruff with fear for her daughter.

Wait. The horse splashing through the stream was white. He picked his way prettily around her furrowed fields, choosing his steps like a dancer. A line of brush separated her winter wheat from herbs and the stallion followed that line. She recognized John's new favorite, Finnvarra, or "white-top," named for an Irish fairy king. But where were the outriders, the archers, hounds? Where was Jacquetta, Pieter? John rode alone in the darkness, sliver of moon picking out his Lincoln green hunting suedes and best yew-bow; dressed thus he often slept several nights in the greenwood without anyone looking for him.

Kathryn lowered the gun. Those shoulders, that posture could never belong to anyone but The Lord of pagan Windsgeat. She handed the gun in through the window to Lissy, crossed sheep-clipped turf, and took Finnvarra by the bit. He gratefully slobbered on her bodice and rubbed his muzzle on her chin. "I received your note. Am I welcome or not, tell me straight out, Woman," ordered his rider.

She peered up at John's face in the faint moonlight. "Very welcome."

He swung down swiftly, landed too hard on his bad ankle. "One forgets one is no longer nineteen and supple as a yew-bow," he managed from between gritted teeth.

Elizabeth came vaulting at him from the kitchen, nearly knocked him over. "Uncle John, Uncle John! You promised me a ride on Finnvarra with you!"

He swung her up into his arms, kissed her with as much affection as if she had been his own. "So I did, but you must wait until tomorrow, horse and rider are tired and dusty. Tomorrow we will ride along the river and you must show me all your favorite fishing places, your aunt Jacqui says you catch many fish."

"Oh, yes, I am much better at fishing than Latin! Mama, may I stay up?"

"No, darling. It is off to bed for you now. John, come in, I will wake my man to cool Finn down."

"Finn would take his head off. Put Lissy to bed, I will be in soon enough."

She had Elizabeth in bed in no time at all, then flew out to the shed. John had walked Finnvarra to cool him down and now stood stripping the stallion of his tack. Kathryn wordlessly began taking pieces from him and wiping them down, ending with the blanket spread over the half-door. "You do that remarkable well," John observed, currycombing the stallion. Finnvarra showed appreciation by sucking on his master's hair; each comb-stroke made the stallion grunt with piglike contentment, tail swishing.

"John, I could never afford my own grooms and stableboys, so I have probably dressed and undressed more horses than *you* have."

He shrugged. "Your note was very kind. Why did you not deliver it in person?"

Lantern light put a soft yellow glow on the scene: horse leaning on master's shoulder, munching oats; John currying slowly, with a feel for what his mount liked. Hens nested sleepily in the rafters, winking down at them while Gray Jenny snorted flirtatiously and nibbled Finn's tail.

"I had jams and fruit to put by and the week's bread-baking to do. I have forty pounds of cheese draining on beds of nettles, fifty head of sheep about to lamb too damned early, and the fishpond needs dredging and restocking. I couldn't leave all that to visit you."

He kept combing. "Your dogs barked at me down by the water. You should have them bring the sheep and cattle nearer the house at night, bandits could clean you out."

"I know, and I need to burn the grass away from the house so chimney sparks find no tinder out there."

"How many men do you have?"

"One shepherd, one cattle drover, and the old man who watches the place for me. I cleared another ten acres this year; I know that sounds ridiculous to a man who owns Windsgeat, but I am proud of my work here. It is such fecund land."

She liked the smells in here: straw, fresh oats in the manger, hen-feathers, horse-breath, and John's velvety new suedes. There was something intimate, almost sexual about being closeted with him and the animals by lantern-light, talking farmer business equal-to-equal.

Kathryn remembered the kiss on her nape many months ago and fairly sizzled.

John took a hoofpick from his baggage next, tapped Finn's knee until it obligingly bent. Kathryn took her own pick from a nail on the wall, and when he had finished, she knelt and did Finn's other forefoot. "It is nice like this, away from Court," John murmured. "I feel more like myself here, out of the stiff clothes and false manners. And it is wonderful how cozy you look in that old wool gown with no stays or corseting, so much more bending, softer. And I always did like your hair worn loose like that, with just a kerchief over it.

You are pink-faced from the cold, let me finish his hooves and we must get you inside to the fireplace."

Then they were kneeling side-by-side, arms brushing as John worked. She looked at the powerful shoulders, straining all the seams of his leather doublet, and tenderness overwhelmed her; she laid her cheek against his back. "Oh, John, John. . . . What a pair of old farmers we have become, we will be discussing seed prices next."

"Gladly. It is better than who-is-sleeping-with-whom and which treaties did which king break today, or who has been arrested. There is something more real about being close to animals and the earth. Something so *basic*. Holy, really. Home is always holy to me."

"I never felt at home anywhere until I owned my own land," she said, closing her eyes, feeling his back-muscles ripple against her cheek through supple leather.

"You never leaned on me before, not physically, not for friendship or love. I like it."

"You forget the day Anne miscarried and we leaned together."

"That is true, I had forgotten. Kathryn? You asked to be my friend again in your brief note but you gave an intimation of more."

She eased her arms around his still-slender waist, thought how wonderfully well he was aging. "Hush, John, must you always talk so much? Let some things happen without debating them to death."

"I think you should know"—he was leaning back against her now—"that if Thomas Seymour ever so much as breathes on you again, life as he knows it is *over*."

"I had to pretend he was you."

He turned, knelt, drew her to him. All at once he was kissing her eyelids, the corners of her trembling mouth. Unbuttoning the throat of her high-necked shift, he rested cool cheek and fingertips against the pulsing blue veins. They remained like that awhile, unmoving, eyes closed in comfort with the moment. "Not here," she murmured finally. "Horses lie down at unexpected times."

He stood, picked her up, tucked her head under his chin. She carried the lantern, he carried her; they said nothing all across the yard and inside the house. Her loaves steamed on the table as they passed, the loaded guns lying on either side; Tansy had saved the week's bread.

She spoke once, to direct him upstairs, then fell silent again. A low glow came from the fireplace in her bedchamber, the curtains had been drawn back on the tall, slender, woman-graceful bed. Eavesdropping Tansy had prepared it all for them. To his surprise, John saw his old sable-lined cloak from the Val d'Or spread atop the turned-back top sheet and blankets. As he bent to set her on the bed's edge, he touched the cloak. "Skins are still supple," he marveled.

"So is mine. See if it is not," she teased.

He sat next to her a moment, circled her throat with one scarred hand. "So it is. I never saw the Woodville bed up close before." The varnish had blackened with age, obscuring finer features of its gargoyles and plants. He ran a finger along the main design, tracing pennyroyal, a powerful abortificant, twined with mandrake for eroticism and chamomile for fecundity. Mandrake, the most dangerous, magical, and seductive of roots—"So Grandmother was a witch after all," he marveled.

Kathryn watched him slip from bed, kneel at her feet, and remove her wooden farm clogs. He reached higher, untied her garters and rolled off her rough woolen work hose. There was mud all along her hem, flour on her arms, nose, and apron; she smelled of her customary ginger-and-rosewater along with bread dough, Finn-sweat, straw, and the evergreen boughs she stored her wool gown on to keep insects away. Honest farm-smells; he supposed he stank of horse-sweat and dusty leather himself. Not like France where she came to him in a prettily-scented cloud, a stranger to tragedy; this new Kathryn was older, harder, more honest, and yet far more elusive. He had no idea how she felt about him in her heart, but her body shook all over when he touched her bare legs in removing those stockings.

Does she love me again or is it mere fondness and rutting? he wondered and felt suddenly awkward.

She pushed at his chest with one bare, chilly foot. "Are you down there praying? I am cold, John, and worse. Come back to my arms."

He stood, unhooking his doublet. The shirt was next. She stood with him, pulled it off over his head. Kathryn lightly ran both hands up his marred arm, asked, "What are all those funny little scars from?"

"I put my arm through a window the day I heard you had divorced, and there I was, newly married. She knew, she understood; I think I started loving her from that day on, though it took me a long time to recover from you."

"Never recover from me again, John."

The sight of his half-naked body maddened her. With an inarticulate moan, Kathryn leaned against him, hands pressed to his velvety skin. She said, "I do not care what you do to me so long as you do it all night long."

She lay back, drew him with her. Feathery kisses to each other's hair, throats, faces—his open mouth on hers, the only warmth in the whole cold room. John undressed her slowly, a garment at a time until she lay naked beneath him, gasping and shuddering with excitement. There was a sunburnt V along her throat where she had worn her high, outdated shift-neck open; anyone could see that, he realized, but he was the only one who knew how white the rest of her body was.

He had never seen a woman so excited, and he had hardly begun to handle her. She arched out like a cat for him, took his hands and ran them all over her body. Kathryn's breath came in pants; he realized that she was, incredibly, within seconds of peaking already.

His mouth at her throat, shoulder, breast—she broke in a series of quick little shocks, moaning out his name. By the time he finished kissing his way down her body and lay between her legs, she was climbing again; he made her crash so hard that she screamed as if struck.

At last he eased into her, the shock of it intense for both of them. Kathryn bit his shoulders, thrashed, almost fought him; he had to pin her wrists gently to the headboard to keep her from hurting both of them. Moving slowly, repetitive strokes . . . When she was calmer, he unexpectedly placed his hands under her rump, pushed up, began to thrust savagely.

"Look at me," he crooned. She focused her eyes on that cool opal stare, found mind and heart in the madness of freed flesh. "*This is real magic*," he said. "Welcome home."

Kathryn took his craggy face between her hands, kissed his grimace of pleasure wide open. *Welcome, home*, she thought. Love, not houses, made for a nest; the man, not the land, was home. And, *Home is alwys holy*, he had said.

The Woodville bed, accustomed to Kathryn's many celibate years, squawked and complained throughout. John found a particular motion that made the entire bed rock and floor creak; they worked on that one until it hurt.

"I love you, I love you, Kathryn. . . ."

Half-crushed beneath him, she dug all ten fingers into his back, would not let him move away afterward.

"I am smothering you," he protested weakly.

"You may grind me down into this mattress until you break every bone of my body, but you must not go away just yet."

He made a sleepily pleased sound into her neck. "I am a very good hand at mending fences and chopping firewood. . . ."

"You are a better hand with the mistress of the house. Lissy may have to wait a few days for that ride on Finnvarra."

All that night he tried to draw three common words from her. He had cried it out himself and meant it, but Kathryn said only his name. There had never been a woman John could not win that one phrase from in bed, if he applied himself with half as much enthusiasm as he had tonight, but Kathryn would not give him that satisfaction. Sexually she was his ultimate experience, wanton in a way she had never been at twenty, but emotionally she left him hungry.

He stayed when he should not have, worked the farm with her. Hitched his finest horse to her plow, dug stones out of the fields, planted more winter wheat. Shored up a sagging corner of the house, split kindling, nose-ringed her evil-tempered black bull before he killed someone. Plucked chickens, delivered lambs, killed a calf for veal. In the evenings he taught Lissy French and Flemish love-songs at the lute, then tucked her in early and carried her mother off to the Woodville bed.

Jacquetta would fall down laughing when he told her. He worked like the lowliest farmhand and felt himself complete for it, a part of the fields and burbling white stream. At Windsgeat he was overlord, overseer, Over-All; here the land knew him as partner, not master, and made him work accordingly. Not since the days after Kenneth de Gael's death when, hardly more than a boy, he had sold his sword's services across Europe, had he worked so hard. Had he been a typical lord he would have been lost in the wildness of Vamplate Manor's lands, but John had always taken part in the planting, reaping, slaughtering, birthing of new stock at Windsgeat; as an independent duchy and the largest baronial estate in all of England, his home required nothing outside itself to survive.

But that was Windsgeat the estate, not Windsgeat the man. John watched Kathryn's slender form as she went about her work, felt all the craving of youth upon him so that he took her wherever the mood struck—in the fields, the shed, kitchens, fishing knee-deep in the stream. Once he threw down the plow-reins from his neck, ordered Finnvarra to stay put, and rolled Kathryn, seed-bag and all, into the nearest furrow.

It came to him that five weeks had passed and she had not once answered his declarations of love in kind. There returned to him also the lure of his own things about him, the luxuries of Windsgeat, how fine she would look at his imported table, or riding his best horses, or in his fancy bed at night. How his boys and Jacquetta would love to have her there, and how the place would seem alive to him again, rejoicing in her presence.

That night in bed she turned into the shelter of his shoulder, said, "Well, John?"

"I would marry you."

"Thank you, but no. I would function poorly with my head off my shoulders, makes it difficult to count embroidery stitches."

He ground his teeth audibly in the dark. "Then we shall marry in secret."

"No. The priest or witnesses could be tortured and forced to talk. I will not risk my lands and daughters for some marriage lines on a piece of paper."

Damn her, damn the woman! "You sound as if I am not good enough to marry, Milady."

"Plenty good enough, John. But no one is good enough to die for at this stage of my life."

"Will you go through a pagan handfasting with me, then?"

He felt, rather than saw her shrug unconcernedly in the dark bed. "Well, then, what are you going to do, Kathryn? Suppose a child comes of this, what then? You will go to the Tower for it; Plantagenet heiresses who are cousins to kings do not bear bastards and wander England to tell of it. Or do you mean to keep on playing me off against Thomas Seymour?"

"John, I have already told you he was only because I saw no honorable way to have *you*. I will keep faith with you as long as you with me and not one moment after; for as long as I am your sole mistress you shall be my sole . . . *partner*."

He had not expected a woman of Kathryn's pride to grant him, "*master*," and that seemed as it should be. But he so wanted to hear "my love" and "my husband" from her! "You are a hard, hard woman!" he accused. He put a hand out over her head, touched the carved wooden plants of lust and fertility on the headboard. *Ishtar, Vesta, Rhiannon, All-Mother, I want this woman all my life. How is it right that you should so wholly enslave me and not her? All my days I have honored you and your consorts; why do you fail me now?*

Jacquetta had once told him that the Summer Isles rang with goddesses' hilarity when a man loved harder than the woman in his life.

John threw Kathryn down, pretended he was going to be rough. She only sighed and clung to his neck, twining her legs with his and breathlessly urging him on. Lost in that hot vortex of wounded pride and desire, he could not resist her. "Sleeping in the Woodville's bed has made you a witch," he accused, gasping in between kisses.

"No, sleeping with a *witch* has made me one. Put more magic into me, John . . . now, please! *Now!*"

He had his revenge; he left without warning her about the king's marital intentions. And he missed Henry Tudor by a scant two hours.

Kathryn, radiant, spotted the incoming royal party. Fortunately John's so-recent presence had left the household in good state; her best linens were on the bed, all the rooms aired, swept, dusted, with her second Turkey carpet on the scrubbed wooden floor and the best laid across her one table. Seeing so many horses approach, she pushed her only two box-chairs up to the table with the old farm-man's help, called for Elizabeth to take her last dozen lemons out of the vinegar crock, wring the juice, mix it with honey and water and so make drinks for all. Tansy took Kathryn's handsome white French mourning gown out of the little sandalwood chest where only her best clothes were kept, laced her into it, then bolted downstairs to fetch water for the incoming horses.

Only the king and de Gaels rode in such state, and seeing as John had just left and Jacquetta was too clever to risk interrupting when he romanced, it must be the king. Kathryn grudgingly toted out her silver hair-caul, patted a thin layer of Spanish liquor on her lips and cheek, and, throwing John's old wolf-lined cloak about her shoulders, descended the stairs and so out through the kitchens.

Henry Tudor drank deeply from the cup of honeyed lemon water that Elizabeth Stoneleigh handed up to him. He smacked his lips appreciatively, beamed at the emerging Kathryn. "By God, Madam, you are a handy husbandman with a farm! I hear this place was naught when you took it on."

"It was right fertile land Your Grace gave me; I could not go far wrong with it," she said. But she thought: *What the devil does Great Harry want from me?*

"Tut, woman, fertile land does not grow neat stone-and-wood fences and whitewashed outbuildings! And all of this without a man! Think what she could do with a husband, eh, Lads?" (He addressed the Seymours, she noted.)

Henry dismounted, pulled her up from a formal curtsy and frowned at her hands. "It will never do for a woman of your station to bear such marks of drudgery on her hands. Why, you have worked like a peasant or slave on this place!"

"It pleased me to care for what Your Grace granted me. Will you enter the house? It is simple but clean."

She still had Jack of Norfolk's two old tapestries, this time hanging on the walls of her Great Room, he noted. Still only one damned table, much-mended and splinted, only two chairs, and not a sign of any gilt or silver plate in her two so-plain open-fronted cupboards. Then there was her gown—elegantly cut and styled, but not one stitch of gold on it, nor a single jewel, and he noted her headdress was a cheap silver caul set with glass stones. He thought: *De Gael is not such a niggard as to keep her thus. She has put away all thought of him, else he would have her in Italian brocades and emeralds big as a baby's fists. Not a decent carpet in the place and I will wager she still owns but the one bed I gave her as a wedding gift.*

There was an odd but pleasant air about her today—how did that one biblical phrase translate? "A woman clothed in the sun." Yes, that was it. She fairly glowed; country life had proved beneficial to her. An aura of power about her, too; strange, he had never noticed it before.

"My Lords, you will enjoy the view from the lady's windows while she shows me the gardens," Henry announced, holding his elbow out for Kathryn to lay her hand on.

He is very merry, she thought, *so he has not come to announce the immediate demise of my family. What could he want of me?*

It struck her as she took him out to the herb-beds: He wanted to ask or tell her of some woman. Something Norfolk had said or done made the king realize she was his longest-termed female acquaintance at court and no longer so hostile toward him; he had come to consult with her on his next marriage and thought she might know of some suitable widow or virgin.

Henry planted his duck-billed shoes on either side of her best row of horehound. "Madam, I have come to ask you to wife," he said.

Her knees buckled. She landed on them far harder than she meant to, had one irritated, totally removed thought amidst all this: *Damn! I will never get mud out of velvet this color!*

There must be some way out of this, some excuse. "My Lady," he continued, pleased at having so dazzled her, "I have long thought your virtues overrode your Howard pride and as you are considered a Plantagenet princess (though of course your father was but a king's bastard), I thought—"

There it was. He had opened the trapdoor onto her escape route. "Your Grace, not so virtuous as you expect. I have been meaning to confess to you for some time."

"What, confess! Am I some canting priest, some minister, Madam, that you would so presume to redden my ears with such stuff?" But natural curiosity ran very high in Henry, and when she did not reply, he urged, "Go on, go on, what would you confess?"

"That a king cannot marry a woman so indiscreet with gentlemen at Your Grace's Court."

"*You!*" He flung his head back, bellowing with laughter. "I do not believe you, everyone from Ned Howard on said you are cold as new snow, though perhaps it is just that you have never had a king to thaw you, eh, Sweetheart? Oh, I know all about the gossip concerning you and John but I know your sense of honor, and how greatly he loved that fine little Flemish wife of his."

As king he could marry a woman once divorced and once widowed, for both of her husbands were dead and buried. Her Plantagenet blood would be an asset to the throne while hindering her from most marriages. But a king could not marry an unchaste woman and have the paternity of his sons doubted. "Pray, continue," he ordered, sterner now, for she said nothing to prettily soothe his fears. "Tell me who laid such gentle siege to your virtue, Madam, and how far it went."

She kept her head down, crouching at his feet. "Thomas

Seymour, and it went as far as though we had been man and wife."

"Kathryn, you astonish me! I do not believe you!"

"—and George Boleyn."

He could not find words for several minutes. "You are not making this up from some modest disinclination to be queen? If so, you have no need to tell lies; I will understand if you regard yourself as too passionless or too unimportant or—a king may be merciful and understanding, Lady Whitbourne. And after these many years of our acquaintance, nay, *friendship*, surely you feel something for me."

Did I tell you exactly what I felt, I would be condemned faster than Anne ever was. She remembered she was Norfolk's niece and said, picking her words with extreme care, "Oh, yes, Your Grace. I feel the same awed affection and respect any good subject feels for her sovereign. Which is why I cannot allow you to go on possessing some false image of my chastity and thus endanger the succession to the throne."

Especially as John might have gotten her with child. Had she been a de Gael and not who she was, she would have leapt at the chance to put a child of such heritage on the throne.

Henry turned away from her, unthinkingly trampling the row of horehound. "Thomas Seymour and George Boleyn! You kneel there and tell me that you have slept with my two brothers-in-law!"

He cast his gaze upon the ground for lack of anything better to focus on in his disappointment. That was when he saw it.

"You whore, you Plantagenet bitch! You tell me such lies about those men when all along there is another stands between us! Look you, Madam!"

He seized her by the caul-full of golden-brown hair, dragged her forward and flung her down. At first she saw nothing but the surrounding acres she and John had plowed together, working to break up the earth a final time before winter froze it solid. The ground was therefore freshly thrown-up and easily received impressions of what had passed over it.

Everywhere she saw a series of shallow *V*'s set together to form the Windsgeat *W* that marked all their stock.

Finnvarra had left his unmistakable hoofprints everywhere.

"Do not give me your stories of Boleyn and Seymour, madam!" Henry roared.

"But they are all true, Your Grace!"

"I doubt it. The truth is that you had rather be John de Gael's whore than my wife and queen of all England!"

"It is that I am too old, too obstinate, too unchaste—I have no strong religious leanings and the queen must be a role model to all young women—"

"It is that you are a pride-filled, treacherous, Plantagenet whore! Who is Windsgeat to do this to me? *Who?* Who were his parents?"

She suddenly remembered John referring to Elizabeth Woodville as his grandmother. Did he mean through the Greys, her family by her first husband? Or—

Henry was shaking her so that she bit her tongue, drawing blood. "I do not know! I thought Kenneth de Gael and Jack of Norfolk's daughter Marguerite made him!" she cried out.

My great-grandfather's armor . . . died in it at Bosworth . . . That made him Marguerite Howard's *grand*son, not son. But why did it matter? What had her father tried to tell her of John before he died? Why did it matter to the king now? Henry was looking at her as though he would kill her, he was tearing the hair from her scalp—

"I believe you," Henry whispered, and released her.

Realizing the rage was past, she sat, knees drawn up under the ruined gown. "Your Grace, you would be the unhappiest man in Christendom did you wed me. I have all of Norfolk and Anne's worst traits, you know that now. Do not hate me because my heart lies elsewhere."

"But he sat there with that unfathomable face of his and let me speak of marrying you five weeks ago!"

That explained John's insufferable smugness this morning. He had known what she was about to face, and had refused to warn her, probably considering it a proper reward since she would not admit her love for him.

"*That old fox.*" She said it aloud. "That old fox did not tell me of your confidences in him, nor did he make a move toward me until you had announced your intentions. He must have ridden to me that very night."

She looked so woebegone that Henry found himself unexpectedly chuckling and slapping his thigh. "What a nerve that man has to so cross me! Calm yourself, Cousin, the Tower only awaits if I actually catch you with him. He has duped both of us, we are equal fools in his sight. Well, since I cannot have you, you must advise me on where to seek my next wife. I have had two pious, dull ones with a bad, exciting one in between; I had rather hoped you would be the woman who proved to be somewhere in the middle. You know what I like best in a woman, Kathryn. Spirit but not so much that she wants to be master, a sense of clothing, some musical ability, conversation, a certain beddability . . . Oh, get up, get up, I have enough groveling at Court."

He extended a hand which she covered in grateful kisses before allowing him to pull her up. Henry grumbled, "I will let Windsgeat live because he never grovels. I have tried to break him, it is a contest between us; he bends so prettily, so excessively, but never snaps. God help him the day he does, I will lose all interest in him then. Thomas More never knuckled under, either, and I admired him all the way to the scaffold. 'See me safely up,' he told the guard. 'As for the way down, let me shift for myself.' I like brave men; I suppose if I send de Gael abroad again you will follow this time. A pity I cannot let the pair of you marry, what brats you would make! I wonder, though . . . your Isabella has his exact coloring and you were at the Val d'Or when Windsgeat bribed my wife into letting him come along . . . You know, a lesser woman would never have so braved my wrath and told me the truth as you have. She would have married me, let men walk about smirking that they had been lovers to the queen. You have never lacked nerve, though, have you, Kathryn? Not much. What a wife you would make!"

"A pity you could not have married Jacquetta de Gael twenty years ago," she answered ruefully. "Now *there* is beauty and spirit enough."

They walked along, her hand in honored place on his extended elbow once more. "I know, Kathryn," he agreed. "All woman pale after her. Say, she is half-Flemish and so was that bonny little baroness of Windsgeat's. Perhaps I should look to the Low Countries for my next bride, those two are so handsome."

"If I may be so bold . . . ? Windsgeat has spent much time there, you could ask him about the women."

Henry liked that idea. "First, though, I will ride back to his estates with a bridegroom's face on, tell him you have said yes. How he will squirm! Then I will tell him that it is a good thing you are chaste, else I would have to execute your old lovers. And after that I will predict in detail my upcoming wedding night with you. Oh, to make him sweat at last! To torture him with no weapons but words, to lead him so merry a dance! What do you think of my plan, Madam?"

"To it, Your Grace," she said. They laughed together. *Squirm?* she thought. *He will froth at the mouth!* "You will eventually tell him you jest, Lord?"

"Yes, and then I will let him know about the hoofprints and he will sweat so mightily as to have appeared dry before! Then on to talks of buxom blonde Flemish women; they must be starved for good men there, if they all are the size of that wicked little Master van der Hüm. I tell you what, Lady Whitbourne: when I marry again, you must come back to Court at once. If I get some foreigner you must study her language and help me woo her. Meanwhile—" Looking about him at the land and house she had worked so hard on. "Meanwhile you are still on full salary as lady-in-waiting; I will tell people I came to have you advise me on suitable brides, so they do not gossip. Of course, you could draw me up a list of eligible Englishwomen—I have Councillors, spies, ambassadors to tell me of foreigners. Now I must go back to my new palace."

They were nearly to the horses, all muzzle-deep in their water buckets. Courtiers came spilling out of Kathryn's house, Thomas Seymour giving her panicked glances. "New palace? Are you remodeling again, Your Grace?" she asked.

"No, no, building from the ground up this time. I intend to call it Nonsuch, as there shall be nonesuch like it. By the by, I had nearly forgotten. This was to be your betrothal gift, but as a certain fox has outfoxed us both, it shall be your reward for honesty."

He drew a long brocade box from his coat, placed it across her hands. Kathryn received it, kneeling, let him lift the lid, showing her Anne Boleyn's coronation pearls—five waist-length strands, each creamy, golden-pink pearl near the size of a cherry.

"Fasten those on Lady Whitbourne for me, would you, Tom?" the king asked the younger Seymour, whose hands shook uncontrollably in obeying. "By the way, Tom, do you know what the penalty is for a queen to have had lovers before her marriage? Penalty for the lovers, I mean?"

They then rode away, Henry mercilessly harassing the terrified man.

Tansy and Elizabeth came racing out to where Kathryn stood, straight-spined, smiling after the royal party. Anne's pearls lay heavy around her neck. She thought, *Were I a true Howard I would have agreed to marry him. But the first time I contradicted him or shrank away from roughness or inconsideration in bed . . .* She had watched him bury three wives, one of heartbreak, one of false accusations and the third of breeding; she would not be queen of England, not abandon her freedom, private *life,* and John.

The pearls dragged at her throat, bit into her neck. "Are we in trouble? I saw you kneel and cry out, lass!" Tansy exclaimed, forgetting her mistress was no longer a little girl in need of her mothering.

"No, we are not in trouble." Kathryn yanked at the necklace.

"Mama, what did he want?"

"Advice on his next queen. Tansy—these pearls—get them off me! They were Anne Boleyn's, they strangle me!"

She was perspiring as the old woman had to break the clasp to free her; the ropes of golden pearls lay hot and dangerous along her breast. She felt better already for having them off. "Jacquetta has a jeweler's agent in France, perhaps he can peddle these for me at the French Court. We will be able to have real stables built, and a henhouse . . . new dresses for Lissy and Isabella and you, Tansy. A second table, some horses—"

King Henry was right, John was no niggard. If he intended to keep her in state as his mistress—and she knew he did—she would soon be a very wealthy woman. Funny that facing riches after years of hardship no longer seemed the important thing.

"*I have not told him I love him!*" she murmured, thick-throated.

"Who, Mama? The king?"

"Neh, Child, your Uncle John," Tansy answered wisely, watching her mistress. Kathryn stood with hands clasped one-over-the-other on her breast, face aglow, the pearls gleaming along the length of her gown. All that velvet ruined and clutching those damned unlucky pearls, to boot! Tansy gently pried Kathryn's hands loose from them.

Elizabeth started laughing. "What is it?" Tansy asked.

"I will wager we go to Windsgeat for Christmas if Mama is in love with Uncle John."

"I will wager you have not finished your chores for the day, my fine little lady. Let us hurry back inside, leave your mother to think."

The king's traveling party became a dot in the distance, finally disappeared. But Kathryn continued to stand on the stream's bank, staring toward distant Windsgeat where her love would sleep tonight and dream of her.

PART FOUR

ANNE OF CLEVES
(The Part Assigned)

"Yet I have lived.
So much stands safe beyond recall.
I grudge not life its joys,
I have tasted one and all,
Nor e'er refrained my hand
From pleasures within reach . . .
The part assigned me I have played
On this life's stage
In costume fitted to the time and to my age . . .
As from a king's great feast,
I go not with ill grace
Though after me one come,
And take the abandoned place."

—Pierre de Ronsard, 1524–1585 (trans. Curtis H. Page)—

"God Send Me Well To Keep."

—motto of Anne of Cleves

31
Duchy of Cleves, Germany
Summer 1538

"I haff no desire to marry," the Duke of Cleves' sister said in very fair English. Lolling back on her curtained bed, she popped another anise comfit into her favorite maidservant's open mouth.

The girl giggled. "Who does the duke expect you to marry?"

"Some French duke, I belief. Haff anodder, Mein Dear."

"You had best hope for that French duke, Milady—they say Great Harry of England hunts a new bride, too."

"Ach, and der he goes, with dree of dem buried already. No, I will not let my brudder marry me off to some horrid and hairy man, especially not one who murders his wives. I like it too much *here*, where *you* are, Mein Dear."

Reaching into the sweets-jar for another comfit, she closed the bed-curtains around the two of them.

Master Hans Holbein, Court painter to His Grace King Henry of England, Ireland, and Wales, woke smiling this spring morning. He had been told that Lady Whitbourne's Vamplate Manor was a bare little place and so had gone reluctantly there to attend the baroness, who wrote him so gently worded a letter.

But upon arrival he found himself in a well-feathered nest. Workmen were finishing with a last coat of gleaming whitewash on the big stone house; one explained to him that they had just enlarged the place and were anxious to cover up signs that the stone did not match. Around him one thousand acres grew lush and crowned with crops; there were five hundred sheep in the river-marsh, perhaps as many cattle at the stream behind miles of stone fence.

The inside of the house had been worked on, too. The scent of fresh-cut wood and varnish told him all the splendid oak paneling was new. The floors, which he expected to be of beaten earth from what the king had said, were laid in herringbone parquetry patterns or chessboard black-and-white marble. Windows had many panes of glass such as only a very great lady could afford; her Great Room was set up as a dining hall, with a breathtaking sea-sphinx table, two dozen box-chairs, and pretty Italian mantles at each fireplace.

Scarlet and blue Turkey carpets, expensive wolf, marten, and ermine pelts had been flung on the floors to be walked upon. Open cupboards sparkled with enameled Venetian glassware and gilt dishes. Solid gold, too, not plated; he picked up one bowl and was amazed at its weight.

The flower-named housekeeper (*Rose? Pansy? no, no—Tansy*, he thought), stiff with the dignity of her new position, showed him about the house. There were seven bedchambers, each with a wonderful Renaissance bed. Coverlets, even in Holbein's guest room, were of cloth of gold lined with sheepskin or fox; all the bedclothes were of softest beaten linen with foot-wide bands of blackwork embroidery, already called Holbein-work in honor of his detailed painting of it.

He had been misinformed. Kathryn Chase lived like an empress in exile.

Master Holbein emerged from his rooms next day after washing in a cloisonné basin the size of a manger. Everywhere he saw bustling servants, each in a gold-and-black livery that took him a while to place. He was seated and served breakfast at the sea-sphinx table with as much state and deliberation as though he were a visiting lord, and the food was better than King Henry's.

The baroness herself finally entered, apologizing for not having met with him earlier. That was when he realized whose livery her servants wore and whose jeweled portrait hung at her throat.

Baron Windsgeat was keeping her.

The gown she had chosen for the sitting was rich black-on-gold figured velvet, crisp, unbending, with gold braid around all edges. The shift below, peeking only at wrists and for an inch above the gown's low neck, was of silk so sheer as to be almost invisible. It lay like a sheen of thinnest perspiration on her gleaming flesh. The delicate golden embroidery and seed pearls appeared to be sitting directly on her skin.

Her French hood was heavy black velvet over gold-and-black striped tissue, crusted with thumbnail-sized pearls and diamonds; the portrait at her neck was his own work of last year, surrounded in diamonds with a fringe of teardrop-shaped pearls at the bottom. Baron Windsgeat, he well recalled, had been an inscrutable sitter; he wondered whether it was love of the man or his money that drew this pretty, delicate-looking woman to him.

She fussed with her headdress a moment, calling her housekeeper to pin up both tails of the hood with two diamond brooches big enough to buy another manor house and lands. Then she sat back, perfectly still for him.

What skin she had! Almost translucent, but not sickly-pale; this woman walked in the sun, for there was a golden gleam about her face and that long throat that would be difficult not to elongate excessively on paper. She worked her hands together awhile, her only sign of nervousness, and Holbein noted they were rough in comparison to the rest of her. So she had guided her own plow until this recent wealth came upon her. To keep from drawing attention to her hands, the only ring she wore was a thin gold wire, one of graduated circles on the ring finger of her right hand; in his homeland that signified a country handfasting on one of the old, forbidden feast days from before Christian times.

"Tell me all the gossip of Court, Master Holbein," she urged.

He thought, *They will be much more interested in hearing of* you, *Dear Lady!*

"The king is about to send me abroad to paint several candidates for the marriage-bed," he answered, outlining the long oval of her face. Nice face, rather pretty despite the sloping nose and slenderness. He worked in chalk crayon, not silverpoint, for she had very delicate coloring and he wanted to catch it well on this first portrait, which he would then take back to Court and use as basis for a later oil painting. Lucky for her she looked so good in Windsgeat's colors; black-and-gold flattered a woman with gold-brown hair, golden-white skin, black brows, and those astounding, too-blue eyes. Why, she seemed prettier to him by the moment, and he had thought her quite plain at Court.

"I hear you will go to France, Sweden, the Low Countries, and Cleves," she said.

"Yes, Cleves is a small German duchy but threatens to unite with the emperor Charles against King Henry, so he considers a wedding with one of the duke's sisters."

Her hands clasped protectively across her abdomen. Though her belly was flat as a tabletop, Holbein had painted too many women not to recognize the position as indicative of a just-discovered pregnancy. Judging by her face, she was thrilled by the knowledge, too. So she was in this affair for de Gael's love, not his money.

What a subtle smile, very sweet, very unconscious, and not for his sake at all. The kind of smile da Vinci excelled at, not really there until the viewer studied it awhile. "Can you hold that pose with your neck, Milady?" he asked.

"Oh, yes, it is very comfortable." As they made small talk about people at Court, he noticed her hands sometimes strayed to the miniature at her throat, stroking it as though her forbidden lover might feel the caress. From time to time her eyes closed langorously. Conversation rambled to an unnoticed halt as she half-dozed in one stray sunbeam coming through the shutters. Her heart was beating very hard against her stiffened bodice, making it leap; the least sound from outside made her start in her chair. When her dogs barked, the portrait at her throat gave a spastic jerk. *She is expecting Windsgeat today,* the artist told himself and sighed. The light was so excellent, her mood so lovely—if he could only finish this first sketch! The French hood he sketched was still no more than a sickle-moon shape at the back of the face-oval, the swan-neck a graceful curve, the neckline perfectly, evenly portrayed. He had even caught the hands folded over her belly, though nothing was detailed yet.

Hooves along the riverbank. By now the portrait was rattling on her delicate collarbones, teardrop pearls dancing. He told himself, *Windsgeat must be nearly as good a lover as my wife theorizes, damn her!*

Hans Holbein gave up, laid his chalk down. "We can work on this some more later," he informed her.

She vaulted out of her chair in a flash of petticoats and finely-knit hose with flowers embroidered up each leg. Little flat velvet shoes, with cutout figures of mermaids—a pearl popped from somewhere as she ran, rolled across the floor, vanished into the deep silk pile of a Turkey carpet.

The door flew open in front of her as servants heard her crying for them to turn out and meet His Lordship. Holbein grinned to himself, thinking that this would be something to watch. He strolled over to the window that looked out on the river, observed as some twenty riders clattered into the yard. At their head trotted a white stallion who went straight up to Lady Whitbourne, butted his head against her bodice. She blushingly ducked her face, fed him some tidbit while Holbein studied the rider.

Same ramrod spine, same masterful hands on the reins.

People said he and the king had been born the same year, but Henry Tudor was growing fat, unhealthy; this man still looked an athlete. Even at this distance Holbein recognized Genoese silk velvet with intricate figures burnt into it—twenty pounds the ell, more than an average laborer made in ten years' time. Apparently Lady Whitbourne was not choosing her lover's fabrics yet, for His Lordship had elected to buy the velvet in a shade of yellow that had shrieked its presence from clear across the river and stream both.

The short, slashed Flemish breeches and long, lynx-lined cloak were of more of the same velvet. *The man looks like a mustard-pot in collision with a bunch of marigolds*, Holbein thought, and covered his eyes a moment to rest them.

The white horse, puffed with his own importance, showily pawed the ground while de Gael dismounted and threw the reins to a boy. The couple greeted each other very quietly, not touching in front of so many witnesses; the archers went to water their mounts, serving girls brought ale out so that onlookers drifted away with them in knots of five and six.

Holbein watched with keen interest. Alone now, the tall baron lifted Lady Whitbourne's chin with one gloved forefinger; she ducked her head, stared at her feet. He queried, she responded, blushing furiously. Windsgeat took off his hat, plum-sized diamond and all, and hurled it into the air. The lady found herself embraced, kissed passionately, then tenderly picked up and carried inside as though she might break.

The artist barely had time to seat himself at the sea-sphinx table and pick up his chalk again. He was busily putting in the sleeves of her gown when they entered, walking arm-in-arm.

"Master Holbein," John greeted him. The artist rose, found his hand wrung as if by an equal. He had always heard that Windsgeat could be a damnably engaging man when he wished to be, but he had heretofore seen no proof of it. The pale blue, almost colorless eyes, seeming to squint because of deep laughlines—the funny front teeth, sincere mouth, and earnest handshake—yes, very engaging indeed. He could see why all women at Court longed to be the third Baroness Windsgeat. "Can you do My Lady justice?" de Gael was asking him, breathless as a boy with his first love.

"Yes. Her coloring is very English, very fair, but I will not overpower it."

Lord and Lady sat in the sun-flooded windowseat together, foreheads nearly touching as they talked. No one had told

Holbein to leave the room, and Lady Whitbourne was nearly in her earlier position, so he kept working. The figure on paper had a bodice and pendant now. Eyes and nose came next; he left the mouth out because it was too hard to draw while the subject talked so animatedly. There, he had the basics—now if he could only catch Windsgeat like that, sitting like a lad with one knee up, both hands clasped on it, listening to his lady-love. The man's look was so unguarded, so loving. Very different from the stiff-necked, almost suspicious Court miniature at Her Ladyship's neck. Another minute and Windsgeat threw back his head and laughed. That was good, the hair falling back like so. He had good hair for an old man of seven-and-forty, very thick and still quite chestnut in hue, though there was gray streaked all through it.

A totally different man than at Court. Holbein drew quickly, lest the spell of intimacy be broken or they remember his presence. Oh, this was going to be good, so good. The moment of laugh, the head back—hands on knee—the whole, unrehearsed pose. Lady Whitbourne's swan-neck at an angle toward him, eyes alight, the smile not so subtle or elusive this time—

Windsgeat grabbed her suddenly and twined necks with her like a mating stallion, both of them laughing and totally oblivious to the artist. Hans Holbein took up his papers and box of chalks and went for a walk. There was no sign of them when he returned but he heard a rhythmic creaking of bed boards from upstairs.

All that week he worked on the drawings, for they sat for him each morning when the light was best. He worked out the colors he would need to use, made detailed notes to himself, and started off for the continent one fine day. France, the Low Countries, and Cleves next, and none of those women would be as easy to draw as Lady Whitbourne. Especially in Cleves; ambassadors said the two prospective brides were so thickly dressed and veiled that it was impossible to make out any features whatsoever.

Richly paid, Hans Holbein rode along, thinking that it would be months before he could escape the king's assignment and finally finish the Whitbourne-Windsgeat portraits.

Kathryn watched him go. "John, where do you think the king will marry?"

"Hell, I hope."

"We were very indiscreet."

"But Holbein is wholly trustworthy. You notice that he told

us no scandalous details of personal lives, only very broad political news. I pay him for his talent as well as the ability to keep his mouth shut. Come here, you."

He caught her by the waist, tucked her head under his chin. "Let us go back upstairs and become even more certain that you are pregnant."

32
Duchy of Cleves
July 1539

The unsmiling woman sat without complaint for five straight hours.

God's Wounds, she is lively as a corpse! King Henry will think her on the way to her own funeral, Holbein thought, throwing his chalk down so that it broke. Anne of Cleves neither flinched at the sound nor glanced about to see what had caused it. "By Christ, she is stiffer than *Windsgeat* was when I first painted him at Court! Who the devil *is* this woman, some long-lost de Gael?" he demanded of his apprentice.

As they spoke in English, he presumed she could not understand him, for the few times he and she exchanged greetings or instructions, it was always in their native German. "At least she is well dressed, Master," pointed out the boy, indicating Anne's deep crimson velvet with its pearls and bullion.

"Yes, it is a beautiful dress; I have painted most of the king's brides in red velvet at one time or another—*if* this one will be a bride. She is not an unattractive woman, but that funereal face! 'Do not flatter these women, Hans, paint them as in life,' King Henry said, and so I shall. He wanted reality? Here it comes, down to the ten thousandth seed pearl on that hideous little cap. Completely covers her hair. What color do you suppose it is?"

The boy shrugged, picked up the broken chalk pieces, and placed them in Holbein's walnut box. "I do not know, master. Her eyes are quite brown but her brows are so finely plucked that they give no clue to the rest. A true, rich brown perhaps, though not too dark. Not as deep as this walnut box of yours, I would venture to guess. The duke of Cleves is worried, by the way; he has heard King Harry's interest in a French bride was much stimulated by your portraits done there."

"I know, I know. He so liked the portraits that he demanded all the marital candidates be trotted to Calais for his viewing. Christ, Boy, did you hear what François the First said? 'Does he zeenk zees are marriageable noblewomen or mares to be trotted to ze market? We do not treat our women zo een Fronze!' "

A delicate snort from across the room. Holbein's head jerked up but all he saw was the princess of Cleves heartily blowing her nose into a fine lawn handkerchief. Was she hiding a laugh? If so, it meant she comprehended English. But why would she wish no one to know that?

He was suddenly sorry he had insulted her pearled cap.

Kathryn's summons to return to Court life arrived in December of 1539.

She had known all along that her part-time life here with John could not continue forever; some day the king would find a wife and she would be required to join the royal household once more. So her initial reactions were disappointment and resignation at the summons. No surprise in the news; she had known all along. And yet to return to Court knowing she and John would have to feign indifference or a passionless friendship . . .

Several days after the summons came, she began to grow excited about it. Back to Court, the center of new politics, adventure! Now she would find out whether those gown sketches Master Holbein sent her were truly as up-to-date as he claimed. After so long, she would get to see all of her old friends at Court—and a few familiar enemies, too, like Jane Parker, George Boleyn's widow.

Best of all—oh, so much the best—she would be able to bring her daughters to Court if work could be found for them. Maybe the little princesses would be recalled to Court and her girls could serve them once more. Oh, that would be nice. And in a few years' time Jacquetta's Wilhelmina could come to Court; John's boys were already there. They often visited with their father; thinking of them saddened her. They were so dear to her—tall, dashing Payne and dependable Francis. And John—they had all so openly lived together as a family that she could not comprehend acting like mere acquaintances with them now. If only the king would let them marry! Isabella had been born a bastard but bore no stigma as such because Kathryn had been married to Ned at the time; what would become of precious little Cecily, the newborn baby, as she grew? For now she could be sent to Windsgeat with her Aunt Jacquetta, but eventually . . .

An abortion would be hard to conceal at Court, where the laundresses knew everything. At night she would always have to go to John's rooms, for men were expected to have love affairs without anyone thinking the worse of them. Whereas if word got out that she had male company every night, she would become a target for every lecher at Court, as well as find herself sent away in disgrace.

If people asked where she had gained all her fine clothes, stock, and servants, she would tell them from selling Anne Boleyn's pearls and cleverly investing. They might or might not believe her.

Kathryn set to furious work with her sewing women. New livery for her personal servants who must not wear the de Gael colors at Court. Finish the three sets of new sheets for her Woodville bed; what riches, more than one patched set of sheets from her first wedding! Finish up smocks, shifts, gowns, and headdresses for herself, Isabella, and Elizabeth. In the stable, men were mending harness, grooming her horses; in the kitchen her cook was baking food for the trip, storing perishables in vinegar or butter.

Fodder for the horses and pack mules, sun-dried fruit going into little leather bags . . . which jewels to take? Kathryn took all of them, daring to flaunt her new wealth. As far as she and John were concerned, they were husband and wife, though they must not allow themselves to use those terms lest they someday slip in the wrong company. Funny that John, the pagan, still talked about becoming "really and truly married" even after the greenwood handfasting, while Kathryn, who had no particular religious leanings, found that she regarded him in all ways as her legal mate.

Anne of Cleves was landing at Deal then traveling overland to Rochester. Kathryn, already in Kent and therefore closer to Rochester than the Court at Hampton, decided not to travel toward London as ordered. "How ridiculous, all the way there and back again! I will not do it and wear out my horses and porters. I shall go straight to Rochester Castle and meet the Court there," she told Tansy.

"You had better ride the bay," her maidservant answered.

Kathryn thought regretfully of the delicate white mare John had given her, christened Val d'Or; she rode like a summer breeze but was too blatant a pronouncement with her snowy hide. She nodded at Tansy. The bay it was.

She arrived on Christmas Eve. The governor of the castle told her no one had arrived from Hampton Court, then took Kathryn to the top of the one-hundred-and-twenty-foot tall castle keep and pointed. "See those torches? A monstrous large traveling party, been watching them coming from Deal the last hour or so. And, My Lady, I do not have the servants or supplies yet from King Henry to prepare anything, while here comes the king's betrothed princess of Cleves!"

"No tapestries, no carpets? No *food*? A good thing I packed furniture and linens for a year at Court."

He looked on in admiring amazement as she bunched up her brocade skirts and flew down the stairs three at a time. He later told friends, "The last time I saw ankles like that, they were on a sixteen-year-old. I would marry Lady Whitbourne for her ankles in a thrice!"

Kathryn all but set fire to the castle staff and her own servants. "You six, unload my best bed, it is in the first cart you will come to. My lord governor, the best bedchamber is—? You scullery maids, take water, soap, and scrub brushes up there, wash the floor and windows and lay down my rush mats with the carpets over them." She called her chief steward to supervise the rest of the unpacking, ordering all her best household furnishings placed in Anne of Cleves' rooms.

Two dozen brooms started flying. Buckets of sudsy water splashed here and there, shutters were thrown wide to admit fresh, icy air. Every stick of wood in Rochester town was purchased and stacked in the many fireplaces. Tansy went to buy herbs for strewing and bagging to keep out fleas and moths while Kathryn's cook and her assistants rushed to wake the castle's kitchen staff and put them to work.

At least the stables had been cleaned recently. She ordered fresh fodder put out for the incoming horses, and water drawn from the well for them to drink and people to wash in; people never drank water if they could help it. Every fish in the courtyard fishpond must be netted and cleaned, stuffed with something, *anything*. Her cook was yelling for the biggest pike in the pond, her housekeeper was fetching cheeses and old fruit from the cellar and setting the latter to simmer in a pot of wine. Women were cutting up burlap bags and hastily stitching them into smaller squares for sachets, the butcher had arrived with a cart of fresh-slaughtered lambs. Tapestries and carpets were hung out of windows, beaten brutally. Rats ran squealing to safety in the paneling, Tansy yelled for candles—

The bed was put together, waiting to receive Kathryn's down-filled mat that stacked atop sacks of straw and dried clover. More feather padding on top of that, her best, crispest blackwork sheets—the fox coverlets and thick wool blankets edged in satin cording—pine needles and lavender buds on all the woven rush mats—the scent of lamb basted in rosemary and butter, turned slowly on a high spit—

Kathryn directed servants, swept floors, made beds, chased dogs outside. Carried in five stablecats who, backs humped, tails like shepherds' crooks, sprang to depopulate Rochester Castle of rodents.

Hooves clattered, halberds and swords rattled. Horses snorted and blew as the traveling party arrived from Cleves. *No time to change my gown*, Kathryn thought, untying her apron and patting her hair. She was glad Tansy had talked her into wearing her new mink-colored velvet while traveling; the color and short nap showed little dirt nor did it rumple much. Not formal enough, of course, but killingly fashionable with its too-long skirts that trailed down so prettily from her sidesaddle; she took precious minutes to hunt her casque of jewels, piling on all three topaz-and-gold chains and her new brown French hood. There had been no time for a servant to unbutton her out of her flesh-snug doeskin gloves, so she took a dagger and sliced them off.

She was halfway down the stairs when she realized she had no shoes on. They were muddy so she had kicked them off before climbing up on the Woodville bed to adjust the damask bed-drapes. Kathryn fled like a doe, leapt at the shoes, sprinted back down the steps with one in each hand.

They were already in the Great Hall. She skidded to a halt, holding her shoes, listening to throaty German laughter at the sight of her. There seemed only one way to get over such a thing; she did not struggle to pull her shoes on, only disdainfully threw them down, went straight up to a tall woman in gorgeous brocades, and knelt. "No, no," the governor whispered, "that is not her!"

This one in the crimson velvet, then; she had heard that was what Anne of Cleves wore in her betrothal portrait. "No, no, Baroness; no, Governor!" came a warning hiss. She glanced up, saw Lord Admiral Wriothesely shaking his head while the

Germans tittered and gossiped. Wriothesely grabbed each of them, pulled them down with him at the feet of—

—a scrubmaid. That was Kathryn's first horrified thought. Men's cheap old riding boots, a filthy hem matted with mud, and horse-manure. Bidden to rise, she could hardly find the heart to do so. Monstrously fat. Wait—no, not really, the hands were slender enough and the face small, not too rounded. But the badly made dress, all its seams crooked, was so puffed and padded as to make the woman appear a leviathan.

"Your Grace, I am Lady Whitbourne. You were not expected so early, the king's party from Hampton Court has not yet arrived," she told Anne of Cleves, trying to keep her voice steady. But what Kathryn thought was: *I must make her a new gown at once, tonight, before the king arrives! Or he will ride, shrieking, for Scotland!*

"The governor and I have tried to prepare for you, however hastily—" What to say? One did not scold a king's prospective bride (or had they already been married by proxy? She had not thought to ask anyone). One did not say: *Why was your baggage not sent on ahead?*

And oh, God's Horns, to use the de Gaels' favorite oath, the king was going to fall over when he saw this woman! For one thing she must be in her thirties, too old to be starting a family successfully. And she knew nothing about grooming or—Kathryn stepped back, barely controlling an urge to scratch—cleanliness. Anne of Cleves' hair was worn down in token of her virgin status, but it lay clumped in a dank tangle, evidence of being neither washed nor brushed in a long time. Anne was scratching herself all over with a complete lack of inhibition, even opening her gown to pick a flea off her breasts. The governor nearly swooned from shock; Kathryn had to furtively grab his arm to steady him.

The Lord Admiral who had accompanied Anne from Calais looked none too steady himself. Kathryn thought the German ladies-in-waiting all homely as crows and outrageously dressed, but at least they looked better than Anne. What had the king said those many months ago at Vamplate Manor? . . . "*a sense of clothing, music.*" Well, this woman had better at least play the virginals or the king was going to drop of apoplexy.

Kathryn, observing Anne approach the heaped trestle table with glee, thought: *And* that *is going to sleep in my bed tonight? Saints! I will never get the fleas out afterward!*

* * *

Next day Kathryn girded her soul as if for battle. She had Tansy lace her into a well cut but comfortable gown of crimson kersey-mere, perfect for the bending, stooping, and stretching involved in measuring and cutting a gown, and ordered two men to follow her with the twenty yards of gold tissue she had planned on lining her new bed-hangings with. Staggering beneath the weight, they obeyed. "Set it here; you may not follow me into Her Grace's rooms. Thank you," she announced stiffly, and knocked.

Ladies-in-waiting often slept three abed at Court for warmth and to save room, but there were yet dozens of empty rooms in Rochester Castle, and Anne's bedchamber had not one but three fireplaces. English ladies also slept in their shifts when bedding together; as a buxom serving wench opened the door a crack, Kathryn saw Anne and her two favorites sitting up in bed, bare-breasted. She was none too certain what they had been engaged in the moment before she entered.

Fortunately she had studied German as a child and could even sing in it, so she required no interpretor though she had to proceed slowly, thinking each phrase out. "Your Grace, I have come to offer my services in making you a gown to wear for the king. Also I hear you have no English and perhaps I could help you with some small-talk to please him."

Anne answered her in the Low German of Cleves. "Thank you, Lady, I have plenty clothes and no English whatsoever and find that suits me well. You will excuse us now?"

The door banged shut in her face.

Sighing, Kathryn sat down on the roll of gold tissue. She could already imagine the king's voice: *What, Madam? You had her in your keeping thus many hours and did not bathe and clothe her?*

A good thing she was an Englishwoman; Jacquetta said Roman matrons in the Caesars' time had been required to open their own veins when facing dishonor. *I will not die for that girl-loving cow,* she thought and, standing, kicked the bundle of cloth. Then a flea bit her wrist, made her slap and dig at it with her nails. Looking at the ensuing red mark, she wistfully thought, *Though maybe if I scratched at my wrists hard enough I could be dead before Great Harry arrives—?*

She went kicking and swearing on her way.

It was not five hours later that the king and five bosom companions showed up, all of them cloaked and hooded in servants' livery. Thinking them actual servants, Kathryn did not start to dive into the nearest privy until far too late.

"*Cousin!*" the king hailed her lustily, throwing back his hood. He kissed her on each blanched cheek, shook her between his hands until she rattled like dried meat in an old nutshell. Over his shoulder she saw John, Norfolk, and three other men she did not know cast off their hoods.

"Come, come, Madam! We have ridden ahead of the others to see her. . . . Where is the bride?" Henry Tudor demanded. She gave a bleat of fear, gestured in the proper direction with one limp finger. Oblivious to her state, the king loped merrily off.

"What is wrong?" John demanded.

"She—she—do not go in there, I pray you! And keep my uncle out. Ugly—horribly dressed, no English—naked girls on top of her—fleas, fleas, and more fleas—"

Norfolk did what any self-respecting Court Councillor would do in such a situation: offered to hide in the privy with her. But John caught them both, dragged them on after the king. When they entered, the other Englishmen were standing on one side side of the room, German women on the other. "What happened?" Norfolk murmured to Thomas Wriothesely the Lord Admiral.

"He pretended to be a messenger to get an unguarded look at her. Then he fell back in horror. He gathered himself back up, approached, announced himself, tried to embrace her. Then *she* fell back in horror!"

A bull had gotten loose in the courtyard and now ran tossing the king's greyhounds and upsetting carts. Anne of Cleves, dirty skirts drawn immodestly to her knees, sat cross-legged in the window bay, picking her teeth with a stick and cheering the bull on.

There ensued long, taut minutes of silence. Then the king said, in a voice quavering with emotion, "I want one man here to tell me, is there a single reason why I should not draw and quarter Hans Holbein myself—at *once*!"

Six sets of shoulders shrugged in unison. Six heads shook "no." "And yet," Thomas Wriothesely attempted timidly, "when I first met the lady she did entirely resemble that painting. It did not flatter her at all unduly, Your Grace, I swear it."

The king's little blue-gray eyes flared wide open. "*And yet there is such a thing as artistic license!*" Wriothesely wailed, and fled.

Henry, two years older, fatter, and crankier than when Kathryn had seen him last, pointed wildly at Anne. "When the stones of a castle are so befouled, one may at least burn them clean! But what can be done for *her*?"

Anne, grinning out the window, showily scratched her rump with the tooth-stick and spat messily on the floor.

The king fell back into Norfolk's arms. The others trampled each other heading out the door. But Henry was still king, game leg and all; only he could grab four men of such rank and shove them out of his way in order to charge out the door first.

Kathryn froze. She could have sworn Anne of Cleves smiled when Henry spoke those last words, was almost certain the woman understood English.

Anne, catching the puzzled reflection in the nearest window, turned and regarded her evenly. Then winked and blew a kiss.

Kathryn barreled after the men. She and John collided with a smack of bone and flesh, raced down the gallery hand-in-hand. "In here—the privy!"

They leapt in, shut the door behind, turned and saw Norfolk playing cards alone on the cold stone floor. "Sit down," he directed. John fanned his cloak out on the floor for the three of them. They all sat, Norfolk reshuffling and dealing for three. They set to playing. John, looking around himself, muttered, "Gives a whole new meaning to Privy Councillor, eh, Norfolk?"

"You said it, Windsgeat. I know you must be holding that Ten of Cups, Niece, you may as well discard now and get it over with."

"Look more closely when you deal next time, Uncle. I have no tens and no cups."

"You must have the hand I meant to deal John!"

Two hands later, Norfolk was lamenting, "We are doomed, all doomed. John here told him how beautiful women of the Low Countries are, I urged him to take a foreign bride for reasons of state. And you, Kat, were with her all the eve and morning and did not magically make her neat, clean, or a beauty. We are all as doomed as the Poles."

Kathryn sucked her breath in. "Uncle, what has happened to the Poles?"

"The king is cleaning house of Plantagenets. Executed a few Poles, a few Courtenays. Geoff Pole got off by incriminating his entire family; his mother, old Margaret, Countess of Salisbury, is still in the Tower while his brother Reginald remains in Rome, unable to come home. Suits Reg to be in the clergy, though it's a piss-poor time to be a Papist Englishman . . . whole crop of them are attaindered."

"Have you heard from the Boleyns?" she asked as John laid down the Ten of Cups and picked up the pile. "For so long I did not write or try to visit because I was angry with my uncle for not begging off the Council condemning his own daughter . . . I miss Aunt Elizabeth."

Norfolk's eyes warned her before he spoke; Elizabeth had been his favorite sibling. "Well, they are all at rest now, Niece. I think losing Anne and George broke their mainsprings."

Eleven years ago she had borne her own little Elizabeth, named for her beloved aunt. "So many die, Uncle!" she burst out. John's comforting hand gripped her knee, a surprising gesture in Norfolk's presence. The doughty old campaigner did not miss it. His eyes flickered, then he said, "Tut, tut, what are you, forty? Wait until you are my age, Kathryn, you will seem the last lone tree in the forest to yourself. There, there, at least Tom and Bess lived to see their Nan crowned queen, that is no sight to belittle."

The door creaked open; they all gasped. "Speaking of queens, do you think he will still marry Cleves?" Thomas Wriothesely whispered, squeezing in. "I have another pack of cards and I hate Imperial—will you play Triumph with me, Lady Whitbourne, while Windsgeat and Norfolk cheat without us?"

They were engrossed in their games and gossip when there came a furtive tap at the door. "Not unless you have ale enough for yourself and four more!" Norfolk said in a hiss.

"I will be right back," promised the voice, footsteps fading away.

"Uncle, who was that?"

"John Dudley, newly appointed Master of the Queen's Horse. That is, if we are going to have a queen after all. Windsgeat, do you think . . ."

Dudley was back in minutes with a whole hamper of cheese, bread, and port. No tankards, so they passed the bottles around from hand-to-hand; unwatered, it made them all very merry. A riotous five-handed game of Tarocchi was in progress when there came one last knock at the privy door.

"Is there room enough to hide one more?" dolefully asked the king.

33

Kathryn had two days to turn twenty yards of gold tissue into a Court gown. Every woman in Rochester Castle was turned out to help, and a few brought in from town besides. Anne of course ruined the gown's effect by refusing to bathe, be deloused, or have her hair tended, but the gown proved that Kathryn had at least tried.

They rode on to formally meet the king at Blackheath. Kathryn and her servants loitered at the end of the long procession, linens and carpets flapping furtively from muleback in hopes that the freezing air would drive creatures out of them. All her possessions had been returned her imbued with various tenacious inhabitants; *"Der German Vermin!"* Norfolk had announced, and Kathryn fell about his neck, laughing.

She rode along now, listening to Anne and her favorites chattering in their gutteral German. "Gott in Himmel! Who is that one with the big shoulders? He should be king," one of them said, and pointed at John's long back.

"If he were king I would like men better," Anne said, not knowing John fluently spoke and understood German. "If he were king, I would even sleep with him! And often!"

"A man! And in a red-and-green doublet, at that—oh, Anne, how could you? Ick, ick!"

Red-eared, John spurred Finnvarra on ahead.

Anne continued, "He has a beautiful mouth for a man, I will wager he knows a few tricks with it. Nearly as many as you bad girls!"

Kathryn, glaring, thought, *If I chucked my money purse at the back of her head, I could drop her like a stone*!

Never mind that King Henry had specifically ordered a "big bride," saying that he was a large person himself; upon seeing the bridal party ride toward him now, he lamented to the Seymour brothers, "She looks like a gold tissue *barn*!"

At his elbow the French ambassador, Marillac, twisted his moustache. "Your Grace, the ladies-in-waiting gossip that she is very slender without the padded coats and cloaks. And she has very little wrists."

That night at the feast, Marillac repeated his assertion at the table. "I still say she is thin under all that stuff." Then his eye fell upon Kathryn at the next table. "But *that!* That is the slenderest woman in all of England! I think she needs some weight on her." He puffed out his chest. "How about my one hundred and fifty pounds?"

John, who could not very well challenge the ambassador to a duel, settled for sticking his foot out each time Marillac passed. As the Frenchman was an incorrigible mingler and gossip and could not long remain in one place, John had plenty of opportunities. On the fourth pass, limping because of bruised shins, Marillac landed in Norfolk's soup. "It is that big *Anglais*, I will swear he trips me!" came the wail from amidst scallions and broth.

Norfolk fished him out. "Yon big Anglais wants to marry the lady in question and has been forbidden to by the king. And as she is my niece, may I suggest that *this* side of the table is not safe for you, *either*?"

Henry Tudor slapped an interpretor on the back. "Ask your mistress how she likes England."

The question was put to Anne of Cleves. She shrugged, went on eating with dirty hands, elbows planted squarely on the table. When she noticed Henry watching her in horrified fascination, she grinned, wiped her nose across both hands. "That is not a princess, that is some great Flemish mare!" Henry snapped.

Marillac said to Norfolk, "So your niece is unmarried? And a widow, I hear. Perhaps she would like a fine, lusty Frenchman between her—"

John de Gael was one of the few men at Court big enough to knock a box-chair over backward getting out of it. As John's goblet was still in his hand, Norfolk seized the opportunity to spring out of his chair, too, holding his own goblet aloft. "Yes, Windsgeat, I agree! A toast to Their Graces' marital bliss!"

Henry Tudor looked daggers at the two of them. Everyone rose; Marillac found himself at armpit-level next to tall John. "Perhaps, Milord Anglais, I am over-hasty in summing up the charms of a particular lady?" the ambassador attempted.

A chorus of toasts to Henry and Anne.

"Or perhaps, M'sieur Français, you are a wizard at the

tiltyard that you can so openly insult the virtue of high-born ladies?" John asked.

Remembrance flared up in Marillac's panicked eyes. "Are you the big Anglais who unhorsed three royal *ducs* at the Val d'Or twenty years ago?"

There were no more unchivalrous comments about women from the French ambassador that night.

Kathryn observed the exchange though she was not close enough to hear it. *Oh, dear, someone must have said something about me or Jacquetta or even a complete stranger. John cannot stand to hear women spoken of with disrespect.*

"Pardon me, Cousin. You *are* my cousin—?"

That voice—almost like Anne or Mary Boleyn's, very lovely—chiming, like crystal. Kathryn turned on the bench she sat, saw a very young woman in brown sarcenet. The long, slightly hooked nose and thin lips proclaimed her a Howard, though her voluptuous little body had been inherited elsewhere. Brown-haired, clever-eyed . . . with that appearance, how could she so make Kathryn think of swarthy, tall, flat-chested Anne Boleyn? "Are you one of my dead uncle Edmund's girls?" she asked at last.

"Yes, I am the other Catherine Howard."

"They still call me Kathryn Chase, though I was Lady Howard for some years . . . have you a post at Court?"

She offered her hand, felt the strength and spark in the girl's grip. "Yes, Norfolk has gotten me on as maid of honor. Of course, it all depends on whether that German cow is going to be made queen or not."

Kathryn dropped the other Catherine's hand. Jane Parker leaned over, said, "I will wager she is never queen."

The new girl laughed indiscreetly. "And I wager she will. He dare not break the German alliance just yet, though in a while . . ." She familiarly leaned on Jane's shoulder. In the almost four years since she had helped send Anne and George Boleyn to the block, no one had befriended Jane; when Kathryn coolly suggested her cousin go back to her place, Jane moved over on the bench, made an empty space which she patted. "No, come sit down, Mistress Catherine! There is always room for a friend."

Catherine Howard came over in a flash of lifted skirts, exposing her legs to the garters before settling cozily between Jane and Kathryn. "Do you think the Cleves mare is a virgin?" she demanded, tearing up tidbits of chicken from Jane's plate and nibbling at them.

Jane faltered. "With men, perhaps. But you should see how she and her German ladies lie piled in bed together, it looks—well, most lascivious."

"Speaking of lascivious—" Catherine giggled. "Who is that magnificent old man over there? The one with the huge shoulders, and awful yellow doublet; I could certainly withstand a sustained gallop with *him*!"

"I suggest you go back to your own place, Cuz."

The women all looked up to the head of the table to see who had spoken. It was Norfolk's daughter Mary, Duchess of Richmond, widow of the king's bastard. "And why should I?" Catherine Howard asked boldly. "Does he belong to you or one of these other la—why, look, you have made our other cousin blush, Mary."

"I am 'Milady Richmond' to *you*," Mary Howard announced coldly as Kathryn resentfully stabbed her slab of porpoise.

"Your nieces do not appear to be getting along, Norfolk," pointed out John Dudley, passing with a filled plate for his wife.

"Probably just some fuss about rank. Little Catherine has no business sitting with women of their station, related or no. You know how—" Norfolk stopped; Dudley wandered off. Oh, no. The king was keeping his chair drawn as far back from Anne's as possible. *Not one more disastrous marriage!* Norfolk thought. But he was the most loyal man in the realm; if Henry Tudor had his mind set upon this marriage, then he, Thomas Howard, must not contradict him in it. By now his nieces were quibbling audibly—the king looked glum and Anne of Cleves ate like an entire forestful of swine—something must be done to cheer the king—

"Your Grace, tell us of this splendid new palace you are hard at building," he urged. "Nonsuch, as you call it. I hear you are funding it with—" God, God, what a blunder! He had nearly said "plunder from the monasteries"! "With, ah, goods rightfully owed you by some abbeys and Canterbury Cathedral."

Goods taken when the Dissolution of Monasteries Act was passed. Abbeys, churches, cathedrals—all were sacked. Twenty-four cartloads of stuff had been taken from Canterbury alone, Saint Thomas Beckett's bones scattered that there should be no more idolatry and worship of relics.

Henry started in on the golden onion domes Nonsuch would have, the many long galleries and gardens. His old leg wound had become an open ulcer now and it did him good to get his mind off it and onto his favorite subject next to women or hunting—building.

Anne of Cleves, nodding into her salad, was suddenly poked awake by one of her German women. "Did you see the one with the legs go over the bench?"

"I certainly did."

"She looked at you and winked, though you missed it. Shall I get her name for you?"

Anne brightened. "Please do." *Ho,* she thought, *Court life may be fine stuff after all, with such a buxom little baggage about me!*

The king of England lay next to his "Great Flemish Mare" and thought of his other wives.

Jane, now—Jane had been nearly perfect. A little jumpy and dull as dishwater, but his word was law to her; she hung as if suspended from each syllable. And submissive and sweet in bed! . . . His Jane would never have embarrassed him as he had been embarrassed today; for the wedding procession this uncouth German bride had taken up her pretty coronet of pearls and diamonds and stuck stalks of rosemary all over it. "Fertility, ja?" she had asked, and brayed with mulelike laughter. He had thought: *Fertile? With her?*

Anne, now, his other Anne . . . a bitch, a shrew, a termagant. But spirited and beautifully dressed, always in one breathtaking outfit or another. The curved French hoods, heaps of pearls about the delicate throat . . . the nightgown she had worn over her shift the night of her investiture to the peerage, thirteen yards of black satin setting off her raven hair and eyes . . . She had ridden and hunted like Diana, danced like Terpsichore, played virginals and lute, and sung to him late at night when he was weary and could not sleep for the cares of his high office.

Catherine of Aragon. Even that unbending old woman had snuggled him adoringly, called him My Lord or Your Grace, cooed herself to sleep against his shoulder. Catherine had always made him feel so very *male,* so mighty. And such shirts she had sewn him; only Windsgeat could afford shirts to equal them. She had dressed and carried herself with a queen's dignity. But this thing next him in bed . . . !

Henry had tried. After the taunts of Anne Boleyn, after George reading the forbidden word "*impotent*" in the courtroom, he had still been able to perform with his sweet Jane.

The times he had been unable to play the stallion for the Boleyn had been because of her shrewish temper putting him off the urge. So tonight when he found himself hardly able to embrace this stinking, itching, belching *thing* he did not at once blame himself.

But he should not have let Cromwell and the others talk him into this damned German alliance. Gawky, dumpy, braying—where was his blonde beauty, where another Jacquetta or Margrethe de Gael? How could those two magnificent examples come from the same region—same *world*!—as Anne of Cleves?

He closed his eyes, clamped them shut against the sight of her lying there in her hideous shift. Jesu! Would he have to hear that word again? *Impotent*. It was a lie. With a fine woman he was certain he could make love the whole night through. *Any* man, he thought, would be appalled at this bride of his. "Impotent" would have only stung at twenty, but it cut to the soul now at nine-and-forty. Not his fault, he insisted to himself as she began to snore with bearlike sounds. The more he insisted it was not his fault, the more he convinced himself that he had never tried, that she had so disinterested him he had never attempted the climb.

Better to forget that she had giggled at the sight of him undressed. Far better to pretend she had not hummed impatiently as her ladies left him to his wooing, that she had not tapped her foot, picked at the cuticle of her nail.

When he had rolled onto her, desperately trying to provoke some reaction from either of them with this last and greatest effort, she had wilted him with a sister's fond "*Gute Nacht, Heinrich*." He had then been unable to flog himself on to service her. The fact that she had fallen asleep with him so poised for action had not helped matters.

Henry Tudor sat, bumping his head on a bedpost. Swearing, he swung his heavy legs over the side of the bed, winced as the bad one sent pains shooting into his hip. *God's Wounds, but I have aged, to be thus employed on my wedding night!* he told himself. But no, it was the woman's fault. Unattractive, dirty, uncouth . . . he had never tried, they would lie who cried him impotent. He had simply not been . . . *interested*, that was all.

He should have married Christina of Sweden, even if she *had* refused him on the grounds that she had one head, not two, and therefore could not spare one for him. Or Mary of Guise, but he had lingered in the courtyards of indecision until she wed his nephew, James of Scotland. He should have married anyone—oh, anyone but Anne the Second! One Catherine, one Jane, two Annes—*I should never have repeated so disastrous a name,* he thought. Difficult to avoid, though, when every woman of the era was a Jane, Catherine, Margaret, Elizabeth, or Mary.

Henry yanked on his ermine-lined nightgown, fumbled for and found his cane. As he started across the cold floor it came to him that he did not want any of the usual sycophants or even that amusing John Dudley, whose father's head had been lopped off at his own father's orders. No, he wanted a good fight before winning at cards tonight, wanted one who would not beg and bow. Windsgeat was his age and might be equal-glad of company this night; Windsgeat it would be.

The guards bowed, astonished as the king left his bridal chamber. He toddled past, wincing as each step jolted his leg. Normally only dukes would have had apartments so near his, but John amused him, so the best-born mere baron in England was tucked in between Norfolk and Suffolk.

Henry bashed the outer door open with one whack of his cane. Pieter van der Hüm rolled over in bed, giving Henry a flash of some woman's long honey hair: "Who in de—*Your Grace*!" the little Fleming exclaimed.

The woman burrowed under the sheets. Van der Hüm sprang, stark-naked, from the bed and tried to block Henry's path. "Your Grace—Sire—"

There were scuffling noises from behind the next door where Windsgeat slept. Henry noticed that the low fire suddenly flamed bright with the admission of air into the room; the inner door leapt on its hinges. Laughing, he flung Pieter back and entered.

"Wake up, John—or are you already up, man? I could swear I hear someone scuttling about in here."

He fumbled for a candlestick near the door, found it, flung it to Pieter, and ordered it lit. By its light he saw John de Gael sitting up in bed, hair askew, coverlets amuck. Yet the man looked unruffled as only a de Gael could at such moments. It did not escape Henry's attention that the frosty blue de Gael squint was unblinking, nor that there was no top sheet on the bed.

"I—I—" stammered Pieter van der Hüm behind him.

"A table, some cards, and wine," the king ordered the Fleming. "Good morrow, John, you look entirely too serene.

When your sister appeared thus it always boded ill for the world's virtue. Where are your cards?"

John stepped majestically from bed. *And well might that whoreson be unashamed of appearing naked at his age,* Henry thought enviously. *He still has as flat a stomach as a boy in training for war.*

John threw on a sable-lined robe of some glaring copper-gold-green-and-silver brocade. "Windsgeat, you could make a blind man wince," the king observed, throwing a hand up to shade his eyes.

"Do you think so, Your Grace? And here I was regretting not trimming it in violet satin. I let Holbein talk me out of it, he made the funniest noises when I suggested it."

"Like gagging?" Henry asked.

"Why, very like it, now that you mention as much . . . Pieter, get some clothes on, you are running in circles flapping your arms and everything else. Wake the others, tell them I want my sphinx table, all the hippocras I brought, the glass-lined cloisonné goblets, several lute and vielle players, and a woman-singer. Fetch my gargoyle chairs, place the singers outside the door, and stir up the fire. *Now!*"

Henry never knew how van der Hüm did it, but the little Fleming had it all in five minutes: table, cards, chairs, wine in exquisite goblets, a roaring fire, discreet musicians outside the door performing "Stand Auf, Katterlein," as the cards were dealt.

"Do you beat them regularly, to have such service?" Henry asked, signaling Pieter to wait.

"No, I pay them too much. They get used to it and fear if they become sloppy or slothful that they will no longer be able to live in the style to which they are accustomed. Pieter, for example, collects porcelains from Cathay. He could not do that in the employ of most lords. Now! *Go away, Pieter.*"

A sharp glance passed between master and servant. Enjoying himself hugely, Henry held his hand out in an unmistakable gesture. It halted half-dressed Pieter in his tracks. "Yes, I believe you must treat your servants very well for them to have women in their rooms at night."

"Well, I do not *geld* them, Your Grace, despite rumor."

". . . she had uncommon hair, near the color of Jacquetta's."

The blue de Gael squint never wavered. "Your Grace, it is unthinkable," John said calmly, making a subtle hand movement that backed Pieter out of the room and shut the door behind him.

"What, that she would bed someone base-born? Oh, how mighty you de Gaels feign being! And then there is the matter of the woman you yourself were with not five minutes ago."

John clapped a hand to his chest. "*Woman?* You underestimate the effect age has had on me; I was asleep."

Henry surveyed the room. "Under the bed is the most obvious place, which is why I doubt she is here. You are too clever for that. The garderobe, perhaps? No, no, you would not put a gentle lady in with your chamber pots and boots—and I believe she *must* be a lady, you are too proud to make love below your own rank. *John!* Is my fair cousin Kat behind one of Jack of Norfolk's tapestries?"

De Gael's jawline was very white. "You wound me, Your Grace," John said.

"Ahh, so you sent her out the window wearing only a sheet, and here we are, three stories up. I believe I shall keep you all night at cards, John, wondering whether she has slipped to the bricks below."

"*Tom?*" asked the duke of Norfolk's mistress, Bess Holland. "Tom, wake up, I am freezing and there is someone else in bed with us!"

"Oh, let him sleep. Sorry I had to come in through the window and admit so much cold air," Kathryn said, "but yours is the closest room to John's."

"Is that you, Kat? Jacquetta was through here a minute ago!"

Norfolk sat, roared out, "Are you goddamned women having a political meeting on top of me as I sleep?"

Kathryn, wrapping her sheet tighter, scrambled across Bess and on out. She spent the next hour dodging from window bay to alcove to chapel, avoiding other people making midnight assignations. From this doorway to that, hiding in the shadows from patroling men-at-arms—one was coming straight toward her. She twisted the doorknob, fell into the nearest room.

"Cousin Kathryn! Is that you? Shut the door," she heard Catherine Howard say in her musical voice. A man swore, bedboards creaked; bare feet slapped across marble floors in the dark and out through the next doorway. Then a candle flickered to life. Kathryn, listening to the guards stop for a chat outside the door, remained as she was.

Catherine Howard, bare-breasted, bounced merrily on the

bed. "Well! So Lady Prim-and-Pure had a lover of her own this night! Or do you always traipse about in that ever-so-fetching bed sheet? And who walked in on you?"

Time to distract her with gossip. "The king did."

"On his wedding night? She must have proved a disappointment. And you, my haughty cousin . . . I take it you were with the owner of the brightest doublets at Court? A wonderful old man with great huge shoulders who walks as though he would stomp over Great Harry himself? You had best be nicer to me, else I will start screaming that there is an intruder in my room. Then those guards will come in here and you will be the talk of the Court."

Kathryn rewrapped the sheet more modestly, brought an edge of it over her head to veil her features. "Scream away, you whining little bitch!" she dared, and, flinging wide the door, stepped out of the room. She had expected laughter, not that the two men would shriek "*Ghost!*" and, dropping their halberds, flee. So she had an uninterrupted stroll back to her own apartments.

Hours later, Tansy admitted an apologetic John. He sat at the foot of the Woodville bed, watched Kathryn blink irritably at him in the sudden candlelight. " '*Oh, no, love,*' " she savagely mimicked his voice. " '*Not under the bed, he will look there first thing. On the window ledge.*' Window ledge! I am frozen half to death, I had to come in through Norfolk's bed—Catherine Howard is trying to blackmail me—half the damned Court thinks I am a ghost—"

"So you are cold? I will warm you," he offered. But the first thing he did was walk across the room and bolt the door.

"What are you doing?"

"Trying to get some sleep," John said, and fell across the bed fully dressed and face-first. He was asleep before he landed.

At least he was on her feet, which were still very cold.

Upon discovering herself pregnant that spring, Kathryn requested leave from Court, claiming she needed tend her estates.

It was denied. She would always wonder whether it was because the new queen was amused by her—which Anne did seem to be—or whether it was because the king suspected her and John and wanted to catch them.

Telling no one, she gathered what she needed all that week, mixed herself a potion. When, later that evening, nothing had happened, she mixed and took a second, stronger dose. It was not an exact science for her as for Jacquetta and Isabella, she guessed at the portions required.

Elizabeth Stoneleigh found her. The girl returned from her lute lesson, and found her mother strewn across the floor, hemorrhaging from nostrils, mouth, and womb. She woke Tansy, ran to fetch John.

He entered and bent over the convulsed body at the bed. Even before Tansy brought him the empty bottle to sniff, he had guessed. "Pennyroyal. No one but Jacquetta can safely mix this stuff for abortions. Lissy, run, fetch Pieter. Send him for your aunt 'Quetta at once."

Something to dilute the poison, first. He could not remember whether milk or water was preferred, so sent Tansy to bring both. His darling, beloved Kathryn, so hot, shuddering and twitching in his arms. Clammy, foul-smelling sweat—

That was it, get her up and walking. Sweat the poison out of her system. She still kept his old sable-lined cloak, so he dug it out of the parquetry trunk, wrapped her in it, made her pace the room with him. It was more like dragging than walking her; she hung on his shoulder, scarce able to put one foot before the other.

"That is My Lady! Come on, Kathryn, you must not give up, must not die on me. Oh, damn you for not telling me, I could have helped! Why did she do it, Tansy? Why?"

"She was refused permission to leave Court."

"I could have gone to the king, bought her way out. Faked a message from Isabella at Vamplate Manor, done something, damn it, *anything!* Walk, Kathryn, walk! Why did she not tell me?"

Ladling warm lemon water with honey down her throat, making her walk, walk . . . where-oh-where was Jacqui? Jacqui and her magic red leather casque, Jacqui with her healer's touch and priestess-prayers. *Hurry, Sister, oh, hurry!*

Tansy was walking her now while Elizabeth mixed the lemon water and John resentfully jabbed at the fire and fed it more wood.

"*John!*"

Kathryn was screaming out his name, holding her arms open to him. Then she was sliding toward the floor in a dead faint as he leapt to catch her—

"You have nearly killed her," Jacquetta said within seconds of her arrival. "The stuff should have been vomited out; diluting it does not have much effect. All your walking did was hasten the stuff into her system and increase the bleeding. Dear Goddess, my Kathryn! I do not know if I can save her!"

She sent everyone out and bolted the door.

For a while he sat on the hearth with Elizabeth sobbing in his arms. "I do not want Mama to go away like Papa did . . . oh, Uncle John, I beg you! Do not let her go!" Later, she was angry with him, pulled away. "You gave her a baby and killed her—I hate you, I hate you, I—" She ran sobbing from the room.

"I will get her," Pieter said, starting up from the windowsill.

"No, no, this is between Lissy and me, I will go catch her."

Outside the stars hung suspended on a black velvet night. No wind blew the courtyard's banners or fruit trees, nothing stirred or appeared to live. Looking about himself, John realized that he had forgotten the heartbroken little girl and had instinctively sought the nearest thing to a greenwood for his offering.

He opened scarred, capable hands to the sky. "I have always been thine," he told the night. "I walked the paths you showed me, I kept your laws, held the forest and god-path sacred above all else. That was the bargain made between you and me, that we should aid each other."

He waited for the sign that always came. But this time it was missing; no wisp of the blue god-mist, no breath of the Wild Hunt's wind at nape or brow, like an icy kiss.

He could not wait. Jacquetta said Kathryn was dying. So he held his hands up higher, lifted his face to the utter blackness. "She is not some forest beast, some creature of yours that I should ask you to succor her. I ask it of The Lady now instead, for She guards all woman-secrets: a woman near death of an aborted child is in Her hands, not yours or mine, Lord Herne."

He had never knelt to the All-Mother before, never asked her help. He was a man; such things belonged to Jacquetta. As soon as he bent to the damp ground, the hair at his nape prickled; he remembered then that She was whimsical, often false and cruel, and that Her fees were always paid in blood. Very well, then. Let fall what may upon him; he opened his shirt to bare his heart, show his sincerity. No matter what She did to him, it would not be allowed to affect Windsgeat—Hraeg's Geat, Woden's Path—and it would save his Kathryn.

A life for a life. Thinking it his own, he drew his dagger, carelessly cut his hand to bring blood. Pressed his gory palm to the Mother-Ground to seal the contract. *Herne will resent it*, he thought, but there seemed no other choice.

The wind came up then in a blast of fury. Blew the banners straight out, twisted slender fruit-trees and broke their boughs. Hurled black clouds across the stars, showed him a brief slice of silver moon.

John's hair whipped straight out behind him. In the breaking of wood and windows flying open, he heard a child cry out. Turning, he saw Elizabeth on the ground behind him. God's Horns, she must have heard the entire prayer! Even his eldest son did not know the family religion yet; Isabella only knew because she had been born possessing The Knowledge.

He caught up the girl, shielded her from the dry storm with his own body. Glass sprayed him, bits of wood struck. At last he reached the doors, fought his way in from the wild garden.

The storm ceased. "She will live now," he told the child. They opened their eyes again. The silver sickle moon was deceptively serene, as though she had won some struggle from her place in the velvet night. But had she? he wondered.

Elizabeth slid through his arms, ran to see how her mother fared. But John remained as he was, clinging to the wall for support. He had invoked powers he had never stretched toward before, abandoning the god of his fathers to do so. He had turned his back on the thing he had been taught to hold dearest.

So it was entirely fitting that Herne the Hunter should reply in kind.

34

April 1540

Catherine Howard stuck her pretty lower lip out. "But, Your Grace, I have no right to approach you, nobody asked me to."

"*However*—?" Henry urged her on. He found her the freshest, most sparkling new creature at Court, radiant and shockingly impudent amidst so many boring old faces.

"But I thought you might be especially sweet and allow my poor, dear cousin, the other Kathryn Howard, to go home."

"*Sweet*." None had called him sweet for a long time. She had her pretty little brown-and-cream head down, glancing up at him from the corners of her eyes. And oh, how prettily she rocked on her little heels, making her full taffeta skirts rustle and sway about her! The stiffest of buckram bodices did not flatten her as it did other women at Court; no, she had lush, round breasts spilling over the top of that sparkling blue fabric. *What a lively little thing, and such unthinking coquetry! I will wager she has no idea what effect she has on a man*, Henry thought, delighted. If only she did not have the Howard nose and chin of his first Anne. Sometimes the resemblance was unsettling.

He found his powers of speech again. "Do you mean Lady Whitbourne? Why, what ails the baroness your cousin?"

She glanced furtively about the Presence Chamber, made a show of reluctance. Henry, intrigued, crooked a finger and signaled her nearer. She climbed the dais, leaned over and showed him all of her breasts. "It is only *love*, Your Grace," she crooned, switching her skirts with both hands.

Her perfume filled his head. The rose-tipped breasts rubbing against the silver bodice edging—*only love*—

"Your cousin shall be allowed to return home," he gasped out. "Now, dear girl, tell me about yourself."

She sat at his feet, allowing him a further view of that sumptuous young bosom. "Well, I am but a poor country girl, Your Grace, and ignorant of the ways of Court. I was raised by Norfolk's old mother . . . I do come to find a husband, my uncle says Howards are very hot-blooded and he would see me married before some tried to drag me into disgrace. Of course I do not really know what he means—something to do with *men* I suppose. . . ."

There was a medallion bouncing just at cleavage-level; she played with it, shifted it so that the long chains below it fell down between her breasts and she had to languidly fish them out. Then she played with the pendant some more, letting its golden fringe stroke all over her nearly-bared bosom. "Do *you* think Howards are hot-blooded?" she asked, and here came another of those looking-up-through-her-long-eyelashes glance.

It escaped him that she had not been granted permission to sit in the royal presence. She was doing it somehow, and yet when he worked one of his feet under her skirts she acted shocked and confused. An innocent Howard, was it really possible? Hot as any mare in season and bewildered by it . . . well, some young rakehell would jump on her and that would be that . . . Henry allowed himself to think of what it would be like making love to this fresh-faced little virgin. So fresh, so gently perfumed. No fleas, greasy hair, or snoring *here*. She had delightful little Howard hands with perfectly straight fingers and one inexpensive ring which she played with in a manner guaranteed to madden any man: sliding it up and down on her finger, up and down, at times furiously, then slower, biting her lip each time before she spoke. Then he would have to urge her to continue with her life story, though he was not hearing a word of it.

"You are a pretty child," he said at last. "How is it that Howard men are so foul and their womenfolk so fair? Now tell me what manner of husband you want and I will look around for you, little Catherine. You of course will want some strapping young colt who can dance all night."

She opened her eyes very wide. "Oh, no, Your Grace. I should prefer a mature man, an older man with much to teach me about the ways of life and . . . other things. I do not want wanton dancing and such foolishness. No, not I; how content I would be nursing my beloved, quietly sewing by the fire while he read to me or instructed me on the king's new religion! I have so much to learn, Your Grace, and no one to teach a foolish young woman like myself. Why, my husband's pains would be mine and his triumphs, too; how I would hasten to heal him in any illness!"

Henry, leg swollen and stinking with a varicose ulcer, found such notions delightful and pressed her for more.

Kathryn, carried in a litter between two sets of mules, lay comfortably back against heaped pillows and furs. "But, John, Catherine Howard does not even like me! Why should she go to the king for this writ excusing me from court?"

He nudged Finnvarra forward to walk alongside the litter. "Because family business makes an excellent excuse for a private audience?" he guessed correctly.

"She is *where*?" Norfolk roared at his mistress.

Bess Holland took another nibble of pigeon pie. "Sitting at the king's feet every day, prattling about husbands and love and nursing the ill."

That a niece of his should so aspire without consulting him

incensed the old warrior. He hammered on the table with both fists, made wine leap from goblets. "Mistress, yes. Wife, never! I will not go through one more hunt-and-chase with a niece of mine, watching her bait the king, lure the king—I will throttle that ingratiating little—"

"So de Howard girl has started it," Anne of Cleves mused aloud and in excellent English. "*Good.* Den I will give her dat diamond brooch of Sampson as I promised. Now please have dis note sent to Lady Whitbourne at Windsgeat."

"The English, you speak it so much better than before. But you made mistake: *Whitborne,* not *Windsgeat* is where de lady lives," one of her German girls said.

"But I *meant* Windsgeat! You do not dink she traveled all de way to Kent in her condition? Of course not. It would kill her. Handsome-John-of-de-Outrageous-Doublets took her home wid him. You will see dat my note reaches her. Oh, und take dis ruby pin, too. She is a good person, Lady Whitbourne; she knows I speak de English und has not told anyone. I want her to get better und shake up all my lazy ladies, und I tell her so in de note."

She grinned to herself, thinking of the other brooch she had tempted Catherine Howard with. *Good*. Now that fat old monster would take a mistress and leave *her*, Anne, alone.

She turned to appreciatively watch the swaying walk of her favorite as the girl crossed the room.

Kathryn returned to a very altered Court three weeks later. Catherine Howard was suddenly the favorite maid-of-honor, with full Lady-of-the-Bedchamber privileges; all others had been virtually excluded. King Henry was openly flirting with her, Norfolk was almost imbecilic with panic, and John Dudley was in a foul mood. "How can I be Master of Horse to a queen who acts afraid of the beasts, Windsgeat?" he demanded one afternoon.

The other John considered it. "But that is the whole point, Dudley. I think Anne of Cleves only *acts* afraid."

Thomas Cromwell, who had chosen the king's bride, slunk about in terror. He was Chief Councillor of Henry's court, having risen from nowhere to the rank of Lord Privy Seal and Earl of Essex in a few short years, but he was out of favor now. He was especially nervous because whenever there was political turmoil, the king chose a victim to throw the people, and word had just come of unrest in the North. This time around, Cromwell feared he, who had wound the scarlet sin-cords about the horns of so many other scapegoats, was about to be so marked himself.

When Norfolk heard that rumor confirmed by the king, he vigorously agreed. He and Cromwell were old enemies. In their plays for power, Norfolk had married his daughter to the king's now-dead bastard, and Cromwell his son to one of Jane Seymour's sisters back when Jane was queen.

Norfolk had Bishop Stephen Gardiner's assistance in tightening the cords on Cromwell's horns. This unholy duo formed their plans, chose the sacrificial offering, and began coaching Catherine Howard in more ladylike, less obvious methods of enticing the king's interest. But she must not be so blatant about a crown as Anne Boleyn, whom she had never known; she must act surprised and a little dismayed when the king asked her to wife, as they became sure he must.

By June Henry was seeking a divorce. Unlike Wolsey, Cromwell was arrested at the Council, not at the dinner table; there was no pear to fall from his fingers, only a quill dipped in ink that ran like old, black blood along his best coat. He had made the Cleves marriage and was not now hastening to undo it, so he was arrested on a host of improbable charges.

Kathryn heard the news from John. *How could Norfolk not tell me,* she thought, hurt. Then, more alarming: *Oh, no! I must warn the queen!*

She found Anne of Cleves in the courtyard with a gardener, pointing to various flowers and making him name and spell them so she could write it all down in a little leatherbound book. She was dressed like a German hausfrau, not English queen: wooden clogs over her shoes to protect them in the mud, many-pleated wool dress with two lines of plain black trim at the hem. A stiff, winged, wholly unflattering white cap, with a piece of similar stuff that she called a *goller* over her back and shoulders. She wore her hair down because no one had the courage to tell her that it was a daily insult to the king, to so remind him and the world that she retained her virginity.

"Your Grace, I must speak with you," Kathryn announced hurriedly.

"Kat'rin, vat ist?"

She leaned forward at this show of blankness, whispered, "*Alone,* Your Grace. It is very urgent!"

"How urgent?"

"Your life may be at stake."

The black leather book struck the garden path. Kathryn, stooping and retrieving it, saw Anne frantically waving the gardener away. "*Gott in Himmel!* Tell me what you mean!"

"The king wants to divorce you to marry Catherine Howard."

Anne paled grotesquely. "Marry? *Marry?* She was only to be his mistress!"

"He is going to send you to Richmond while he makes his plans. Once you are there, Wriothesely and Charles Brandon—he that is Duke of Suffolk—will be sent to obtain your agreement. If you do not give it—"

"But I will, I will! I never vish to marry any man, let alone dis hulking king of yours!"

"But you must not appear too eager or it will insult him, and when his pride is hurt he is capable of *anything*. Continue acting foolish and innocent, tell them, wide-eyed, that you are amenable to whatever the king wishes. He must not think you oppose the divorce."

"How could it be a divorce when it vas never a marriage? Oh, dese men, dey so confuse me! Women are so much more fortright! You have not told me how you come by dis news. Your lover?"

Kathryn nodded. "Vell, dat is good, he is a nice man and seems trustworthy. As he is very high on de king's Council dese days, he would hear de trute at meetings and such. Please, Kat'rin, you must come to Richmond wid me and help me find de right dings to say! My ladies are no good at handling you English, and everyone dinks I do not speak de tongue."

"Or dance, sing, make music, hunt, or any of the other things you probably do. Why the lies?"

"To make me ugly in his eyes. Dear Gott, when I am unmarried I will bade in scented water drice a day and wear such pretty dings! Come to Richmond and stand up for me to dese two-faced lords."

"But if there is indeed going to be a new queen, the king will order me to remain at Court."

Anne burst out, "How can she so betray me? Mistress, yes, but to aspire so high! Gott help me, but I was fool to her; I luff the girl."

Funny to hear those words from one woman about another. But she had heard Arthur speak thus of boys; was it any odder women should have a form of the same vice? "Richmond is lovely," Kathryn soothed. "You will like it, though it is rather old-fashioned. Wonderful, wonderful gardens, you will delight in them. And the prettiest copper-clad onion towers in the world."

Anne considered it, dragged a dirty hand across her eyes. "Why do you help me, knowing you and I are two so-different types of women?"

"Well, because you are queen. And—and maybe because I liked helping you keep secrets from the king. What will you do if the king divorces you?"

"And does not cut off mine head, you mean? Stay here, I hope. Maybe brother William will be too ashamed of me to take me home, I hope. He would only try to remarry me, and I do not wish that."

"If I may, Your Grace—" Kathryn bit her lip a moment. "Why did you marry King Henry, then?"

"Ach, William dreatened to turn me out, penniless, into de streets. All I haff ever wanted is a place of my own where I can ride and garden, haff a few good friends about me. Not all dis Courtly talk, political maneuvers, and lies. And executions! *Gott!* Just a place of my own . . ."

Kathryn considered it. "Ask for Richmond as part of the divorce settlement, King Henry never goes there any more. You will have your privacy, your gardens and horses and friends. And it is so near the river you will indeed be able to bathe every day!"

Several days later she received a letter from Richmond. "Dear Lady Whitborne," Anne had written in her own hand, "I very well like it here at Richmond. Fourteen towers in the royal apartments alone, most splendid. Did you know each have five stories? I climb to the top and look out on all the world thanks be to you. Otherwise I should thought that divorce leads to execution and so refuse it, thereby *truly* leading to my death. I told Suffolk that I would be very pleased 'to be regarded as the king's good sister now.' Is too much, do you think? Sometimes I overdo. Please wear the jewel, I know you ride and hunt well. With much affection, A. of C., which is much in debte to you."

"The jewel" was an enameled solid gold brooch of Diana. Her bodice was formed by an enormous baroque pearl and she aimed a diamond-and-pearl longbow. Kathryn loved the little goddess, pinned it on all her riding hats, but John claimed it gave him the shudders and repeatedly insisted it was bad luck, a bad omen, and she should not wear it. But as he did not explain himself, she balked at following his whims;

he had never told her about his bargain with the Wild Hunt's goddess in the garden when she lay dying.

Catherine Howard blocked Kathryn's horse with hers at the next Windsor hunt. "What ho, Lady Whitbourne! I see by the queen's jewel upon your cap that you are not adverse to, shall we say, certain German vices? And you acting so prudish, even though losing Windsgeat's bastard this April!"

"Where I sleep or do not sleep is no affair of yours, Madam. Though of course I could tell a few tales of a man in your bedchamber late one night—tales that could prevent you from becoming queen."

The girl paled. "Peace, Cuz! You must not be such a wretch—remember how I got you excused from Court to recover? We Howards must always help one another, we must stay friends!"

Kathryn's white mare, Val d'Or, whinnied excitedly. Glancing up, both women saw another Windsgeat White approaching through the mossy oaks. Thinking it might be John, her heart leapt in her breast. But it was Payne, his oldest son, with the same chestnut hair and crook-toothed smile, though Payne's eyes were a black-blue like his mother's. He was handsomer than his father, Kathryn disloyally admitted. John was attractive, John had a smouldering presence, but there was an irregularity of feature to him; Payne was an unmarred Apollo.

"I have seen him at Court. Who is he? He puts me in mind of your lover," Catherine Howard said, clutching the reins to her bosom.

"John's son, Payne. You play a risky game with the king. Cuz, are you sure you would not prefer a fine boy like Payne? Of course he is slightly younger than you, but he is very clever, a wonderful rider and dancer and . . ."

Catherine was not listening. The dappled sunlight brought out the red of Payne's chestnut hair as he approached; he was not so craggy-faced as his father, nor so muscular, and his eyes made her think of only the very best and brightest sapphires.

He doffed his hat, and rode slowly up to them. His colt bumped noses with Val d'Or. "Good day, Aunt Kathryn, Milady Howard."

So he had noticed her! "Am I too late for the hunt?" he inquired with a dazzling smile. Seeing no answer forthcoming, he told Kathryn, "I saw your son James the other day on the river, we . . . had words." So that explained the dark shadow under his left eye—there had been a fight.

"Please stay away from him, Payne, he has sworn to kill your father and Pieter."

Catherine Howard was regarding him with such a palpitating bosom and dilated pupils that she reminded Kathryn of a twitch-tailed cat about to spring at the juiciest pigeon it had ever seen. "Ride on ahead," Catherine Howard suggested to her.

"Go to the devil," Kathryn answered evenly. Angered, her young cousin spurred her horse on ahead, though Kathryn noted she did not go far.

Turning, Kathryn saw admiration in Payne's eyes. "Never be alone with her," she warned. "She is going to be the new queen. A love affair with her will be deemed treasonous. So! Tell me what you have been doing lately and whether or not you will be going to Sorbonne and the university there."

He was so dear to her that she never stopped thinking of him as her real son and James as some evil changeling. She loved his brother, too, though Francis was more like Margrethe—slow-speaking, gentle, wryly humorous. Payne was all fire and energy.

I wish he were my son, she thought as he spoke. Lissy had just been sent to join Elizabeth Tudor's household and Isabella had been with Mary Tudor two years this last time, never at Court longer than a few days. Cecily, reared at Windsgeat, did not recognize Kathryn and in fact once called Jacquetta "Mama" by mistake, hearing Jacquetta's Wilhelmina address her as such.

"What hurts you?" Payne asked suddenly.

She had not realized she was blinking back tears. "I am wishing I was not cursed by this damned Plantagenet blood. Wishing I could be with your father and all our children and bear babies openly, with no fear of the Tower. Payne, you are so dear to me—promise me you will always obey the king, swear to me that you will not do anything to endanger yourself or your family."

He cocked an eyebrow at her. "Why do you women always think you alone feel pain, Aunt Kathryn? Why do you think men do not know worry and fretting and lying awake night after night with fear for the ones they love? I watched Mother die by inches and have spent these last three years worrying you and Father would marry and go to the block for it. But do you know what the worst pain of all was? That I fell so deeply in love with Isabella before anyone thought to tell me she was my sister."

Her mouth sagged.

Payne finished, "So if I wish to sleep with the future queen of England or anyone else in the whole damned world, I shall! Because none of it matters; why not have something real, actual, physical to lie awake about instead of those maybe's and what-if's?"

She knew he was not angry with her, it was only youth and frustration speaking. He put his spurs to his colt, made the animal leap after the loitering Catherine Howard.

Surprise made Kathryn dull. All she could think was how angry John would be that spurs had been used on his best colt.

PART FIVE

CATHERINE HOWARD
(The Secret Imparted)

"The secret thought imparted
With such trust;
The wanton talk,
The divers change of ploy.
The friendship sworn
And promises kept so just,
Wherewith we passed the winter nights away."

—Henry Howard, Earl of Surrey—
Executed by Henry VIII—

"No Other Will But His."
—motto of Catherine Howard—

35

28 July, 1540

She was little Catherine Howard, who had been nobody and no thing. Well, she was about to marry a king. What a difference that would make! They would all look twice now, would they not? Aye, and stare and stare.

They would look at her many fine gowns and furs, at the jewels the old fool heaped on her. Properties, horses, lap dogs, carts, and litters. Henry gave her all the wardrobes and trinkets of her predecessors, with the exception of Anne of Cleves, and who wanted her disgusting old rags, anyway?

Little Catherine Howard, the nobody, the orphan! How clever she had been to play on Norfolk's sympathies and family pride with her many letters until he got her invited to Court. Virtuous little Catherine, she had passed herself off as. Well, none in this Court knew her for what she was, she had left all witnesses in the north. Any who could testify that she had always been a voluptuary with the knowledge of how to please herself and later a man—no, they were all living in obscurity in the savage North.

It had been awhile since she had shown a man what she knew. Since the king's interest in her had been piqued, Catherine had been forced to be first discreet, then celibate. Anne of Cleves had only been her second female and that had been exciting, but her appetite for men had not been quenched.

No time for such thoughts now, she told herself, pressing her thighs together to stop their trembling. Today was her wedding morning, she must sit while her ladies tried the headdresses of all those old, dead queens on her. But all she could think was that she wanted Windsgeat's son so badly she feared she must die of it.

In the Tower, Thomas Cromwell knelt to his confessor, poured out his iniquities for the last time.

"I do not like the ones that look like dog kennels! Get me one of my Boleyn cousin's French hoods!" Catherine Howard snapped at last. Jane Parker raced to obey.

"Here, your hair needs to be a little different with a

French Hood," Kathryn softly suggested, taking up the queen-to-be's brushes and tending her. "The center part like so, and the hair drawn down lower in back . . ."

Jane Parker dug in a sandalwood trunk carved with *H*'s and *A*'s. From its depths she drew out a costly creation of pearls, rubies, and brocade stretched over buckram and wire. "She only wore this two or three times, he might not know it. I always thought it the prettiest thing I had ever seen."

"Why, so it is," Catherine greeted the headdress. "Here, give it to me, you old people are so slow with such things. Bother Harry if he *does* recognize it, I shall not leave anything this lovely hidden away in a box. Hm! Quite flattering to the Howard nose, but I suppose that is why the Boleyn liked them. Say, Cuz, where did you get that sloping nose? You have not the family nose or chin."

She held up her hand mirror to Kathryn. "I look very like the Chases, I hear," Kathryn answered musingly.

"What? Fairies left you, Cuz, to have such an uptilted nose. Or perhaps witches did it. I hear witches do it very well, Cuz."

Kathryn's ears reddened. *I hope to God this is my last wedding day with a bride of Great Harry's. Every year I get closer to boxing a queen's ears!* She handed the mirror back.

Catherine Howard kissed her own reflection in it. "I shall love being queen," she said. Then, thinking of Payne de Gael, she shivered sensuously.

Thomas Cromwell, former Lord Privy Seal, former earl Essex, knelt saying his last penance.

"I have not enough necklaces on!" Catherine Howard cried out in wounded surprise. "Bring me more, bring me all those old, boring queens' jewels! I want Anne Boleyn's coronation pearls."

Jane Parker leaned forward. "The queen of France wears them these days, Your Grace. Lady Whitbourne sold them to her."

Bitch! Kathryn thought. *She was always jealous of me and George Boleyn.*

Catherine Howard twisted on the backless bench that allowed her ladies to reach her hair and headdress. "Cuz! What did you do to earn those pearls from my bridegroom?" she asked. Her laughter rippled prettily, little silvery sounds.

"If you really wish to know, ask the king," Kathryn shot

back. She grabbed the nearest jewel-chest, yanked out a necklace with six gaudy gold chains and a fringe of medallions, the largest of which was hand-sized.

"Oh, Cuz! It is monstrous, it is appalling. I must wear it or die! Put it on me, please. No, no, never mind, give me the damned thing. Turning forty must make a woman slow as a tortoise; can you move no faster?"

Kathryn allowed herself the brief but satisfying fantasy of her hands closing about that plump little white neck. Catherine Howard stood. "There! How do I look? I think I am finally ready. Poor Harry, to wait so long."

On Tower Green, the headsman took a few practice swings with his axe. Not bad, not bad at all. He adjusted his mask and waited.

Henry Tudor puffed his chest out as the buxom little bride approached the altar. Another short one, like Jane who died giving him his only prince. Well, this one would give him princes aplenty, to judge by those curved hips, that white bosom. Such tiny women never made him feel hulking, but rather big and masterful, protective of them. Tall women unnerved him, for they seemed unnatural; surely God did not mean for Woman to look her Master so nearly in the eye as Kathryn, Jacquetta, and both Annes had done him on plenty of occasions.

He did not hear the sound of his twenty-four-year-old daughter grinding her teeth. "She is nearly five years my junior!" hissed Mary Tudor.

"I know, Milady, I know," soothed Isabella Howard.

"This is his fifth marriage while I am four-and-twenty and he will not let me wed! I hate that mincing Howard peahen of his—hate her, hate her!"

"You have another new mama," Elizabeth Stoneleigh whispered.

Elizabeth Tudor, just shy of her seventh birthday, answered, "I so fear that some day I may call one of them by the other's name."

"Then just to be safe, call all of them 'Mother,' " Lissy suggested.

Thomas Cromwell finished his speech, knelt down on the scaffold. He fitted his neck in the groove. There was time to reflect upon both the shortness of years and the smoothness of the wood cradling his head. How many lives before his had ended on these few inches of age-hardened wood? How much ambition, how much passion snuffed out here?

Thomas Howard, Duke of Norfolk, pushed his chair back from Anne Boleyn's gold leaf writing desk. "By God," he said to his son Henry, Earl of Surrey. "I never liked Cromwell but now that I have read these, his ledgers, I see how he held the king's spending in check. That is the real reason he is dying, not the Cleves marriage. Without him I do not see how England can avoid going bankrupt. *I* cannot stand up to King Henry and tell him 'no,' else I will find *myself* on Tower Green next."

". . . man and wife," finished Bishop Stephen Gardiner.

On Tower Green, the axe came whooshing down.

Catherine Howard whispered, with downcast eyes and bewitching smile, "Husband—may I sometimes call you Husband, and not always Your Grace? I already like being married to you." She fit her tiny hand in his big, hot one, gave a timid squeeze that captivated him. So shy, so modest! And yet so fond of him that she was bold enough to hold his hand in public.

The executioner held Cromwell's head aloft. "Thus perish all enemies of the king!" he cried out.

No one cheered. He thought that very odd.

Catherine Howard made up her mind to be a very good queen and she was. People marveled that a girl not yet twenty could seem so regal on state occasions and yet so merry when hostessing feasts and greeting ambassadors. She went with the king on his usual summer progress and suddenly he seemed to come alive again, to drop years and pounds because of her presence.

She had him in the saddle at dawn, riding three hours a day and then dancing vigorously well into the night. He showered her with jewels, gowns, properties—not merely the leavings of his other wives, but new things as well. In fact he so enjoyed her company that he chose to be chiefly alone with her for some months; the Court, disbanded for the progress, was not recalled to Hampton Court until almost Christmas.

That autumn Kathryn returned to her estates as a farmwife. But there was no farm husband; after several months together at Windsgeat, she and John quarreled again about marrying. It started when he told her his workmen still waited, after twenty years, to finish their marriage bed . . . She was no sooner to Vamplate Manor than she missed him terribly, lying awake at night hungry for his body against hers, his deep voice singing her to sleep in the shelter of his arms. His laughter, his companionship, the lovemaking . . . the day they halter-broke the new foals, the day he took her to the wool sheds and taught her how to clip sheep, as any good farmwife ought to know. How he made her laugh that day!

At least she had little Cecily with her, from the time of the king's new marriage until her return to Court at Christmas. The little girl was blonde as could be: "Where does she come by that flaxen hair? There is none such in my family," Kathryn had mused. John had taken the child up, kissed the bright hair and murmured, "It is the Woodville hair, more silver than gold . . ."

"But my father was but a bastard of Edward the Fourth's and no blood of Elizabeth Woodville. John—John, you called Elizabeth Woodville your grandmother once. What did you mean?"

That had begun the argument. It had progressed on to his anger that their children were bastards and not liable to inherit after Payne and Francis; he had used all his wiles to try and draw from her the word that would call a priest to Windsgeat. That word, she told him, was still *No*. "Does your religion mean so little to you, then?" she had cried out. "We married according to its rites and that is good enough for me, no one will call me traitor for a right-handed ring in the greenwood! Why does the Christian legal ritual mean so much to you? Have you deserted your faith?"

John had gone very pale; looking back, she wondered why.

Now she was home without him and pregnant again. She could not return to court but must dawdle here until after the new year, making pleas of crop trouble, lost stock, the stream flooding. Anything to forestall a royal command to return, great-bellied, and stand thus before the whole court. "Are ye goin' to tell Windsgeat this time?" Tansy demanded.

"No, I—I want to surprise him."

She gave birth to John's son four months early. He was

born dead and afterward, lying in a haze of agony, it seemed funny to her that a dead child was harder to birth than a live one. Tansy, muttering to herself, sent a boy riding hard for Windsgeat. As she could not write and the message was verbal, all of its urgency remained intact; John killed Circe, the fastest horse in his stables, riding to Kathryn.

He found her lying frail and thin, skin a waxy yellow compared to the white sheets. She felt light when lifted into his lap, light as the eleven-year-old Kathryn he had carried so many lifetimes ago. "No more children. No more," he said, kissing her cool brow. "I will not have you a martyr to breeding."

"I want a son of yours!"

"Of what use would he be? I have sons already, and no boy-child could replace Cecily and Isabella in my affections. No, nor even Lissy, for all that she is not really mine. It is the same way you feel about Payne and Francis . . . No more children, Kathryn. You are too precious to die of childbearing, I will not have it. Jacquetta has potions to keep you from conceiving and you know as well as I that there are plenty of pleasant past-times in bed that do not lead to children. I will not further endanger you."

It was pleasant lying thus against his chest. He had come straight away from Windsgeat without tying his shirt, so she could get her entire face and hands on warm, bare flesh. So safe here, so warm. Nothing ever seemed to threaten her in John's arms. "I am sorry I was too proud to apologize," she said, draping a weak arm about his neck. He always smelled so good—horse, leather, silk, *home*.

"About what, that stupid quarrel? We were both in the wrong, though I was by far the worse. No, what angers me is that you think childbearing is a thing all unto yourself and no damned business of mine. You will not keep secrets again from me, or I will go and never return."

He started halfway up from the bed, made her sob out his name. "No, John! I swear I will tell you the truth next time!"

"I do not believe you. You have a poor opinion of men, you think we are all unfeeling knaves who do not care if our women die of loving us."

He put on his angry face, chin out, fist on hip. She clung to him, swore it was not so, said she would never hide secrets from him in the future. Only then did he sit back down with her in his lap. "Did you get all that, Tansy?" he asked.

The muffled voice on the other side of the door called out, "Yes, Milord, and I will hold her to it, you can depend on me."

Kathryn wearily gasped out, "You are—why, were you a woman I would call you a *bitch*, Windsgeat!"

"Call me what you will, we will make no children for two years."

"Two years! In two years I might be past childbearing, John! Do not try and make me agree to this!"

"If you do not, I am out the door, Woman. I will not be your murderer."

She feigned weeping to fool him. But as she was not a habitual weeper, he spotted the lie and gruffly ordered her to stop. She did. "You will not leave me, John, I know you will not," she predicted.

"Oh, I will remain your friend. But there will be nothing else between us, I will never come to your bed again."

Could he do that? She thought of the long nights, the fierce passion. Even the nights without lovemaking there was talking in the dark, laughter, singing her to sleep. Would John go to another woman? At his age women were still fascinated by him, from Norfolk's estranged wife to the new queen. Word would soon be out that Windsgeat and Whitbourne were no longer lovers; he would have to fight ladies off with a sword in each hand.

Jealousy smote her. "All right, damn you, I swear it!"

He kicked his boots off, let his heavy cloak slide to the floor. Got under the covers with her, drew her head to his chest, and began singing.

"Es taget vor dem holze:
Stand auf, Katterlein!
Die jager hurnen stolze;
Stand auf, Katterlein, holder Buehl!
Heiho, du bist mein und ich bin dein:
Stand auf, Katterlein!"

(It is dawn in the holly—Get up, Kathryn!
The hunters are blowing their horns;
Awaken, Kathryn, my darling!
Hi-ho, you are mine and I am yours:
Get up, Kathryn.)

"Not two years," she said sleepily, purring against his throat. "Make it eighteen months and I will sign the contract."

"Eighteen months? All right, but only if you are healthy,

fat, and round as our new queen by then. I want to see little rolls on your belly and cheeks like a chipmunk."

(Jacquetta had once chased her through Windsgeat, pelting her with French pastries and shouting, "Woman, to make you gain weight a person would have to nail meat to your arms!")

"Is the queen pregnant yet?" she asked, settling deeper into his arms.

"No, not yet. Nor will you be for the next year and a half." Eighteen months was a long time, it seemed as far away as one hundred years. He glanced down at her, saw that she slept with a smile on her thin face. Look at all those bones! Fairly stuck up through her flesh, they did. He must fatten her up, have Tansy make thick soups and stews, scraped cheese and sweet cream desserts, and as much bread as she could hold.

John kissed the top of her head, noticed gray hairs. When had they first trespassed on the ashy gold-brown he knew so well? She always wore a headdress or caul at court, he only saw her head uncovered in bed and by candlelight. Now, in daylight, he saw that the silver hairs grew in all over. It had never occurred to him that she might age, might fear it and the loss of her fertility. How it would hurt her to be denied a last child! But they had so many others, and loved them all. All except James.

He kissed the bony throat and limp hands, heard her sigh in her sleep. One year and a half. No time at all. He had no idea how topsy-turvy the world could become in eighteen months.

Smiling to himself, he softly sang one more time, "It is dawn in the greenwood . . . I am yours, you are mine, Kathryn."

It was Windsgeat's finest Christmas—or Yule, the Winter Solstice, to give it the old name. Tiny Cecily walked from Kathryn to John without falling, it was obvious from Isabella's conversation that she was closer than ever to Mary Tudor, and Lissy was enjoying life with the other Tudor daughter. Isabella taught Payne and Francis the latest dance from Spain, brought to England by the Spanish ambassador, and John took all the children on a treasure hunt throughout the house.

Afterward, Jacquetta, trembling with emotion, shyly ducked her head and said there was an announcement to be made.

Pieter cleared his throat twice, wrung his hat between his hands, and told John he wished to marry Jacquetta.

John seized the little Fleming and tossed him into the air as he might have a child. Astonished, Pieter came down hugging him; the two men were uproarious the rest of the evening and had to be put to bed by the servants. "I have never seen John drink like that before," Kathryn observed.

Jacquetta sighed. "Pieter was so nervous. I had to rehearse him for days, he kept wanting to ask John's permission. I had to tell him, 'Look: Windsgeat is half mine and I am no man's chattel.' He was afraid John would not want his servant marrying so far above himself. As if I could find a better man!"

It would not be fitting for Pieter to pick up after John now. Once the initial joy wore off, John realized he was without the best bodyservant a man could have, and he hired and fired replacements at a rate of two a week.

After the Yule, he and Kathryn rode toward Hampton Court, Val d'Or daintily picking her way through the snow at Finnvarra's side. "Why, that mare is pregnant, and I have kept her apart! How is that possible?" John demanded.

"I put her in with Finn some months back. You will not let me conceive but you cannot stop my mare, John de Gael!"

"One of these days I am going to lose my temper with you, Woman. And then—watch out!"

"I am terrified. See me tremble," she answered, and clapped a gloved hand over her yawning mouth.

The holidays were still in progress at Hampton Court. Kathryn was surprised to find the queen ensconced amidst a fresh crop of maids of honor. "What is going on here? Why so many new girls?" she asked Jane Parker, Lady Rochford.

Jane, polishing the queen's many hand mirrors, shrugged. "Her Grace has many sisters and half-sisters—there were ten children in all—and aunts and girlhood friends from, oh, let me see, Lambeth House and Horsham up North. None of them very exceptional, I wonder that the king so lets her flood us with them. Even boys she knew have come to beg positions."

Two days later John's sons returned to Court. Catherine Howard was perky as a kitten that night at feast, tickling the king under his chins with her wheel-shaped feather fan and feeding him delicacies from her dish. Kathryn heard him laugh as he had at eighteen with Catherine of Aragon. Remembering the lean, athletic boy of thirty-one years ago, she thought that if he had kept the old queen she would still be sitting dutifully at his side, stitching blackwork shirts of finest lawn and warning him not to hunt with a headcold. Her eyes misted over. Thank gods the old queen had never lived to see what the beautiful boy became—a self-besotted tyrant, obese, obscene, with murderous rages, letting this mincing minx lead him by the nose. Catherine of Aragon dead of neglect and shameful treatment, Anne executed on false charges, Jane dead for lack of proper care in childbed—where had Catherine Howard gotten up the courage to marry so cold a man? Oh, he seemed fond now, but in a few years if there were no sons . . .

Just listen to the old fool, carrying on as if he were once again gorgeous Prince Hal, not this gruesome old hulk whose bad leg stank and whose carnal appetites were the butt of every filthy joke in Europe. No dignity, no mercy, always blaming a Cromwell or a Wolsey for what went wrong in his government and then executing him.

She could not help comparing him to John, who was his same age within a few weeks. All his servants, even the lowliest stable-boy and milkmaid at Windsgeat liked working for John. Even those who did not love him respected him, and they were all pleased to take his orders, knowing they were never unfair. She guessed that he was far more than their employer and an aristocrat; to them he was The Lord, god-on-earth, representative of the very force of Nature which fed and housed them. They all seemed to know and accept the Old Religion at Windsgeat; understood that The Lord and The Land were one and that John would willingly die to keep their farms green and their livestock producing young.

Kathryn had finally noticed how different his attitude was even from lords ranked far higher than him; they had to demand the respect due their titles while John never noticed, always taking it for granted. She had never met anyone but kings with that attitude and it confused her. Just how high-born *was* John? And how could he be a grandson of Elizabeth Woodville's without openly acknowledging himself a child of one of her Grey offspring? Yet if he was, why hide and deny it? John never lied, that much she was certain of. If asked something he did not wish to answer he would say outright that he had no intention of responding, or else he would dance evasions all the day, but when he looked her in the eye and said he was not descended from Elizabeth Woodville's first family, she believed him.

Last night she approached Norfolk on the subject. He had grumbled, "Sweet Mary Mother, must you pry so? Is it not enough for you that he is the most dangerous man in England?"

"Dangerous to whom?"

"All of us and the Tudors! You should know that, since King Harry executed Margaret Pole and her family last year. With two bastard daughters, one little son and the Treasury empty, he is unsure of his throne once again and Plantagenet heads always roll at such a time. Be thankful if he does not send for your James as well. And meanwhile you and de Gael are—tut, tut, niece! You live most dangerously!"

"He *claims* he is a de Gael, but—"

"He is, he is, can you not see the resemblance between him and Kenneth's Jacquetta? Not that they are true brother and sister . . . But the rest of his blood—God forbid that de Gael should ever force me to make a choice, him or Harry Tudor! I loathe and fear the man but the pull of blood and loyalty is very strong."

So there the mystery lay as it always had, bigger than ever.

Meanwhile, Mary Tudor had been banished from Court, for after her kind treatment by Jane Seymour and Anne of Cleves, she found that the latest stepmother detested her. "Those Howard women! They have always hated me," Mary shrilled, packing to leave Hampton Court. "Anne Boleyn made my life a misery, this new bitch eyes me as though she would tear my heart out—and I hate Howard women, too!"

"Oh, no," Isabella answered, brow puckered with concern. "My Lady Mother has always been fond of you and I am Howard myself—"

"Oh, come, Isabella, you are the spitting image of Windsgeat, we all know that. Besides, only your grandmother Joanna was a Howard, and she was thrown out of my household years ago, I do not even know if she lives."

"She does. My mother sends Joanna money every month. She must be one thousand years old and living on spite."

That had made the banished lady laugh and think that exile to the country would not be so glum with Isabella at her side.

Meanwhile in the Great Hall, Kathryn sat dawdling with her food and staring across the room at John, wondering who he really was.

Around her Hampton Court blazed with color and scent. Pine boughs and mistletoe hung from the hammerbeam ceiling, fireplaces blazed with fruitwood and incense. Too many wassails were being drunk to various healths; ale, metheglin, hippocras, and port flowed like brightly colored water. A great number of people woke next to complete strangers in the morning while men of sixty cavorted with girls of sixteen in admiration of the royal example.

Kathryn spent the night embroidering because Norfolk wanted to talk politics with John. The night after, it was John and the Seymours; on the next four nights, the entire council drank themselves insensible in John's apartments on his too-excellent French malmsey. Had Anne of Cleves not arrived for the New Year's celebrations, thus distracting everyone from politics, not a wife or mistress at court could have gotten with child over the holidays, and it would have been John's fault.

Anne of Cleves claimed she came to celebrate having met the king on this day one year ago, but she could not resist a conspirator's wink at Kathryn as she said so. Kathryn, winking back, knew she had come to celebrate her freedom and visit betwitching little Catherine Howard.

Anne brought two matched mares she had bought from John, half-Arabian with trappings of purple velvet and leather in what she imagined an equally Arabic mode. The former queen herself stunned the court by appearing in a rust-colored German gown, finely pleated all around, with sectioned sleeves fastened by ribbons over puffs of sheer gold tissue. Her hat, too, was German, puffed, slashed, and swaying with gorgeous plumes. She was squeakingly clean, smelled of gillyflowers and musk, and her hair—which turned out to be yellow when clean—was worn up in neat, glossy coils. There was even a faint hint of Spanish liquor coloring her cheeks and lips.

"My good brother!" Anne greeted the king, kissing his be-ringed hands with a show of much reverence. "And my good sister, the queen of England!" She kissed Catherine Howard's hand with rather more gusto, Kathryn observed with a grin. Then the flustered-looking Henry found himself seated at the dinner table with a chattering wife on either side. "Man, man," Norfolk observed to John, "I would not be in his duck-billed slippers for aught! One wife is bloody well enough!"

French Ambassador Marillac entered, bowed low. He stepped carefully over John's extended foot, bowed again, announced a gift from his master, François the First of France. "Very well, then, sir, fetch it in," Henry ordered, glad of the break in tension. He felt like a puppy trapped between two gorgeously-furred cats; pretty creatures, but, oh, the claws! They were carrying on like long-lost sisters, he could hardly breathe or speak without them trampling over his words to urge each other on to some new, tittering cleverness. And when had that great Flanders mare of his gotten *pretty*?

Marillac backed away from the dais, bowing. This time he forgot John's foot, went sprawling through Norfolk's heaped platter. "Goddamn it, Windsgeat!" the duke roared, leaping up. "Could you not aim him at someone else just this once?"

John dusted Marillac off with the offer of a new doublet, and booted him on his way.

Shrill-voiced, grease-splattered, the ambassador returned in a moment with three men behind wheeling in enormous meat pies. "What is this?" Henry asked, smacking his lips.

Marillac spoke excellent English but did not understand the language's nuances as his royal master did. "His Majesty the king of France bids me tell you that these were made from the largest boar ever killed in France. He added," Marillac tweeted, faithfully reciting what he had been taught, "that it made him quite think of you two at the Field of Cloth of Gold."

He was delighted to see that for some reason all the English found that very funny. The king in particular was snorting and stomping with laughter. "Oh, sir, that is rich, rich! Stay for some of this meat pie, partake of me and François the First, the two biggest boors in Christendom! Come hither, Marillac!"

Cher Dieu! What King François had told him to say could have been taken as a mortal insult! Marillac made a flying leap over John's equally flying foot and came gracefully down. "Oh, all right. If you want to dance, then *dance*," the king said, and yelled for his musicians to begin.

At first Henry danced with each of his queens but he had hunted in the morning, which pained his sore leg. So he retired to sit on the sidelines and drink, which ended in his being carried to bed while Catherine Howard and Anne of Cleves danced in each other's arms all the night.

Kathryn found herself partnered, first with her uncle, then Wriothesely, and finally John Dudley, Master of the Horse. Dudley's company she appreciated, for he was frank and quick-witted, while there was something unsettling about Wriothesely. She could not quite put her finger on it.

"Windsgeat is looking daggers at me," Dudley told her during their third turn around the marble floor. "He is famed for keeping his temper in the Council Chamber when even Norfolk is swearing and sweating, but he is not so cool about love. Is it true you two have married in secret?"

"I love my neck slightly better than I love John, so what do you think, Master Dudley? I am no fool, I obey the king." She could not resist a counterthrust. "And what about you? Is it true you mean to marry your seven-year-old son to Elizabeth Tudor?"

By the time he regained his tongue, he had missed three steps of the dance, and so fouled the entire line following them. There were breathy *boo*'s made in his direction, one lord saying that anyone who could not step properly with so light a dancer as Lady Whitbourne needed lessons. Dudley did not even notice that he had been insulted. "By God, Madam," he said and wiped his brow. "I heard the de Gaels have an excellent spy system, but this—!"

He forgot she had daughters at two Court households, neither with her surname. "I am not so bound-up with Windsgeat that I lack sources of my own," she said.

"Well, I must hasten to deny this rumor about my son Robert, just as you deny your own marriage reports."

She was leading the dance in all senses. This was a delight, after such dear but overpowering men as John and Norfolk; Kathryn found herself choosing her movements with extreme care and whipping Dudley around as though she, not he, were the man. "Ahh, but Master Dudley, there is a difference between us," she pointed out. "You see, *I* am telling the *truth*!"

There came a crash nearby, followed by a splash. Marillac, heading toward Kathryn with a gleam in his eye, had just been intercepted into the nearest wine fountain. John de Gael pointed at his guilty right foot. "*Stop that!*" he ordered severely, and held out his hand to help Marillac up.

The ambassador shook his head. "No, no, I hate dancing, anyway, Milord. I prefer drinking—see?" He stuck his head under the spout, let wine run over him like bath water.

John Dudley shook like a leaf. "Pardon me, Lady Whitbourne, but my wife will never forgive me if I let Windsgeat do that to *my* best doublet! Farewell!"

Her own John reclaimed her, held her possessively and showed her who would lead any dance she had with *him*. "How dare you be jealous, you know my heart is all yours," she scolded.

"Ahh, but other men are not so sure about your *body*."

He was a good dancer for a big man, very light on his feet as long as he did not dance too long on that old ankle injury. She held his hand tighter as he took her through the intricate maze of steps, and said, "I think this is as married as I want to feel to so jealous a man."

He threw her up higher than he needed to, pretended he was not going to catch her quickly enough. Kathryn came squealing down into his arms. "If you tease me, My Lady, I shall throw you even higher next time and leave you in the rafters. If we are ever *really* married, I will teach you to dance with other men! I will make you go veiled like a Muslim woman and for breakfast I shall serve you roasted popinjays like Marillac."

"Then king's permission or nay, you will never get further than a greenwood handfasting with *me*, Windsgeat. I will be master and mistress of my own fate, you will not."

He was holding her indecently close for the dance. She was fluttering in his arms like a trapped bird, peeking around him to see if anyone noticed. But the hour was late, the king gone, the queen oblivious to all but Anne of Cleves. Candles had gone out and couples were leaving hand-in-hand.

Kathryn opened her mouth to protest, had it silenced with a violent kiss. Although she would never admit it, she liked John's jealousy. And God help any woman she caught *him* dancing with! Though of course they had to choose other partners to keep up appearances.

He finally stopped kissing the breath out of her and led her away. "There goes Father with Aunt Kathryn," Francis de Gael noted, chin in hands. "I think she is the prettiest lady in the whole Court, even prettier than Aunt 'Quetta."

Payne, elbows on the long table, watched Anne of Cleves and Catherine Howard giggle together, dance closer, finally leave the room. "No," he said so softly that Francis hardly heard him. "No, there is no one in the world prettier than the queen."

36

That winter the king's leg ulcer flared up again, reducing life at Court to a crawl. Kathryn and John retired to Vamplate Manor. Francis went north to visit aunts, cousins, and the irascible "Doctor Tom," John's full brother.

Payne de Gael had hardly been separated from his brother in all his life. Good old steadfast Francis; what to do without him? Shorn of his constant companion, he wandered back to Court. Newly seventeen and grown out of his infatuation with Isabella, he was restless, handsome, and tempermental. And the young queen was so sweet, so flirtatious that she outshone the many pretty girls who strove for his attention.

He had competition, though, for Catherine Howard's attention: her favorite cousin on her mother's side, Thomas Culpepper, had come to Court. Catherine began to play them off one against the other, and if she ever took either young man to bed, none knew, though many surmised.

She dazzled the females of the Court, too, especially little Elizabeth Tudor who hardly remembered her own mother and had spent years shunted from one lonely country house to the next. Bastardized, ignored, stripped of her titles for Prince Edward's sake, Elizabeth now had a home with her father and this queen who was her dead mother's cousin. It seemed a fairy tale to sit with them at dinner, to go riding with the queen, to sew with her, pray with her. And such clothes she finally had, after so many years of hand-me-ups, hand-me-downs, mending, patching, thrice-turned gowns! Such shifts and gowns she had from the queen, and always many niceties from her sister, Mary, now that Mary had money, too. Mary always gave her little bags of coins to play cards with, and prettily worked bed linens, clothes—she had a splendid new yellow satin dress from her sister, exquisitely flattering to a milky-skinned redhead such as Elizabeth was.

Since Elizabeth Tudor was at Court, so was almost twelve-year-old Elizabeth Stoneleigh. Copper-haired as any Tudor, with her father's long green eyes, Lissy was already referring all marriage offers to her mother's authority. She adored her

Uncle John while feeling vaguely mistrustful of him, knowing her mother had been forbidden to marry him, realizing her mother must bear the shame of his bastards. Yet he treated Lissy herself with affection and delight, as though she were his own, and had presented her with a half-Barb, half-Welsh mountain pony of the same hue as her hair.

Francis de Gael, back from York, leaned on the fence next to his tall father one afternoon at Windsgeat, watching Lissy put her filly through her paces. "Father, may I ask you a question? A very personal one?"

He was too big to have his hair ruffled any more, so John settled for clapping the boy on the shoulder. "Yes, of course, Francis."

"Is Lissy your daughter?"

"No she is not. Why?"

Any other thirteen-year-old boy would have blushed furiously. "Because if you and Aunt Kathryn and the king allow it, I should like to marry Lissy some day."

The Plantagenet bloodline come home at last! If not through sons of John's own, then through his grandsons. "You will have to wait until both of you are of suitable age, Francis. And then you will have to wait for a year when the king is not busy lopping off Plantagenet heads. If you can wait and if you are still interested, then I will approach His Grace for you. Hopefully he will see that you and Lissy are no danger to him."

No danger! For centuries before the first de Gael came to England there had existed a family whose sole purpose was to guard the god-path running like a seam of emerald-green magic through the heart of this country. Then the de Gaels acquired the priesthood and one day, without meaning to, the Divine Kingship. For exactly four hundred and forty-one years the de Gaels had been trying to shove the responsibility off on the blood-kings of England, and now there were these damned Tudors to deal with.

John swallowed hard as Francis turned back to the fence. No danger! Not when Henry the Seventh repealed the Act making young Edward the Fifth and his brother Richard, Duke of York, legitimate again? Not when two-faced, conniving, magnificent Kenneth de Gael, his grandfather, had agreed to infanticide while all the time—

His sons should have been told years ago. But Payne was too hot-headed, too liable to hurl the information at those who injured him. While Francis—oh, Francis was a rock and unexcitable, but by accident of birth he was not the one who would inherit Windsgeat and its manifold secrets. *I should have told Jacquetta years ago,* John thought. The torture could not yet be invented that would wring the news from Jacquetta. She had the right both as his beloved 'sister' and as goddess-on-earth to know who he was, but he had never been able to bring himself to so endanger her. Norfolk knew but Norfolk still accepted the Tudor claim. All others were dead without passing on the secret, he thought.

It never struck him that, while Lord Hal Chase had died without telling anyone, he had left behind papers for his son, Arthur—papers inherited by James Howard along with Arthur's armor, clothing, writing desk, and horse.

"Messenger," Francis said suddenly, pointing to Windsor knoll. A boy in no recognizable livery on a poorly-bred horse rode toward them, courier's satchel flapping across his saddle. He rode straight to John, tugged his forelock by way of salute as he wore no hat to remove in a lord's presence. "I was to wait for a reply, Milord," he said, and took out a sealed envelope for John.

Jack of Norfolk's old lions, though this was not Thomas, Duke of Norfolk's writing. He broke the patch of flame-red wax, read: *I know who you are and who your grandfather Kenneth really killed. For a position at Court and ten thousand marks I will bide silence. If not for yourself, then to save my mother and your bastards I believe you will pay. Do not threaten me in this matter, or the information will be published.*

No name, no signature. But the reference to Kathryn and the arrogant Howard lions told him James was the writer.

He squinted up into the sun. "Tell your master that I will commit nothing to paper, Boy. And that I will need a few days to gather my resources and make reply. Tell him that."

"What is it?" Francis asked, trying to read over his father's arm.

John did not hear him. Ten thousand gold marks! He crumpled the letter. The pope's own ransom had not been so much! So great a sum could only be gotten two ways: utterly strip the house or sell off the lands. Deprive his people of their sacred god-path or sell every jewel, carpet, chair—it was no choice at all. The land was their bond with the Old Dark Ones. Of course there were his foreign properties . . . his broodstock . . .

Kathryn, Jacquetta, the children. Pieter. Thousands of rolling green acres, a house full of priceless possessions. The blue-green ley line stretching from Windsgeat to eternity. God, gods, he was the only de Gael Lord in the family book to have been so honored by the gods as to reach fifty and live. How could he break that trust? He could not. He must do what he had never done before—ask the aid and advice of another human being.

He turned to Francis. "You must to Whitehall for me, I cannot trust a hireling. Tell the Duke of Norfolk in strictest privacy that circumstance forces me to call in the bargain made between his father and Kenneth de Gael. Do you have that? Say 'Kenneth,' not 'my grandfather' or 'my father's father,' because that would be misleading. He would not know what you meant. Go, Boy—and go at once!"

He kissed Francis, told him to take the wily Finnvarra.

Up on the hill, wild Cernunnos trumpeted and raked the ground with a mighty hoof. *I know,* John thought, looking at that harbinger of magick. *We are both too old for the job and so feel Windsgeat threatened.*

The duke arrived, furious and frightened. "Why here, Man?" he demanded without a word of greeting.

"Because no where else can we ride into the middle of so many flat, treeless acres, eighty yards from the nearest hiding places. Remount, Tom, we are going to the middle of Windsgeat's plain to talk."

The next day James Howard had an important secretarial post under Norfolk's tutelage. Norfolk rode to Howard House and bargained for John, as a result of which James received not one huge amount but a weekly stipend that, in some years, would amount to more than he had originally requested. A weekly amount John could hide by juggling figures in the family ledgers; sell off a few cattle here, let the southernmost fifty acres go, part with this jewel or that.

As Kathryn thought the state of her womb none of his business, so he thought being blackmailed none of hers. Nor Jacquetta's; his sister would simply send someone to kill James, and who knew where the information would go then? *I should have thrashed him and let him go. But I thought Kathryn would die because of being so incarcerated and I let my rage deal with him accordingly. I let Pieter*—hurt *him.*

John did not fool himself into thinking James would settle for an allowance and position. No, there would follow little public rudenesses that grew into abuse he could not respond to in kind. Then demands for more money and finally,

Windsgeat itself. That must not be. He must find where James had hidden the incriminating papers and have them—and him—destroyed. But how could he murder a child of Kathryn's?

That following month Howard House began receiving a new roof and new flooring. A stylish long gallery was added, courtesy of John's largest sapphire being purchased by the king of France. Soon after, James was riding a very fine Windsgeat White and dressing splendidly, with much spending cash. Fathers began considering him as a possible husband to their daughters.

John called on him at Court, demanded to know what proof he had. James, lolling in his chair, said, "It must be very frustrating for you, Windsgeat. You want those papers but you dare not send some hireling to look for them, because then they would also become privy to the information, requiring you buy them off or murder them. I know full-well that you and van der Hüm have burgled my house twice and gone through my Court apartments with a fine comb to no avail. I have not thought how best to strike back at *him*, by the way, though I will. The things that man could do with a hot fireplace poker and not leave a mark were amazing; I lost the use of my voice for eight months, did you know that? He burned the power of speech from me."

He watched as John started from the room with a gesture of defeat. "Wait up, Windsgeat, there is more. I want to tell you what I know in full detail so you will know how much more I am worth than the paltry amount you grant me each week."

Passersby saw John's white jawline as he left and leapt out of his way. He brushed a guard once, sent the man spinning. But as none at Court had ever seen Windsgeat openly angry before, the guard said nothing, only retrieved his halberd and scuttled back to his post.

James followed John, making overly-familiar small talk with him to gall him in front of observers. By the time John barreled into his apartments, chalk-faced with rage, James was walking with an arm flung about his shoulders as a best friend might.

Francis rose from his fireside chair. "Father—"

John's forefinger jabbed at the door. He said only one word and he did not repeat himself. "*Go!*" At that thunderous decree every servant in his chambers ran. Francis, though, faltered, having something to tell John. A glance from his fierce father warned him; the boy dropped his Latin primer and left without saying John had a visitor.

James observed all of this with amusement, watched John kick the two outer doors shut. "Inside," John said hoarsely, pointing to the bedchamber where his sea-sphinx table still stood with chairs poised from a card-game the night before. The room was damnably chill; swearing, he banged the windows shut, whirled to face James.

"A little hippocras, Windsgeat? I have so developed a taste for the stuff, never could afford it before. Now then, where were we?"

"Wait while I search the room."

John looked under the bed, in its hangings, behind his tapestries. Opened all chests and the door to the garderobe before he was satisfied. "Very well, we are alone. Even the inner walls of Whitehall are two feet thick; pray, begin."

James plopped himself into the best chair, a hideous, ancient green thing awrithe with gargoyles and votive maidens. It was so old that the beasts forming its arms had been rubbed faceless; John did not know where it came from or how old it was.

"Wait on me, Windsgeat. I want that hippocras served in one of your fine enameled glass goblets from Venice, I hear they cost five marks a stem and are fragile as eggshells."

John was almost too angry to focus, but he opened the bottle, poured, served James, and stood back as muddy boots landed atop the sea-sphinx table, spurs and all. Metal grated into rare, burled wood.

"I will begin the story," James said pleasantly, "at a rather disastrous battle called Bosworth Field. There your great-grandfather Jack of Norfolk died fighting for Richard Plantagenet and there also perished Kenneth de Gael's father. Kenneth was the next Duke Windsgeat and was wounded, but not severely. He stood in danger of losing his title, his lands, house, and life to the victor, Henry Tudor. But our Kenneth was an opportunist, was he not, John? I may call you 'John,' may I not? Like a friend?

"Anyway, Kenneth-the-opportunist, instead of fleeing, forced himself to think of Windsgeat. I do not know why; granted, it is gloriously fertile land but only land all the same; I had rather keep a sound neck than a few green acres, myself. He did not ride for a boat to France or Flanders where he had kin, friends; he went straight to Henry Tudor and boldly offered his services, thereby striking a hellish deal—hellish even by de Gael standards, which, granted, are pretty low. 'Take my title in an outer show of punishment but grant my land status as an independent duchy and I will give you all you desire to sit securely on the throne of England.' Can you imagine the nerve of the man? He had fought on the losing side and now thought to bargain with the victor and new king!"

Here James held his goblet out for a refill. But when John began to pour, James snatched his hand back, deliberately dropped the gold-and-red goblet to the marble floor. Pieces flew; dark red wine flowed across John's best table and silk carpet. Still he made no protest, only fetched another goblet, another bottle. This time James took the goblet and drank deeply, continuing his tale.

"I suppose King Henry said something to de Gael along the lines of, 'You are a madman and about to die.' But Kenneth said, probably: 'You wish to marry the princess Elizabeth Plantagenet, yes? But that will not strengthen your claim to the throne, for she was bastardized along with all Edward Fourth's offspring when it was discovered the king had married their mother only after precontracting himself to another woman.' He then told Henry that to marry the princess he must reverse the Titulus Regulus declaring the children bastard. Old Henry Tudor had no sense of humor but I will wager he laughed at that and protested that Edward's sons would then be rightful kings of England.

"De Gael apparently said, 'Yes, Your Grace, then they must die.' According to a fascinating document I now possess, de Gael did not even use hirelings, but went to accomplish the deed personally after drawing up papers with Surrey, Buckingham, and young Lord Hal Chase, Edward the Fourth's favorite bastard."

John licked his parched lips. "So Kenneth de Gael killed the Little Princes. I do not care who knows that, it does not affect me."

"Do not speak unless told to! I am not through with my story. . . . So Kenneth kills Richard, Duke of York, and turns to the boy-king, Edward the Fifth. But looking at him I suppose he realizes his own sickly, whining son, Robert, is about the young king's age and coloring. For some reason you de Gaels are madly superstitious about Plantagenets; has something to do with your witchcrafts, I am guessing. So there he stands looking upon the face of the rightful king of England who is twelve years old and probably pissing himself with fear. Think of it, my dear John: the king of England, helpless in Kenneth's hands, and Kenneth suddenly wavering because he has so long been a rabid Plantagenet supporter, as are all his kin. This boy was his *king*!"

James took a sip, dawdled his goblet along the table's edge. "Kenneth apparently murdered his own son who was dying anyway, and left him in Edward the Fifth's place. Then he took the rightful king away to one of his properties. Married him to his daughter, Cecily, so their heirs would be legitimate. There must have been miscarriages, stillbirths, because it was 1492 before you were born, with Doctor Tom following in '93. By that time Edward was a liability, perhaps he sickened and died or Kenneth did away with him, raised you as his own son. Which makes you, John Howard Plantagenet, rightful and legal-born king of England. All hail, Your Grace." He raised his goblet in mocking salutation.

"Of course, I do not know the rest of the details that Kenneth was fool enough to let others in on, but for some reason Norfolk knows and Arthur Chase left papers from his father that he had never opened. For poor old Norfolk to know the truth and not dare tell Tudor makes him guilty of the most heinous of treasons; should you ever marry your double cousin, my mother, your sons will be undoubted kings. I wager that right now poor old Norfolk is stomping and swearing on his father's grave for having gotten him into so great a mess as this; I am squeezing *him* for money, too."

John was in total control of himself again. He mused, "You should not push Norfolk too far. He chooses to regard Tudor as the right-born king; if you apply too much pressure he is like as not to go to Great Harry and tell all. Whereas that would send the three of us to the block, it would leave at least some of the Howard kin alive, and that matters more to Norfolk than all the money you can wring from him. Family is all-important to him; be forewarned. And the plan was never Kenneth's, but that of Red Emma, his mother. But Henry the Eighth would not deal with a woman, so . . ."

James let the second goblet drop. Steepling his fingertips, he said, "I have more. Signed statements from chambermaids, ladies-in-waiting, and so forth proving your eldest son the lover of the queen of England. So you see, I have you boxed in, old man. You cannot win, I have you coming and going. The rightful king of England, at my mercy!"

"Then pray, continue. I wish to hear the terms."

"Terms? There are no terms. I will have Windsgeat. There

is no debate there. But I will be generous; before I give the documents to the king, I will allow you without my bitch of a mother to fly across the Channel to safety in some foreign land. But I want Pieter van der Hüm and the Book of Shadows placed in my keeping, to protect myself against assassination. You understand, Milord."

James stood, took the bottle in hand. "A good hippocras, but I expected better of you. Five days from now you will meet me at Windsor. You know that string of ponds, the Windles? Be at the Windsgeat side of the middle-most pond an hour before sunset. And, John? Have Pieter and the Book. And the necessary deeds of ownership."

He went on out.

Only then did Kathryn let herself down from the outside window ledge. John had forgotten they were to meet in his rooms; she had climbed out the window at hearing him approach with a companion. Now she felt her way along the decorative stone edging until she reached Norfolk's apartments and so entered. All the while, her brain raced—*John, king of England! And James threatening to ruin them all. . . . He is my son, it is my responsibility to stop him. But how?*

One fact remained with her: she must be at the middle-most of the Windles just before sunset five days from now. James was taking everything with him and leaving John with nothing more to lose; did he realize how dangerous that made John?

Or her?

37

Henry Tudor thought he had never seen so fine an autumn. He and the queen had gone on his longest summer progress of the reign, riding clear to York amidst such splendor and pomp as had not been seen a-traveling since the Field of Cloth of Gold.

Catherine Howard rode home at his side, fighting down an inner knot of worry. She had been married to Fat Harry over a year now and showed no sign of pregnancy, for she had taken potions to prevent it. A child would interfere with riding, hunting, dancing, having a handsome figure; she thought pregnant women monstrous things to behold.

Yesterday Norfolk had taken her by the shoulders, shaken her until her French hood fell away and her brown hair streamed. "You had better bear a prince to save the house of Howard, Niece! You do not know what calamities face us otherwise! Stop your witch's ways, your potions, your less fertile ways of fornication! Give England and our king an heir! Only then can the Howards survive."

She had shrugged unconcernedly, taking another bite of apple. "The king is still madly in love with me and already has a son. He does not care whether I breed or not."

Yet now she worried. The king's affections were easily swayed; witness the scant three years it had taken Anne Boleyn to topple from throne to grave.

When Catherine looked in any of her many hand mirrors, she saw the same self Henry had so fallen in love with—voluptuous, full of fire and vitality. Leaning forward she kissed her reflection lingeringly. *Let them go on wondering what I do after the old king lies a-snoring*, she thought, satisfied. Henry still called her his rose without a thorn, still begged for a single kiss, showered her with gifts. The rose would branch off for him soon enough; she pondered one pregnancy four or five years down the road for safekeeping. Her enemies thought her a fool but she knew she was not, despite the heat with which she kissed Thomas Culpepper and Payne de Gael.

Upon return to Hampton Court she lolled in bed until noon, eating gingered plums and trying to think if she lacked much in life at present.

She noted, even in her happiness, that her cousin Kathryn was marvelous tense these days. "You are nervous, Sweet Cuz, and that irritates me. I want nothing to disturb my contentment of mind, do you hear me? Lady Rochford, see my cousin out."

Kathryn went. As the door closed behind her, she heard Jane Parker say, "It is disgraceful the way she continues whoring with Windsgeat, at her age!"

The queen laughed prettily, filigree silver sounds over crystal.

Whore. Where were the prickles of conscience or pain that word should have brought her? Kathryn twisted the graduated gold circles on her finger, kissed them as she walked. It was the fifth day after James's meeting with John and the Windsgeat apartments already stood deserted; she grimly dressed for the hunt and left Tansy wondering.

She was at the stables seeing Val d'Or saddled when Francis de Gael caught up to her. "Aunt Kathryn, where are you going? Father said I was to keep you here at Court."

Panting from his run, he stepped back. The look in her eyes said she would knock him down and walk over him if necessary—his gentle Aunt Kathryn! "Wait and I will come, too," he blurted out, signaling a boy to bring his Hermes from the stall.

"You are *not* coming with me."

"What, let you ride out alone? Father would skin and stuff me did you so much as get a scratch due my lack of vigilance!"

But she did not wait after he lifted her to the gilt sidesaddle, only touched up Val d'Or and cantered on ahead.

The day was cool, brisk, gray. Hampton Court seemed ominously quiet. What was it about today that seemed so haunted? The wondering what John would do at the Windles? No, no, something bigger, something tainted with time . . . *The night the dead ride*, Jacquetta had called it. All Hallow's. *Samhain*, John said last year. He had pronounced it 'sowun,' like the Scots word for oat-husk porridge. *And why not?* he had asked. *They eat it in autumn after harvest when the fruit of the oat is gone and husks are all that's left before the winter's reaping*.

John, her John. He had not confided in her about this blackmailing and she knew it was not from mere petty spite about her concealing pregnancies from him. No, John was so totally panic-stricken for the first time in his life that he could not bring himself to involve her, and had gone over her head to Norfolk. And those two did not even like each other; what odd bedfellows fear made of old politicians.

Her John, her lover and beloved . . . If he lost Windsgeat or had to flee England she would go with him this time. Banishment, exile, a price on their heads; she would not lose John a second time. Why, oh, why had she ever borne James? Better that she had aborted him and not John's son, better that he had died a-birthing than become this monster threatening all she held dear.

"Aunt Kathryn, Aunt Kathryn!"

Francis on Hermes caught up to her, eyed the longbow and quiver across her slender back. "You are not going hunting at all, are you? You are going to—I do not know what, but your face is like stone. I must tell you, Father is gone, too. He rode away not a quarter-hour ago. The funny thing is, not five minutes after, I saw the duke of Norfolk in pursuit, riding like a storm-wind. What would Father and Norfolk be doing together? They are not social outside of Council Chambers, as a rule."

It was so gray and sunless that Kathryn wondered how she would be able to tell the onset of sundown. She clucked to Val d'Or, who smartened her pace.

It was a deeper gray when they rode down off the river barge, saw the liveoaks and willows lining the bank. Trees grew thicker here, greener; it was always the sign, even before spotting the turrets of Windsor Castle, that they were nearing home.

The sky overhead now boiled with clouds, mottled lavender and black. Their horses' manes and tails stood straight out in the wind; Kathryn lost the plumes from her little French riding cap. "Look at the river," Francis said suddenly. He pointed out an uncommon sight to her—whitecaps on the Thames. But Kathryn had just seen something far more interesting: a powerfully built man heavily cloaked and hooded, on a white stallion. A man on a bay rode alongside him.

She slapped the reins along Val d'Or's startled neck. "*Go!*" she cried; the mare all but flew. Francis pursued, heart thudding with foreboding.

Kathryn crossed the Virginia Water that connected the Windles downstream, where she would not be seen. She splashed daintily across, holding Val d'Or back to keep her quiet. Wait—there, up ahead. A flash of white tail. She climbed laboriously from the saddle, gave Val d'Or's reins to Francis. "My boy, my darling boy," she said to him, eyes shining. "As you love me and your father, wait here. I am going to spy on him, Francis, going to try and help him, though I do not know how. You must swear to remain here. Please, Francis! You must not overhear!"

He reluctantly agreed. But not a minute later, a hand clapped over his mouth. "*Not a sound!*" was hissed in his ear. "Hush you!"

Kathryn went on foot, safely hued from discovery in her Lincoln green riding velvets and brown cloak. Where there were trees, she walked behind them; where none, she crawled along the ground. There were no decent-sized trees near the meeting place, nor any brush that would shield a man, but she was child-slim and dressed for concealment; she managed to creep close enough to listen.

The three men stood arguing, their horses unconcernedly cropping grass. "Kenninghall!" Norfolk spat out. "My best house! As for the money—lad, it will leave me nothing. *Nothing!*"

"It leaves your life. Windsgeat, I do not see you toting anything so large as your family Book of Shadows—my assurance of further safety."

John made no reply. This was terrible, she could not bear the tension. Jacquetta, John, Pieter, Norfolk, everyone's children, cousins, siblings—James would take them all down. New residents for the Bloody Tower, fresh heads over Tower Gate. Why did one of them not kill him? *Oh, dear God!* she found herself praying. *Let them forget my feelings in the matter and kill my son, my only son!*

It struck her what she had asked.

Kathryn lay full-length in the grass, dry-heaving while the quarrel resumed.

At last she wiped her face on her sleeve, sat up. They were arguing in circles, it would do no good. John and Norfolk had their backs to the stone wall of James's implacable hatred and greed; they must give him everything they had fought to protect and build all their lives, or they must perish. *God's Horns!* she thought wildly. *How poorly men read other men; can they not see James means exactly what he says? He has no need of counterbids when he holds all the cards; they have no queens or trumps to offer him.*

Only one Plantagenet king.

Kathryn rose from the brush, dusted her skirts. She was nearly to the men before they saw her. John and Norfolk cried out her name but James only smiled cynically. "Good day, Mother. I trust Windsgeat told you all about this."

"No, I was on the window ledge the other day. I thought it was the king coming in with him and so hid." She found a button she had missed on her green suede riding gloves with their many stylish perforations, tended it with a nonchalance the men found maddening. "Well, Son? I am waiting."

"For what?"

"To hear what all this ridiculous behavior is about. You are not in this for the money but for the hatred, the sense of power. What have I done that you should so strike at me through the men I love best?"

John and Norfolk stared at her as though she had gone mad. But James burst out with, "You loved the Goddamned de Gaels! You always loved them!" It erupted from him in a red-faced haze of resentment, brought one fist up to shake at her. "You cheated on my father, made a fool of him! Bore this man's bastards, let me be carted hither and yon like a chestful of old clothes! But de Gael's bastards are rarely parted from you; oh, how you love him and his heretic brood! Always so close to his sister, too, so that people said you slept with her as well. Nowhere can I hold my head up, for you have been the scandal of this Court since before I was born!"

Kathryn smiled wryly. "You must be the only man in the world twenty-six years old and shocked that your mother has a love-life. James, your father and I should not have married, for I loved him while he mocked me. But I stayed with him for your sake—yours and Adam's. You do not remember, but I *had* to let you be taken from me, else we all would have ended in the Tower. And I did not fling you unfeelingly to strangers, I gave you into my dear uncle's keeping before your father took you back to Howard House. I suckled you myself, to the great consternation of your father and the whole Court; I was never away from you by choice. When I could have stayed in France with John I chose to come home for my sons. I made all your clothes myself, I played with you—you used to ride my back when I picked flowers at the river and sometimes you fell asleep like that with your arms around my neck."

She reached for him but he struck her hands away. Thunder crackled in the distance; no sun remained.

Francis and Jacquetta crept closer through the underbrush.

"Windsgeat was not bad enough—George Boleyn and the Seymours! Did you think I would not hear what a whore you were?" James shouted.

"Oh, James, stop," she said wearily. "You are too old to stand hurling insults at your mother, who loved you so greatly."

"How could I insult so infamous a woman? You were whore to any that asked and I have had my face rubbed in it these twenty-some years! Oh, my father told me all about it—"

"Your father was a lying, cheating wastrel," John cut in. "*He* was the one, not your mother. She kept to her wedding vows long after Ned Howard whored, drank, and gambled away your inheritance."

"You lie!" James shouted. "My father was a saint—I knew my father, he was the most wonderful—" He stopped, breathing like an exhausted runner. "This is everyone's last chance. I want van der Hüm, the Book, and the estate deeds now. Right now! Or I ride to the king with everything, I publish all those papers."

No one moved. "So be it, then!" he exclaimed, and, grabbing his reins, remounted.

Kathryn ran to him, caught at his leg. "Please, Jamey, let us be a family again—we will talk, I will help you get over this rage and misdirected pain—" she hoped to reach the suffering little boy in him, whose whining voice she still seemed to hear. But James only brought his foot out of the stirrup, kicked her savagely in the head.

She fell into John's arms, her cap and caul torn away by the blow. "I pray you, stop him," she whispered.

Thunder rumbled in the distance, from across the Thames. "I will see you all broken—I will see you crawling!" James shrieked into the rising wind. "Archbishop Cranmer already has the papers concerning Payne and the queen—Catherine Howard was very unchaste before her marriage, did any of you fools know that? And for a fee, her maids have all been delighted to say the activity continued afterward as well. Anything to strike at you, Windsgeat; I want to see you bleed for your son the way I bled for my father!"

His horse wheeled twice before he could straighten it out. Lightning streaked across the sky; the river valley far behind them echoed with the ensuing thunder. In that sound, none heard Jacquetta cry out with fear.

"Five thousand marks and a thousand acres!" John called out, crushing Kathryn to his broad chest. "Think of it, Howard! You could live like a prince anywhere in Europe!"

"How easy it all is," James jeered. "I nudge one card marked 'Windsgeat' and all fall down. There is the Catherine Howard card that will take Payne with it and my mother, for ladies-in-waiting are always accused of procuring for the queen; there is the Norfolk card, too—oh, how easy it all is!"

He sank his spurs into the horse's ribs up to the rowels. Screaming, the animal leapt forward.

Kathryn raised her aching head, wiped blood out of one eye. "John—Uncle—stop him! You must stop him!"

John answered, in a small, faint voice, "I cannot. I bargained once to save your life, I offered my own. Here stands the sacrifice."

Was he mad? What did he mean? She watched James's Windsgeat White wade through the Windles, come out on the other side. "Uncle, stop him or we are all dead!" she shouted.

Norfolk brought his pistol out, hands shaking. His fingers jerked spastically at the string of the powder bag. "I cannot! I cannot kill family!" he cried out in anguish. "I helped you rear that boy!"

James was halfway to the trees now. If he reached them, he could never be stopped.

Kathryn, feeble-minded with panic, stared from John to Norfolk and back again. The men she loved most; how would it feel to see their heads on pikes? Her John, her John, her life, her love . . . Her three beautiful daughters would never leave the Tower, never marry, know love, bear children. Men-at-arms would drag her ancient, almost-forgotten mother from her cottage in Wales . . . Jacquetta and Pieter would probably die, too. No one would believe they did not know the secret of John's birth. And John's brothers and sisters up North; the Tower for them, too, whom she had never met.

John. Jacquetta, Lissy, Cecily, Isabella, *Norfolk*. Francis, Pieter.

She did not think of herself. Her own death was unavoidable. She had lived beneath the axe's shadow so long that theirs was a comfortable old enmity; one did not feel the death-blow unless it was sloppy and required a second or third. She had Anne Boleyn's long, slender neck; she would present an easy target. Her own death mattered little at the moment. But to face the fall of the Howards and de Gaels—! With no one to guard the god-path, the ribbon of fertility, England would parch and wither; *When Windsgeat falls, so falls England*. Somehow the entire country mattered less than her three laughing girls and John.

Norfolk, the father of her heart. Jacquetta, her soul's sister.

John . . . oh, John.

James crested the low ridge. Beyond lay the sheltering trees. Kathryn slung her yew-bow from her shoulder. It was capable of bringing down a full-grown stag at three hundred yards and James was well within that range.

She slipped her carved jade thumb-guard on. Fitted the arrow to the polished horn nock. Drew the bowstring back with her thumb, in the Turkish style Jacquetta had taught her so long ago. *I loved you*, she thought, as if from a great distance. *My eldest-born; how I loved you! But you hated me from the cradle on, as if some dark, hideous thing crawled inside of you, devoured the James I bore. I tried to be a good mother; you would not allow me the same, foolish mistakes all parents make*.

Her shoulders shook with the strain of holding the bow taut for so long in perfecting the aim. She called on some hidden reserve of strength, steadied herself. *Good-bye, my darling, my little curly-haired boy! Good-night forever, my changeling child!*

She loosed the arrow.

A second arrow, black and gold, flew with it. Arched over her head, struck home an instant behind hers. But then, Jacquetta's timing had always been superb.

The Windsgeat White reared as its rider slumped. Kathryn, dry-eyed, released a second arrow and a third while James slid from the saddle. He toppled, dead, to the turf.

She emptied her quiver into him until he lay quilled like a hedgehog.

There were no more arrows. Kathryn went on reaching into her gilt leather quiver, aiming nonexistent arrows and letting them fly. Drawing the string to her ear, aiming, releasing. John and Norfolk ran past her, unheeding; she watched them splash through the pond, and strike out for that unmoving figure in the grass.

"Easy, darling," said a husky female voice at her ear. Jacquetta took hold of Kathryn's yew-bow, lowered it. "*Kathryn*. Get a grip on yourself, we have things to do. While they bury him we must ride to Howard House and find those papers. I have sent Francis on to fetch Pieter from Windsgeat so he can rob Cranmer's offices. Only you know Howard House well enough to direct me through every cranny and cubbyhole. Please, Kathryn!—if you must break down, do not break down yet! There is still much at stake."

38

There were two more murders that night. The second was because Pieter could not silence James's servant in Cranmer's offices any other way.

Jacquetta committed the third. She had the barest outline of the story first from Francis, who had listened from the brush behind Kathryn, then from John and Norfolk. She shook Kathryn into some semblance of life, shoved her onto her uncle's bay, and rode double with her to Howard House. There Jacquetta was discovered breaking in by James's valet and so she cut his throat with John's voyding knife.

Kathryn was useless. She sat blank-visaged in the window

bay, barely answering questions Jacquetta asked about hidey-holes and closets, loose floorboards, cupboards with false tops. Instead of the incriminating papers themselves, Jacquetta found addresses of bankers and agents in France, and determined to send her husband for them; she could trust no one else and Pieter was a man of remarkable talents when it came to skullduggery.

So her 'brother' was King of England. Somehow not surprising, knowing John, though she had always presumed his sense of mastery came from being The Lord of their ancient religion. So they were not even brother and sister but cousins of some sort, or worse—she must be his aunt, though he was the elder.

Jacquetta stifled an hysterical laugh as she stuffed the addresses in her bodice. How weird it all was. *What if I have missed something?* she asked herself. *One single line of writing on one scrap of paper, some addresses that look meaningless except to a confederate of James'?*

She had a thought as she led the dazed Kathryn out. Why not destroy all the evidence? She and Kathryn had ridden cloaked and hooded on Norfolk's sturdy bay, leaving the incriminating Windsgeat Whites with the men. Suppose she was to burn the place down, thus destroying all evidence? James could even be presumed dead in the fire. It would certainly save dragging his valet out for burial in the garden.

Jacquetta planted Kathryn at the door, said as if to a child: "*Stay*." It worked, she sank down where indicated.

Jacquetta shamelessly burgled the house first. Took two little red Turkey carpets, a tiny Flemish tapestry, some crystal-handled knives, and a fortune in John's gold from the desk.

Howard House was old, the wood dry. It went up like a pitch torch, catching the trail of papers and linens she had strewn throughout the place. Now to lead Kathryn away—*Acquiescent as a child,* she thought worriedly. Boost her up onto the horse, ride back for her mare Val d'Or or—no, wait. Brilliant inspiration. Kathryn was supposed to attend the queen tonight as every night, Francis had told her, worried that she would be missed. Jacquetta would ride her into Court, say she had fallen from her horse while hunting. There was a nasty cut over her eye, a swollen place where James had kicked her. It made a wonderful excuse for Kathryn's absence as well as her dazed condition.

Only once did Jacquetta look back. By then, flames were leaping up like streaks of saffron to a rain-swollen sky. It seemed fitting to her that she had lit such a fire on Samhain night, one of the major fire festivals of the pagan year. The night the old summer stubble was burnt in the fields, to be plowed under as fertilizer on the morrow, the ground then planted with winter wheat. The night fires were lit in imitation of the sun's brightness, for thus the ancients had thought to call it back from its long winter journey.

Left hand outstretched, she saluted the fire that took all male de Gaels in the end, and blessed it for its warmth and cleansing powers. Then she saw Kathryn to Hampton Court.

Tansy took Kathryn from her, agreed to the hunting accident story. "I do not know what has happened, Countess, but I see by your face there is trouble afoot so get you on back to Windsgeat. I will see to her ladyship."

No one had bothered to tell Jacquetta about Catherine Howard, or that it meant arrest and execution for Kathryn to be at court.

Tansy undressed her and put her to bed. Found her still awake, staring blank-eyed and unresponsive in the morning. Bathed her, dressed her, took her to the queen's chambers to explain the accident and beg leave to put her to bed until she was better. "Oh, leave her, she will come to herself shortly," Catherine Howard said, and shoved her cousin into the nearest chair.

The unshed storm waters of the night before had left the young queen on edge. She was very short with all her ladies, even Jane Parker, her favorite. Her temper was such that she had not gone to hear Mass with the king and his Councillors, but had remained in her chambers to sulk and eat peppermint comfits.

Kathryn still sat with the same blank expression as Cranmer slipped into the chair next to Henry's at Mass, handed him several folded sheets of paper detailing the queen's past. Henry glanced at them, eyes growing large with wonderment. Next rage creased the royal face, then agony; Henry flung the papers down with a muffled cry, crumpled against Archbishop Cranmer's shoulder.

Kathryn was still in her chair as the king was led, weeping, from the chapel. Cranmer took him to his offices, related more; Henry agreed to ride to a meeting of his lords to decide what must be done.

"Why, there goes my husband," said Catherine Howard, nose to the window. "Why does he ride away without telling me? I must see what is happening."

She, Jane, and the others picked up their trailing skirts and ran out. Forgotten, Kathryn still sat as the chamberers entered, blowing out the expensive candles to save them for reuse. They all looked at her queerly but none thought to examine or move her. So she sat in gray woolen darkness as the day progressed, ignored, unknowing.

"Do you wish Norfolk present at this meeting, Your Grace?" Cranmer asked the king as they rode.

A pause of nearly one-half mile. "Oh, yes, Cranmer. I would see that old fox's face. Windsgeat's, too."

John and Norfolk came prepared. As everyone knew how much they disliked each other, complicity did not occur to the Court. It seemed a marvel to all but Henry that each should bring him information so closely related to the other's, and each condemn a member of his own family. "You are in a rare humor to so doom your own son, Windsgeat," Henry snapped.

John, who believed Payne on a ship bound for relatives in the Low Countries, said, "I but serve my king."

"Serve? When you let your son and heir impale himself upon my rose with no thorns? By God, de Gael, you will sit in judgment upon your own son or I will arrest and execute your entire family and sow your estate with salt, is that clear?"

"Your Grace," John said hoarsely, and bowed, not overdoing it for once.

Henry looked for the familiar whitened jawline and did not find it. "Close all ports," he suddenly ordered, and there it was, that one, subtle sign of panic on Windsgeat's face—a taut jaw.

"You showman, you viper! You could well afford to bring me such news, knowing your son on some ship! Wriothesely! Close every port, stop every ship! If young de Gael escapes I will have your head alongside his on Tower Gate!"

This, then, was the sacrifice his gods demanded of him, John thought. Not himself but his son in exchange for Kathryn's life. For a moment the whole Council Chamber swam before him. He wobbled, thrust out a hand to steady himself. There. Better. He unbuckled his sword belt, laid the full scabbard across the council table. "I surrender myself to your captain of the guard," he said. Dry words, dry throat, dry whisper; what did it matter when he stood to lose so much?

Henry sneered.

"Oh, no, Windsgeat. If you are under arrest you will not

be able to sit on the Council convicting your son of treason. I would prefer seeing your face as that happens to having your head on a pike; the difference in pain will be wonderful to behold. Go home and remain there until I send for you, or, by Christ, I will burn that place to the ground with your witch-sister in it!"

He swung on Norfolk next. "What a traitorous, adulterous nest of bitches you Howards have reared! Spare me your line about turning traitor when Tottenham turns French; I have heard it too much, Tom! Catherine . . . oh, my little Catherine, my rose with no thorns. Sweet little girl who bounced on my knee and called me 'Darling.' The most beautiful, most precious treasure in all my kingdom, and I find she is a whore!"

Both meaty fists crashed down across the table. He stooped so low his head struck his hands; when his cap slipped off, the startled councillors saw that he was nearly bald. "My little girl, my rose," Henry said and wept. "No . . . no . . ."

John and Norfolk sickly awaited dismissal or arrest. The king shouted, "Fetch me my sword, I will cut off her head myself!" Tears came from the small blue-gray eyes; folds of flesh along the oxlike neck trembled. "I will erase this disgrace myself, I will cut her down in her false prime! Yes, and all of you, too, for urging me on to so many ill-conditioned wives! I wish she may have as much grief in death as she may yet have in life—arrest her, I say! *Arrest the queen!*"

He slid to his knees against the table.

In the uproar that followed, John and the duke of Norfolk staggered out, unnoticed. They reached a fountain in the yard, sat gulping air and splashing their faces. "*Kathryn,*" John said suddenly. "God's Horns, Norfolk—what will become of my Kathryn?"

"Where is he? Where is my husband?" Catherine Howard demanded again.

"I tell you, Your Grace, he was at Mass last time I saw him," repeated a steward. Another man said no, he had left; a third said he had returned to the chapel.

Glancing out the window, the queen saw a captain of the guard leading a small troop of men across the courtyard. Voices whispered and jabbered in the long gallery and stairwells. ". . . her secretary Dereham has not been seen this morning, nor her cousin Culpepper."

"I know. Word is, they have been arrested."

"They are coming for the queen. What do you think it could be?"

"The queen? You are mad, Great Harry dotes on her very shadow."

"Perhaps they mean the other Kathryn Howard—Lady Whitbourne. Perhaps she and Windsgeat married after all."

"Do not be a fool, Kathryn Chase was never called Kathryn Howard."

Yes, that was it. The queen pressed a hand to her heaving bosom. They meant her cousin. "D you hear?" she asked Lady Rochford. "They have come to arrest Cousin Kathryn. She must have married John in secret and someone found out. The priest was finally caught, racked, and confessed. Poor woman, she will go to the Tower now. Jane, help them out; show them where my cousin is."

The Long Gallery lay between Catherine and the chapel. *I can make it*, she shakily insisted to herself. *If Harry is back at his prayers, I can reach him ahead of all this vile gossip. He can never resist me, I will be saved*. But as Jane picked up her skirts and started away, a crowd welled up the Long Gallery at the queen.

"Your Grace, what news of the king?"

"Pardon me, Your Grace, but what news of your cousin and secretary, Dereham?"

"Your Majesty, we heard—"

"Catherine Howard, queen of England," the captain of the guard said to Jane Rochford.

"This way, to be sure," Jane babbled, affecting to have misunderstood. Somewhere before her, she knew a tiny figure struggled to part that sea of bodies and reach the chapel. "This way, this way," Jane chattered wildly, and led the troop in to where Kathryn sat, frozen.

"But that is Lady Whitbourne," he said.

"Oh, no, her first married name was Howard, Lady Kathryn Howard. This is the woman you have come for."

"No, Madam, she is Kathryn Chase; we come for the queen of England and you. You are Jane Parker Boleyn, Lady Rochford, are you not?"

Jane ducked under his arm, ran screaming into the gallery. "Run to the king, Your Grace! *Oh, my Catherine! Run!*"

Ahead, the little figure in gold velvet clawed her way through the crowd. Fled shrieking and babbling down the portrait-hung gallery. "*Henry!*" she screamed. "Henry, Husband, save me! Your Grace, Your Grace—*God in heaven, Harry, save me!*"

The men-at-arms sprinted after her, caught her at the chapel doors. She fought like a Fury, came away kicking, punching. Swearing they would lose their heads for so mishandling the Queen of England, Ireland, Wales and France. Blood came from her nostrils as she struggled; her eyes started nearly from their sockets. Her French hood with its thousand black pearls toppled from her head, rolled to the ground where souvenir hunters ripped it to tatters.

"That pearl is mine, give it to me!"

"I had it first!"

"Let go, goddamn you!"

Catherine Howard was dragged, wailing and keening, from the corridor. The captain ordered a guard, "See to it that her women are gathered up and questioned. And Lady Whitbourne, too, though she is bruised and black-eyed, looks to have been struck rather violently on the head. She is sitting dazed and confused in the queen's chambers; I pray you, be not too rough with the poor woman."

But no one knew what to do with her. He ended by gently scooping her up and carrying her himself.

Eight-year-old Elizabeth Tudor said to Elizabeth Stoneleigh, "My father has arrested my mother the queen and your mother as well. Oh, Lissy—will we both lose our mothers this time? Everybody leaves me, Father takes them all—everyone leaves me—"

Sobbing, Lissy said, "I will not leave my princess!" Not an hour later the guard removed her to her mother's cell in the Tower.

Young Elizabeth Tudor feared they would come for her next. She wrote three brief letters in her lovely, long-handed scrawl: one warning her sister Mary, one addressed to The Lord of Windsgeat, and one to her great-uncle Norfolk, appraising them all of the situation. Her only pocket money was two groats for card-playing; she had to tear the pearls off her best cap to bribe messengers into carrying such dangerous writings.

The courier reached Mary Tudor minutes ahead of the king's guard. He went straight to the slender, pale, would-be heir, flung himself at her feet. She read the letter, sent him out the side door with a money purse. "Queen Catherine Howard is arrested and her ladies also," she said grimly. "Isabella, they have your mother, they will come for you, too.

Someone get her food, someone clothing—saddle a horse—Godspeed, my dearest Isabella! Fly now, I hear troops! I will stall them as best I can."

One woman raced into the kitchens, threw an apron on the table. Placed two bottles of ale in it, topped by a round of soft cheese, two small loaves, a pigeon pie. She then tied up the ends of the apron, making a sling for Isabella to throw around her neck.

Isabella herself grabbed her jewel casque, emptied it down her bodice knowing the stiff, cinched-in waist would prevent her losing the larger pieces. Someone threw a fur-lined cloak about her shoulders, another friend pressed a dagger into her hand. Food slung around her neck, she lunged out the rear doors.

No. Must not look suspicious. She did not run but sauntered across the green to the stables, swinging her arms and acting utterly unconcerned. Once inside, she seized a bridle from a nail in the wall, whistled softly to rouse Dôn. "Up, my girl. Hold still for blanket and saddle—open your mouth for this bit, that is my sweet girl—"

The color. They would be looking for a girl on a Windsgeat White. But they were men and outweighed her, being half-armored besides; Dôn was dead Circe's fastest filly, and speed now mattered more than anonymity.

Isabella climbed up the stall door, straddled the mare. "Hee-*yah*!" she cried out, and dug her soft-shod heels in.

The filly flew. Clean-limbed, ghost-pale, she burst out the open doors. Took the hedge, the low stone wall. Shot straight at the troop's riderless, unguarded horses. Isabella rode at them shrieking, flapping arms and reins. They scattered before her, ran in all directions as she mowed through their midst. Not a trooper caught his horse quickly.

There could be no stopping at Windsgeat in case it was guarded. She took a barge, a ferry, left two false trails, and rode on light-headed with terror.

Three hours up the riverbank to Kent she caught a glimmer of fabric in the brush, saw familiar black-and-gold. The de Gael livery, and plenty of it. She stopped long enough to hide it better, spurred on ahead. Several minutes later she came up behind a long line of empty carts and coatless riders following one familiar blond head. "Pieter! Pieter!"

He reached out as she rode abreast of him. They clasped hands. "Elizabeth Tudor warned me," both said at once.

Isabella added, "We must save something for my mother in case she lives!"

"Dat is why I am here. I will disband her household dat her servants do not report any falsehoods to de king's men. Everyding dat can fit in dose carts will go on to John's brudder at York; de livestock will be driven into de marsh where soldiers will not wish to follow."

"Cecily—the baby—they think she is a de Gael and not Mother's. If Windsgeat falls—"

"She left dis morning for Flanders. Lady . . ." Pity sparked in his eyes, and sympathy for all ensuing losses they would share. "Isabella, we will be lucky if de Lord and your mudder live. But dere can be no saving Payne if dey catch him at de ports and I dink dey will; we could not find him to warn him until very late dis morning. Payne will probably die, Milady."

"I *know* he will!" she said with a seeress's sudden knowledge. Squeezing her eyes shut, she forced back tears.

They rode on in silence.

39

Henry Tudor could not bear the thought of his Rose With No Thorns in the Bloody Tower, so she went to crenellated Syon House instead. Edward Seymour, brother to the dead Jane, was only too glad to loan it for the current queen's imprisonment; better that she die with no issue than that there should be other sons to vie with his nephew Edward for the crown.

Jane Parker went mad at Syon House. She went to the scaffold uncertain who she was or what had happened, recognizing only the shadow of the great axe waiting to sever her thin thread of life. All the world turned white for her as the blindfold was knotted over her head; puzzled, she thought she heard George and Anne Boleyn laughing. There came a sound as of metal whistling through the air, then she knew no more.

(There were rumors among the Tower guards that the two Boleyns now rested easier in their arrow cases beneath the paving stones of Saint Peter in Chains chapel.)

I had rather be Harry's countess than Hal's queen! Anne Boleyn had once cried to Kathryn. Catherine Howard, the morning of her execution, murmured to no one in particular that she had rather die Culpepper or de Gael's sweetheart than Great Harry's wife.

Dereham, who had sinned with her before marriage but not after, could not be forced even by the rack to say that he had committed adultery with her. The most that could be wrung, cracked, split, and bled from him was that he had wanted to sleep with her but did not. Nor did Culpepper, a lover from her girlhood days, or Payne confess, each staunchly insisting to the end that they and she were innocent. Only Payne, being a peer's son, was spared torture; the others went to the scaffold hardly able to walk unaided.

All made pretty speeches at the end in a bid to spare their families the king's wrath. Payne forgave the executioner, spoke forgiveness to his father with his eyes.

When his head was held aloft, John, forced to witness, fainted dead away. All the crowd murmured at this; Windsgeat, the Iron Baron, so stricken! They had thought him incapable of feeling, to so sit in judgment on his own son; now they all remembered Thomas Boleyn in the same situation and wondered, had they condemned him unfairly, too?

Short, voluptuous Catherine Howard was buried next to long, slender Anne Boleyn in Saint Peter's chapel. If the cousin-ghosts walked in the night to discuss their mutual husband, only the guard on the green knew, and so far he claimed only to have seen George Boleyn's shade, looking for his head.

The king's men could not find Isabella Howard anywhere. Vamplate Manor had been stripped bare before they arrived; not one carpet, goblet, or hen remained for their perusal. Deep cart tracks ran north and toward the coast while hoofprints of cattle, horses, and sheep trailed off toward the marshlands. Orders were given for Isabella's arrest but countryfolk always thrilled to an outlaw, and she was suddenly a female Robin Hood, fighting the king's tyranny, protected by miles of holy greenwood. People helped by shipping her stock for her, selling and buying until she had only the very finest left in her herd and could move through Kent more easily, never staying more than one night in a place. The forest hid her, then the marshes, and chalk cliffs; she was reported a dozen places at once and all of them false.

At Richmond, Anne of Cleves received a message, bundled up a bag of warm clothing and letters, and sent her messenger speeding to the flatlands near Old Maidstone. In return,

Isabella asked her to invest Kathryn's money from her livestock and Anne did.

John de Gael ordered all the trees on his estate cropped in mourning and rode his many acres looking like a gaunt specter of himself. His mistress-wife was in the Tower, mad, along with Lissy; old Joanna Chase had died being dragged from Wales to join them. His son and heir was dead, Isabella was vanished in the eastern wetlands, and the ship bearing little Cecily had been lost crossing the Channel.

"You did it, Your Grace. You broke Windsgeat at last, he is a shadow of the man we knew," Thomas Wriothesely proudly told the king.

"God, Man, d'you think I wanted that? He was my only fit enemy, my only real friend! Do you think I would rejoice at beating a high-spirited horse to death, or kicking my hound 'till it lay bleeding across my feet?" the king cried out. "Get away from me, you do not understand—none of you understand me but John, and I have murdered his soul!"

The royal palaces closed down, for the king was in no mood for company. Chambermaids who cleaned Hampton Court reported that the long gallery seemed full of a violent wind sometimes, as though someone rushed by them; one woman claimed she saw Catherine Howard run past her, arms out, empty mouth frozen open in a scream that never came.

The artist Holbein died that year. Kathryn and John's oil portraits had long hung at Windsgeat but now Holbein's children, hoping for added payment, sent the delicate chalk drawings. Jacquetta thanked and paid them, tucked the drawings away in the huge Book of Shadows.

Her brother's iron will, hardly bent before now, lay shattered before her. "How can we help him?" she asked Pieter. "*How*?"

"We can do nothing but pack away Payne's things and wait to see if Kathryn lives."

Daily they watched him go out to the forest and ask his gods if it was time for the Green King to die. But the offer of sacrifice when they had already taken so much from him went unheeded; Windsgeat and thus England remained verdant and The Lord alive, though wounded to the heart.

On the day that John Dudley visited Elizabeth Tudor's household to check on the maintenance ledgers, he brought her friend, his son of her same age, Robert. Two of her father's wives had been executed for adulteries no one could prove, one other had died of childbirth, and one of a broken heart. Men therefore fascinated and repulsed her, for if a husband could murder his wives at will and shut his daughters away like shirts in a wardrobe, then what was love but stark, unreasoning terror?

"I will never marry," she told Robert Dudley after another night of nightmares in which Catherine Howard ran screaming down Hampton Court's long gallery.

He thought she was joking. He continued to think so for thirty-odd years until it occurred to him that she would bend her knee to no man after her father, allow no one the mastery to marry, slander, discard, and murder her.

Mary Tudor, smothered beneath the weight of overaged virginity and fear for her own head, cried out, "Will he never send Isabella back or let poor Lady Whitbourne from the Tower? And Sweet Jesu, will he never let me marry? I am six-and twenty, my best years gone, and still he keeps me from children and a husband! Am I to remain forever in this in-between existence, neither here nor there? May I never know happiness? Oh, the children I will never have—oh, my Isabella!"

While at Windsgeat John de Gael waited . . . and waited . . .

Her name came to her one day. A copper-haired child had been calling her Mother for some while (weeks? months? she did not know time); visitors said "Lady Whitbourne." To the old, somehow familiar serving woman she was "Milady," but that did not help. Everyone was Milady to a woman of that class.

Then a brown-haired woman with German clothes and a German accent visited. "Ach, mein Kat'ryn, what have dey done to you? *Liebchen*, where is your sparkle, your speech? Oh, Lissy! Have dey tortured her?"

"No. She had been like this ever since the day Aunt Jacquetta brought her to Court from a riding accident."

"Do you receive the food I send? You are not hungry or cold or—"

"Look about you, Milady; you and Uncle John keep us very well now. In the beginning we were shut in the dark and starved, but your intercession saved us. I watch over Mother as she watched over me when I was little."

Sobbing now. The German woman was kissing her hands, calling her Dear Kat'ryn. Was she Kat'ryn, then? Oh, yes, she remembered now; she was Catherine Howard and they were going to cut off her head.

Dull, slow, she looked down at her hands, clutched by the nice German lady. Long hands, resting on bony knees; she could make out sharp bones through her skirts. Catherine Howard had never been bony in her life—therefore she must be some other kind of Catherine. Not Catherine of Aragon, was she?

Another day it came to her that she was approximately forty-two years old and her monthly courses had ceased. A child, she had longed to give someone another child. Who? Was the pretty, green-eyed girl her daughter? Well, there would be no more without her monthly blood.

Turning her head, she saw lovely things about her, familiar things. Rich bedding, linens, tapestries. A table mounted on four dog-headed, woman-breasted sea-sphinxes. A bed: *JG*'s and *EW*'s on the headboard.

That night she sat up in the bed screaming for her son, Payne. The girl and maidservant grabbed her, told her it was all right and that Payne was not her son. "But he is! Payne is my son and my son is dead! I saw him die—I killed him with my hunting bow!"

It was the first time she had spoken since being arrested. After that she forgot how to form words again, and could not even read the books they gave her. But sewing remained; her stitches were still tiny, exacting, precise. One chill winter morning as she sat before the fire mending it seemed to her she heard a commotion outside. Rising from her chair, she pushed a tapestry back to look out the window.

An execution. She knew the scene at once. They were killing her father. No, no, she had watched her father's death from the ground, not up high like this. Whose, then? Someone she loved, she thought.

"God's sake! Lady Elizabeth, get her away from that window, today is the day the men die! Milady Kat, come away from there!"

Stubborn, she dug her fingers into the broad stone sill, clung so that they could not move her. And so she saw her love, her life, climb the steps, make his speech, lay his head on the block. *John*. She remembered his name now, stood whispering it. "John, oh, John—my John, oh Jesu! Do not kill my John, my John—"

The axe fell, the chestnut head was held aloft. At the other end of the scaffold a big man, with hair of the same hue though muchly grayed, crumpled in a faint.

"Mother, that was Payne just died! John is all right! Come

away from there, Mama, you cannot help the dead. John is safe, John is alive. It was Payne died."

Payne was her son. No, no, something was wrong here. Her son was dead. Were all her sons gone? Yes, they must be. There had been a sweet little one, dead of the stinking Sweat. There was Payne, who was not born of her body but had been given her by his mother: *Take care of my sons, Kat'rin, they are yours now.*

She began to remember why she was insane. Too many executions, too much living in fear, loving where it was forbidden. And murdering her last son.

When it was announced months later that Kathryn had finally regained her senses, Archbishop Cranmer was sent to confess her. He expected details of complicity in choosing the dead queen's lovers, awaited details of her fornications and politicking with the de Gaels and old Norfolk. "Confess? Why should I, I have done nothing wrong," she said with a child's unnervingly innocent stare.

Stephen Gardiner, the wily, the dangerous, was sent to her next. "But, Milady Whitbourne, even madwomen sin," he said, and waited.

She wanted to respond that there was no sin in her world, that she was free of that notion now. But he would not understand. So Kathryn said, "All right then, I will confess. Confess that I do not like you and your woman-hating god. So stoke up the fires and prepare my stake; I am not afraid."

That excessively blue, cornflower stare unnerved him. He told the king he deemed her still mad. But John Dudley visited her and found her clear-minded and able of speech. The Seymours came next, Thomas because he was fond of her, and tight-lipped, unlovable Edward because, with Norfolk and Windsgeat banished from Court, he had become the king's pillar of state.

"What did you think of her?" Thomas asked later, as they leaned over the White Tower's battlements to watch the sun setting.

"She is sound as a gold mark. But it is very dangerous for her to have lost her belief in sin; Gardiner will burn her for it, if he can. It will be a very bad thing should we English continue the burnings; public recantation was good enough in the old days. At any rate, the dowager Lady Whitbourne is a political liability now, so I am glad you did not marry her."

"She was too clever, Edward; a man likes to be able to fool

a woman sometimes. Which is why I have my eye on quite another type of woman."

"Some silly, prattling young thing? Like her daughter, the inheriting Lady Whitbourne?"

"No, no, Kate is thirty, a sober individual much unused to passion and frivolity. She has been married to two ancient men, and has much property."

Edward Seymour considered it, watched as encroaching night painted the lime-washed Tower rose and peach. "You must mean Lady Latimer—little Anne Parr's sister."

He caught himself thinking: *A wrong woman for brother Tom. But a sturdy, dull, dependable, book-learned widow would be perfect for His Grace. She will not be adulterous like the Howards nor make him dance and hunt himself to death.*

How grateful aching, gimping old Harry Tudor would be for a solid and trustworthy woman to lean on in his declining years! No more skirt-twitching minxes, no more games, flirts, and whores. Lady Latimer, while no beauty, was not ugly, either; she would prove no gross Anne of Cleves. Entirely too good a woman to waste on brother Tom.

He clapped Thomas on the shoulder. "I think we should pay a respectful call on Lady Latimer. Maybe drag the king along to take him out of himself and his miseries. He will appreciate the thoughtfulness."

It was not the first time cold-blooded Edward won out over his younger brother.

Elizabeth Stoneleigh was almost fourteen before she was released into John's custody. She ran, sobbing, to his arms, and he held her until she had cried herself dry. When he lifted her into the saddle of her half-Barb pony, she was surprised to note both that she had outgrown her mount and that John did not lift her so lightly as he used to. Seated above his head level, she saw that his chestnut hair was half-silver. His back was still straight as an arrow, though she noted the old ankle injury had him noticeably limping in public for the first time. The ice-blue eyes and their deep laughlines had not aged; only the many silver hairs and dragging walk gave him away. And the black doublet—to see Uncle John dressed plainly as a priest hurt her beyond endurance.

"Come," he said simply. "Let us go home to Windsgeat."

At Vamplate Manor the hard-cleared fields went back to

brush. Pigeons roosted in the gorgeous hammerbeam ceiling, foxes ran in empty, echoing rooms. Shutters blew open, admitting rain, snow, sun. It was the king's property and banned; none went there now.

Deserted Hever Castle was reported haunted by a tall, thin woman with the Howard nose and a shrill laugh. *Anne Boleyn walks*! country folk cried. Thus Isabella found sanctuary and a garden in which to grow, distill, and bottle her herbs.

Kathryn was forty-three years old when the king signed her release. "My poor old cousin has suffered enough and can be of no danger to me now. The laundress says she is incapable of breeding sons for Windsgeat; let him take her home, if he is still so inclined," Henry told Edward Seymour. "And these papers—I will give her lands back."

When the Windsgeat servants were admitted to her Tower rooms to begin dismantling the furniture and take down the tapestries, Kathryn knew she still had a home. Courteously handed into a new lynx-lined velvet coat, buttoned into fan-tailed doeskin gauntlets, she thought: *How well he remembers me! My love of lynx fur, the exact color of velvet I like best. But I am very changed and so must he be.*

They had let her walk on the Green these last months and she had gone around and around by the hour as her father and brother had done before her. Stretching stiff muscles, pushing herself on to some semblance of trimness, of youth—*He will not find me attractive. I am an old woman,* she thought with a last, despairing glance at the hand mirror. Womanlike, she thought only of her own shortcomings, did not consider that John might age, too.

She did not know him at once. His back was to her, for he was supervising the loading of the carts. What very broad shoulders that silver-haired man had, she thought. And then something about the still-arrogant stance seemed familiar and she saw threads of red-brown in his hair.

But chiefly, the somber black doublet fooled her. John had never worn anything so tasteful in his life; she found herself smiling sadly.

He turned, came toward her at a halting pace. "My Kathryn," he said, and kissed her cheek. They held hands a long minute in the clatter and bustle of the carts. "Vamplate Manor is not ready for you. Your belongings are only now being returned from my brother in York. Jacqui and I would like you to stay with us at Windsgeat."

"Yes, I hear my house and lands are deserted."

"You are in luck, though. You were not attaindered and the king has returned all deeds to your property. Your house and outbuildings still stand, intact."

"I suppose I should fall on my knees in gratitude before the throne. Not today; my knees are too stiff. To Windsgeat then, Dear."

They rode like two fond old acquaintances with no flesh to make them recall baser things. She spoke only once, to say, "You never wrote."

"Kathryn, my entire family nearly went to the Tower. There were spies in my household staff; you were not capable of reading until these last few months. Only Anne of Cleves dared visit you and smuggle messages; did you not notice how the food I sent was always cut into, the fruits and vegetables sliced open lest they conceal messages? Gods! I have lived under such fear since they took you and my boy! I do not know why Tudor did not kill me as well. He held me and all my riches in his hand and did not close his fist; I wonder why."

Upon leaving the greenwood she saw that all the trees surrounding Windsgeat manor house had been cropped as a sign of mourning. It must have taken weeks. Only the passing of a very great lord was so marked, but she knew John had ordered it done out of fatherly sorrow, not notice that the heir to Windsgeat lay dead. But not buried; de Gael men, Jacquetta once told her, were always burned instead. Only their women, their priestesses, entered earth.

John gave her rooms apart from his, not knowing how much of their relationship would resume. He lay awake that night, hands behind his head on the pillows, thinking, wondering. A flicker of light suddenly crossed the hatched-marked moonshadows thrown across his floor by mullioned windows; he sat up, hopeful as a boy of twenty. "*Kathryn*?" He breathed it like an invocation.

The slender, pale shape paused in the doorway. "May I come in and talk, John?"

"We could *always* talk to one another, you know that." He started up for his fur-lined robe, remembered suddenly that it might no longer be proper to lunge out of bed naked in front of her. They had been apart a long time and he did not know what she needed from him—passion or compassion or both. So he sat back, arms defensively folded.

Kathryn set the candle on his leather trunk, perched delicately at the foot of the bed. "Tell me," she said. "Tell me *everything*, John! Tell me about the trial, tell me about Payne. I want to hear what you have done this eighteen months, every detail, how the crops have grown, which mares have foals. Who is important at Court now, who is out of favor. Jacqui, Francis, Pieter. Every single thing that has happened—tell me *all* of it!"

It helped both of them. They wept together about Payne, laughed wryly because the totally unremarkable-seeming Francis had, in the tiltyard, unhorsed both Pieter and John in the same hour. She heard how the lands of Windsgeat river valley did, which crops were best, how Val d'Or's second colt by Finnvarra had been bridle-trained and that wicked old Cernunnos still ran free.

He had not talked so intimately with anyone in her absence. That strangling welter of feelings was released now; finding himself emptied of much grief and his first sense of real, lasting defeat, he returned the favor. "And now tell me about your journey back from wherever your mind went," he said flatly.

"I was mad, John, say it: *Kathryn was mad*. I could not accept killing James or coming so close to losing you and all the rest of my family. So I retreated into some blank corner of my being and crouched there on and off for a year."

She had worked her way up to his knees by now; while her story progressed she moved a little more, inches at a time. Then his arms were open and she lay across his chest. "My hairline has crept back since you saw me last," he admitted. "And I have gone *very* silver."

"John, I am beginning to sag in places that never existed before. How can anyone as thin as me *sag*?"

"Did you think you would stay twenty and I, twenty-nine, forever?" He rumpled her hair, kissed it. "Sometimes you and I forget we are just *people*, Kathryn. We expect to go on forever and we are irritated at being reminded of our own mortality. You know—I sorrowed for so long that I was one vast, aching knot of pain. And after that I became numb. No feelings, no reactions. Just drawing breath, eating, riding—poor Finn, I nearly wore him out. And then one day I began returning to life, began to feel hunger, lust, anger, all the normal emotions again."

"And did you have women then?" she asked, twining her fingers in his chest hair.

"What a question! I should throw you out of my bed for

asking. Of course not. I keep faith with those I love; I keep faithful to my wife."

She tried to make light of the thing that caused a lump in her throat. "John, I am past childbearing. That means we need not rely on potions or restraint or anything else; no need to fear. I am barren as a stone!"

He took her face between his hands, and smiling, shook his head at her. "Do you think I only love you for that? I love our children but it is a relief to have you out of danger at last. But I know it hurts you. There, my love, there . . ."

He was kissing her hair now, then her forehead. The eyelids she closed to golden candlelight and the gracefully aging male beauty of him. Her cheek, her ear, and at last, her mouth. Oh, dear God. To think she had lived without this, to think she had lain without him night after night! It did not seem possible.

It was better than at twenty. Then it had been new to her, for she had not known what appetites her body held. But now—to have lived with this hunger—

John was saying something in between kisses. Did the man never stop talking? "Kathryn, love . . . oh, Kathryn . . ."

She bit his shoulders, sucked the leaping pulse at the hollow of his throat. Shuddered as he unfastened her shift, drew it down to her waist. His warm hands caressed her face, shoulders, breasts. At that she cried out, cupping her hands over his and urging him to be less gentle. *Biting*. He was biting her neck too hard, she liked it. Quick, sharp little bites that made her gasp, cry out as if in protest. But when he stopped, she pushed his head back where it had been.

Laughing, John laid her back against the pillows. Pushed her hem all the way up. His strong hands parted her legs, moved up. With that one touch she crashed, cried out. Embarrassed at her own ease of response, she started away from him. "Stop that," John scolded. "Do you think it is an insult to either of us?"

He drew her back. This time the feeling was not hit-and-run like lightning but slower, easier, building step by step. He was touching her everywhere, kissing her face, then body all over. Hip, thighs, the burning place between. Such gentleness, the light, stroking touch of mouth and fingertips—

The long peak brought her arching up against him, soundless, contorted. Then she drew him up by the shoulders, wordlessly beseeched him to fill her. John put his hands under her rump, pushed her up to meet him.

They had kept their feelings locked inside too long; neither made a sound. There was something savage about it, Kathryn thought, opening her eyes to the sight of one broad, bare shoulder, golden in the candlelight. Gods, what a magnificent man! How had she ever won him?

It was too good. He was killing her, she could not stand any more. Sensing her panic, he slacked pace; at once her short fingernails pressed crescent moons in his shoulderblades. She did not have to say "more" or "please" to make him understand that was what she meant. They continued together, violent with need; now she was gasping, crying out with each thrust. "I love you, I love you . . ." Perspiration put a glistening layer on their skin, making them slide together. He had never lasted this long at twenty-nine, she thought. It was too much, too—*there*. Gods! A whole little chain of inner explosions, making her moan into his neck.

No, not finished. She bit his shoulder, drew blood. Could she still—? She certainly could. Kathryn managed to bring her legs up around his waist, drag him past the breaking point.

John yelled so loudly the servants came running. Suddenly the room was full of candles and embarrassed faces. Kathryn, laughing, sagged down into the mattress beneath him. She heard Jacquetta cry out, "What is—"

The whack of Pieter's hand on his wife's shapely rump. "All right, everyone, out, out. No one is killing John—except wid love."

The door banged shut. John and Kathryn collapsed, laughing. She finally rolled him over, sat on his stomach tickling him. "Did I really *yell*?" John asked.

"Like someone had just made off with your most garish doublet."

"My doublets! Why does no one like my doublets? I think them very fine," he huffed.

She settled back into his arms. Loud clothes were part of the man, she would never change that. *I wonder, would I have loved him had he been decently dressed, or did the very horror of his clothes dazzle me*?

Then again . . . had he worn normal clothes she would not have been able to see him entering her life from so far off.

"Lady Isabella Howard," the herald announced. The few people in the Presence Chamber gasped.

Henry Tudor gasped, too. Good, the little wretch had

come to beg forgiveness! Probably straight from the wilds of Kent where his men had been pursuing her legend for months; he pictured her ragged, gaunt, dispirited. But how odd she should walk right in here, and no sign of those who arrested her.

It was not until she entered alone and looking like an empress that he realized she had not been captured. No, she had chosen to enter Court on her own.

And *Doux Jesu,* but she was gorgeously garbed! Sheer gold-and-blue tissue over flesh-colored satin, and a French hood stiff with jewels. The sapphire at her throat was big enough to gag a horse, and she wore a ring on every finger.

John de Gael's unfathomable eyes looked back at Henry from her face. He had never been certain before that she was John's daughter; now the knowledge seemed undeniable. The same chestnut hair, too, though she was not built like a de Gael woman but, rather, like her arrow-straight mother.

She did not prostrate herself. Instead she went straight up the dais as quickly as if invited, knelt on the top step at his feet. Stretched her arms up beseechingly.

He had not thought of the three-year-old Isabella in many years. She conjured that image now of her other self begging him wordlessly with that same save-me-hold-me gesture.

It was witchcraft and Henry knew it. Thus had Jacquetta called him, put images in his head. But there was no sexual invitation in Isabella's magic, and he knew that had he ordered her head struck off on the spot, her expression would not change. She had neither Kathryn's stubbornness nor John's arrogant pride; she was only Isabella to whom nothing was straight-black or straight-white and it made her small difference how he responded. If she did not prostrate herself as her mother did, it was not from any sense of self-importance, but because she simply did not feel so inclined.

The child of three, wordless, serene even with those outheld beseeching arms. The little girl who said she would obey him in all things. "You have cost me much time and money, Lady Howard," he grumbled.

"Catherine Howard meant nothing to me; I had no intention of dying or letting my mother lose her possessions because of her. In my place you would have done no less and would, I suspect, have been far bolder. A regular Robin Hood, I think; you would have taken to humiliating and robbing the king's men, which I never did. You always wore Lincoln green and a bow well, Your Grace."

He could not fight a reluctant grin. She knew Robin Hood was one of his heroes, knew he could never resist flattery. His expression said, *I know what you are doing and a good job of it, too*. Hers answered, *I expected you to know and would have been disappointed had you remained unaware*.

"You are very like your father," he mused, and they both knew which man he meant.

Isabella allowed herself a smile that, like any of John's, was brief but sincere. "Grant me, Your Grace, that I at least pick my clothes better."

He tapped a finger on his chin before pointing at her. "I do not feel so certain about that. Your blue-and-gold is not subtle."

"I wanted you to see me coming from a distance."

He threw his balding head back, laughed until his hat slid half-off. "Oh, you are clever, Isabella Howard! How well you know your Courtly repartee, how well you judge your political victims! Tell me, are you as good a judge of women?"

She lowered her arms. "Why, Your Grace? What do you wish to know about Lady Latimer?"

Edward Seymour bent the silver cup he was holding. Damn her! Beating him to the draw! He had never liked her mother; now he liked Isabella less.

Hearing laughter from the Presence Chamber, people peeked in. Was that not the outlawed Isabella Howard sitting at the king's feet, laughing and gossiping with him about marital prospects?

The word spread: Kathryn Chase and her daughters were coming back into favor.

PART SIX

CATHERINE PARR
(No Years My Own)

"Ahh, me! When thinking of the years,
The vanished years, alas, I do not find
Among them all one day
That was my own!"

—Michelangelo
Buonarroti—

"Then Mordred fell,
But like a prince he fell,
And as a branch of great Pendragon's graft.
His life breathes out,
His eyes forsake the sun. . . ."

—anonymous, *The Mis-
Fortunes of Arthur*—

40

Whitehall Palace
Autumn 1543

"I am sorry, Kate, but I do not know where it is. There is not a chamberer or laundress that I know left from my days at court. Old Mistress Stonor is all that remains, that was once Mother of the Maids. I tell you, if the dowager Lady Whitbourne does not return and straighten things out, you and I shall remain lost as babes in the woods. I am surprised you do not recall her, she is Isabella Howard's mother."

Mistress Herbert—still plain Anne Parr to her beloved sister—made a fool's cross-eyed face. Her sister Catherine Parr, now queen of England, responded in kind and stuck her tongue out as well. Both women burst out laughing. "Will I like her? I cannot bear one more dragon like Mistress Stoner!" the new queen exclaimed.

"Oh, Kate, you will love old Lady Whitbourne. She is not giddy or flirtatious or lazy like so many of these useless women we have about us. I do not believe she went mad in the Tower of London, everyone said she had a bump on the head before they took her away, and you remember that time I was six and fell out of the tree? I was addled for days! Plus her son disappearing when his house burned and worrying she would be beheaded, why, it would be enough to make anyone with a bump to the head not speak for months. But if she comes back here and you find her the least little bit mad, why, chuck her out. But I remember her as the soul of strength and dependability back when Jane Seymour and I were maids of honor together."

From Anne's description, Catherine Parr expected a mousy nobody with a twitch at unexpected times, starting at loud noises. Perhaps Lady Whitbourne talked to herself, or—

"Goodness, what is that fuss in the courtyard?" she asked, setting down her prayer book. "They seem all a-bustle out there."

"Someone has arrived, let us go see."

"You trot along without me, Anne, I must finish translating this from the Latin. Whoever is arriving, I hope he or she knows where the bed-linens are!"

Anne left her at a trot; the queen returned to her prayers. But concentrate though Catherine tried, she could not get from Latin to the vernacular with such a ruckus just outside her window. So at last she surrendered to curiosity, set her book down, and crossed the room to press her nose to the glass.

Two dozen men in black-and-gold livery were dismounting from fine gray horses. In their midst a chestnut-haired boy sprang from a white colt's back, rushed to the side of a horse twin to his own. *Glorious beasts,* Catherine thought, noting the little wedge-shaped heads and plumed tails of both white mounts.

The woman he handed down from the mare was thin and magnificent. A little French hood entirely covered in pearls and sapphires showed much of her ashy light brown hair; her blue-gray velvet gown's sheen proclaimed itself purest Genoese silk. The sleeves were so cunning, the queen noted, hardly more than one square of gold-fishnetting-over-blue tied on the forearm, with another at the upper arm. Jeweled ribbons tied those squares, with puffs of gold tissue shift hanging out in between.

Her neckline was stiff with many pearls; she wore a necklace so intriguing that Catherine Parr opened the window and leaned out for a better look. Sweet Savior! A triple strand of blue champlevé enameled plaques hung nearly to her knees; the queen had seen something like that in a Byzantine empress's picture. There was also a choker of cherry-sized sapphires and many rings. Her short-sleeved coat was blue-and-gold brocade lined with gold tinsel, and the boy was rushing to fling a massive velvet cloak lined with lynx fur about her slender shoulders.

To Catherine Parr's surprise, her sister Anne and this splendid creature were embracing with much chattering and laughter, each presenting a subtley painted cheek to be kissed. Then the servants, packmules, and long line of carts pulled up to the stairs to unload. A heavy table supported by four dog-faced sea-sphinxes was coming out of the first cart, and she had never seen its like.

The queen stopped a porter. "Who is that woman?"

"Kathryn Chase—the dowager Baroness Lady Whitbourne, Your Grace," he answered and bowed before moving off. Why, she did not look at all mad or priggish! In fact she looked absolutely charming.

Anne brought Kathryn to her. "Your Grace," the newcomer said, and curtsied so gracefully she must have been born doing it.

"I see you have been doing this for some years, Lady Whitbourne," the queen greeted her, extending a hand to haul Kathryn back up.

"Thank you, Your Grace. The curtsies still come easy; it is the getting back up that grows hard with age. I am so pleased to be called back to Court, for I have heard nothing but pleasantries about working under you. That will be a marveled-at change; there have been some hard mistresses in this place."

She was very frank, the queen liked that and so smiled. "Yes, His Grace is fond of saying that he had three dull, safe wives, two bad, exciting ones, and now hopes I fall somewhere in the middle!"

Kathryn hoped she would, too. The new queen was thirtyish, plainish, but so animated as to give an impression of prettiness. She spoke quickly, directly, and with an unthinking musical lilt to her voice; *I will wager she sings beautifully,* Kathryn thought. *She is reported to be intelligent and pious, and though she had no children by her two old husbands, she is still young enough to give King Henry a duke of York.*

"In what manner may I aid Your Grace?" she asked. "Mistress Herbert" (funny to call little Anne Parr that!) "tells me I may be of some special assistance."

"I—they—oh, dear, I have never been queen before," Catherine Parr said, uncertain where to start. "Anne and I do not know where to place the dukes and barons, and I cannot find linens for the royal bed—this palace has been closed down for so long. Everything is in the wrong place, I know nothing of Court protocol or how many maids of honor go in a bed or—" She halted, and gave a perplexed sigh that said the whole thing was beyond her management.

"Your Grace, if I may suggest . . . ? Your sister has spent a good many years at court, she would be an excellent Head Lady of the Bedchamber, which is your innermost sanctum. Only your very favorites go there, along with several ladies that you do not have to like, but who possess such high rank they cannot be ignored. That way Anne will have final word over who approaches you. That way you will be able to *sleep*. She will also be less subject to bribes than others; a stranger might pocket the money and let any number of folk in to pester you with requests. Old Mistress Stoner will be excellent flogging the chambermaids into line, she has a memory that never lags when it come to names, faces, and how many acres of floor one girl can scrub in an hour."

"She was Mother of the Maids, was she not? Well, then, I should like you to take that title now, Lady Whitbourne," Catherine Parr said.

Kathryn bit her lip a moment. What a splendid office to have, and how she had longed for it! "But I cannot, though it is a very kind offer, Your Grace," she forced herself to say. "The Mother of Maids, having so many unmarried girls in her care, must have an unblemished reputation."

The queen laid an already-fond hand on her arm. "My Lady, I could never believe ill of you. Pray, know that I will not hear gossips' lies."

"But they tell the truth, Your Grace. The king will not allow me to marry Baron Windsgeat so we handfasted in the woods and I live almost openly as his mistress. You see why I cannot mother the maids. However, I will be delighted to take some lesser title, say, Household Advisor, for I think I still know which garderobe all the chamber pots are stored in and which apartments His Grace best likes and how many doors down Dudley and the Seymours go. What we will need to begin work is a complete inventory of Bridewell, Bayard's Castle, the Tower, Greenwich—we must send for the Household Inventory Clerks and find out where all the royal belongings are so you and King Henry can decide what you want *where*. Also, riding in, I noticed that the stables are a mess, so you must have your secretary write John Dudley to come at once or all your mares will get with foal by the least desirable stallions. Dudley is an excellent Master of Horse."

"You are now my private secretary. No one can object to that, and if they do, they can—they can—" Catherine Parr tried to think of a frightening enough fate to condemn such blackguards to. "They can go to the king! He likes you again, and as he is lord and master here, his opinion is all that counts."

She squared her shoulders, looked capable of fistfighting for both Kathryn's reputation and the king's position of power. *Oh, Harry Tudor!* Kathryn thought, hiding a grin. *Methinks you picked a proper queen at last*.

It was a greatly changed Court. Following the new queen's lead, necklines crept up, trimmings became less garish. Only Kathryn continued to parade like a peacock, for it pleased John no end.

Instead of dancing all evening, making love through the night, and leaping to the saddle at dawn, ladies-in-waiting found themselves expected to study Holy Scripture and classical literature, brush up on their longhand, shorthand, needlework, Latin, and philosophy.

The king's daughters returned to court. With Mary Tudor came Isabella, at twenty-three now firmly ensconced in her state as the oldest non-royal virgin at Court. It comforted Mary to have her companionship, though the two of them were very different—Mary, desperate to wed, and Isabella with her vow of perpetual virtue.

Elizabeth Tudor, age ten, returned with the breathtaking fourteen-year-old Lissy. Men from ten to eighty began making utter fools of themselves to catch the attention of Kathryn's youngest daughter. But she seemed oblivious to it all, which puzzled her mother.

At first Elizabeth Tudor hung back from her new stepmother. She confessed to Lissy that she would not love again only to see it end on the block; she was very stiff with Catherine Parr. But when the king boxed the child's ears, the queen cried out, "Please, Your Grace! She is not rude or obstinate, only afraid of your glory and majesty and my unfamiliarity. Why, I am a stranger to her and you seem some glittering being from myth or country legend! She does not know you well enough to think you flesh-and-blood; no, you are a symbol to her of England's might and God's power! I pray you, be tender with Bess for she is your adoring daughter."

Phrased like that he could not remain angry. Especially when Catherine so-gently lifted his bad leg to her lap. That always comforted him more than plopping it on some cold hassock or bench; her warmth seemed to thaw him, for though she was not sensual and hot, she was affection itself and utterly biddable. It was the first time since Catherine of Aragon that he had been treated with the awe due God's annointed representative on earth, and he liked that in his corpulent, near-crippled old age.

People were surprised that he called John back to Court, for while they were the same age, John was still a magnificent figure of a man, unbowed by time, handsome enough to turn women's heads. His astounding vitality and powers of attraction were expected to incense the king's touchy pride, so it was a further surprise when John moved back into the king's inner circle as though he had never been gone. There was no magic involved except that of nostalgia, for few of Henry's favorites remained who could recall the past in such vivid detail, tell such stories of their younger days.

At other times Henry regarded the other man's straight warrior-body with an envy that verged on maniacal. Easy for Windsgeat to ride miles a day and dance with his mistress at night! Easy for a man with two nearly sound legs to stride along like a stallion; he no longer jousted at Court but Henry heard John still aimed a lance in his own private tiltyard. At least he had the pleasure of also hearing that Windsgeat's sole son and heir unhorsed him frequently. That would slow the old man down.

And there were the gifts. Every time Henry thought he could no longer face a man of his own years whose hairline had hardly shifted and whose stomach looked flat as a boy's, John presented him with something so delicious he was overwhelmed. Gemmy bits of harness, voiceless Arabian hunting hounds, Damascene swords of state. An intricately carved chair on poles for when the royal leg was too puffed with infection to allow walking. Pies which, when cut into, released swarms of exotic songbirds to tweet from the rafters all through a meal. Weird and rare fruits never before seen in England, smuggled from foreign ports by ship, camelback, and yak-caravan.

Oh, the man's taste was princely except in his own clothes. It made Henry grin that after all her years with him, Kathryn could still not get John into anything tamer than a violet-and-green brocade doublet garnished with yellow satin ribbon and fifty-seven matched cabuchon rubies. And the feathered hat that went with it would dazzle a blind man. A hundred pink ostriches must be running mother-naked through Africa even now.

From time to time Henry considered clapping John in the Tower on one pretext or another. But then it would return to him how he and John had ridden with the Wild Hunt and he would fear injuring him. To be sure, owning Windsgeat would vastly enrich the royal coffers. But sometimes he found himself awake at night, wondering if he was only King of England and alive because John de Gael allowed it.

So he slept and dreamed of Windsgeat the Green, Windsgeat the Eternal. And he wondered who would die first, the Green King or the annointed king.

That winter, John's most remarkable gift to date arrived from the North. It was tall, stocky, craggy-faced, and blond as a Fleming, though most of the blond had gone to silver and the beard was white as snow. Tiny round spectacles perched at the end of the craggy Howard-de Gael nose; the ice-blue eyes peering through them could have been John's, Jacquetta's, or even Isabella's.

"Your Grace, I am Doctor Thomas Gale. My brother Windsgeat says you have need of me."

Henry reared up from his bed of agony on one elbow. "Who the devil let you into my bedchamber, sir!"

"Your wife the queen."

"Gale! You made the name more English! Then you are Gale the radical, Gale the madman who is against cauterizing with pitch and hot irons! Gale the lunatic who says not to amputate unless there are red stripes from the wound, a great stink, and the infection is spreading toward the body proper. What then, have you come to cut off my leg?"

Doctor Tom calmly opened his bags, began laying things out on the nearest sandalwood chest. "Searing wounds kills the victim. Since I have initiated the practice of washing my hands, boiling my tools, and using herb oils in place of hot irons, I find my patients live and prosper. I lose only those who have shed too much blood or suffered too great a shock to the system before I arrived."

"What, then you are probably against bleeding, too! A radical and no doubt a heretic like the rest of the de Gaels!"

Doctor Tom was lighting candles and balancing little metal tripods over them with bottles of oil suspended above the flames. "No, I am Christian, which is why John and I settled my share of the family property in money, not land, and he wrote me out of the inheritance. Neither of us bears a grudge; a man does what he thinks is right and no more."

The man was bossy as his brother, imperiously ordering chamberers here and there: "You there! Bring me buckets of water, as many as will fill His Grace's deepest wooden bath. Send me someone from the kitchens and I will tell them what meals to prepare."

He flung the bedclothes back, began unwrapping the king's leg without so much as a by-your-leave. "Sir, you are most saucy with your sovereign! But if you can heal me—" Henry sputtered.

"I cannot. But I can make you much better."

Henry lay back, groaning. "Now you will want to poke and prod, stick knives in to drain it."

"Not unless it is absolutely necessary. I intend to place the leg in exceedingly hot water, soak the ill humors out. Then it will be washed repeatedly with aqua vitae and soaked and soaked again. Pew, these bandages are foul. You must have the world's worst physicians. You should have Doctor Butts horsewhipped or, at the least, sent East to study medicine with those who know it."

"East? Sorbonne? Milan?" the king queried eagerly.

"Arabia, Persia. *Egypt*."

The bandages were off now; porters and chamberers brought buckets and poked up the fire. Henry shook his head disbelievingly. "And have you been those places, sir?"

"Yes, my brother sent me. It was part of the arrangement when he wrote me out of his will. I was glad to get away from those heathen rituals."

"Yes, I can see where having one's brother run around the countryside naked come every full moon would be an annoyance. He must have paid you dear to come south."

"Oh, he did. But I am worth every last pence, mark, and groat. I so prefer being paid in gold to trading in stock and lands, it has such a final sound in a wooden trunk!"

Windsgeat must have paid him excessively for the amount to require more room than provided by a leather pouch.

One month later, when the humorless doctor left, Henry was well enough to dance, hunt, and stride about the palace again. But there was so much to do, so many places that he could not see while wasting an hour a day standing in hot water up to his groin. So within a week the varicose ulcer was poisoning his whole leg again.

41

Catherine Parr's two great expenses as queen were the royal children and shoes.

She was Henry's busiest queen, wearing out twenty-some pairs of shoes her first year to wife, and more the second. Each year after that, she gave up and bought replacements by the dozen, for she flittered up and down stairs all day, in and out of gardens, stables, chapels, and poorhouses where she made her donations and fed the ill, aged, and impoverished. Then back to her house, back to the palace, run to nurse the king. Run out again later, visit prisoners in the Tower, run back . . .

"That woman must have calf-muscles like a battle charger," John surmised.

Catherine adored the royal children (as she thought of them, though Mary was but few years her junior) and continually fussed over their diets, religious interests, companions. But she did not do so in any annoying or busybody way, only poured affection and concern on them. Prince Edward and little Elizabeth basked under such treatment though Mary was slower to come around.

As the queen was no great needleworker, she did not make the childrens' shifts and shirts herself as her predecessors had done, but rather played music with them, discussed religious books and ancient philosophers. She was glad there were still a few women like Kathryn around who remembered the secret stitches in every blackworked Holbein portrait and could put their twins into body-linen for Mary, Elizabeth, and Edward.

The king's leg was bad again but he still went a-warring to Boulogne for three months and left Catherine Parr as regent to prove his faith in her ability. Letters detailing his pain drove her into correspondence with many doctors in England and abroad, and so it was inevitable that she should invite famed herbalist and midwife Jacquetta de Gael back to Court. Jacquetta sent an exquisitely-worded refusal, resplendent with thank-you's and pardon-me's, and a whopping diamond brooch attached. It was unheard-of that anyone should refuse to attend Court, but then, Catherine had always heard that the de Gaels were a law unto themselves. She asked John why he did not order his sister to Court and was taken aback when so big and masterful a man, so feared a political opponent as Windsgeat, asked, "Your Grace—a mere man give orders to a de Gale woman? Brother or not, she would have my liver on a platter! I will warrant you the king himself never dared tell my sister 'Jump,' or how high."

While the king was yet in France he summoned John to join and advise him on counting the French war. John hesitated. "Go on, man, what is it?" Henry roared.

"I beg you do not do it. You will lose, Your Grace."

Lose? He was Great Harry of England, he never lost!

Henry rose from his sickbed, broke his lead-weighted walking stick across John's right shoulder. With a loud snapping of bones, The Lord of Windsgeat went down.

Henry, weeping, fell to one knee at his side. "See what you have made me do!" he raged at his other lords. "The rest of you obsequious liars tell me 'Go on, go on to war and ruin.' Then I hear the truth and it so unhinges me that I strike down my only loyal and honest lord! Oh, John, lean on me! Can you not get up?"

The shoulder never really mended. Pieter rebroke it for him when he returned home, but not all Jacquetta and Thomas's skills could reset it properly. "The blow chipped bones, John, and that cannot be helped. We have made it straighter, is all," Jacquetta told him.

Thomas his brother eased him into a black silk sling. "They are old bones and brittle, John. Admit that your tiltyard days are over and return to the Council chamber, you may yet be of some use there. Of course, in the end you will roast in hell, so what you do on earth does not matter."

"That is my Tom, always cheerful! Thank you for your tender concerns, for which Jacquetta no doubt had to pay you handsomely. Now take your crucifixes of that tormented being away from here; Windsgeat is for the living. And crippling the sacrificial king is always a sacred act, so I will bear with it as best I may."

Following Kathryn's advice, John selected John Dudley as the least detestable of the Seymour-Seymour-Wriothesely-and-Dudley faction at Court, and made friends with him. These were the men now running England under Henry and he must carefully place himself within their sphere if he wished to protect his family, for the new faction was avaricious, and brutal to its opponents.

Now that he wore the black sling and his hair had gone stark silver, John found the king no longer had trouble looking him up and down. Women still turned around when John walked by, but Kathryn would always be the only one with cause to know his supposedly crippled arm was remarkably able in bed. It took him months before he could write, read, eat, and caress with that hand, but he was John: when he made up his mind to be obeyed, even so badly injured a limb dared not disobey.

He still made Kathryn late for chapel more mornings than not. It made her the envy of every woman at Court, caused people to regard John as more of a legend than ever, and embarrassed the queen no end. "Oh, Husband, can you not let them marry?" she begged repeatedly.

"Wife, you jest. I know, if Windsgeat does not, that Lady Whitbourne is capable of breeding again; laundresses are marvelous spies! She can still make him a Plantagenet son, which must not be. This way, if he gets her with child again, I will catch them; she will not leave my court under any pretext from now on, or they will both end in the Tower."

As Kathryn could not leave to tend Vamplate Manor, Isabella and even John occasionally went for her. The last time this was necessary, John was gone two weeks. By the time he returned she was so anxious for him that she was late for chapel three mornings running. All the maids of honor then regarded John with superstitious awe.

"It is appalling that the king allows their affair to so openly continue," Edward Seymour protested to his brother. "How does Windsgeat do it?"

"With a great deal of zeal; I have the room next to his," Thomas answered sourly.

The third morning, Kathryn came vaulting down the gallery toward chapel at a dead run. She discovered that she was so late she had missed services altogether and now must fly on to find the sewing circle that discussed religion with the king and queen each morning. It did not occur to her that, the day being so fair, the ladies would retire to a sunnier room to sit; as she raised her hand to tap at the royal Presence Chamber, she heard the king say, "By God, sir! I will not be preached at by my own wife! A good hearing it is when women act as clerks; a fine comfort, in my old age, to be corrected as though I were some errant schoolboy! Corrected on a point of faith by a mere woman! Who does she think she is—if I did not stand it from the pope, why thinks she I will bear it from a female?"

"A good thing Your Grace made that provision in the Act of Succession's renewal at marrying the queen."

"Eh? Which proviso, there were so many."

Kathryn froze, hand still raised. She heard Bishop Stephen Gardiner, the heretic-hater, answer, "For the succession of young Edward your son followed by whatever heirs you may have by this, 'or any other queen.' "

Her blood seemed to congeal within her. Gods! John had not been back at Court for the marriage, he could not know about those words. She must tell him, warn the queen. Gardiner continued, ". . . there is of course the matter of that Askew woman, Your Grace. Wriothesely gave her several good turns on the rack himself, but he could get no information out of her other than that Anne Parr—Mistress Herbert—had made her some gifts of money and food. The queen's sister, supporting a known heretic! It is as near you as that, Your Grace."

Oh, no, no. Little Anne Parr had somehow incriminated the queen.

The king asked, "Stephen, do you think this matter bears further investigation?"

She stayed only to hear the "yes" before creeping away from the door. It took most of an hour to find Francis de Gael and send him for his father; another few minutes before she located the queen and her ladies. They had returned to the chapel, which had them all so preoccupied that it was easy to slide onto the chair next to Anne Parr's, tug at her sleeve, and point to the door. Mystified, Anne followed.

Kathryn took her into the middle of the Long Gallery, the only place she could think of where they could see all approaches and so hush themselves in time. Anne, curious as a kitten, waited with mouth ajar.

"Gardiner is investigating Anne Askew, the woman preacher. She is in the Tower being tortured and has confessed only that you have supported her. Beware of Wriothesely—he is racking her himself." Anne gasped but Kathryn continued, "The queen and probably all of her ladies are going to be investigated. Your sister must burn all suspect books she holds, must have no more theological disputes with the king, for he is infuriated at thinking she doubts his rightness, his authority. Harry Tudor never could bear a woman who did not think her place twenty paces behind him! I have served all six of his queens, Anne, I know the man. Trust me!"

Hard to believe the king could so conspire behind Catherine Parr's back when he sat that night with his leg in her lap, laughing and tweaking her cheek. Hard to believe for everyone, but especially the queen, who thought old Lady Whitbourne was reverting to her Tower madness and so did nothing. How could the king threaten her and be so openly sweet? Faugh, it was impossible. Not her Harry.

It took John de Gael to make her confront reality.

The document was signed by both king and Council. As the ladies-in-waiting were under strict surveillance those weeks, Kathryn and John had avoided each other; he who had been forced to condemn his own son to death had now signed with other Council members the writ that would send Catherine Parr to the Tower for investigation.

He could not simply walk up to the queen and tell her what had happened. But his mistress was the queen's secretary; what more natural than that after a two-week separation he should break and carelessly, openly seek her out?

She was seated at the gold leaf desk that had once been Anne Boleyn's, the queen dictating a letter to her. ". . . and furthermore, good brother, we would desire that you . . ." The only other women in the room were two vielle-playing Howard cousins and Anne Parr, every one of the lot loyal to Queen Catherine. Even so, John was not blatant, only saying, "Pardon me, Your Grace, but I would like to speak to your secretary on private matters."

Leaning just so, he let the fateful writ drop out of his sling onto Kathryn's lap. She picked it up to hand back, glimpsed the rows of signatures and gasped. "Your Grace, quickly!" she urged, holding the writ out.

The Howard cousins hesitated with their vielles and bows. Catherine Parr read, eyes growing white-rimmed in horror. Her mouth was opening to scream—

John lunged at her, covered her mouth with his hand. She fought mindlessly, kicking, biting until blood ran down his wrist. Nails raked his face, caught the corner of his eye.

"What the devil!" Anne Parr cried out, and started for the guard.

Kathryn felled her with one swing of her writing box. The two Howards froze. She hissed, "Do not say a word. We are all facing the Tower; that document is our death writ, conveying us to the Tower for questioning about heresy and then probably the block. Play the vielles, damn you! Play them! No one must suspect anything is wrong!"

Bows scraped strings, breaking one. The songs were discordant a moment, then the Howard blood triumphed. They played.

The queen sagged, unclamped her teeth from John's hand. He let her slide through his arms to the nearest chair, then yanked his sling back on. "I must go. Say something shrill, loud, and insulting; I will answer in kind and thus we may blame my wounds on a lover's quarrel."

She could think of nothing harsh she wanted to say to her John. Desperately casting about for something to fling at him, her gaze caught Anne Parr. "You bitch!" she shouted, and slapped her hands together loudly. "Take that!" *Smack!* "And that! I will teach you to meddle with my lover! And you, Windsgeat—you faithless, you monster—" Smack, shout, a denial from John. Now loud sobbing from her as John retrieved the letter and bolted out the door. When the guard looked in he saw Anne Parr flat on the floor, Kathryn over her with a triumphant expression, and the queen sunk down in a chair with her hands clamped over her mouth. Baron Windsgeat had gone by with a bloodied face nursing a badly bitten hand. A ladies' fist-fight did not seem state business so the guard ducked back out. But oh, what gossip it would make!

Ann was groggily sitting up now. She heard the whole story, was sent to the window to watch for approaching troops. Kathryn knelt before the queen. "Your Grace, you must regain control. Do you hear me? You must fly to the king, cry and act weak. Tell him you did not mean to question his word—"

At the window, Anne was suddenly saying, "I know a good song of Windsgeat's, Lady Whitbourne! Care to hear it?" She was singing "Es Taget vor dem Walde," which everyone knew was John's favorite song. After a moment's fumbling, the Howard girls joined in.

What in Heaven was Anne singing so loudly for? Kathryn glanced up, saw her old friend making frantic hand gestures.

> "Der jager hurnen stolze,
> *Stand auf, Katterlein*, holder buehl!"

The hunter's horns are blowing—get up, Kathryn! She stood, raced to Anne's side. Wriothesely and a company of men had accosted John on his way across the garden. They demanded the writ. John was holding it and making small talk, gesturing with it so Thomas Wriothesely could not quite seize it. A question was asked; John, with a guileless face, silently pointed in the opposite direction from where the queen and her ladies were. To the far end of the palace, out past the tennis courts. He had just bought the troop a fruitless hour's chase, though he could no longer stall his opponent from taking the deadly document.

"Too late, too late," the queen was mumbling.

Kathryn leapt at her, shook her shoulders until the queenly gable headdress toppled to the ground, spilling gems. "Listen to me! The king cannot resist a combination of flattery and a direct appeal. Tell him you are troubled by your conscience, tell him you are confused about religion—oh, Jesu, Lady, tell him anything! I have *children* to protect! Make him think you were merely fishing for his true beliefs—Anne, get a paintpot, she is pale as sheets."

Catherine Parr fought for control and won. "Y-yes, you are right. Fetch my hair brushes—no, not the gable headdress, a French hood. My red gown, quickly. Sweet Savior, if I never coquetted before I must learn now. If it save our heads I must act stupid and gullible as any child, but oh, how it hurts me to appear thus to any man. I have studied my Scripture, I know whereof I spoke to him those many times. But because I am fashioned smaller and weaker than him—hurry, the gown!"

"I will go follow the troop and cause delays, if necessary," Anne whispered, and sprinted out.

Kathryn blotted the queen's damp eyes, used combs, Spanish liquor, and the smallest corset she could find on such short notice. Made the queen's waist tiny, strapped her into her crimson velvet. Wiped most of the red liquor off lest the queen look too suspiciously unlike herself. Tied the curved cap on, pinned up the tails at the last minute because Henry so often expressed admiration for a pretty neck.

When she and the Howards were done, a queen of England stood before them, regal, fearless, equal to any man and superior to most. She left them at a brisk pace; the Howards fled elsewhere but Kathryn followed. "The gardens, Your Grace! I saw him carried out in his pole-chair!"

Wait a moment. She had children to protect and so ran back to the gold desk. *If I am not with you in one half-hour, send Tansy to my daughters and them all across the Channel,* she wrote. "Take this to Francis de Gael in the Windsgeat apartments, he will be there with his Latin tutor at this hour," she told the guard, and gave him a gold mark to speed him along. To be safe, she sealed all edges of the note with red wax; Francis would know if the man had read it.

She had to know. Could not desert another queen as she had done Catherine of Aragon and been forced to do the others. If she heard what happened between Henry and the queen she would be forewarned and forearmed and more likely to lead her family to safety. So she raised her hem and ran blindly through the gardens until she heard Henry's booming voice. Then, dropping to the herb-rows, Kathryn inched along to the safety of a nearby yew-hedge.

Catherine Parr knelt with her head on the king's knee. She

sobbed out, "And I cannot eat or sleep for distress at so having forgotten myself as to preach at you! I am so clumsy, Husband; all I meant was that you correct me, teach me properly. You seemed so distraught with your bad leg that I thought I must distract you and have my knowledge increased all at the same time. I did not mean to argue, Husband—I mean, Your Grace."

He stiffly replied, "You behaved as a doctor of theology, Kate. You did not ask instruction but gave it Us—no, no, *thrust* it upon Us. Most unwomanly behavior!"

"Oh, it was, it was! I but meant to hear your opinion, the true opinion of enlightened men everywhere! That way perhaps I could better aid my lord in teaching his children how to love, fear, and serve God! Oh, please let me send for my confessor that I may rid myself of the sins of pride and argumentativeness!"

Kathryn peered through the thick foliage, saw the queen stroking and kissing Henry's hand. "Teach me now, Husband! Tell me how and where I have erred, show me the truth! I am only a poor, foolish woman and you my master!"

I would vomit did I not think she was saving our lives, Kathryn told herself grimly.

"You will not preach at me further, Wife?" Henry demanded.

"How could I? Only teach me the right things!"

"Why, then, you and I are as good of friends as we ever were, Sweetheart," the king said. Kissing Catherine, he raised her to his lap.

The tramp-tramp of marching feet approached. Terror-stricken, Kathryn rolled under the nearest stone bench, thanking Heaven that she had worn green today and so was garden-colored. If she lay very still and did not move, she might later make it to the stables and so to Flanders, where Jacquetta had kin—

"What is the meaning of this, Sir?" Henry was shouting.

The marching sounds smartly ceased. "Your Grace," said the unfortunate Thomas Wriothesely, "I come on your orders to arrest the queen and her ladies-in—"

A shriek, a soft thud of woman-flesh onto deep turf. There came the creak of a thickly padded chair, then Henry Tudor cried out, "By God, Sir, you have made the queen my wife faint! You are a knave, to so terrify and belabor my Kate—have you frightened her to death, I will have you skinned and pickled like an eel! Get out—*get out!*" The walking-cane struck the astounded Wriothesely many times.

Two men-at-arms leapt over yew-hedge and stone bench in fleeing, but Kathryn did not move. Only when the king and queen had gone did she venture out in time to stop Francis in his flight to warn her daughters.

Catherine Parr was so grateful at having her life saved by Kathryn's quick-thinking that she offered her a safe passage from Court for as long as she wished. "But the king says you must be examined by Doctor Butts and some midwives to prove you are not pregnant."

Kathryn shivered. "If I go I will never come back. I froze under that bench today, Your Grace, my mind nearly snapped again. I cannot live this way; I want my farm, my lands, my firm stone walls about me with one notch to aim my lance from. Yes, I will agree to the examinations, only allow me to go home to my Vamplate."

Two days later she sat at the head of a long line of carts and pack mules waving good-bye to John and the queen.

That last year, John was not able to leave Court much to see her, lest in his absence the other Council members find some reason to turn on him.

But he visited the mistress of Vamplate Manor often enough to have her great with child by the end of 1546.

Epilogue

The Vamplate
1547

In February, John de Gael came riding through Kathryn's fields shouting like a boy.

She heard his voice, ran slipshod from the house whipping off her apron, patting her hair back into its caul. Behind her, nervous servants waited for the signal to fetch horses and mules: she had been prepared for instant flight ever since leaving Court.

Finnvarra was lathered up and steaming. John's black silk sling flapped, empty, in the wind while his best fox cloak stood straight out behind him. Straight through frozen furrows, hooves striking sparks of iron on ice—

He reined in, slid down into her arms. "Get your blue silk velvet out of the sandalwood chest."

She was so huge with child that he could hardly wrap his arms around her. "John, have you lost your mind? What has happened? Are we in danger? Is—"

"The king is dead and I will not marry a woman in a linsey-woolsey work smock! Run in there and put on your sapphires, Sweetheart, the priest is not an hour behind me, and my carpenters are hurrying to finish up the marriage bed from nigh thirty years ago!"

She led him inside as someone took Finn away. "Start at the beginning, John."

"Well, your cousin Henry Howard was arrested alongside your uncle of Norfolk—Norfolk's mistress, Bess Holland, was forced to invent disloyalties of him. I think I can save the old man but not the son. He has been executed, Kathryn, I am sorry. Dudley and the Seymours are grappling for the reins of power and will keep the king's death secret some days now."

Kathryn shook her head. "God rest that confusing, cruel, fascinating old wreck of a man! You and I will work together to save Norfolk, we both owe him much. Now tell me what this babble of marriage means."

He swung her up in his arms, kissing her face, her throat, her hard, so-pregnant belly. "It means I need no longer hide that papal dispensation for cousins to marry; God's Horns, I have been sitting on the thing eleven years now, and the newer dispensation, these twelve months! Dudley and the Seymours were so busy grappling for regency of Edward Tudor that it was easy to slip in behind their backs, bribe everyone else on the Council, and show them all those signatures granting that you and I marry at last. Here it is, darling, look at all the names!"

From his blinding blue-and-red coat he pulled a long document a-dangle with dozens of red wax seals. Kathryn could not believe it and as he set her down, stood reading it over and over and over and—"John," she said, hand to her belly, "if that priest rides very quickly we may actually have a legitimate child at last."

"Yes, I know, a Duke of York to back up Francis."

"John, you are not paying attention. I was about to add: but, if the priest does *not* hurry . . ."

The next contraction that rippled across her belly was evident even through her clothing. "*Oho,*" said John worriedly. "Can you not push back or something—?"

"John, this is not a game of tug rope in the village, I—oh, oh! That was a very strong one!"

So many mingled feelings. Marriage at last after so many desperate years—the child coming—marriage, the old king dead . . .

"Why are you weeping?" he asked, picking her up and starting to the Woodville bed upstairs. "Are you in too great of pain?"

"No, no," she murmured into his reassuring shoulder. "I was crying because I will never be a lady-in-waiting again. My whole life has been spent waiting *on* someone, waiting *for* someone. Waiting for you, waiting on the queens. So many years in service, so little time my own! And I am sad because the glorious boy-king turned into a rotting hulk who should have perished years ago but lingered to make my life a Hell. And the lives of so many others, too . . . Oh, hold me, John. I have loved you so long, I am frightened at the thought of finally marrying you. Hold me!"

She insisted on the blue velvet dress and her best French hood and was still up and walking when the priest arrived. But during the last vows she sank, screaming triumphantly, to a crouch. And so Jack de Gael, "Black Pope" of the Jesuits, was born narrowly legitimate by some three or four minutes.

"That was very close, *Wife*," John observed, tying off the cord.

"You should have thought of that before you impregnated me, *Husband,*" she gasped out.

Later, lying back against heaped down pillows nursing her last child, she frowned. "John? Where will young King Edward get such ladies as me, such courtiers as you?" For she knew he would try to retire from Court life now, take her to Windsgeat to live the rest of their lives without separation.

"We are not a dying breed, we are good for years yet if Edward Tudor needs us. And you forget the children, Sweetheart. They will make all our mistakes of blood and temperament, but perhaps Edward will be a more merciful king than his father and so they will serve him well."

Enfield House, London.

Elizabeth and Edward Tudor could not believe the news. They clung together, weeping first for grief, then for fear of the many greedy Council members waiting to take charge of them, jerk them about like bait before the populace of England and Courts of Europe. They were yet children; they could be ordered about, abused, forced to marry or divorce where it suited Dudley and the Seymours. Made to sign writs condemning old friends—*At least I am only a bastard now,* Elizabeth thought. *At worst they will send me to the Tower. But my brother, my prince—the things they will make him do!*

Kill her and Mary, perhaps. Sign their death warrants.

"Jesu, are those brats still wailing in there? This has been going on two hours," Edward Seymour snapped. "You, there—the maid of honor."

Something familiar about that gorgeous young woman. Long green cat eyes, hair like a Tudor—one of Great Harry's bastards, maybe. He snapped his fingers at her. "Go in there and shut those brats up."

It was not until she had entered the chamber and softly shut the door behind her that he realized who she was. Young Lady Whitbourne, Stoneleigh's girl by Kathryn Chase. Christ, what a beauty, and baroness in her own right. Rich, too. Mayhaps Thomas could marry her.

The children were quieter immediately. Wonderful what

women were good for even outside of bed; another few hours to calm them down was all she had, then he had to take them away. Crying children were not a speciality of Seymour's, he was better with brothers. And his own, Thomas, was proving trouble. Wanted to marry the widowed queen, the fool! Well, heads were expendable, especially those of fools, related or not.

In the shuttered room, Lissy knelt near the children. "Your Grace, Milady, how may I help?"

" 'Your Grace?' " Edward burst out. "Oh no, no—I am *king* now!" He staggered toward her, flung his arms around her neck. "My uncle Ned will kill me, I know he will! Me and Bessy and old Norfolk—oh, I do not know what to do! I do not wish to be king!"

He was king of England, Ireland, Wales, and Calais but he was also a panic-struck nine-year-old boy whose worshiped father had just died. Lissy picked him up, carried him upstairs to the monstrously big bed and tucked him in. Elizabeth Tudor, older than Edward and too self-conscious to so cling to Lissy's neck, settled for clutching her hand instead. The two young women sat on the edge of the bed, watched the boy drift off toward a sleep born of exhaustion and nerves.

"Oh, Lissy! I am so glad you are here!" Elizabeth Tudor whispered.

"Will you . . . will you stay with us?" Edward asked, beginning to nod.

Lissy said proudly, "You may depend on me. I am a lady-in-waiting: I will *always* be here."

Special Offer
Buy a Bantam Book
for only 50¢.

Now you can have Bantam's catalog filled with hundreds of titles plus take advantage of our unique and exciting bonus book offer. A special offer which gives you the opportunity to purchase a Bantam book for only 50¢. Here's how!

By ordering any five books at the regular price per order, you can also choose any other single book listed (up to a $5.95 value) for just 50¢. Some restrictions do apply, but for further details why not send for Bantam's catalog of titles today!

Just send us your name and address and we will send you a catalog!

BANTAM BOOKS, INC.
P.O. Box 1006, South Holland, Ill. 60473

Mr./Mrs./Ms. ______________________
(please print)

Address ______________________

City ______________ State ______________ Zip ______
FC(A)—10/87

Please allow four to six weeks for delivery.